I0662822

The Captives by Hugh Walpole

Sir Hugh Seymour Walpole, CBE was born in Auckland, New Zealand, on March 13th, 1884.

His parents had moved to New Zealand in 1877, but his mother, Mildred, unable to settle there, eventually persuaded her husband, Somerset, an Anglican clergyman, to accept another post, this time in New York in 1889. Walpole's early years involved being educated by a Governess until, in 1893, his parents decided he needed an English education and the young Walpole was sent to England.

He first attended a preparatory school in Truro. He naturally missed his family but was reasonably happy. A move to Sir William Borlase's Grammar School in Marlow in 1895, found him bullied, frightened and miserable.

The following year, 1897, the Walpole's returned to England and Walpole was moved to be a day boy at Durham School. His sense of isolation increased. His refuge was the local library and reading.

From 1903 to 1906 Walpole studied history at Emmanuel College, Cambridge and there, in 1905, had his first work published, the critical essay "Two Meredithian Heroes".

Walpole was also attempting to cope with and come to terms with his homosexual feelings and to find "that perfect friend".

After a short spell tutoring in Germany and then teaching French at Epsom in 1908 he found the desire to fully immerse himself in the literary world. He moved to London to become a book reviewer for The Standard and to write fiction in his spare time. In 1909, he published his first novel, The Wooden Horse. The book received good reviews but sold little.

Better was to come in 1911 when he published Mr Perrin and Mr Traill. In early 1914 Henry James wrote an article for The Times Literary Supplement surveying the younger generation of British novelists. Walpole was greatly encouraged that one of the greatest living authors had publicly ranked him among the finest young British novelists.

As war approached, Walpole realised that his poor eyesight would disqualify him from service and accepted an appointment, based in Moscow, reporting for The Saturday Review and The Daily Mail. Although allowed to visit the front in Poland, these dispatches were not enough to stop hostile comments at home that he was not 'doing his bit' for the war effort.

Walpole was ready with a counter; an appointment as a Russian officer, in the Sanitar. He explained they were "part of the Red Cross that does the rough work at the front, carrying men out of the trenches, helping at the base hospitals in every sort of way, doing every kind of rough job".

During a skirmish in June 1915 Walpole rescued a wounded soldier; his Russian comrades refused to help and this meant Walpole had to carry one end of a stretcher, dragging the man to safety. He was awarded the Cross of Saint George. By late 1917 it was clear to Walpole, and the authorities, that his work was at an end. In London Walpole joined the Foreign Office and remained there until resigning in February 1919. For his wartime work he was awarded the CBE in 1918.

Walpole continued to write and publish and now also began a career on the highly lucrative lecture tour in the United States.

In 1924 Walpole moved to a house, Brackenburn, near Keswick in the Lake District. Although he maintained a flat in Piccadilly, Brackenburn was to be his main home for the rest of his life.

At the end of 1924 Walpole met Harold Cheevers, who soon became his friend and constant companion and remained so for the rest of his life; "that perfect friend".

Hollywood, in the shape of MGM, invited him in 1934 to write the script for a film of David Copperfield. He also had a small acting role in the film.

In 1937 Walpole was offered a knighthood. He accepted although Kipling, Hardy, Galsworthy had all refused. "I'm not of their class... Besides I shall like being a knight," he said.

Unfortunately his health was undermined by diabetes made worse by the frenetic pace of his life. Sir Hugh Seymour Walpole, CBE died of a heart attack at Brackenburn, aged 57 on June 1st, 1941. He was buried in St John's churchyard in Keswick.

Index of Contents

PART I

BEGINNING OF THE JOURNEY

CHAPTER I

DEATH OF THE REV. CHARLES CARDINAL

Death leapt upon the Rev. Charles Cardinal, Rector of St. Dreots in South Glebeshire, at the moment that he bent down towards the second long drawer of his washhand-stand; he bent down to find a clean collar. It is in its way a symbol of his whole life, that death claimed him before he could find one.

At one moment his mind was intent upon his collar; at the next he was stricken with a wild surmise, a terror that even at that instant he would persuade himself was exaggerated. He saw before his clouding eyes a black pit. A strong hand striking him in the middle of his back flung him contemptuously forward into it; a gasping cry of protest and all was over. Had time been permitted him he would have stretched out a hand towards the shabby black box that, true to all miserly convention, occupied the space beneath his bed. Time was not allowed him. He might take with him into the darkness neither money nor clean clothing.

He had been told on many occasions about his heart, that he must not excite nor strain it. He allowed that to pass as he allowed many other things because his imagination was fixed upon one ambition, and one alone. He had made, upon this last and fatal occasion, haste to find his collar because the bell had begun its Evensong clatter and he did not wish to-night to be late. The bell continued to ring and he lay his broad widespread length upon the floor. He was a large and dirty man.

The shabby old house was occupied with its customary life. Down in the kitchen Ellen the cook was snatching a moment from her labours to drink a cup of tea. She sat at the deal table, her full bosom pressed by the boards, her saucer balanced on her hand; she blew, with little heaving pants, at her tea to cool it. Her thoughts were with a new hat and some red roses with which she would trim it; she looked out with little shivers of content at the falling winter's dusk: Anne the kitchen-maid scoured the pans; her bony frame seemed to rattle as she scrubbed with her red hands; she was happy because she was hungry and there would be a beef-steak pudding for dinner. She sang to herself as she worked.

Upstairs in the dining-room Maggie Cardinal, the only child of the Rev. Charles, sat sewing. She hoard the jangling of the church hell; she heard also, suddenly, with a surprise that made her heart beat for a moment with furious leaps, a tapping on the window-pane. Then directly after that she fancied that there came from her father's room above the thud of some sudden fall or collapse. She listened. The bell swallowed all other noise. She thought that she had been mistaken, but the tapping at the window began again, now insistent; the church bell suddenly stopped and in the silence that followed one could hear the slight creak of some bough driven by the sea-wind against the wall.

The curtains were not drawn and where the curve of the hill fell away the sky was faintly yellow; some cold stars like points of ice pierced the higher blue; carelessly, as though with studied indifference, flakes of snow fell, turning grey against the lamp-lit windows, then vanishing utterly. Maggie, going to the window, saw a dark shapeless figure beyond the glass. For an instant she was invaded by the terror of her surprised loneliness, then she remembered her father and the warm kitchen, then realised that this figure in the dark must be her Uncle Mathew.

She went out into the hall, pushed back the stiff, clumsy handle of the door, and stepped on to the gravel path. She called out, laughing:

"Come in! You frightened me out of my life."

As he came towards her she felt the mingled kindness and irritation that he always roused in her. He stood in the light of the hall lamp, a fat man, a soft hat pushed to the back of his head, a bag in one hand. His face was weak and good-tempered, his eyes had once been fine but now they were dim and blurred; there were dimples in his fat cheeks; he wore on his upper lip a ragged and untidy moustache and he had two indeterminate chins. His expression was mild, kindly, now a little ashamed, now greatly indignant. It was a pity, as he often said, that he had not more control over his feelings. Maggie saw at once that he was, as usual, a little drunk.

"Well," she said. "Come in, Uncle. Father is in church, I think," she added.

Uncle Mathew stepped with careful deliberation into the hall, put his bag on a chair, and began a long, rambling explanation.

"You know, Maggie, that I would have sent you a post card if I had had an idea, but, upon my soul, there I was suddenly in Drymouth on important business. I thought to myself on waking this morning—I took a room at the 'Three Tuns'—'Why, there are Charles and Maggie whom I haven't seen for an age.' I'd have sent you a telegram but the truth is, my dear, that I didn't want to spend a penny more than I must. Things haven't been going so well with me of late. It's a long story. I want your father's advice. I've had the worst of luck and I could tell you one or two things that would simply surprise you—but anyway, there it is. Just for a night I'm sure you won't mind. To-morrow or the day after I must be back in town or this thing will slip right through my fingers. These days one must be awake or one's simply nowhere."

He paused and nodded his head very solemnly at her, looking, as he did so, serious and important.

It was thus that he always appeared, "for one night only," but staying for weeks and weeks in spite of the indignant protests of his brother Charles who had never liked him and grudged the expense of his visits. Maggie herself took his appearance as she did everything else in her life with good-tempered philosophy. She had an affection for her uncle; she wished that he did not drink so much, but had he made a success of life she would not have cared for him as she did. After all every one had their weaknesses ...

She steered her uncle into the dining-room and placed him on a chair beside the fire. In all his movements he attempted restraints and dignity because he knew that he was drunk but hoped that his niece, in spite of her long experience of him, would not perceive it. At the same time he knew that she did perceive it and would perhaps scold him about it. This made him a little indignant because, after all, he had only taken the tiniest drop—one drop at Drymouth, another at Liskane station, and another at "The Hearty Cow" at Clinton St. Mary, just before his start on his cold lonely walk to St. Dreot's. He hoped that he would prevent her criticism by his easy pleasant talk, so on he chattered.

She sat down near him and continuing to sew smiled at him, wondered what there was for dinner and the kind of mood that her father would be in when he found his dear brother here.

Maggie Cardinal, at the time, was nineteen years of age. She was neither handsome nor distinguished, plain indeed, although her mild, good-natured eyes had in their light a quality of vitality and interest that gave her personality; her figure was thick and square—she would be probably stout one day. She moved like a man. Behind the mildness of her eyes there was much character and resolve in her carriage, in the strong neck, the firm breasts, the mouth resolute and determined. She had now the fine expectation of her youth, her health, her optimism, her ignorance of the world. When these things left her she would perhaps be a yet plainer woman. In her dress she was not clever. Her clothes were ugly with the coarse drab grey of their material and the unskilful workmanship that had created them. And yet there would be some souls who would see in her health, her youth, the kind sympathy of her eyes and mouth, the high nobility of her forehead from which her hair was brushed back, an attraction that might hold them more deeply than an obvious beauty.

Uncle Mathew although he was a silly man was one of these perceptive souls, and had he not been compelled by his circumstances to think continually about himself, would have loved his niece very dearly. As it was, he thought her a fine girl when he thought of her at all, and wished her more success in life than her "poor old uncle" had had. He looked at her now across the fireplace with satisfaction. She was something sure and pleasant in a world that swayed and was uncertain. He was drunk enough to feel happy so long as he was not scolded. He dreaded the moment when his brother Charles would appear, and he strove to arrange in his mind the wise and unanswerable word with which he would defend himself, but his thoughts slipped just as the firelight slipped and the floors with the old threadbare carpet.

Then suddenly the hall door opened with a jangle, there were steps in the hall, and Old Timmie Carthewe the sexton appeared in the dining-room. He had a goat's face and a body like a hairpin.

"Rector's not been to service," he said. "There's Miss Dunnett and Mrs. Giles and the two Miss Backshaws. I'm feared he's forgotten."

Maggie started up. Instantly to her mind came the memory of that fancied sound from her father's room. She listened now, her head raised, and the two men, their eyes bleared but their noses sniffing as though they were dogs, listened also. There were certain sounds, clocks ticking, the bough scraping on the wall, a cart's echo on the frozen road, the maid singing far in the depths of the house. Maggie nodded her head.

"I'll go and see," she said.

She went into the hall and stood again listening. Then she called, "Father! Father!" but there was no answer. She had never in all her life been frightened by anything and she was not frightened now; nevertheless, as she went up the stairs, she looked behind her to see whether any one followed her.

She called again "Father!" then went to his door, pushed it open, and looked in. The room was cold with a faint scent of tallow candle and damp.

In the twilight she saw her father's body lying like a shadow stretched right across the floor, with the grey dirty fingers of one hand clenched.

After that events followed swiftly. Maggie herself had no time nor opportunity for any personal emotion save a dumb kind of wonder that she did not feel more. But she saw all "through a glass darkly." There had been first that moment when the sexton and Uncle Mathew, still like dogs sniffing, had peered with their eyes through her father's door. Then there had been the summoning of Dr. Bubbage from the village, his self-importance, his continual "I warned him. I warned him. He can't say I didn't warn him," and then (very dim and far away) "Thank you, Miss Cardinal. I think I will have a glass if you don't mind." There had been cook crying in the kitchen (her red roses intended for Sunday must now be postponed) and the maid sniffing in the hall. There had been Uncle Mathew, muddled and confused, but clinging to his one idea that "the best thing you can do, my dear, is to send for your Aunt Anne." There had been the telegram dispatched to Aunt Anne, and then after that the house had seemed quite filled with people—ladies who had—wished to know whether they could help her in any way and even the village butcher who was there for no reason but stood in the hall rubbing his hands on his thighs and sniffing. All these persons Maggie surveyed through a mist. She was calm and collected and empty of all personality; Maggie Cardinal, the real Maggie Cardinal, was away on a visit somewhere and would not be back for a time or two.

Then suddenly as the house had filled so suddenly it emptied. Maggie found that she was desperately tired. She went to bed and slept instantly. On waking next morning she was aware that it was a most beautiful winter's day and that there was something strange in the air. There came to her then very slowly a sense of her father. She saw him on the one side, persistently as she had found him in his room, strange, shapeless, with a crumpled face and a dirty beard that seemed to be more dead than the rest of him. On the other side she saw him as she had found him in the first days of her consciousness of the world.

He must have been "jolly" then, large and strong, laughing often, tossing her, she remembered, to the ceiling, his beard jet-black and his eyebrows bushy and overhanging. Once that vigour, afterwards this horror. She shook away from her last vision of him but it returned again and again, hanging about her over her shoulder like an ill-omened messenger. And all the life between seemed to be suddenly wiped away as a sponge wipes figures off a slate. After the death of her mother she had made the best of her circumstances. There had been many days when life had been unpleasant, and in the last year, as his miserliness had grown upon him, his ill-temper at any fancied extravagance had been almost that of an insane man, but Maggie knew very little of the affairs of other men and it seemed to her that every one had some disadvantage with which to grapple. She did not pretend to care for her father, she was very lonely because the villagers hated him, but she had always made the best of everything because she had never had an intimate friend to tell her that that was a foolish thing to do.

It was indeed marvellous how isolated her life had been; she knew simply nothing about the world at all.

She could not pretend that she was sorry that her father had died; and yet she missed him because she knew very well that she was now no one's business, that she was utterly and absolutely alone in the universe. It might be said that she could not be utterly alone when she had her Uncle Mathew, but, although she was ignorant of life, she knew her Uncle Mathew ... Nevertheless, he did something to remove the sharp alarm of her sudden isolation. Upon the day after her father's death he was at his very best, his kindest, and most gentle. He was rather pathetic, having drunk nothing out of respect to the occasion; he felt, somewhere deep down in him, a persistent exaltation that his brother Charles was dead, but he knew that it was not decent to allow this feeling to conquer him and he was truly anxious to protect and comfort his niece so well as he was able. Early in the afternoon he suggested that they should go for a walk. Everything necessary had been done. An answer to their telegram had been received from his sister Anne that she could not leave London until that night but would arrive at Clinton St. Mary station at half-past nine to-morrow morning. That would be in good time for the funeral, a ceremony that was to be conducted by the Rev. Tom Trefusis, the sporting vicar of Cator Hill, the neighbouring parish.

The house now was empty and silent. They must escape from that figure, now decent, clean, and solemn, lying upon the bed upstairs. Mathew took his niece by the hand and said:

"My dear, a little fresh air is the thing for both of us. It will cheer you up."

So they went out for a walk together. Maggie knew, with a deep and intimate experience, every lane and road within twenty miles' radius of St. Dreot's, There was the high-road that went through Gator Hill to Clinton and then to Polwint; here were the paths across the fields to Lucent, the lanes that led to the valley of the Lisp, all the paths like spiders' webs through Rothin Wood, from whose curve you could see Polchester, grey and white, with its red-brown roofs and the spires of the Cathedral thrusting like pointing fingers into the heaven. It was the Polchester View that she chose to-day, but as they started through the deep lanes down the St. Dreot's hill she was startled and disturbed by the strange aspect which everything wore to her. She had not as yet realised the great shock her father's death had been; she was exhausted, spiritually and physically, in spite of the deep sleep of the night before. The form and shape of the world was a little strained and fantastic, the colours uncertain, now vivid, now vanishing, the familiar trees, hedges, clouds, screens, as it were, concealing some scene that was being played behind them. But beyond and above all other sensations she was conscious of her liberty. She struggled against this; she should be conscious, before everything, of her father's loss. But she was not. It meant to her at present not so much the loss of a familiar figure as the sudden juggling, by an outside future, of all the regular incidents and scenes of her daily life, as at a pantomime one sees by a transformation of the scenery, the tables, the chairs, and pictures the walls dance to an unexpected jig. She was free, free, free—alone but free. What form her life would take she did not know, what troubles and sorrows in the future there might be she did not care—to-morrow her life would begin.

Although unsentimental she was tender-hearted and affectionate, but now, for many years, her life with her father had been a daily battle of ever-increasing anger and bitterness. It may be that once he had loved her; that had been in those days when she was not old enough to love him ... since she had known him he had loved only money. She would have loved him had he allowed her, and because he did not she bore him no grudge. She had always regarded her life, sterile and unprofitable as it was, with humour until now when, like a discarded dress, it had slipped behind her. She did not see it, even now, with bitterness; there was no bitterness for anything in her character.

As they walked Uncle Mathew was considering her for the first time. On the other occasions when he had stayed in his brother's house he had been greatly occupied with his own plans—requests for money (invariably refused) schemes for making money, plots to frighten his brother out of one or other of his possessions. He had been frankly predatory, and that plain, quiet girl his niece had been pleasant company but no more. Now she was suddenly of the first importance. She would in all probability inherit a considerable sum. How much there might be in that black box under the bed one could not say, but surely you could not be so relentless a miser for so long a period without accumulating a very agreeable amount. Did the girl realise that she would, perhaps, be rich? Uncle Mathew licked his lips with his tongue. So quiet and self-possessed was she that you could not tell what she was thinking. Were she only pretty she might marry anybody. As it was, with that figure ... But she was a good girl. Uncle Mathew felt kind and tender-hearted towards her. He would advise her about life of which he had had a very considerable experience, and of which, of course, she knew nothing. His heart was warm, although it would have been warmer still had he been able to drink a glass of something before starting out.

"And what will you do now, my dear, do you think?" he asked.

They had left the deep lanes and struck across the hard-rutted fields. A thin powder of snow lay upon the land, and under the yellow light of the winter sky the surface was blue, shadowed with white patches where the snow had fallen more thickly. The trees and hedges were black and hard against the white horizon that was tightly stretched like the paper of a Japanese screen. The smell of burning wood was in the air, and once and again a rook slowly swung its wheel, cutting the air as it flew. The cold was so pleasantly sharp that it was the best possible thing for Uncle Mathew, who was accustomed to an atmosphere of hissing gas, unwashen glasses, and rinds of cheese.

Maggie did not answer his question but herself asked one.

"Uncle Mathew, do you believe in religion?"

"Religion, my dear?" answered her uncle, greatly startled at so unusual a question. "What sort of religion?"

"The kind of religion that father preached about every Sunday—the Christian religion."

"To tell you the truth, my dear," he answered confidentially, "I've never had much time to think about it. With some men, you see, it's part of their lives, and with others—well, it isn't. My lines never ran that way."

"Was father very religious when he was young?"

"No, I can't say that he was. But then we never got on, your father and I. Our lines didn't run together at all. But I shouldn't have called him a religious man."

"Then all this time father has been lying?"

Her uncle gazed at her apprehensively. He did not wish to undermine her faith in her father on the very day after his death, but he was so ignorant about her, her thoughts and beliefs and desires, that he did not know what her idea of her father had been. His idea of him had always been that he was a dirty, miserly scoundrel, but that was not quite the thing for a daughter to feel, and there was an innocence and simplicity about Maggie that perplexed him.

"I can't truly say that I ever knew what your father's private feelings were. He never cared for me enough to tell me. He may have been very religious in his real thoughts. We never discussed such things."

Maggie turned round upon him.

"I know. You're pretending. You've said to yourself, 'I mustn't tell her what I think about her father the very day after his death, that isn't a pleasant thing to do.' We've all got to pretend that he was splendid. But he wasn't—never. Who can know it better than I? Didn't he worry mother until she died? Didn't he lead me an awful life always, and aren't I delighted now that he's dead? It's everything to me. I've longed for this day for years, and now we've got to pretend that we're sorry and that it would be a good thing if he were alive. It wouldn't be a good thing—it would be a bad thing for every one. He was a bad man and I hated him."

Then, quite suddenly, she cried. Turning away from her uncle she folded her face in her arms like a small child and sobbed. Standing, looking at her bent shoulders, her square, ugly figure, her shabby old hat with its dingy black ribbon, pushed a little to the side of her head, Uncle Mathew thought that she was a most uncomprehensible girl. If she felt like that about her father why should she cry; and if she cried she must surely have some affection for his memory. All he could say was:

"There, there, my dear—Well, well. It's all right." He felt foolish and helpless.

She turned round at last, drying her eyes. "It's such a shame," she said, still sobbing, "that that's what I shall feel about him. He's all I had and that's what I feel. But if you knew—if you knew—all the things he did."

They walked on again, entering Rothin Wood. "He never tried to make me religious," she went on. "He didn't care what I felt. I sat in the choir, and I took a Sunday-school class, and I visited the villagers, but I, myself—what happened to me—he didn't care. He never took any trouble about the church, he just gabbled the prayers and preached the same old sermons. People in the village said it was a scandal and that he ought to be turned out but no one ever did anything. They'll clean everything up now. There'll be a new clergyman. They'll mend the holes in the kitchen floor and the ceiling of my bedroom. It will be all new and fresh."

"And what will you do, Maggie?" said her uncle, trying to make his voice indifferent as though he had no personal interest in her plans.

"I haven't thought yet," she said.

"I've an idea," he went on. "What do you say to your living with me? A nice little place somewhere in London. I've felt for a long time that I should settle down. Your father will have left you a little money—not much, perhaps, but just enough for us to manage comfortably. And there we'd be, as easy as anything. I can see us very happy together."

But he did not as yet know his niece. She shook her head.

"No," she said. "I'm going to live with Aunt Anne and Aunt Elizabeth. We wouldn't be happy, Uncle, you and I. Our house would always be in a mess and there are so many things that I must learn that only another woman could teach me. I never had a chance with father."

He had entered upon this little walk with every intention of settling the whole affair before their return. He had had no idea of any opposition—her ignorance of the world would make her easy to adapt. But now when he saw that she had already considered the matter and was firmly resolved, his arguments deserted him.

"Just consider a moment," he said.

"I think it will be best for me to live with the aunts," she answered firmly. "They have wished it before. Of course then it was impossible but now it will do very well."

He had one more attempt.

"You won't be happy there, my dear, with all their religion and the rest of it—and two old maids. You'll see no life at all."

"That depends upon myself," she answered, "and as to their religion at least they believe in it."

"Yes, your Aunt Anne is a very sincere woman," Uncle Mathew answered grimly.

He was angry and helpless. She seemed suddenly some one with whom it was impossible to argue. He had intended to be pathetic, to paint delightful pictures of uncle and niece sheltering snugly together defended by their affection against a cold and hostile London. His own eyes had filled with tears as he thought of it. What a hard, cold-hearted girl she was! Nevertheless for the moment he abandoned the subject.

That she should go and live with her aunts was not for Maggie in any way a new idea. A number of years ago when she had been a little girl of thirteen or fourteen years of age her father had had a most violent quarrel with his sister Anne. Maggie had never known the exact cause of this although even at that period she suspected that it was in some way connected with money. She found afterwards that her father had considered that certain pieces of furniture bequeathed to the family by a defunct relation were his and not his sister's. Miss Anne Cardinal, a lady of strong character, clung to her sofa, cabinet, and porcelain, bowls, and successfully maintained her right. The Reverend Charles forbade the further mention of her name by any member of his household. This quarrel was a grievous disappointment to Maggie who had often been promised that when she should be a good girl she should go and stay with her aunts in London. She had invented for herself a strange fascinating picture of the dark, mysterious London house, with London like a magic cauldron bubbling beyond it. There was moreover the further strangeness of her aunt's religion. Her father in his anger had spoken about "their wicked blasphemy," "their insolence in the eyes of God," "their blindness and ignorant conceit." Maggie had discovered, on a later day, from her uncle that her aunts belonged to a sect known as the Kingscote Brethren and that the main feature of their creed was that they expected the second coming of the Lord God upon earth at no very distant date.

"Will it really happen, Uncle Mathew?" she asked in an awe-struck voice when she first heard this.

"It's all bunkum if you ask me," said her uncle. "And it's had a hardening effect on your aunts who were kind women once, but they're completely in the hands of the blackguard who runs their chapel, poor innocents. I'd wring his neck if I caught him."

All this was very fascinating to Maggie who was of a practical mind with regard to the facts immediately before her but had beyond them a lively imagination. Her life had been so lonely, spent for the most part so far from children of her own age, that she had no test of reality. She did not see any reason why the Lord God should not come again and she saw every reason why her aunts should condemn her uncle. That London house swam now in a light struck partly from the wisdom and omniscience of her aunts, partly from God's threatened descent upon them.

Aunt Anne's name was no longer mentioned in St. Dreot's but Maggie did not forget, and at every new tyranny from her father she thought to herself—"Well, there is London. I shall be there one day."

As they walked Maggie looked at her uncle. What was he really? He should be a gentleman and yet he didn't look like one. She remembered things that he had at different times said to her.

"Why, look at myself!" he had on earlier days, half-maudlin from "his drop at the 'Bull and Bush,'" exclaimed to Maggie, "I can't call myself a success! I'm a rotten failure if you want to know, and I had most things in my favour to start with, went to Cambridge, had a good opening as a barrister. But it wasn't quick enough for me. I was restless and wanted to jump the moon—now look at me! Same with your father, only he's put all his imagination into money—same as your aunts have put theirs into religion. We're not like ordinary people, us Cardinals."

"And have I got a lot of imagination too?" Maggie had asked on one occasion.

"I'm sure I don't know," her uncle had answered her. "You don't look to me like a Cardinal at all—much too quiet. But you may have it somewhere. Look out for a bad time if you have."

Today Maggie's abrupt checking of his projects had made him sulky and he talked but little. "Damn it all!" he had started out with the most charming intentions towards the girl and now look at her! Was it natural conduct in the day after she had lost her only protector? No, it was not. Had she been pretty he might have, even now, forgiven her, but today she looked especially plain with her pale face and shabby black dress and her obstinate mouth and chin. He was uneasy, too, about the imminent arrival of his sister Anne, who always frightened him and made him think poorly of the world in general. No hope of getting any money out of her, nor would Charles have left him a penny. It was a rotten, unsympathetic world, and Uncle Mathew cursed God as he strutted sulkily along. Maggie also had fallen into silence.

They came at last out of the wood and stood at the edge of it, with the pine trees behind them, looking down over Polchester. On this winter's afternoon Polchester with the thin covering of snow upon its roofs sparkled like a city under glass. The Cathedral was dim in the mist of the early dusk and the sun, setting behind the hill, with its last rays caught the windows so that they blazed through the haze like smoking fires. Whilst Maggie and her uncle stood there the bells began to ring for Evensong, and the sound like a faint echo seemed to come from behind them out of the wood. In the spring all the Polchester orchards would be white and pink with blossom, in the summer the river that encircled the city wall would run like a blue scarf between its green sloping hills—now there was frost and snow and mist with the fires smouldering at its heart. She gazed at it now as she had never gazed at it before. She was going into it now. Her life was beginning at last. When the sun had left the windows and the walls were grey she turned back into the wood and led the way silently towards home.

The house that night was very strange with her father dead in it. She sat, because she thought it her duty, in his bedroom. He lay on his bed, with his beard carefully combed and brushed now, spread out upon the sheet. His closed eyes and mouth gave him a grave and reverend appearance which he had never worn in his life. He lay there, under the flickering candle-light, like some saint who at length, after a life of severe discipline, had entered into the joy of his Lord. Beneath the bed was the big black box.

Maggie did not look at her father. She sat there, near the dark window, her hands folded on her lap. She thought of nothing at all except the rats. She was not afraid of them but they worried her. They had been a trouble in the house for a long time past, poison had been laid for them and they had refused to take it. They had had, perhaps, some fear of the Reverend Charles, at any rate they scampered and scurried now behind the wainscoting as though conscious of their release. "Even the rats are glad," Maggie thought to herself. In the uncertain candle-light the fancy seized her that one rat, a very large one, had crept out from his hole, crawled on to the bed, and now sat on the sheet looking at her father. It would be a horrible thing did the rat walk across her father's beard, and yet for her life she could not move. She waited, fascinated. She fancied that the beard stirred a little as though the rat had moved it. She fancied that the rat grew and grew in size, now there were many of them, all with their little sharp beady eyes watching the corpse. Now there were none; only the large limbs outlined beneath the spread, the waxen face, the ticking clock, the strange empty shape of his grey dressing-gown hanging upon a nail on the wall. Where was her father gone? She did not know, she did not care—only she trusted that she would never meet him again—never again. Her head nodded; her hands and feet were cold; the candle-light jumped, the rats scampered ... she slept.

When it was quite dark beyond the windows and the candles were low Maggie came downstairs, stiff, cold, and very hungry. She felt that it was wrong to have slept and very wrong to be hungry, but there it was; she did not pretend to herself that things were other than they were. In the dining-room she found supper laid out upon the table, cold beef, potatoes in their jackets, cold beetroot, jelly, and cheese, and her uncle playing cards on the unoccupied end of the table in a melancholy manner by himself. She felt that it was wrong of him to play cards on such an occasion, but the cards were such dirty grey ones and he obtained obviously so little pleasure from his amusement that he could not be considered to be wildly abandoning himself to riot and extravagance.

She felt pleasure in his company; for the first time since her father's death she was a little frightened and uneasy. She might even have gone to him and cried on his shoulder had he given her any encouragement, but he did not speak to her except to say that he had already eaten. He was still a little sulky with her.

When she had finished her meal she sat in her accustomed chair by the fire, her head propped on her hands, looking into the flame, and there, half-asleep, half-awake, memories, conversations, long-vanished scenes trooped before her eyes as though they were bidding her a long farewell. She did not, as she sat there, sentimentalise about any of them, she saw them as they were, some happy, some unhappy, some terrifying, some amusing, all of them dead and passed, grey and thin, the life gone out of them. Her mind was fixed on the future. What was it going to be? Would she have money as her uncle had said? Would she see London and the world? Would she find friends, people who would be glad to be with her and have her with them? What would her aunts be like? and so from them, what about all the other members of the family of whom she had heard? She painted for herself a gay scene in which, at the door of some great house, a fine gathering of Cardinals waited with smiles and outstretched hands to welcome her. Then, laughing at herself as she always did when she had allowed her fancy free rein, she shook her head. No, it certainly would not be like that. Relations were not like that. That was not the way to face the world to encourage romantic dreams. Her uncle, watching her surreptitiously, wondered of what she was thinking. Her determined treatment of him that afternoon continued to surprise him. She certainly ought to make her way in the world, but what a pity that she was so plain. Perhaps if she got some colour into her cheeks, dressed better, brushed her hair differently—no, her mouth would always be too large and her nose too small—and her figure was absurd. Uncle Mathew considered that he was a judge of women.

He rose at last and, rather shamefacedly, said that he should go to bed. Maggie wondered at the confusion that she detected in him. She looked at him and he dropped his eyes.

"Good night, Uncle Mathew."

He looked at her then and noticed by her white face and dark-lined eyes what a strain the day had been to her. He saw again the figure in the shabby black hat sobbing in the lane. He suddenly put his arms about her and held her close to him. She noticed that he smelled of whisky, but she felt his kindness, and putting her hand on his fat shoulder kissed once more his cheek.

When he had left her, her weariness came suddenly down upon her, overwhelming her as though the roof had fallen in. The lamp swelled before her tired eyes as though it had been an evil, unhealthy flower. The table slid into the chairs and the cold beef leered at the jelly; the pictures jumped and the clock ran in a mad scurry backwards and forwards.

She dragged her dazed body up through the silent house to her bedroom, undressed, was instantly in bed and asleep.

She slept without dreams but woke suddenly as though she had been flung into the midst of one. She sat up in bed, knowing from the thumping of her heart that she was seized with panic but finding, in the first flash, no reason for her alarm. The room was pitch black with shadows of light here and there, but she had with her, in the confusion of her sleep, uncertainty as to the different parts of the room. What had awakened her? Of what was she frightened? Then suddenly, as one slits a black screen with a knife, a thin line of light cracked the darkness. As though some one had whispered it in her ear she knew that the door was there and the dark well of uncertainty into which she had been plunged was suddenly changed into her own room where she could recognise the window, the chest of drawers, the looking-glass, the chairs. Some one was opening her door and her first thought that it was of course her father was checked instantly by the knowledge, conveyed again as though some one had whispered to her, that her father was dead.

The thin line of light was now a wedge, it wavered, drew back to a spider's thread again, then broadened with a flush of colour into a streaming path. Some one stood in the doorway holding a candle. Maggie saw that it was Uncle Mathew in his shirt and trousers.

"What is it?" she said.

He swayed as he stood there, his candle making fantastic leaps and shallows of light. He was smiling at her in a silly way and she saw that he was drunk. She had had a horror of drunkenness ever since, as a little girl, she had watched an inebriated carter kicking his wife. She always, after that, saw the woman's bent head and stooping shoulders. Now she knew, sitting up in bed, that she was frightened not only of Uncle Mathew, but of the house, of the whole world.

She was alone. She realised her loneliness in a great flash of bewilderment and cold terror as though the ground had suddenly broken away from her and she was on the edge of a vast pit. There was no one in the house to help her. Her father was dead. The cook and the maid were sunk in heavy slumber at the other end of the house. There was no one to help her. She was alone, and it seemed to her that in the shock of that discovery she realised that she would always be alone now, for the rest of her life.

"What is it, Uncle Mathew?" she said again. Her voice was steady, although her heart hammered. Some other part of her brain was wondering where it was that he had got the drink. He must have had a bottle of whisky in his room; she remembered his shyness when he said good-night to her.

He stood in the middle of the floor, swaying on his feet and smiling at her. The flame of the light rose and fell in jerks and spasms.

"I thought," he said, "I'd come—to see m'little Maggie, m'little niece, jus' to talk a lill bit and cheer her up—up." He drew nearer the bed. "She'll be lonely, I said—lonely—very—aren't you—lonely Maggie?"

"It's very late," she said, "and you're dropping grease all over the floor with that candle. You go back to bed, uncle. I'm all right. You go back to bed."

"Go back? No, no, no. Oh no, not back to bed. It'll soon be mornin'. That'll be jolly-jolly. We'll talk—together till mornin'."

He put the candle on a chair, nearly falling as he did so, then came towards her. He stood over her, his shirt, open at the neck, protuberating over his stomach, his short thick legs swaying. His red, unshaven face with the trembling lips was hateful to her.

Suddenly he sat on the edge of her bed and put his hands out towards her. He caught her hair.

"My little Maggie—my little Maggie," he said.

The fright, the terror, the panic that seized her was like the sudden rising of some black figure who grew before her, bent towards her and with cold hard fingers squeezed her throat. For an instant she was helpless, quivering, weak in every bone of her body.

Then some one said to her:

"But you can manage this."

"I can manage this," she answered almost aloud.

"You're alone now. You mustn't let things be too much for you."

She jumped out of bed, on the farther side away from her uncle. She put on her dressing-gown. She stood and pointed at the door.

"Now, uncle, you go back to your room at once. It's disgraceful coming in the middle of the night and disturbing every one. Go back to bed."

The new tone in her voice startled him. He looked at her in a bewildered fashion. He got up from the bed.

"Why, Maggie—I only—only—"

He stared from her to the candle and from the candle back to her again.

"Now go," she repeated. "Quick now."

He hung his head. "Now you're angry—angry with your poor ole uncle—poor ole uncle." He looked at her, his eyes puzzled as though he had never seen her before.

"You're very hard," he said, shaking his head. He stumbled towards the door—"Very hard," he repeated, and went out, his head still hanging.

She heard him knock his foot against the stairs. Soon there was silence.

She blew out the candle and went back to bed. She lay there, her heart, at first, throbbing, her eyes straining the darkness. Then she grew more tranquil. She felt in her heart a strange triumph as though already she had begun life and had begun it with success. She thought, before she sank deep into sleep, that anything would yield to one did one only deal sensibly with it ... After all, it was a fine thing to be alone.

CHAPTER II

AUNT ANNE

In the morning, however, she discovered no fine things anywhere. The hours that had elapsed since her father's death had wrought in him a "sea-change." He had gained nobility, almost beauty. She wondered with a desolate self-criticism whether during all those years she had been to blame and not he. Perhaps he had wished for sympathy and intimacy and she had repulsed him. His little possessions here and there about the house reproached her.

Uncle Mathew had a bad headache and would not come down to breakfast. She felt indignant with him but also indulgent. He had shown himself hopelessly lacking in good taste, and good feeling, but then she had never supposed that he had these things. At the same time the last support seemed to have been removed from her; it might well be that her Aunt Anne would not care for her and would not wish to have her in her house. What should she do then? Whither should she go? She flung up her head and looked bravely into the face of Ellen, the cook, who came to remove the breakfast, but she had to bite her lip to keep back the tears that WOULD come and fill her eyes so that the world was misty and obscure.

There was, she fancied, something strange about Ellen. In HER eyes some obscure triumph or excitement, some scorn and derision, Maggie fancied, of herself. Had the woman been drinking? ...

Then there arrived Mr. Brassy, her father's solicitor, from Cator Hill. He had been often in the house, a short fat man with a purple face, clothes of a horsy cut, and large, red, swollen fingers. He took now possession of the house with much self-importance. "Well, Miss Maggie" (he blew his words at her as a child blows soap-bubbles). "Here we are, then. Very sad indeed—very. I've been through the house—got the will all right. Your aunt, you say, will be with us?"

"My aunt from London. Miss Anne Cardinal. I expect her in half an hour. She should have arrived at Clinton by the half-past nine train."

"Well, well. Yes—yes—indeed, your uncle is also here?"

"Yes. He will be down shortly."

"Very good, Miss Maggie. Very good."

She hated that he should call her Miss Maggie. He had always treated her with considerable respect, but to-day she fancied that he patronised her. He placed his hand for a moment on her shoulder and she shrank back. He felt her action and, abashed a little, coughed and blew his nose. He strutted about the room. Then the door opened and Ellen the cook looked in upon them.

"I only wished to see, Miss, whether I could do anything for you?"

"Nothing, thank you," said Maggie.

"Been with you some time that woman?" said Mr. Brassy.

"Yes," said Maggie, "about five years, I think."

"Hum! Hum—name of Harmer."

"Yes. Harmer."

"Not married?"

"No," answered Maggie, wondering at this interest.

"Not so far as you know."

"No. She's always Miss Harmer."

"Quite so—quite so. Dear me, yes."

Other people appeared, asked questions and vanished. It seemed to have been all taken out of her hands and it was strange how desolate this made her. For so many years she had had the management of that house, since her fourteenth birthday, indeed. Ugly and dilapidated though the place had been, it had grown, after a time, to belong to her, and she had felt as though it were in some way grateful to her for keeping it, poor thing, together. Now it had suddenly withdrawn itself and was preparing for the next comer. Maggie felt this quite definitely and thought that probably it was glad that now its roof would be mended and its floors made whole. It had thrown her off ... Well, she would not burden it long.

There were sounds then of wheels on the gravel. The old dilapidated cab from Clinton with its ricketty windows and moth-eaten seats that smelt of straw and beer was standing at the door, the horse puffing great breaths of steam into the frozen air. Her aunt had arrived. Maggie, standing behind the window, looked out. The carriage door opened, and a figure, that seemed unusually tall, appeared to straighten itself out and rose to its full height on the gravel path as though it had been sitting in the cab pressed together, its head upon its knees.

Then in the hall that was dark even on the brightest day, Aunt Anne revealed herself as a lady, tall indeed, but not too tall, of a fine carriage, in a black rather shabby dress and a black bonnet. Her face was grave and sharply pointed, with dark eyes—sad rather, and of the pale remote colour that the Virgin in the St. Dreot's east end window wears. Standing there in the dusky hall, quietly, quite apart from the little bustle that surrounded her, she seemed to Maggie even in that first moment like some one wrapt, caught away into her own visions.

"I paid the cabman five shillings," she said very softly. "I hope that was right. And you are Maggie, are you?"

She bent down and kissed her. Her lips were warm and comforting. Maggie, who had, when she was shy, something of the off-hand manner of a boy, said:

"Yes. That's all right. We generally give him four and six."

They went into the dining-room where was Mr. Brassy. He came forward to them, blowing his words at them, rubbing his hands:

"Miss Cardinal—I am honoured—my name is Brassy, your brother's lawyer. Very, very sad—so sudden, so sudden. The funeral is at twelve. If there is anything I can do—"

Miss Cardinal did not regard him at all and Maggie saw that this annoyed him. The girl watched her aunt, conscious of some strange new excitement at her heart. She had never seen any one who in the least resembled this remote silent woman. Maggie did not know what it was that she had expected, but certainly it had not been this. There was something in her Aunt's face that recalled her father and her uncle, something in the eyes, something in the width and height of the forehead, but this resemblance only accentuated the astounding difference. Maggie's first impression was her ultimate one—that her aunt had strayed out of some stained-glass window into a wild world that did not bewilder her only because she did not seriously regard it. Maggie found herself wondering who had fastened her aunt's buttons and strings when she rose in the morning, how had she ever travelled in the right train and descended at the right station? How could she remember such trifles when her thoughts were fixed on such distant compelling dreams? The pale oval face, the black hair brushed back from the forehead, the thin hands with long tapering fingers, the black dress, the slender upright body—this figure against the cold bright winter sunlight was a picture that remained always from that day in Maggie's soul.

Her aunt looked about her as though she had just awaked from sleep. "Would you care to come up to your room?" asked Maggie, feeling the embarrassment of Mr. Brassy's presence.

"Yes, dear, thank you—I will," said Miss Cardinal. They moved from the room, Aunt Anne walking with a strange, almost clumsy uncertainty, halting from one foot to the other as though she had never learnt to trust her legs, a movement with which Maggie was to become intensely familiar. It was as though her aunt had flown in some earlier existence, and had never become accustomed to this clumsier earthly fashion.

The spare bedroom was a bright room with a broad high window. The view was magnificent, looking over the hill that dropped below the vicarage out across fields and streams to Cator Hill, to the right into the heart of the St. Dreot Woods, to the left to the green valley through whose reeds and sloping shadows the Lisp gleamed like a burnished wire threading its way to the sea. There was a high-backed old-fashioned chair by the window. Against this Miss Cardinal stood, her thin body reflected, motionless, as though it had been painted in a long glass behind her. She gazed before her.

Maggie saw that she was agitated, passionately moved. The sun catching the hoar-frost on the frozen soil turned the world to crystal, and in every field were little shallows of blue light; the St. Dreot Woods were deep black with flickering golden stars.

She tried to speak. She could not. Tears were in her eyes. "It is so long ... since I ... London," she smiled at Maggie. Then Maggie heard her say:

The Lord is my shepherd; therefore can I lack nothing.

He shall feed me in a green pasture; and lead me forth beside the waters of comfort.

He shall convert my soul, and bring me forth in the paths of righteousness, for His Name's sake.

Yea, though I walk through the valley of the shadow of death, I will fear no evil; for thou art with me, they rod and thy staff comfort me.

Thou shalt prepare a table before me against them that trouble me: thou hast anointed my head with oil, and my cup shall be full.

But thy loving—kindness and mercy shall follow me all the days of my life; and I will dwell in the house of the Lord for ever.

There was a pause—then Maggie said timidly, "Won't you take off your bonnet? It will be more comfortable." "Thank you, my dear." She took off her bonnet and laid it on the bed. Then she resumed her stand at the window, her eyes lost in the sunny distance. "I did wrong," she said, as though she were speaking to herself. "I should not have allowed that quarrel with your father. I regret it now very deeply. But we always see too late the consequences of our proud self-will." She turned then.

"Come here, dear," she said.

Maggie came to her. Her aunt looked at her and Maggie was deeply conscious of her shabby dress, her rough hands, her ugly boots. Then, as always when she was self-critical, her eyes grew haughty and her mouth defiant.

Her aunt kissed her, her cool, firm fingers against the girl's warm neck.

"You will come to us now, dear. You should have come long ago."

Maggie wanted to speak, but she could not.

"We will try to make you happy, but ours is not an exciting life."

Maggie's eyes lit up. "It has not," she said, "been very exciting here always." Then she went on, colour in her cheeks, "I think father did all he could. I feel now that there were a lot of things that I should have done, only I didn't see them at the time. He never asked me to help him, but I wish now that I had offered—or—suggested."

Her lips quivered, again she was near tears, and again, as it had been on her walk with Uncle Mathew, her regret was not for her father but for the waste that her life with him had been. But there was something in her aunt that prevented complete confidence. She seemed in something to be outside small daily troubles. Before they could speak any more there was a knock on the door and Uncle Mathew came in. He stood there looking both ashamed of himself and obstinate.

He most certainly did not appear at his best, a large piece of plaster on his right cheek showing where he had cut himself with his razor, and a shabby and tight black suit (it was his London suit, and had lain crumpled disastrously in his hand-bag) accentuating the undue roundness of his limbs; his eyes blinked and his mouth trembled a little at the corners. He was obviously afraid of his sister and flung his niece a watery wink as though to implore her silence as to his various misdemeanours.

Brother and sister shook hands, and Maggie, as she watched them, was surprised to feel within herself a certain sympathy with her uncle. Aunt Anne's greeting was gentle and kind but infinitely distant, and had something of the tenderness with which the Pope washes the feet of the beggars in Rome.

"I'm so glad that you were here," she said in her soft voice. "It must have been such a comfort to Maggie."

"He has been, indeed, Aunt Anne," Maggie broke in eagerly.

Her uncle looked at her with great surprise; after his behaviour of last night he had not expected this. Reassured, he began a voluble explanation of his movements and plans, rubbing his hands together and turning one boot against the other.

He had a great deal to say, because he had seen neither of his sisters for a very long time. Then he wished to make a good impression because Maggie, the heiress, would be of importance now. What an idiot he had been last night. What had he done? He could remember nothing. It was evident that it had been nothing very bad—Maggie bore him no grudge—good girl, Maggie. He felt affectionate towards her and would have told her so had her aunt not been present. These thoughts underlay his rambling history. He was aware suddenly that his audience was inattentive. He saw, indeed, that his sister was standing with her back half-turned, gazing on to the shining country beyond the window. He ceased abruptly, gave his niece a wink, and when this was unsuccessful, muttering a few words, stumbled out of the room.

The whole village attended the funeral, not because it liked the Rev. Charles, but because it liked funerals. Maggie was, in all probability, the only person present who thought very deeply about the late Vicar of St. Dreot's. The Rev. Tom Trefusis who conducted the ceremony was a large red-faced man who had played Rugby football for his University and spent most of his energy over the development of cricket and football clubs up and down the county. He could not be expected to have cared very greatly for the Rev. Charles, who had been at no period of his life and in no possible sense of the word a sportsman. As he conducted the service his mind speculated as to the next vicar (the Rev. Tom knew an excellent fellow, stroke of the Cambridge boat in '12, who would be just the man) the possibility of the frost breaking in time for the inter-county Rugby match at Truxe, the immediate return of his wife from London (he was very fond of his wife), and, lastly, a certain cramp in the stomach that sometimes "bowled him over" and of which the taking of a funeral—"here to-day and gone to-morrow"—always reminded him.

"Wonder how long I'll last," he thought as he stood over the grave of the Rev. Charles and let his eyes wander over the little white gravestones that ran almost into the dark wall of St. Dreot Woods as though they were trying to hide themselves. "Wish the frost 'ud break—ground'll be as hard as nails." The soil fell, thump, thump upon the coffin. Rooks cawed in the trees; the bell tolled its cracked note. The Rev. Charles was crammed down with the soil by the eager spades of the sexton and his friend, who were cold and wanted a drink.

Maggie, meanwhile, watched the final disappearance of her father with an ever-growing remorse. Ever since her declaration to her uncle during their walk yesterday this new picture of her father had grown before her eyes. She had already forgotten many, many things that might now have made her resentful or at least critical. She saw him as a figure most disastrously misunderstood. Without any sentimentality in her vision she saw him lonely, proud, reserved, longing for her sympathy which she denied him. His greed for money she saw suddenly as a determination that his daughter should not be left in want. All those years he had striven and his apparent harshness, sharpness, unkindness had been that he might pursue his great object.

She did not cry (some of the villagers curiously watching her thought her a hard-hearted little thing), but her heart was full of tenderness as she stood there, seeing the humped grey church that was part of her life, the green mounds with no name, the dark wood, the grey roofs of the village clustered below the hill, hearing the bell, the rooks, the healthy voice of Mr. Trefusis, the bark of some distant dog, the creak of some distant wheel.

"I missed my chance," she thought. "If only now I could have told him!"

Her aunt stood at her side and once again Maggie felt irritation at her composure. "After all, he was her brother," she thought. She remembered the feeling and passion with which her aunt had repeated the Twenty-third Psalm. She was puzzled.

A moment of shrinking came upon her as she thought of the coming London life.

Then the service was over. The villagers, with that inevitable disappointment that always lingers after a funeral, went to their homes. The children remained until night, under the illusion that it was Sunday.

Maggie spent the rest of the day, for the most part, alone in her room and thinking of her father. Her bedroom, an attic with a sloping roof, contained all her worldly possessions. In part because she had always been so reserved a child, in part because there had been no one in whom she might confide even had she wished it, she had always placed an intensity of feeling around and about the few things that were hers. Her library was very small, but this did not distress her because she had never cared for reading. Upon the little hanging shelf above her bed (deal wood painted white, with blue cornflowers) were The Heir of Redclyffe, a shabby blue-covered copy, Ministering Children, Madame How and Lady Why, The Imitation of Christ, Robinson Crusoe, Mrs. Beeton's Cookery Book, The Holy Bible, and The Poems of Longfellow. These had been given her upon various Christmasses and birthdays. She did not care for any of them except The Imitation of Christ and Robinson Crusoe. The Bible was spoilt for her by incessant services and Sunday School classes; The Heir of Redclyffe and Ministering Children she found absurdly sentimental and unlike any life that she had ever known; Mrs. Beeton she had never opened, and Longfellow and Kingsley's Natural History she found dull. For Robinson Crusoe she had the intense human sympathy that all lonely people feel for that masterpiece. The Imitation pleased her by what she would have called its common sense. Such a passage, for example: "Oftentimes something lurketh within, or else occurreth from without, which draweth us after it. Many secretly seek themselves in what they do, and know it not."

"They seem also to live in good peace of mind, when things are done according to their will and opinion; but if things happen otherwise than they desire, they are straightway moved and much vexed."

And behind this common sense she did seem to be directly in touch with some one whom she might find had she more time and friends to advise her. She was conscious in her lonely hours, that nothing gave her such a feeling of company as did this little battered red book, and she felt that that friendliness might one day advance to some greater intimacy. About these things she was intensely reserved and she spoke of them to no human being.

Even for the books for whose contents she did not care she had a kindly feeling. So often had they looked down upon her when she sat there exasperated, angry at her own tears, rebellious, after some scene with her father. No other place but this room had seen these old agonies of hers. She would be sorry after all to leave it.

There were not many things beside the books. Two bowls of blue Glebeshire pottery, cheap things but precious, a box plastered with coloured shells, an amber bead necklace, a blue leather writing-case, a photograph of her father as a young clergyman with a beard and whiskers, a faded daguerreotype of her mother, last, but by no means least, a small black lacquer musical-box that played two tunes, "Weel may the Keel row" and "John Peel,"—these were her worldly possessions.

She sat there; as the day closed down, the trees were swept into the night, the wind rose in the dark wood, the winter's moon crept pale and cold into the sky, snow began to fall, at first thinly, then in a storm, hiding the moon, flinging the fields and roads into a white shining splendour; the wind died and the stars peeped between the flakes of whirling snow.

She sat without moving, accusing her heart of hardness, of unkindness. She seemed to herself then deserving of every punishment. "If I had only gone to him," she thought again and again. She remembered how she had kept apart from him, enclosed herself in a reserve that he should never break. She remembered the times when he had scolded her, coldly, bitterly, and she had stood, her face as a rock, her heart beating but her body without movement, then had turned and gone silently from the room. All her wicked, cold heart that in some strange way cared for love but could not make those movements towards others that would show that it cared. What was it in her? Would she always, through life, miss the things for which she longed through her coldness and obstinacy?

She took her father's photograph, stared at it, gazed into it, held it in an agony of remorse. She shivered in the cold of her room but did not know it. Her candle, caught in some draught, blew out, and instantly the white world without leapt in upon her and her room was lit with a strange unearthly glow. She saw nothing but her father. At last she fell asleep in the chair, clutching in her hand the photograph.

Thus her aunt found her, later in the evening. She was touched by the figure, the shabby black frock, the white tired face. She had been honestly disappointed in her niece, disappointed in her plainness, in her apparent want of heart, in her silence and moroseness. Mathew had told her of the girl's outburst to him against her father, and this had seemed to her shocking upon the very day after that father's death. Now when she saw the photograph clenched in Maggie's hand tears came into her eyes. She said, "Maggie! dear Maggie!" and woke her. Maggie, stirring saw her aunt's slender figure and delicate face standing in the snowlight as though she had been truly a saint from heaven.

Maggie's first impulse was to rise up, fling her arms around her aunt's neck and hug her. Had she done that the history of her life might have been changed. Her natural shyness checked her impulse. She got up, the photograph dropped from her hand, she smiled a little and then said awkwardly, "I've been asleep. Do you want me? I'll come down."

Her aunt drew her towards her.

"Maggie, dear," she said, "don't feel lonely any more. Think of me and your Aunt Elizabeth as your friends who will always care for you. You must never be lonely again."

Maggie's whole heart responded. She felt its wild beating but she could do nothing, could say nothing. Her body stiffened. In spite of herself she withdrew herself. Her face reddened, then, was pale.

"Thank you, aunt," was all she could say.

Her aunt moved away. Silently they went downstairs together.

At about ten the next morning they were seated in the dining-room—Aunt Anne, Uncle Mathew, Maggie, and Mr. Brassy. Mr. Brassy was speaking:

"I'm afraid, Miss Cardinal, that there can be no question about the legality of this. It has been duly witnessed and signed. I regret extremely ... but as you can well understand, I was quite unable to prevent. With the exception of a legacy of 300 Pounds Sterling to Miss Maggie Cardinal everything goes to Miss Ellen Harmer, 'To whom I owe more than I can ever possibly—'"

"Thank you," interrupted Aunt Anne. "This is, I think, the woman who has been cook here during the last four years?"

"About five, I think," said Mr. Brassy softly.

Uncle Mathew was upon his feet, trembling.

"This is monstrous," he stuttered, "absolutely monstrous. Of course an appeal will be made—undue influence—the most abominable thing."

Maggie watched them all as though the whole business were far from herself. She sat there, her hands folded on her lap, looking at the mantelpiece with the ugly marble clock, the letter clip with old soiled letters in it, the fat green vase with dusty everlastings. Just as on the night when her uncle had come into her room she had fancied that some one spoke to her, so now she seemed to hear:

"Ah, that's a nasty knock for you—a very nasty knock."

Her father had left all his money, with the exception of 300, Pounds Sterling to Ellen the cook; Maggie did not, for a moment, speculate as to the probable total amount. Three hundred pounds seemed to her a very large sum—it would at any rate give her something to begin life upon—but the thing that seized and held her was the secret friendship that must have existed between her father and Ellen—secret friendship was the first form that the relationship assumed for her. She saw Ellen, red of face with little eyes and a flat nose upon which flies used to settle, a fat, short neck, the wheezings and the pantings, the stumping walk, the great broad back. And she saw her father—first as the tall, dirty man whom she used to know, with the shiny black trousers, the untidy beard, the frowning eyes, the nails bitten to the quick, the ragged shirt-cuffs—then as that veiled shape below the clothes, the lift of the sheet above the toes, the loins, the stomach, the beard neatly brushed, the closed yellow eyelids, the yellow forehead, the rats with their gleaming eyes. In a kind of terror as though she were being led against her will into some disgusting chamber where the skulls were stale and the sights indecent, she saw the friendship of those two—Ellen the cook and her father.

Young, inexperienced though she was, she was old already in a certain crude knowledge of facts. It could not be said that she traced to their ultimate hiding-place the relations of her father and the woman, but in some relation, ugly, sordid, degraded, she saw those two figures united. Many, many little things came to her mind as she sat there, moments when the cook had breathlessly and in a sudden heat betrayed some unexpected agitation, moments when her father had shown confusion, moments when she had fancied whispers, laughter behind walls, scurrying feet. She entwined desperately her hands together as pictures developed behind her eyes.

Ah! but she was ashamed, most bitterly ashamed!

The rest of the interview came to her only dimly. She knew that Uncle Mathew was still upon his feet protesting, that her aunt's face was cold and wore a look of distressed surprise as though some one had suddenly been rude to her.

From very, very far away came Mr. Brassy's voice: "I was aware that this could not be agreeable, Miss Cardinal. But I am afraid that, under the circumstances, there is nothing to be done. As to undue influence I think that I should warn you, Mr. Cardinal, that there could be very little hope ... and of course the expense ... if I may advise you ..."

The voice sank away again, the room faded, the air was still and painted; like figures on a stage acting before an audience of one Maggie saw those grotesque persons ...

She did not speak one word during the whole affair.

After a time she saw that Mr. Brassy was not in the room. Her aunt was speaking to her:

"Maggie, dear—I'm so very sorry—so very sorry. But you know that you will come to us and find a home there. You mustn't think about the money—"

With a sudden impulse she arose, almost brushing her aunt aside.

"Ah! that's not it—that's not it!" she cried. Then, recovering herself a little, she went on—"It's all right, Aunt Anne. I'm all right. I'm going out for a little. If I'm not back for lunch, don't wait. Something cold, anything, tell Ellen—"

At the sudden mention of that name she stopped, coloured a little, turned away and left the room. In the hall she nearly ran against the cook. The woman was standing there, motionless, breathing deeply, her eyes fixed upon the dining-room. When she saw Maggie, she moved as though she would speak, then something in the girl's face checked her. She drew back into the shadow.

Maggie left the house.

The brother and sister, remaining in the room, walked towards one another as though driven by some common need of sympathy and protection against an outside power. Mathew Cardinal felt a genuine indignation that had but seldom figured in his life before. He had hated his brother, always, and never so greatly as at the moments of the man's reluctant charity towards him. But now, in the first clean uplift of his indignation, there was no self-congratulation at the justification of his prophecies.

"I knew him for what he was. But that he could do this! He meant it to hurt, too—that was like him all over. He had us in his mind. I wish I'd never taken a penny from him. I'd rather have starved. Yes, I would—far rather. I've been bad enough, but never a thing like that—"

His sister said quietly:

"He's dead, Mathew. We can do nothing. Maggie, poor child ..."

He approached for an instant more nearly than he had ever done. He took her hand. There were tears in his eyes.

"It's good of you, Anne—to take her."

She withdrew her hand—very gently.

"I wish we'd taken her before. She must have had a terrible time here. I'd never realised ..."

He stood away from her near the window, feeling suddenly ashamed of his impetuosity.

"She's a strange girl," Anne Cardinal went on. "She didn't seem to feel this,—or anything. She hasn't, I think, much heart. I'm afraid she may find it a little difficult with us—"

Mathew was uncomfortable now. His mood had changed; he was sullen. His sister always made him feel like a disgraced dog. He shuffled on his feet.

"She's a good girl," he muttered at last, and then with a confused look about him, as though he were searching for something, he stumbled out of the room.

Meanwhile Maggie went on her way. She chose instinctively her path, through the kitchen garden at the back of the village, down the hill by the village street, over the little bridge that crossed the rocky stream of the Dreot, and up the steep hill that led on to the outskirts of Rothin Moor. The day, although she had no eyes for it, was one of those sudden impulses of misty warmth that surprise the Glebeshire frosts. The long stretch of the moor was enwrapped by a thin silver network of haze; the warmth of the sun, seen so dimly that it was like a shadow reflected in a mirror, struck to the very heart of the soil. Where but yesterday there had been iron frost there was now soft yielding earth; it was as though the heat of the central fires of the world pressed dimly upward through many miles of heavy weighted resistance, straining to the light and air. Larks, lost in golden mist, circled in space; Maggie could feel upon her face and neck and hands the warm moisture; the soil under her feet, now hard, now soft, seemed to tremble with some happy anticipation; the moor, wrapped in its misty colour, had no bounds; the world was limitless space with hidden streams, hidden suns.

The moor had a pathetic attraction for her, because not very long ago a man and a woman had been lost, only a few steps from Borhedden Farm, in the mist—lost their way and been frozen during the night. Poor things! lovers, perhaps, they had been.

Maggie felt that here she could walk for miles and miles and that there was nothing to stop her; the clang of a gate, a house, a wall, a human voice was intolerable to her.

Her first thought as she went forward was disgust at her own weakness; once again she had been betrayed by her feelings. She could remember no single time when they had not betrayed her. She recalled now with an intolerable self-contempt her thoughts of her father at the time of the funeral and the hours that followed. It seemed to her now that she had only softened towards his memory because she had believed that he had left her money—and now, when she saw that he had treated her contemptuously, she found him once again the cruel, mean figure that she had before thought him.

For that she most bitterly, with an intensity that only her loneliness could have given her, despised herself. And yet something else in her knew that that reproach was not a true one. She had really softened towards him only because she had felt that she had behaved badly towards him, and the discovery now that he had behaved badly towards her did not alter her own original behaviour. She did not analyse all this; she only knew that there were in her longings for affection, a desire to be loved, an aching for companionship, and that these things must always be kept down, fast hidden within her. She realised her loneliness now with a fierce, proud, almost exultant independence. No more tears, no more leaning upon others, no more expecting anything from anybody. She was not dramatic in her new independence; she did not cry defiance to the golden mist or the larks or the hidden sun; she only walked on and on, stumping forward in her clumsy boots, her eyes hard and unseeing, her hands clasped behind her back.

Her expectation of happiness in her opening life that had been so strong with her that other day when she had looked down upon Polchester was gone. She expected nothing, she wanted nothing. Her only thought was that she would never yield to any one, never care for any one, never give to any one the opportunity of touching her. At moments through the mist came the figure of the cook, stout, florid, triumphant. Maggie regarded her contemptuously. "You cannot touch me," she thought. Of her father she would never think again. With both hands she flung all her memories of him into the mist to be lost for ever ...

She came suddenly upon a lonely farm-house. She knew the place, Borhedden; it had often been a favourite walk of hers from the Vicarage to Borhedden. The farmer let rooms there and, because the house was very old, some of the rooms were fine, with high ceilings, thick stone walls, and even some good panelling. The view too was superb, across to the Broads and the Molecatcher, or back to the Dreot Woods, or to the dim towers of Polchester Cathedral. The air here was fine—one of the healthiest spots in Glebeshire.

The farm to-day was transfigured by the misty glow; cows and horses could be faintly seen, ricks burnt with a dim fire. Somewhere dripping water falling on to stone gave a vocal spirit to the obscurity. The warm air seemed to radiate about the house like a flame that is obscured by sunlight.

The stealthy movements of the animals, the dripping of the water, were the only sounds. To Maggie the house seemed to say something, something comforting and reassuring.

Standing there, she registered her vow that through all her life she would care for no one. No one should touch her.

Had there been an observer he might have found some food for his irony in the contemplation of that small, insignificant figure so ignorant of life and so defiant of it. He would have found perhaps something pathetic also. Maggie thought neither of irony nor of pathos, but turned homewards with her mouth set, her eyes grave, her heart controlled.

As she walked back the sun broke through the mist, and, turning, she could see Borhedden like a house on fire, its windows blazing against the sky.

It was natural that her aunt should wish to return to London as soon as possible. For one thing, Ellen the cook had packed her clothes and retired to some place in the village, there to await the departure of the defeated family. Then the house was not only unpleasant by reason of its atmosphere and associations, but there were also the definite discomforts of roofs through which the rain dripped and floors that swayed beneath one's tread. Moreover, Aunt Elizabeth did not care to be left alone in the London house.

Uncle Mathew left on the day after the funeral. He had one little last conversation with Maggie.

"I hope you'll be happy in London," he said.

"I hope so," said Maggie.

"I know you'll do what you can to help your aunts." Then he went on more nervously. "Think of me sometimes. I shan't be able to come and see you very often, you know—too busy. But I shall like to know that you're thinking about me."

Maggie's new-found resolution taken so defiantly upon the moor was suddenly severely tested. She felt as though her uncle were leaving her to a world of enemies. She drove down her sense of desolation, and he saw nothing but her quiet composure.

"Of course I'll think of you," she answered. "And you must come often."

"They don't like me," he said, nodding his head towards where Aunt Anne might be supposed to be waiting. "It's not my fault altogether—but they have severe ideas. It's religion, of course."

She suddenly seemed to see in his eyes some terror or despair, as though he knew that he was going to drop "this time"—farther than ever before.

She caught his arm. "Uncle Mathew, what are you going to do? Where will you live? Take my three hundred pounds if it will help you. I don't want it just now. Keep it for me."

He had a moment of resolute, clear-sighted honesty. "No, my dear, if I had it it would go in a week. I can't keep money; I never could. I'm really better without any. I'm all right. You'll never get rid of me— don't you fear. We've got more in common than you think, although you're a good girl and I've gone to pieces a bit. All the same there's plenty worse than me. Your aunt, for all her religion, is damned difficult for a plain man to get along with. Most people would find me better company, after all. One last word, Maggie."

He bent down and whispered to her. "Don't you go getting caught by that sweep who runs their chapel up in London. He's a humbug if ever there was one—you mark my words. I know a thing or two. He's done your aunts a lot of harm, and he'll have his dirty fingers on you if you let him."

So he departed, his last kiss mingled with the usual aroma of whisky and tobacco, his last attitude, as he turned away, that strange confusion of assumed dignity and natural genial stupidity that was so especially his.

Maggie turned, with all her new defiant resolution, to face the world alone with her Aunt Anne. Throughout the next day she was busied with collecting her few possessions, with her farewells to the one or two people in the village who had been kind to her, and with little sudden, almost surreptitious visits to corners of the house, the garden, the wood where she had at one time or another been happy.

As the evening fell and a sudden storm of rain leapt up from beneath the hill and danced about the house, she had a wild longing to stay—to stay at any cost and in any discomfort. London had no longer interest, but only terror and dismay. She ran out into the dark and rain-drenched garden, felt her way to an old and battered seat that had seen in older days dolls' tea-parties and the ravages of bad-temper, stared from it across the kitchen-garden to the lights of the village, that seemed to rock and shiver in the wind and rain.

She stared passionately at the lights, her heart beating as though it would suffocate her. At last, her clothes soaked with the storm, her hair dripping, she returned to the house. Her aunt was in the hall.

"My dear Maggie, where have you been?" in a voice that was kind but aghast.

"In the garden," said Maggie, hating her aunt.

"But it's pouring with rain! You're soaking! You must change at once! Did you go out to find something?"

Maggie made no answer. She stood there, her face sulky and closed, the water dripping from her. Afterwards, as she changed her clothes, she reflected that there had been many occasions during these three days when her aunt would have felt irritation with her had she known her longer. She had always realised that she was careless, that when she should be thinking of one thing she thought of another, that her housekeeping and management of shops and servants had been irregular and undisciplined, but until now she had not sharply surveyed her weaknesses. Since the coming of her aunt she had been involved in a perfect network of little blunders; she had gone out of the room without shutting the door, had started into the village on an errand, and then, when she was there, had forgotten what it was; there had been holes in her stockings and rents in her blouses. After Ellen's departure she had endeavoured to help in the kitchen, but had made so many mistakes that Aunt Anne and the kitchen-maid had been compelled to banish her. She now wondered how during so many years she had run the house at all, but then her father had cared about nothing so that money was not wasted. She knew that Aunt Anne excused her mistakes just now because of the shock of her father's death and the events that followed it, but Maggie knew also that these faults were deep in her character. She could explain it quite simply to herself by saying that behind the things that she saw there was always something that she did not see, something of the greatest importance and just beyond her vision; in her efforts to catch this farther thing she forgot what was immediately in front of her. It had always been so. Since a tiny child she had always supposed that the shapes and forms with which she was presented were only masks to hide the real thing. Such a view might lend interest to life, but it certainly made one careless; and although Uncle Mathew might understand it and put it down to the Cardinal imagination, she instinctively knew that Aunt Anne, unless Maggie definitely attributed it to religion, would be dismayed and even, if it persisted, angered. Maggie had not, after all, the excuse and defence of being a dreamy child. With her square body and plain face, her clear, unspeculative eyes, her stolid movements, she could have no claim to dreams. With a sudden desolate pang Maggie suspected that Uncle Mathew was the only person who would ever understand her. Well, then, she must train herself.

She would close doors, turn out lights, put things back where she found them, mend her clothes, keep accounts. Indeed a new life was beginning for her. She felt, with a sudden return to the days before her walk on the moor, that if only her aunts would love her she would improve much more rapidly. And then with her new independence she assured herself that if they did not love her she most certainly would not love them ...

That night she sat opposite her aunt beside the fire. The house lay dead and empty behind them. Aunt Anne was so neat in her thin black silk, her black shining hair, her pale pointed face, a little round white locket rising and falling ever so slowly with the lift of her breast. There were white frills to her sleeves, and she read a slim book bound in purple leather. Her body never moved; only once and again her thin, delicate hand ever so gently lifted, turned a page, then settled down on to her lap once more. She never raised her eyes.

The fire was heavy and sullen; the wind howled; that old familiar beating of the twigs upon the pane seemed to reiterate to Maggie that this was her last evening. She pretended to read. She had found a heavy gilt volume of Paradise Lost with Dore's pictures. She read these words:

Beyond this flood a frozen Continent Lies dark and wilde, beat with perpetual storms Of whirlwind and dire hail; which on firm land Thaws not, but gathers heap, and ruin seems Of ancient pile; all else deep snow and ice, A gulf profound as that Serbonian bay Betwixt Damiata and Mount Casius old, Where armies whole have sunk; the parching Air Burns froze, and cold performs the effect of Fire.

Further again, words caught her eye.

Thus roving on In confused march forlorn, th' adventurous Bands With shuddering horror pale, and eyes aghast Viewed first their lamentable lot, and found No rest; through many a dark and drearie Vaile They passed, and many a Region dolorous. O'er many a frozen, many a fiery Alpe, Rocks, Caves, Lakes, Fens, Bogs, Dens and shades of death, A Universe of death, which God by curse Created evil, for evil only good Where all life dies, death lives, and nature breaks Perverse, all monstrous, all prodigious things, Abominable, inutterable, and worse Than Fables yet have feigned, or fear conceived, Gorgons, and Hydras, and Chimaeras dire.

She did not care for reading, most especially she did not care for poetry, but to-night she saw the picture. Up to the very bounds of the house this waste country, filled with beasts of prey, animals with fiery eyes and incredible names, the long stretch of snow and ice, the black water with no stars reflected in it, the wind.

A coal crashed in the fire; she gave a little cry.

"My dear, what is it?" said Aunt Anne. Then, with a little shake of her shoulders, she added: "There's a horrid draught. Perhaps you forgot to close the kitchen-door when you came away, Maggie dear."

Maggie flushed. Of course she had forgotten. She left the room, crossed the hall. Yes, there was the door, wide open. She locked it, the place was utterly cold and desolate. She closed the door, stood for a moment in the little hall.

"I don't care what's going to happen!" she cried aloud. So ended her life in that house.

CHAPTER III

THE LONDON HOUSE

It was strange after this that the start on the London journey should be so curiously unexciting; it was perhaps the presence of Aunt Anne that reduced everything to an unemotional level. Maggie wondered as she sat in the old moth-eaten, whisky-smelling cab whether her Aunt Anne was ever moved about anything. Then something occurred that showed her that, as yet, she knew very little about her aunt. As, clamping down the stony hill, they had a last glimpse at the corner of the two Vicarage chimneys, looking above the high hedge like a pair of inquisitive lunatics, Maggie choked. She pressed her hands together, pushed her hair from her face and, in so doing, touched her black hat.

"Your hat's crooked, Maggie dear," said her aunt gently. The girl's hot hands clutched the soft packet of sandwiches and a little black handbag that yesterday Aunt Anne had bought for her in the village. It was a shabby little bag, and had strange habits of opening when it was not expected to do so and remaining shut when something was needed from it. It gaped now and, just as the cab climbed Cator Hill, it fell forward and flung the contents on to the floor. Maggie, blushing, looked up expecting a reproof. She saw that her aunt's eyes were fixed upon the view; as upon the day of her arrival, so now. Her face wore a look of rapture. She drank it in.

Maggie also took the last joy of the familiar scene. The Vicarage, like a grey crouching cat, lay basking on the green hill. The sunlight flooded the dark wood; galleons of clouds rolled like lumbering vessels across the blue sky.

"It's lovely, isn't it?" whispered Maggie.

"Beautiful—beautiful," sighed her aunt.

"I've always loved just this view. I've often walked here just to see it," Maggie said.

Aunt Anne sat back in her seat.

"It's been hard for me always to live in London. I love the country so."

"So do I," said Maggie, passionately.

For a moment they were together, caught up by the same happiness.

Then Aunt Anne said:

"Why, your bag, dear! The things are all about the place."

Maggie bent down. When she looked up again they had dipped down on the other side of the hill.

Maggie had only once in all her life been in a train, but on this present occasion she did not find it very thrilling. It was rather like being in anything else, and her imagination exercised itself upon the people in the carriage rather than the scenery outside. She was at first extremely self-conscious and fancied that every one whispered about her. Then, lulled by the motion of the train and the warmth, she slept; she was more deeply exhausted by the events of the last week than she knew, and throughout the day she slumbered, woke, and slumbered again.

Quite suddenly she awoke with a definite shock to a new world. Evening had come; there were lights that rushed up to the train, stared in at the window, and rushed away again. On every side things seemed to change places in a general post, trees and houses, hedges and roads, all lit by an evening moon and wrapt in a white and wavering mist. Then the town was upon them, quite instantly; streets ran like ribbons into grey folds of buildings; rows of lamps, scattered at first, drew into a single point of dancing flame; towers and chimneys seemed to jump from place to place as though they were trying to keep in time with the train; a bell rang monotonously; wreaths of smoke rose lazily against the stars and fell again.

When at last she found herself, a tiny figure, standing upon the vast platform under the high black dome, the noise and confusion excited and delighted her. She rose to the waves of sound as a swimmer rises in the sea, her heart beat fast, and she was so eagerly engaged in looking about her, in staring at the hurrying people, in locating the shrill screams of the engines, in determining not to jump when the carriages jolted together, that her little black bag opened unexpectedly once more and spilled a handkerchief, a hand-mirror, a paper packet of sweets, a small pair of scissors, and a shabby brown purse upon the station-floor. She was greatly confused when an old gentleman helped her to pick them up. The little mirror was broken.

"Oh! it's bad luck!" she cried, staring distressfully at the old man. He smiled, and would have certainly been very agreeable to her had not Aunt Anne, who had been finding their boxes and securing a cab, arrived and taken Maggie away. "You shouldn't speak to strange gentlemen, dear," said Aunt Anne.

But Maggie did not listen. It was characteristic of Anne Cardinal that she should secure the only four-wheeler in the station, rejecting the taxi-cabs that waited in rows for her pleasure. Had Maggie only known, her aunt's choice was eloquent of their future life together. But Maggie did not know and did not care. Her excitement was intense. That old St. Dreot life had already swung so far behind her that it was like a fantastic dream; as they rumbled through the streets, the cries, the smells, the lights seemed arranged especially for her. She could not believe that they had all been, just like this, before her arrival. As with everything, she was busy imagining the World behind this display, the invisible Circle inside the circle that she saw.

They came into the Strand, and the masses of moving people seemed to her like somnambulists walking without reason or purpose. She felt as though there would suddenly come a great hole in the middle of the street into which the cab would tumble. The noise seemed to her country ears deafening, and when, suddenly, the lighted letters of some advertisement flashed out gigantic against the sky, she gave a little scream. She puzzled her aunt by saying:

"But it isn't really like this, is it?"

To which Aunt Anne could only say:

"You're hungry and tired, dear, I expect."

With one last outrending scream the whole world seemed to fling itself at the window, open because Aunt Anne thought the cab "had a smell." "Oosh—O O S H." "OOSH." ... Maggie drew back as though she expected some one to leap in upon them. Then, with that marvellous and ironical gift of contrast that is London's secret, they were suddenly driven into the sleepiest quiet; they stumbled up a street that was like a cave for misty darkness and muffled echoes. The cab's wheels made a riotous clatter.

A man posting a letter in a pillar-box was the only figure in the street. The stars shone overhead with wonderful brilliance, and a little bell jangled softly close at hand. All the houses were tall and secret, with high white steps and flat faces. A cat slipped across the street; another swiftly followed it.

St. Dreot's seemed near at hand again and Ellen the cook not so far away. Maggie felt a sudden forlornness and desolation.

"What a very quiet street!" she whispered, as though she were afraid lest the street should hear.

They stopped before one of the flat-faced houses; Aunt Anne rang the bell, and an old woman with a face like a lemon helped the cabman with the boxes. Maggie was standing in a hall that smelt of damp and geraniums. It was intensely dark, and a shrill scream from somewhere did not make things more pleasant.

"That's Edward the parrot," said Aunt Anne. "Take care not to approach him too closely, dear, because he bites."

Then they went upstairs, Maggie groping her way and stumbling at the sharp corners. The darkness grew; she knocked her knee on the corner of something, cried out, and a suddenly opened door threw a pale green light upon a big picture of men in armour attacking a fortified town beneath a thundery sky. This picture wavered and faltered, hung as it was upon a thin cord strained to breaking-point. Maggie reached the security of the room beyond the passage, her shoulders bent a little as though she expected to near at every instant the crashing collapse of the armoured men. Her eyes unused to the light, she stumbled into the room, fell into some one's arms, felt that her poor hat was crooked and her cheeks burning, and then was rebuked, as it seemed, by the piercing cry of Edward the parrot from the very bowels of the house.

She stammered something to the man who had held her and then let her go. She was confused, hot and angry. "They'll think me an idiot who can't enter a room properly." She glared about her and felt as though she had been taken prisoner by some strange people who lived under the sea. She was aware, when her eyes were accustomed to the dim light, that the entrance of herself and her aunt had interrupted the conversation of three people. Near the fireplace sat a little woman wearing black mittens and a white lace cap; standing above her with his arm on the mantelpiece was a thin, battered-looking gentleman with large spectacles, high, gaunt features and a very thin head of hair; near the door was the man against whom Maggie had collided. She saw that he was young, thick-set and restless. She noticed even then his eyes, bright and laughing as though he were immensely amused. His mouth opened and closed again, his eyes were never still, and he made fierce dumb protests with his body, jerking it forward pulling it back, as a rider strives to restrain an unruly horse. Maggie was able to notice these things, because during the first moments her Aunt Anne entirely held the stage. She advanced to the fireplace with her halting movement, embraced the little lady by the fire with a soft and unimpassioned clasp.

"Well, Elizabeth, here we are, you see," turned to the thin gentleman saying, "Why you, Mr. Magnus! I thought that you were still in Wiltshire!" then from the middle of the room addressing the stout young man: "I'm very glad to see you, Mr. Warlock."

Maggie fancied that the three persons were nervous of her aunt; the stout young man was amused perhaps at the general situation, but Mr. Magnus by the fireplace showed great emotion, the colour mounting into his high bony cheeks and his nostrils twitching like a horse's. Maggie had been always very observant, and she was detached enough now to notice that the drawing-room was filled with ugly and cumbrous things and yet seemed unfurnished. Although everything was old and had been there obviously for years, the place yet reminded one of a bare chamber into which, furniture had just been piled without order or arrangement. Opposite the door was a large and very bad painting of the two sisters as young girls, sitting, with arms encircled, in low dresses, on the seashore before a grey and angry sea, and Uncle Mathew as a small, shiny-faced boy in tight short blue trousers, carrying a bucket and spade, and a smug, pious expression. The room was lit with gas that sizzled and hissed in a protesting undertone; there was a big black cat near the fire, and this watched Maggie with green and fiery eyes.

She stood there by the door tired and hungry; she felt unacknowledged and forgotten.

"I know I shall hate it," was her thought; she was conscious of her arms and her legs; her ankle tickled in her shoe, and she longed to scratch it. She sneezed suddenly, and they all jumped as though the floor had opened beneath them.

"And Maggie?" said the little lady by the fireplace.

Maggie moved forward with the awkward gestures and the angry look in her eyes that were always hers when she was ill at ease.

"Maggie," said Aunt Anne, "has been very good."

"And she's tired, I'm sure," continued the little lady, who must of course be Aunt Elizabeth. "The journey was easy, dear. And you had no change. They gave you footwarmers, I hope. It's been lovely weather. I'm so glad to see you, dear. I've had no photograph of you since you were a baby."

Aunt Elizabeth had a way, Maggie thought, of collecting a number of little disconnected statements as though she were working out a sum and hoped—but was not very certain—that she would achieve a successful answer. "Add two and five and three and four ..." The statements that she made were apparently worlds apart in interest and importance, but she hoped with good fortune to flash upon the boards a fine result. She was nervous, Maggie saw, and her thin shoulders were a little bent as though she expected some one from behind to strike her suddenly in the small of the back.

"She's afraid of something," thought Maggie.

Aunt Elizabeth had obviously not the strong character of her sister Anne.

"Thank you," said Maggie, looking, for no reason at all, at Mr. Magnus, "I slept in the train, so I'm not tired." She stopped then, because there was nothing more to say. She felt that she ought to kiss her aunt; she thought she saw in her aunt's small rather watery eyes an appeal that she should do so. The distance, however, seemed infinite, and Maggie had a strange feeling that her bending down would break some spell, that the picture in the passage would fall with a ghostly clatter, that Edward the parrot would scream and shriek, that the gas would burst into a bubbling horror, that the big black cat would leap upon her and tear her with its claws.

"Well, I'm not afraid," she thought. And, as though she were defying the universe, she bent down and kissed her aunt. She fancied that this act of hers produced a little sigh of relief. Every one seemed to settle down. They all sat, and conversation was general.

Mr. Magnus had a rather melancholy, deprecating voice, but with some touch of irony too, as though he were used to being called a fool by his fellow-beings, but after all knew better than they did. He did not sound at all conceited; only amused with a little gentle melancholy at his own position.

"I'm glad to see you so well, Miss Cardinal," he said with an air of rather old-fashioned courtesy. "I had been afraid that it might have exhausted you. I only came to welcome you. I must return at once. I have an article to finish before midnight."

Aunt Anne smiled gently: "No, I'm not tired, thank you. And what has happened while I have been away?"

"I have been away too, as you know," said Mr. Magnus, "but I understand that your sister has been very busy—quite a number—"

Aunt Elizabeth said in her trembling voice: "No. No—Anne—I assure you. Nothing at all. As you know, the Bible Committee wanted to discuss the new scheme. Last Tuesday. Mr. Warlock, Mr. Simms, young Holliday, Miss Martin, Mary Hearst. And Sophie Dunn. AND Mr. Turner. Nothing at all. It was a wet day. Last Tuesday afternoon."

"Your mother is quite well, I hope, Mr. Warlock?" said Aunt Anne, turning to the young man. "Yes—she's all right," he answered. "Just the same. Amy wants you to go and see her. I was to give you the message, if you could manage to-morrow sometime; or she'd come here if it's more convenient. There's something important, she says, but I don't suppose it's important in the least. You know what she is."

He spoke, laughing. His eyes wandered all round the room and suddenly settled on Maggie with a startled stare, as though she were the last person whom he had expected to find there.

"Yes. To-morrow afternoon, perhaps—about three, if that would suit her. How is Amy?"

"Oh, she's all right. As eager to run the world as ever—and she never will run it so long as she shows her cards as obviously as she does. I tell her so. But it's no good. She doesn't listen to me, you know."

Aunt Anne, with the incomparable way that she had, brushed all this very gently aside. She simply said: "I'm glad that she's well." Then she turned to the other gentleman:

"Your writing's quite satisfactory, I hope, Mr. Magnus."

She spoke as though it had been a cold or a toothache.

He smiled his melancholy ironical smile. "I go on, you know, Miss Cardinal. After all, it's my bread and butter."

Maggie, looking at him, knew that this was exactly the way that he did not regard it, and felt a sudden sympathy towards him with his thin hair, his large spectacles and his shabby clothes. But her look at him was the last thing of which she was properly conscious. The wall beyond the fireplace, that had seemed before to her dim and dark, now suddenly appeared to lurch forward, to bulge before her eyes; the floor with its old, rather shabby carpet rose on a slant as though it was rocked by an unsteady sea; worst of all, the large black cat swelled like a balloon, its whiskers distended like wire. She knew that her eyes were burning, that her forehead was cold, and that she felt sick. She was hungry, and at the same time was conscious that she could eat nothing. Her only wish was to creep away and hide herself from every one.

However, through all her confusion she was aware of her determination not to betray to them that she was ill. "If only the cat wouldn't grow so fast, I believe I could manage," was her desperate thought. There was a roaring in her ears; she caught suddenly from an infinite distance the voice of the stout young man—"She's ill! She's fainting!"

She was aware that she struggled to face him with fierce protesting eyes. The next thing she knew was that she lay for the second time that afternoon in his arms. She felt that he laid her, clumsily but gently, upon the sofa; some one sprinkled cold water on her forehead. Deep down in her soul she hated and despised herself for this weakness before strangers. She closed her eyes tightly, desiring to conceal not so much the others as herself from her scornful gaze. She heard some one say something about a cup of tea, and she wanted it suddenly with a desperate, fiery desire, but she would not speak, no, not if they were to torture her with thirst for days and days—to that extent at least she could preserve her independence.

She heard her Aunt Elizabeth say something like: "Poor thing—strain—last week—father—too much."

She gathered all her energies together to say "It hasn't been too much. I'm all right," but they brought her a cup of tea, and before that she succumbed. She drank it with eager greed, then lay back, her eyes closed, and slowly the bars of hot iron withdrew from her forehead. She slept.

She woke to a room wrapped in a green trembling twilight. She was alone save for the black cat. The fire crackled, the gas was turned low, and the London murmur beyond the window was like the hum of an organ. There was no one in the room; she felt, as she lay there, an increasing irritation at her weakness. She was afraid too for her future. Did she faint like this at the earliest opportunity people would allow her no chance of earning her living. Where was that fine independent life upon which, outside Borhedden Farm, she had resolved? And these people, her aunts, the young man, the thin spectacled man, what would they think of her? They would name it affectation, perhaps, and imagine that she had acted in such a way that she might gain their interest and sympathy. Such a thought sent the colour flaming to her cheeks; she sat up on the sofa. She would go to them at once and show them that she was perfectly strong and well.

The door opened and Aunt Elizabeth came in, very gently as though she were going to steal something. She was, Maggie saw now, so little as to be almost deformed, with a soft pale face, lined and wrinkled, and blue watery eyes. She wore a black silk wrapper over her shoulders, and soft black slippers. Alice in Wonderland was one of the few books that Maggie had read in her childhood; Aunt Elizabeth reminded her strongly of the White Queen in the second part of that masterpiece.

"Oh, you're not asleep, dear," said Aunt Elizabeth.

"No, I'm not," said Maggie. "I'm perfectly all right. I can't think what made me behave like that. I've never done such a thing before. I'm ashamed!"

"It was very natural," said Aunt Elizabeth. "You should have had some tea at once. It was my fault. It's late now. Nine o'clock. My sister suggests bed. Supper in bed. Very nice, I always think, after a long journey. It will be fine to-morrow, I expect. We've had beautiful weather until this morning, when it rained for an hour. Chicken and some pudding. There's a little Australian wine that my sister keeps in the house for accidents. I liked it myself when I had it once for severe neuralgia."

She suddenly, with a half-nervous, half-desperate gesture, put out her hand and took Maggie's. Her hand was soft like blanc-mange; it had apparently no bones in it.

Maggie was touched and grateful. She liked this little shy, frightened woman. She would do anything to please her.

"Don't think," she said eagerly, "that I've ever fainted like that before. I assure you that I've never done anything so silly. You mustn't think that I'm not strong. I'm strong as a horse—father always said so. I've come to help you and Aunt Anne in any way I can. You mustn't think that I'm going to be in the way. I only want to be useful."

Aunt Elizabeth started and looked at the door. "I thought I heard something," she said. They both listened.

"Perhaps it was the parrot," said Maggie.

Aunt Elizabeth smiled bravely.

"There are often noises in an old house like this," she said. The black cat came towards them, slowly, with immense dignified indifference. He swung his tail as though to show them that he cared for no one. He walked to the door and waited; then followed them out of the room.

Maggie found that her bedroom was a room at the top of the house, very white and clean, with a smell of soot and tallow candle that was new and attractive. There was a large text in bright purple over the bed—"The Lord cometh; prepare ye the way of the Lord." From the window one saw roofs, towers, chimneys, a sweeping arc of sky-lights now spun and sparkled into pathways and out again, driven by the rumble behind them that never ceased, although muffled by the closed window.

They talked together for a little while, standing near the window, the candle wavering in Aunt Elizabeth's unsteady hand.

"We thought you'd like this top room. It's quieter than the rest of the house. Sometimes when the sweep hasn't been the soot tumbles down the chimney. You mustn't mind that. Thomas will push open the door and walk in at times. It's his way."

"Thomas?" said Maggie bewildered.

"Our cat. He has been with us for many years now. Those who know say that he might have taken prizes once. I can't tell I'm sure. If you pull that bell when you want anything Martha will come. She will call you at half-past seven; prayers are in the dining-room at a quarter past eight. Sometimes the wind blows through the wall-paper, but it is only the wind."

Maggie drew back the curtains that hid the glitter of the lights.

"Were those great friends of yours, those gentlemen this evening?"

"The one who wears spectacles, Mr. Magnus—yes, he is a very old friend. He is devoted to my sister. He writes stories."

"What, in the papers?"

"No, in books. Two every year."

"And the other one?"

"That is young Mr. Warlock—he is the son of our minister."

"Does he live near here?"

"He lives just now with his parents. Of late years he has been abroad."

"He doesn't look like the son of a minister," said Maggie.

"No, I'm afraid—" Aunt Elizabeth suddenly stopped. "His father has been minister of our chapel for twenty years. He is a great and wonderful man."

"Where is the chapel?"

"Very near at hand. You will see it to-morrow. To-morrow is Sunday."

There was a long pause. Maggie knew that now was the time when she should say something friendly and affectionate. She could say nothing. She stared at her aunt, then at a long mirror that faced her bed, then at the lighted sky. She felt warmly grateful, eager to show all the world that she would do her best, that she was ready to give herself to this new life with all her soul and strength—she could say nothing.

They waited.

At last her aunt said:

"Good-night, dear Maggie."

"Good-night, Aunt Elizabeth."

She stole away, leaving the candle upon the chest of drawers; the cat followed her, swinging his tail.

Left alone, Maggie felt the whole sweep of her excitement. She was exhausted, her body felt as though it had been trampled upon, she was so tired that she could scarcely drag her clothes from her, but the exaltation of her spirit was beyond and above all this. Half undressed she stood before the long mirror. She had never before possessed a long looking-glass, and now she seemed to see herself as she really was for the first time. Was she very ugly and unattractive? Yes, she must be with that stumpy body, those thick legs and arms, that short nose and large mouth. And she did not know what to do to herself to make herself attractive. Other girls knew but she had never had any one who could tell her. Perhaps she would make girl friends now who would show her.

But, after all, she did not care. She was herself. People who did not like her could leave her—yes they could, and she would not stir a finger to fetch them back.

Then, deep down in her soul, she knew that she wanted success, a magnificent life, a great future. Nay more, she expected it. She had force and strength, and she would compel life to give her what she wanted. She laughed at herself in the glass. She was happy, almost triumphant, and for no reason at all.

She went to her windows and opened them; there came up to her the tramping progress of the motor-omnibuses. They advanced, like elephants charging down a jungle, nearer, nearer, nearer. Before the tramp of one had passed another was advancing, and then upon that another—ceaselessly, advancing and retreating.

In her nightdress she leaned out of the window, poised, as it seemed to her, above a swaying carpet of lights.

Life seemed to hold every promise in store for her.

She crossed to her bed, drew the clothes about her and, forgetting her supper, forgetting all that had happened to her, her journey, her fainting, the young man, Edward the parrot, she fell into a slumber as deep, as secure, as death itself.

CHAPTER IV

THE CHAPEL

Maggie woke next morning to a strange silence. Many were the silent mornings that had greeted her at St. Dreots, but this was silence with a difference; it was the silence, she was instantly aware, of some one whose very soul was noise and tumult. She listened, and the sudden chirping of some sparrows beyond her window only accentuated the sense of expectation. She had never, in all her days, been so conscious of Sunday.

She was almost afraid to move lest she should break the spell.

She lay in bed and thought of the preceding evening. Her fainting fit seemed to her now more than ever unfortunate; it had placed her at a disadvantage with them all. She could imagine the stout young man returning to his home and saying: "Their niece has arrived. Seems a weak little thing. Fainted right off there in the drawing-room." Or her aunts saying anxiously to one another: "Well, I didn't know she was as delicate as that. I hope she won't be always ill," ... and she wasn't delicate—no one stronger. She had never fainted before. The silliness of it!

The next thing that disturbed her was the comfort and arrangement of everything. Certainly the drawing-room had not been very orderly, full of old things badly placed, but this bedroom was clean and tidy, and the supper last night, so neat on its tray with everything that she could want! She could feel the order and discipline of the whole house. And she had never, in all her life, been either orderly or disciplined. She had never been brought up to be so. How could you be orderly when there were holes in the bedroom ceiling and the kitchen floor, holes that your father would never trouble to have mended?

Her aunts would wish her to help in the house and she would forget things. There passed before her, in that Sunday quiet, a terrible procession of the things that she would forget. She knew that she would not be patient under correction, especially under the correction of her Aunt Anne. Already she felt in her a rebellion at her aunt's aloofness and passivity. After all, why should she treat every one as though she were God? Maggie felt that there was in her aunt's attitude something sentimental and affected. She hated sentiment and affectation in any one. She was afraid, too, that Anne bullied Aunt Elizabeth. Maggie was sorry for Aunt Elizabeth but, with all the arrogance of the young, a little despised her. Why did she tremble and start like that? She should stand up for herself and not mind what her sister said to her. Finally, there was something about the house for which Maggie could not quite account, some uneasiness or expectation, as though one knew that there was some one behind the door and was therefore afraid to open it. It may have been simply London that was behind it. Maggie was ready to attribute anything to the influence of that tremendous power, but her own final impression was that the people in this house had for too long a time been brooding over something. "It would do my aunts a lot of good to move somewhere else," she said to herself. "As Aunt Anne loves the country so much I can't think why she doesn't live there." There were many things that she was to learn before the end of the day.

Her thoughts were interrupted by a little whirr and clatter, which, thin and distant though it was, penetrated into her room. The whirr was followed by the voice, clear, self-confident and cheerful, of a cuckoo. Maggie was in an instant out of bed, into the passage and standing, in her nightdress, before a high, old cuckoo-clock that stood at the top of the stairs. The wooden bird, looking down at her in friendly fashion, "cuckooed" eight times, flapped his wings at her and disappeared. It is a sufficient witness to Maggie's youth and inexperience that she was enraptured by this event. It was not only that she had never seen a cuckoo-clock before; she had, for that matter, never heard of the existence of such a thing. It gave her greater happiness than any bare mechanical discovery could have done. The bird seemed to have come to her, in the friendliest way, to remove some of the chilly passivity of the house. Her greatest fear since her arrival had been that this was a house "in which nothing was ever going to happen," and that "she would never get out of it." "It will be just as it has been all my life, seeing nothing, doing nothing—only instead of father it will be the aunts." The bird seemed to promise her adventure and excitement. To most people it would have been only a further sign of an old-fashioned household far behind the times. To Maggie it was thrilling and encouraging. He would remind her every hour of the day of the possibility of fun in a world that was full of surprises. She heard suddenly a step behind her and a dry voice saying:

"Your hot water, Miss Maggie."

She turned round, blushing at being caught staring up at a cuckoo-clock like a baby in her nightdress, to face the wrinkled old woman who the night before had brought her, with a grudging countenance, her supper. Maggie had thought then that this old Martha did not like her and resented the extra work that her stay in the house involved; she was now more than ever sure of that dislike.

"I thought I was to be called at half-past seven."

"Eight on Sundays," said the old woman. "I hope you're better this morning, miss."

Maggie felt this to be deeply ironical and flushed.

"I'm quite well, thank you," she said stiffly. "What time is breakfast on Sundays?"

"The prayer-bell rings at a quarter to nine, miss."

They exchanged no more conversation.

At a quarter to nine a shrill, jangling bell rang out and Maggie hurried down the dark staircase. She did not know where the dining-room was, but by good chance she caught sight of Aunt Elizabeth's little body moving hurriedly down the passage and hastened after her. She arrived only just in time. There, standing in a row before four chairs, their faces red and shining, their hands folded in front of them, were the domestics; there, with a little high desk in front of her, on the other side of the long dining-room table was Aunt Anne; here, near the door, were two chairs obviously intended for Aunt Elizabeth and Maggie.

Maggie in her haste pushed the door, and it banged loudly behind her; in the silent room the noise echoed through the house. It was followed by a piercing scream from Edward, whom, Maggie concluded, it had awakened. All this confused her very much and gave her anything but a religious state of mind.

What followed resembled very much the ceremonies with which her father had been accustomed to begin the day, except that her father, with one eye on the bacon, had gabbled at frantic pace through the prayers and Aunt Anne read them very slowly and with great beauty. She read from the Gospel of St. John: "These things I command you, that ye love one another ..."; but the clear, sweet tones of her voice gave no conviction of a love for mankind.

Maggie looking from that pale remote face to the roughened cheeks and plump body of the kitchen-maid felt that here there could be no possible bond. When they knelt down she was conscious, as she had been since she was a tiny child, of two things—the upturned heels of the servants' boots and the discomfort to her own knees. These two facts had always hindered her religious devotions, and they hindered them now. There had always been to her something irresistibly comic in those upturned heels, the dull flat surfaces of these cheap shoes. In the kitchen-maid's there were the signs of wear; Martha's were new and shining; the house-maid's were smart and probably creaked abominably. The bodies above them sniffed and rustled and sighed. The vacant, stupid faces of the shoes were Aunt Anne's only audience. Maggie wondered what the owners of those shoes felt about the house. Had they a sense of irritation too or did they perhaps think about nothing at all save their food, their pay and their young man or their night out? The pain to her knees pierced her thoughts; the prayers were very long?—Aunt Anne's beautiful voice was interminable.

Breakfast was quiet and silent. Edward, who received apparently a larger meal on Sundays than at ordinary times, chattered happily to himself, and Maggie heard him say complacently, "Poor Parrot?—Poor Parrot. How do you do? How do you do?"

"Service is at eleven o'clock, dear," said Aunt Anne. "We leave the house at ten minutes to eleven."

Maggie, not knowing what to do with the hour in front of her, went up to her bedroom, found the servant making the bed, came down into the drawing-room and sat in a dark corner under a large bead mat, that, nailed to the wall, gave little taps and rustlings as though it were trying to escape.

She felt that she should be doing something, but what? She sat there, straining her ear for sounds. "One always seems to be expecting some one in this house," she thought. The weather that had been bright had now changed and little gusts of rain beat upon the windows. She thought with a sudden strange warmth of Uncle Mathew. What was he doing? Where was he? How pleasant it would be were he suddenly to walk into that chilly, dark room. She would not show him that she was lonely, but she would give him such a welcome as he had never had from her before. Had he money enough? Was he feeling perhaps as desolate amongst strangers as she? The rain tickled the window-panes. Maggie, with a desolation at her heart that she was too proud to own, sat there and waited.

She looked back afterwards upon that moment as the last shivering pause before she made that amazing plunge that was to give her new life.

The sound of a little forlorn bell suddenly penetrated the rain. It was just such a bell as rang every Sunday from chapels across the Glebeshire moors, and Maggie knew, when Aunt Elizabeth opened the door and looked in upon her, that the summons was for her.

"Oh! my dear (a favourite exclamation of Aunt Elizabeth's) and you're not ready. The bell's begun. The rain's coming down very hard, I'm afraid. It's only a step from our door. Your things, dear, as quick as you can."

The girl ran upstairs and, stayed by some sudden impulse, stood for a moment before the long mirror. It was as though she were imploring that familiar casual figure that she saw there not to leave her, the only friend she had in a world that was suddenly terrifying and alarming. Her old black dress that had seemed almost smart for the St. Dreot funeral now appeared most desperately shabby; she knew that her black hat was anything but attractive.

"What do I care for them all!" her heart said defiantly. "What do they matter to me!"

She marched out of the house behind the aunts with her head in the air, very conscious of a hole in one of her thin black gloves.

The street, deserted, danced in the rain; the little bell clanged with the stupid monotony of its one obstinate idea; the town wore its customary Sunday air of a stage when the performance is concluded, the audience vanished and the lights turned down. The aunts had a solemn air as though they were carrying Maggie as a sacrifice. All these things were depressing.

They turned out of their own street into a thin, grey one in which the puddles sprang and danced against isolated milk-cans and a desolate pillar-box. The little bell was now loud and strident, and when they passed into a passage which led into a square, rather grimy yard, Maggie saw that they had arrived. Before her was a hideous building, the colour of beef badly cooked, with grey stone streaks in it here and there and thin, narrow windows of grey glass with stiff, iron divisions between the glass. The porch to the door was of the ugliest grey stone with "The Lord Cometh" in big black letters across the top of it. Just inside the door was a muddy red mat, and near the mat stood a gentleman in a faded frock-coat and brown boots, an official apparently. There arrived at the same time as Maggie and her aunts a number of ladies and gentlemen all hidden beneath umbrellas. As they stood in the doorway a sudden scurry of wind and rain drove them all forward so that there was some crush and confusion in the little passage beyond the door. Waterproofs steamed; umbrellas were ranged in dripping disorder against the wall. The official, who talked in a hushed whisper that was drowned by the creaking of his boots, welcomed them all with the intimacy of an old acquaintance. "Oh, Miss Hearst—terrible weather—no, she's not here yet." "Good morning, Mrs. Smith—very glad you're better. Yes, I spoke to them about the prayer-books. They promised to return them this morning ..." and so on. He turned, pushed back a door and led the way into the chapel. The interior was as ugly as the outside. The walls were of the coldest grey stone, broken here and there by the lighter grey of a window. Across the roof were rafters built of that bright shining wood that belongs intimately to colonial life, sheep-shearing, apples of an immense size and brushwood. Two lamps of black iron hung from these rafters. At the farther end of the chapel was a rail of this same bright wood, and behind the rail a desk and a chair. In front of the rail was a harmonium before which was already seated a stout and expectant lady, evidently eager to begin her duties of the day. The chapel was not very large and was already nearly filled. The congregation was sitting in absolute silence, so that the passing of Maggie and her aunts up the aisle attracted great attention. All eyes were turned in their direction and Maggie felt that she herself was an object of very especial interest.

Aunt Anne walked first and took what was obviously her own regular seat near the front. Maggie sat between her two aunts. She could not feel for the moment anything but a startled surprise at the ugliness of the building. She had entered at different times the Glebeshire chapels, but their primitive position and need had given them the spirit of honest sincerity. Here she had expected she did not know what. Always from those very early days when she had first heard about her aunts she had had visions of a strange illuminated place into which God, "riding on a chariot clothed in flames," would one day come. Even after she had grown up she had still fancied that the centre of her aunts' strange, fantastic religion must be a strange, fantastic place. And yet now, as she looked around her, she was not, to her own surprise, disappointed. She was even satisfied; the "wonder" was not in the building. Well, then, it must be in something "inside," something that she had yet to discover. The chapel had the thrilling quality of a little plain deal box that carries a jewel.

She examined then the people around her. Women were in a great majority, a man scattered forlornly amongst them once and again. She discovered at once the alert eyes of young Mr. Warlock. He was seated in the side aisle with a thin, severe-looking woman beside him. He stared straight in front of him, wriggling sometimes his broad back as though he were a dog tied by a chain. Some one else very quickly claimed Maggie's attention; this was a girl who, in the seat behind Mr. Warlock, was as noticeable in that congregation as a bird-of-paradise amongst a colony of crows. She was wearing a dress of light blue silk and a large hat of blue with a grey bird in the front of it.

Her hair, beneath the hat, was bright gold, her cheeks were the brightest pink and her eyes sparkled in a most lovely and fascinating manner. She was immensely interesting to Maggie, who had never, in her life, dreamed of anything so dazzling. She was very restless and animated and self-conscious. There sat at her side a stout and solemn woman, who was evidently from a strange, almost ironical likeness her mother. The young lady seemed to regard both the place and the occasion as the greatest joke in the world. She flung her eyes from one to another as though inviting some one to share her merriment.

Amongst that black-garbed assembly the blue dress shone out as though it would attract everything to itself. "She's very pretty," thought Maggie, who was more conscious of her shabby clothes than ever. But her chief feeling was of surprise that so brilliant a bird had been able to penetrate into the chapel at all. "She must be a stranger just come out of curiosity." Then the girl's eyes suddenly met Maggie's and held them; the brilliant creature smiled and Maggie smiled in return. She looked afterwards at Aunt Anne, but Aunt Anne, buried in her book of devotions, had seen nothing.

Suddenly, after a strange wheeze and muffled scream, the harmonium began. Every one looked up expectantly; Mr. Warlock, alone, appeared from a door at the right of the screen and took his place behind the desk.

He stood for a moment facing them before he took his place. He was a man of great size, old now but holding himself absolutely erect. He was dressed in a plain black gown with a low, white collar and a white tie. This long gown added to his height, but the width of the shoulders and neck, and the carriage of his head showed that he was a man built on a noble scale. His hair was snow-white and he wore a beard, that was in startling contrast against his black gown. His cheeks were of high colour, his eyes blue; he was older than Maggie had expected and must, she thought, be over seventy. His whole bearing and behaviour was of a man who had enjoyed great physical health. His expression was mild and simple, dignified but not proud, utterly unconscious of self, earnest and determined, lacking in humour perhaps. There was nothing in the least theatrical about him and yet he conveyed an impression that was startling and dramatic. His was a figure that would have been noticed anywhere, if only for its physical health and shining cleanliness. Maggie felt that to many people there his entrance was a sensation, sought for and expected by them. So startling was the impression that he made upon herself that she wondered that the chapel was not crowded by an excited throng. She liked him at once, felt that she would be at ease with him as she had never been with anybody in her life. And yet behind this there was perhaps some subtle sense of disappointment. He was not mysterious, he did not seem very clever; he was only an old man, magnificently preserved. There was no fear nor wonder in her attitude to him. He could not convince her, she thought, of things that she herself had not seen.

He knelt and prayed for a moment before his desk, then he rose and, with his hands resting on the wood before him, said: "Let us offer thanks to Almighty God that He has kept us in safety and in health during the past week." They all knelt down. He prayed then, in a voice that was soft and clear and that hid behind the words a little roughness of accent that was not unpleasant. His prayer was extempore, and he addressed God intimately and almost conversationally. "Thou knowest how we are weak and foolish, our faults are all known to Thee and our blunders are not hid, therefore we thank Thee that Thou hast not been impatient with us, but, seeing that we are but little children in Thy hands, hast deemed the thunderbolt too heavy for our heads and the lightning too blinding for our eyes. With humble hearts we thank Thee, and pray that Thou wilt keep us mindful of Thy coming, that we may be found watching, with our loins girt and our lamps lit, waiting in prayer for Thy dreadful day..."

During this prayer Maggie was conscious of a strange excitement. She knelt with her eyes tightly closed, but through the darkness she felt as though he were addressing her alone. She seemed to approach him, to feel his hands upon her shoulders, to hear his voice in her ears. When she rose at the ending of the prayer it was as though she had definitely passed through some door into a new room. Then, rising, she was conscious that the laughing eyes of the young lady in blue were again trying to hold her own. She refused to look—she coloured, hanging her head so that her eyes should not be caught.

For some time she was unaware of the progress of the service. Then the clear emphasis of his voice caught again her attention. "Our lesson for to-day," he said, "is from the Fortieth Chapter of Isaiah." He proceeded to read:

Comfort ye, comfort ye my people, saith your God.

Speak ye comfortably to Jerusalem, and cry unto her, that her warfare is accomplished, that her iniquity is pardoned: for she hath received of the Lord's hand double for all her sins.

The voice of him that crieth in the wilderness, Prepare ye the way of the Lord, make straight in the desert a highway for our God.

Every valley shall be exalted, and every mountain and hill shall be made low: and the crooked shall be made straight, and the rough places plain:

And the glory of the Lord shall be revealed, and all flesh shall see it together: for the mouth of the Lord hath spoken it.

The voice said, Cry. And he said, What shall I cry? All flesh is grass, and all the goodliness thereof is as the flower of the field:...

The grass withereth, the flower fadeth; but the word of our God shall stand for ever.

O Zion, that bringest good tidings, get thee up into the high mountain; O Jerusalem, that bringest good tidings, lift up thy voice with strength; lift it up, be not afraid; say unto the cities of Judah, Behold your God!

Behold, the Lord God will come with strong hand, and his arm shall rule for him; behold, his reward is with him, and his work before him.

He shall feed his flock like a shepherd; he shall gather the lambs with his arm, and carry them in his bosom, and shall gently lead those that are with young.

How many times had Maggie heard the reading of those words. They brought instantly back to her her father's voice, the strange snuffling hurry with which he hastened to the end, his voice hesitating a little as his wandering eye caught the misbehaviour of some small boy in the choir.

Now the words were charged with a conviction that was neither forced nor adopted for dramatic effect. It was as though a herald read some proclamation for his master who was approaching the gates of the city. The hymns and prayers that followed seemed to have no importance. The hymns happened on that day to be familiar ones that Maggie had always known: "As pants the hart for cooling streams," "Just as I am, without one plea" and "Jerusalem the golden." These were sung, of course, slowly, badly and sentimentally, the harmonium screaming in amazing discords, and the deep and untuneful voices of some members of the congregation drowning the ladies and placing a general discord upon everything. Especially distressing was Aunt Elizabeth, who evidently loved to sing hymns but had little idea of melody or rhythm, and was influenced entirely by a copious sentiment which overflowed into her eyes and trembled at the tips of her fingers.

All this was as naive and awkward as is always the singing of English hymns in English churches by English citizens. The chapel, which had seemed before to be rising to some strange atmosphere of expectation, slipped back now to its native ugliness and sterility. The personality was in the man and in the man alone.

Maggie looked about her, at the faces of the women who surrounded her. They were grey, strained, ugly in the poor light of the building. The majority of them seemed to be either servant-girls or women who had passed the adventurous period of life and had passed it without adventure. When the time for the sermon arrived Mr. Warlock prayed, his head bowed, during a moment's silence, then leaning forward on his desk repeated some of the words of his earlier reading:

Prepare ye the way of the Lord, make straight in the desert a highway for our God. Every valley shall be exalted, and every mountain and hill shall be made low: and the crooked shall be made straight, and the rough places plain: ... say unto the cities of Judah, Behold your God!...

What followed was practical, eloquent, the preaching of a man who had through the course of a long life addressed men of all kinds and in all places. But behind the facility and easy flow of his words Maggie fancied that she detected some urgent insistence that came from the man's very heart. She was moved by that as though he were saying to her personally, "Don't heed these outward words of mine. But listen to me myself. There is something I must tell you. There is no time to lose. You must believe me. I will compel your belief. Follow me and I will show what will transform your life." He concluded his sermon with these words:

"And what of our responsibility? We may compare ourselves, I think, to men who, banded together on some secret service, wait for the moment when they are to declare themselves and, by that action, transform the world. Until that moment comes they must lead their ordinary daily lives, seem as careless of the future as their fellows, laugh and eat and work and play as though nothing beyond the business of the day were their concern. But in their hearts is the responsibility of their secret knowledge. They cannot be as other men knowing what they do, they cannot be to one another as they are to other men with the bond of their common duty shared between them. Much has been given them, much will be demanded of them; and when the day comes it will not be the events of that day that will test them but the private history, known only to themselves and their Master, of the hours that have preceded that day."

"I tell you what I have often told you before from this same place, that beside the history of the spirit the history of the body is nothing—and that history of the spirit is no easy, tranquil progress from birth to death, but must rather be, if we are to have any history at all, a struggle, a wrestling, a contest, bloody, unceasing, uncertain in its issue from the first hour until the last. This is no mere warning spoken from the lips only by one who, from sheer weekly necessity, may seem to you formal and official; it is as urgent, as deeply from the heart as though it were a summons from a messenger who has come to you directly from his Master. I beg of you to consider your responsibility, which is greater than that of other men. We are brothers bound together by a great expectation, a great preparation, a great trust. We are in training for a day when more will be demanded of us than of any other men upon the earth. That is no light thing. Let us hold ourselves then as souls upon whom a great charge is laid."

When he had ended and knelt again to pray Maggie felt instantly the inevitable reaction. The harmonium quavered and rumbled over the first bars of some hymn which began with the words, "Cry, sinner, cry before the altar of the Lord," the man with the brown, creaking boots walked about with a collection plate, an odour of gas-pipes, badly heated, penetrated the building, the rain lashed the grey window-panes. Maggie, looking about her, could not see in the pale, tired faces of the women who surrounded her the ardent souls of a glorious band. Their belief in the coming of God had, it seemed, done very little for them. It might be true that the history of the soul was of more importance than the history of the body, but common sense had something to say.

Her mind went back inevitably to St. Dreot's church, her father, Ellen the cook. That was what the history of the spirit had been to her so far. What reason had she to suppose that this was any more real than that had been? Nevertheless, when at the end of the sermon she left the building and went once more into the soaking streets some sense of expectation was with her, so that she hastened into her aunt's house as though she would find that some strange event had occurred in her absence.

Nothing, of course, had occurred.

During the afternoon the rain ceased to fall and a dim, grey light, born of an intense silence, enveloped the town. About three o'clock the aunts went out to some religious gathering and Maggie was left to herself. She discovered in Aunt Elizabeth's bedroom a bound volume of Good Words, and with this seated herself by the drawing-room fire. Soon she slept.

She was awakened by a consciousness that some one was in the room and, sitting up, staring through the gloom, heard a movement near the door, a rustle, a little jingle, a laugh.

"Is any one there?" said a high, shrill voice.

Maggie got up.

"I'm here," she said.

Some one came forward; it was the girl of the blue dress who had smiled at Maggie in chapel. She held out her hand—"I hope you don't think me too awful. My name's Caroline Smith. How do you do?"

They shook hands. Maggie, still bewildered by sleep, said, stammering, "Won't you sit down? I beg your pardon. My aunts—"

"Oh, it isn't the aunts I wanted to see," replied Miss Smith, laughing so that a number of little bracelets jingled most tunefully together. "I came to see you. We smiled at one another in chapel. It was your first time, wasn't it? Didn't you think it all awfully quaint?"

"Won't you sit down?" said Maggie again, "and I'll ring for the lamp."

"Oh! don't ring for the lamp. I like the dusk. And we can make friends so much better without a lamp. I always say if you want to know anybody really well, don't have a light."

She seated herself near the fire, arranging her dress very carefully, patting her hair beneath her hat, poking her shoes out from beneath her skirts, then withdrawing them again. "Well, what do you think of it all?"

Maggie stared. She did not know what to say. She had never met any one in the least like this before.

"I do hope," Miss Smith went on, "that you don't think me forward. I daresay you do. But I can't bear wasting time. Of course I heard that you were coming, so then I looked out for you in chapel to-day. I thought you looked so nice that I said to mother, 'I'll go and see her this very afternoon.' Of course I've known your aunts for ages. I'm always in and out here so that it isn't as bad as it seems. They'll all be back for tea soon and I want to have a talk first."

"Thank you very much," was all that Maggie could think of to say.

"You've come to live here, haven't you?" continued Miss Smith. "I'm so glad. I think you look so nice. You don't mind my saying that, do you? I always tell people what I think of them and then one knows where one is. Now, do tell me—I'm simply dying to know—what do you think of everything?"

"Well," said Maggie, smiling, "I only arrived here yesterday. It's rather difficult to say."

"Oh! I know. I saw Mr. Magnus this morning and he told me that he met you. He said you were ill. You don't look ill."

"It was very silly of me," said Maggie, "I don't know what made me faint. I've never done such a thing before."

"I used to faint simply heaps of times when I was a kid," said Miss Smith, "I was always doing it. I had all sorts of doctors. They thought I'd never grow up. I'm not very strong now really. They say it's heart, but I always say it can't be that because I've given it all away." Here Miss Smith laughed immoderately.

"Weren't they the most terrible set of frumps at chapel this morning?"

She did not wait for an answer, but went on: "Mr. Warlock's all right, of course. I think he's such a fine-looking man, don't you? Of course he's old now, but his beard's rather attractive I think. He's a duck, but isn't that harmonium ghastly? I can't think why they don't buy an organ, they're most awfully rich I know, and do simply nothing with their money."

"Why do you go," said Maggie, "if you think it all so dreadful?"

"Oh! I have to go," said Miss Smith, "to please mother. And one has to do something on Sunday, and besides one sees one's friends. Did you notice Martin Warlock, Mr. Warlock's son, you know. He was sitting quite close to me."

"He was here yesterday afternoon," said Maggie quietly.

"Oh, was he really? Now that is interesting. I wonder what he came for. He scarcely ever comes here. Did you like him?"

"I didn't speak to him," said Maggie.

"Of course he's only been here a little time. He's Mr. Warlock's only son. He's lived for years abroad and then the other day his aunt died and left him some money so he came home. His father simply adores him. They say—but of course I don't know. Don't quote me—that he's been most awfully wild. Drink, all sorts of things. But of course they'll say anything of anybody. I think he's got such an interesting face, don't you?"

"I don't think," said Maggie, "that you ought to say those things of any one if you don't know they're true."

"Oh! what a darling you are!" said Miss Smith. "You're perfectly right—one oughtn't. But every one does. When you've lived up here a little while you will too. And what does it matter? You're sure to hear it sooner or later. But that's right. You keep me straight. I know I talk far too much. I'm always being told about it. But what can one do? Life's so funny—one must talk about it. You haven't seen Miss Avies and Mr. Thurston yet, have you?"

"No," said Maggie. "Not unless I saw them in Chapel this morning."

"Ah! they're the ones," said Miss Smith. "No, they weren't there to-day. They're away on a mission. They make things hum. They quarrel with Mr. Warlock because they say he isn't noisy enough. Mr. Thurston's awful and Miss Avies isn't much better. You'll have them on to you soon enough. But of course I'm not one of the Inside Ones."

"Inside Ones?" asked Maggie.

"Yes, the real ones. They'll be at you after a time and ask you if you'll join them. The congregation this morning was just anybody who likes to come. But the real brethren have to swear vows and be baptized and all sorts of things. But that's only if you believe God's really coming in a year or two. Of course I don't, although sometimes it makes one quite creepy—all down one's spine. In case, after all, He really should come, you know."

"Are my aunts inside?" asked Maggie.

"Of course they are. Miss Anne Cardinal's one of the chief of them. Miss Avies is jealous as anything of her, but your aunt's so quiet that Miss Avies can't do anything. I just love your aunts. I think they're sweet. You will be a friend of mine, won't you? I like you so much. I like your being quiet and telling me when I talk too much. I sound silly, I know, but it's really mother's fault, as I always tell her. She never brought me up at all. She likes me to wear pretty things and doesn't care about anything else. Poor mother! She's had such a time with father; he's one of the most serious of all the Brethren and never has time to think about any of us. Then he's in a bank all the week, where he can't think about God much because he makes mistakes about figures if he does, so he has to put it all into Sunday. We will be friends, won't we?"

It came to Maggie with a strange ironic little pang that this was the first time that any one had asked for her friendship.

"Of course," she said.

Miss Smith's further confidences were interrupted by the aunts and behind them, to Maggie's great surprise, Mr. Warlock and his son. The sudden descent of these gentlemen upon the still lingering echoes of Miss Caroline Smith's critical and explanatory remarks embarrassed Maggie. Not so Miss Smith. She kissed both the aunts with an emphasis that they apparently appreciated for they smiled and Aunt Anne laid her hand affectionately upon the girl's sleeve. Maggie, watching, felt the strangest little pang of jealousy. That was the way that she should have behaved, been warm and demonstrative from the beginning—but she could not.

Even now she stood back in the shadows of the room, watching them all with large grave eyes, hoping that they would not notice her.

With Mr. Warlock and his son also Miss Smith seemed perfectly at home, chattering, laughing up into young Warlock's eyes, as though there were some especial understanding between them. Maggie, nevertheless, fancied that he, young Warlock, was not listening to her. His eyes wandered. He had that same restlessness of body that she had before noticed in him, swinging a little on his legs set apart, his hands clasped behind his thick broad back. He had some compelling interest for her. He had had that, she now realised, since the first moment that she had seen him. It might be that the things that that girl had told her about him increased her interest and, perhaps her sympathy? But it was his strange detached air of observation that held her—as though he were a being from some other planet watching them all, liking them, but bearing no kind of relation to them except that of a cheerful observer—it was this that attracted her. She liked his thick, rough untidy hair, the healthy red brown of his cheeks, his light blue eyes, his air of vigour and bodily health.

As she waited she was startled into consciousness by a voice in her ear. She turned to find the elder Mr. Warlock beside her.

"You will forgive my speaking to you, Miss Cardinal. I saw you at our Chapel this morning."

His great height towered above her short clumsy figure; he seemed to peer down at her from above his snowy beard as though he were the inhabitant of some other world. His voice was of an extreme kindliness and his eyes, when she looked up at him, shone with friendliness. She found herself, to her own surprise, talking to him with great ease. He was perfectly simple, human and unaffected. He asked her about her country.

"I spend my days in longing to get back to my own place—and perhaps I shall never see it again. I was born in Wiltshire—Salisbury Plain. My great-grandfather, my grandfather, my father, they all were ministers of our Chapel there before me. They had no thought in their day of London. I have always missed that space, the quiet. I shall always miss it. Towns are not friendly to me."

She told him about St. Dreots, a little about her father.

"Ah, you're lucky!" he said. "You'll return many times before you die—and you'll find no change there. Those places do not change as towns do."

They were standing apart from the others near the window. He suddenly put his hand on her arm, smiling at her.

"My dear," he said. "You don't mind me saying 'My dear,' but an old man has his privileges—will you come and see us whenever you care to? My wife will be so glad. I know that at first one can be lonely in this great place. Just come in when you please."

He took her hand for a moment and then turned back to Aunt Anne, who was now pouring out tea at a little table by the fire.

Martin Warlock, as his father moved away, came across to her, She had known that he would do that as though something had been arranged between them. When he came to her, however, he stood there before her and had nothing to say. She also had nothing to say. His eyes searched her face, then he broke out abruptly.

"Are you better?"

"I'm all right," she answered him brusquely. "Please don't say anything about yesterday. It was an idiotic thing to do."

"That's what I came about to-day—to see how you were," he answered her, his eyes laughing at her. "I should never have dreamed of coming otherwise, you know. I saw you in chapel this morning so I guessed you were all right, but it seemed such bad luck fainting right off the minute you got here."

"I've never fainted in my life before," she answered.

"No, you don't look the sort of girl who'd faint. But I suppose you've had a rotten time with your father and all."

His eyes still searched for hers. She determined that she would not look at him; her heart was beating strangely and, although she did not look, she could in some sub-conscious way see the rough toss of his hair against his forehead; she could smell the stuff of his coat. But she would not look up.

"You're going to live here, aren't you?"

"Yes," she said.

"I've only just come back," he went on.

"I know," she said.

"Oh! of course; that girl," jerking his head in the direction of the tea-table and laughing. "She told you. She's been here this afternoon, hasn't she? She chatters like anything. Don't you believe half she says."

There was another pause. The voices at the tea-table seemed to come from very far away.

Then he said roughly, moving a very little nearer to her:

"I'm glad you've come."

At that she raised her eyes, her cheeks flushed. She looked him full in the face, her head up. Her heart thundered in her breast. She felt as though she were at the beginning of some tremendous adventure—an adventure enthralling, magnificent—and perilous.

PART II

THE CHARIOT OF FIRE

CHAPTER I

THE WARLOCKS

There is beyond question, in human nature, such a thing as an inherited consciousness of God, and this consciousness, if inherited through many generations, may defy apparent reason, all progress of vaunted civilisations, and even, it may be suggested, the actual challenge of death itself.

This consciousness of God had been quite simply the foundation of Mr. Warlock's history. In the middle of the eighteenth century it expressed itself in the formula of John Wesley's revival; the John Wesley of that day preached up and down the length and breadth of Westmoreland, Cumberland, Northumberland, Durham, and being a fighter, a preacher and a simple-minded human being at one and the same time, received a large following and died full of years and honours.

It was somewhere about 1830 that this John's grandson, James Warlock, Martin's grandfather, broke from the main body and led his little flock on to the wide spaces of Salisbury Plain. James Warlock, unlike his father and grandfather, was a little sickly man with a narrow chest, no limbs to speak of and a sharp pale face. Martin had a faded daguerreotype of him set against the background of the old Wiltshire kitchen, his black clothes hung upon him like a disguise, his eyes burning even upon that faded picture with the fire of his spirit. For James Warlock was a mystic, a visionary, a prophet. He walked and talked with God; in no jesting spirit it was said that he knew God's plans and could turn the world into a blazing coal so soon as he pleased. It was because he knew with certainty that God would, in person, soon, descend upon the earth that he separated from the main body and led his little band down into Wiltshire. Here on the broad gleaming Plain they prepared for God's coming. Named now the Kingscote Brethren after their new abode, they built a Chapel, sat down and waited. Then in 1840 the prophet declared that the Coming was not yet, that it would be in the next generation, but that their preparations must not be relaxed. He himself prepared by taking to himself a wife, a calm untroubled countrywoman of the place, that she might give him a son whom he might prepare, in due course, for his great destiny. John, father of Martin, was born, a large-limbed, smiling infant, with the tranquillity of his mother as well as something of the mysticism of his father.

Upon him, as upon his ancestors, this consciousness of God had most absolutely descended. Never for a moment did he question the facts that his father told to him. He grew into a giant of health and strength, and those who, in those old days, saw them tell that it was a strange picture to watch the little wizened man, walking with odd emotional gestures, with little hops and leaps and swinging of the arms beside the firm long stride of the young man towering above him.

When young John was twenty-three years of age his father was found dead under a tree upon a summer's evening. His expression was of a man challenging some new and startling discovery; he had found perhaps new visions to confront his gaze. They buried him in Kingscote and his son reigned in his stead.

But they were approaching new and modern times. These old days, of simple faith and superstition were passing never to return. There were new elements in the Kingscote company of souls and these elements demanded freer play both of thought and action. They argued that, as to them alone out of all the world the time and manner of God's coming was known, they should influence with their activities some wider sphere than this Wiltshire village.

John Warlock clung with all his strength to the old world that he knew, the world that gave him leisure and quiet for contemplation. He had no wish to bring in converts, to stir England into a frenzy of terror and anticipation. God gave him no command to spread his beliefs; even his father, fanatic though he had been, had cherished his own small company of saints as souls to whom these things, hidden deliberately from the outside world, had especially been entrusted.

So long as he could he resisted; then when he was about forty, somewhere around 1880, the Kingscote Brethren moved to London. In this year, 1907, John Warlock was sixty-seven and the Kingscote Brethren had had their Chapel in Solomon's Place, behind Garrick Street, for twenty-seven years. In 1880 John Warlock had married Amelia, daughter of Francis Stephens, merchant. In 1881 a daughter, Amy, was born to them; in 1883, Martin; they had no other children. Martin was at the time of Maggie's arrival in London twenty-four years of age.

Upon a certain fine evening, a fortnight after Martin Warlock's first meeting with Maggie, he arrived at the door of his house in Garrick Street, and having forgotten his latch-key, was compelled to ring the old screaming bell that had long survived its respectable reputable days. The Warlocks had lived during the last ten years in an upper part above a curiosity shop four doors from the Garrick Club in Garrick Street. There was a house-door that abutted on to the shop-door and, passing through it, you stumbled along a little dark passage like a rabbit warren, up some crooked stairs, and found yourself in the Warlock country without ever troubling Mr. Spencer, the stout, hearty, but inartistic owner of the curiosity shop.

On the present occasion, after pulling the bell, Martin stared down the street as though somewhere in the dim golden light of its farthest recesses he would find an answer to a question that he was asking. The broad sturdy strength of his body, the easy good-temper of his expression spoke of a life lived physically rather than mentally. And yet this was only half true. Martin Warlock should at this time have been a quite normal young man with normal desires, normal passions, normal instincts. Such he would undoubtedly have been had he not had his early environment of egotism, mystery and clap-trap—had he, also, not developed through his childhood and youth his passionate devotion to his father. The religious ceremonies of his young days had made him self-conscious and introspective and, although during his years abroad he had felt on many occasions that he was completely freed from his early bondage, scenes, thoughts and longings would recur and remind him that he was celebrating his liberty too soon. The licences that to most men in their first youth are incidental and easily forgotten engraved themselves upon Martin's reluctant soul because of that religious sense that had been driven in upon him at the very hour of his birth. He could not sin and forget. He sinned and was remorseful, was impatient at his remorse, sinned again to rid himself of it and was more remorseful still. The main impulse of his life at this time was his self-distrust. He fancied that by returning home he might regain confidence. He longed to rid himself of the conviction that he was "set aside" by some fate or other, call it God or not as you please. He thought that he hurt all those whom he loved when his only longing was to do them good. He used suddenly to leave his friends because he thought that he was doing them harm. It was as though he heard some Power saying to him: "I marked you out for my own in the beginning and you can't escape me. You may struggle as you like. Until you surrender everything shall turn to dust in your hands." He came back to England determined to assert his independence.

He gazed now at the placidity of Garrick Street with the intensity of some challenging "Stand and Deliver!" All that the street had to give for the moment was a bishop and an actor mounting the steps of the Garrick Club, an old lady with a black bonnet and a milk-jug, a young man in a hurry and a failure selling bootlaces. None of them could be expected to offer reassurance to Martin—none of these noticed him—but an intelligent observer, had such a stranger to Garrick Street been present, might have found that gaze of interest. Martin's physical solidity could not entirely veil the worried uncertain glance that flashed for a moment and then, with a little reassuring sigh, was gone.

The door opened, a girl looked for a moment into the street, he passed inside. Having stumbled up the dark stairs, pushed back their private entrance, hung up his coat in the little hall, with a deliberate effort he shook off the suspicions that had, during the last moments, troubled him and prepared to meet his mother and sister.

Because he had a happy, easy and affectionate temperament absence always gilded his friends with gifts and qualities that their presence only too often denied. His years abroad had given him a picture of his mother and sister that the few weeks of his return had already dimmed and obscured. His mother's weekly letters had, during ten long years, built up an image of her as the dearest old lady in the world. He had always, since a child, seen her in a detached way—his deep and permanent relations had been with his father—but those letters, of which he had now a deep and carefully cherished pile, gave him a most charming picture of her. They had not been clever nor deep nor indeed very interesting, but they had been affectionate and tender with all the gentleness of the figure that he remembered sitting in its lace cap beside the fire.

After three weeks of home life he was compelled to confess that he did not in the least understand his mother. His intuitions about people were not in fact of a very penetrating character.

His mother appeared to all her world as a "sweet old lady," but even Martin could already perceive that was not in the least what she really was. He had seen her old hands tremble with suppressed temper on the very day after his arrival; he had seen her old lips white with anger because the maid had brought her the wrong shawl. Old ladies must of course have their fancies, but his mother had some fixed and fierce purpose in her life that was quite beyond his powers of penetration. It might of course have something to do with her attachment to his father. Attached Martin could see that she was, but at the same time completely and eternally outside her husband's spiritual life. That might have been perhaps in the first place by her own desire—she did not want "to be bothered with all that nonsense." But certainly all these years with him had worked upon her: she was not perhaps so sure now that it was all "nonsense." She wanted, it might be, a closer alliance with him, which she could not have because she had once rejected the chance of it. Martin did not know; he was aware that there was a great deal going on in the house that he did not fathom. Amy, his sister, knew. There was an alliance between his mother and his sister deep and strong, as he could see—he did not yet know that it was founded very largely on dislike and fear of himself.

How fantastic these theories of fire and passion must seem, he amused himself by considering, to any one who knew his mother only from the outside. She was sitting to-day as always in her little pink and white chintz drawing-room, a bright fire burning and a canary singing in a cage beside the window. The rest of the house was ugly and strangely uninhabited as though the Warlocks had merely pitched their tents for a night and were moving forward to-morrow, but this little room, close, smelling of musk and sweet biscuits (a silver box with lemon-shaped biscuits in it stood on a little table near the old lady), with its pretty pink curtains, its canary, and its heavy and softly closing door, was like a place enclosed, dedicated to the world, and ruled by a remorseless spirit of comfort.

Mrs. Warlock was only sixty years of age, but she had, a number of years ago, declared herself an invalid, and now never, unless she drove on a very fine afternoon, left the house. Whether she were truly an invalid nobody knew; she presented certainly a most healthy appearance with her shell-pink cheeks, her snow-white hair, her firm bosom rising and falling with such gentle regularity beneath the tight and shining black silk that covered it, her clear bright eyes like shining glass. She always sat in a deep arm-chair covered with the chintz of the curtains and filled with plump pillows of pink silk. A white filmy shawl was spread over her knees, at her throat was a little bright coquettish blue bow that added, amazingly, to the innocent charm of her old age. On her white hair, crinkled and arranged as though it were some ornament, not quite a wig but still apart from the rest of her body, she wore a lace cap. She was fond of knitting; she made warm woollen comforters and underclothing for the children of the poor. She was immensely fond of conversation, being of an inquisitive nature. But above all was she fond of eating. This covetousness of food had grown on her as her years had increased. The thought of foods of various kinds filled many hours of her day, and the desire for pleasant things to eat was the motive of many of her most deliberate actions. She cherished warmly and secretly this little lust of hers. None of the family was aware of the grip that the desire had upon her nor of the speed with which the desire was growing. She did not ask directly for the things that she liked, but manoeuvred with little plots and intrigues to obtain them. The cook in the Warlock household had neither art nor science at her disposal, but as it happened old Mrs. Warlock lusted after very simple things. She loved rice-pudding; her heart beat fast in her breast when she thought of the brown crinkly skin of the rich warm milk of a true rice-pudding; also she loved hot buttered toast, very buttery so that it soaked your fingers; also beef-steak pudding with gravy rich and dark and its white covering thick and heavy; she also loved hot and sweet tea and the little cakes that Amy sometimes bought, red and yellow and pink, held in white paper—also plum-pudding, which, alas! only came at Christmastime and wedding-cake, which scarcely ever came at all.

This vice, of which she was almost triumphantly conscious as though it were a proof of her enduring vitality, she clutched eagerly to herself. She did not wish that any human being should perceive it. Of her husband she was not afraid—it would never possibly occur to him that food was of importance to any one; Amy might discover what she pleased, she was in strong alliance with her mother and would never betray her.

Her fear was of Martin. She feared very deeply his influence upon her husband. During Martin's absence she and Amy had managed very successfully to have the house as they wished it; John Warlock, the master, had been too deeply occupied with the affairs of the soul to be concerned also with the affairs of the body.

She had, she believed, exercised an increasing influence over him. She had always loved him with a fierce and selfish love, but now, when he was nearly seventy, and to both of them only a few years of earthly ambition could remain, she desired, with all the urgent ferocity of a human being through whose fingers the last sands of his opportunity are slipping, to seize and hold and have him entirely hers. He had always eluded her; although he had once certainly loved her with, at any rate, a semblance of earthly passion, his spiritual life had always come between them, holding him from her, helping him to escape when he pleased, tantalising, sometimes maddening too. She was certainly now not so ready to dismiss that spiritual life as once she had been. She was herself an old heathen; for herself she believed in nothing but her earthly appetites and desires, but for him and for others there might be something in it, ... and perhaps some day some dreadful thing would occur ... a chariot of Fire descend upon the Chapel and some sort of a fierce and hostile God deliver judgment; she only hoped that she would be dead before then.

Meanwhile she and Amy had, undoubtedly, during these last years, increased their influence over him. He was not aware of it, but as he was growing now older and weaker—he had had trouble with his heart—he inevitably depended more upon them. The old lady began to count upon her triumph. Then came Martin's return.

She had forgotten Martin. It is true that she had written to him every week during his long absence, but her letters had been all part of the "dear old lady" habit which was put on by her just as an actress prepares herself, nightly, for a character in which she knows she is the greatest possible success. "Thank you very much, Mrs. Smith ... No, we've not heard from Martin now for three weeks. Careless boy! I always write myself every week so that he may have at any rate one little word from home ..."

She had never felt that she had any real share in his life; he had always belonged to his father; nor was she a woman who cared about children. Martin had long ago become to her simply an opportunity for further decoration. Since his return it had been quite another affair. In one moment she had seen her power over her husband shrivel and disappear. Martin was home again. Martin must be here, Martin must be there; Martin must see this, Martin must do this. She had seen before in earlier days the force of her husband's passion when it was roused. There was something now in his reception of their son that terrified her. She had at once perceived that Amy was as deeply moved as she. The girl, plain, awkward, silent, morose, had always adored her father, but she had never known how to approach him. She was not clever, she had not been able to enter into his life although she would have done anything that he desired of her. What she had suffered during those early years when, as a little ugly girl, she had watched her brother, accepted, received into the Brotherhood, praised for his wisdom, his intimacy with God, his marvellous saintly promise, praised for these things when she had known all his weaknesses, how he had slipped away to a music-hall when he was only fourteen and smoked and drank there, how he had laughed at Mr. Thurston's dropping of his "h's" or at Miss Avies' prayer meetings! No one ever knew what in those years she had thought of her brother. Then, after Martin had flung it all away and escaped abroad, she had begun, slowly, painfully, but with dogged persistence, to make herself indispensable to her father; Martin she had put out of her mind. He would never return, or, at least, the interval of his departure should have been severe enough to separate him for ever from his father ...

In a moment's glance, in a clasp of the hand, in a flash of the eye, she had seen that love leap up in her father's heart as strong as ever it had been. Every day of Martin's residence in the house had added fire to that love. She was a good woman; she struggled hard to beat down her jealousy. She prayed. She lay for hours at night struggling with her sins. If Martin had been worthy, if he had shown love in return, but, from the bottom of her soul, as the days increased she despised him—despised him for his light heart, his care of worldly things, his utter lack of comprehension of their father, his scorn, even now but badly concealed, of all the sanctities that she had in reverence.

Therefore she drew near to her mother and the two of them watched and waited ...

His mother was knitting. She lifted to him her pink wrinkled face and, her spectacles balanced on the end of her nose, smiled the smile of the dearest old lady in the world.

"Well, dear, and have you had a pleasant day?"

"All right, mother, thank you. Funny thing; met a man in the street, hadn't seen for five years. Saw him last in Rio—Funny thing. Well, we lunched together. Not a bad fellow—Seen a thing or two, he has."

Mrs. Warlock counted her stitches. "Fourteen, fifteen, sixteen ... How nice for you, dear. What was his name?"

"Thompson ... I say," Martin suddenly raised his head as though he heard something, "where's Amy?"

"Changing. She's been paying a call on the Miss Cardinals. Thought it would be polite because of the new niece.—Six, seven, eight and nine..."

"What did she think of her?"

"Of whom, dear?"

"Of the niece."

"Oh, I don't think she liked her very much. She said that she was plain and silent—and looked cross, Amy thought."

"Oh yes, Amy would." His face, as was his way when he was vexed, flushed very slowly, the deeper red rising through the red-brown until, ceasing in the middle of his forehead, it left a white line beneath his hair. "She isn't cross a bit."

"I don't know, dear. It isn't my opinion. I only tell you what Amy said. People here don't seem to like her. Mrs. Smith was telling me yesterday that she's so difficult to talk to and seems to know nothing about anything, poor girl."

"Mrs. Smith!" He swung his body on his hips indignantly. "A lot she knows about anything! I hate that woman and her chattering daughter."

"Well, dear, I don't know, I'm sure; Mrs. Smith always seems to me very kind."

He looked at her as though he had suddenly remembered something.

"I say—is it true what Amy says, that I woke you up this morning when I went out by banging my door?"

"I'm sure you didn't.—Amy shouldn't say such things. And if you did what does it matter? I sleep so badly that half an hour more or less makes very little difference."

"Well, she says so—" He went on, dropping his voice: "I say, mother, what's the matter with Amy? Why's she so sick with me? I haven't done anything to offend her, have I?"

"Of course not. What a silly boy you are, Martin! Nine, ten, eleven ... There! that's enough for this evening. I'll finish it in another day. You mustn't mind Amy, Martin. She isn't always very well."

The door opened and Amy came in. She was a tall gaunt woman who looked a great deal older than her brother. She did not make the best of herself, brushing her thin black hair straight back from her bony forehead. She had a habit of half closing her eyes when she peered at some one as though she could not see. She should, long ago, have worn spectacles, but from some strange half-conscious vanity had always refused to do so. Every year her sight grew worse. She was wearing now a dress of black silk, very badly made, cut to display her long skinny neck and bony shoulders. She wore her clothes as though she struggled between a disdain for such vanities and a desire to appear attractive. Her manner of twisting her eyelids and wrinkling her nose gave her a peevish expression, but, behind that, there was a hint of pathos, a half-seen glimpse of a soul that desired friendship and affection. She was very tall and there was something masculine in the long angularity of her limbs. She offered a strange contrast to the broad and ruddy Martin. There was, however, something in the eyes of each—some sudden surprised almost visionary flash that came and went that showed them to be the children of the same father. To Mrs. Warlock they bore no resemblance whatever. Amy stopped when she saw her brother as though she had not expected him to be there.

"Well, Martin," she said—then came forward and sat in a chair opposite her mother.

"Mr. Thurston's coming to suppar," she said.

Martin frowned. "Oh, hang it, what for?" he cried.

"He's taking me to Miss Aries' Bible meeting," Amy answered coldly. "What a baby you are about people, Martin. I should have thought all your living abroad so much would have made you understanding. But you're like the rest. You must have every one cut to the same pattern."

Martin looked up for a moment as though he would answer angrily; then he controlled himself and said, laughing: "I suppose I have my prejudices like every one else. I daresay Thurston's a very good sort of fellow, but we don't like one another, and there's an end of it, Everybody can't like everybody, Amy—why, even you don't like every one."

"No, I don't," she answered shortly.

She looked for an instant at her mother. Martin caught the glance that passed between them, and suddenly the discomfort of which he had been aware as he stood, half an hour before, in the street, returned to him with redoubled force. What was the matter with everybody? What had he done?

"Well, I'll go and change," he said.

"Dinner will be ready in ten minutes, dear," said his mother.

"I'll be in time all right," he said.

At the door he almost ran into Mr. Thurston. This gentleman had been described, on some earlier occasion, by an unfriendly observer as "the Suburban Savonarola." He was tall and extremely thin with a bony pointed face that was in some lights grey and in others white. He had the excited staring eyes of a fanatic, and his hair now very scanty, was plastered over his head in black shining streaks. He wore a rather faded black suit, a white low collar and a white bow tie. He had a habit, at moments of stress, of cracking his fingers. He had a very pronounced cockney accent when he was excited, at other times he struggled against this with some success.

He passed from brooding silences into sudden bursts of declamation with such abruptness that strangers thought him very eloquent. When he was excited the colour ran into his nose as though he had been drinking, and often his ears were red. His history was simple. The son of a small draper in Streatham, he had at an early age joined himself to an American Revivalist called Harper. When after some six years of successful enterprise Mr. Harper had been imprisoned for forgery, young William Thurston had attached himself to a Christian Science Chapel in Hoxton. Then, somewhere about 1897, he had met Miss Avies at a Revivalist Meeting in the Albert Hall and, fascinated by her ardent spirit, transferred his services to the Kingscote Brethren.

He had now risen to a position of great importance in the Chapel; it was known that he disagreed profoundly with his leader on some vital questions, and it was thought that he might at a later date definitely secede and conduct a party of his own.

Certainly he had exceptional energies and gifts of exhortation and invective not to be despised. Martin politely wished him "Good evening" and escaped to his room.

As he changed his clothes he tried to translate into definite facts his vague discomfort. One, he hated that swine Thurston. Two, Amy was vexed with him (What strange impossible creatures women were!). Third—and by far the most important of them all—his father wanted to talk to him. He knew very well that this talk had been preparing for him ever since his return from abroad. He dreaded it. Oh! he dreaded it most horribly!

He loved his father but with a love that had in it elements of fear, timidity, every possible sort of awkwardness. Moreover he was helpless. Ever since that first day when as a tiny child of four or five he had awakened to behold that figure, enormous in a long night-shirt, summoning God in the middle of the night with a candle flickering fantastic shadows on to the wall behind them, Martin had been weak as putty in his father's hands. Against other men he could stand up; against that strange company of fears, affections, superstitions, shadowy terrors, dim expectations that his father presented to him he could do nothing.

Well—that conversation had to come some time. He must show that he was a man now, moulded by the world with his own beliefs, purposes, resolves. But if he did not love him, how much easier it would be!

When he went downstairs he found the old man in the little pink drawing-room—he looked tired and worn. Martin remembered with alarm the things that he had heard recently about his father's heart. He glanced up and the older man's hand fastened on his shoulder; they stood there side by side. After a few minutes they all went in to supper.

Mr. Thurston's nose was flushed with the success of the mission from which he had just returned. He had been one of a number whose aim it had been during the preceding week to bring light and happiness into the lives of the inhabitants of Putney. They had been obviously appreciated, as the collection for the week had amounted to between seventy and eighty pounds. A proper share of this fine result Mr. Thurston naturally appropriated to his own efforts. His long tapering fingers were not so clean as they might have been, but this did not prevent him from waving them in the air and pointing them at imaginary Putney citizens whom he evoked in support of his statements.

"We 'ad a reelly thumpin' meeting on Thursday—Town Hall—One for the women in the small 'all hand one for the men in the Main Hall. Almost no opposition you might say, and when it came to the Hymn singing it fairly took the roof off. A lot of 'em stopped afterwards—one lad of eighteen or so is coming over to us 'ere. Butcher's apprentice. Says 'e's felt the Lord pressing him a long way back but the flesh held him. Might work him up into a very useful lad with the Lord's help. Thank you, Mrs. Warlock, I will try a bit more of that cold beef if you don't mind. Pretty place, Putney. Ever been there, Mr. Warlock? Ah, you should go—"

Amy Warlock listened with the greatest interest; otherwise, it must be confessed, Mr. Thurston's audience was somewhat inattentive. Mr. Warlock's mind was obviously elsewhere; he passed his hand through his beard, his eyes staring at the table-cloth. Mr. Thurston, noticing this, tried another topic.

"What 'ave you heard, Mrs. Warlock, about the new Miss Cardinal? I 'aven't seen her yet myself."

Mrs. Warlock, who had just given herself a little piece of beef, some potato and some spinach, and was arranging these delicacies with the greatest care upon her plate, just smiled without raising her eyes. Amy answered—

"I've seen her. I was there this afternoon. I can't say that I found her very interesting. Plain-ugly in fact. She never opened her mouth all the afternoon. Caroline Smith tells me that she knows nothing at all, seen nothing, been nowhere. Bad-tempered I should think."

"Dear, dear," said Mr. Thurston with a gratified sigh, "is it so reelly?"

Martin looked across at his sister indignantly. "Trust one woman about another," he said. "Just because she doesn't chatter like a magpie you concluded she's got nothing to say. It's even conceivable that she found you dull, Amy."

Amy looked at him with a strange penetrating glance that in some undefined way increased his irritation. "It's quite possible," she said quietly. "But I don't think even you, Martin, can call her handsome. As to her intelligence, she never gave me a chance of judging."

"I've been there several times," said Martin hotly. "I like her immensely." He felt as soon as he had spoken that it had been a foolish thing to say. He saw Mr. Thurston smile. In the pause that followed he felt as though he had with a gesture of the hand flung a stone into a pool of chatter and scandal whose ripples might spread far beyond his control. At that moment he hated his sister.

"I didn't know you knew her so well, dear," said his mother.

"I don't know her," he said, "I've only seen her three times. But she ought to be given her chance. It can't be much fun for her coming here where she knows no one—after her father suddenly dying. I believe she was all alone with him."

He had expected his father to defend her. He remembered that he had apparently liked her. But his father said nothing. There was an awkward and uncomfortable pause. After supper Mr. Thurston rubbed his hands, helped Amy Warlock into her cloak, said to the company in general:

"Good night. Should be a very full meeting to-night ... Well, well ... Thank you for your kindness, Mrs. Warlock, I'm sure."

The door was closed, Mrs. Warlock retired into her bedroom; the house was left to Martin and his father.

Mr. Warlock's room was hideous. It opened, somewhat ironically, out of Mrs. Warlock's pink drawing-room. A huge and exceedingly ugly American roll-top desk took up much of the room. There were bookshelves into which books had been piled. Commentaries on the Bible, volumes of sermons, pamphlets, tattered copies of old religious magazines. A bare carpet displayed holes and rents. The fireplace was grim with dirty pieces of paper and untidy shavings. In the midst of this disorder there hung over the mantelpiece, against the faded grey wall-paper, a fine copy of Raphael's "Transfiguration." Mr. Warlock lighted a candle and the flame flickered with changing colours upon the picture's surface. It had been given to John Warlock many years before by an old lady who heard him preach and had been, for a week, converted, but on his demand that she should give her wealth to the poor and fling aside her passion for Musical Comedy, left him with indignation. The picture had remained; it hung there now crooked on its cord.

John Warlock was unconscious of the dust and disorder that surrounded him. His own passion for personal cleanliness sprang from the early days with his father, to whom bodily cleanliness had been part of a fanatical mysticism. Partly also by reason of that early training, sloth, drunkenness, immorality, had no power over him. And of the whole actual world that surrounded him he was very little conscious except that he hated towns and longed always for air and space.

So that the windows were open one room was to him as another.

He had often, during his work with the members of his community, been conscious of his ignorance of the impulses and powers that went up to make the ordinary sensual physical life of the normal man. His own troubles, trials, failures were so utterly of another kind that in this other world his imagination refused to aid him. This had often deeply distressed him and made him timid and shy in his dealings with men and women. It was this, more than anything else, that held him back from the ambition to proselytise. How could he go forth and challenge men's souls when he could not understand nor feel their difficulties? More and more as his years advanced had he retired into himself, into his own mystical world of communion with a God who drew ever nearer and nearer to him. He humbled himself before men; he did not believe himself better than they because he had not yielded to their temptations; but he could not help them; his tongue was tied; he was a man cut off from his fellows and he knew it.

He had never felt so impatient of his impotence as he did to-night. For ten years he had been waiting for this interview with his son, and now that it was come he was timid and afraid as though he had been opposed by a stranger. He had always known that Martin would return. It had been his one worldly ambition and prayer to have him at his side again. When he had thought and dreamt of the time that was coming, he had thought that it would be simple enough to win the boy back to the old allegiance and faith to which he had once been bound. Meanwhile the boy had grown into a man; here was a new Martin deep in experiences, desires, ambitions of which his father could have no perception. Even in the moment that he was aware of the possibility of losing his son he was aware also of the deep almost fanatical resolve to keep him, to hold him at all costs.

This was to be the test of his whole earthly life. He seemed, as he sat there, looking across at his boy, to challenge God Himself to take him from him. It was as though he said:

"This reward at least I have a right to ask. I demand it ..."

Martin, on his side, was conscious of a profound discomfort. He had, increasingly as the years had passed, wished to take life easily and pleasantly. Suddenly now another world rose up before him. Yes, another world. He was not fool enough to dismiss it simply because it did not resemble his own. Moreover it had been once his, and this was increasingly borne in upon him. But it all seemed to him now incredibly old, childish and even fantastic, as though here, in the middle of London, he had suddenly stepped into a little wood with a witch, a cottage and a boiling cauldron. Such things could not frighten, of course—he was no longer a child—and yet because he had once been frightened some impression of alarm and dismay hovered over him.

During all his normal years abroad he had forgotten the power of superstition, of dreams and omens; he knew now, as he faced his father, that the power was real enough.

They talked for a little while of ordinary things; the candle flame jumped and fell, the shavings rustled strangely in the fireplace, the "Transfiguration" swung a little on its cord, the colour still lingering at its heart as the rest of the room moved restlessly under the ebb and flow of black shadows. Then the candle suddenly blew out.

"A lamp will be better," said Mr. Warlock.

He left the room and Martin sat there, in the darkness, haunted by he knew not what anticipations. The light was brought, they drew closer together, sitting in the little glossy pool, the room pitch dark around them.

"Well, Martin," at last Mr. Warlock said, "I want to hear so many things. Our first time together alone."

"There isn't very much," Martin tried to speak naturally and carelessly. "I wrote about most things in my letters. Pretty rotten letters I'm afraid." He laughed.

"And now—what do you intend to do now?"

"Oh, I don't know—Look around for a bit."

There was another long pause. Then Mr. Warlock began again. "When I ask about your life, my boy, I don't mean where you've lived, how you've earned your living—I do know all that—you've been very good about writing. But your real life, what you've been thinking about things, how you feel about everything ..."

"Well, father—I don't know. One hadn't much time for thinking, you know. No one did much thinking in Rio. When I was in the Bermudas there was a fellow ..."

"Yes, but tell me about yourself."

Then, with a desperate effort, he broke out:

"Father, you'll be badly disappointed in me. I've been feeling it coming all the time. I can't help it. I'm just like any one else. I want to have a good time. One's only young once. I'm awfully sorry. I want to please you in any way I can, but—but—it's all gone—all that early part. It's simply one's childhood that's finished with."

"And it can't come back?" his father said quietly.

"Never!" Martin's voice was almost a cry as though he were defying something.

"We are very weak against God's will," his father said, still quietly as though it were not he that was speaking but some voice in the shadow behind him. "You are not your own master, Martin."

"I am my own master," Martin answered passionately. "I have been my own master for ten years. I've not done anything very fine with my life, I know. I'm just like any one else—but I've found my feet. I can look after myself against anybody and I'm independent—of every one and of everything."

His father drew a little closer to him.

"Of course," he said, "I was not so foolish as to expect that you would come back to us just as you left us. I know that you must have your own life—and be free—so much as any of us are free at all ..." Then after a little pause. "What are your plans? What are you going to do?"

"Well," answered Martin, hesitating, "I haven't exactly settled, you know. I might take a small share in some business, go into the City. Then at other times I feel I shouldn't like being cooped up in a town after the life I've led. Sometimes, this last month, I've felt I couldn't breathe. It was though, are you, all the chimneys were going to tumble in. When you're out on a field you know where you are, don't you? So I've thought it would be nice to have a little farm somewhere in the South, Devonshire or Glebeshire ... And then I'd marry of course, a girl who'd like that kind of life and wouldn't find it dull. There'd be plenty of work—a healthy life for children right away from these towns ... That's my sort of idea, father, but of course one doesn't know ..."

Martin trailed off into inconsequent words. It was as though his father were waiting for him to commit himself and would then suddenly leap upon him with "There! Now, you've betrayed yourself. I've caught you—" and he had simply nothing to betray, nothing to conceal.

But anything was better than these pauses during which the threats and anticipations piled up and up, making a monstrous figure out of exactly nothing at all.

It was not enough to tell himself that between every father and son there were restraints and hesitations, a division cleft by the remembrance of the time when one had commanded and the other obeyed. There were other elements here—for one the element of an old affection that had once been at the very root of the boy's soul and was now in the strangest way creeping back to him, as an old familiar, but forgotten form might creep out of the dark and sit at his feet and clasp his knees.

"Well," said John Warlock. "That's very pleasant. You must feel very grateful to your aunt Rachel, Martin; she's given you the opportunity of doing what you like with your life. She spoke to me about it before she died."

"She spoke to you about it?"

"Yes. She told me that she did it because she wanted to bring you back to me. She knew of my love for you. We often talked of you together. She was a faithful servant of God. She believed that God meant to bring you, through her, back into His arms."

"I might not have come," Martin said with a sudden anger that surprised himself. "She made no conditions. I might have gone on with my life there abroad. I am free to lead my own life where and how I please."

"Quite free." His father answered gently. "But she knew that you would come. Of course you are your own master, Martin—"

"No, but it must be quite clear," Martin cried, the excitement rising in him as he spoke. He leaned forward almost touching his father's chair. "I'm not bound to any one by this money. It was awfully jolly of Aunt Rachel. I'll never forget her—but I'm free. I haven't got to say that I believe things when I don't, or that I think things that she thought just because she did ... I don't want to hurt you, father, but you know that it must have seemed to me pretty odd coming back after all these years and finding you, all in the same place, doing the same things, believing in the same things—just like years ago. I've seen the world a bit, I can tell you—Russia, China, Japan, America, North and South, India. You believe as far as you can see. What are you to think when, in every country that you come to, you see people believing in different things? They can't all be right, you know."

His father said nothing.

"But each thinks he's right—and each hates the other. Then, when I came back and saw a fellow like that man Thurston preaching and laying down the law, well, it seemed odd enough that any one could be taken in by it. I hope I don't hurt you, father ... only that's what you want, isn't it ... to have it out quite plainly? ..."

His father, still very gently and hesitating as though he found it difficult to catch the words that he wished (his voice had still the remoteness of some one speaking, who was far from them both), said:

"You'll think it odd, Martin, when you know how often I have to preach and speak in public, that I should find it hard to talk—but I never, with any man alone, could find words easily. I know so little. It is God's punishment for some selfish nervousness and shyness in me, that even now when I am an old man I cannot speak as one man to another. There was once, I remember, a young man who had heard me preach and was moved by my words and begged to see me in private. He came one evening; he was tempted to commit a terrible sin. He depended upon me to save him and I could say nothing. I struggled, I prayed, but it was incredible to me that any man could be tempted to such a thing. I spoke only conventional words that meant nothing. He went away from me, and his lost soul is now upon me and will always be ... but, Martin, what I would say beyond everything is—do not let us separate. Be free as you must be free, as you should be free—but stay with me—remain with me. I am an old man; I have longed for you as I think no other father can ever have longed for his son. They tell me that I cannot live many more years. God chooses His time. Be with me, Martin, for a little while even though I may seem old to you and foolish. Perhaps things will come back to you that you have long forgotten. You were once pledged and it was a vow that is not easily removed—but it is enough for the present if you will be with me a little, give me some of your time—give the old days a chance to come back." He laid his hand upon his son's.

The sudden touch of the dry, hot, trembling skin filled Martin's heart with the strangest confusion of affection, embarrassment and some familiar pathos. In just that way ten years before he had felt his father's hand and had thought: "How old he's getting! ... How I shall miss him! ... I hope nothing happens to him!" In the very balance of his father's sentences and the deliberate choice of words there had been something old-fashioned and remote from all the life and scramble of Martin's recent years. Now he took his father's hand in his own strong grasp and said gruffly:

"That's all right, father ... I'm not going while you want me ... You and I ... always ... it's just the same now."

But even as he spoke he felt as though he were giving some pledge that was to involve him in far more than he could see before him. Then, with a happy sense that the sentimental part of the conversation was over, he began to talk about all kinds of things. He let himself go and even, after a while, began to feel the whole thing really jolly and pleasant. His father wanted waking up. He had been here so long, with all these awful frumps, brooding over one idea, never getting away from this Religion.

Martin began to imagine himself very cleverly leading his father into a normal natural life, taking him to see things, making him laugh; it would do his health a world of good.

Then, quite suddenly, the old man said:

"And what do you remember, Martin, of the old days here, the days when you were quite small, when we lived in Mason Street?"

What did Martin remember? He remembered a good deal. He was surprised when he began to think ... "Did he remember ..." his father suggested a scene, a day—yes, he remembered that. His father continued, as though it had been for his own pleasure.

The scenes, the hours returned with a vividness and actuality that thronged the room.

He could see Mason Street with its grocer's shop at the corner, its Baths and Public Library, the sudden little black dips into the areas as the houses followed one another, the lamp-post opposite their window that had always excited him because it leaned inwards a little as though it would presently tumble. He remembered the fat short cook with the pink cotton dress who wheezed and blew so when she had to climb the stairs. He remembered the rooms that would seem bare enough to him now, he supposed, but were then filled with exciting possibilities—a little round brown table, his mother's work-box with mother-of-pearl shells upon the cover, a stuffed bird with bright blue feathers under a glass case, a screen with coloured pictures of battles and horses and elephants casted upon it. He remembered the exact sound that the tinkling bell made when it summoned them to meals, he remembered the especial smell of beef and carpet that was the dining-room, he remembered a little door of coloured glass on the first landing, a cupboard that had in it sugar and apples, a room full of old books piled high all about the floor upon the dry and dusty boards ... a thousand other things came crowding around him.

Then, as his father's voice continued, out from the background there came his own figure, a small, pale, excited boy in short trousers.

He was immensely excited—that was the principal thing. It was evening, the house seemed to swim in candlelight and smoke through which things could be seen only dimly.

Something wonderful was about to happen to him. He was in a state of glory, very close to God, so close that he could almost see Him sitting with His long white beard in the middle of a cloud, watching Martin with interest and affection. He was pleased with Martin and Martin was pleased with himself. At the same time as his pleasure he was aware that the stuff of his new black trousers tickled his knees and that he was hungry.

He saw his small sister Amy for a moment and expressed quite effectively by a smile and nod of the head his immeasurable superiority to her ...

They, he and his father, drove in a cab to the Chapel. Of what followed then he was now less aware. He remembered that he was in a small room with two men, that they all took off their clothes (he remembered that one man, very stout and red, looked funny without his clothes), that they put on long white night-shirts, that his was too long for him and that he tripped over it, that they all three walked down the centre of the Chapel, which was filled with eyes, mouths and boots, and that he was very conscious of his toe-nails, which had never been exposed in public before, that they came to a round stone place filled with water and into this after the two men he was dipped, that he didn't scream from the coldness, of the water although he wanted to, that he was wrapped in a blanket and finally carried home in an ecstasy of triumph.

What happiness followed! The vitality of it swept down upon him now, so that he seemed never to have lived since then. He was the chosen of God and every one knew it. What a little prig and yet how simple it had all been, without any consciousness of insincerity or acting on his part. God had chosen him and there he was, for ever and ever safe and happy.

It was not only that he was assured that when the moment arrived he would have, in Heaven, a "good time"—it was that he was greatly exalted, so that he gave his twopence a week pocket-money to his school-fellows, never pulled Amy's hair, never teased his mother's canary. He had been aware, young though he was, of another life. He prayed and prayed, he went to an endless succession of services and meetings. There was Mr. Bates, one of the leading brethren then, who loved him and spoilt him ... above all, through and beyond it all, there was his father, who adored him and whom he adored.

That adoration—of God, of his father, of life itself! Was it possible that a small boy, normal and ordinary enough in other ways, could feel so intensely such passions?

The dark room was crowding him with figures and scenes. A whole world that he had thought dead and withered was beating—urgently, insistently, upon his consciousness.

In another instant he did not know what surrender, what acknowledgement he might have made. It seemed to him that nothing in life was worth while save to receive again, in some fashion, that vitality that he had once known.

The door was flung open; a stream of light struck the dark; the shadows, memories, fled, helter-skelter, like crackling smoke into the air.

Amy stood in the doorway, blinking at him, scowling. He knew, for some undefined reason, that he could not meet his father's eyes. He jumped up and walked to the window.

CHAPTER II

EXPECTATION

Maggie developed marvellously during her first weeks in London. It could not truthfully be said that her aunts gave her great opportunity for development; so far as they were concerned she might as well have been back in the green seclusion of St. Dreots.

It is true that she accompanied her Aunt Elizabeth upon several shopping expeditions, and on one hazardous afternoon they penetrated the tangled undergrowth of Harrods' Stores; on all these occasions Maggie was too deeply occupied with the personal safety and happiness of her aunt to have leisure for many observations.

Aunt Elizabeth always started upon her shopping expeditions with the conviction that something terrible was about to happen, and the expectation of this overwhelming catastrophe paralysed her nerves. Maggie wondered how it could have been with her when she had ventured forth alone. She would stand in the middle of the street hesitating as to the right omnibus for her to take, she was often uncertain of the direction in which she should go. She would wave her umbrella at an omnibus, and then when it began to slacken in answer to her appeal, would discover that it was not the one that she needed, and would wave her umbrella furiously once more. Then when at last she had mounted the vehicle she would flood the conductor with a stream of little questions, darting her eyes angrily at all her neighbours as though they were gathered there together to murder her at the earliest opportunity. She would be desperately confused when asked to pay for her ticket, would be unable to find her purse, and then when she discovered it would scatter its contents upon the ground. In such an agony would she be at the threatened passing of her destination that she would spring up at every pause of the omnibus, striking her nearest neighbour's eye or nose with her umbrella, apologising nervously, and then, because she thought she had been too forward with a stranger, staring fiercely about her and daring any one to speak to her. Upon the day that she visited Harrods' she spent the greater part of her time in the lift because she always wished to be somewhere where she was not, and because it always went up when she wished it to go down and down when she wished it to go up. Maggie, upon this eventful occasion, did her best, but she also was bewildered, and wondered how any of the attendants found their way home at night. Before the end of the afternoon Aunt Elizabeth was not far from tears. "It isn't cutlery we want. I told the man that it was saucepans. They pay us no attention at all. You aren't any help to me, Maggie." They arrived in a room filled with performing gramophones. This was the final blow. Aunt Elizabeth, trembling all over, refused either to advance or retreat. "Will you please," said Maggie very firmly to a beautifully clothed young man with hair like a looking-glass, "show us the way to the street?" He very kindly showed them, and it was not until they were in the homeward omnibus that Aunt Elizabeth discovered that she had bought nothing at all.

Nevertheless, although Maggie collected but little interesting detail from these occasions, she did gather a fine general impression of whirling movement and adventure. One day she would plunge into it— meanwhile it was better that she should move slowly and assemble gradual impressions. The solid caution that was mingled in her nature with passionate feeling and enthusiasm taught her admirable wisdom. Aunt Anne, it seemed, never moved beyond the small radius of her home and the Chapel. She attended continually Bible-meetings, prayer-meetings, Chapel services. She had one or two intimate friends, a simple and devout old maid called Miss Pynchon, Mr. Magnus, whom Maggie had seen on the day of her arrival, Mr. Thurston, to whom Maggie had taken an instant dislike, and Amy Warlock. She visited these people and they visited her; for the rest she seemed to take no exercise, and her declared love for the country did not lead her into the Parks. She was more silent, if possible, than she had been at St. Dreots, and read to herself a great deal in the dark and melancholy drawing-room. Although she talked very little to Maggie, the girl fancied that her eye was always upon her. There was a strange attitude of watchfulness in her silent withdrawal from her scene as though she had retired simply because she could see the better from a distance.

She liked Maggie to read the Bible to her, and for an hour of every evening Maggie did this. For some reason the girl greatly disliked this hour and dreaded its approach. It was perhaps because it seemed to bring before her the figure of her father, the words as they fell from her lips seemed to be repeated by him as he stood behind her. Nothing was more unexpected by her than the way that those last days at St. Dreots crowded about her. They should surely have been killed by the colours and interests of this new life. It appeared that they were only accentuated by them. Especially did she see that night when she had watched beside her father's dead body ... she saw the stirring of the beard, the shape of the feet beneath the sheet, the flicker of the candle. Apart from this one hour of the day, however, she was happy, excited, expectant. What it was that she expected she did not exactly know, but there were so many things that life might now do for her. One thing that very evidently it did not intend to do for her was to make her tidy, careful, and a good manager. Old Martha, the Cardinal servant, was her sworn enemy, and, indeed, with reason. It seemed that Maggie could not remember the things that she was told: lighted lamps were left long after they should have been extinguished, one night the bathroom was drowned in water by a running tap, her clothes were not mended, she was never punctual at meal-times. And yet no one could call her a dreamy child. She could, about things that interested her, be remarkably sharp and penetrating. She had a swift and often successful intuition about characters; facts and details about places or people she never forgot. She had a hard, severe, entirely masculine sense of independence, an ironic contempt for sentimentality, a warm, ardent loyalty and simplicity in friendship. Her carelessness in all the details of life sprang from her long muddled years at St. Dreots, the lack of a mother's guidance and education, the careless selfishness of her father's disregard of her. She struggled, poor child, passionately to improve herself. She sat for hours in her room working at her clothes, trying to mend her stockings, the holes in her blouses, the rip of the braid at the bottom of her skirt. She waited listening for the cuckoo to call that she might be in exact time for luncheon or dinner, and then, as she listened, some thought would occur to her, and, although she did not dream, her definite tracking of her idea would lead her to forget all time. Soon there would be Martha's knock on the door and her surly ill-tempered voice:

"Quarter of an hour they've been sitting at luncheon, Miss."

And her clothes! The aunts had said that she must buy what was necessary, and she had gone with Aunt Elizabeth to choose all the right things. They had, between them, bought all the wrong ones. Maggie had no idea of whether or no something suited her; a dress, a hat that would look charming upon any one else looked terrible upon her; she did not know what was the matter, but nothing became her!

Her new friend, Caroline Smith, laughing and chattering, tried to help her. Caroline had very definite ideas about dress, and indeed spent the majority of her waking hours in contemplation of that subject. But she had never, she declared, been, in all her life, so puzzled. She was perfectly frank.

"But it looks AWFUL, Maggie dear, and yesterday in the shop it didn't seem so bad, although that old pig wouldn't let us have it the way we wanted. It's just as it is with poor mother, who gets fatter and fatter, diet herself as she may, so that she can wear nothing at all now that looks right, and is only really comfortable in her night-dress. Of course you're not FAT, Maggie darling, but it's your figure—everything's either too long or too short for you. You don't mind my speaking so frankly, do you? I always say one's either a friend or not, and if one's a friend why then be as rude as you please. What's friendship for?"

They were, in fact, the greatest possible friends. Maggie had never possessed a girl-friend before. She had, in the first days of the acquaintance, been shy and very silent—she had been afraid of going too far. But soon she had seen that she could not go too far and could not say too much. She had discovered then a multitude of new happinesses.

There was nothing, she found, too small, too unimportant to claim Caroline's interest. Caroline wished to know everything, and soon Maggie disclosed to her many things that she had told to no other human being in her life before. It could not honestly be said that Caroline had many wise comments to make on Maggie's experiences. Her attitude was one of surprised excitement. She was amazed by the most ordinary incidents and conversations. She found Maggie's life quite incredible.

"You must stop me, Maggie, if I hurt your feelings. But really! ... Why, if poor father had treated me like that I'd have gone straight out of the house and never come back. I would indeed ... Well, here you are now, dear, and we must just see each other as often as ever we can!"

They made a strange contrast, Maggie so plain in her black dress with her hair that always looked as though it had been cut short like a boy's, her strong rough movements, and Caroline, so neat and shining and entirely feminine that her only business in the world seemed to be to fascinate, beguile and bewilder the opposite sex. Whatever the aunts may have thought of this new friendship, they said nothing. Caroline had her way with them as with every one else. Maggie wondered often as to Aunt Anne's, real thoughts. But Aunt Anne only smiled her dim cold smile, gave her cold hand into the girl's warm one and said, "Good afternoon, Caroline. I hope your father and mother are well." "They're dears, you know," Caroline said to Maggie; "I do admire your Aunt Anne; she keeps to herself so. I wish I could keep to myself, but I never was able to. Poor mother used to say when I was quite little, 'You'll only make yourself cheap, Carrie, if you go on like that. Don't make yourself cheap, dear.' But what I say is, one's only young once and the people who don't want one needn't have one."

Nevertheless there were, even in these very early days, directions into which Maggie did not follow her new friend. Young as she was in many things, in some ways she was very old indeed. She had been trained in another school from Caroline; she felt from the very first that upon certain questions her lovely friend was inexperienced, foolish and dangerously reckless. On the question of "men," for instance, Maggie, with clear knowledge of her father and her uncle, refused to follow Caroline's light and easy excursions. Caroline was disappointed; she had a great deal to say on the subject and could speak, she assured Maggie, from a vast variety of experience: "Men are all the same. What I say is, show them you don't care 'that' about them and they'll come after you. Not that I care whether they do or no. Only it's fun the way they go on. You just try, Maggie."

But Maggie had her own thoughts. They were not imparted to her friend. Nothing indeed appeared to her more odd than that Caroline should be so wise in some things and so foolish in others. She did not know that it was her own strange upbringing that gave her independent estimates and judgments.

The second influence that, during these first weeks, developed her soul and body was, strangely enough, her aunt's elderly friend, Mr. Magnus. If Caroline introduced her to affairs of the world, Mr. Magnus introduced her to affairs of the brain and spirit.

She had never before known any one who might be called "clever." Her father was not, Uncle Mathew was not; no one in St. Dreots had been clever. Mr. Magnus, of course, was "clever" because he wrote books, two a year.

But to be an author, was not a claim to Maggie's admiration. As has been said before, she did not care for reading, and considered that the writing of books was a second-rate affair. The things that Mr. Magnus might have done with his life if he had not spent it in writing books! She regarded him with the kind indulgence of an elder who watches a child brick-building. He very quickly discovered her attitude and it amused him. They became the most excellent friends over it. She on her side very quickly discovered the true reason of his coming so often to their house; he loved Aunt Anne. At its first appearance this discovery was so strange and odd that Maggie refused to indulge it. Love seemed so far from Aunt Anne. She greeted Mr. Magnus from the chill distance whence she greeted the rest of the world—she gave him no more than she gave any one else—But Mr. Magnus did not seem to desire more. He waited patiently, a slightly ironical and self-contemptuous worshipper at a shrine that very seldom opened its doors, and never admitted him to its altar. It was this irony that Maggie liked in him; she regarded herself in the same way. Their friendship was founded on a mutual detachment. It prospered exceedingly.

Maggie soon discovered that Mr. Magnus was very happy to sit in their house even though Aunt Anne was not present. His attitude seemed to be that the atmosphere that she left behind her was enough for him and that he could not, in justice, expect any more. Before Maggie's arrival he had had but a slender excuse for his continual presence. He could not sit in the empty drawing-room surveying the large and ominous portrait of the Cardinal childhood, quite alone save for Thomas, without seeming a very considerable kind of fool. And to appear that in the eyes of Aunt Anne, who already regarded mankind in general with pity, would be a mistake.

Now that Maggie was here he might come so often as he pleased. Many was the dark afternoon through the long February and March months that they sat together in the dim drawing-room, Maggie straining her eyes over an attempted reform of some garment, Mr. Magnus talking in his mild ironical voice with his large moon-like spectacles fixed upon nothing in particular.

Mr. Magnus did all the talking. Maggie fancied that, all his life, he had persisted in the same gentle humorous fashion without any especial attention as to the wisdom, agreement or even existence of his audience. She fancied that all men who wrote books did that. They had to talk to "clear their ideas." She raised her eyes sometimes and looked at him as he sat there. His shabby, hapless appearance always appealed to her. She knew that he was, in reality, anything but hapless, but his clothes never fitted him, and it was impossible for him to escape from the Quixotic embarrassments of his thin hair, his high cheek-bones, his large spectacles. His smile, however, gave him his character; when he smiled—and he was always smiling—you saw a man independent, proud, wise and gentle. He was not a fool, Mr. Magnus, although he did love Aunt Anne.

To a great deal that he said Maggie paid but little attention; it was, she felt, not intended for her. She had, in all her relations with him, to struggle against the initial disadvantage that she regarded all men who wrote books with pity. She was not so stupid as not to realise that there were a great many fine books in the world and that one was the better for reading them, but, just because there were, already, so many fine ones, why write more that would almost certainly be not so fine? He tried to explain, to her that some men were compelled to write and could not help themselves.

"I wrote my first book when I was nineteen. One morning I just began to write, and then it was very easy. Then everything else was easy. The first publisher to whom I sent it accepted it. It was published and had quite a success. I thought I was made for life. Anything seemed possible to one. After all, so far as one's possibilities went one was on a level with any one—Shakespeare, Dante, any one you like. One might do anything... . I published a book a year, after that, for ten years—ten years ten books, and then awoke to the fact that I was nothing at all and would never be anything—that I would never write like Shakespeare, and, a matter of equal importance, would never sell like Mrs. Henry Wood. Not that I wished to write like any one else. I had a great idea of keeping to my own individuality, but I saw quite clearly that what I had in myself—all of it—was no real importance to any one. I might so well have been a butcher or baker for all it mattered. I saw that I was one of those unfortunate people—there are many of them—just in between the artists and the shopkeepers. I was an artist all right, but not a good enough one to count; had I been a shopkeeper I might have sold my goods."

"Well, then, here's your question, Miss Cardinal. Why on earth did I go on writing? ... Simply because I couldn't help myself. Writing was the only thing in the world that gave me happiness. I thought too that there might be people, here and there, unknown to me who cared for what I did. Not many of course—I soon discovered that outside the small library set in London no one had ever heard of me. When I was younger I had fancied that that to me fiery blazing advertisement: "New Novel by William Magnus, author of ..." must cause men to stop in the street, exclaim, rush home to tell their wives, 'Do you know Magnus' new novel is out?'—now I realised that by nine out of every ten men and five out of every ten women the literary page in the paper is turned over with exactly the same impatience with which I turn over the betting columns. Anyway, why not? ... perfectly right. And then by this time I'd seen my old books, often enough, lying scattered amongst dusty piles in second-hand shops marked, 'All this lot 6d.' Hundreds and hundreds of six-shilling novels, dirty, degraded, ashamed ... I'd ask, sometimes, when I was very young, for my own works. 'What's the name? What? Magnus?—No, don't stock him. No demand. We could get you a copy, sir...' There it is. Why not laugh at it? I was doing perhaps the most useless thing in the world. A commonplace little water-colour, hung on a wall, can give happiness to heaps of people; a poor piece of music can do a thousand things, good and bad, but an unsuccessful novel—twenty unsuccessful novels! A whole row, with the same history awaiting their successors ... 'We welcome a new novel by Mr. William Magnus, who our readers will remember wrote that clever story ... The present work seems to us at least the equal of any that have preceded it.' ... A fortnight's advertisement—Dead silence. Some one in the Club, 'I see you've written another book, old man. You do turn 'em out.' A letter from a Press Agency who has never heard of one's name before, 'A little sheaf of thin miserable cuttings.' ... The Sixpenny Lot ... Ouf! And still I go on and shall go on until I die. Perhaps after all I'm more justified than any of them. I'm stripped of all reasons save the pleasure, the thrill, the torment, the hopes, the despairs of the work itself. I've got nothing else out of it and shall get nothing ... and therefore I'm justified. Now do you understand a little, Miss Cardinal?"

She half understood. She understood that he was compelled to do it just as some men are compelled to go to race meetings and just as Uncle Mathew was compelled to drink.

But she nevertheless thought it a dreadful pity that he was unable to stop and interest himself in something else. Then he could see it so plainly and yet go on! She admired and at the same time pitied him.

It seemed, this private history of Mr. Magnus, at first sight so far from Maggie's immediate concerns, her new life, her aunts, the Chapel and the Chapel world. It was only afterwards, when she looked back, that she was able to see that all these private affairs of private people radiated inwards, like the spokes of a wheel, towards the mysterious inner circle—that inner circle of which she was already dimly aware, and of which she was soon to feel the heat and light. She was, meanwhile, so far impressed by Mr. Magnus' confidences that she borrowed one of his novels from Caroline, who confided to her that she herself thought it the dullest and most tiresome of works. "To be honest, I only read a bit of it—I don't know what it's about. I think it's downright silly."

This book bore the mysterious title of "Dredinger." It was concerned apparently with the experiences of a young man who, buying an empty house in Bloomsbury, discovered a pool of water in the cellar. The young man was called Dredinger, which seemed to Maggie an unnatural kind of name. He had an irritating habit of never finishing his sentences, and the people he knew answered him in the same inconclusive fashion. The pool in the cellar naturally annoyed him, but he did nothing very practical about it, allowed it to remain there, and discussed it with a Professor of Chemistry. Beyond this Maggie could not penetrate. The young man was apparently in love with a lady much older than himself, who wore pince-nez, but it was an arid kind of love in which the young man discovered motives and symptoms with the same dexterous surprise with which he discovered newts and tadpoles in the cellar-pond. Maggie bravely attacked Mr. Magnus.

"Why didn't he have men in to clear up the pond and lay a new floor?" she asked.

"That was just the point," said Mr. Magnus. "He couldn't."

"Why couldn't he?"

"Weakness of character and waiting to see what would happen."

"He talked too much," she answered decisively. "But are there houses in London with ponds in them?"

"Lots," said Mr. Magnus. "Only the owners of the houses don't know it. There is a big pond in the Chapel. That's what Thurston came out of."

This was beyond Maggie altogether. An agreeable thing, however, about Mr. Magnus was that he did not mind when you disliked his work. He seemed to expect that you would not like it. He was certainly a very unconceited man.

A more important and more interesting theme was Mr. Magnus' reason for being where he was. What was he doing here? What led him to the Chapel doors, he being in no way a religious man?

"It was like this," he told her. "I was living in Golders Green, and suddenly one morning I was tired of the country that wasn't country, and the butcher boy and the postman. So I moved as far into the centre of things as I could and took a room in St. Martin's Lane close at hand here. Then one evening I was wandering about, a desolate Sunday evening when the town is given over to cats. I suddenly came across the Chapel. I like going into London churches by chance, there's always something interesting, something you wouldn't expect. The Chapel simply astonished me. I couldn't imagine what they were all about, it wasn't the ordinary London congregation, it was almost the ordinary London service and yet not quite; there was an air of expectation and even excitement which is most unusual in a London church. Then there was Warlock. Of course one could see at once that he was an extraordinary man, a kind of prophet all on his own; he was as far away from that congregation as Columbus was from his crew when he first sighted the Indies."

"I've met one or two prophets in my time, and their concern has always been with their audience first, themselves second and their vision last. Warlock is the other way round. He should have been a hermit, not the leader of a community. Well, it interested me. I came again and again ... I'm going to stay on now until the end."

"The end?" asked Maggie.

"The end of myself or the Chapel, whichever comes first. I wrote a story once—a very bad one—about some merchants—why merchants I don't know—who were flung on a desert island. It was all jungle and desolation, and then suddenly they came upon a little white Temple. It doesn't matter what happened afterwards. I've myself forgotten most of it, but I remember that the sailors used the Temple in different ways to keep their hopes and expectations alive. Their expectations that one day a ship would come and save them ... and so far as I remember they became imaginative about the Temple, and fancied that the Unknown God of it would help them to regain their private affairs: one of them wanted to get back to his girl, another to his favourite pub, another to his money-making, another to his collection of miniatures. And they used to sit and look at the Temple day after day and expect something to happen. When the ship came at last they wouldn't go into it because they couldn't bear to think that something should happen at last and they not be there to see it. Oh yes, one of them went back, I remember. But his actual meeting with his girl was so disappointing in comparison with his long expectation of it in front of the Temple that he took the next boat back to the island ... but he never found it again. He travelled everywhere and died, a disappointed man, at sea."

Mr. Magnus was fond of telling little stories, obscure and pointless, and Maggie supposed that it was a literary habit. On this occasion he continued to talk quite naturally for his own satisfaction. "Yes, one can make oneself believe in anything. I have believed in all sorts of things. In England, of course, people have believed in nothing except that things will always be as they always have been—a useful belief considering that things have never been as they always were. In the old days, when the Boer War hadn't interfered with tradition, it must have seemed to any one who wasn't a young man pretty hopeless, but now I don't know. Imagination's breaking in ... Warlock's a prophet. I've got fascinated, sitting round this Chapel, as badly as any of them. Yes, one can be led into belief of anything."

"And what do you believe in, Mr. Magnus?" asked Maggie.

"Well, not in myself anyway, nor Thurston, nor Miss Avies ... But in your Aunt perhaps, and Warlock. The only thing I'm sure of is that there's something there, but what it is of course I can't tell you, and I don't suppose I shall ever know. The story of Sir Galahad, Miss Cardinal—it seems mid-Victorian to us now—but it's a fine story and true enough."

Maggie, who knew nothing of mid-Victorianism, was silent.

He ended with: "Mind you decide for yourself. That's the great thing in life. Don't you believe anything that any one tells you. See for yourself. And if there's something of great value, don't think the less of it because the people who admire it aren't worth very much. Why should they be? And possibly after all it's only themselves they're admiring ... There's a fearful lot of nonsense and humbug in this thing, but there's something real too ..."

He changed his note, suddenly addressing himself intently to her as though he had a message to deliver.

"Don't think me impertinent. But your Aunt Anne. See as much of her as you can. She's devoted to you, Miss Cardinal. You mayn't have seen it—she's a reserved woman and very shy of her feelings, but she's spoken to me ... I hope I'm not interfering to say this, but perhaps at first you don't understand her. She loves you, you're the first human being I do believe that she's ever loved."

What was there then in Maggie that started up in rebellion at this unexpected declaration? She had been sitting there, tranquil, soothed with a happy sense that her new life was developing securely for her in the way that she would have it. Suddenly she was alert, suspicious, hostile.

"What has she said to you?" she asked quickly, frowning up at him and drawing back as though she were afraid of him. He was startled at the change in her.

"Said?" he repeated, stammering a little. "Why only ... Nothing ... except that she cared for you and hoped that you would be happy. She was afraid that it would all be strange for you at first ... Perhaps I have been interfering ..."

"No," Maggie interrupted quickly. "Not you. Only I must lead my own life. I must, mustn't I? I don't want to be selfish, but I can begin for myself now. I have a little money of my own—and I MUST make my own way. I don't want to be selfish," she repeated, "but I must be free. I don't understand Aunt Anne. She never seems to care for me. I want to do everything for her I can, but I don't want to be under any one ever any more."

She was so young when she said this that he was suddenly moved to an affectionate fatherly tenderness—but he knew her now too well to show it.

"No, you mustn't be selfish," he answered her almost drily. "We can't lead our lives quite alone, you know—every step we take we affect some one somewhere. Your aunt doesn't want your liberty—she wants your affection."

"She wants to make me religious," Maggie brought out, staring at Mr. Magnus.

"Ah, if you see that, you don't understand her," he answered. "How should you—yet? She cares so deeply for her religion that she wishes naturally any one whom she loves to share it with her. But if you don't—"

"If you don't?" cried Maggie, springing up from her seat and facing him.

"I'm sure she would wish to influence no one," he continued gravely. "You've seen for yourself how apart her life is. She is too conscious of the necessity for her own liberty—"

"It isn't liberty, it's slavery," Maggie caught him up passionately. "Do you suppose I haven't watched all these weeks? What does her religion do but shut her off from everything and everybody? Is she kind to Aunt Elizabeth? No, she isn't, and you know it. Would she care if we were all of us buried in the ruins of this house to-morrow? Not for a single moment. And it's her religion. I hate religion. I hate it! ... and since I've been in this house I've hated it more and more. You don't know what it was like with father. I don't think of it now or talk of it, but I know what it made of HIM. And now it's the same here, only it takes them in a different way. But it's the same in the end—no one who's religious cares for any one.

And they'd make the same of me. Aunt Anne would—the same as she's made of Aunt Elizabeth. They haven't said much yet, but they're waiting for the right moment, and then they'll spring it upon me. It's in the house, it's in the rooms, it's in the very furniture. It's as though father had come back and was driving me into it. And I want to be free, I want to lead my own life, to make it myself. I don't want to think about God or Heaven or Hell. I don't care whether I'm good or bad.... What's the use of my being here in London and never seeing anything. I'll go into a shop or something and work my fingers to the bone. They SHAN'T catch me. They SHAN'T ... If Uncle Mathew were here ..."

She broke off suddenly, breathless, staring at Mr. Magnus as though she had not been aware until now that he was in the room. To say that her outburst astonished him was to put it very mildly indeed. She had always been so quiet and restrained; she had seemed so happy and tranquil.

He blushed, pushed his spectacles with his fingers, then finally stammered:

"I'd no idea—that—that you hated it so much."

She was quiet and composed again. "I don't hate it," she answered very calmly. "Only they shan't tie me—no one shall. And in the house it's as though some one were watching behind every door. It used to be just the same at home. When people think a lot about religion something seems to get into a place. Why, truly, Mr. Magnus, I've wondered once or twice lately, in spite of myself, whether they mayn't be right after all and God's going to come in a chariot and set the world on fire."

"It sounds silly, but when you see the way Aunt Anne and Mr. Warlock believe things it almost makes them true."

Maggie finally added: "You mustn't think me selfish. I'm very very grateful for all their kindness. I'm very happy. It's all splendid compared with what life used to be at home—but I fancy sometimes that the aunts think I'm just going to settle down here for ever and be like them—and I'm not—I'm afraid of Aunt Anne."

"Afraid of her?" said Mr. Magnus. "Ah, you mustn't be that."

"She has some plan in her head. I know she has—"

"No plan is set except for your good," said Mr. Magnus.

"I don't want any one to bother about my good," answered Maggie. "I can look after that for myself."

This little conversation revealed Maggie to Mr. Magnus in an entirely new light. He had thought her, until now, a good simple girl, entirely ignorant of life and eager to be taught. The sudden discovery of her independence distressed him. He left the house that afternoon with many new points to consider.

Meanwhile Maggie had kept from him the true root of the matter. She had said nothing of Martin Warlock. She had said nothing, even to herself, about him, and yet the consciousness of her meeting with him was always with her as a fire smoulders in the hold of a ship, burning stealthily through the thick heart of the place, dim and concealed, to burst suddenly, with a touch of the wind, into shining flame.

It was after her talk to Mr. Magnus that she suddenly saw that Martin Warlock was always in her thoughts, and then, because she was Maggie and had never been deceitful to herself or to any one else, she faced the fact and considered it. She knew that she was ignorant of the world and of life, that she knew nothing about men and, although she had many times fancied to herself what love must be like, she did not tell herself now that it was love that had come to her.

She saw him as a desirable companion; she thought that he would make a most interesting friend; she would like to make her experiences of life with him at her side. She would be free and he would be free, but they would exchange confidences.

And then because she was very simple and had learnt nothing of the difference between the things that decent girls might do and the things they might not she began to consider the easiest way of meeting him. She intended to go to him simply as one human being to another and tell him that she liked him and hoped that they would often see one another. There were no confused issues nor questions of propriety before Maggie. Certainly she was aware that men took advantage of girls' weakness—but that was, as in the case of Uncle Mathew, when they had drunk too much—and it was the fault of the girls, too, for not looking after themselves. Maggie felt that she could look after herself anywhere. She was more afraid, by far, of her Aunt Anne than of any man.

It happened on the very day after that conversation with Mr. Magnus that Aunt Anne said at luncheon:

"I think, Maggie dear, if you don't mind, that you and I will pay a call on Mrs. Warlock this afternoon. You have not been there yet. To-day will be a very good opportunity."

Maggie's mind flew at once to her clothes. She had been with Caroline Smith to that young lady's dressmaker, a thin and sharp-faced woman whose black dress gleamed with innumerable pins. Maggie had been pinched and measured, pulled in here and pulled out there. Then there had been afternoons when she had been "fitted" under Caroline's humorous and critical eye. Finally the dress had been delivered, only two days ago, in a long card-board box; it waited now for the great occasion.

The great occasion had, in the guise of the Warlock family, surely arrived. Maggie's heart beat as she went up to her room. When at last she was wearing the dress, standing before her mirror, her cheeks were red and her hands shook a little.

The dress was very fine—simple of course and quite plain, but elegant as no dress of Maggie's had ever been elegant. There surely could not anywhere be a more perfect black dress, and yet, as Maggie gazed, she was aware that there was something not quite right. She was always straightforward with herself; yes, the thing that was not quite right was her own stupid shape. Her figure was too square, her back was too short, her hands too large. She had a moment of acute disgust with herself so that she could have torn the dress from her and rushed into her old obscure and dingy black again. Of what use to dress her up? She would always look wrong, always be awkward and ungainly ... tears of disappointment gathered slowly in her eyes. Then her pride reasserted itself; she raised her head proudly and laughed at her anxious gaze. There was still her new hat. She took it from the bed and put it on, sticking big pins into it, moving back from the mirror, then forward again, turning her back, standing on her toes, suddenly bowing to herself and waving her hand.

She was caught thus, laughing into the mirror, by old Martha, who pushed her sour face through the door and said: "They've been waiting this long time for you, Miss."

"All right, Martha," Maggie answered sharply, annoyed that she should be found, posturing and bowing, by the woman. "Why didn't you knock?"

"I did knock, Miss. You were that occupied you didn't hear me." The old woman was grinning.

Maggie went downstairs, her heart still beating, her cheeks still flushed. She did hope that Aunt Anne would be pleased. Aunt Anne, although she never said anything about clothes, must, of course, notice such things, and if she loved Maggie as Mr. Magnus said she did, then she would "show her approval." The girl stood for a moment on the bottom step of the staircase looking at her aunt who was waiting for her in the little dark hall.

"Well, dear—I'm waiting," she said.

The burning eyes of Thomas the cat watched from the deep shadows.

"I'm so sorry. I was dressing," said Maggie.

Her aunt said nothing more and they left the house.

Maggie, as always when she walked with Aunt Anne, was aware that they made a strange couple, she so short and the other so tall, she with her sturdy masculine walk, her aunt with her awkward halting movement. They went in silence.

Maggie longed for a word of approval; a short sentence such as "How nice you're looking, Maggie," or "I like your dress, Maggie," or "That's a new dress, dear—I like it," would be enough. After that Maggie felt that she could face a multitude of wild and savage Warlocks, that she could walk into the Warlock drawing-room with a fine brave carriage, above all, that she would feel a sudden warm affection for her aunt that would make all their future life together easy.

But Aunt Anne said nothing. She looked exactly as she had looked upon her first appearance at St. Dreots, so thin and tall, with her pale tapering face and her eyes staring before her as though they saw nothing.

Maggie, as they turned up into Garrick Street, said:

"I hope you like my new dress, aunt."

Aunt Anne turned to her for a moment, smiled gently and then vaguely, as though her mind were elsewhere, answered:

"I liked your old dress better, dear."

Maggie's face flamed; her temper flared into her eyes. For a moment she had wild thoughts of breaking into open rebellion. She hated her dress, she hated London, above all, she hated Aunt Anne. That lady's happy unconsciousness that anything had occurred drove the girl into furious irritation. Well, it was hopeless then, Mr. Magnus could say what he pleased, her aunt did not care for her—she would not mind did she fall dead in the street before her. The words in Maggie's mind were: "You don't look at me.

I'm not a human being to you at all. But I won't live with you. I'll go my own way. You can't keep me if you never speak to me nor think of me." But in some dark fashion that strange impassivity held her. Aunt Anne had her power ...

They climbed the dim crooked staircase behind the antiquary's wall. They rang the Warlock bell and were admitted. Maggie did not know what it was that she had expected, but it was certainly not the pink, warm room of Mrs. Warlock.

The heavy softly closing door hemmed them in, the silent carpet folded about their steps; the canary twittered, the fire spurted and crackled. But at once the girl's heart went out to old Mrs. Warlock; she looked so charming in her white cap and blue bow, her eyes were raised so gently to Maggie's face and her little hand was so soft and warm.

The meeting between Anne Cardinal and Mrs. Warlock was very gracious. Aunt Anne gravely pressed the old lady's hand, looked at her with her grave distant eyes, then very carefully and delicately sat down.

Amy Warlock came in; Maggie had met her before and disliked her. Conversation dealt decently and carefully with the weather, the canary and Maggie's discovery of London. Maggie was compelled to confess that she was afraid that she had not discovered London at all. She felt Amy Warlock's sharp eyes upon them all and, as always when she was in company that was, she thought, suspicious of her, she became hot and uncomfortable, she frowned and spoke in short, almost hostile, sentences.

"They're laughing at my new clothes," she thought, "I wish I'd worn my old ones ... and anyway these hurt me." She sat up very stiffly, her hands on her lap, her eyes staring at the little bright water-colour on the wall opposite. Mrs. Warlock, like a trickling, dancing brook, continued her talk:

"Of course there's the country. I was brought up as a girl just outside Salisbury ... So many, many years ago—I always tell my boy that I'm such an old woman now that I don't belong to his world at all. Just to sit here and see the younger generation go past. Don't regret your youth, Miss Cardinal. You'll want it back again one day. I said to Martin only yesterday ..."

Neither Aunt Anne nor Amy Warlock had anything to say, so that quite suddenly on the entrance of tea, conversation dropped. They all sat there and looked at one another. There was a large silver tray with silver tea-things upon it and a fat swelling china dish that held hot buttered toast. There was a standing wicker pyramid containing bread and butter, plates of little yellow and red cakes, shortbread and very heavy plum cake black with currants.

Mrs. Warlock had ceased all conversation, her eyes were fixed upon the preparations for tea. The door opened and John Warlock and his son came in.

Maggie's eyes lighted when she saw Martin Warlock. She behaved as she might have done had she been in her own room at St. Dreots. She sprang up from her chair and stood there, smiling, waiting for him. First his father shook hands with her, then Martin came and stood beside her, laughing.

His face was flushed and he seemed excited about something, but she felt nothing save her pleasure at meeting him, and it was only when he had moved on to her aunt that she was conscious once more of Amy Warlock's eyes, and wondered whether she had behaved badly in jumping up to meet him.

As she considered this her anger and her confusion at her anger increased. She saw that Martin was talking to her aunt and did not look at her. Perhaps he also had thought her forward; of course that horrid sister of his would think everything that she did wrong. But did he? Surely he understood. She wanted to ask him and then wanted to go home and leave them all. She saw that her teacup was trembling in her hand. She steadied it upon her knee and then her knee began to quiver, and all the time Amy Warlock watched her. She thought then that she must assert herself and show that she was not confused nor timid, so she began in a high-strained voice to talk to Mrs. Warlock. She told Mrs. Warlock that she found Harrods' a confusing place, that she had not yet visited Westminster Abbey, that her health was quite good, that she had no brothers and no sisters, that she could not play the piano, and that she was afraid that she never read books.

It was after the last of these interesting statements that she was suddenly aware of the sound of her own voice, as though it had been a brazen gong beating stridently in the vastness of a deserted Cathedral. She saw the old lady take two pieces of buttered toast from the china dish, hold them tenderly in her hand and fling them a swift, bird-like glance before she devoured them; during that moment's vision Maggie discovered what so many people of vaster experience both of life and of Mrs. Warlock had never discovered; namely, that the old lady cared more for her food than her company. Maggie was suddenly less afraid of the whole family. She looked up then at Martin as though she thus would prove her new courage and, he glancing across at the same moment, they smiled. He left his father's side and, coming over to her, sat down close to her. He dropped his voice in speaking to her.

"I've been wanting to see you," he said.

"Why?" she asked him.

"Well," he answered, smiling at her as though he wanted to tell her something privately. "I feel as though we'd got a lot to tell one another ... I'm a stranger here really quite as much as you."

"No, you're not," she said. "You can't be so MUCH a stranger anywhere because you've been all over the world and are ready for anything."

"And you?"

"I don't seem to manage the simplest things. Aunt Elizabeth and I get lost the moment we move outside the door ... Do you like my dress?" she asked him.

"Why!" he said, obviously startled by such a question. "It's—it's splendid!"

"No, you know it isn't," she answered quickly, dropping her voice into a confidential statement. "It's all wrong. I thought you'd know why as you've been everywhere. Caroline Smith helped me to choose it, and it looked all right until I wore it. It's me ... I'm hopeless to fit. Caroline says so. I don't care about clothes—if only I looked just like anybody else I'd never bother again—but it's so tiresome to have taken so much trouble and then for it to be all wrong."

Martin was then aware of many things—that this was a strange unusual girl, that she reassured him as to her interest, her vitality, her sincerity as no girl had ever done before, that his sister was aware of their intimate conversation and that she resented it, and that he must see this girl again and as soon as possible. He was as liable as any young man in the world to the most sudden and most violent enthusiasms, but they had been enthusiasms for a pretty face, for a sensual appeal, for a sentimental moment. Here there was no prettiness, no sensuality, no sentiment. There was something so new that he felt like Cortez upon his peak in Darien.

"It's all right," he reassured her urgently. "It's all right. I promise you it is. The great thing is to look yourself. And you'll never be the least like any one else." He meant that to be the first open declaration of his own particular discovery of her, but he was aware that his sentence could have more than one interpretation. Uncomfortably conscious then of his sister's regard of them, he looked up and said:

"Amy, Miss Cardinal's been telling me how confusing London is to her. You've got as good an idea of London as any one in the world. You should take her to one or two places and show her things."

Amy Warlock, every line of her stiff body firing at them both her hostility, answered:

"Oh, I don't think Miss Cardinal would care for me as a guide. I shouldn't be able to show her interesting things. We have scarcely, I should fancy, enough in common. Miss Cardinal's interests are, I imagine, very different from my own."

The tone, the words, fell into the sudden silence like a lighted match into water. Maggie, her head erect, her voice, in spite of herself, trembling a little, answered:

"Why, Miss Warlock, I shouldn't think of troubling you. It's very kind of your brother, but one must make one's discoveries for oneself, mustn't one? ... I am already beginning to find my way about."

After that the tea-party fell into complete disruption. Maggie, although she did not look, could feel Martin's anger like a flame beside her. She was aware that Aunt Anne and Mr. Warlock were, like some beings from another world, distant from the general confusion. Her one passionate desire was to get up and leave the place; to her intense relief she heard Aunt Anne's clear voice:

"I think, Mrs. Warlock, we must be turning homewards. Shall I send you those papers about the Perteway's Mission? ... Such splendid work. I think it would interest you."

It was as though a hole had suddenly opened in the floor of the neat little drawing-room and they were all hurrying to leave without, if possible, tumbling into it. There was a general shaking of hands.

Mrs. Warlock said kindly to Maggie:

"Do come soon again, dear. It does an old lady good to see young faces."

Martin was near the door. He almost crushed Maggie's hand in his: "I must see you—soon," he whispered.

Free from the house Maggie and her aunt walked home in complete silence. Maggie's heart was a confusion of rage, surprise, loneliness and pride. No one had ever behaved like that to her before. And what had she done? What was there about her that people hated? ... Why? ... Why? She felt as though, in some way, it had all been Aunt Anne's fault. Why did not Aunt Anne speak? Well, if they all hated her she would go on her own way. She did not care.

But alone in her room, her face, indignant, proud, quivering, surprising her in the long mirror by its strangeness, and causing her to feel, because it did not seem to belong to her, more lonely than ever, she burst out:

"I can't stand it. I CAN'T stand it. I'll get away ... so soon as ever I can!"

CHAPTER III

MAGGIE AND MARTIN

That moment in her bedroom altered for Maggie the course of all her future life. She had never before been, consciously, a rebel; she had, only a week before, almost acquiesced in the thought that she would remain in her aunts' house for the rest of her days; now Mr. Magnus, the Warlocks, and her new dress had combined to fire her determination. She saw, quite suddenly, that she must escape at the first possible moment.

The house that had been until now the refuge into which she had escaped became the jumping-off place for her new adventure.

Until now the things in the house had been there to receive her as one of themselves; from this moment they were there to prevent, if possible, her release. She felt everything instantly hostile. They all—Thomas the cat, Edward the parrot, the very sofas and chairs and cushions—were determined not to let her go.

She saw, more than ever before, that her aunts were preparing some religious trap for her. They were very quiet about it; they did not urge her or bully her, but the subtle, silent influence went on so that the very stair-carpet, the very scuttles that held the coal, became secret messengers to hale her into the chapel and shut her in there for ever. After her first visit there the chapel became a nightmare to her—because, at once, she had felt its power. She had known—she had always known and it had not needed Mr. Magnus to tell her—that there was something in this religion—yes, even in the wretched dirt and disorder of her father's soul—but with that realisation that there was indeed something, had come also the resolved conviction that life could not be happy, simple, successful unless one broke from that power utterly, refused its dictates, gave no hearing to its messages, surrendered nothing—absolutely nothing—to its influence. Had not some one said to her once, or was it not in her little red A Kempis, that "once caught one might never escape again"?

She would prove that, in her own struggle and independence, to be untrue. The chapel should not have her, nor her father's ghost, nor the dim half-visualised thoughts and memories that rose like dark shadows in her soul and vanished again. She would believe in nothing save what she could see, listen to nothing that was not clear and simple before her. She was mistress of her own soul.

She did not, in this fashion, think things out for herself. To herself she simply expressed it that she was going to lead her own life, to earn her own living, to fight for herself; and that the sooner she escaped this gloomy, damp, and ill-tempered house the better. She would never say her prayers again; she would never read the Bible again to herself or any one else; she would never kneel on those hard chapel kneelers again; she would never listen to Mr. Warlock's sermons again—once she had escaped.

Meanwhile she said nothing at all to herself about Martin Warlock, who was really at the root of the whole matter.

She began at once to take steps. Two years before this a lady had paid, with her sister, a short visit to St. Dreots and had taken a great liking to Maggie. They had made friends, and this lady, a Miss Katherine Trenchard, had begged Maggie to let her know if she came to London and needed help or advice. Miss Trenchard divided her life between London and a place called Garth in Roselands in Glebeshire, and Maggie did not know where she would be now—but, after some little hesitation, she wrote a letter, speaking of the death of her father and of her desire to find some work in London, and directed it to Garth.

Now of course she must post it herself—no allowing it to lie on the hall-table with old Martha to finger it and the aunts to speculate upon it and finally challenge her with its destiny.

On a bright evening when the house was as dark as a shut box and an early star, frightened at its irregular and lonely appearance, suddenly flashed like a curl of a golden whip across the sky, Maggie slipped out of the house. She realised, with a triumphant and determined nod of her head, that she had never been out alone in London before—a ridiculous and shameful fact! She knew that there was a pillar-box just round the corner, but because she had a hat upon her head and shoes upon her feet she thought that she might as well post it in the Strand, an EXCITING river of tempestuous sound into which she had as yet scarcely penetrated. She slipped out of the front door, then waited a moment, looking back at the silent house. No one stirred in their street; the noise of the Strand came up to her like wind beyond a valley. She must have felt, in that instant, that she was making some plunge into hazardous waters and she must have hesitated as to whether she would not spring back into the quiet house, lock and bolt the door, and never go out again. But, after that one glance, she went forward.

She had never before in her life been on any errand alone, and at this evening hour the Strand was very full. She stood still clinging to the safe privacy of her own street and peering over into the blaze and quiver of the tumult. In the Strand end of her own street there were several dramatic agencies, a second-hand book and print shop with piles of dirty music in the barrow outside the window, a little restaurant with cold beef, an ancient chicken, hard-boiled eggs and sponge cakes under glass domes in the window; everywhere about her were dim doors, glimpses of twisting stairs, dusty windows and figures flitting up and down, in and out as though they were marionettes pulled by invisible strings to fulfil some figure.

These were all in the dusk of the side-street; a large draper's with shirts and collars and grinning wax boys in sailor suits caught with its front windows the Strand lamps. It was beside the shop that Maggie stood for an instant hesitating. She could see no pillar-box; she could see nothing save the streams of human beings, slipping like water between the banks of houses.

She hesitated, clinging to the draper's shop; then, suddenly catching sight of the pillar-box a few yards down the street, she let herself go, had a momentary sensation of swimming in a sea desperately crowded with other bodies, fought against the fierce gaze of lights that beat straight upon her eyes, found the box, slipped in the letter, and then, almost at once, was back in her quiet quarters again.

She turned and, her heart beating, hurried home. The house door was still ajar. She pushed it back, slipped inside, caught her breath and listened. Then she closed the door softly behind her, and with that little act of attempted secrecy realised that she was now a rebel, that things could never be, for her, the same again as they had been a quarter of an hour ago. That glittering crowd, the lamps, the smells, the sounds, had concentrated themselves into a little fiery charm that held her heart within a flaming circle. She felt the most audacious creature in the world—and also the most ignorant. Not helpless—no, never helpless—but so ignorant that all her life that had seemed to her, a quarter of an hour ago, so tensely crowded with events and crises was now empty and barren like the old straw-smelling cab at home. She did not want to offend her aunts and hurt their feelings, but she was a living, breathing, independent creature and she must go her own way. Neither they nor their chapel should stop her—no, not the chapel nor any one in it.

She was standing, motionless, in the dark cold hall, wondering whether any one had heard her enter, when she was suddenly conscious of two eyes that watched her—two steady fiery eyes suspended as it seemed in mid air. She realised that it was the cat. The cat hated her and she hated it. She had not realised that before, but now with the illumination of the lighted street behind her she realised it. The cat was the spirit of the chapel watching her, spying upon her to see that she did not escape. The cat knew that she had posted her letter and to whom she had posted it. She advanced to the bottom of the stair and said: "Brr. You horrid thing! I hate you!" and instantly the two fiery eyes had vanished, but now in their place the whole house seemed to be watching, so silent and attentive was it—and the odour of damp biscuits and wet umbrellas seemed to be everywhere.

Just then old Martha came out with a lamp in her hand, and standing upon a chair, lit the great ugly gas over the middle of the door.

"Why, Miss Maggie," she said in her soft, surprised whisper, looking as she always did, beyond the girl, into darkness.

"I've been out," said Maggie, defiantly.

"Not all alone, miss?"

"All alone," said Maggie. "Why not? I can look after myself."

"Well, there's your uncle waiting in the drawing-room—just come," said the old woman, climbing down from the chair with that silent imperturbable discontent that always frightened Maggie.

"Uncle Mathew! Here! in this house!" Maggie, even in the moment of her first astonishment, was amazed at her own delight. That she should ever feel THAT about Uncle Mathew! Truly it showed how unhappy she had been, and she ran upstairs, two steps at a time, and pushed back the drawing-room door.

"Uncle Mathew!" she cried.

Then at the sight of him she stood where she was. The man who faced her, with all his old confusion of nervousness and uneasy geniality, was, indeed, Uncle Mathew, but Uncle Mathew glorified, shabbily glorified and at the same time a little abashed as though she had caught him in the act of laying a mine that would blow up the whole house. He was wearing finer clothes than she had ever seen him in before—a frock coat, quite new but fitting him badly, so that it was buttoned too tightly across his stomach and loose across the back. He had a white flower in his button-hole, and a rather soiled white handkerchief protruded from his breast-pocket. One leg of his dark grey trousers had been creased in two places, and there were little spots of blood on his high white collar because he had cut himself shaving. His complexion was of the same old suppressed purple, but his little eyes were bright and shining and active; they danced towards Maggie. His scanty locks had been carefully brushed over his bald head, and his hands, although they were still puffed and swollen, were whiter than Maggie had ever seen them.

But it was in the end his attitude of confused defiance that made her pause. What had he been doing, or what did he intend to do? He was prosperous, she could see, and knowing him as she did, she was afraid of his prosperity. She had never in her life realised so clearly as she did now that he was a wicked old man—and still she was glad to see him. He was an odd enough creature in that room, and that, she was aware, pleased her.

"Well, my dear," he said very genially, as though they met again after an hour's parting, "how are you? I'm very glad to see you—looking so well too. And quite smart. Your aunts dressed you up. I thought I must look at you. I'm staying just round the corner, and my first thought was 'I wonder how she's getting on in all that tom-foolery. You bet she's keeping her head.' And so you are. One can see at a glance."

She went up to him, kissed him, and smelt whisky and some scent that had geraniums in it. He put his arm round her, with his old unsteady gesture, and held her to him for a moment, then patted her back with his large, soft hand.

"Your aunt's a long time. I've been waiting half an hour."

"They've been to some meeting." She stood looking at him with her fine steady gaze that had always made him afraid of her, and did so, to his own surprise, again now. He had thought that his clothes would have saved him from that; his fingers felt at his button-hole. Looking at him she said:

"Uncle, I want to get away—out of this—at once. No, they aren't horrid to me. Every one's been very kind. But I'm afraid of it all—of never getting out of it—and I want to be independent ..." She stopped with a little breathless gasp because she heard the hall-door close. "Ah, they're here! Don't tell them anything. We'll talk afterwards ..."

His eyes glittered with satisfaction. "I knew you would, my dear. I knew you wouldn't be able to stand it ... I'll get you out of it ... Trust me!"

The door opened and Aunt Anne came in. She had been prepared by Martha for her visitor, and she came forward to him now with the dignity and kindly patronage of some lady abbess receiving the miscreant and boorish yokel of a neighbouring village. And yet how fine she was! As Maggie watched her, she thought of what she would give to have some of that self-command and dignity and decision. Was it her religion that gave her that? Or only her own self-satisfaction? No; there was something behind Aunt Anne, something stronger than she, something that Mr. Warlock also knew ... and it was this something that Uncle Mathew met with his own hostility as he looked up now at his sister and greeted her:

"Why, Mathew! You never told us. I would have hurried back, and now Elizabeth, I'm afraid, has gone on to see some friends. She will be so disappointed. But at least you've had Maggie to entertain you."

A quick glance was exchanged between uncle and niece.

"Yes," he said, "we've had a talk, Anne, thank you. And it doesn't matter about Elizabeth, because I'm staying close here in Henrietta Street, and I'll be in again if I may. I just looked in to ask whether Maggie might come and have dinner with me at my little place to-night. It's a most respectable place—I'll come and fetch her, of course, and bring her back afterwards."

Of course Aunt Anne could not refuse, but oh! how Maggie saw that she wanted to! The battle that followed was silent. Uncle Mathew's eyes narrowed themselves to fiery malicious points; he dropped them and moved his feet restlessly on the soft carpet.

"Quite respectable!" he repeated.

Aunt Anne smiled gently. "Why, of course, Mathew. I know you'll look after Maggie. It will be a change for her. She's been having rather a dull time here, I'm afraid."

Then there was silence. Maggie wanted to speak, but the words would not come, and she had the curious sensation that even if she did find them no one would hear them.

Then Uncle Mathew suddenly said good-bye, stumbled over his boots by the door, shot out, "Seven o'clock, Maggie"—and was gone.

"Well, that will be nice for you, Maggie," said Anne, looking at her.

"Yes," said Maggie. "You don't mind, do you?"

"No dear, of course not."

"What do you want me to do?" Maggie broke out desperately. "I know I'm not satisfying you and yet you won't say anything. Do tell me—and I'll try—anything—almost anything ..."

Then the sudden memory of her own posted letter silenced her. Was that readiness to do "anything"? Had that not been rebellion? And had she not asked Uncle Mathew to help her to escape? The consciousness of her dishonesty coloured her cheek with crimson. Then Aunt Anne, very tenderly, put her hand on her shoulder.

"Will you really do anything—for me, Maggie—for me?" Her voice was gentle and her eyes had tears in them. "If you will—there are things very close to my heart—"

Maggie turned away, trembling. She hung her head, then with a sudden movement walked to the door.

"You must tell me," she said, "what you want. I'll try—I don't understand."

Then as though she was aware that she was fighting the whole room which had already almost entrapped her and that the fight was too much for her, she went.

When she came to her own room and thought about her invitation she wished, with a sudden change of mood, that she had a pretty frock or two. She would have loved to have been grand to-night, and now the best that she could do was to add her coral necklace and a little gold brooch that years ago her father had given her, to the black dress that she was already wearing. She realised, with a strange little pang of loneliness, that she had not had one evening's fun since her arrival in London—no, not one— and she would not have captured to-night had Aunt Anne been able to prevent it.

Then as her mind returned back to her uncle she felt with a throb of excited anticipation that perhaps after all this evening was to prove the turning-point of her life. Her little escape into the streets, her posting of the letter, had been followed so immediately by Uncle Mathew's visit, and now this invitation!

"No one can keep me if I want to go," and the old cuckoo-clock outside seemed to tick in reply:

"Can no one keep her if she wants to go?"

She finished her preparations; as she fastened the coral necklace round her neck the face of Martin Warlock was suddenly before her. He had been perhaps at her elbow all day.

"I like him and I think he likes me," she said to the mirror. "I've got one friend," and her thought still further was that even if he didn't like her he couldn't prevent her liking him.

She went down to the drawing-room and found Uncle Mathew, alone, waiting for her.

"Here I am, Maggie," he said. "And let's get out of this as quick as we can."

"I must go and say good-night to the aunts," she said.

She went upstairs to Aunt Anne's bedroom. Entering it was always to her like passing into a shadowed church after the hot sunshine—the long, thin room with high slender windows, the long hard bed, of the most perfect whiteness and neatness, the heavy black-framed picture of "The Ascension" over the bed, and the utter stillness broken by no sound of clock or bell—even the fire seemed frozen into a glassy purity in the grate.

Her aunt was sitting, as so often Maggie found her, in a stiff-backed chair, her hands folded on her lap, staring in front of her. Her eyes were like the open eyes of a dead woman; it was as though, with a great effort of almost desperate concentration, she were driving her vision against some obstinate world of opposition, and the whole of life had meanwhile stayed to watch the issue.

A thin pale light from some street lamp lay, a faintly golden shadow, across the white ceiling.

Maggie stood by the door.

"I've come to say good-night, aunt."

"Ah, Maggie dear, is that you?" The pale oval face turned towards her.

"You won't be very late, will you?"

"Hadn't I better have a key, not to bother Martha?"

"Oh, Martha won't have gone to bed."

Maggie felt as though her whole evening would be spoilt did she know that Martha was waiting for her at the end of it.

"Oh, but it will be such a pity—"

"Martha will let you in, dear. Come and kiss me; I hope that you'll enjoy yourself."

And then the strangest thing happened. Maggie bent down. She felt a tear upon her cheek and then the thin strong arms held her, for an instant, in an almost threatening embrace.

"Good-night, dear aunt," she said; but, outside the room, she had to stand for a moment in the dark passage to regain her control; her heart was beating with wild unreasoning terror. Although she had brushed her cheek with her hand the cold touch of the tears still lingered there.

Outside the house they were free. It looked so close and dark behind them that Maggie shivered a little and put her arm through her uncle's.

"That's all right," he said, patting her hand. "We're going to enjoy ourselves."

She looked up and saw Martin Warlock facing her. The unexpected meeting held both of them silent for a moment. To her it seemed that he had risen out of the very stones of the pavement, at her bidding, to make her evening wonderful. He looked so strong, so square, so solid after the phantom imaginations of the house that she had left, that the sight of him was a step straight into the heart of comfort and reassurance.

"I was just coming," he said, looking at her, "to leave a note for Miss Cardinal—from my father—"

"She's in," Maggie said.

"Oh, it wasn't to bother her—only to leave the note. About some meeting, I think."

"We're just going out. This is my uncle—Mr. Warlock."

The two men shook hands.

Mathew Cardinal smiled. His eyes closed, his greeting had an urgency in it as though he had suddenly made some discovery that gratified and amused him. "Very glad to meet you—very glad, indeed, sir. Any friend of my niece's. I know your father, sir; know him and admire him."

They all turned down the street together. Uncle Mathew talked, and then, quite suddenly, stopping under a lamp-post as though within the circle of light his charm were stronger, he said:

"I suppose, Mr. Warlock, you wouldn't do me the great, the extreme, honour of dining with myself and my niece at my humble little inn to-night? A little sudden—I hope you'll forgive the discourtesy—but knowing your father—"

Martin looked straight into Maggie's eyes.

"Oh, please do!" she said, her heart beating, as it seemed, against her eyes so that she dropped them.

"Well—" he hesitated. "It's very good of you, Mr. Cardinal—very kind. As a matter of fact I was going to dine alone to-night—just a chop, you know, somewhere—if it's really not inconvenient I'll be delighted—"

They walked on together.

As they passed into Garrick Street, she knew that she had never in all her life been so glad to be with any one, that she had never so completely trusted any one, that she would like to be with him often, to look after him, perhaps, and to be looked after by him.

Her feeling for him was almost sexless, because she had never thought, as most girls do, of love and the intrigue and coquetry of love. She was so simple as to be shameless, and at once, if he had asked her then in the street to marry him she would have said yes without hesitation or fear, or any analysis. She would like to look after him as well as herself—there were things she was sure that she could do for him—and she would be no burden to him because she intended, in any case, to lead her own life. She would simply lead it with a companion instead of without one.

He must have felt as he walked with her this trust and simplicity. She was certainly the most extraordinary girl whom he had ever met, and he'd met a number ...

He could believe every word she said; he had never known any one so direct and simple and honest, and yet with that she was not a fool, as most honest girls were. No, she was not a fool. He would have given anything to be as sure of himself ...

She was plain—but then was she? As they passed beneath the light of a street lamp his heart gave a sudden beat. Her face was so GOOD, her eyes so true, her mouth so strong. She was like a boy, rather— and, of course, she was dressed badly. But he wanted to look after her. He was sure that she knew so little of the world and would be so easily deceived ...But who was he to look after any one?

He knew that she would trust him utterly, and trust him not only because she was ignorant of the world, but also because she was herself so true. At the thought of this trust his heart suddenly warmed, partly with shame and partly with pride.

They walked very happily along laughing and talking. They turned into Henrietta Street, misty with lamps that were dim in a thin evening fog, and at the corner of the street, facing the Square, was Uncle Mathew's hotel. It was a place for the use, in the main, of commercial gentlemen, and it was said by eager searchers after local colour, to have retained a great deal of the Dickens spirit. In the hall there was a stout gentleman with a red nose, a soiled waiter, a desolate palm and a large-bosomed lady all rings and black silk, in a kind of wooden cage. Down the stairs came a dim vapour that smelt of beef, whisky and tobacco, and in the distance was the regular click of billiard-balls and the brazen muffled tones of a gramophone. Uncle Mathew seemed perfectly at home here, and it was strange to Maggie that he should be so nervous with Aunt Anne, his own sister, when he could be so happily familiar with the powdered lady in the black silk.

"We're to have dinner in a private room upstairs," said Uncle Mathew in a voice that was casual and at the same time important. He led the way up the stairs.

Maggie had read in some old bound volume at home a very gruesome account of the "Life and Misdeeds of Mr. Palmer, the Rugeley Poisoner." The impression that still remained with her was of a man standing in the shadowy hall of just such an hotel as this, and pouring poison into a glass which he held up against the light. This picture had been vividly with her during her childhood, and she felt that this must have been the very hotel where those fearful deeds occurred, and that the ghost of Mr. Palmer's friend must, at this very moment, be writhing in an upstairs bedroom—"writhing," as she so fearfully remembered, bent "like a hoop."

However, these reminiscences did not in the least terrify her; she welcomed their definite outlines in contrast with the shadowy possibilities of her aunts' house. And she had Martin Warlock ... She had never been so happy in all her life.

A dismal little waiter with a very soiled shirt and a black tie under his ear, guided them down into a dark passage and flung open the door of a sitting-room. This room was dark and sizzling with strange noises; a gas-jet burning low was hissing, some papers rustled in the breeze from the half-opened window, and a fire, overburdened with the weight of black coal, made frantic little spurts of resistance.

A white cloth was laid on the table, and there were glasses and knives and forks. A highly-coloured portrait of her late Majesty Queen Victoria confronted a long-legged horse desperately winning a race in which he had apparently no competitors. There was a wall-paper of imitation marble and a broken-down book-case with some torn paper editions languishing upon it. Beyond the open window there was a purple haze and a yellow mist—also a bell rang and carts rattled over the cobbles. The waiter shut out these sights and sounds, gave the tablecloth a stroke with his dirty hand, and left the room.

They continued their cheerful conversation, Martin laughing at nothing at all, and Maggie smiling, and Uncle Mathew stroking his mouth and sharpening his eyes and standing, in his uneasy fashion, first on one leg and then on the other. Maggie realised that her uncle was trying to be most especially pleasant to young Warlock. She wondered why; she also remembered what he had said to her about Martin's father ... No, he had changed. She could not follow his motives as she had once been able to do. Then he had simply been a foolish, drunken, but kindly-intentioned old man.

Then Mr. Warlock on his side seemed to like her uncle. That was an extraordinary thing. Or was he only being friendly because he was happy? No, she remembered his face as he had joined them that evening. He had not been happy then. She liked him the more because she knew that he needed help ... The meal, produced at last by the poor little waiter, was very merry. The food was not wonderful—the thick pea-soup was cold, the sole bones and skin, the roast beef tepid and the apple-tart heavy. The men drank whiskies and sodas, and Maggie noticed that her uncle drank very little. And then (with apologies to Maggie) they smoked cigars, and she sat before the dismal fire in an old armchair with a hole in it.

Martin Warlock talked in a most delightful way about his travels, and Uncle Mathew asked him questions that were not, after all, so stupid. What had happened to him? Had Maggie always undervalued him, or was it that he was sober now and clear-headed? His fat round thighs seemed stronger, his hands seemed cleaner, the veins in his face were not so purple. She remembered the night when he had come into her room. She had been able to manage him then. Would she be able to manage him now?

After dinner he grew very restless. His eyes wandered to the door, then to his watch, then to his companions; he smiled uneasily, pulling his moustache; then—jumping to his feet, tried to speak with an easy self-confidence.

"I must leave you for a quarter of an hour ... A matter of business, only in this hotel. Downstairs. Yes. A friend of mine and a little matter. Urgent. I'm sure you'll forgive me."

For a moment Maggie was frightened. She was here in a strange hotel in a strange room with a man whom she scarcely knew. Then she looked up into young Warlock's face and was reassured. She could trust him.

He stood with his arm on the shabby, dusty mantelpiece, looking down upon her with his good-natured kindly smile, so kindly that she felt that he was younger than she and needed protection in a world that was filled with designing Uncle Mathews and mysterious Aunt Annes and horrible Miss Warlocks.

He, on his side, as he looked down at her, was surprised at his own excitement. His heart was beating, his hand trembling—before this plain, ordinary, unattractive girl! Unattractive physically—but not uninteresting. One of the most interesting human beings whom he had ever met, simply because she was utterly unlike any one else. He felt shame before her, because he knew that she would believe every word that he said. In that she was simple, but "he would be bothered if she was simple in anything else." She had made up her mind—he knew it as well as though she had told him—to trust him absolutely, and he knew well enough how little he was to be trusted. And because of that faith and because of that trust he felt that she was more reliable than he could have believed that changing fickle human being would ever be. How secure he might feel with her!

Then, as he thought that, he realised how troubled he was about his life at home during the last weeks. Amy hated him, his mother hid herself from him, and his father's love frightened him. Already he had found himself telling lies to avoid the chapel services and the meetings with Thurston and the rest. His father's love for him had something terrible in it, and, although he returned it, he could not live up to that fire and heat.

No; he saw that he would not be able to remain for long at home. On the other hand, go back to the old wandering life he would not. He had had enough of that and its rotten carelessness and shabbiness. What a girl this would be to settle down with somewhere! So strange that she would be always interesting, so faithful that she would be always there! Nor was he entirely selfish. Her childishness, her ignorance, appealed to him for protection. She had no one but those old aunts to care for her, she was poor and rebellious and ignorant. Warlock was kind-hearted beyond the normal charity of man—much of his weakness came from that very kindness.

As he saw which way he was going he tried to pull himself back. He could not protect her—he had the best of reasons for knowing why. He could do her nothing but harm ... and yet he went on.

He took a chair close to her and sat down. He, who had known in his time many women, could see how happy she was. That happiness excited him. Suddenly he held her hand. She did not remove it.

"Look here," he began, and he was surprised at the hoarseness of his voice, "your uncle will be back in a moment, and we never have a chance of being alone. I've wanted to talk to you ever since I first saw you."

He felt her hand move in his. That stir was so helpless that he suddenly determined to be honest.

"I think you'll trust me, won't you?" he asked.

"Yes," she said.

"Well, you mustn't," he went on hurriedly, his eyes on the door. "I'm not worse, I suppose, than other men, but all the same I'm not to be trusted. And when I say I'm not to be trusted I mean that I myself don't know whether I'll keep my word from one minute to another. I'm sure you don't know very much about men. I could see it at once from the way you spoke."

She looked up, her clear, unconfused, unquestioning eyes facing him.

"I knew my father well," she said. "We were quite alone for years together. And then Uncle Mathew—"

"Oh, your father, your uncle," he answered quickly. "They don't count. What I mean is that you mustn't think men are scoundrels just because they act badly. I swear that nine out of ten of them never mean to do any harm."

"And they think they're speaking the truth at the time. But anything 'does' for them and then they're in a mess, and all they think about is how to get out of it. Then it's every man for himself ..."

Maggie shook her head.

"I've always known that I'd have to manage for myself," she said. "I've never expected any one to do anything for me, so I'm not likely to be disappointed now."

He moved a little closer to her and held her hand more firmly; even as he did so something in his heart reproached him, but now the reproach was very far away, like an echo of some earlier voice.

"Do you know you're a wonderful girl?" he said. "I knew you were from the first moment I saw you. You're the most independent person I've ever known. You can't guess how I admire that! And all the same you're not happy, are you? You want to get out of it, don't you?"

She thought for a little while before she nodded her head.

"I suppose as a fact." she said, "I do. If you want to know—and you mustn't tell anybody—I've posted a letter to a lady whom I met once who told me if ever I wanted anything to write to her. I've asked her for some work. I've got three hundred pounds of my own. It isn't very much, I know, but I could start on it ... I don't want to do wrong to my aunts, who are very kind to me, but I'm not happy there. It wouldn't be true to say I'm happy. You see," she dropped her voice a little, "they want to make me religious, and

I've had so much of that with father already. I feel as though they were pressing me into it somehow, and that I should wake up one morning and find I should never escape again. There's so much goes on that I don't understand. And it isn't only the chapel. Aunt Anne's very quiet, but she makes you feel quite helpless sometimes. And perhaps one will get more and more helpless the longer one stays. I don't want to be helpless ever—nor religious!" she ended.

"Why, that's just my position," he continued eagerly. "I came home as happily as anything. I'd almost forgotten all that had been when I was a boy, how I was baptized and thought I belonged to God and was so proud and stuck up. That all seems nonsense when you're roughing it with other men who think about nothing but the day's work. Then I came home meaning to settle down. I wanted to see my governor too. I've always cared for him more than any one else in the world ... but I tell you now I simply don't know what's going on at home. They want to catch me in a trap. That's what it feels like. To make me what I was as a kid. It's strange, but there's more in it than you'd think. You wouldn't believe the number of times I've thought of my young days since I've been home. It's as though some one was always shoving them up in front of my face. All I want, you know, is to be jolly. To let other people alone and be let alone myself. I wouldn't do any one any harm in the world—I wouldn't really. But it's as though father wanted me to believe all the things he believes, so that he could believe them more himself. Perhaps it's the same with your aunt ..." Then he added, "But they're sick people. That explains a lot."

"Sick?" asked Maggie.

"Yes. My governor's got heart—awfully bad. He might go off at any moment if he had a shock. And your aunt—don't you know?"

"No," said Maggie.

"Cancer. They all say so. I thought you'd have known."

"Oh!" Maggie drew in her breath. She shuddered. "Poor Aunt Anne! Oh, poor Aunt Anne! I didn't know."

She felt a sudden rush of confused emotion. A love for her aunt, desire to help her, and at the same time shrinking as though she saw the whole house which had been, from the first, unhappy to her was now diseased and evil and rotten. The hot life in her body told her against her moral will that she must escape, and her soul, moving in her and speaking to her, told her that now, more than ever, she must stay.

"Oh, poor, poor Aunt Anne," she said again.

He moved and put his arm around her. He had meant it simply as a movement of sympathy and protection, but when he felt the warmth of her body against his, when he realised how she went to him at once with the confidence and simplicity of a child, when he felt the hot irregular beat of her heart, his own heart leapt, his arm was strengthened like a barrier of iron against the world.

He had one moment of desperate resistance, a voice of protest calling to him far, far away. His hand touched her neck; he raised her face to his and kissed her, once gently, kindly, then, passionately again and again.

She shivered a little, as though surrendering something to him, then lay quite still in his arms.

"Maggie! Maggie!" he whispered.

Then she raised her head and herself kissed him.

There was a noise on the door. They separated; the door opened and in the sudden light a figure was visible holding a glass.

For a blind instant Maggie, returning from her other world, thought it the figure of Mr. Palmer of Rugeley.

It was, of course, Uncle Mathew.

CHAPTER IV

MR. CRASHAW

Uncle Mathew saw Maggie back to her door, kissed her and left her. On their way home he did not once mention Martin Warlock to her.

He left her as he heard the bolt turn in the door, hurrying away as though he did not want to be seen. Maggie went in to find old Martha with her crabbed face watching her sourly. But she did not care, nothing could touch her now. Even the old woman, cross with waiting by the fading kitchen fire, noticed the light in the girl's eyes. She had always thought the girl hard and ungracious, but now that face was soft, and the mouth smiling over its secret thoughts, and the eyes sleepy with happiness.

Maggie could have said: "I'm wild with joy, Martha. I know what love is. I had never thought that it could be like this. Be kind to me because it's the greatest night of my life."

Martha said: "There's some milk hotted for you, Miss, and some biscuits. There on the table by the stairs."

"Oh, I don't want anything, Martha, thank you!"

"Your aunt said you was to have it."

Maggie drank it down, Martha watching her. Then she went upstairs softly, as though her joy might awaken the whole house. She lay wide-eyed on her bed for hours, then fell into a heavy sleep, deep, without dreams.

When, in the quieter light of the morning, she considered the event, she had no doubts nor hesitations. She loved Martin and Martin loved her. Soon Martin would marry her and they would go away. Her aunt would be sorry of course, and his father, perhaps, would be angry, but the sorrow and anger would be only for a little while. Then Martin and she would live happily together always—happily because they were both sensible people, and her own standard of fidelity and trust was, she supposed, also his. She did not think very deeply about what he had said to her; it only meant that he wanted to escape from his family, a desire in which she could completely sympathise. She had loved him, as she now saw, from the first moment of meeting, and she would love him always. She would never be alone again, and although Martin had told her that he was weak, and she knew something about men, she was aware that their love for one another would be a thing apart, constant, unfaltering, eternal. She had read no modern fiction; she knew nothing about psychology: she was absolutely happy ...

And then in that very first day she discovered that life was not quite so simple. In the first place, she wanted Martin desperately and he did not come; and although she had at once a thousand sensible reasons for the impossibility of his coming, nevertheless strange new troubles and suspicions that she had never known before rose in her heart. She had only kissed him once; he had only held her in his arms for a few moments ...She waited, looking from behind the drawing-room curtains out into the street. How could he let the whole day go by? He was prevented, perhaps, by that horrible sister of his. When the dusk came and the muffin-man went ringing his bell down the street she felt exhausted as though she had been running for miles ...

Then with sudden guilty realisation of the absorption that had held her all day she wondered how much her aunt had noticed.

During the afternoon when she had been watching the streets from behind the curtain Aunt Elizabeth had sat sewing, Thomas the cat lumped before the fire, the whole room bathed in afternoon silence. Maggie had watched as though hypnotized by the street itself, marking the long squares of light, the pools of shadow, the lamp-posts, the public-house at the corner, the little grocer's shop with cases of oranges piled outside the door, the windows on the second floor of the dressmaker's, through which you could see a dummy-figure and a young woman with a pale face and shiny black hair, who came and glanced out once and again, as though to reassure herself that the gay world was still there.

The people, the horses and carts, the cabs went on their way. Often it seemed that this figure must be Martin's—now this—now this ... And on every occasion Maggie's heart rose in her breast, hammered at her eyes, then sank again. Over and over she told to herself every incident of yesterday's meeting. Always it ended in that same wonderful climax when she was caught to his breast and felt his hand at her neck and then his mouth upon hers. She could still feel against her skin the rough warm stuff of his coat and the soft roughness of his cheek and the stiff roughness of his hair. She could still feel how his mouth had just touched hers and then suddenly gripped it as though it would never let it go; then she had been absorbed by him, into his very heart, so that still now she felt as though with his strong arms and his hard firm body he was around her and about her.

Oh, she loved him! she loved him! but why did he not come? Had he been able only to pass down the street and smile up to her window as he went that would have been something. It would at least have reassured her that yesterday was not a dream, an invention, and that he was still there and thought of her and cared for her ...

She pulled herself together. At the sound of the muffin-man's bell she came back into her proper world. She would be patient; as she had once resolved outside Borhedden Farm, so now she swore that she would owe nothing to any man.

If she should love Martin Warlock it would not be for anything that she expected to get from him, but only for the love that she had it in her to give. If good came of it, well, if not, she was still her own master.

But more than ever now was it impossible to be open with her aunts. How strange it was that from the very beginning there had been concealments between Aunt Anne and herself. Perhaps if they had been open to one another at the first all would have been well. Now it was too late.

Tea came in, and, with tea, Aunt Anne. It was the first time that day that Maggie had seen her, and now, conscious of the news that Martin had given her, she felt a movement of sympathy, of pity and affection. Aunt Anne had been in her room all day, and she seemed as she walked slowly to the fire to be of a finer pallor, a more slender body than ever. Maggie felt as though she could see the firelight through her body, and with that came also the conviction that Aunt Anne knew everything, knew about Martin and the posted letter and the thoughts of escape. Maggie herself was tired with the trial of her waiting day, she was exhausted and was beating, with all her resolve, against a disappointment that hammered with a thundering noise, somewhere far away in the recesses of her soul. So they all drew around the fire and had their tea.

Aunt Anne, leaning back in her chair, her beautiful hands stretched out on the arms, a fine white shawl spread on her knees, asked Maggie about last night.

"I hope you enjoyed yourself, dear." "Very much, Aunt Anne. Uncle Mathew was very kind."

"What did you do?"

Maggie flushed. It was deceit and lies now all the time, and oh! how she hated lies! But she went on:

"Do you know, Aunt Anne, I think Uncle Mathew is so changed. He's younger and everything. He talked quite differently last night, about his business and all that he's doing. He's got his money in malt now, he says."

"Whose money?" asked Aunt Anne.

"His own, he says. I never knew he had any. But he says yes, it's in malt. It's not a nice hotel, though, where he lives."

"Not nice, dear?"

"No, I didn't like it. But it's only for men really of course."

"I think he'd better take you somewhere else next time. I'll speak to him. By the way, Maggie dear, Martha tells me you went out yesterday afternoon all alone—into the Strand. I think it would be better if you were to tell us."

Maggie's cheeks were hot. She set back her shoulders.

"How does Martha know?" she asked quickly. "I only went for a moment—only for a little walk. But I'm grown up, Aunt Anne. Surely I can go out by myself if ..." she stopped, looking away from them into the fire.

"It isn't that, dear," Aunt Anne said very gently. "It's only that you've been so little a time in London that you can't know your way about yet. And London's a strange place. It might be unpleasant for you alone. I'd rather that you told us first."

Then Maggie delivered her challenge.

"But, aunt, I won't be always here. I'm going off to earn my living soon, aren't I?"

Aunt Elizabeth drew her breath in sharply. Aunt Anne said quietly:

"You are free, dear, quite free. But whilst I am not quite myself—I don't want to be selfish, dear—but you are a great comfort to us, and when I am stronger certainly you shall go ... even now if you wish, of course ... but my illness."

Even as she spoke—and it was the first time that she had ever mentioned her illness—she caught at her breast and pressed her hand there as though she were in great pain. Maggie sprang to her side. She caught the girl's hand with hers and held her. Maggie could feel her swift agonized breathing. Then with a little sigh the moment had passed. Maggie still knelt there looking up into her aunt's face.

Martha's voice was heard at the door.

"Mr. Martin Warlock, Miss. Could you see him? ..."

"Yes, Martha," said Aunt Anne, her voice calm and controlled. "Ask him to come up."

She had abandoned so completely any idea that he might still come that she could not now feel that it was he. She withdrew from her aunt's side and stood in the shadow against the wall.

Although her heart beat wildly her whole mind was bent upon composure, upon showing nothing to her aunts, and on behaving to him as though she scarcely knew him, but so soon as he entered the room some voice cried in her: "He is mine! He is mine!" She did not stir from her wall, but her eyes fastened upon him and then did not move. He was wearing the same clothes as yesterday; his tie was different, it had been black and now it was dark blue. He looked quiet and self-possessed and at his ease. His rough stiff hair was carelessly brushed as always; good-humour shone from his eyes, he smiled, his walk had the sturdy broad strength of a man who is absolutely sure of himself but is not conceited. He seemed to have no trouble in the world.

He greeted the aunts, then shook hands with Maggie. He gave her one glance and she, suddenly feeling that that glance had not the things in it that she had wanted, was frightened, her confidence left her, she felt that if she did not have a word alone with him she would die.

He sat down near Aunt Anne.

"No, thank you, I won't have any tea," he said. "We're dining very early to-night because Father and Amy have a meeting right away over Golders Green way somewhere. It's really on a message from him that I came."

He did not look at her, placed like a square shadow against the dusky wall. He sat, leaning forward a little, his red-brown hand on his knee, his leg bulging under the cloth of his trouser, his neck struggling behind his collar—but his smile was pleasant and easy, he seemed perfectly at home.

"My father wonders whether you will mind some friends of Miss Avies sitting with you in your pew to-morrow evening. She has especially asked—two of them ... ladies, I believe. But it seems that there will be something of a crowd, and as your pew is always half empty— He would not have asked except that there seems nowhere else."

Aunt Anne graciously assented.

"But, of course, Mr. Warlock, Maggie will be going with us, but still there will be room. Mr. Crashaw is going to speak after all, I hear. I was afraid that he would have been too ill."

Martin laughed. "He is staying with us, you know, and already he is preparing himself. He's about the oldest human being I've ever seen. He must be a hundred."

"He's a great saint," said Aunt Anne.

"He's always in a terrible temper though," said Martin. "He mutters to himself—and he eats nothing. His room is next to mine, and he walked up and down all night talking. I don't know how he keeps alive."

Perhaps Aunt Anne thought Martin's tone irreverent. She relapsed into herself and seemed suddenly, with a spiritual wave of the hand, to have dismissed the whole company.

Martin took his leave. He barely touched Maggie's hand, but his eyes leapt upon hers with all the fire of a greeting too long delayed. His lips did not move, but she heard the whisper "Soon!" Then he was gone.

Soon! She felt as though she could not wait another instant but must immediately run after him, follow him into the street, and make clear his plans both for himself and her.

Then, continuing her struggle of the long day, she beat into herself endurance; she was in a new world, in a world with roads and cities, mountains, rivers, seas and forests that had to be traversed by her, to be learnt and remembered and conquered, and for the success of this she must have her own spirit absolutely aloof and firm and brave. She loved him. That must be enough for her, and meanwhile she need not lose her common sense and vision of everyday life ...But meanwhile it hurt. She was now twice as lonely as she had been before because she did not know what he intended to do, and always with her now there was something strange and unknown that might at any moment be stronger than she.

But by next morning she had conquered herself. She would see him at Chapel that night and perhaps have a word with him, and so already she had arrived at her now lover's calendar of dates and seasons. There was the time before she would see him and the time after—no other time than that.

The trouble that weighed upon her most heavily was her deceitfulness to the aunts. Fifty times that day she was on the edge of speaking and telling them all, but she was held back by the vagueness of her relations to Martin. Were they engaged? Did he even love her? He had only kissed her. He had said nothing. No, she must wait, but with this definite sense of her wickedness weighing upon her—not wickedness to herself, for that she cared nothing, but wickedness to them—she tried, on this day, to be a pattern member of the household, going softly everywhere that she was told, closing doors behind her, being punctual and careful. Unhappily it was a day of misfortune, it was one of Aunt Anne's more worldly hours and she thought that she would spend it in training Maggie. Very good—but Maggie dropped a glass into which flowers were to have been put, she shook her pen when she was addressing some envelopes so that some drops of ink were scattered upon the carpet, and, in her haste to be punctual, she banged her bedroom door so loudly that Aunt Anne was waked from her afternoon nap.

A scene followed. Aunt Anne showed herself very human, like any other aunt justly exasperated by any other niece.

"I sometimes despair of you, Maggie. You will not think of others. I don't wish to be hard or unjust, but selfishness is the name of your greatest weakness."

Maggie, standing with her hands behind her, a spot of ink on her nose and her short hair ruffled, was hard and unrepentant.

"You must send me away," she said; "I'm not a success here. You don't like me."

Aunt Anne looked at Maggie with eyes that were clear and cold like deep unfriendly waters. "You mustn't say that. We love you, but you have very much to learn. To-night I shall speak to Miss Avies and arrange that you go to have a talk with her sometimes. She is a wise woman who knows many things. My sister and I are not strong enough to deal with you, and we are weakened perhaps by our love for you."

"I don't want to go to-night," Maggie said, then she burst out: "Oh, can't I lead an ordinary life like other girls—be free and find things out for myself, not only go by what older people tell me—earn my living and be free? I've never lived an ordinary life. Life with Father wasn't fair, and now—"

Aunt Anne put out her arm and drew her towards her. "Poor Maggie ... Aren't you unfair to us? Do you suppose really that we don't love you? Do you think that I don't understand? You shall be free, afterwards, if you wish—perfectly free—but you must have the opportunity of learning what this life is first, what the love of God is, what the companionship of Him is. If after you have seen you still reject it, we will not try to keep you. But it is God's will that you stay with us for a time."

"How do you know that it is God's will?" asked Maggie, melted nevertheless, as she always was by any sign of affection.

"He has told me," Aunt Anne answered, and then closed her eyes.

Maggie went away with a sensation of being tracked by some stealthy mysterious force that was creeping ever closer and closer upon her, that she could only feel but not see. For instance, she might have said that she would not go to Chapel to-night, and she might have taken her stand upon that. And yet she could not say that. Of course she must go because she must see Martin, but even if she had known that he would not be there she would have gone. Was it curiosity? Was it reminiscence? Was it superstition? Was it cowardice? Was it loneliness? All these things, perhaps, and yet something more than they ...

All through the afternoon of the lovely November day she anticipated that evening's services as though it were in some way to be a climax. She knew that it was to be for all of them an especial affair. She had heard during the last days much discussion of old Mr. Crashaw. He was an old man with, apparently, a wonderful history of conversions behind him. His conversions had been, it seemed, of the forcible kind, seizing people by the neck and shoving them in; he was a fierce and militant kind of saint; he believed, it seemed, in damnation and eternal hell fire, and could make you believe in them too; his accent was on the tortures rather than the triumphs of religion.

But Maggie had other thoughts, in this, outside Mr. Crashaw. She had never lost the force of that first meeting with Mr. Warlock; she had avoided him simply because she was afraid lest he should influence her too much, but now after her friendship with Martin she felt that she could never meet old Mr. Warlock frankly again. What he would say to her if he knew that she meant to take his son away from him she knew well enough. On every side there was trouble and difficulty. She could not see a friend anywhere unless it was Caroline, whom she did not completely trust, and Mr. Magnus, whom her deception of her aunt would, she knew, most deeply distress. Meanwhile she was being pushed forward more and more into the especial religious atmosphere of the house, the Chapel and the Chapel sect. Of no use to tell herself that this was only a tiny fragment of the whole world, that there, only five yards away from her, in the Strand, was a life that swept past the Chapel and its worshippers with the utmost, completest indifference. She had always this feeling that she was caught, that she could only escape by a desperate violent effort that would hurt others and perhaps be, for herself, a lasting reproach. She wanted so simple a thing ... to be always with Martin, working, with all this confusing, baffling, mysterious religion behind her; this simple thing seemed incredibly difficult of attainment.

Nevertheless, when they started that evening for the Chapel she felt, in spite of herself, a strange almost pleasurable excitement. There was, in that plain, ugly building some force that could not be denied. Was it the force of the worshippers' belief? Was it the force of some outside power that watched ironically the efforts of those poor human beings to discover it? Was it the love of a father for his children? No, there was very little love in this creed—no more than there had been in her father's creed before. As she walked along between her aunts her brain was a curious jumble of religion, Martin, and how she was ever going to learn to be tidy and punctual.

"Well, I won't care," was the resolution with which she always brought to an end her discussions and misgivings. "I'm myself. Nobody can touch me unless I let them."

It was a most lovely evening, very pale and clear with an orange light in the sky like the reflection of some far distant towering fire. The air was still and the rumble of the town scarcely penetrated into their street; they could hear the ugly voice of the little Chapel bell jangling in the heart of the houses, there was a scent of chrysanthemums from somewhere and a very faint suggestion of snow—even before they reached the Chapel door a few flakes lazily began to fall.

Maggie was thinking now only of Martin. There was a gas-lamp already lighted in the Chapel doorway, and this blinded her eyes. She had hoped that he would be there, waiting, so that he might have a word with her before they went in, but when they were all gathered together under the porch she saw with a throb of disappointment that he was not there. She saw no one whom she knew, but it struck her at once that here was a gathering quite different from that of the first time that she had come to the Chapel. There seemed to be more of the servant class; rather they were older women with serious rapt expressions and very silent. There were men too, to-night, four or five gathered together inside the passage, standing gravely, without a word, not moving, like statues. Maggie was frightened. She felt like a spy in an enemy's camp, and a spy waiting for an inevitable detection, with no hope of securing any news. As she went up the aisle behind her aunts her eyes searched for Martin. She could not see him. Their seat was close to the front, and already seated in it were the austere Miss Avies and two lady friends.

Maggie was maliciously pleased to observe that Miss Avies had not expected these additions to her number and was now in danger of an uncomfortable squashing; there was, indeed, a polite little struggle between Miss Avies and Aunt Anne as to who should have the corner with a wooden arm upon which to rest. Miss Avies' two friends, huddled and frightened like fledglings suddenly surprised by a cuckoo, stirred Maggie's sympathy. She disliked Miss Avies from the very first moment. Miss Avies had a pale, thin, pointed face with no eyebrows, grey eyes dim and short-sighted, and fair colourless hair brushed straight back under a hard, ugly black hat.

At the same time she was nervous, emotional, restless; something about her was always moving—her lips, her hands, her shoulders, her eyes. She was fierce and hostile and ineffectual, one felt, so long as she was by herself. Maggie did not, of course, notice all this at the time, but in after years she always looked back on the pale, thin, highly-strung Miss Avies as the motive of most of the events that followed this particular evening. It was as though she felt that Miss Avies' weight, not enough in itself to effect any result, when thrown into the balance just turned everything in one direction. It had that result, at any rate, upon Maggie herself.

She soon lost, however, consideration of Miss Avies in the wider observation of the Chapel and its congregation. It was, as it had been on the occasion of her first visit to it, stuffy, smelling of gas and brick and painted wood, ugly in its bareness and unresponsiveness—and, nevertheless, exciting. The interior of the building had the air of one who has watched some most unusual happenings and expects very shortly to watch them again. Even the harmonium seemed to prick up its wooden ears in anticipation. And to-night the congregation thrilled also with breathless expectation. As Maggie looked round upon them she could see that they were throbbing with the anticipation of some almost sensuous delight. By now they had filled the Chapel to its utmost limits, but there was not one human being there who did not seem to have the appearance of having been especially selected from other less interesting human beings. It was not that the forces that surrounded her were especially interesting, but she felt that all of them had taken on some especial dramatic character from the occasion. Such personalities as Aunt Anne and Miss Avies were in any case vivid and dramatic, but to-night Aunt Elizabeth and the placidly rotund Mrs. Smith, who was sitting in the front row with her mouth open, and simple little Miss Pyncheon, Aunt Anne's friend, were remarkable and exceptional.

Then suddenly Maggie caught sight of Martin. He was sitting in the extreme right next the wall; his ill-tempered sister was next to him. Maggie could only see his head and shoulders, but she realised at once that he had been, for a long time, trying to catch her eye. He smiled at her an intimate peculiar smile that sent the blood flooding to her face and made her heart beat with happiness. At the moment of her smiling she realised that Miss Avies' dim eye was upon her. What right had Miss Avies to watch over her? She set back her shoulders, sat up stiffly, and tried to look as old as she might—that was not, unhappily, very old. That smile exchanged with Martin had made her happy for ever. Miss Avies was of less than no importance at all ...

The little bell ceased its jangling, the harmonium began a quavering prelude, and from a door at the back, behind the little platform and desk, three men entered: first Mr. Thurston; then a little crooked man who must, Maggie knew, be Mr. Crashaw; finally, in magnificent contrast, Mr. Warlock. A quiver of emotion passed over the Chapel—there was then a hushed expectant pause.

"Brothers and sisters, let us pray," said Mr. Thurston.

Maggie had not seen him before; she wondered what strange chance had led him and Mr. Warlock to work together. In every movement of the body, in every tone of the voice, Thurston showed the professional actor—his thoughts were all upon himself and the effect that he was making. So calculated was he in his attitude that his eyes betrayed him, having in their gleam other thoughts, other intentions very far away from his immediate business in the Chapel. Maggie, watching him, wondered what those thoughts were. His voice was ugly, as were all his movements; his sharp actor's face, with the long rather dirty black hair, the hooked nose, the long dirty fingers which moved in and out as though they worked of themselves—all these things were false and unmoving. But behind his harsh voice, gross accent and melodramatic tone there was some power, the power of a man ambitious, ruthless, scornful, self-confident. He did not care a snap of his fingers for his congregation, he laughed at their beliefs, he made use of their credulity.

"Oh God," he prayed, his voice now shrill and quivering and just out of tune, so that it jarred every nerve in Maggie's body, "Thou seest what we are, miserable sinners not worthy of Thy care or goodness, sunk deep in the mire of evil living and evil 'abits, nevertheless, oh God, we, knowing Thy loving 'eart towards Thy sinful servants, do pray Thee that Thou wilt give us Thy blessing before we leave this Thy 'ouse this night; a new contrite 'eart is what we beg of Thee, that we may go out into this evil world taught by Thee to search out our ways and improve our thoughts, caring for nothing but Thee, following in Thy footsteps and making ready for Thy immediate Coming, which will be in Thine own good time and according to Thy will."

"This we pray for the sake of Thy dear Son, our Lord Jesus Christ, who died for our sins upon the bloody Cross."

"Amen."

From between her hands Maggie watched those two strange eyes wandering about the Chapel, picking up here a person, there a person, wondering over this, wondering over that, and always, in the end, concerned not about these things at all but about some other more ultimate loneliness, fear or expectation, something that set him apart and made him, as are all men in the final recesses of their spirit, as lonely as though he were by himself on a desert island.

The thrill of anticipation faded through the Chapel as Thurston continued his prayer. He had not to-night, at any rate, power over his audience—the thing that they were waiting for was something that he could not satisfy. A restlessness was abroad; coughing broke out once, twice, then everywhere; chairs creaked, sighs could be heard, some one moved to the door. Thurston seemed to realise his failure; with a sudden snap of impatience he brought prayer to an end and rose to his feet.

"We will sing," he said, "No. 341. 'Bathed in the blood of the Lamb.'"

The singing of the hymn roused the excitement of the congregation to even more than its earlier pitch. The tune was a moving one, beginning very softly, beseeching God to listen, then, more confident, rising to a high note of appeal:

By all Thy sores and bloody pain Come down and heal our sins again;

falling, after that, to a note of confidence and security in the last refrain:

By the blood, by the blood, by the blood of the Lamb We beseech Thee—

In spite of the crudity of the words and the simplicity of the tune Maggie had tears in her eyes. The whole Chapel was singing now, singing as though the sins of the world could be redeemed only by the force and power of this especial moment. Maggie was caught up with the rest. She found herself singing parts of the second verse, then in the third she was carried away, had forgotten herself, her surroundings, even Martin. There was something real in this, something beyond the ugliness of the Chapel and its congregation. She remembered what Mr. Magnus had said: "If there's something of great value, don't think the less of it because the people, including yourself, who admire it, aren't worth very much. Why should they be?"

She looked for a moment at Aunt Anne and saw her in an ecstasy, singing in her cracked tuneless voice, a smile about her lips and in her eyes, that gazed far, far beyond that Chapel. Maggie felt the approach of tears; she stopped singing—softly the refrain of the last verse came:

By the blood, by the blood, by the blood of the Lamb We beseech Thee!

The hymn over, Mr. Warlock read the Bible and then offered up a long extempore prayer. Strangely enough Mr. Warlock brought Maggie back to reality—strangely because, on an earlier occasion, he had done exactly the opposite. She realised at once that he was not happy to-night. Before, he had been himself caught up into the mood that held the Chapel; to-night he was fighting against a mood that was then outside him, a mood with which he did not sympathise and in which he could not believe.

She saw that he was unhappy, he spoke slowly, without the spontaneity and force that he had used before; once he made a long pause and you could feel throughout the Chapel a wave of nervous apprehension, as though every one were waiting to see whether he would fight his way through or not. Maggie felt her earlier emotion sentimental and false, it was as though he had said to her: "But that's not the true thing; that's cheap sham emotion. That's what they're trying to turn our great reality into. I'm fighting them and you must help me."

He was fighting them. She could imagine Mr. Thurston's scornful lip, hidden now by his hands. As Mr. Warlock went on with his dignified sentences, his restraint and his reverence, she could fancy how Thurston was saying to himself: "But what's the good of this? It's blood and thunder we want. The old feller's getting past his work. He must go."

But it was Mr. Warlock's reality of which she was afraid. As he continued his prayer she felt all her old terror return, that terror that she had known on the night her father died, during the hours that she had watched beside his dead body, at the moment when she had first arrived at the house in London, during her first visit to the Chapel, when she had said good-night to her aunt before going out with Uncle Mathew ... And now Mr. Warlock was sweeping her still farther inside. The intensity of his belief forced hers. There was something real in this power of God, and you could not finish with it simply by disregarding it. She felt, as she had felt so often lately, that some one was suddenly going to rise and demand some oath or promise from her that she, in her panic, would give her word and then would be caught for ever.

"By the love of Thy dear Son, Our Lord Jesus Christ, and by the promise of Thy second coming, we beseech Thee" ... finished Mr. Warlock.

During all this time the atmosphere of the Chapel had been growing hotter and hotter and closer and closer. It had always its air of being buried deep under ground, bathed in a kind of sunken heat that found its voice in the gas that hissed and sizzled overhead; near the door was a long rail on which coats might be hung, and now these garments could be seen, swaying a little to and fro, like corpses of condemned men.

The bare ugliness of the building with its stone walls, its rows of wooden seats, its grey windows, its iron-hung gas-lamps, its ugly desk and platform, was veiled now in a thin steaming heat that rose mistily above the heads of the kneeling congregation and seemed to hide strange shapes and shadows in its shifting depths. Every one was swimming in an uncertain world; the unreality grew with the heat. Maggie herself, at the end of Mr. Warlock's prayer, felt that her test of a real solid and unimaginative world was leaving her. She was expectant like the rest, as ready to believe anything at all.

Out of the mist rose Mr. Crashaw. This was a little old man with a crabbed face and a body that seemed to have endured infernal twistings in some Inquisitioner's torture-chamber. Maggie learnt afterwards that he had suffered for many years from intolerable rheumatism, but to-night the contortions and windings of the body with which he climbed up onto the platform, and then the grimaces that he made as his large round head peered over the top of the desk, might have struck any less solemn assemblage as farcical. He wore an old shiny black frock coat and a white rather grimy tie fastened in a sharp little bow. His face was lined like a map, his cheeks seamed and furrowed, his forehead a wilderness of marks, his scanty hair brushed straight back so that the top of his forehead seemed unnaturally shiny and bald; his hands, with which he clutched the side of his desk, were brown and wrinkled and grasping like a monkey's. His eyes were the eyes of a fanatic, but they were not steady and speculative like Warlock's or glowing and distant like Aunt Anne's, but rather angry and restless and pugnacious; they were the eyes of a madman, but of a madman who can yet calculate upon and arrange his position in the world. He was mad for his own purposes, and could, for these same purposes, bind his madness to its proper bounds.

He seemed to Maggie at first rather pathetic with his little twisted body and his large round head. Very soon it was emotions quite other than pity that she was feeling. She saw at once that he was a practised preacher, and she who had, with the exception of Mr. Warlock, never heard a fine preacher, was at once under the sway of one of the ablest and most dramatic orators of his time. His voice was sweet and clear, and seemed strange enough coming from that ugly and malevolent countenance. Only the head and the grasping hands could be seen, but sometimes the invisible body was driven with such force against the desk that it seemed that it must fling the thing over, down into the congregation.

"My brothers and sisters," he began, "I have come to-night to give you a warning, and this warning is given to you not as the expression of a personal opinion but as the declaration of an assumed fact. Disregard it or not as you please, but I shall have done my duty in pointing out to you the sure and certain meaning of my message."

"I, a sinner like the rest of you, live nevertheless in the fear of hell fire. Hell fire has become, I think, to many of the present generation a mockery and a derision. I come to tell you that it is no mockery, that it as surely lies there, a blazing furnace, in front of us as though we saw it with our own eyes ..."

With his own eyes he had surely seen it. They were fixed now in a frenzy of realisation upon some distant vision, and, with a shiver, the Chapel followed his gaze. It is easy enough to laugh at bare and conventional words stripped of the atmosphere and significance of their original surroundings. The merest baby in this twentieth century can laugh at the flames of hell and advance a string of easy arguments against the probability of any such melodramatic fulfilment of the commonplace and colourless lives that the majority of us lead, but Maggie was in no mood to laugh that night.

Before five minutes had passed she found herself shivering where she sat. The Chapel was convicted of Sin, and of Sin of no ordinary measure. The head that rested like a round ball on the surface of the desk thrust conviction into every heart: "You think that you may escape, you look at your neighbours, every one of you, and say, 'He is worse than I. I am safe,' but I tell you that not one man or woman here shall be secure unless he turn instantly now to God and beg for mercy..."

As he continued he did indeed bear the almost breathless urgency of one who has been sent on in advance to announce the imminence of some awful peril. No matter what the peril might be; simply through the Chapel there passed the breath of some coming danger. Impossible to watch him and not realise that here was a man who had seen something with his own eyes that had changed in a moment the very fabric of his life. Thurston might be a charlatan who played with the beliefs of his dupes, Warlock might be a mystic whose vision was in the future and not in the past—Crashaw knew.

He painted, quietly, without fine words but with assurance and conviction, his belief in the punishment of mankind. God was almost now upon the threshold of their house. He was at the very gates of their city, and with Him was coming a doom as sure and awful as the sentence of the earthly judge on his earthly victim.

"Punishment! Punishment! ... We have grown in this careless age to laugh at punishment. A future life? There is no future life. God? There is no God! Even were He to come upon us we could escape from Him. We could make a very good case for ourselves. This world is safe, secure, founded upon our markets, our treasuries, our laws and commandments, our conventions of decent behaviour, our police and our ministers. God cannot touch us. We are secure ... I tell you that at this very moment this earth in which you trust is trembling under you, at this instant everything in which you believed is undermined and is betraying you. You have been given your opportunity—you are refusing it—and God is upon you."

His voice changed suddenly to tones of a marvellous sweetness. He appealed, pleaded, implored. The ugliness of his face and body was forgotten, he was simply a voice issuing from space, sent to save a world.

"And we here—the few of us out of this huge city gathered together here—it is not too late for us. Let us surrender ourselves. Let us go to Him and say that we are His, that we await His coming and obey His law ... Brothers and sisters, I am as you are, weak and helpless and full of sin, but come to Him, come to Him, come to Him! ... There is help for us all, help and pity and love. Love such as none of us have ever known, love that cannot fail us and will be with us until eternity!"

He stepped out from behind the desk, stood before them all with his little stunted, twisted body, his arms held out towards them. There followed then an extraordinary scene—from all over the Chapel came sobs and cries. A man rose suddenly from the back of the building and cried aloud, "Lord, I believe! Help Thou mine unbelief." One of the women who had come with Miss Avies fell upon her knees and began to sob, crying hysterically: "Oh God, have mercy! God have mercy!" Women pressed up the two aisles, some of them falling on their knees there where they had stood, others coming to the front and kneeling there. Somewhere they began to sing the hymn that had already been sung that evening, a few voices at first, then more, then all singing together:

"By the blood, by the blood, by the blood of the Lamb We beseech Thee!"

Everywhere now women were crying, the Chapel was filled with voices, sobs, cries and prayers.

Mr. Crashaw stood there, motionless, his arms outstretched.

Maggie did not know what she felt. She seemed deprived of all sensation on one side, and, on the other, fear and excitement; both joy and disgust held her. She could not have told any one what her sensations were; she was trembling from head to foot as though with cold. But behind everything she had this terror, that at any moment she might be drawn forward to do something, to give some pledge that would bind her for all her life. She felt as though some power were urging her to this, and as though the Chapel and every one in it was conscious of the struggle.

What might have happened she would never know. She felt a touch on her sleeve, and, turning round, saw Aunt Anne's eyes looking up at her out of a face that was so white and the skin of it so tightly drawn that it was like the face of a dead woman.

"I'm in great pain, Maggie. I think you must take me home," she heard her aunt say.

Aunt Anne took her arm, they went out followed by Aunt Elizabeth. The fresh evening air that blew upon Maggie's forehead seemed suddenly to make of the Chapel a dim, incredible phantom; faintly from behind the closed door came the echo of the hymn. The street was absolutely still—no human being was in sight, only an old cab stationed close at hand waiting for a possible customer; into this they got. The pale, almost white, evening sky, with stars in sheets and squares and pools of fire, shone with the clear radiance of glass above them. Maggie could see the stars through the dirty windows of the cab.

They were quite silent all the way home. Aunt Anne sitting up very straight, motionless, her fingers still on Maggie's arm.

Inside the house there was Jane. She seemed at once to under-stand, and, with Aunt Elizabeth, led Aunt Anne up the dark stairs.

They disappeared, leaving Maggie alone in the hall, whose only sound was the ticking clock from the stairs and only light the dim lamp above the door.

CHAPTER V

THE CHOICE

She waited for some time alone in the hall listening for she knew not what. Her departure from the Chapel had been too abrupt to allow her in a moment to shake off the impression of it—above all, the impression of Mr. Crashaw standing there, his arms stretched out to her, his eyes burning her through and through with the urgent insistence of his discovery.

She was tired, her head ached horribly, she would have given everything at that moment for a friend who would care for her and protect her from her own wild fears. She did not know of what she was afraid, but she knew that she felt that she would rather do anything than spend the night in that house. And yet what could she do? How could she escape? She knew that she could not. Oh! if only Martin would come! Where was he? Why could he not carry her off that very night? Why did he not come?

She gazed desperately about her. Could she not leave the house there and then? But where should she go? What could she do without a friend in London? She stood there, clasping and unclasping her hands, looking up at the black stairs, listening for some sound from above, fancying a ghost in every darkening corner of the place.

Then her common sense reasserted itself. It was something, at any rate, that she was out of the Chapel, away from Mr. Crashaw's piercing eyes, Mr. Thurston's rasping voice, Mr. Warlock's reproachful melancholy. She felt this evening as though by struggling with all her strength she could shut the gates upon new experiences that were fighting to enter into her soul, but must, at all costs to her own happiness, be defeated. No such thing as ghosts, no such thing as a God, be He kind, tender, cruel or loving—nothing but what one can see, can touch, can confront with one's physical strength. She had been to a service at a Methodist chapel, her aunt had been ill, to-morrow there would be daylight and people hurrying down the street about their business, work and shops and food and sun ... No such thing as ghosts! Nothing but what you can see!

"And I'll get some work without wasting a minute," she thought, nodding her head. "In a shop if necessary—or I could be a governess—and then when he is free, Martin will be with me."

She climbed on a chair and turned down the hall-gas as she had seen Martha do. She went to the door and slipped the chain into its socket and turned the lock. She listened for a moment before she started upstairs, she saw Mr. Crashaw's eyes in the dark—she heard his voice.

"Punishment! Punishment!..."

She suddenly started to run up the black stairs, stumbled, ran faster through the passage under the picture of the armed men, arrived at last in her room, breathless.

During her undressing she stopped sometimes to listen. Her aunt's bedroom was on the floor below hers, and she certainly could hear nothing through the closed doors, and yet she fancied, as she stood there, that the sound of sobbing came up to her and, twice, a sharp cry.

"I suppose I'm terribly selfish," she thought, "I ought to want to go and help Aunt Anne, and I don't." No, she didn't. She wanted to run away from the house, miles and miles and miles. She climbed into bed and thought of her escape. If Miss Trenchard did not answer her letter, then she could go off to Uncle

Mathew, greatly though she disliked the thought of that; then she could live on her three hundred pounds and look about until she found work or Martin came for her.

But so ignorant was she of the world that she did not in the least know how she could get her three hundred pounds. But Uncle Mathew would know. She thought of him standing in the doorway at the hotel, holding up a glass, then she thought of Martin, and so fell asleep.

She woke suddenly to find some one standing in her open doorway and holding up a candle. That some one was old Martha, looking strange enough in a nightdress, her scanty grey hairs untidily about her neck and a dirty red shawl over her shoulders. Maggie blinked at the light and sat up in bed.

"What is it?" she asked.

"It's your aunt, Miss—Miss Anne. She's very bad. She wants you to go to her."

Maggie got out of bed, put on her dressing-gown and slippers and followed the servant.

As she hurried along the dark passage she was still only half-awake; her soul had not returned into her body, but her body was awake and vibrating with the knowledge that the soul was soon coming to it, and coming to it with great news, with the consciousness of a marvellous experience. For at the instant when Martha awoke her she had been dreaming of Martin, dreaming of him physically, so that it was his body against hers, his hand hot and dry in hers cool and soft, his cheek rough and strong against hers smooth and pale. There had been no sentimentality or weakness in her dream. They had been confident and sure and defiant together, and it had been real life for her, so real that this dream life in which now she moved down the shadowy passage was about her as green water is about one when one swims under waves.

It was only slowly, as the cold air of the house at night cleared her eyes and her throat and her breast, that she came to the world consciousness again and surrendered her lover back to the shades and felt a sudden frightened fear lest, after all, she should never really know that ecstasy of which she had just been dreaming.

Nevertheless it was still with a great consciousness of Martin that she entered her aunt's bedroom. Before she entered she turned round for a moment to Martha.

"What must I do?" she asked. "What will she want me to do?"

"It's only," said Martha, "if the pains come on very bad, to give her some drops. They're in a little green bottle by her bed. Five drops ... yes, miss, five drops in a little green bottle. Only if the pains is very bad. She's brave—wonderful. I'd 'ave sat up till morning willing, and so of course would Miss Elizabeth. But she seemed to want you, miss."

They were like two conspirators whispering there in the dark. The room within was so still. Maggie very softly pushed back the door and entered. She walked a few steps inside the room and hesitated. There was no sound in the room at all, utter stillness so that Maggie could hear her own breathing as though it were some one else at her side warning her. Then slowly things emerged, the long white bed first, afterwards a shaded lamp beside it, a little table with bottles, a chair—beyond the circle of lighted shadow there were shapes, near the window a high glass, a dark shade that was the dressing-table, and faint grey squares where the windows hung.

In the room was a strange scent half wine, half medicine, and beyond that the plain tang of apples partially eaten, a little smell of oil too from the lamp—very faintly the figure of the Christ above the bed was visible. Maggie moved forward to the bed, then stopped again. She did not know what to do; she could see a dark shadow on the pillow that must she knew be her aunt's hair, and yet she did not connect that with her aunt. The room was cold and, she felt, of infinite space. The smell of the wine and the medicine made her shy and awkward as though she were somewhere where she should not be.

There came a little sigh, and then a very quiet, tired voice.

"Maggie, is that you?"

"Yes, Aunt Anne."

She came very close to the bed, and suddenly, as though a curtain had been drawn back, she could see her aunt's large eyes and white sharp face.

"It was very good of you, dear, to come. I felt ashamed to wake you up at such an hour, but I wanted you. I felt that only you must be with me to-night. It was a call from God. I felt that it must be obeyed. Sit down, dear. There, on that chair. You're not cold, are you?"

Maggie sat down, gathering her dressing-gown close about her. She was not even now drawn right out of her dream, and the room seemed fantastic, to rise and fall a little, and to be filled with sound, just out of hearing. For a time she was so sleepy that she nodded on her chair, and the green lamp swelled and quivered and the very bed seemed to sway in the dark, but soon the cold air cleared her head, and she was wide awake, staring before her at the grey window-panes. Her aunt did not for a long time speak again. Maggie sat there her mind a maze of the Chapel, old Crashaw, Miss Avies, and Martin. Slowly the cold crept into her feet and her hands, but her head now was burning hot. Then suddenly her aunt began to talk in a dreamy rather lazy voice, not her natural daily tone which was always very sharp and clear. She talked on and on; sometimes her sentences were confused and unfinished, sometimes they seemed to Maggie to have no meaning; once or twice the voice dropped so low that Maggie did not catch the words, but always there was especial urgency behind the carelessness as though every word were being spoken for a listener's benefit—a listener who sat perhaps with pencil and notebook somewhere in the dark behind them.

"So sorry ... so sorry, Maggie dear ... so sorry," the words ran up and down. "I hadn't meant to take you away before the service was over. Elizabeth could have ... sometimes my pain is very bad and I have to lie down, you know. But it's nothing—nothing really—only I'm glad, rather, that you should share all our little troubles, because then you'll know us better, won't you? Dear Maggie, there's been something between us all this time, hasn't there? Ever since our first meeting—and it's partly been my fault. I wasn't good at first, I wanted to be kind, but I was stiff and shy. You wouldn't think that I'm shy? I am, terribly. I always have been since I was very little, and just to enter a room when other people are there makes me so embarrassed ... I remember once when mother was alive her scolding me because I wouldn't come in to a tea-party. But I couldn't; I stood outside the door in an agony, doing everything to make myself go in—but I couldn't ... But now I've come to love you, dear, although of course you have your faults. But they are faults of your age, carelessness, selfishness. They are nothing in the eyes of

God, who understands all our weaknesses. And you must learn to know Him, dear. That is my only prayer now. If I am taken, if I go before the great day—if it be His will—then I pray always, now that I may leave you in my place, waiting for Him as I have waited, trusting Him as I have trusted ... you saw to-night what it means to us, what it must mean to any one who has listened. There were times, years ago, when I had not turned to God, when I did not care, when I thought of earthly love ... God drew me to Himself ... You too must come, Maggie—you must come. You mustn't stay outside—you are asked, you are invited—perhaps you will be compelled ..."

The voice sank: Maggie's teeth chattered in her head from the cold, and her foot had gone to sleep. She felt obstinate and rebellious and frightened, she could not think clearly, and the words that came from her, suddenly, seemed to her not to be her own.

"Aunt Anne, I want to do everything that you and Aunt Elizabeth think I should, but I must be myself, mustn't I? I'm grown up now; I've got my three hundred pounds and I don't think I want to be religious. I'm very grateful to you and Aunt Elizabeth, but I'm not a help to you much, I'm afraid. I know I'm very careless, I do want to be better, and that's all the more reason, perhaps, why I should go out and earn my own living. I'd learn more quickly then. But I do love you and Aunt Elizabeth ..."

She broke off; she did not love them. She knew that she did not. The only human being in all the world whom she loved was Martin. Nevertheless there did come to her suddenly then a new tenderness for her aunt; the actual sight of her pain in the Chapel had deeply touched her and now her eagerness for escape was mingled with a longing to be affectionate and good.

But Aunt Anne did not seem to have heard.

"Are you sure you're not cold, dear?"

"No, aunt."

Their hands touched.

"But you are. Put that rug over you. That one at the end of the bed. I'm quiet now. I think perhaps I shall sleep a little."

"Is there anything I can do?"

"Perhaps turn the lamp down, dear. That's it. A little more. Now, if you'd just raise my pillow. There, behind my head. That's the way! Why, what a good nurse you are!"

Maggie, as tenderly as she could, turned the pillow, patted it, placed it beneath her aunt's head. She was close against her aunt's face, and the eyes seemed suddenly so fierce and urgent, so insistent and powerful, that seeing them was like the discovery of some blazing fire in an empty house. Most of all, they were terrified eyes. Maggie went back to her chair. After that, she sat there during the slow evolution of Eternity; Eternity unrolled itself before her, on and on and on, grey limitless mist and space, comfortless, lifeless, hopeless. She had been for many weeks leading a thoroughly unwholesome life in that old house with those old women. She did not herself know how unhealthy it had been, but she knew that she missed the wide fields and downs of Glebeshire, the winds that blew from the sea round Borhedden, the air that swirled and raced up and down the little stony strata of St. Dreot. Now she had been kept indoors, had had no fun of any kind, had looked forward to Mr. Magnus as her chief diversion. Then Martin had come, and suddenly she had seen how dangerously her life was hemming her in. She was losing courage. She would soon be afraid to speak for herself at all; she would soon ...

In a panic at these thoughts, and feeling as though some one was trying to push her down into a coffin whilst she was still alive, she began hurriedly to speak, although she did not know whether her aunt were asleep or no.

"I think I ought to tell you, Aunt Anne, that I wrote a letter some days ago and posted it myself. It was to a lady who knew Father once in Glebeshire, and she said that if ever I wanted help I was to write to her, and so—although perhaps I oughtn't to have done it without asking you first, still I was afraid you mightn't want me to—so I sent it. I wouldn't like to hurt your feelings, Aunt Anne, and it isn't that I'm not happy with you and Aunt Elizabeth, but I ought to be earning my own living, oughtn't I? And I've only got my three hundred pounds, haven't I? I'm not complaining, but I don't know about anything yet, do I? I can't even find my way when I'm out with Aunt Elizabeth. And I'm afraid I'll never be really good enough to be religious. Perhaps if Father'd wanted me to be I might be now, but he never cared ... I hope you won't be angry, Aunt Anne, but I didn't like to-night—I didn't really. When I was there I thought that soon I'd begin to cry like the others, but it was only because every one else was crying—not because I wanted to. I hope you won't be angry, but I'm afraid I'll never be religious as you and Aunt Elizabeth want me to be; so don't you think it will be better for me to start learning something else right away?"

Maggie poured all this out and then felt immense relief. At last she was honest again; at last she had said what she felt, and they knew it and could never say that she hadn't been fair with them. She felt that her speech had cleared the air in every kind of way. She waited for her aunt's reply. No sound came from the bed. Had her aunt heard? Perhaps she slept. Maggie waited. Then timidly, and softly she said:

"Aunt Anne ... Aunt Anne ..."

No reply. Then again in a whisper:

"Aunt Anne ... Aunt Anne ..."

Supposing Aunt Anne ... Maggie trembled, then, commanding herself to be calm, she bent towards the bed.

"Aunt Anne, are you asleep?"

Suddenly Aunt Anne's face was there, the eyes closed, the mouth, the cheeks pale yellow in the faint reflection from the lamp. There was no stir, no breath.

"Aunt Anne, Aunt Anne," Maggie whispered in terror now. Then she saw that her aunt was sleeping; very, very faintly the sheets rose and fell and the fingers of the hand on the coverlet trembled a little as though they were struggling to wake.

Then Aunt Anne had heard nothing after all. But it might be that she was pretending, just to see what Maggie would say.

"Aunt Anne," whispered Maggie once more and for the last time. Then she sat back on her seat again, her hands folded, staring straight in front of her. After that she did not know for how long she sat there in a state somewhere between dream and reality. The room, although it never lost its familiarity, grew uncouthly strange; shapes grey and dim seemed to move beneath the windows, humping their backs, spinning out into long limbs, hands and legs and gigantic fingers. The deadest hour of the night was come; the outside world seemed to press upon the house, the whole world cold, thick, damp, lifeless, like an animal slain and falling with its full weight, crushing everything beneath it. Perhaps she slept— she did not know. Martin seemed to be with her, and against them was Aunt Anne, her back against the door, her hands spread, refusing to let them pass. The room joined in the struggle, the floor slipped beneath their tread, the curtain swayed forward and caught them in its folds, the lamp flickered and flickered and flickered ...

She was awake suddenly, quite acutely aware of danger. She rubbed her eyes, turned, and in the dim shadow saw her aunt sitting up in bed, her body drawn up to its intensest height, her hands pressing down, flat upon the bed. Her eyes stared as though they would break down all boundaries, but her lips trembled like the lips of a little child.

"Aunt Anne, what is it?" Maggie whispered.

"It's the pain—" Her voice was far away as though some one were speaking from the passage outside the door. "It's the pain ... I can't ... much more ..."

Maggie remembered what Martha had told her about the drops. She found the little green bottle, saw the glass by the side of it.

Suddenly she heard Aunt Anne: "Oh no ... Oh no! God I can't ... God, I can't ... I can't."

Maggie bent over the bed; she put her hand behind her aunt's back and could feel the whole body quivering, the flesh damp beneath the night-dress. She steadied her, then put the glass to her lips.

The cry was now a little whisper. "No more ... I can ... no more." Then more softly still: "Thy will, oh Lord. As thou wilt—Our Father, which art in Heaven, Hallowed ... Hallowed ... Hallowed..."

She sank down on to her pillows.

"Is it better?" Maggie asked.

Her aunt caught her hand.

"You mustn't leave me. I shan't live long, but you must stay with me until I go. Promise me! Promise me!"

"No, I can't promise," said Maggie.

"You must stay. You must stay."

"No I can't promise." Then suddenly kneeling down by the bed she put her hand on the other's arm: "Aunt Anne, I'll do anything for you—anything—to make you better—if I can help ... but not a promise, I can't promise."

"Ah, but you will stay," Aunt Anne's whisper trembled with its certainty.

That seemed the climax of the night to Maggie then. She felt that she was indeed held for eternity by the house, the Chapel, and something beyond the Chapel. The scent of the medicine, the closeness of the room, the darkness and the sickness, seemed to close all about her ... She was at the bottom of a deep well, and she would never get out, she would never get out ...

The door slowly, very softly opened, and old Martha looked in.

"She's been very bad," whispered Maggie.

"Ay, I heard something. That's why I came. You gave her the drops?"

"Yes."

"She'll sleep a bit now. I'll take your place, Miss Maggie. It's time you went back to your bed."

Maggie crept away.

She came down to breakfast to find the house bathed in sunlight and the parrot singing hoarsely "And her golden hair was hanging down her back." Aunt Elizabeth was there, cheerful and almost merry in her bird-like fashion. The world was normal, ghosts out of fashion, and this morning was the day on which the silver was cleaned. This last was Maggie's business, and very badly she did it, never being "thorough," and having a fatal habit of thinking of other things. Porridge, eggs and bacon, marmalade—

"And—her golden hair was hanging—" croaked Edward.

"Your aunt won't come down this morning, Maggie. She's much better. The sun's shining. A little walk will be a good thing. I'll buy the calico that Anne talked about. Your aunt's better."

Maggie felt ashamed of herself. What desperate silly feelings had she allowed last night? How much she had made of that service, and how weak she was to give way so easily!

"I'll clean the silver," she thought. "I'll do it better than ever"—but unfortunately she had a hole in her stocking, and Aunt Elizabeth, like a sparrow who has found a worm, told her about it.

"Mr. Crashaw's coming to tea this afternoon," she concluded.

"That's why Anne's staying in bed—to be well enough." The stocking and Mr. Crashaw dimmed a little of the morning's radiance, but behind them was the thought, "Martin must come to-day. It was like a message his look last night." She even sang to herself as she scrubbed at the silver.

They spent a domestic morning. Aunt Elizabeth did not go for her walk, but instead stayed in the dining-room and, seated at the end of the long dining-table, her head just appearing above the worn and soiled green table-cloth, tried to discipline the week's household accounts. She worked sucking one finger after another and poking her pencil into her ears.

"One pound, three shillings—ham, ham, ham—?"

At one moment she invited the cook to assist her, and that lady, crimson from the kitchen fire, bared arms akimbo, stated that she was not only the most economical woman in London, but was also, thanks to her upbringing, one of the most sober and virtuous, and if Miss Cardinal had anything to say against—

Oh no! Aunt Elizabeth had nothing to say against, only this one pound, three shillings—

Well, the cook couldn't help that; she wasn't one to let a penny out of her fingers where it shouldn't go.

So the morning hummed along; luncheon-time came, the silver was all cleaned, the stockings changed, and there was roast chicken. Thomas, with his wicked eyes, came slowly, majestically upon the scene—but even he was not sinister to-day, being interested in his own greed rather than other persons' sins.

All this time Maggie refused to think. Martin would come, then she would see.

Martin ... Martin ... Martin ... She went up into her bedroom and whispered the name over and over to herself whilst she tried to mend her stocking. She flung the stocking down and gazed out of the window on to a world that was all golden cloud and racing watery blue. The roofs swam like floating carpets in the sun, detached from the brick and mortar beneath them, carried by the racing clouds. It was only at that sudden gaze that she realised that she was a prisoner. All her alarm came back to her.

"Why can't I go out? I'll put on my hat and just walk out. No one can stop me. No one ..."

But she knew that she could not. Something more must happen first. She turned from the window with a little shudder, finished very clumsily her stocking, and as the cuckoo clock struck halfpast three went down to the drawing-room.

There to her surprise, she found Caroline Smith. The events of the last few days had, a little, dimmed Caroline from her memory. She had not seen Caroline for a fortnight. She did not know that she especially wanted to see Caroline now. However, it was very certain that Caroline wanted to see her. The young woman was dressed in rose-coloured silk that stood out from her slim body almost like a crinoline, and she had a straw funnel-shaped hat with roses perched on the side of her lovely head. She kissed Maggie many times, and then sitting down with her little sharp black shoes poked out in front of her, she ran on:

"It's been too bad, Maggie, dear; it's simply ages since we had a moment, isn't it, but it hasn't been my fault. Father's been ill—bronchitis—and I've had to help Mother. Father's been so happy, he's just been able to lie in bed for days and think about God. None of those tiresome people at the Bank to interrupt him, and chicken and jelly as much as he liked. He was so unhappy yesterday when he had to go back to work, poor dear ... But, Maggie, I hear you were at the service last night. How did you like it?"

"Like it?" said Maggie. "I don't know that it's a thing one likes, exactly."

"Doesn't one? I don't know. I'm not one of the Inside Saints, you know, and I wouldn't be if they wanted me to be. But you're one now, they say, and I never would have thought it. You don't look a bit like one, and I shouldn't have dreamt that you'd ever stand that sort of thing. You look so matter-of-fact."

Maggie was on the point of bursting out that she was not an Inside Saint, and would never be one, when caution restrained her. She had learnt already that her gay young companion was not as trustworthy as best friends ought to be.

"It was the first time, last night," she said.

"Yes, I know, and Miss Cardinal was ill and had to come away in the middle, didn't she? It must have been a simply awful meeting, because Mother came back as limp as anything. She'd been crying buckets, and has a dreadful headache to-day. I suppose Mr. Crashaw gave it them. I've never heard him, but I've seen him. Horrid old monkey—I hope Miss Cardinal's better to-day."

"Yes, thank you," said Maggie. "She's better."

"Well, that's a good thing. I'm so glad. And you, you darling, what did you think of it all? I'm sure you didn't cry buckets. I can see you sitting there as quiet as anything, like a little Quaker. I'd like to have gone just to have seen you. I hear Martin Warlock was there too. Was he?"

"He was," said Maggie.

"Fancy that! I wonder what he went for. His father made him, I expect. You know they say he's getting on awfully badly at home and that there are quarrels all the time. I don't know, of course, but his sister can't stand him. She's always showing her feelings—not very good taste, I think, but Mr. Thurston eggs her on. They'll be making a match of it one day, those two ... I say, Maggie—" Caroline drew her chair close. "I'll give you a secret. You won't tell any one, will you?"

"Certainly not—if you tell me not to," said Maggie.

"Well, Martin Warlock and I—ever since he came back. Oh! I don't say it's anything really. But he's attracted by me and would like to go farther. He'll be asking me to marry him one of these days, and then I'll have fun. He would have done the other day if I'd let him. I like him rather, don't you? He's getting a bit fat, of course, but he's got nice eyes, and then he's a real man. I like real men. But there, you'll be thinking me coarse, I know you will. I'm not coarse really, only impulsive. You don't like me, honestly, if it were known. Oh no! you don't! I can tell. I always know. But I don't care—I love you. You're a darling—and what I say is if you love some one, just love them. Never mind what they think. Don't you agree with me? But you wouldn't. You wouldn't think of loving anybody. But I'm not really bad—only careless, Mother says—"

What Mother said could not be known, because the door opened and Martha announced Mr. Crashaw. The old man, leaning on a walking stick, came forward and greeted Maggie and Caroline with good-temper and amiability. He was indeed in day-time a very mild old man, and it was difficult for Maggie to believe that this was the same who last night had frightened her out of her wits and led her to the edge of such strange suspicions. He was more than ever like a monkey, with his bony brown forehead, protuberant eyes and large mottled nose, and he sat there all huddled up by his rheumatism, a living example of present physical torments rather than future spiritual ones. It was apparent at once that he liked pretty young women, and he paid Caroline a number of flattering attentions, disregarding Maggie with a frankness that witnessed to a life that had taught one lesson at least, never on any occasion to waste time. Maggie did not mind—it amused her to see her terror of the night before transformed into a mere serenading crippled old gentleman, and to see, too, the excited pleasure with which Caroline accepted even such decayed attentions as these. But what was it that had persuaded her last night? Why did she now spend her time half in one world and half in another? Which world was the real one?

Aunt Anne very soon joined them, and this quiet, composed figure only added to Maggie's scorn of her last night's terrors. Was this the same who had struggled with such agony, who had made Maggie feel that she was caught in a trap and imprisoned for ever?

The sun beat hotly upon the carpet. Caroline's rose-coloured silk shone and glowed, the tea was poured out, and there was chatter about the warm winter that it was and how time passed, and how fashions changed, and how you never saw a four-wheeler now, and what they were turning Kingsway into, and what they were turning the Law Courts out of, and even once, by Mr. Crashaw, a word about the Lyceum Theatre, where some one was playing the Merchant of Venice, which was a fine play and could do no one any harm.

"But I daresay," said Mr. Crashaw, "that this young lady here goes to nothing but plays every night of her life."

"Why, Mr. Crashaw," said Caroline, tossing her head. "If that's the kind of life you fancy I lead you're completely mistaken. Theatres indeed! Never do I put so much as the tip of my nose inside one. Father thinks they're wrong and so does Mother say she does, although I know she likes them, really; but any way that doesn't matter because I never have a moment to myself—sitting at home sewing, that's the way I spend my days, Mr. Crashaw."

It was the very last way she really spent them, as Maggie perfectly well knew. It is not to be supposed that Mr. Crashaw either was deceived. However, he gave a wicked wink with the eye that was least rheumatic and said something about "a beautiful young lady like Miss Smith wasted on sewing and darning," and Caroline smiled and said something about "one day perhaps"—and Aunt Anne looked remotely benevolent. What did she think of all this, Maggie wondered? What did she think of her great preacher, her prophet, wasting the few hours of life that remained to him over such a business? They had some secret understanding, perhaps, as though they said to one another, "We know, you and I, what are our real intentions beneath all this. We only do what we must."

Understanding or no, Mr. Crashaw sprang up with unexpected activity when Caroline departed and announced his intention of conducting her to her door. He made his adieus and then hobbled along after the rose-coloured silk as though this was his last chance of warming his hands at the flame of life.

When they were gone, Aunt Anne said:

"I am going back to bed, Maggie, dear. Martha will send me up some supper later. Elizabeth has gone to Lambeth to see a friend, so make yourself busy until seven, dear. If I want anything I'll ring."

When she was left alone in the darkening room she stood there thinking. Why should she not go out and find Martin? She did not care what any one thought. She would go to his house and ask for him. She had waited and waited ... She wanted him so, she wanted him so desperately!

Then Martha opened the door and announced him, yes, really announced him, saying: "It's young Mr. Warlock, Miss, and he says if your aunts isn't in you'll do."

"Ask him to come up, Martha," said Maggie, and then held herself there, rooted, where she stood so that she should not run to him and fling her arms round his neck. She felt at once with that quick perception that was hers, in spite of her ignorance of life, that this was no moment for love-making, and that he wanted something quite other from her.

He closed the door behind him, looked round the room, didn't come to her, but stayed where he was.

"I've been trying to see you all day," he said. "How long have we got alone do you think?" She never took her eyes from his face. "Until seven probably. Aunt Elizabeth's in Lambeth and Aunt Anne's in bed."

"That's luck." He drew a breath of relief, then moved over to the fireplace. "Maggie, I've come to say we mustn't see one another any more."

Some one, some vast figure shadowy behind her, moved suddenly forward and caught her in his arms and his embrace was deadly cold. She stood where she was, her hands at her side, looking steadfastly at him.

"Why?" she said. "Because—because—the fact is, I've been wrong altogether. Maggie, I'm not the sort of man for you to have anything to do with. You don't know much about life yet, do you? I'm about the first man you've ever met, aren't I? If you'd met another man before me, you'd have cared for him as much."

She said nothing and he seemed to be confused by her steady gaze, because he looked down and continued to speak as though to himself:

"I knew at once that there was danger in our meeting. With other girls they can look after themselves. One hasn't any responsibility to them. It's their own affair, but you believe every word a fellow says. And if we'd been friends it wouldn't have mattered, but from the very first we weren't that—we were something more."

"You were so different from any other girl. I've wanted to be good to you from the beginning, but now I see that if we go on I shall only be bad. It all comes in the end to my being bad—really bad—and I want you to know it."

"I don't know," said Maggie, "that I've thought very much whether you're good or bad. And it doesn't matter. I can look after myself."

"No, you can't," he said vehemently, making a step towards her and then suddenly stopping. "That's just it—you can't. I've been thinking all the time since the other evening when we were together, and I've seen that you believe every word I say and you trust me. I don't mean to tell lies—I don't know that I'm worse than most other men—but I'm not good enough for you to trust in all the same. I've been knocking about for years, and I suppose I've had most of my idealism knocked out of me. Anyway I don't believe in most people, and you still do. I'm not going to be the one to change you."

"Perhaps I know more about life than you think," said Maggie.

"No, how can you? You've never had a chance of seeing any of it. You'd get sick of me in no time. I'm moody and selfish and bad-tempered. I used to drink a bit too. And I can't be faithful to women. I might think I was going to be faithful to you and swear I would be—and then suddenly some one would come along. I thought for a bit I'd just go on with you and see what came of it. You're so unusual, you make me want to be straight with you; but I've seen it wouldn't be fair. I must just slip out of your path and you'll forget me, and then you'll meet a much better man than I and be happy. I'm queer—I have funny moods that last for days and days sometimes. I seem to do every one harm I come in touch with. There's my father now. I love him more than any one in the world, and yet I make him unhappy all the time. I'm a bad fellow to be with—"

He stopped suddenly, looked at her and laughed. "It isn't any good, Maggie ... You haven't any idea what a sweep I am. You'd hate me if you really knew."

She looked steadily back at him. "We haven't much time," she said, speaking with steady, calm conviction as though she had, for years, been expecting just such a conversation as this, and had thought out what she would say. "Aunt Elizabeth can come back earlier than she said. Perhaps I shall say something I oughtn't to. I don't care. The whole thing is that I love you. I suppose it's true that I don't know anything about men, but I'd be poor enough if my love for you just depended on your loving me back, and on your being good to me and all the rest of it. I've never had any one I could love until you came, but now that you have come it can't be anything that you can do that can alter it. If you were to go away I'd still love you, because it's the love in me that matters, not what I get for it. Perhaps you'll make me unhappy, but anyway one will be unhappy some of the time."

She went up to him and kissed him. "I know Caroline Smith or some one would be very shocked if they thought I'd said such things to you, but I can't help what they say."

He had a movement to catch her and hold her, but he kept himself off, moved away from her, turning his back to her.

"You don't understand ... you don't understand," he repeated. "You know nothing about men, Maggie, and you know nothing about me. I tell you I wouldn't be faithful to you, and I'd be drunk sometimes, and I'd have moods for days, when I'd just sulk and not speak to a soul. I think those moods some damned sort of religion when I'm in them, but what they really are is bad temper. You've got to know it, Maggie. I'd be rotten to you, however much I wanted not to be."

"That's my own affair," she answered. "I can look after myself. And for all the rest, I'm independent and I'll always be independent. I'll love you whether you're good to me or bad."

"Well, then," he suddenly wheeled round to her, "you'd better have it ... I'm married already."

She took that with a little startled cry. Her eyes searched his face in a puzzled fashion as though she were pursuing the truth. Then she said like a child who sees some toy broken before its eyes:

"Oh, Martin!"

"Yes. Nobody knows—not a soul. It was a mad thing—four years ago in Marseille I met a girl, a little dressmaker there. I went off my head and married her, and then a month later she ran off with a merchant chap, a Greek. I didn't care; we got on as badly as anything ... but there you are. No one knows. That's the whole thing, Maggie. I thought at first I wouldn't tell you. I was beginning to care for you too much, as a matter of fact, and then when your uncle asked me to dinner, I told myself I was a fool to go. Then when I saw how you trusted me, I thought I'd be a cad and let it continue, but somehow ... you've got an influence over me ... You've made me ashamed of things I wouldn't have hesitated about a year ago. And the funny thing is it isn't your looks. I can say things to you I couldn't to other women, and I'll tell you right away that there are lots of women attract me more. And yet I've never felt about any woman as I do about you, that I wanted to be good to her and care for her and love her. It's always whether they loved me that I've thought about ... Well, now I've told you, you see that I'd better go, hadn't I? You see ... you see."

She looked up at him.

"I've got to think. It makes a difference, of course. Can we meet after a week and talk again?"

"Much better if I don't see you any more. I'll go away altogether—abroad again."

"No—after a week—"

"Much better not."

"Yes. Come here after a week. And if we can't be alone I'll give you a letter somehow ... Please, Martin—you must."

"Maggie, just think—"

"No—after a week."

"Very well, then," he turned on her fiercely. "I've been honest. I've told you. I've done all I can. If I love you now it isn't my fault."

He left the room, not looking at her again. And she stood there, staring in front of her.

CHAPTER VI

THE PROPHET IN HIS OWN HOME

Martin walked into the street with a confused sense of triumph and defeat, that confusion that comes to all sensitive men at the moment when they are stepping, against their will, from one set of conditions into another. He had gone into that house, only half an hour ago, determined to leave Maggie for ever—for his good and hers. He came back into the street realising that he was now, perhaps for the first time, quite definitely involved in some relation with her—good, bad, safe, dangerous he did not know—but involved. He had intended to tell her nothing of his marriage—and he had told her. He had intended to treat their whole meeting as something light, passing, inconsiderable—he had instead treated it as something of the utmost gravity. He had intended, above all, to prove to himself that he could do what he wished—he had found that he had no power.

And so, as he stepped through the dim gold-dust of the evening light he was stirred with an immense sense of having stepped, definitely at last, across the threshold of new adventure and enterprise. All kinds of problems were awaiting solution—his relation to his father, his mother, his sister, his home, his past, his future, his sins and his weaknesses—and he had meant to solve them all, as he had often solved them in the past, by simply cutting adrift. But now, instead of that, he had decided to stay and face it all out, he had confessed at last that secret that he had hidden from all the world, and he had submitted to the will of a girl whom he scarcely knew and was not even sure that he liked.

He stopped at that for a moment and, standing in a little pool of purple light under the benignant friendliness of a golden moon new risen and solitary, he considered it. No, he did not know whether he liked her—it was interest rather that drew him, her strangeness, her strength and loneliness, young and solitary like the moon above him—and yet—also some feeling softer than interest so that he was suddenly touched as he thought of her and spoke out aloud: "I'll be good to her—whatever happens, by God I'll be good to her," so that a chauffeur near him turned and looked with hard scornful eyes, and a girl somewhere laughed. With all his conventional dislike of being in any way "odd" he walked hurriedly on, confused and wondering more than ever what it was that had happened to him. Always before he had known his own mind—now, in everything, he seemed to be pulled two ways. It was as though some spell had been thrown over him.

It was a lovely evening and he walked slowly, not wishing to enter his house too quickly. He realised that he had, during the last weeks, found nothing there but trouble. And if Maggie wished, in spite of what he had told her, to go on with him? And if his father, impatient at last, definitely asked him to stay at home altogether and insisted on an answer? And if his gradually increasing estrangement with his sister broke into open quarrel? And if, strangest of all, this religious business, that in such manifestations as the Chapel service of last night he hated with all his soul, held him after all?

He was in Garrick Street, outside the curiosity shop, his latchkey in his hand. He stopped and stared down the street as he had done once before, weeks ago. Was not the root of all his trouble simply this, that he was becoming against his will interested, drawn in? That there were things going on that his common sense rejected as nonsense, but that nevertheless were throwing out feelers like the twisting threats of an octopus, touching him now, only faintly, here for a second, there for a second, but fascinating, holding him so that he could not run away? Granted that Thurston was a charlatan, Miss Avies a humbug, his sister a fool, his father a dreamer, Crashaw a fanatic, did that mean that the power behind them all was sham? Was that force that he had felt when he was a child simply eager superstition? What was behind this street, this moon, these hurrying figures, his own daily life and thoughts? Was there really a vast conspiracy, a huge involving plot moving under the cardboard surface of the world, a plot that he had by an accident of birth spied upon and discovered?

Always, every day now, thoughts, suspicions, speculations were coming upon him, uninvited, undesired, from somewhere, from some one. He did not want them he wanted only the material physical life of the ordinary man. It must be because he was idling. He would get work at once, join with some one in the City, go abroad again ... but perhaps even then he would not escape. Thoughts like those of the last weeks did not depend for their urgency on place or time. And Maggie, she was mixed up in it all. He was aware, as he hesitated before opening the door, of the strangest feeling of belonging to her, not love, nor passion, not sentiment even. Only as though he had suddenly realised that with new perils he had received also new protection.

He went upstairs with a feeling that he was on the eve of events that would change his whole world.

As Martin climbed to the top of the black crooked staircase he was conscious, as though it had been shown him in a vision, that he was on the edge of some scene that might shape for him the whole course of his future life. He had been aware, once or twice before, of such a premonition, and, as with most men, half of him had rejected and half of him received the warning. To-day, however, there were reasons enough for thinking this no mere baseless superstition. With Maggie, with his father, with his sister, with his own life the decision had got to be taken, and it was with an abrupt determination that he would end, at all costs, the fears and uncertainties of these last weeks that he pushed back the hall-door and entered. He noticed at once strange garments hanging on the rack and a bright purple umbrella which belonged, as he knew, to a certain Mrs. Alweed, a friend of his mother's and a faithful servant of the Chapel, stiff and assertive in the umbrella-stand. There was a tea-party apparently. Well, he could not face that immediately. He would have to go in afterwards ... meanwhile ...

He turned down the passage, pushed back his father's door and entered. He paused abruptly in the doorway; there, standing in front of the window facing him, his pale chin in the air, his legs apart, supercilious and self-confident, stood Thurston. His father's desk was littered with papers, rustling and blowing a little in the breeze from the window that was never perfectly closed.

One candle, on the edge of the desk, its flame swaying in the air was the only light. Martin's first impulse was to turn abruptly back again and go up to his room. He could not speak to that fellow now, he could not! He half turned. Then something stopped him:

"Halloo!" he said. "Where's father?"

"Don't know," said Thurston, sucking the words through his teeth. "I've been wanting him too."

"Well, as he isn't here—" said Martin fiercely.

"No use me waiting? Quite so. All the same I'm going to wait."

The two figures were strangely contrasted, Martin red-brown with health, thick and square, Thurston pale with a spotted complexion, dim and watery eyes, legs and arms like sticks, his black clothes shabby and his boots dusty.

Nevertheless at that moment it was Thurston who had the power. He moved forward from the window. "Makes you fair sick to see me anywhere about the 'ouse, doesn't it? Oh, I know ... You can't kid me. I've seen from the first. You fair loathe the sight of me."

"That's nothing to do with it," said Martin uneasily. "Whether we like one another or not, there's no need to discuss it."

"Oh, isn't there?" said Thurston, coming a little closer so that he was standing now directly under the light of the candle. "Why not? Why shouldn't we? What's the 'arm? I believe in discussing things myself. I do really. I've said to myself a long way back. 'Well, now, the first time I get 'im alone I'll ask him why 'e does dislike me. I've always been civil to him,' I says to myself, 'and yet I can't please him—so I'll just ask him straight.'"

Martin shrugged his shoulders; he wanted to leave the room, but something in Thurston held him there.

"I suppose we aren't the sort to get on together. We haven't got enough in common," he said clumsily.

"I don't know about that," Thurston said in a friendly conversational tone. "I shouldn't wonder if we've got more in common than you'd fancy. Now I'll tell you right out, I like you. I've always liked you, and what's more I always shall. Whatever you do—"

"I don't care," broke in Martin angrily, "whether you like me or not."

"No, I know you don't," Thurston continued quietly. "And I know what you think of me, too. This is your idea of me, I reckon—that I'm a pushing, uneducated common bounder that's just using this religious business to shove himself along with; that's kidding all these poor old ladies that 'e believes in their bunkum, and is altogether about as low-down a fellow as you're likely to meet with. That's about the colour of it, isn't it?"

Martin said nothing. That was exactly "the colour of it."

"Yes, well," Thurston continued, a faint flush on his pale cheeks. "Of course I know that all right. And I'll tell you the idea that I might 'ave of you—only might 'ave, mind you. Why, that you're a stuck-up ignorant sort of feller, that's been rolling up and down all over Europe, gets a bit of money, comes over and bullies his father, thinks 'e knows better than every one about things 'e knows nothing about whatever—"

"Look here, Thurston," Martin interrupted, stepping forward. "I tell you I don't care a two-penny curse what a man like—"

"I only said might, mind you," said Thurston, smiling. "It's only a short-sighted fool would think that of you really. And I'm not a fool. No, really, I'm not. I've got quite another idea of you. My idea is that you're one of us whether you want to be or not, and that you always will be one of us. That's why I like you and will be a friend to you too."

"I tell you I don't want your damned friendship," Martin cried. "I don't want to have anything to do with you or your opinion or your plans or anything else."

"That's all right," said Thurston. "I quite understand. It's natural enough to feel as you do. But I'm afraid you'll 'ave to 'ave something to do with me. I'm not quite what you think me, and you're not quite what you think yourself. There's two of each of us, that's the truth of it. I may be a sham and a charlatan, one part of me, I don't know I'm sure. I certainly don't believe all your governor does. I don't believe all I say and I don't say all I think. But then 'oo does? You don't yourself. I'll even tell you straight out that when I just came into the business I laughed at the lot of 'em, your father and all. 'A silly lot o' softs they are,' I said to myself, 'to believe all that nonsense.' But now—I don't know. When you've been at this game a bit you scarcely know what you do believe, that's the truth of it. There may be something in it after all. Sometimes ... well, it 'ud surprise you if you'd seen all the things I have. Oh, I don't mean ghosts and spirits and all that kind of nonsense. No, but the kind of thing that 'appens to people you'd never expect.

You're getting caught into it yourself; I've watched you all along. But that isn't the point. The point is that I'm not so bad as you think, nor so simple neither. And life isn't so simple, nor religion, nor love, nor anything as you think it. You're young yet, you know. Very young."

Martin turned back to the door.

"All very interesting, Thurston," he said. "You can think what you like, of course. All the same, the less we see of one another—"

"Well," said Thurston slowly, smiling. "That'll be a bit difficult—to avoid one another, I mean. You see, I'm going to marry your sister."

Martin laughed. Inside him something was saying: "Now, look out. This is all a trap. He doesn't mean what he says. He's trying to catch you."

"Going to marry Amy? Oh no, you're not."

Thurston did not appear to be interested in anything that Martin had to say. He continued as though he were pursuing his own thoughts. "Yes ... so it'll be difficult. I didn't think you'd like it when you heard. I said to Amy, 'E won't like it,' I said. She said you'd been too long away from the family to judge. And so you have, you know. Oh! Amy and I'll be right enough. She's a fine woman, your sister."

Martin burst out:

"Well, then, that settles it. It simply settles it. That finishes it."

"Finishes what?" asked Thurston, smiling in a friendly way.

"Never you mind. It's nothing to do with you. Has my father consented?"

"Yes ... said all 'e wanted was for Amy to be 'appy. And so she will be. I'll look after her. You'll come round to it in time."

"Father agrees ... My God! But it's impossible! Don't you see? Don't you see? I ..."

The sudden sense of his impotence called back his words. He felt nothing but rage and indignation against the whole set of them, against the house they were in, the very table with the papers blowing upon it and the candle shining ... Well, it made his own affair more simple—that was certain. He must be off—right away from them all. Stay in the house with that fellow for a brother-in-law? Stay when ...

"It's all right," said Thurston, moistening his pale dry lips with his tongue. "You'll see it in time. It's the best thing that could 'appen. And we've got more in common than you'd ever suppose. We 'ave, really. You're a religious man, really—can't escape your destiny, you know. There's religious and non-religious and it doesn't matter what your creed is, whether you're a Christian or a 'Ottentot, there it is. And if you're religious, you're religious. I may be the greatest humbug on the market, but I'm religious. It's like 'aving a 'are lip—you'll be bothered with it all your life."

But what more Thurston may have said Martin did not hear: he had left the room, banging the door behind him. On what was his indignation based? Injured pride. And was he really indignant? Was not something within him elated, because by this he had been offered his freedom? Thurston marry his sister? ... He could go his own way now. Even his father could not expect him to remain.

And he wanted Maggie—urgently, passionately. Standing for a moment there in the dark passage he wanted her. He was lonely, disregarded, despised.

They did not care for him here, no one cared for him anywhere—only Maggie who was clear-eyed and truthful and sure beyond any human being whom he had ever known. Then, with a very youthful sense of challenging this world that had so grossly insulted him by admitting Thurston into the heart of it, he joined the tea-party. There in the pink, close, sugar-smelling, soft atmosphere sat his mother, Amy, Mrs. Alweed and little Miss Pyncheon. His mother, with her lace cap and white hair and soft plump hands, was pouring tea through a strainer as though it were a rite. On her plate were three little frilly papers that had held sugary cakes, on her lips were fragments of sugar. Amy, in an ugly grey dress, sat severely straight upon a hard chair and was apparently listening to Miss Pyncheon, but her eyes, suspicious and restless, moved like the eyes of a newly captured animal. Mrs. Alweed, stout in pink with a large hat full of roses, smiled and smiled, waiting only for a moment when she could amble off once again into space safe on the old broad back of her family experiences, the only conversational steed to whose care she ever entrusted herself. She had a son Hector, a husband, Mr. Alweed, and a sister-in-law, Miss Alweed; she had the greatest confidence in the absorbed attention of the slightest of her acquaintances. "Hector, he's my boy, you know—although why I call him a boy I can't think—because he's twenty-two and a half—he's at Cambridge, Christs College—well, this morning I had a letter ..." she would begin. She began now upon Martin. His mind wandered. He looked about the little room and thought of Thurston. Why was he not more angry about it all? He had pretended to be indignant, he had hated Thurston as he stood there ... But had he? Half of him hated him. Then with a jerk Thurston's words came back to him: "There's two of each of us, that's the truth of it." "Two of each of us ..." Sitting there, listening to Mrs. Alweed's voice that flowed like a river behind him, he saw the two figures, saw them quite clearly and distinctly, flesh and blood, even clothes and voices and smile. And he knew that all his life these two figures had been growing, waiting for the moment when he would recognise them. One figure was the Martin whom he knew—brown, healthy, strong and sane; a figure wearing his clothes, his own clothes, the tweeds and the cloths, the brogues and the heavy boots, the soft untidy hats; the figure was hard, definite, resolute, quarrelling, arguing, loving, joking, swearing all in the sensible way. It was a figure that all the world had understood, that had been drunk often enough, lent other men money, been hard-up and extravagant and thoughtless. "A good chap." "A sensible fellow." "A pal." "No flies on Warlock." That was the kind of figure. And the life had been physical, had never asked questions, had never known morbidity, had lived on what it saw and could touch and could break ... And the other figure! That was, physically, less plainly seen. No, there it was, standing a little away from the other, standing away, contemptuously, despising it, deriding it. Fat, soft, white hanging cheeks, wearing anything to cover its body, but shining in some way through the clothes, so that it was body that you saw. A soft body, hands soft and the colour of the flesh pale and unhealthy. But it was the eyes that spoke: the mouth trembled and was weak, the chin was fat and feeble, but the eyes lived, lived—were eager, fighting, beseeching, longing, captive eyes!

And this figure, Martin knew, was a prey to every morbid desire, rushed to sensual excess and then crept back miserably to search for some spiritual flagellation. Above all, it was restless, as some one presses round a dark room searching for the lock of the door, restless and lonely, cowardly and selfish, but searching and sensitive and even faithful, faithful to something or to some one ... pursued also by something or some one. A figure to whom this world offered only opportunities for sin and failure and defeat, but a figure to whom this world was the merest shadow hiding, as a shade hides a lamp, the life within. Wretched enough with its bad health, its growing corpulence, its weak mouth, its furtive desires, but despising, nevertheless, the strong, healthy figure beside it. Thurston was right. Men are not born to be free, but to fight, to the very death, for the imprisonment and destruction of all that is easiest and most physically active and most pleasant to the sight and touch ...

"And so Hector really hopes that he'll be able to get down to us for Christmas, although he's been asked to go on this reading party. Of course, it's simply a question as to whether he works better at home or with his friends. If he were a weak character, I think Mr. Alweed would insist in his coming home, but Hector really cares for his work more than anything. He's never been very good at games; his short sight prevents him, poor boy, and as he very justly remarked, when he was home last holidays, 'I don't see, mother, how I am going to do my duty as a solicitor (that's what he hopes to be) if I don't work now. Many men regard Cambridge as a time for play. Not so I.'"

"But I hope that if Hector comes home this Christmas he'll attend the Chapel services. The influence your father might have on such a boy as Hector, Mr. Warlock, a boy, sensitive and thoughtful ... I was saying, Miss Pyncheon, that Hector—"

Miss Pyncheon was the soul of good-nature—but she was much more than that. She was by far the most sensible, genial, and worldly of the Inside Saints; it was, in fact, astonishing that she should be an Inside Saint at all.

Of them all she impressed Martin the most, because there was nothing of the crank about her. She went to theatres, to the seaside in the summer, took in The Queen, and was a subscriber to Boots' Circulating Library. She dressed quietly and in excellent taste—in grey or black and white. She had jolly brown eyes and a dimple in the middle of her chin. She was ready to discuss any question with any one, was marvellously broad-minded and tolerant, and although she was both poor and generous, always succeeded in making her little flat in Soho Square pretty and attractive.

Her chief fault, perhaps, was that she cared for no one especially—she had neither lovers nor parents nor sisters nor brothers, and to all her friends she behaved with the same kind geniality, welcoming one as another. She was thus aloof from them all and relied upon no one. The centre of her life was, of course, her religion, but of this she never spoke, although strangely enough no one doubted the intensity of her belief and the reality of her devotion.

She was a determined follower of Mr. Warlock; what he said she believed, but here, too, there seemed to be no personal attachment. She did not allow criticism of him in her own presence, but, on the other hand, she never spoke as though it would distress her very greatly to lose him. He was a sign, a symbol ... If one symbol went another could be found.

To Martin she was the one out-standing proof of the reality of the Chapel. All the others—his sister, Miss Avies, Thurston, Crashaw, the Miss Cardinals, yes, and his father too, were, in one way or another, eccentric, abnormal, but Miss Pyncheon was the sane every-day world, the worldly world, the world of drinks and dinners, and banks and tobacconists, and yet she believed as profoundly as any of them. What did she believe? She was an Inside Saint, therefore she must have accepted this whole story of the Second Coming and the rest of it. Of course women would believe anything ... Nevertheless ...

He scarcely listened to their chatter. He was forcing himself not to look at his sister, and yet Thurston's news seemed so extraordinary to him that his eye kept stealing round to her to see whether she were still the same. Could she have accepted him, that bounder and cad and charlatan? He felt a sudden cold chill of isolation as though in this world none of the ordinary laws were followed. "By God, I am a stranger here," he thought. It was not until after dinner that night that he was alone with his father. He had resolved on many fine things in the interval. He was going to "have it out with him," "to put his foot down," "to tell him that such a thing as Thurston's marriage to his sister was perfectly impossible." And then, for the thousandth time since his return to England he felt strangely weak and irresolute. He did wish to be "firm" with his father, but it would have been so much easier to be firm had he not been so fond of him. "Soft, sentimental weakness," he called it to himself, but he knew that it was something deeper than that, something that he would never be able to deny.

He went into his father's study that night with a strange dismal foreboding as though he were being drawn along upon some path that he did not want to follow. What was his father mixed up with all this business for? Why were such men as Thurston in existence? Why couldn't life be simple and straightforward with people like his father and himself and that girl Maggie alone somewhere with nothing to interfere? Life was never just as you wanted it, always a little askew, a little twisted, cynically cocking its eye at you before it vanished round the corner? He didn't seem to be able to manage it. Anyway, he wasn't going to have that fellow Thurston marrying his sister.

He found his father lying back in his arm-chair fast asleep, looking like a dead man, his long thin face pale with fatigue, his eyelids a dull grey, his mouth tightly closed as though in a grim determination to pursue some battle. And at the sight of him thus worn out and beaten Martin's affection flooded his heart. He stood opposite his father looking at him and loving him more deeply than he had ever done before.

"I will take him away from all this," was his thought, "these Thurstons and all—out of all this ... We'll go off abroad somewhere. And I'll make him fat and happy."

Then his father suddenly woke up, with a start and a cry: "Where am I?" ... Then he suddenly saw Martin. "Martin," he said, smiling.

Martin smiled back and then began at once: "Father, this isn't true about Thurston, is it?"

He saw, as he had often done before, that his father had to call himself up from some world of vision before he could realise even his surroundings. Martin he recognised intuitively with the recognition of the spirit, but he seemed to take in the details of the room slowly, one by one, as though blinded by the light.

"Ah—I've been dreaming," he said, still smiling at Martin helplessly and almost timidly. "I'm so tired these days—suddenly—I usen't to be ..." He put his hand to his forehead, then laid it on Martin's knee, and the strength and warmth of that seemed suddenly to fill him with vigour.

"You're never tired, are you?" he asked as a child might ask an elder.

"Very seldom," answered Martin, "I say, father, what is all this about Thurston?"

"Thurston ... Why, what's he been doing?"

"He says he's engaged to Amy." The disgust of the idea made Martin's words, against his will, sharp and angry.

"Does he? ... Yes, I remember. He spoke to me about it."

"Of course it's simply his infernal cheek ..."

Mr. Warlock sighed. "I don't know, I'm sure. Amy seemed to wish it."

Martin felt then more strongly than before the Something that drove him. It said to him: "Now, then ... here's a thing for you to make a row about—a big row. And then you can go off with Maggie." But, on the other hand, there was Something that said: "Don't hurt him. Don't hurt him. You may regret it all your life if ..."

If what? He didn't know. He was always threatened with regretting things all his life. The blow was always going to fall. And that pleasant very British phrase came back to him, "He would put his foot down"—however—he was very angry—very angry.

He burst out: "Oh, but that's absurd, father. Impossible—utterly. Thurston in the family? Why, you must see yourself how monstrous it would be. Amy's got some silly, sentimental whim and she's got to be told that it won't do. If you ask me, I don't think Amy's improved much since I was away. But that's not the question. The idea of Thurston's disgusting. You can't seriously consider it for a minute..."

"Why is Thurston disgusting, my boy?"

Martin hated to be called "my boy"—it made him feel so young and dependent.

"You've only got to look at him!" Martin jumped up, disregarding his father's hand, and began to stamp about the room. "He's a cad—he's not your friend, father. He isn't, really. He'd like to out you from the whole thing if he could. He thinks you're old-fashioned and behind the times, and all he thinks about is bringing in subscriptions and collecting new converts. He's like one of those men who beat drums outside tents in a fair ... He's a sickening man! He doesn't believe in his religion or anything else. I should think he's crooked about money, and immoral probably too. You're much too innocent, father. You're so good and trustful yourself that you don't know how these fellows are doing you in. There's a regular plot against you and they'd be most awfully pleased if you were to retire. They're not genuine like you. They simply use the Chapel for self-advertisement and making money. Of course there are some genuine ones like the Miss Cardinals, but Thurston's an absolute swindler ..."

He stopped short at that. He had said more than he had intended and he was frightened suddenly. He swung round on his heel and looked at his father.

"Come here, Martin." He came across the room. "Closer. Now, tell me. We're good friends, aren't we?"

"Of course, father."

He put his hand on his son's shoulder. "Do you know that I love you more than anything in the whole world? More, I'm sometimes terribly afraid, than God Himself. I can't help myself. I love you, Martin, so that it's like hunger or thirst ... It's the only earthly passion that I've ever had. And I'll tell you another thing. It's the one terror of my earthly life that you'll leave me. Now that I've got you back I'm afraid every time you go out of the house that you'll run away, round the corner, and never come back again. I love you and I'm not going to let you go again.—Not until—until—the Time has come ... What does it matter to you and me what Thurston and Amy do? God will come and He will find us both together— you and I—and He will take us up and keep us together and we shall never be separated any more ... I love your strength, Martin, your happiness, your youth—all the things I've never had. And you're not going to leave me, not though Amy married a hundred Thurstons ..."

Mr. Warlock's grip on his son's shoulder was iron.

Martin bent down and sat on the arm of his dusty leather chair to bring himself on to the same level. He put his arm round his father and drew him close to him. Maggie, Life, Money, Adventure—everything seemed to draw away from him and he saw himself, a little boy, pattering on bare feet down the aisle towards the font—just as though a spell had been cast over him.

They sat close together in silence. Then slowly the thought of Thurston came back again. Martin drew away a little.

"All the same, father," he said, "Thurston mustn't marry Amy."

"They're only engaged. There's no question of marriage yet."

"Then they are engaged?" Martin drew right away, standing up again.

"Oh, yes, they're engaged."

"Then I'm not going to stand it. I tell you I won't stay here if Thurston marries Amy."

Mr. Warlock sighed. "Well then, let's leave it, my boy. I daresay they'll never marry."

"No. I won't have it. It's too serious to leave."

His father's voice was sharper suddenly.

"Well, we won't talk about it just now, Martin, if you don't mind."

"But I must. You can't leave a thing like that. Thurston will simply own the place ..."

"I tell you, Martin, to leave it alone." They were both angry now.

"And I tell you, father, that if you let Thurston marry Amy I leave the house and never come back again."

"Isn't that rather selfish of you? You've been away all these years. You've left us to ourselves. You come back suddenly without seeing how we live or caring and then you dictate to us what we're to do. How can you expect us to listen?"

"And how can you expect me to stay?" Martin broke into a torrent of words: "I'm miserable here and you know that I am. Mother and Amy hate me and you're always wrapped up in your religion. What kind of a place is it for a fellow? I came back meaning that you and I should be the best pals father and son have ever been, but you wouldn't come out with me—you only wanted to drag me in. You tell me always to wait for something. To wait for what? I don't know. And nobody here does seem to know. And I can't wait for ever. I've got to lead my own life and if you won't come with me I must go off by myself—"

He was following his own ideas now—not looking at his father at all. "I've discovered since I've been home that I'm not the sort of fellow to settle down. I suppose I shall go on wandering about all my days. I'm not proud of myself, you know, father. I don't seem to be much good to any one, but the trouble is I don't want to be much better. I feel as though it wouldn't be much good if I did try. I can't give up my own life—for nobody—not even for you—and however rotten my own life is I'd rather lead it than some one else's."

He stopped and then went on quietly, as though he were arguing something out with himself: "The strange thing is that I do feel this place has got a kind of a hold on me. When you remind me of what I was like as a kid I go right back and feel helpless as though you could do anything with me you like. All the same I don't believe in this business, father—all this Second Coming and the rest of it. We're in the Twentieth Century now, you know, and everybody knows that that kind of thing is simply impossible. Only an old maid or two ... Why, I don't believe you believe in it really, father. That's why you're so keen on making me believe. But I don't; it's no use. You can't make me. I don't believe there's any God at all. If there were a God he'd let a fellow have more free will ..."

He was interrupted by an extraordinary cry. He turned to see his father standing, one hand pressed back on the chair, his face white, his eyes black and empty, like sightless eyes.

"Martin! That's blasphemy! ... Take care! Take care! ... Oh, my son, my son! ..."

Then he suddenly collapsed backwards, crouching on to the chair as though he were trying to flee from some danger. Martin sprang towards him. He caught him round the body, holding him to him—something was leaping like a furious animal inside his father's breast.

"What is it?" he cried, desperately frightened.

"It's my heart," Warlock answered in a voice very soft and distant. "Bad ... Excitement ... Ring that bell ... Amy ..."

A moment later Amy entered. She came quickly into the room, she said nothing—only gave Martin one look.

She gave her father something from a little bottle, kneeling in front of him.

At last she turned to her brother. "You'd better go," she said. "You can do nothing here."

Miserable, repentant, feeling as though he had no place in the world and yet eager too to defend himself, he left the room.

CHAPTER VII

THE OUTSIDE WORLD

Maggie had a week.

She did not need it. From the first half-hour after Martin's leaving her her mind was made up. This question of marriage did not, on further reflection, very greatly disturb her. She had known, in her time, a number of married people and they had been invariably unhappy and quarrelsome. The point seemed to be that you should be, in some way, near the person whom you loved, and she had only loved one person in all her life, and intended never to love another. Even this question of love was not nearly so tangled for her as it would be for any more civilised person. She knew very little about marriage and only in the most sordid fashion about sexual relations which were definitely connected in her mind with drunken peasants and her father's cook. They had nothing at all to do with Martin.

The opinion of the world was an unknown factor in her vision, she only knew of the opinion of her aunts and Miss Warlock and with these she was already in rebellion.

She would have been in great trouble had she supposed that this woman still loved Martin and needed him, but that, from what Martin had said, was obviously not so. No, it was all quite clear. They would escape together, out of this tangle of unnatural mysteries and warnings, and live happily for ever after in the country.

As to Martin's self-portrait, that did not greatly distress her. She had never supposed that he or any one else was "good." She had never known a "good" person. Nor did it occur to her, in her pristine state of savagery, that you loved any one the less for their drawbacks. She would rather be with Martin at his worst than with any one else at their best—that was all.

Half-an-hour was enough time to settle the whole affair. She then waited patiently until the end of the week. She did not quite know how she would arrange a meeting, but that would, she expected, arrange itself.

Two events occurred that filled her mind and made the week pass quickly. One was that she received an answer to her adventurous letter, the other was a remarkable conversation with Miss Caroline Smith. The answer to her letter was lying on her plate when she came down to breakfast, and Aunt Elizabeth was watching it with an excited stare.

It read as follows:

14 BRYANSTON SQUARE.

Dear Miss CARDINAL,

Of course I remember you perfectly. I wondered whether you would write to me one day. I am married now and live most of the year in London. Would you come and see me at Bryanston Square? I am nearly always at home at tea-time. If you are free would you perhaps come next Friday?

It will be so nice to see you again.

Yours sincerely,

KATHERINE MARK. "You've got a letter, dear. Your aunt isn't quite so well this morning, I'm afraid. Scrambled eggs."

"Yes," she looked her aunt in the face without any confusion. How strangely her decision about Martin had altered her relationship now to every one! What did it matter whether any one were angry? "I ought to have told you, Aunt Elizabeth. I wrote about a fortnight ago to a lady who came once to see us at home. She was a Miss Trenchard then. She said that if ever I wanted any help I was to write to her. So I have written—to ask her whether she can find me any work to do, and she has asked me to go and see her."

"Work," said Aunt Elizabeth. "But you won't go away while your aunt's so ill."

Wouldn't she? Maggie didn't know so much about that.

"I want to be independent," said Maggie, trying to fix Aunt Elizabeth's eyes. "It isn't fair that I should be a burden to you."

"You're no burden, dear." Aunt Elizabeth looked uneasily round the room. "Your aunt depends on you."

"Depends on me for what?"

"For everything."

"Then she oughtn't to, Aunt Elizabeth, I've said it again and again. I'm not fit for any one to depend on. I'm forgetful and careless and untidy. You know I am. And I'm different from every one here. I'm very grateful to Aunt Anne, but I'm not good enough for her to depend on."

Aunt Elizabeth blinked nervously.

"She's got very little. You mustn't take away all she has."

"I'm not all she has," answered Maggie, knowing that she was becoming excited and cross. "I don't belong to any one except myself." "And Martin" her soul whispered. Then she added, suddenly moved by remorse as she looked at Aunt Elizabeth's meek and trembling face, "You're so good to me, both of you, and I'm so bad. I'll give you anything but my freedom."

"You talk so strangely, dear," said Aunt Elizabeth. "But there are so many things I don't understand."

Maggie took the letter up to her bedroom and there read it a number of times. It all seemed wonderful to her, the stamped blue address, the rich white square notepaper, and above all the beautiful handwriting. She thought of her own childish scrawl and blushed, she even sat down, there and then, at her dressing-table and, with a pencil, began to imitate some of the letters.

On Friday! To-day was Tuesday. Bryanston Square. Wherever was Bryanston Square, and how would she find it? She determined to ask Caroline Smith.

She had not long to wait for her opportunity. On Wednesday evening about half-past five Miss Smith poked her head into the Cardinal drawing-room to discover Maggie sitting with her hands on her lap looking down on to the street.

"Are your aunts anywhere?" asked Caroline.

"No," said Maggie. "Aunt Anne's in bed and Aunt Elizabeth's at Miss Pyncheon's."

"That's right," said Caroline, "because I haven't seen you, darling, for ages."

"The day before yesterday," said Maggie.

"You're a literal pet," said Caroline kissing her. "I always exaggerate, of course, and it's so sweet of you to tell me about it." She rushed off to the fire and spread out her blue skirt and dangled her feet.

"Isn't it cold and dark? You funny dear, not to have the blinds down and to sit staring into the beastly street like that ... I believe you're in love."

Maggie came to herself with a start, got up and slowly went over to the fire.

"Caroline, where's Bryanston Square?"

"Oh, you pet, don't you know where Bryanston Square is?" cried Caroline suddenly fixing her bright eyes upon Maggie with burning curiosity.

"If I did I wouldn't ask," said Maggie.

"Quite right—neither you would. Well, it's near Marble Arch."

"But I don't know where the Marble Arch is."

"Lord!" cried Caroline. "And she's been in London for months. You really are a pet. Well, what you'd better do is to get into the first taxi you see and just say 'Bryanston Square.'"

How stupid of her! She might have thought of that for herself.

"Is there a park near Bryanston Square?" she asked.

"Yes. Of course—Hyde Park."

"And is it open at six?"

"Of course. You can't shut Hyde Park."

"Oh!"

Maggie pursued her thoughts. Caroline watched her with intense curiosity.

"What do you want with a Park, you darling?" she asked at last.

"Oh, nothing," said Maggie, slowly. Then she went on, laughing: "I've been asked out to tea—for the first time in my life. And I'm terribly frightened."

"How exciting!" said Caroline clapping her hands. "Who's it with?"

"It's a Mrs. Mark. She was a Miss Trenchard. She used to live in Glebeshire. She's going to find me some work to do."

"Work!" cried Caroline. "Aren't you going to stay with your aunts then?"

"I want to be independent," said Maggie slowly.

"Well!" said Caroline, amazed.

Could Maggie have seen just then into Miss Smith's mind and could she only have realised that, with Miss Smith, every action and intention in the human heart pivoted upon love-affairs and love-affairs only, she might have been warned and have saved much later trouble. She was intent on her own plans and was thinking of Caroline only as a possible agent.

"Caroline," she asked, "would you take a note for me to some one?"

"Of course," said Caroline. "Who is it?"

"Martin Warlock," said Maggie.

At the name she suddenly blushed crimson. She knew that Caroline was looking at her with eager curiosity. She suspected then that she had done something foolish and would have given anything to recall her words, but to recall them now seemed only to make it the more suspicious.

"It's only something his sister wanted to know," she said casually. "I thought you'd be seeing him soon. I hardly ever do."

"Yes, I'm going up there to-night," said Caroline staring at Maggie. "Well, I'll give it you before you go," then she went on as casually as she could. "What's been happening lately?"

"Of course you know all about the excitement," said Caroline sitting back in the faded arm-chair with her blue dress spread all about her like a cloud.

"What excitement?" said Maggie, pulling herself up, with a desperate struggle, from her own private adventures.

"What! you don't know?" Caroline exclaimed in an awed whisper.

"Know what?" Maggie asked, rather crossly, repenting more and more of asking Caroline to carry her note.

"Why, where DO you live? ... All about Mr. Warlock and his visions!"

"I've heard nothing at all," said Maggie.

This was unexpected joy to Caroline, who had never imagined that there would be any one so near the Inner Saints as Maggie who yet knew nothing about these recent events.

"Do you really know nothing about it?"

"Nothing," said Maggie.

"Aren't you wonderful?" said Caroline. "What happened was this. About three weeks ago Mr. Warlock had a vision in the middle of the night. He saw God at about three in the morning."

"How did he see God?" asked Maggie, awed in spite of herself.

Caroline's voice dropped to a mysterious whisper. "He just woke up and there God was at the end of the bed. Of course he's not spoken to me about it, but apparently there was a blaze of light and Something in the middle. And then a voice spoke and told Mr. Warlock that on the last night of this year everything would be fulfilled."

"What did He mean?" asked Maggie.

"Different people think He meant different things," said Caroline. "Of course there's most fearful excitement about it. Mr. Warlock's had two since."

"Two what?" asked Maggie.

"Two visions. Just like the first. The blazing light and the voice and telling him that the last night of the year's to be the time." Caroline then began to be carried away by her excitement. She talked faster and faster. "Oh! You don't know what a state every one's in! It's causing all sorts of divisions. First there are all his own real believers. Miss Pyncheon, your aunts, and the others. My father's one. They all believe every word he says. They're all quite certain that the last day of this year is to be the time of the Second Coming. They won't any of them, look a minute further than that. Father doesn't care a bit now what mother does with the money because, he says, we shan't want any next year. Mother isn't so sure so she's taking as much care of it as ever, and of course it's nice for her now to have it all in her own hands. They're all of them doing everything to make themselves ready. It doesn't matter how aggravating you are, father never loses his temper now. He's so sweet that it's maddening. Haven't you noticed how good your aunts are?"

"They're always the same," said Maggie.

"Well. I expect they're different really. Then there's the middle-class like Mr. Thurston and Miss Avies who pretend to believe all that Mr. Warlock says, but of course, they don't believe a word of it, and they hope that this will prove his ruin. They know there won't be any Second Coming on New Year's Eve, and then they think he will be finished and they'll be able to get rid of him. So they're encouraging him to believe in all this, and then when the moment comes they'll turn on him!"

"Beasts!" said Maggie suddenly.

"Well, I daresay you're right," said Caroline. "Only it does make me laugh, all of it. Thurston and Miss Avies have all their plans made, only now they're quarrelling because Thurston wants to marry Amy Warlock and Miss Avies meant him to marry her!"

"Is Mr. Thurston going to marry Miss Warlock?" cried Maggie.

"So they say," said Caroline again watching Maggie curiously. "Well, anyway, Miss Avies is the strongest of the lot really. I'd back her against anybody. I'm terrified of her myself, I tell you frankly. She'd wring any one's neck for twopence. Oh yes, she would! ... Then there are the third lot who simply don't believe in Mr. Warlock's visions at all and just laugh at him. People like Miss Smythe and Mrs. Bellaston. A lot of them are leaving the chapel. Mr. Warlock won't listen to anybody. He's getting stranger and stranger, and his heart's so bad they say he might die any day if he had a shock. Then he's always quarrelling with Martin."

Caroline suddenly stopped. She looked at Maggie.

"Martin's a terrible trial to his father," she said.

But Maggie was secure now.

"Is he?" she asked indifferently. Then she added slowly, "What do you believe, Caroline?"

"What do I believe?"

"Yes, about Mr. Warlock's visions."

"Oh, of course, it's only because he's ill and prays for hours without getting off his knees, and won't eat enough, that he sees things. And yet I don't know. There may be something in it. If I were on my knees for weeks I'd never see anything. But I'll be terribly sorry for Mr. Warlock if the time comes and nothing happens. He'll just have to go."

They sat a little longer together and then Caroline said: "Well, darling, I must be off. Where's that note?" She hesitated, looking at Maggie with a wicked gleam in her pale blue eyes. "You know, Maggie, I can't make up my mind. I've had an offer of marriage."

"I'm so glad, Caroline," said Maggie.

"Yes, but I don't know what to do. It's a man—Mr. Purdie. His father's ever so rich and they've got a big place down at Skeaton."

"Where's that?" asked Maggie.

"Oh, don't you know? Skeaton-on-Sea. It's a seaside resort. I've known William for a long time. His father knows father. He came to tea last week, and proposed. He's rather nice although he's so silent."

"Why don't you marry him then?" asked Maggie.

"Well, I know Martin Warlock's going to ask me. It's been getting closer and closer. I expect he will this week. Of course, he isn't so safe as William, but he's much more exciting. And he's got quite a lot of money of his own."

Strange, the sure, confident, happy security that Maggie felt in her heart at this announcement.

"I should wait for Martin Warlock," she said. "He'd be rather fun to marry."

"Do you think so?" answered Caroline. "Do you know, I believe I will. You're always right, you darling ... Only suppose I should miss them both. William won't wait for ever! Got that note, dear?"

Maggie was defiant. She would just show the creature that she wasn't afraid of her. She'd give her the note and she might imagine what she pleased.

She got a pencil and a piece of paper and wrote hurriedly.

The week is up on Friday. Will you meet me that evening at a quarter past six under the Marble Arch? MAGGIE.

The boldness, the excitement of this inflamed her. It was so like her to challenge any action once she was in it by taking it to its furthest limit. She put it in an envelope and wrote Martin's name with a flourish.

"There!" she said, giving it to Caroline.

"Thank you," said Caroline, and with a number of rather wet and elaborate kisses (Maggie hated kissing) departed.

But her afternoon was not yet over; hardly had Caroline left when the door was opened and Miss Avies was shown in. Maggie started up with dismay and began to stammer excuses. Miss Avies brushed them aside.

"It doesn't matter," she said. "You'll do as well—even, it may be, better."

A strange woman Miss Avies! Maggie had, of course, seen her at Chapel, but this was the first time that they had been alone together. Miss Avies was like a thin rod of black metal, erect and quivering and waiting to strike. Her long sallow face was stiff, not with outraged virtue, or elaborate pride, or burning scorn, but simply with the accumulated concentration of fiery determination. She was the very symbol of self-centred energy, inhuman, cold, relentless. Her hair was jet black and gleamed like steel, and she had thick black eyebrows like ink-marks against her forehead of parchment. Her eyes were dead, like glass eyes, and she had some false teeth that sometimes clicked in her mouth. She wore a black dress with no ornament and thin black gloves.

She did not seem, however, to Maggie unkindly, as she stood there, looking about the room rather short-sightedly. (She would not wear glasses. Could it have been vanity?) She was not hostile, nor scornful, nor even patronising ... but had Maggie been struck there, dead at her feet she would not have moved a step to help her. Her voice was ugly, with a crack in it, as though it needed oil. Maggie, as she looked at her, did not need to be told that she did not believe in Mr. Warlock's mysticism. She came across and shook Maggie's hand. Her touch was cold and stiff and a little damp like that of a wet stone.

"Sorry your Aunt's out," she said, "but I can talk to you for a while." She looked at Maggie for a moment. Then she said:

"Why don't you clear out of all this?"

The voice was so abrupt and the words so unexpected that Maggie jumped.

"Why don't I?" she repeated.

"Yes, you," said Miss Avies. "You've no place here in all this business. You don't believe in it, do you?"

"No," said Maggie.

"And you don't want to use it for something you do believe in?"

"No," said Maggie. "Well then, clear out."

Maggie, colouring a little, said:

"My aunts have been very good to me. I oughtn't to leave them."

"Fiddlesticks," said Miss Avies. "Your life's your own, not your aunts'."

She sat down and stayed bolt upright and motionless near the fire; she flung a thin dark shadow like a stain on the wall. There was a long pause between them. After that abrupt opening there seemed to be nothing to say. Maggie's thoughts also were elsewhere. She was wishing now passionately that she had not given that note to Caroline.

Suddenly Miss Avies said, "What do you do with yourself all day?"

Maggie laughed. "Try and make myself less careless, Miss Avies."

Miss Avies replied, "You'll never make yourself less careless. We are as we are."

"But don't you think," said Maggie, "that one can cure one's faults?"

"One gets rid of one only to make room for another ... But that doesn't matter. The point is that one should have an ambition. What's your ambition, child?"

Maggie didn't answer. Her ambition was Martin, but she couldn't tell Miss Avies so.

At last, after a long pause, as Miss Avies still seemed to be waiting, she answered:

"I suppose that I want to earn my living—to be independent."

"Well, leave this place then," said Miss Avies. "There's no independence here." Then added, as though to herself. "They think they're looking for the face of God ... It's only for themselves and their vanity they're looking."

Maggie said, to break another of the long pauses that seemed to be always forming between them:

"I think every one ought to earn their own living, don't you?"

Miss Avies shook her head. "You're very young—terribly young. I've got no advice to give you except to lead a healthy life somewhere away from these surroundings. We're an unnatural lot here and you're a healthy young creature ... Have you got a lover?"

Maggie smiled. "I've got a friend," she said. Miss Avies sighed. "That's more than I've got," she said.

"Not that I've time for one," she added. She got up. "I won't wait for your aunt," she said, "I've left a note downstairs ... You clear out as soon as you can, that's my advice to you."

She said good-bye, looking into Maggie's clear eyes. She was suddenly less inhuman, the touch of her hand was warmer.

"Don't you cheat yourself into believing in the Deity," she said, and was gone.

When Friday arrived Maggie had not seen Caroline again, and she could not tell whether the note had been safely delivered or no. She was not sure what she had better do. Caroline might hare done anything with the note, torn it up, burnt it, lost it, forgotten it altogether. Well, that was a risk that Maggie must take. If he did not appear she would wait a little while and then come away. They must soon meet in any case. They had all their lives before them.

Aunt Anne was up again—very, very pale now and so thin that the light seemed to shine through her making her more of a stained window saint than ever.

Maggie told her about the visit, Aunt Anne looked at her curiously. She seemed so weak and frail that Maggie suddenly felt warm maternal love. Rather shyly she put her hand upon her aunt's: "I won't go away until you're better—"

Aunt Anne nodded her head.

"I know you won't, dear," she said. "Don't be out late to-day. We shall be anxious about you."

Maggie had made a promise and was terrified when she thought of it. Suppose her aunt did not get better for years and years?

People often had long lingering illnesses with no apparent change in their condition. To Maggie a promise was an utterly final thing. She could not dream that one ever broke one's word. She trembled now when she thought of what she had done. She had been entrapped after all and by her own free will.

In her little room as she was putting on her hat she suddenly prayed to a God, of whom she knew nothing, that her aunt might get better soon.

She started out on her great adventure with a strange self-assurance as though loving Martin had given her the wisdom of all the ages.

Turning down the street towards the Strand she found almost at once a taxi-cab drawn up, as though it had been waiting there especially for her like an eloping coach in a romantic tale. A fat red-faced fellow with a purple nose, a cloth cap and a familiar vague eye, as though he always saw further than he intended, waited patiently for her to speak.

Boldly, as though she had done such things all her life, she said, "Fourteen Bryanston Square." Then she slipped in and was hidden from the gay world. She sat there, her hands on her lap staring at the three crimson rolls in the neck of her driver. She was thinking of nothing, nothing at all. Did she struggle to think? Only words would come, "Martin," or "Bryanston Square," or "cab," again and again, words that did not mean anything but physical sensations. "Martin" hot fire at the throat, "Bryanston Square" an iron rod down the spine, and "cab" dust and ashes in the eyes.

She tried to look at herself in the little mirror opposite her, but she could only catch the corner of her cheek and half her hat. But she minded less about her appearance now. If Martin could love her it did not matter what others thought—nevertheless she pulled her hat about a little and patted her dress. The cab stopped and she felt desperately lonely. Did any one care about her anywhere? No, no one. She could have cried with pity at the thought of her own loneliness.

"One and sixpence, Miss," said the cabman in so husky a voice.

She gave it to him.

"What's this?" he asked, looking at it.

"One and sixpence," she answered timidly, wondering at his sarcastic eye.

"Oh well, o' course," he said, looking her all over.

She knew instinctively that he demanded more. She found another sixpence. "Is that enough?" she asked.

He seemed ashamed.

"If I 'adn't a wife sick—" he began.

She ran up the high stone steps and rang a bell. The episode with the driver had disturbed her terribly. It had shown in what a foreign world she was. All her self-confidence was gone. She had to take a pull at herself and say: "Why, Maggie, you might be ringing the dentist's bell at this moment."

That helped her, and then the thought of Martin. She saw his boyish smile and felt the warm touch of his rough hand. When the maid was there instead of the green door, she almost said: "Is Martin in?"

But she behaved very well.

"Mrs. Mark?" she said in precisely the voice required.

The maid smiled and stood aside. And then into what a world she entered! A world of comfort and reassurance, of homeliness and kindliness, without parrots and fierce-eyed cats and swaying pictures of armoured men—a world of urbanity and light and space. There was a high white staircase with brown etchings in dark frames on the white walls. There was a thick soft carpet and a friendly fat grandfather clock. Many doors but none of them mysterious, all ready to be opened.

She climbed the staircase and was shown into a room high and gaily coloured and full of flowers. She saw the deep curtains, blue silk shot with purple, the chairs of blue silk and a bowl of soft amber light hanging from the ceiling. A mass of gold-red chrysanthemums flamed against the curtains. Several people were gathered round a tea-table near the fire.

She stood lost on the thick purple carpet under the amber light, all too brilliant for her. She had come from a world of darkness, owl-like she must blink before the blaze. Some one came forward to her, some one so kind and comforting, so easy and unsurprised that Maggie suddenly felt herself steadied as though a friend had put an arm around her. Before she had felt: "This light—I am shabby." Now she felt, "I am with friendly people." She was surprised at the way that she was suddenly at her ease.

Mrs. Mark was not beautiful, but she had soft liquid eyes and her hand that held Maggie's was firm and warm and strong.

"Let me introduce you," said Mrs. Mark. "That is Miss Trenchard, and that Mr. Trenchard. This is my husband. Philip, this is Miss Cardinal."

Miss Trenchard must be forty, Maggie thought. She was plump and thick-set, with a warm smile. Then Mr. Trenchard was a clergyman—he would be stout were he not so broad. His face was red, his hair snowy white, but he did not look old.

He smiled at Maggie as though he had known her all his life. Then there was Mr. Mark, who was stocky and thick, and reminded Maggie of Martin, although his face was quite different, he looked much cleverer and not such a boy; he was not, in fact, a boy at all. "I'm sure he thinks too hard," decided Maggie, who had habits of making up her mind at once about people.

"Well, there's no one to be frightened about here," she decided. And indeed there was not! It was as though they had all some especial reason for being nice to her. Perhaps they saw that she was not in her own world here. And yet they did not make her feel that. She drank in the differences with great gulps of appreciation, but it was not they who insisted.

Here were light and colour and space above all—rest. Nothing was about to happen, no threat over their heads that the roof would fall beneath one's feet, that the floor would sink. No sudden catching of the breath at the opening of a door, no hesitation about climbing the stairs, no surveillance by the watching

Thomas, no distant clanging of the Chapel bell. How strange they all seemed, looking back from this safe harbour. The aunts, the Warlocks, Thurston, Mr. Crashaw, Caroline—all of them. There the imagination set fire to every twig—here the imagination was not needed, because everything occurred before your eyes.

She did not figure it all out in so many words at once, but the contrast of the two worlds was there nevertheless. Why had she been so anxious, so nervous, so distressed? There was no need. Had she not known that this other world existed? Perhaps she had not. She must never again forget it ...

Katherine Mark was so kind and friendly, her voice so soft and her interest so eager, that Maggie felt that she could tell her anything. But their talk was not to come just yet—first there must be general conversation.

The clergyman with the white hair and the rosy face laughed a great deal in a schoolboy kind of way, and every time that he laughed his sister, who was like a pippin apple with her sunburnt cheeks, looked at him with protecting eyes.

"She looks after him in everything," said Maggie to herself. He was called Paul by them all.

"He's my cousin, you know, Miss Cardinal," said Mrs. Mark. "And yet I scarcely ever see him. Isn't it a shame? Grace makes everything so comfortable for him ..."

Grace smiled, well pleased.

"It's Paul's devotion to his parish ..." she said in calm, happy, self-assured voice, as though she'd never had a surprise in her life.

"I'm sure it isn't either of those things," thought Maggie to herself. "He's lazy."

Lazy but nice. She had never seen a clergyman so healthy, so happy so clean and so kind. She smiled across the table at him.

"Do you know Skeaton?" he asked her. Skeaton! Where had she heard of the place? Why, of course, it was Caroline!

"Only yesterday I heard of it for the first time," she said. "A friend of mine knows some one there."

"Beastly place," said Mr. Mark. "Sand always blowing into your eyes."

Mr. and Mrs. Trenchard got up to go.

He stood a moment holding Maggie's hand. "If ever you come to Skeaton, Miss Cardinal," he said, "we shall be delighted ..." His eyes she noticed were light blue like a baby's. She felt that he liked her and would not forget her.

"Come, Paul," said Miss Trenchard, rather sharply Maggie fancied.

Soon afterwards Philip departed. "Must finish that beastly thing," he assured his wife.

"It's an article," Katherine Mark explained. "He's always writing about politics. I hate them, so he pretends to hate them too. But he doesn't really. He loves them."

"I know nothing about politics," said Maggie with profound truth. "Your husband must be very clever."

"He's better than that," said Katherine with pride; "I hate perfect people, don't you?"

"Oh, indeed I do!" said Maggie from the bottom of her heart. They then came to her particular business.

"I would like to get some work to do," said Maggie, "that would make me independent. I have three hundred pounds of my own."

"What can you do?" asked Katherine.

"I don't know," said Maggie.

"Can you shorthand and type?"

"No, I can't," said Maggie; "but I'll learn."

"Must you be independent soon?" asked Katherine. "Are you unhappy where you are?"

Maggie paused.

"Don't tell me anything you oughtn't to," said Katherine.

"No," answered Maggie. "It isn't that exactly. I'm not happy at home, but I think that's my fault. My aunts are very good. But I want to be free. It is all very religious where I am, and they want me to believe in their religion. I'm afraid I'm not religious at all. Then I don't want to be dependent on people. I'm very ignorant. I know nothing about anything, and so long as I am kept with my aunts I shall never learn."

She stopped abruptly. She had thought suddenly of Martin. His coming had altered everything. How could she say what she wanted her life to be until her relation to him were settled? Everything depended on that.

This sense of Martin's presence silenced her. "If I can feel," she said at last, "that I can ask your advice. I have nobody ... We all seem ... Oh! how can I make you understand properly! You never will have seen anything like our house. It is all so queer, so shut-up, away from everything. I'm like a prisoner ..."

And that is perhaps what she was like to Mrs. Mark, sitting there in her funny ill-fitting clothes, her anxious old-fashioned face as of a child aged long before her time. Katherine Mark, who had had, in her life, her own perplexities and sorrows, felt her heart warm to this strange isolated girl. She had needed in her own life at one time all her courage, and she had used it; she had never regretted the step that she had then taken. She believed therefore in courage ... Courage was eloquent in every movement of Maggie's square reliant body.

"She could be braver than I have ever been," she thought.

"Miss Cardinal," she said, "I want you to come here whenever you can. You haven't seen our boy, Tim, yet—one and a half—and there are so many things I want to show you. Will you count yourself a friend of the house?"

Maggie blushed and twisted her hands together.

"You're very good," she said, "but ... I don't know ... perhaps you won't like me, or what I do."

"I do like you," said Katherine. "And if I like any one I don't care what they do."

"All the same," said Maggie, "I don't belong ... to your world, your life. I should shock you, I know. You might be sorry afterwards that you knew me. Supposing I broke away ..."

"But I broke away myself," said Katherine, "it is sometimes the only thing to do. I made my mother, who had been goodness itself to me, desperately unhappy."

"Why did you do that?" asked Maggie.

"Because I wanted to marry my husband."

"Well, I love a man too," said Maggie.

"Oh, I do hope you'll be happy!" said Katherine. "As happy as I am."

"No," said Maggie, shaking her head, "I don't expect to be happy."

She seemed to herself as she said that to be hundreds of miles away from Katherine Mark and her easy life, the purple curtains and her amber light.

"Not happy but satisfied," she said.

She saw that it was five minutes past six. "I must go," she said.

When they said good-bye Katherine bent forward and kissed her.

"If ever, in your life. I can help in any way at all," she said, "come to me."

"I'll do that," promised Maggie. She coloured, and then herself bent forward and kissed Katherine. "I shall like to think of you—and all this—" she said and went.

She was let out into the outer world by the smiling maid-servant. Bryanston Square was dark with purple colour as though the purple curtains inside the house had been snipped off from a general curtained world. There was a star or two and some gaunt trees with black pointing fingers, and here a lighted window and there a shining doorway; behind it all the rumble of a world that disregarded love and death and all the Higher Catechism.

Maggie confronted a policeman.

"Please, can you tell me where the Marble Arch is?" she asked.

"Straight ahead, Miss," he answered, pointing down the street, "you can't miss it."

And she could not. It soon gleamed white ahead of her against the thick folds of the sky. When she saw it her heart raced in front of her, like a pony, suddenly released, kicking its heels. And her thoughts were so strangely wild! The lovely night, yes, purple like Mrs. Mark's curtains and scented oranges, chrysanthemums, boot-polish and candied sugar.—Oh yes! how kind they had been—nice clergyman, fat a little, but young in spite of his white hair, and Aunt Anne in bed under the crucifix struggling and Mr. Crashaw smiling lustfully at Caroline ... The long black streets, strips of silk and the lamps like fat buttons on a coat, there was a cat! Hist! Hist! A streak of black against black ... and the Chapel bell ringing and Thomas' fiery eyes ...

Behind all this confusion there was Martin, Martin, Martin. Creeping nearer and nearer as though he were just behind her, or was it that she was creeping nearer and nearer to him? She did not know, but her heart now was beating so thickly that it was as though giants were wrapping cloth after cloth round it, hot cloths, but their hands were icy cold. No, she was simply excited, desperately, madly excited.

She had never been excited before, and now, with the excitement, there was mingled the strangest hot pain and cold pity. She noticed that now her knees were trembling and that if they trembled much more she would not be able to walk at all.

"Now, Maggie, steady your knees!" she said to herself. But look, the houses now were trembling a little too! Ridiculous those smart houses with their fine doors and white steps to tremble! No, it was her heart, not the houses ...

"Do I look queer?" she thought; "will people be looking at me?"

Ideas raced through her head, now like horses in the Derby.

"Woof! Poof! Off we go!" St. Dreot's, that square piece of grass on the lawn with the light on it, her clothes, the socks that must be mended, Caroline's silk and the rustle it made, shops, houses, rivers, seas, death—yes, Aunt Anne's cancer ... and then, with a great upward surge like rising from the depths of the sea after a dive, Martin! Martin, Martin! ... For a moment then she had to pause. She had been walking too fast. Her heart jumped, then ran a step or two, then fell into a dead pause ... She went on, seeing now nothing but two lamps that watched her like the eyes of a giant.

She was there! This was a Marble Arch! All by itself in the middle of the road. She crossed to it, first went under it, then thought that he would not see her there so came out and stood, nervously rubbing her gloved hands against one another and turning her head, like a bird, swiftly from side to side. She didn't like standing there. It seemed to make her so prominent. Men stared at her. He should have been there first. He might have known ... But perhaps Caroline never gave him the letter. At that thought her heart really did stop. She was terrified at once as though some one had told her disastrous news. She would not wait very long; then she would go home ...

She saw him. He stood only a little away from her staring about him, looking for her. She felt that she had not seen him for years; she drank in his sturdiness, his boyish face, his air of caring nothing for authority. She had not seen his dark blue overcoat before. He stood directly under a lamp, swaying ever so little on his heels, his favourite, most characteristic, movement. He stood there as though he were purposely giving her a portrait that she might remember for the rest of her days. She was too nervous to move and then she wanted that wonderful moment to last, that moment when she had realised that he had come to meet her, that he was there, amongst all those crowds, simply for her, that he was looking for her and wanting her, that he would be bitterly disappointed did she not come ...

She saw him give a little impatient jerk of the head, the same movement that she had seen him make in Chapel. That jerk set her in motion again, and she was suddenly at his side. She touched his arm; he turned and his eyes lit with pleasure. They smiled at one another and then, without a word, moved off towards the park. He took her arm and put it through his. She felt the warm thick stuff of the blue coat, and beneath that the steady firm beat of his heart. They walked closely together, his thigh pressed against hers, and once and again her hair brushed his cheek. She was so shy that, until they were through the gates of the park, she did not speak. Then she said:

"I was so afraid that Caroline would not give you the note."

"Oh, she gave it me all right." He pressed her arm closer to him. "But I expect that she read it first."

"Oh, is she like that?"

"Yes, she's like that ..."

There was another pause; they turned down the path to the right towards the trees that were black lumps of velvet against the purple sky. There were no stars, and it was liquidly dark as though they ploughed through water. Maggie felt suffocated with heat and persecuted by a strange weariness; she was suddenly so tired that it was all that she could do to walk.

"I'm tired ..." she murmured—"expecting you—afraid that you wouldn't come."

"I believe that I would have come," he answered quite fiercely, "even if I hadn't had the note—I was determined to see you to-night some way. But you know, Maggie, it had better be for the last time ..."

"No," she said, whispering, "it's the first time."

"Let's sit down here," he said. "We're alone all right."

There was no seat near them. The trees made a cave of black above them, and in front of them the grass swept like a grey beach into mist. There was no sound save a distant whirr like the hum of a top that died to a whisper and then was lashed by some infuriated god to activity again.

They sat close together on the bench. She felt his arm move out as though he would embrace her, then suddenly he drew back.

"No," he said, "until we've talked this out we've got to be like strangers. We can't go on, you know, Maggie, and it's no use your saying we can."

She pressed her hands tightly together. "I can convince him better," she thought to herself, "if I'm very quiet and matter-of-fact." So, speaking very calmly and not looking at him, she went on:

"But, Martin, you promised last time that it would depend on me ... You said that if I didn't mind your being married and was willing to take risks that we would go on together. Well, I've thought all about it and I know that I'd rather be miserable with you than happy with any one else. But then I shouldn't be miserable. You seem to think you could make me miserable just as soon as you like. But that depends on myself. If I don't want to be miserable nobody can make me be." She paused. He moved a little closer and suddenly took her hand.

She drew it away and went on:

"Don't think I'm inexperienced about this, Martin. You say I know nothing about men. Perhaps I don't. But I know myself. I know what I want, and I can look after myself. However badly you treated me, it would be you that I was with all the time."

"No, no, Maggie," he answered, speaking rapidly and as though he were fiercely protesting against some one. "It isn't that at all. You say you know yourself—but then I know myself. It isn't only that I'm a rotten fellow. It is that I seem to bring a curse on every one I'm fond of. I love my father, and I've come back and made him miserable. It's always like that. And if I made you miserable it would be the worst thing I ever did ... I don't even know whether I love you. If I do it's different from any love I've ever had. Other women I'd be mad about. I'd go for them whatever happened and got them somehow, and I wouldn't care a bit whether they were happy or no. But I feel about you almost as though you were a man—not sensually at all, but that safe steady security that you feel for a man sometimes ... You're so restful to be with. I feel now as though you were the one person in the world who could turn me into a decent human being. I feel as though we were just meant to move along together; but then some other woman would come like a fire and off I'd go ... Then I'd hate myself worse than ever and be really finished."

Maggie looked at him.

"You don't love me then, Martin?" she asked.

"Yes I do," he answered suddenly, "I keep telling myself that I don't, but I know that I do. Only it's different. It's as though I were loving myself, the better part of myself. Not something new and wildly exciting, but something old that I had known always and that had always been with me. If I went away now. Maggie, I know I'd come back one day—perhaps years afterwards—but I know I'd come back. It's like that religious part of me, like my legs and my arms. Oh! it's not of my own comfort I'm doubting, but it's you! ... I don't want to hurt you, Maggie darling, just as I've hurt every one I loved—"

"I'll come with you, Martin," said Maggie, "as long as you want me, and if you don't want me, later you will again and I'll be waiting for you."

He put his arm round her. She crept up close to him, nestled into his coat and put her hand up to his cheek. He bent down his head and they kissed.

After that there could be no more argument. What had he not intended to press upon her? With what force arid power had he not planned to persuade her? How he would tell her that he did not love her, that he would not be faithful to her, that he would treat her cruelly. Now it was all gone. With a gesture of almost ironic abandonment he flung away his scruples. It was always so; life was stronger than he. He had tried, in this at least, to behave like a decent man. But life did not want him to be decent ...

And how he needed that rest that she gave him! As he felt her close up against him, folded into him with that utterly naif and childish trust that had allured and charmed him on the very first occasion, he felt nothing but a sweet and blessed rest. He would not think of the future. He would not ... HE WOULD NOT. And perhaps all would be well. As he pressed her closer to him, as he felt her lips suddenly strike through the dark, find his check and then his mouth, as he felt her soft confident hand find his and then close and fold inside it like a flower, he wondered whether this once he might not force things to be right. It was time he took things in hand. He could. He must ...

He began to whisper to her:

"Maggie darling ... It mayn't be bad. I'll find out where this other woman is and she shall divorce me. I'll arrange it all. And we'll go away somewhere where I can work, and we won't allow anybody to interfere. After all, I'm older now. The mess I've been in before is because I always make wrong shots ..."

His words ceased. Their hearts were beating too tumultuously together for words to be possible. Maggie did not wish to speak, she could not. She was mingled with him, her heart his, her lips his, her check his ... She did not believe that words would come even though she wished for them. She was utterly happy—so utterly that she was, as it were, numb with happiness. They murmured one another's names.

"Martin."

"Maggie! ..."

At last, dreaming, scarcely knowing what they did, like two children in a dark wood, they wandered towards home.

CHAPTER VIII

PARADISE

Maggie had never really been happy before. She had of course not known this; her adventures in introspection had been very few, besides she had not known what happiness looked like; her father, her uncle, and her aunts were not exactly happy people ...

Now she flung herself without thought or care into a flood of happiness, and as sometimes occurs in life, she was granted by the gods, beneficent or ironic as you please, a period of security when everything menacing or dangerous withdrew and it seemed as though the whole world were in a conspiracy to cheat her into confidence. She was confident because she did not think; she simply did not think at all. She loved Martin and Martin loved her; cased in that golden armour, she confronted her aunts and the house and the world behind the house with a sublime and happy confidence. She loved her aunts now, she loved Martha and the parrot and the cat, and she could not believe that they did not all love her. Because Martin loved her the rest of the world must also do so, and if they did not she would compel them.

For three whole weeks the spell lasted, for three marvellous golden weeks. When she looked back afterwards she wondered that she had not seen many things, warnings, portents, whatever you please to call them. But for three weeks she saw nothing but Martin, and for three weeks he saw nothing but Maggie.

She began her career of defiance at once by informing Aunt Anne that she was now going out every morning to do her shopping. Considering the confinement to the house that her life had always been, this was such a declaration of independence as those walls had never encountered before. But Aunt Anne never turned one of her shining neatly ordered hairs. "Shopping, my dear?" she asked. "Yes," said Maggie, looking her full in the face. "What sort of shopping, dear?" "Oh, I don't know," said Maggie. "There's always something every day."

Maggie had an uncomfortable feeling that her aunt had in some way mysteriously defeated her by this sudden abandonment of all protest, and for a moment the mysterious house closed around her, with its shadows and dim corners and the little tinkling Chapel bell in the heart of it. But the thought of Martin dissolved the shadows, and off she went.

They agreed to meet every morning at eleven o'clock outside Hatchards, the bookseller's, in Piccadilly. They chose that place because you could look into a bookseller's window for quite a long time without seeming odd, and there were so many people passing that no one noticed you. Their habit then was to walk to the corner of the Green Park and there climb on to the top of a motor omnibus and go as far as they could within the allotted time. Maggie never in after life found those streets again. They had gone, she supposed, to Chelsea, to St. John's Wood, to the heart of the city, to the Angel, Islington, to Westminster and beyond, but places during those three weeks had no names, streets had no stones, houses no walls, and human figures no substantiality. They tried on one or two occasions to go by Tube, but they missed the swing of the open air, the rush of the wind, and their independence of men and women. Often he tried to persuade her to stay with him for luncheon and the afternoon, but she was wiser than he.

"No," she said, "everything depends on keeping them quiet. A little later on it will be lovely. You must leave that part of it to me."

She promised him definitely that soon they should go to a matinee together, but she would not give her word about a whole evening. In some strange way she was frightened of the evening, although she had already pledged her word to him on something much more final: "No," she thought to herself, "when the moment comes for me to leave everything, I will go, but he shall know that I am not doing it cheaply, simply for an evening's fun." He felt something of that too, and did not try to persuade her. He hugged his unselfishness; for the first time in his life it seemed to him that he wanted to follow somebody else's will; with the other women it had been so different, if they had not wanted to obey him he had left them. But indeed all through these three weeks they were discovering themselves and one another, and, as though it were part of the general conspiracy, only the best part of themselves. On the top of the 'bus, as they sat close together, their hands locked under his overcoat, the world bumping and jolting, and jogging about their feet, as though indeed public houses and lamp-posts and cinemas and town halls and sweet-shops were always jumping up tiptoe to see whether they couldn't catch a glimpse of the lovers, Martin and Maggie felt that they were really divine creatures, quite modestly divine, but nevertheless safe from all human ravages and earthly failings, wicked and cowardly thoughts, and ambitions and desires.

Indeed, during those three weeks Maggie saw nothing of Martin's weaknesses, his suspicions and dreads, his temper and self-abasement. The nobility that Martin had in him was true nobility, his very weaknesses came from his sharp consciousness of what purity and self-sacrifice and asceticism really were, and that they were indeed the only things for man to live by. During those weeks he saw so truly the sweetness and fidelity and simplicity of Maggie that his conscience was killed, his scruples were numbed. He did not want during those weeks any sensual excitement, any depravity, any license. A quiet and noble asceticism seemed to him perfectly possible. He burst out once to Maggie with: "I can't conceive, Maggie, why I ever thought life complicated. You've straightened everything out for me, made all the troubles at home seem nothing, shown me what nonsense it was wanting the rotten things I was always after."

But Maggie had no eloquence in reply—she could not make up fine sentences; it embarrassed her dreadfully to tell him even that she loved him, and when he was sentimental it was her habit to turn it off with a joke if she could. She wanted terribly to ask him sometimes what he had meant when he said that he didn't love her as he had loved other women. She had never the courage to ask him this. She wondered sometimes why it had hurt her when he had said he loved her as though she were a man friend, without any question of sex. "Surely that's enough for me," she would ask herself, "it means that it's much more lasting and safe." And yet it was not enough.

Nevertheless, during these weeks she found his brotherly care of her adorable, he found her shyness divine.

"Every other woman I have ever been in love with," he told her once, "I have always kept asking them would they ever change, and would they love me always, and all that kind of nonsense. A man always begins like that, and then the time comes when he wishes to God they would change, and they won't. But you're not like that, Maggie, I know you'll never change, and I know that I shall never want you to." "No, I shall never change," said Maggie.

At the very beginning of the three weeks a little incident occurred that was trivial enough at the time, but appeared afterwards as something significant and full of meaning. This incident was a little talk with poor Mr. Magnus. Maggie always thought of him as "poor Mr. Magnus." He seemed so feckless and unsettled, and then he wrote novels that nobody wanted to buy. He always talked like a book, and that was perhaps one reason why Maggie had avoided him during these last months. Another reason had been that she really could not be sure how far he was in the general conspiracy to drive her into the Chapel. He would not do that of his own will she was sure, but being in love with Aunt Anne he might think it his sacred duty, and Maggie was terrified of "sacred duties." Therefore when, three days after that great evening in the park, he caught her alone in the drawing-room, her first impulse was to run away; then she looked at him and found that her love for the world in general embraced him too "if only he won't talk like a book," she thought to herself.

He looked more wandering than ever with his high white collar, his large spectacles, and his thin, dusty hair; the fire of some hidden, vital spirit burnt beneath those glasses, and his face was so kindly that she felt ashamed of herself for having avoided him so often.

"Both the aunts are at Miss Avies'." she said.

"Oh," he said, looking at her rather blankly.

"Perhaps I'll come another time," and he turned towards the door.

"No," she cried. "You won't—I haven't seen you for months."

"That's not my fault," he answered. "I thought we were to have been friends, and you've run away every time you saw the corner of my dusty coat poking round the door."

"Yes," she said, "I have—I've been frightened of every one lately."

"And you're not now?" he asked, looking at her with that sudden bright sharpness that was so peculiarly his.

"No, I'm not," she answered. "I'm frightened of nobody."

He said nothing to that, but stared fixedly in front of him.

"I'm in a bad mood," he said. "I've been trying for weeks to get on with a novel. Just a fortnight ago a young man and a young woman took shelter from the rain in the doorway of a deserted house—they're still there now, and they haven't said a word to one another all that time."

"Why not?" asked Maggie.

"They simply won't speak," he answered her.

"Well then, I should start another story," said Maggie brightly.

"Ah," he said, shaking his head. "What's the use of starting one if you know you're never going to finish it, what's the use of finishing it if you know no one is ever going to read it?" Maggie shook her head.

"You've changed. When I saw you last you told me that you didn't mind whether any one ever read them or not, and that you just wrote them because you loved doing them."

"Every author," said Mr. Magnus gloomily, "says that to himself when he can't sell his books, but it's all vainglory, I'm afraid."

"I can't help being glad," Maggie answered. "There are such interesting things you might do. I can't imagine why any one writes books now when there are so many already in existence that nobody's read."

He wasn't listening to her. He looked up suddenly and said quite wildly:

"It's terrible all this that's going on. You know about it, of course—Warlock's visions I mean and the trouble it's making. I'm outside it and you're outside it, but we're being brought into it all the same— how can we help it when we love the people who are in it? It's so easy to say that it's nonsense, that people ought to be wiser nowadays; that it's hysteria, even insanity—I know all that and, of course, I don't believe for a moment that God's coming in a chariot of fire on New Year's Eve especially for the benefit of Thurston, Miss Avies and the rest, but that doesn't end it—it ought to end it, but it doesn't.

There's more in some people's madness than in other people's sanity, and anyway, even if it's all nonsense it means life or death to your aunt and some of the others, and it means a certain breaking up of all this place. And it probably means the triumph of a charlatan like Thurston and the increase of humbug in the world and the discouragement of all the honest adventurers. I call myself an adventurer, you know, Miss Maggie, although I'm a poor specimen—but I'm damned if it isn't better to be a poor adventurer than to be a fat, swollen, contented stay-at-home who can see just as far as his nose and his cheque-book and might be just as well dead as alive—I beg your pardon," he added suddenly, "for swearing—I'm not myself, I'm not really."

She could see indeed that he was in great agitation of mind, and some of this agitation communicated itself to her. Had she not been selfish in forgetting all this through her own happiness? He was right, she was part of it all, whether she wished or no.

"What do you think," she asked, dropping her voice a little, "is the real truth about it?"

"The real truth"—he looked at her suddenly with a tender, most charming smile that took away his ugliness. "Ah, that's a tremendous question. Part of the truth is that Warlock's been praying so much and eating so little that it would be odd indeed if he didn't see visions of some sort. And part of the truth is that there are a lot of women in the world who'll believe simply anything that you tell them. It's part of the truth, too, that there are scoundrels in the world who will take advantage of anybody's simple trust to fill their pockets. But that's not all," he went on, shaking his head, "no, that's not all. It's part of the truth that there is a mystery, and that human beings will go on searching whatever all the materialists and merchants in the world can try to do to stop them. I remember years ago an old man, a little off his dot, telling my father that he, the old man, was a treasure hunter. He told my father that the world was divided into two halves, the treasure hunters and the Town Councillors, and that the two halves would never join and never even meet. My father, who was a practical man, said that the old idiot should be shut up in an asylum, and eventually I believe he was. 'We'll have him going off one day,' my father said, 'in a cargo boat with a map in his pocket, looking for gold pieces.' But it wasn't gold pieces he was after."

To Maggie it was always irritating the way that Mr. Magnus would wander away from the subject. She brought him back now with a jerk.

"No, but what do you think is going to happen?" she asked him.

"I don't know," he answered. "I can't tell, but I know all my happiness here is coming to an end, and I don't know what I shall do. If I were a strong man I would go out and find all the other treasure hunters, all the vicious ones, and the diseased, and the drunkards and the perverted, and I would try to found some kind of a society so that they should recognise one another all the world over and shouldn't feel so lonely and deserted and hopelessly done for. I don't mean a society for improving them, mind you, or warning them or telling them they'll go to prison if they don't do better, that's none of my business. But it seems to be a solemn fact that you aren't a treasure hunter until there's something wrong with you, until you've got a sin that's stronger than you are, or until you've done something that's disgraceful in the eyes of the world—not that I believe in weakness or in giving way to things. No one admires the strong and the brave more than I do. I think a man's a fool if he doesn't fight as hard as he can. But there's a brotherhood of the dissatisfied and the uneasy and the anxious-hearted, and I believe it's they who will discover the Grail in the end if it's ever going to be discovered at all."

He broke off, then said restlessly: "I think things out, you know, and at last I come to a conclusion, and it ends by being a platitude that all the goody, goody books have said times without number. But all the same that doesn't prevent it from being my discovery. It's nothing to do with goodness and nothing to do with evil, it's nothing to do with strength, and nothing to do with weakness; it simply is that there are some people who want what they can see and no more, and there are others, the baffled, fighting and disordered others, for whom nothing that they can see with their mortal eyes is enough, and who'll be restless all their days with their queer little maps and their mysterious, thumbed directions to some island or other that they'll never reach and never even get a ship for."

He stopped and there was a long silence between them, Maggie was silent because she never knew what to say when he burst into parables and divided mankind, under strange names, into different camps. And yet this time she did know a little what he was after. There was that house of Katharine Mark's the other day, with its comfort and quiet and kind smiling clergyman—and there was this strange place with all of them in an odd quiver of excitement waiting for something to happen. But she couldn't speak to him about that, she couldn't say anything to him at all. He cleared his throat as though he were embarrassed and were conscious that he had been making a fool of himself. Maggie felt that he was disappointed in her. She was sorry for that, but she was as she was.

"Well, I'm glad you're happy," he said, looking at her wistfully. He got up and stood awkwardly looking at her.

"I want you to promise me something," he said, "that's really what I came for. I want you to promise that you won't in any case leave your aunts before the New Year."

She got up, looked at him and gave him her hand.

"Yes," she said. "I promise that."

The year had only a week or two more to run and she was not afraid of that little space of time. He seemed to want to say something more, but after hesitating he suddenly made a bolt for the door and she could hear him stumbling downstairs.

She forgot him almost as soon as he had left the house, but his words nevertheless brought her to consider her aunts. Next morning at breakfast time she had a further reason to consider them. Aunt Elizabeth met her, when she came downstairs, with a very grave face.

"Your aunt's had a terrible night," she said. "She's insisted on coming downstairs—I told her not. She never listens to anything I say."

Maggie could see that something more than ordinary had occurred. Aunt Elizabeth was on the edge of tears, and in so confused a state of mind that she put sugar into her egg, and then ate it with a puzzled air as though she could not be sure why it tasted so strange. When Aunt Anne came in it was plain enough that she had wrestled with demons during the night. Maggie had often seen her before battling with pain and refusing to be defeated. Now she looked as though she had but risen from the dead. It was a ghost in very truth that stood there; a ghost in black silk dress with white wristbands and a stiff white collar, black hair, so tightly drawn back and ordered that it was like a shining skull-cap. Her face was white, with the effect of a chalk drawing into which live, black, burning eyes had been stuck. But it was none of these things that frightened Maggie. It was the expression somewhere in the mouth, in the eyes, in the pale bony hands, that spoke of some meeting with a torturer whose powers were almost omniscient—almost, but not quite. Pain, sheer physical, brutal pain, came into the room hulking, steering behind Aunt Anne's shoulder. It grinned at Maggie and said, "You haven't begun to feel what I can do yet, but every one has his turn. You needn't flatter yourself that you're going to escape."

When Aunt Anne moved now it was with infinite caution, as though she were stalking her enemy and was afraid lest any incautious gesture should betray her into his ambush. No less marked than her torture was her courage and the expectation that sustained that courage. She had her eyes set upon something very sure and very certain. Maggie was afraid to think what that expectation might be. But Maggie had grown during these last weeks. She did not now kiss her aunt and try to show an affection which was not so genuine as she would have liked it to be by nervous little demonstrations. She said gravely:

"I am so sorry, Aunt Anne, that you have had so bad a night. Shall I stay this morning and read to you?"

Even as she spoke she realised with sharp pain what giving up her meeting with Martin meant.

"What were you going to do, dear?" asked Aunt Anne, her eyes seeing as ever far beyond Maggie and the room and the house. As she spoke Thomas, the cat, came forward and began rubbing himself very gently, as though he were whispering something to his mistress, against her dress. Maggie had an impulse, so strong that it almost defeated her, to burst out with the whole truth. She almost said: "I'm going out to meet Martin Warlock, whom I love and with whom I'm going to live." She hated deceit, she hated lies. But this was some one else's secret as well as her own, and telling the truth now would only lead to much pain and distress, and then more lies and more deceit.

So she said:

"I'm going to Piccadilly to get some things for Aunt Elizabeth."

"Yes," said Aunt Elizabeth, "she saves me a great deal of trouble. She's a good girl."

"I know she's a good girl," said Aunt Anne softly.

It was strange to remember the time not so long ago when to run out of the house and post a letter had seemed a bold defiant thing to do threatened with grave penalties. The aunts had changed their plans about her and had given her no reasons for doing so. No reasons were ever given in that house for anything that was done. The more Maggie went out, the more she was drawn in.

On her way to Martin that morning the figure of Aunt Anne haunted her. She felt for a brief moment that she would do anything, yes, even surrender Martin, to ease her aunt's pain. And then she knew that she would not, and she called herself cruel and selfish and felt for an instant a dark shadow threatening her because she was so. But when she saw Martin outside Hatchard's she forgot it all. It was a strange thing that during those weeks they neither of them asked any questions about their home affairs. It was as though they both inwardly realised that there was trouble for them of every kind waiting outside and that they could only definitely realise their happiness by building a wall around themselves. They knew perhaps in their secret hearts, or at any rate Martin knew, that they could not hold their castle for long. But is not the gift of three perfect weeks a great thing for any human being to be given—and who has the temerity, the challenging audacity, to ask with confidence for even so much?

On this particular morning Martin said to her:

"Before we get into the 'bus, Maggie, you've got to come into a shop with me." He was especially boyish and happy and natural that morning. It was strange how his face altered when he was happy. His brow was clear, his eyes were bright, and he had a kind of crooked confident smile that must have won anybody's heart. His whole carriage was that of a boy who was entering life for the first time with undaunted expectation that it could give him nothing but the best and jolliest things. Maggie as she looked at him this morning caught her breath with the astonishing force of her love for him. "Oh, how I'll look after him," was her thought. "He shall never be unhappy again."

They crossed the street together, and stood for a moment close together on the kerb in the middle way as though they were quite alone in the world. She caught his arm and they ran before a charging motor-'bus, laughing. People turned back and looked at them, so happy they seemed. They walked up Bond Street and Martin drew her into a jeweller's. She had never possessed any ornament except her coral necklace in all her life and she knew now for the first time how terribly she liked beautiful things. It was useless of her to pretend that she did not know that he was going to give her something. She did not pretend. A very thin old man, who looked like one of the prophets, drawn out of the wilderness and clothed by the most fashionable of London tailors, looking over their shoulders as he talked to them because he saw at once that they were not customers who were likely to add very much to his shop's exchequer, produced a large tray, full of rings that glittered and sparkled and danced as though they'd been told to show themselves off to the best possible advantage. But for Maggie at once there was only one possible ring. It was a thin hoop of gold with three small pearls set in the middle of it; nothing very especial about it, it was in fact less striking than almost any other ring in the tray. Maggie looked at the ring and the ring looked at Maggie. It was as though the ring said, "I shall belong to you whether you take me or no."

"Now," said Martin with a little catch in his throat, "you make your choice, Maggie." He was not a millionaire, but he did honestly intend that whatever ring she chose she should have.

"Oh," said Maggie, whispering because the shop was so large and the prophet so indifferent, "don't you think you'd better choose?"

At the same time she felt the anxious gaze of the three little pearls upon her.

"No," said Martin, "I want to give you what you'd like."

"I'd like what you'd like," said Maggie, still whispering.

At this banality the prophet made a little impatient movement as though he really could not be expected to stand waiting there for ever. Also a magnificent lady, in furs so rich that you could see nothing of her but her powdered nose, was waving ropes of pearls about in a blasé manner very close to them, and Maggie had a strange, entirely unreasonable fear that this splendour would suddenly turn round and snatch the little pearl ring and go off with it.

"I'd like that one," said Maggie, pointing. She heard the prophet sniff his contempt, but she did not care.

Martin, although he would willingly have given her the most gorgeous ring in the shop, was delighted to find that her taste was so good, and like herself. He had great ideas about taste, some of his secret fears had been lest her strange uncouth upbringing should have caused her to like gaudy things. He could have hugged her before them all when she chose that particular ring, which he had himself noticed as the prettiest and neatest there.

"Just see whether it fits, darling," he said. At the word "darling" the prophet cast another despairing look about the shop, as though he knew well the length of time that lovers could take over these things if they once put their hearts into it. Maggie was ashamed of her stubby finger as she put her hand forward—but the ring fitted exactly.

"That's right," said Martin, "Now we'll have this put into a case."

"How wonderful he is," thought Maggie. Not as other women might have thought, "I wonder how many times he's done this before." Maggie thought then that it would be more proper to retire a little so that she should not know the price—and she stood in the doorway of the shop, looking upon the wind and weather in Bond Street and the magnificent motor car that belonged to the lady with the pearls and a magnificent chauffeur, who was so superior that it was probable that the lady with the pearls belonged to him—and she saw none of these things, but was conscious of herself and Martin wrapt together in a mist of happiness that no outside force could penetrate.

As they walked away from the shop she said: "Of course I won't be able to wear it."

He put the little square box, wrapped in tissue paper, into her hand, and answered: "You can wear it on a ribbon under your dress."

"Oh yes," she whispered, pressing his hand for a moment.

They did not climb on to a 'bus that morning, but walked ahead blindly, blissfully, they did not know whither. They were now in wild days at the end of November and the weather was tempestuous, the wind blowing with a screaming fury and black clouds scudding across the sky like portents. Little heavy drops of rain fell with a sudden urgency as though they were emphasising some secret; figures were swept through the streets and the roar of the wind was so vehement that the traffic seemed to make no sound. And yet nothing happened—no great storm of rain, no devastating flood. It was a day of warning.

They noticed nothing of the weather. It might have been a world of burning sunshine for all they saw of it.

"You know," said Martin, "I've never liked giving any one anything so much as I liked giving you that ring."

"I wish I could give you something too," she said.

"Well, you can," he said. "Some little thing that I'll carry about with me always ... Oh, Maggie!" he went on. "Isn't it strange how easy it is to be good when no one worries you. These last ten days with you I couldn't have done anything wrong if I tried. It isn't fair to say we can help ourselves. We can't. Something just comes along and seizes you and makes you do wrong."

"Oh, I don't know," said Maggie. "Don't let's talk about those things. It's like Mr. Magnus, who says we're treasure hunters or pools of water, or old men in asylums. I don't understand all that. I'm just Maggie Cardinal.—All the same I believe one can do what one wants to. I don't believe people can make one do things."

"Do you think any one could make me not love you if they tried? I shall love you always, whatever happens. I know I shall never change. I'm not one to change. I'm obstinate. Father used to say 'obstinate as a pig.'"

That made her think of the old days at St. Dreot's, just then, as they seemed, so remote. She began to tell him of those old days, of the Vicarage, of the holes in the floor and the ceiling, of her loneliness and the way the villagers used to talk, of her solitary walks and looking down on to Polchester from the hill-top, of her father's sudden death, of Uncle Mathew ...

"He's a funny old codger," said Martin. "What does he do?"

"I don't know," said Maggie. "I really don't know how he lives I'm afraid it's something rather bad."

"I've known men like that," said Martin, "plenty, but it's funny that one of them should be connected with you. It doesn't seem as though you could have anything to do with a man like that."

"Oh, but I like him!" said Maggie. "He's been very kind to me often. When I was all alone after father died he was very good—" She stopped abruptly remembering how he'd come into her bedroom. "Drink's been his trouble, and never having any money. He told me once if he had money he'd never do a thing he shouldn't." "Yes," said Martin. "That's what they always say when they haven't any money, and then when they have any it's worse than ever."

He was thinking, perhaps, of himself. At any rate to stop remorseful thoughts he began to tell her about his own childhood.

"Mine was very different from yours, Maggie," he said. "I wasn't lonely. You don't know what a fuss people made of me. I was conceited, too. I thought I was chosen, by God, out of all the world, that I was different from every one else, and better too. When I was only about nine, at home one Sunday they asked me if I'd say a prayer, and I did, before them all, made it up and went on for quarter of an hour. Lord! I must have been an awful child. And outside the religious time I was as wicked as I could be. I used to go down into the kitchen and steal the food and I'd dress up as a ghost to frighten Amy and I'd break mother's china. I remember once, after we'd had a service in the drawing-room and two girls had gone into hysterics, I stole down into the kitchen in my nightdress to get some jam and I found one of the Elders making love to the cook. They were both so fat and he had his coat and waistcoat off and he was kissing her neck. My word, they were frightened when they saw me standing there! After that I could do what I liked with the cook ... We used to have prayer meetings in the drawing-room, and sometimes father would pray so hard that the glass chandelier would shake and rattle till I used to think it would come down."

"And the funny thing was that one minute I'd be pinching Amy who was kneeling next to me and the next I'd be shaking with religion and seeing God standing right in front of me by the coal-scuttle. Such a mix-up! ... it was then and so it is now. Amy always hated me. She was really religious and she thought I was a hypocrite. But I wasn't altogether. There was something real in it and there still is."

"Didn't you go to school?" asked Maggie.

"No, that was the mistake. They never sent me. Father loved me too much and he wanted to keep me always with him. He tried to teach me himself but I never learnt anything. I always knew I could turn them round my little finger. I always knew he'd rather do anything than make me unhappy. Sometimes we had lovely times together, sitting in the dusk in the front of the fire. Do you know, Maggie, I've never changed in my love for father? I've changed in everything else, but in that never. Yet I've hurt him over and over and over again. I've done things ..." Here he broke off. To-day was to be happy; they must build up their walls faster, faster, faster to keep the world out. He would think of nothing, nothing but the present. The wind blew and the heavy drops of rain fell, one and one and one, slowly between the gusts. Ho drew her close to him.

"Are you cold?"

"No, Martin dear."

"I suppose we should turn back."

"Yes, it's getting late."

"It will seem hours until to-morrow."

"And to me too."

They were at the end of the Green Park. There was no one there. They kissed and clung together and Maggie's hand was warm inside his coat. Then they turned back and entered the real world once more ...

"Now we must have our matinee," Martin said. Maggie could not refuse and besides she herself wanted it so badly. Also the three weeks were drawing to a close, and although she did not know what was in store for them, she felt, in some mysterious way, that trouble was coming.

"Yes, we'll have our matinee," she said.

It was a terrific excitement for her, apart altogether from her love for Martin. She had, of course, never been to a theatre. She could not imagine in the least what it was like. It so happened, by a wonderful chance, that a note came from Katherine Mark asking her to tea. She showed this to the aunts and said that she would accept it. She wrote to Katherine Mark and refused and told Martin that for that Wednesday afternoon she was quite free until at least seven o'clock. She wove these deceits with strong disgust. She hated the lies, and there were many, many times when she was on the edge of confessing everything to the aunts. But the thought of what would follow that confession held her back. She could not make things harder for Martin.

Nevertheless she wondered why when she felt, in herself, no shame al all at the things that she was doing, she should have to lie to cover those things up. But everything in connection with the Chapel seemed to lie.—The place was wrapped in intrigue and double-dealing. How long would it be before she and Martin were out of it all?

She was to meet him by one of the lions in Trafalgar Square. She bought a golden chrysanthemum which she stuck into the belt of her black dress and she wore her coral necklace. She was tired of black. She sometimes thought she would spend all her Three Hundred Pounds on clothes ... To-day, as soon as she was out of the house and had turned the corner into King William Street, she slipped on her ring. She kissed it before she put her glove on. He was waiting there looking like a happy schoolboy, that way that she loved him to look. That slow crooked smile of his, something that broke up his whole face into geniality and friendliness, how she adored him when he looked like that! He was wearing clothes of some rough red-brown stuff and a black knitted tie—

She was carrying something, a little parcel in tissue paper. She pressed it into his hand when they met. He opened it, just like a boy, chuckling, his eyes shining, his fingers tearing the paper in his eagerness. Her present was a round locket of thin plain gold and inside was the funniest little black faded photograph of Maggie, her head only, a wild untidy head of hair, a fat round schoolgirl face—a village snapshot of Maggie taken in St. Dreot's when she was about fifteen.

"It's all I had," she said. "I remembered it the other day and I found it. A travelling photographer took it one day. He came to the village and every one was taken, father and all. It's very bad but it was the only one."

"It's wonderful," said Martin, and truly it was wonderful. It had caught by a marvellous chance, in spite of its shabby faded darkness, the very soul of Maggie. Was it her hair, her untidy hair, or the honesty of her eyes, or the strength and trustiness of her mouth? But then it was to any one who did not know her the bad dim photograph of an untidy child, to any one who did know her the very stamp and witness of Maggie and all that she was. Maggie had spent twenty-five shillings on the locket (she had had three pounds put away from her allowance in her drawer).

It was a very simple locket, thin plain gold round and smooth, but good, and it would last.

"You darling," whispered Martin. "There couldn't have been anything more like you if you'd been taken by the grandest photographer in London."

They started off towards Shaftesbury Avenue where the theatre was, and as they went a funny little incident occurred. They were both too happy to talk and Maggie was too happy even to think. Suddenly she was aware that some one was coming towards her whom she knew. She looked and tugged herself from that world of Martin and only Martin in which she was immersed. It was the large, smiling, rosy-cheeked, white-haired clergyman, Mr. Trenchard. Yes, certainly it was he. He had recognised her and was stopping to speak to her. Martin moved on a little and stood waiting for her. She was confused and embarrassed but pleased too because he seemed glad to see her. He looked the very picture of a well-dressed, kindly, genial friend who had known her all his life. He was wearing a beautifully shining top-hat and his stiff white collar gleamed. Yes, he was glad to see her and he said so. He remembered her name. "Miss Cardinal," he called her. How had she been? What had she been doing? Had she seen Mrs. Mark? He was staying with his sister at Brown's Hotel in Somewhere—she didn't catch the name of the street. His sister would be so glad if she would come and see them one day. Would she come? He wouldn't tie her down, but she had only to write and say she was coming ...

He took her hand and held it for a moment and looked in her eyes with the kindliest friendliest regard. He was glad to have seen her. He should tell his sister ...

He was gone and Maggie really could not be sure what she had said. Something very silly she could be certain. Stupid the pleasure that his few words had given her, but she felt once again, as she had felt in Katherine Mark's drawing-room, the contact with that other world, that safe, happy, comfortable, assured world in which everything was exactly what it seemed. She was glad that he liked her and that his sister liked her. Then she could not be so wild and odd and uncivilised as she often was afraid that she was. She rejoined Martin with a little added glow in her cheeks.

"Who was that?" Martin asked her rather sharply.

She told him.

"One of those humbugging parsons," he said. "He stood over you as though he'd like to eat you."

"Oh, I'm sure he's not a humbug," she answered.

"You'd be taken in by anybody," he told her.

"Oh, no, I shouldn't," she said. "Now forget him."

And they did. By the time they had reached Piccadilly Circus they were once more deep, deep in one another. They were back in their dark and gleaming wood.

The Lyric Theatre was their destination. Maggie drew a breath as they stepped into the hall where there stood two large stout commissionaires in blue uniforms, gold buttons, and white gloves. People pushed past them and hurried down the stairs on either side as though a theatre were a Nothing. Maggie stood there fingering her gloves and feeling lonely. The oil painting of a beautiful lady with a row of shining teeth faced her. There were also some palms and a hole in the wall with a man behind it.

Soon they too passed down the stairs, curtains were drawn back, and Maggie was sitting, quite suddenly, in a large desert of gold and red plush, with emptiness on every side of it and a hungry-looking crowd of people behind a wooden partition staring at her in such a way that she felt as though she had no clothes on. She gave a hurried glance at these people and turned round blushing.

"Why don't they sit with us?" she whispered to Martin.

"They're the Pit and we're the Stalls," he whispered to her, but that comforted her very little.

"Won't people come and sit where we are?" she asked.

"Oh yes; we're early," he told her.

Soon she was more composed and happier. She sat very close to Martin, her knee against his and his hand near to hers, just touching the outside of her palm. Her ring sparkled and the three little pearls smiled at her. As he breathed she breathed too, and it seemed to her that their bodies rose and fell as one body. Without looking directly at him, which would, she knew, embarrass him before all those hungry people behind her, she could out of the corner of her eye see the ruddy brown of his cheek and the hard thick curve of his shoulder. She was his, she belonged to no one else in the world, she was his utterly. Utterly. Ever so swiftly and gently her hand brushed for an instant over his; he responded, crooking his little finger for a moment inside hers. She smiled; she turned round and looked at the people triumphantly, she felt a deep contented rest in her heart, rich and full, proud and arrogant, the mother, the lover, the sister, the child, everything to him she was ...

People came in, the theatre filled, and a hum of talk arose, then the orchestra began to tune, and soon music was playing, and Maggie would have loved to listen but the people must chatter.

When suddenly the lights went down the only thing of which she was conscious was that Martin's hand had suddenly seized hers roughly, sharply, and was crushing it, pressing the ring into the flesh so that it hurt. Her first excited wondering thought then was:

"He doesn't care for me any more only as a friend.—There's the other now ..." and a strange shyness, timidity, and triumph overwhelmed her so that her eyes were full of tears and her body trembling.

But as the play continued she must listen. It was her very first play and soon it was thrilling to her so that she forgot, for a time, even Martin. Or rather Martin was mingled with it, absorbed in it, part of it, and she was there too sharing with him the very action of the story. It was a very old-fashioned play about a little Charity girl who was brought up by a kindly middle-aged gentleman who cared for nothing but books. He brought her up on his own plan with a view to marrying her afterwards. But meanwhile, of course, she saw a handsome young soldier who was young like herself, and she was naturally bored with the studious gentleman. Maggie shared all the feelings of the Charity girl. Had she been brought up, say by a man like Mr. Trenchard and then had met Martin, why, of course, she could have gone only one way.

The soldier was not like Martin, being slim and curled and beautiful, nor was the studious gentleman like Mr. Trenchard, being thin and tall with a face like a monk and a beautiful voice. But the girl was like Maggie, prettier of course, and with artful ways, but untidy a little and not very well educated. At the first interval, when the lights were up and the band was playing and the people walking, Martin whispered:

"Do you like it, Maggie?"

"I love it," she answered.

And then they just sat there, without another word between them, pressed close together.

A little song ran through the play—one of Burns's most famous songs, although Maggie, who had never read anything, did not know that. The verses were:

O my luve's like a red, red rose That's newly sprung in June: O my luve's like the melodie That's sweetly played in tune!

As fair art thou, my bonnie lass, So deep in luve am I: And I will luve thee still, my dear, Till a' the seas gang dry:

Till a' the seas gang dry, my dear, And the rocks melt wi' the sun; I will luve thee still, my dear, While the sands o' life shall run.

And fare thee weel, my only Luve, And fare thee weel a while! And I will come again, my Luve, Tho' it were ten thousand mile.

First the handsome soldier sang this to the Charity girl, and then, because it was a sentimental tune, it was always turning up through the play, and if one of the characters were not singing it the orchestra was quietly playing it. Maggie loved it; she was not sentimental but she was simple, and the tune seemed at once to belong to herself and to Martin by natural right.

As the story developed it became more unreal and Maggie's unerring knowledge of the difference between sense and nonsense refused to credit the tall handsome villainness who confronted the Charity girl at the ball. The Charity girl had no right to be at the ball and people stood about in unnatural groups and pretended not to listen to the loud development of the plot and no one seemed to use any of their faculties. Then at the end, when the middle-aged gentleman nobly surrendered his Charity girl to the handsome soldier, the little tune came back again and all was well.

They came out of the theatre into lights and shadows and mists cabs and omnibuses and crowds of people ... Maggie clung to Martin's arm. It seemed to her, dazzled for an instant, that a great are of white piercing light cut the black street and that in the centre of this arc a tree, painted green, stood, and round the tree figures, dark shapes, and odd shadows danced. She shaded her eyes with her hand. The long shining line of Shaftesbury Avenue ran out, from her feet, into thick clusters of silver lights. The tree had vanished and now there were policemen and ladies in hats and strange mysterious houses. She caught above it all, between the roofs, the pale flat river of the evening sky and in this river stars like golden buttons floated. The moon was there too, a round amber coin with the laughing face stamped upon it.

"What time is it?" she asked Martin.

"Half-past five," he said. "How early the moon rises. It's only climbing now. See the chimney's tossing it about."

"I must get home."

"No, no." He held her arm fiercely. "You must come to tea. That's part of the programme. We have plenty of time before seven o'clock." She knew that she ought to return. Something seemed to tell her, as she stood there, that now was the moment to break this off. But when his hand was on her arm, when he was so close to her, she could not leave him. She would have one hour more ... He took her across the street, down into darkness, up into light. Then they went into a shop, up some stairs, and were suddenly in a little room with a table with a cloth, a window looking out into the lamp-lit square, cherry-coloured curtains and gay hunting pictures on the walls. Martin pushed a bell in the wall and a stout waiter, perspiring, smiling, a napkin in his hand, came to the door. "Tea," said Martin, and he vanished. "It's all right," he said, drawing her to a creaking wicker armchair near the empty fireplace. "No one will interrupt us. They know me here. I ordered the room yesterday." Tea came, but she could not eat anything. In some strange way that moment in the theatre when he had pressed her hand had altered everything. She recognised in herself a new Maggie; she was excited with a thick burning excitement, she was almost sleepy with the strain of it and her cheeks were hot, but her throat icy cold. When she told him that she wasn't hungry, he said, "I'm not either." Then he added, not looking at her, "That fellow won't be back for an hour." He came and stood by her looking down on her. He bent forward over the chair and put his hands under her chin and pressed her face up towards his. But he did not kiss her. Then he took her hands and pulled her gently out of the chair, sat down on it himself, then, still very tenderly, put his arms round her and drew her down to him. She lay back against him, her cheek against his, his arms tight around her. He whispered to her again and again, "Darling ... Darling ... Darling." She felt now so terribly part of him that she seemed to have lost all her own identity. His hands, softly, tenderly passed up and down her body, stroking her hair, her cheeks, her arms. Her mouth was against his cheek and she was utterly motionless, shivering a little sometimes and once her hand moved up and caught his and then moved away again. At last, as it seemed from an infinite distance, his voice came to her, speaking to her. "Maggie, darling," he said, "don't go back till late to-night. You can say that those people asked you to stay to dinner. Your aunts can't do anything. Nothing can happen. Stay with me here and then later we'll go and have dinner at a little place I know ... and then come back here ... come back here ... like this. Maggie, darling, say you will. You must. We mayn't have another chance for so long. You're coming to me afterwards. What does it matter, a week or two earlier? What does it matter, Maggie? Stay here. Let us love one another and have something to think about ... to remember ... to remember ... to remember ..." His voice seemed to slip away into infinity as voices in a dream do. She could not say anything because she was in a dream too. She could only feel his hand stroking her face. He seemed to take her silence for consent. He suddenly kissed her furiously, pressing her head back until it hurt. That woke her. She pushed his arms back and sprang up. Her hands were trembling. She shook her head. "No, Martin. No, not now." "Why not?" He looked at her angrily from the chair. His face was altered, he was frowning, his eyes were dark. "I'm not going to stay now." Her voice shook in spite of herself. With shaking hands she patted her dress. "Why not?" he asked again. "I'm not. I promised the aunts. Not now. It would spoil everything." "Oh, very well." He was furious with her. He wouldn't meet her eyes. "Not now." She felt that she would cry; tears flooded her eyes. "It's been so lovely ... Martin ... Don't look like that. Oh, I love you too much!" She broke off. With a sudden movement she fell at his feet; kneeling there, she drew his hands to her face, she kissed them, the palms of his hands over and over again. His anger suddenly left him. He put his arms round her and kissed her, first her eyes, then her cheeks, then, gently, her mouth. "All right," he said. "Only I feel somehow ... I feel as though our time had come to an end." "But it shan't?" He turned upon her fiercely, held her hands, looked in her face. "Maggie, do you swear that you'll love me always, whatever I am, whatever I do?" "I swear," she answered, gazing into his eyes, "that I'll love you always, whatever you are, whatever you do." Then she went away, leaving him by the table, staring after her. In the street she saw that her chrysanthemum was in pieces, torn and scattered and destroyed. She slipped off the ring and put it into her pocket, then, with forebodings in her heart, as though she did indeed know that her good time was over, she turned towards home. She was right. Her good time was over. That night she was left alone. Martha let her in and, regarding her darkly, said nothing. The aunts also said nothing, sitting all the evening under the green shade of the lamp in the drawing-room, Aunt Anne reading a pamphlet, Aunt Elizabeth sewing. Maggie pretended to read but she saw no words. She saw only the green lamp like a dreadful bird suspended there and Aunt Anne's chiselled sanctity. Over and over again she reasoned with herself. There was no cause for panic. Nothing had happened to change things—and yet—and yet everything was changed. Everything had been changed from that moment when Martin pressed her hand in the theatre. Everything! ... Danger now of every sort. She could be brave, she could meet anything if she were only sure of Martin. But he too seemed strange to her. She remembered his dark look, his frown when she had refused him. Oh, this loneliness, this helplessness. If she could be with him, beside him, she would fear nothing. That night, the first faint suspicion of jealousy, of doubt, an agonising dart of pain at the knowledge of what it would mean to her now if he left her, stirred in her breast. This room was stifling. She got up from her chair, went to the window, looked out between the thick curtains at the dark deserted street. "What is it, Maggie?" "Nothing, Aunt Anne." "You're very restless, dear." "It's close. May I open the door?" "A little, dear." She opened the door and then sat there hearing the Armed Men sway ever so slightly, tap, tap, against the wall in the passage. That night she scarcely slept at all, only tumbling into sudden nightmare dreams when something had her by the throat and Martin was not there. In the morning as soon as she could escape she hurried to Piccadilly. Martin was waiting for her. When she saw him she realised at once that her good time was indeed over. His face was white and strained. He scarcely looked at her but stared anxiously up and down the street.

"What is it?" she asked breathlessly. "Look here, Maggie," he began, still scarcely looking at her. "I must get back at once. I only came to tell you that we must drop our meetings for the next day or two—until it's blown over."

"Until what's blown over," she asked him.

"It's my father. I don't know what exactly has happened. They'll none of them tell me, damn them. It's Caroline Smith. She's been talking to Amy about you and me. I know that because of what Amy said about you at breakfast this morning."

"What did she say?"

"She wouldn't speak out. She hinted. But she admitted that Caroline Smith had told her something. But she doesn't matter. Nothing matters except father. He mustn't be excited just now. His heart's so bad. Any little thing ... We must wait."

She saw that he was scarcely realising her at all. She choked down all questions that concerned themselves. She simply agreed, nodding her head.

He did look at her then, smiling as he used to do.

"It's awfully hard on us. It won't be for more than a day or two. But I must put things right at home or it will be all up. I don't care for the others, of course, but if anything happened to father through me ..." He told her to write to the Charing Cross post-office. He would do the same. In a day or two it would be all right. He pressed her hand and was gone.

When she looked about her the street seemed quite empty although it was full of people. She threw up her head. She wouldn't be beaten by anybody ... only, it was lonely going back to the house and all of them ... alone ... without Martin.

She cried a little on her way home. But they were the last tears she shed.

CHAPTER IX

THE INSIDE SAINTS

Maggie, when she was nearly home, halted suddenly. She stopped as when on the threshold of a room that should be empty one sees waiting a stranger. If at the end of all this she should lose Martin! ...

There was the stranger who had come to her now and would not again depart. She recognised the sharp pain, the almost unconscious pulling back on the sudden edge of a dim pit, as something that would always be with her now—always. One knows that in the second stage of a great intimacy one's essential loneliness is only redoubled by close companionship. One asks for so much more, and then more and more, but that final embrace is elusive and no physical contact can surrender it. But she was young and did not know that yet. All she knew was that she would have to face these immediate troubles alone, that she would not see him for perhaps a week, that she would not know what his people at home were doing, and that she must not let any of these thoughts come up into her brain. She must keep them all back: if she did not, she would tumble into some foolish precipitate action.

When she reached home she was obstinate and determined. At once she found that something was the matter. During luncheon the two aunts sat like statues (Aunt Elizabeth a dumpy and squat one). Aunt Anne's aloofness was coloured now with a very human anger. Maggie realised with surprise that she had never seen her angry before. She had been indignant, disapproving, superior, forbidding, but never angry. The eyes were hard now, not with religious reserve but simply with bad temper. The mist of anger dimmed the room, it was in the potatoes and the cold dry mutton, especially was it in the hard pallid knobs of cheese. And Aunt Elizabeth, although she was frightened by her sister's anger on this occasion, shared in it. She pursed her lips at Maggie and moved her fat, podgy hand as though she would like to smack Maggie's cheeks.

Maggie was frightened—really frightened. The line of bold independence was all very well, but now risks were attached to it. If she swiftly tossed her head and told her aunts that she would walk out of the house they might say "Walk!" and that would precipitate Martin's crisis. She knew from the way he had looked at her that morning that his thoughts were with his father, and it showed that she had travelled through the first stage of her intimacy with him, that she could not trust him to put her before his own family troubles. At all costs she must keep him safe through these next difficult weeks, and the best way to keep him safe was herself to remain quietly at home.

Of all this she thought as she swallowed the hostile knobs of cheese and drank the tepid, gritty coffee.

She followed her aunts upstairs, and was not at all surprised when Aunt Elizabeth, with an agitated murmur, vanished into higher regions. She followed Aunt Anne into the drawing-room.

Aunt Anne sat in the stiff-backed tapestry chair by the fire. Maggie stood in front of her. She was disarmed at that all-important moment by her desperate sensation of defenceless loneliness. It was as though half of herself—the man-half of herself—had left her. She tried to summon her pluck but there was no pluck there. She could only want Martin, over and over again inside herself. Had any one been, ever so hopelessly ALONE before?

"Maggie, I am angry," said Aunt Anne. She said it as though she meant it. Amazing how human this strange aloof creature had become. As though some coloured saint bright with painted wood and tinsel before whom one stood in reverence slipped down suddenly and with fingers of flesh and blood struck one's face. Her cheeks were flushed, her beautiful hands were no longer thin but were hard and active.

"What have I done, aunt?" asked Maggie.

"You have not treated us fairly. My sister and I have done everything for you. You have not made it especially easy for us in any way, but we have tried to give you what you wanted. You have repaid is with ingratitude."

She paused, but Maggie said nothing. She went on:

"Lately—these last three weeks—we have given you complete liberty. I advised that strongly against my sister's opinion because I thought you weren't happy. You didn't make friends amongst our friends, and I thought you should have the chance of finding some who were younger and gayer than we were. Then I thought we could trust you. You have many faults, but I believed that you were honest."

"I am honest!" Maggie broke in. Her aunt went on:

"You have used the liberty we gave you during these weeks to make yourself the talk of our friends. You have been meeting Mr. Martin Warlock secretly every day. You have been alone with him in the Park and at the theatre. I know that you are young and very ignorant. You could not have known that Martin Warlock is a man with whom no girl who respects herself would be seen alone—"

"That is untrue!" Maggie flamed out.

"—and," went on Aunt Anne, "we would have forgiven that. It is your deceit to ourselves that we cannot forget. Day after day you were meeting him and pretending that you went to your other friends. I am disappointed in you, bitterly disappointed. I saw from the first that you did not mean to care for us, now, as well, you have disgraced us—"

Maggie began: "Yes, I have been seeing Martin. I didn't think it wrong—I don't now. I didn't tell you because I was afraid that you would stop me—"

"Then that shows that you knew it was wrong."

"No, Aunt Anne—only that you would think it was wrong. I can only go by myself, by what I feel is wrong I mean. I've always had to, all my life. It would have been no good doing anything else at home, because father—"

She pulled herself up. She was not going to defend herself or ask for pity. She said, speaking finally:

"Yes, I have been out with Martin every day. I went to the theatre with him, too, and also had tea with him."

Maggie could see Aunt Anne's anger rising higher and higher like water in a tube. Her voice was hard when she spoke again—she pronounced judgment:

"We see now that you were right when you said that you had better leave us. You are free to go as soon as you wish. You have, of course, your money, but if you care to stay with us until you have found some work you must now obey our rules. While you remain with us you must not go out unless my sister or I accompany you." Then her voice changed, softening a little. She suddenly raised her hands in a gesture of appeal: "Oh, Maggie, Maggie, turn to God. You have rebelled against Him. You have refused to listen to His voice. The end of that can be only misery. He loves, but He also judges. Even now, within a day, a week, He may come with judgment. Turn to Him, Maggie, not because I tell you but because of the Truth. Pray with me now that He may help you and give you strength."

Because she felt that she had indeed treated them badly and must do just now what they wished, she knelt down on the drawing-room carpet. Aunt Anne also knelt down, her figure stiff like iron, her raised hands once again delicate and ghost-like.

"O Lord God," she prayed, "this Thy servant comes to Thee and prays that Thou wilt give her strength in her struggle with the Evil One. She has been tempted and is weak, but Thou art strong to save and wilt not despise the least of these Thy children."

"Come, O Lord the Father, and take Thy daughter into Thy loving care, and when Thou comest, in all Thy splendour, to redeem the world, I pray that Thou wilt find her waiting for Thee in holiness and meekness of heart."

They rose. Maggie's knees were sore with the stiff carpet. The family group watched her from the wall ironically.

She saw that in spite of the prayer Aunt Anne had not forgiven her. She stood away from her, and although her voice now was not so hard, it had lost altogether the tender note that it used to have.

"Now, Maggie, you must promise us that you will not see Martin Warlock again."

Maggie flushed. "No, aunt, I can't promise that."

"Then we must treat you as a prisoner whilst you are with us."

"If he wants to see me I must see him."

They looked at one another. Aunt Anne was like a man just then.

"Very well. Until you give us your promise we must see ourselves that you do not disgrace us."

There was no more to be said. It was as though a heavy iron door had rolled to.

Aunt Anne passed Maggie and left the room.

Well, then, there was the situation. As she remained in the empty room she felt relief because now she knew where she was.

If only she could keep in touch with Martin then nothing else at all mattered. But that must be, otherwise she felt that she would rush at them all and tread them down and break doors and windows to get at him.

Meanwhile, how they must all have been talking! She felt no especial anger against Caroline Smith. It had been her own fault for trusting that note to her honour. Caroline had no honour, of course. Maggie might have guessed that from the way that she talked about other people. And then probably she herself was in love with Martin ... She sat down, staring in front of her, thinking. They all knew, Amy

Warlock, Mr. Thurston, Miss Avies—knew about that wonderful, marvellous thing, her love for Martin, his for her. They were turning it over in their hands, soiling it, laughing at it, sneering at it. And what were they doing to Martin? At that thought she sprang up and began hurriedly to walk about. Oh, they must leave him alone! What were they saying to him? They were telling him how ridiculous it was to have anything to do with a plain, ugly girl! And he? Was he defending her? At the sudden suggestion of his disloyalty indignation fought in her with some strange, horrible suspicion. Yes, it would come back, that thought. He was weak. He had told her that he was. He was weak. She KNEW that he was. She would not lie to herself. And then at the thought of his weakness the maternal love in her that was the strongest instinct in her character flooded her body and soul, so that she did not mind if he were weak, but only wanted to defend him, to protect him ...

Strangely, she felt more sure of him at that moment when she was conscious of his weakness than she had been when she asserted his strength. Beneath that weakness he would be true to her because he needed her. No one else could give him what she did; he had said so again and again. And it would always be so. He would have to come back to her however often he denied her.

She felt happier then. She could face them all. She had been bad to her aunts, too. She had done them harm, and they had been nothing but goodness to her. Apart from leaving Martin she would do all, these next weeks, to please them.

She went up to her bedroom, and when she reached it she realised, with a little pang of fright, that she was a prisoner. No more meetings outside Hatchards, no more teas, no more walks ... She looked out of the window down into the street. It was a long way down and the figures walking were puppets, not human at all. But the thing to be thought of now was the question of letters. How was she to get them to the Strand Office and receive from them Martin's letters in return? After long, anxious thought there seemed to be only one way. There was a kitchen-maid, Jane, who came every morning to the house, did odd jobs in the kitchen, and went home again in the evening. Maggie had seen the girl about the house a number of times, had noticed her for her rebellious, independent look, and had felt some sympathy with her because she was under the harsh dominion of Martha.

Maggie had spoken to her once or twice and the girl had seemed grateful, smiling in a kind of dark, tearful way under her untidy hair. Maggie believed that she would help her; of course the girl would get into trouble were she discovered, and dismissal would certainly follow, but it was clear enough that she would not in any case be under Martha's government very long. Martha never kept kitchen-maids for more than a month at a time.

She sat down at once and wrote her first letter, sitting on her bed.

DARLING MARTIN—There has been an explosion here. The aunts have told me to give you up. I could not promise them that I would not see you and so I am a prisoner here until I leave them altogether. I won't leave them until after the New Year, partly because I gave a promise and partly because it would make more trouble for you if I were turned out just now. I can't leave the house at all unless I am with one of them, so I am going to try and send the letters by the kitchen-maid here who goes home every day, and she will fetch yours when she posts mine. I'll give her a note to tell the post people that she is to have them. Martin, dear, try and write every day, even if it's only the shortest line, because it is dreadful to be shut up all day, and I think of you all the time and wonder how you are. Don't be unhappy, Martin—that's the one thing I couldn't bear. If you're not, I'm not. There's no reason to be unhappy about me. I'm very cheerful indeed if I know that you are all right. You are all right, aren't you?

I do want to know what happened when you got home. I quite understand that the one thing you must do now is to keep your father well and not let anything trouble him. If the thought of me troubles him, then tell him that you are thinking of nothing but him now and how to make him happy. But don't let them change your feeling for me. You know me better than any of them do and I am just as you know me, every bit. The aunts are very angry because they say I deceived them, but they haven't any right to tell me who I shall love, have they? No one has. I am myself and nobody's ever cared for me except you—and Uncle Mathew, so I don't see why I should think of anybody. The aunts never cared for me really—only to make me religious.

But, Martin, never forget I love you so much I can never change. I'm not one who changes, and although I'm young now I shall be just the same when I'm old. I have the ring and I look at it all the time. I like to think you have the locket. Please write, dear Martin, or I'll find it very difficult to stay quiet here, and I know I ought to stay quiet for your sake.

Your loving,

MAGGIE.

She put it in an envelope, wrote the address as he had told her, and then set out to find Jane. It was four o'clock in the afternoon now and the house, on this winter's day, was dark and dim.

The gas was always badly lit in the passages, spitting and muttering like an imprisoned animal. The house was so quiet when Maggie came out on to the stairs that there seemed to be no one in it. She found her way down into the hall and saw Thomas the cat there, moving like a black ghost along the floor. He came up to her and rubbed himself in his sinister, mysterious way against her dress. When she turned towards the green baize door that led towards the kitchen regions he stood back from her, stole on to the lower steps of the staircase and watched her with steady, unblinking eyes. She pushed the door and went through into the cold passage that smelt of cheese and bacon and damp earth. There seemed to be no one about, and then suddenly the pantry door opened and Jane came out. She stopped when she saw Maggie.

"Where's Martha?" asked Maggie in a low voice.

The whisper seemed to tell Jane at once that this was to be a confidential matter. She jerked with a dirty thumb in the direction of the kitchen.

"In there. Cooking the dinner," she whispered back. She was untidy, there were streaks of black on her face, but her eyes looked up at Maggie with a friendly, roguish glance, as though they had already something in common. Maggie saw that she had no time to lose. She came close to her.

"Jane," she said, "I'm in trouble. It's only you who can help me. Here's a letter that I want posted—just in the ordinary way. Can you do that for me?"

Jane, suddenly smiling, nodded her head.

"And there's something else," Maggie went on. "To-morrow morning, before you come here, I want you to go to the Strand post-office—you know the one opposite the station—and ask for a letter addressed to me. I've written on a piece of paper here that you're to be given any letters of mine. Give it to me somehow when no one's looking. Do you understand?"

Jane nodded her head. Maggie gave her the note and also half-a-crown, but Jane pushed back the money.

"I don't want no money," she said in a hoarse whisper. "You're the only one here decent to me."

At that moment the kitchen door opened and Martha appeared. When she saw Jane she came up to her and said: "Now then, idling again! What about the potatoes?"

She looked at Maggie with her usual surly suspicion.

"I came down for a candle," Maggie said, "for my room. Will you give me one, please?"

Jane had vanished.

Martin, meanwhile, after Maggie left him, had returned home in no happy state. There had leapt upon him again that mood of sullen impatient rebellion that he knew so well—a mood that really was like a possession, so that, struggle as he—might, he seemed always in the grip of some iron-fingered menacing figure.

It was possession in a sense that to many normal, happy people in this world is so utterly unknown that they can only scornfully name it weakness and so pass on their way. But those human beings who have suffered from it do in very truth feel as though they had been caught up into another world, a world of slavery, moral galley-driving with a master high above them, driving them with a lash that their chained limbs may not resist. Such men, if they try to explain that torment, can often point to the very day and even hour of their sudden slavery; at such a tick of the clock the clouds gather, the very houses and street are weighted with a cold malignity, thoughts, desires, impulses are all checked, perverted, driven and counter-driven by a mysterious force. Let no man who has not known such hours and the terror of such a dominion utter judgment upon his neighbour.

To Martin the threat of this conflict with his father over Maggie was the one crisis that he had wished to avoid. But his character, which was naturally easy and friendly and unsuspicious, had confused him. Those three weeks with Maggie had been so happy, so free from all morbidity and complication, that he had forgotten the world outside. For a moment when Maggie had told him that she had given her note to Caroline he had been afraid, but he had been lulled as the days passed and nothing interfered with their security. Now he was suddenly plunged into the middle of a confusion that was all the more complicated because he could not tell what his mother and his, sister were thinking. He knew that Amy had disliked him ever since his return, and that that dislike had been changed into something fiercer since his declared opposition to Thurston. His mother he simply did not understand at all. She spoke to him still with the same affection and tenderness, but behind the words he felt a hard purpose and a mysterious aloofness.

She was not like his mother at all; it was as though some spy had been introduced into the house in his mother's clothing.

But for them he did not care; it was his father of whom he must think. Here, too, there was a mystery from which he was deliberately kept. He knew, of course, that they were all expecting some crisis; as the days advanced he could feel that the excitement increased. He knew that his father had declared that he had visions and that there was to be a revelation very shortly; but of these visions and this revelation he heard only indirectly from others. His father said nothing to him of these things, and at the ordinary Chapel services on Sunday there was no allusion to them. He knew that the Inside Saints had a society and rules of their own inside the larger body, and from that inner society he was quite definitely excluded. Of that exclusion he would have been only too glad had it not been for his father, but now when he saw him growing from day to day more haggard and worn, more aloof from all human society, when lie saw him wrapped further and further into some strange and as it seemed to him insane absorption, he was determined to fight his way into the heart of it. His growing intimacy with Maggie had relieved him, for a moment, of the intensity of this other anxiety. Now suddenly he was flung back into the very thick of it. His earlier plan of forcing his father out of all this network of chicanery and charlatanism now returned. He felt that if he could only seize his father and forcibly abduct him and take him away from Amy and Thurston and the rest, and all the associations of the Chapel, he might cure him and lead him back to health and happiness again.

And yet he did not know. He had not himself escaped from it all by leaving it, and then that undermining bewildering suspicion that perhaps after all there was something in all of this, that it was not only charlatanism, confused and disconcerted him. He was like a man who hears sounds and faint cries behind a thick wall, and there are no doors and windows, and the bricks are too stout to be torn apart.

He had been behind that wall all his life ...

Amy's allusion to Maggie in the morning had been very slight, but had shown quite clearly that she had heard all, and probably more, than the truth. When he returned that morning he found his mother alone, knitting a pink woollen comforter, her gold spectacles on the end of her nose, her fresh lace cap crisp and dainty on her white hair—the very picture of the dearest old lady in the world.

"Mother," he began at once, "what did Amy mean this morning about myself and Maggie Cardinal?"

"Maggie who, dear?" his mother asked.

"Maggie Cardinal—the Cardinal niece, you know," he said impatiently.

"Did she say anything? I don't remember."

"Yes, mother. You remember perfectly well. She said that they were all talking about me and Maggie."

"Did she?" The old lady slowly counted her stitches. "Well, dear, I shouldn't worry about what they all say—whoever 'they' may be."

"Oh, I don't care for that," he answered contemptuously, "although all the same I'm not going to have Amy running that girl down. She's been against her from the first. What I want to know is has Amy been to father with this? Because if she has I'm going to stop it. I'm not going to have her bothering father with bits of gossip that she's picked up by listening behind other peoples' key-holes."

Amy, meanwhile, had come in and heard this last sentence.

"Thank you, Martin," she said quietly.

He turned to her with fury. "What did you mean at breakfast," he asked, "by what you said about myself and Maggie Cardinal?"

She looked at him with contempt but no very active hostility.

"I was simply telling you something that I thought you ought to know," she said. "It is what everybody is saying—that you and she have been meeting every day for weeks, sitting in the Park after dark together, going to the theatre. People draw their own conclusions, I suppose."

"How much have you told father of this?" he demanded.

"I don't know at all what father has heard," she answered.

"You've been that girl's enemy since the first moment that she came here," he continued, growing angrier and angrier at her quiet indifference. "Now you're trying to damage her character."

"On the contrary," she answered, "I told you because I thought you ought to know what people were saying. The girl doesn't matter to me one way or another—but I'm sorry for her if she thinks she cares for you. That won't bring her much happiness."

Then suddenly her impassivity had a strange effect upon him. He could not answer her. He left them both, and went up to his room.

As soon as he had closed the door of his bedroom he knew that his bad time was come upon him. It was a physical as well as a spiritual dominion. The room visibly darkened before his eyes, his brain worked as it would in dreams suggesting its own thoughts and wishes and intentions. A dark shadow hung over him, hands were placed upon his eyes, only one thought came before him again and again and again. "You know, you have long known, that you are doomed to make miserable everything that you touch, to ruin every one with whom you come in contact. That is your fate, and you can no more escape from it than you can escape from your body!"

How many hours of this kind he had known in Spain, in France, in South America. Often at the very moment when he had thought that he was at last settling down to some decent steady plan of life he would be jerked from his purpose, some delay or failure would frustrate him, and there would follow the voice in his ear and the hands on his eyes.

It was indeed as though he had been pledged to something in his early life, and because he had broken from that pledge had been pursued ever since ...

He stripped to the waist and bathed in cold water; even then it seemed to him that his flesh was heavy and dull and yellow, that he was growing obese and out of all condition. He put on a clean shirt and collar, sat down on his bed and tried to think the thing out. To whomsoever he had done harm in the past he would now spare Maggie and his father. He was surprised at the rush of tenderness that came over him at the thought of Maggie; he sat there for some time thinking over every incident of the last three weeks; that, at least, had been a good decent time, and no one could ever take it away from them again. He looked at her picture in the locket and realised, as he looked at it, a link with her that he had never felt with any woman before. "All the same," he thought, "I should go away. She'd mind it at first, but not half as much as she'd mind me later on when she saw what kind of a chap I really was. She'd be unhappy a bit, but she'd soon meet some one else. She's never seen a man yet except me. She'd soon forget me. She's such a kid."

Nevertheless when he thought of beginning that old wandering life again he shrank back. He had hated it—Oh! how he'd hated it! And he didn't want to leave Maggie. He was in reality beginning to believe that with her he might pull himself right out of this morass of weakness and indecision in which he had been wallowing for years. And yet what sort of a life could he offer her? He did not believe that he would ever now be able to find this other woman whom he had married, and until he had found her and divorced her Maggie's position would be impossible. She, knowing nothing of the world, could disregard it, but HE knew, knew that daily, hourly recurrence of alights and insults and disappointments, knew what that life could make after a time of women in such a position; even though she did not mind he would mind for her and would reproach himself continually.

No, it was impossible. He must go away secretly, without telling her ... Then, at that, he was pulled up again by the thought of his father. He could not leave him until this crisis, whatever it might be, was over. A very little thing now might kill him, and at the thought of that possibility he jumped up from his bed and swore that THAT catastrophe at least must be prevented. His father must live and be happy and strong again, and he, Martin, must see to it.

That was his charge and his sacred duty above all else.

Strong in this thought he went down to his father's room. He knocked on the door. There was no answer, and he went in. The room was in a mess of untidiness. His father was walking up and down, staring in front of him, talking to himself.

At the sound of the door he turned, saw Martin and smiled, the old trusting smile of a child, that had been, during his time abroad, Martin's clearest memory of him.

"Oh, is that you? Come in."

Martin came forward and his father put his arm round his neck as though for support.

"I'm tired—horribly tired." Martin took him to the shabby broken arm-chair and made him sit down. Himself sat in his old place on the arm of the chair, his hand against his father's neck.

"Father, come away—just for a week—with me. We'll go right off into the country to Glebeshire or somewhere, quite alone. We won't see a soul. We'll just walk and eat and sleep. And then you'll come back to your work here another man."

"No, Martin. I can't yet. Not just now."

"Why not, father?"

"I have work, work that can't be left."

"But if you go on like this you'll be so that you can't go on any longer. You'll break down. You know what the doctor said about your heart. You aren't taking any care at all."

"Perhaps ... perhaps ... but for a week or two I must just go on, preparing ... many things ... Martin."

He suddenly looked up at his son, putting his hand on his knee.

"Yes, father."

"You're being good now, aren't you?"

"Good, father?"

"Yes ... Not doing anything you or I'd be ashamed of. I know in the past ... but that's been forgotten, that's over. Only now, just now, it's terribly important for us both that you should be good ... like you used to be ... when you were a boy."

"Father, what have people been saying to you about me?"

"Nothing—nothing. Only I think about you so much. I pray about you all the time. Soon, as you say, we'll go away together ... only now, just now, I want you with me here, strong by my side. I want your help."

Martin took his father's hand, felt how dry and hot and feverish it was.

"I'll be with you," he said. "I promise that. Don't you listen to what any one says. I won't leave you." He would like to have gone on and asked other questions, but the old man seemed so worn out and exhausted that he was afraid of distressing him, so he just sat there, his hands on his shoulders, and suddenly the white head nodded, the beard sank over the breast and huddled up in the chair as though life itself had left him; the old man slept.

During the next four days Martin and Maggie corresponded through the fair hands of Jane. He wrote only short letters, and over them he struggled. He seemed to see Maggie through a tangled mist of persons and motives and intentions. He could not get at the real Maggie at all, he could not even get at his real feelings about her. He knew that these letters were not enough for her, he could feel behind her own a longing for something from him more definite, something that would bring her closer to him. He was haunted by his picture of her sitting in that dismal house, a prisoner, waiting for him, and at last, at the end of the four days, he felt that he must, in some way or other see her. Then she herself proposed a way.

"To-morrow night (Friday)," she wrote, "the aunts are going to a meeting. They won't return until after eight o'clock. During most of that time Martha will be in the kitchen cooking, and Jane (who is staying late that night) has promised to give me a signal. I could run out for quarter of an hour and meet you somewhere close by and risk getting back. Jane will be ready to let me in. Of course, it may fail, but things can't be worse than they are ... I absolutely forbid you to come if you think that this can make anything worse for you at home. But I MUST see you, Martin ... I feel to-night as though I couldn't stand it any longer (although I've only had five days of it!), but I think that if I met you, really you, for only five minutes, I could bear it then for weeks. Let me know if you agree to this, and if so where we could meet about 7.30."

The mere thought of seeing her was wonderful. He would not have believed a month ago that it could have come to mean so much to him.

He wrote back:

"Yes. At the corner of Dundas Street, by the Pillar Box, 7.30."

He knew that she had been to that dark little street with her aunts to see Miss Pyncheon.

The night, when it came, was misty, and when he reached the place she was at once in his arms. She had been there more than five minutes, she had thought that he was not coming. Martha had nearly caught her ...

He kissed her hair and her eyes and her mouth, holding her to him, forgetting everything but her. She stayed, quiet, clinging to him as though she would never let him go, then she drew away.

"Now we must walk about or some one will see us," she said.

"We've only got five minutes. Martin, what I want to know is, are you happy?"

"Yes," he said.

They walked like ghosts, in the misty street.

"Well, then I am," she said. "Only your letters didn't sound very happy."

"Can you hold on till after the New Year?" They were walking hand in hand, her fingers curled in his palm.

"Yes," she said. "If you're happy."

"There are troubles of course," he said. "But I don't care for Amy and the rest. It's only father that matters. I can't discover how much he knows. If I knew that I'd be much happier. We'll be all right, Maggie, if nothing happens to him."

With a little frightened catch in her throat she asked him:

"How do you mean, if anything happens to him?"

"If anything happened to him—" she could feel his hand stiffen round hers; "through me—then—why then—I'd leave you—everything—I'd have to."

"Leave me! ... Oh Martin! No!"

"I'd go. I'd go—I don't know where to. I don't know what I'd do. I'd know then that I must leave every one alone, always, for ever—especially you."

"No. You'd need me more than ever."

"You don't understand, Maggie. I'd be impossible after that. If father suffered through me that would be the end of it—the end of everything."

"Martin, listen." She caught his arm, looking up, trying to see his face. "If anything like that did happen that would be where you'd want me. Don't you see that you COULDN'T harm me EXCEPT by leaving me?"

"You can reason it as you like, Maggie, but I know myself. I know the impulse would be too strong—to go away and hide myself from everybody. I've felt it before—when I've done something especially bad. It's something in me that I've known all my life." Then he turned to her: "But it's all right. Nothing shall happen to the old man. I'll see that it doesn't. We've only got to wait a fortnight, then I'll get him away for a holiday. And once he's better I can leave him. It WILL be all right. It SHALL."

Then he bent down to her. "You know, Maggie, I love you more, far more than I ever thought. Even if I went away you'd be the only one I'd love. I never dreamt that I'd care for any one so much."

He felt her tremble under his hand when he said that.

She sighed. "Now I can go back," she said. "I'll say that over to myself again and again."

They stayed a little longer, he put his arms round her again and held her so close to him that she could feel his heart throbbing. Then when they had kissed once more she went away.

She returned safely. Jane opened the door for her, mysteriously, as though she enjoyed her share in the conspiracy. Maggie sped upstairs, and now with Martin's words in her ears, had enough to stiffen her back for the battle.

The next move in the affair was on the following afternoon when Maggie, alone in the drawing-room, beheld Caroline Smith in the doorway.

"She's got cheek enough for anything," was Maggie's first thought, but she was not aware of the true magnificence of that young woman's audacity until she found her hand seized and her cheek kissed.

Caroline, in fact, had greeted her with precisely her old spontaneous enthusiasm.

"Maggie, darling, where have you been all these days—but WEEKS it is indeed! You might at least have sent me just a word. Life simply hasn't been the same without you! You pet! ... and you look tired! Yes, you do. You've been overworking or something, all because you haven't had me to look after you!"

Maggie gravely withdrew, and standing away from the shining elegance of her friend said:

"Caroline—I want to know something before we go any further. What I want to know is—why did you read that note that I asked you to give to Martin Warlock?"

Caroline stared in amazement. "My dear, what IS the matter? Are you ill or something? Oh, you are. I can see you are! You poor darling! Read your note? What note, dear?"

"The note I gave you a month ago—one evening when you were here."

"A note! A month ago. My dear! As though I could ever remember what I did a MONTH ago! Why, it's always all I can manage to remember what I did yesterday. Did you give me a note, dear?"

Maggie began to be angry. "Of course I did. You remember perfectly well. I gave it to you for Martin Warlock. You let him have it, but meanwhile you read it, and not only that but told everybody else about it."

Caroline's expression changed. She was suddenly sulky. Her face was like that of a spoilt child.

"Well, Maggie Cardinal, if you call that being a friend! To say that I would ever do such a thing!"

"You know you did!" said Maggie quietly.

"Read your letters? As though I'd want to! Why should I? As though I hadn't something more interesting to do! No thank you! Of course you have been getting yourself into a mess. Every one knows that. That's why I came here to-day—to show you that I was a REAL friend and didn't mind WHAT people said about you! When they were all talking about you last night, and saying the most DREADFUL things, I defended you and said it wasn't really your fault, you couldn't have told what a rotten sort of a man Martin Warlock was—"

"That's enough," said Maggie. "I don't want your defence, thank you. You're mean and deceitful and untrue. You never have been a friend of mine, and I don't want ever to see you again!"

Caroline Smith was horrified. "Well, upon my word. Isn't that gratitude? Here am I, the only person in this whole place would take any trouble with you! When the others all said that you were plain and stupid and hadn't anything to say for yourself I stuck to you. I did all I could, wasting all my time going to the dressmaker with you and trying to make you look like something human, and this is the way you repay me! Well, there's a lesson for me! Many's the time mother's said to me, 'Carry, you'll just ruin yourself with that kind heart of yours, laying yourself out for others when you ought to be seeing after yourself. You've got too big a heart for this world.' Doesn't it just show one? And to end it all with accusing me of reading your letters! If you choose to sit in the park after dark with a man who everybody knows—"

"Either you're going to leave this room or I am," said Maggie.

"Thank you!" said Caroline, tossing her head. "I haven't the slightest desire to stay, I assure you! Only you'll be sorry for this, Maggie Cardinal, you will indeed!"

With a swish of the skirts and a violent banging of the door she was gone.

"The only friend I had," thought Maggie.

The next development was an announcement from Aunt Anne that she would like Maggie to accompany her to a meeting at Miss Avies'. Aunt Anne did not explain what kind of a meeting it would be, and Maggie asked no questions. She simply replied that she would go. She had indeed by this time a very considerable curiosity of her own as to what every one thought was going to happen in ten days' time. Perhaps this meeting would enlighten her. It did.

On arriving at Miss Avies' gaunt and menacing apartment she found herself in the very stronghold of the Inside Saints. It was a strange affair, and Maggie was never to see anything quite like it again. In the first place, Miss Avies' room was not exactly the place in which you would have expected to discover a meeting of this kind.

She lived over a house-agent's in John Street, Adelphi. Her sitting-room was low-ceilinged with little diamond-paned windows. The place was let furnished, and the green and red vases on the mantelpiece, the brass clock and the bright yellow wallpaper were properties of the landlord. To the atmosphere of the place Miss Avies, although she lived there for a number of years, had contributed nothing.

It had all the desolate forlornness of a habitation in which no human being has dwelt for a very long time; there was dust on the mantelpiece, a melancholy sputtering of coal choked with cinders and gasping for breath in the fireplace, stuffy hot clamminess beating about the unopened windows. Along the breadth of the faded brown carpet some fifty cane-bottomed chairs were pressed tightly in rows together, and in front of the window, facing the chairs, was a little wooden table with a chair beside it, on the table a glass of water and a Bible.

When Maggie and her aunts entered the chairs were almost all occupied and they were forced to sit at the end of the last row but one. The meeting had apparently not yet begun, and many heads were turned towards them as they took their places. Maggie fancied that the glances directed at herself were angry and severe, but that was very possibly her imagination. She soon recognised people known to her—Miss Pyncheon, calm and placid; Mrs. Smith, Caroline's mother, very stout, hot, and self-important; Amy Warlock, proud and severe; and Miss Avies herself standing, like a general surveying his forces, behind the table.

The room was draughty and close and had a confused smell of oil-cloth and geraniums, and Maggie knew that soon she would have a headache. She fancied that already the atmosphere was influencing the meeting. From where she sat she could see a succession of side faces, and it was strange what a hungry, appealing look these pale cheeks and staring eyes had. Hungry! Yes, that's what they all were. She thought, fantastically, for a moment, of poor Mr. Magnus's Treasure Hunters, and she seemed to see the whole of this company in a raft drifting in mid-ocean, not a sail in sight and the last ship's biscuit gone.

They were not, taken altogether, a very fine collection, old maids and young girls, many of them apparently of the servant class, one or two sitting with open mouths and a vacancy of expression that seemed to demand a conjurer with a rabbit and a hat. Some faces were of the true fanatic cast, lit with the glow of an expectancy and a hope that no rational experience had ever actually justified. One girl, whom Maggie had seen with Aunt Anne on some occasion, had especially this prophetic anticipation in the whole pose of her body as she bent forward a little, her elbows on her knees her chin on her hands, gazing with wide burning eyes at Miss Avies. This girl, whom Maggie was never to see again hung as a picture in the rooms of her mind for the rest of her life—the youth, the desperate anxiety as of one who throws her last piece upon the gaming-table, the poverty of the shabby black dress, the real physical austerity and asceticism of the white cheeks and the thin arms and pale hands—this figure remained a symbol for Maggie. She used to wonder in after years, when fortune had carried her far enough away from all this world, what had happened to that girl. But she was never to know.

There were faces, too, like Miss Pyncheon's, calm, contented, confident, old women who had found in their religion the panacea of all their troubles. There were faces like Mrs. Smith's, coarse and vulgar, out for any sensation that might come along, and ready instantly to express their contempt if the particular "trick" that they were expecting failed to come off; other faces, again, like Amy Warlock's, grimly set upon secret thoughts and purposes of their own, faces trained to withstand any sudden attack on the emotions, but eager, too, like the rest for some revelation that was to answer all questions and satisfy all expectations.

Maggie wondered, as she looked about her, how she could have raised in her own imagination, around the Chapel and its affairs, so formidable an atmosphere of terror and tyrannic discipline. Here gathered together were a few women, tired, pale, many of them uneducated, awaiting like children the opening of a box, the springing into flower of a dry husk of a seed, the raising of the curtain on some wonderful scene. Maggie, as she looked at them, knew that they must be disappointed, and her heart ached for them all, yes, even for Amy Warlock, her declared enemy. She lost, as she sat there, for the moment all sense of her own personal history. She only saw them all tired and hungry and expectant; perhaps, after all, there WAS something behind it all—something for which they had a right to be searching; even of that she had not sure knowledge—but the pathos and also the bravery of their search touched and moved her. She was beginning to understand something of the beauty that hovered like a bird always just out of sight about the ugly walls of the Chapel.

"Whatever they want, poor dears," she thought, "I do hope they get it."

Miss Avies opened the meeting with an extempore prayer: then they all stood up and sang a hymn, and their quavering voices were thin and sharp and strained in the stuffy close-ceilinged room. The hymn, like all the other Chapel hymns that Maggie had heard, had to do with "the Blood of the Lamb," "the sacrifice of Blood," "the Blood that heals." There was also a refrain:

And, when Thou comest, Lord, we pray That Thou wilt spare Thy sword, Or on that grim and ghastly day Who will escape the Lord? WHO will escape the Lord?

There were many verses to this hymn, and it had a long and lugubrious tune, so that Maggie thought that it would never end, but as it proceeded the words worked their effect on the congregation, and at the last there was much emotion and several women were crying.

Then they all sat down again and the meeting developed a very business-like side. There was a great deal of discussion as to dates, places, appointments, and Maggie was amused to discover that in this part of the proceedings Mrs. Smith had a great deal to say, and took a very leading place.

The gathering became like any other assemblage of ladies for some charitable or social purpose, and there were the usual disputes and signs of temper and wounded pride; in all those matters Miss Avies was a most admirable and unflinching chairman.

Then at last the real moment came. Miss Avies got up to speak. She stood there, scornful, superior, and yet with some almost cynical appeal in her eyes as though she said to them: "You poor fools! No one knows better than I the folly of your being here, no one knows better than I how far you will, all of you, be from realising any of your dreams. Tricked, the lot of you!—and yet—and yet—go on believing, expecting, hoping. Pray, pray that I may be wrong and you may be right."

What she actually said was as follows: "This will be our last meeting before the end of the year. What will come to all of us before we all meet again no one can say, but this we all know, that we have, most of us, been living now for many years in expectation. We have been taught, by the goodness of God, to believe that we must be ready at any moment to obey His call, and that call may come, in the middle of our work, of our prayers, of our love for others, of our pursuit of our own ambitions, and that whenever it does come we must be ready to obey it. We have been told by our great and good Master, who has been set over us for our guidance by God Himself, that that call may now be very near. Whatever form it may take we must accept it, give up all we have and follow Him. That is understood by all of us. I will not say more now. This is not the time for any more directions from me. We must address ourselves, each one of us, to God Himself, and ask Him to prepare us so that we may be as He would have us on the day of His coming. I suggest now before we part that we share together in a few minutes of private prayer." They all rose, and Maggie, before she knelt down, caught a sudden glimpse of the pale girl whom she had noticed earlier standing for a moment as though she were about to make some desperate appeal to them all. Some words did indeed seem to come from her lips, but the scraping of chairs drowned every other sound. Nevertheless that figure was there, the hands stretched out, the very soul struggling through the eyes for expression, the body tense, sacred, eloquent, like the body of some young prophetess. Then all were on their knees, and Maggie, too, her face in her hands, was praying. It was, perhaps, the first time in her life that she had actively, consciously, of her own volition prayed. The appeal formed itself as it were without her own agency.

"God—if there is a God—give me Martin. I care for nothing else but that. If You will give me Martin for my own always, ever, I will believe in You. I will worship You and say prayers to You, and do anything You tell me if You give me Martin. Oh God! I ought to have him. He is mine. I can do more for him than any one else can—I can make him happy and good. I know I can. God give him to me and I will be your slave. God, give me Martin—God, give me Martin."

She rose, as it were, from the depths of the sea, from great darkness and breathlessness and exhaustion. For a moment she could not see the room nor any detail, but only one pale face after another, like a pattern on a wall, hiding something from her.

She stood bewildered beside her aunts, not hearing the strains of the last hymn nor the quaver of Aunt Anne's trembling voice beside her.

"God, give me Martin," was her last challenge in the strange pale silence that floated around her. Then suddenly, as though she had pushed open a door and gone through, she was back in the world again, a flood of sound was about her ears, and in front of her the red face of Mrs. Smith, her mouth wide open, like the mouth of an eager fish, singing about "the Blood of the Lamb" with unctuous satisfaction ...

CHAPTER X

THE PROPHET

The year 1907 had four more days of life: it crept to its grave through a web and tangle of fog. It was not one of the regular yellow devils who come and eat up London, first this part, and then that, then disgorge a little, choking it all up only to snap at it and swallow it down all bewildered a quarter of an hour after. This was a cobweb fog spun, as it might be, by some malignant central spider hidden darkly in his lair. The vapouring-like filmy threads twisted and twined their way all over London, and for four days and nights the town was a city of ghosts. Buildings loomed dimly behind their masks of silver tissue, streets seemed unsubstantial, pavements had no foundation, streams of water appeared to hang glittering in mid-air, men and horses would suddenly plunge into grey abysses and vanish from sight, church-bells would ring peals high up in air, and there would be, it seemed, no steeple there for them to ring from. As the sun behind the fog rose and set so the mist would catch gold and red and purple into the vapours, strange gleams of brass and silver as though behind its web armies flaunting their colours were marching through the sky; down on the very earth itself horses staggered and stumbled on the thin coating of greasy mud that covered everything; men opened their doors to look out on to the world, and instantly into the passages there floated such strange forms and shadows in misty shape that it seemed as though the rooms were suddenly invaded by a flock of spirits.

Sometimes for half an hour the fog lifted and bright blue sky gleamed like a miraculous lake suddenly discovered in the heart of the boundless waste, then vanished again. Suddenly, with a whisk of the immortal broom, the web was torn, the spider slain, the world clear once more—but, in the obscurity and dusk, 1907 had seen his chance and vanished.

Warlock, long before this, had lost consciousness of external sights and sounds. He could not have told any one when it was that the two worlds had parted company. For many many years he had been conscious of both existences, but during his youth and middle-age they had seemed to mingle and go along together. He had believed in both equally and had been a citizen of both. Then gradually, as time passed, he had seemed to have less and less hold upon the actual physical world. He saw it suddenly with darkened vision; his wife and daughter, and indeed all human beings, except in so far as they were souls to be saved for the Lord, became less and less realities. Only Martin was flesh and blood, to be loved and longed for and feared for just as he had always been. All the physical properties of life— clothes, food, household possessions, money—became of less and less importance to him. Had Amy not watched over him he would have been many days without any food at all, and one day he come into the living-room at breakfast-time clothed in a towel. All this had come upon him with vastly increased power during the last months. In Chapel, and whenever he had work to do in connection with the Chapel, he was clear-headed and practical, but in things to do with this world he was now worse than a child.

He was conscious of this increasing difficulty to deal with both worlds. It was because one world—the world of God—was opening out before him so widely and with so varied and thrilling a beauty that there was less and less time to be spared for the drab realities of physical things.

All his life he had been preparing, and then suddenly the call had come. Shortly after Martin's return he had known in Chapel, one evening, that God was approaching. It had happened that that day, owing to his absorption in his work, he had eaten nothing, and there had come to him, whilst praying to the congregation, a sensation of faintness so strong that for a moment he thought he would fall from his seat. Then it had passed, to give way to a strange, thrilling sense of expectancy. It was as though a servant had opened the door and had announced: "My master is coming, sir—" He had felt, indeed, as though he had been lifted up, in the sheet of Paul the Apostle, to meet his God. There had been the most wonderful sense of elevation, a clearing of light, a gentler freshness in the air, a sudden sinking to remoteness of human voices and mundane sounds. From that moment in the Chapel life had been changed for him. He never seemed to come down again from that mysterious elevation. Human voices sounded far away from him; he could be urged, only with the greatest difficulty, to take his food, and he frequently did not recognise members of his own congregation when they came to see him. He waited now, waited, waited, for this visitation that was approaching him. He could have no doubts of it.

Then one night he woke from a deep sleep. He was conscious that his room was filled with a smoky light; in his heart was such an ecstasy that he would have thought that the joy would kill him.

Something spoke to him, telling him to prepare, that he had been chosen, and that further signs would come to him. He fell on his knees beside the bed and remained there in a trance until daylight. He had heard the voice of God, he had seen His light, he had been chosen as His servant. Some weeks later a second visitation came to him, similar to the first, but telling him that at the last hour of the present year God would come in His own person to save the world, and that he must make this known to a few chosen spirits that they might prepare …

The whole brotherhood then was at length justified; they alone, out of all men in the world, had believed in the Second Coming of the Lord, and so God had chosen them. He had no doubt at all about his visions at this time. They seemed to him as real and sure as the daily traffic of the streets and the monotonous progress of the clock.

Eagerly, with the confident resolution of a child, he told his news to the leaders of the Chapel, Thurston, Miss Avies, and one or two others. Then a special meeting of the Inside Saints was called and, in the simplest language, he described exactly what had occurred. He did not at first perceive the effect that his news had. Then, dimly, through the mist of his prayers and ecstasies, he realised that his message had created confusion. There was in the first place the question as to whether the whole congregation should be told. He found that he could not decide about this, and when he left the judgment to Thurston, Thurston told him that, in his opinion, "the less that they knew about it the better." It was then that the first suspicion came to him as to whether some of the Saints "doubted." He questioned Thurston as to the effect of this message upon the Saints. Thurston explained to him that "many of them had been very troubled. They had not expected It to come so soon." Thurston explained that they were, after all, only poor human clay like the rest of mankind, and to prepare for a Second Coming in general, something that might descend upon the world, say, in a hundred years' time, was very different from a Judgment that might be expected, definitely, in about three weeks. One or two of them, in fact, had left the Chapel. Others begged for some clearer direction: "Give it them a bit more clearly, Master. Tell 'em a few facts what the Lord God looked like and 'ow He spoke and in what kind of way He was coming. Supposing He wasn't to come after all …"

It was then that the trouble that had been smouldering for so long between Thurston and the Master burst into flame. For half an hour the Master lost his temper like an ordinary human being. Thurston said very little but listened with a quiet and sarcastic smile. Then he went away. Warlock was left in a torment of doubt and misery. That night he was in his room, until the dawn, on his knees, wrestling with God. He accused himself because, during these latter months, he had removed himself from human contact with his congregation. He had been so intent upon God that he had forgotten his flock. Now he hardly knew how to approach them. The thought of a personal interview with the Miss Cardinals, or Miss Pyncheon, or Mr. Smith filled him with a strange shy terror. He seemed to have nothing more to say to them, and he blamed himself bitterly because he had been intent upon his own salvation rather than theirs.

Thurston's words sent him groping back through the details of the visions. And there were no details. For himself there had been enough in the light, the ecstasy, the contact, but these others who had not themselves felt this, nor seen its glory, demanded more.

He began then, in an agony of distress, to question himself as to whether he had not dreamt his visions. He wrestled with God, beseeching Him to come again and give him a clearer message. Night after night passed and he waited for some further vision, but nothing was granted him. Then he thought that perhaps he himself was now cursed for leaving God. God had come to him and revealed Himself to him in unmistakable signs, and yet he was doubting Him and demanding further help.

As the weeks passed he perceived more and more clearly that there was every kind of division and trouble in the Chapel. Many members left and wrote to him telling him why they had done so. In his own household he felt that Amy no longer gave him any confidence. She attended to him more carefully than before, watched over him as though he were a baby, but made no allusion to the services or the Chapel or any meeting. He seemed, as the weeks passed, to be lonelier and lonelier, and he looked upon this as punishment for his own earlier selfishness. He was pulled then two ways. On the one hand it seemed to him that he would only hear God's full message if he withdrew further and further from the world, on the other he felt that he was letting his followers slip away from him now at the very moment when he should be closest to them, advising, helping, encouraging. This divided impulse was a torture, and as the weeks went on he ate less and less and slept scarcely at all. He had been for a long time past in delicate health owing to the weakness of his heart, and now he began to look strange indeed, with his bright gaunt face with its prominent cheek-bones, his eyes straining to see beyond his actual vision, his flowing white beard. His doctor, a cheerful, commonplace little man, a member of the Chapel, although not a Saint, tried to do his best with him, but his visits only led to scenes of irritation, and Warlock obeyed none of his commands. After a visit on the afternoon of Christmas Eve he took Amy aside:

"Look here," he said, "unless you keep a stricter eye on your father than you have been doing he'll be leaving you altogether."

She looked up at him with that odd dark impassivity that seemed to remove her so deliberately from her fellow-beings.

"It's very well to talk like that," she said. "But how is any one to have any control over him? He listens to nothing that we say, and if we insist he's in a frenzy of irritation."

"Can your mother do nothing?" the doctor asked.

"Mother?" Amy smiled. "No, mother can do nothing."

"Well," said the doctor, "any sudden shock will kill him—I warn you."

When the fog came down upon the city Warlock was already in too thick a fog of his own to perceive it.

He was sure now of nothing. It seemed as though all the spirits of the other world now were taunting him, but he felt that this was the work of the Devil, who wished to destroy his faith before the Great Day arrived. He thought now that the Devil was closely pursuing him, and he seemed to hear first his taunting whisper and then the voice of God encouraging him: "Well done, my good and faithful servant."

He had lost now almost all consciousness of what he really expected to happen when the Day arrived, but he was dimly aware that if nothing happened at all his whole influence with his people would be gone. Nevertheless this did not trouble him very greatly; the congregation of the Chapel seemed now dimly remote. The only human being who was not remote was Martin; his love for his son had not been touched by his other struggles, it had been even intensified. But the love had grown a terror, ever increasing, lest Martin should leave him. He seemed to hear dimly, beyond the wall of the mysterious world into whose regions he was ever more deeply passing, sentences, vague, without human agency, accusing Martin of sins and infidelities and riotous living. Sometimes he was tempted to go further into this and challenge Martin's accusers, but fear held him back. Martin had been a good son since his return to England, yes, he had, and he had forsaken his evil ways and was going to be with his father now until the end, his last refuge against loneliness. Every one else had left him or was leaving him, but Martin was there. Martin hadn't deceived him, Martin was a good boy ... a good boy ... and then, as it seemed to him, with Martin's hand in his own he would pass off into his world of strange dreams and desperate prayer and hours of waiting, listening, straining for a voice ...

During that last night before New Year's Eve an hour came to him when he seemed to be left utterly alone. Exhausted, faint, dizzy with want of sleep and food, he knelt before his bed; his room seemed to be filled with devils, taunting him, tempting him, bewildering and blinding him. He rose suddenly in a frenzy, striking out, rushing about his room, crying ... then at last, exhausted, creeping back to his bed, falling down upon it and sinking into a long dreamless sleep.

They found him sleeping when they came to call him and they left him. He did not wake until the early afternoon; his brain seemed clear and his body so weak that it was with the greatest difficulty that he washed and put on some clothes.

The room was dark with the fog; lamps in the street below glimmered uncertainly, and voices and the traffic of the street were muffled. He opened his door and, looking out, heard in the room below Martin's voice raised excitedly. Slowly he went down to meet him.

Martin also had reached, on that last day of the year, the very end of his tether. During the last ten days he had been fighting against every weakness to which his character was susceptible. With the New Year he felt that everything would be well; he could draw a new breath then, find work somewhere away from London, have Maggie perhaps with him, and drive a way out of all the tangle of his perplexities. But even then he did not dare to face the future thoroughly. Would his father let him go? Was he, after all his struggles, to give way and ruin Maggie's position and future? Could he be sure, if he look her away with him, that then he would keep straight, and that his old temptations of women and drink and general restlessness would be conquered? Perhaps. There had never been a surer proof that his love for Maggie was a real and unselfish love than his hesitation on that wretched day when he seemed utterly deserted by mankind, when Maggie seemed the only friend he had in the world.

Everything was just out of reach, and some perverse destiny prevented him from realising any desire that had a spark of honesty and decency in it. It was not wonderful that in the midst of his loneliness and unhappiness he should have been tempted back to the old paths again, men, women, places that for more than three months now he had been struggling to abandon.

All that day he struggled with temptation. He had not seen Maggie for a week, and during the last three days he had not heard from her, the adventurous Jane having defied the aunts and left.

At luncheon he asked about his father, whom he had not seen for two days.

"Father had a very bad night. He's asleep now."

"There's something on to-night, isn't there?" he asked.

"There's a service," Amy answered shortly.

"Father oughtn't to go," he went on. "I suppose your friend Thurston can manage."

Amy looked at him. "Father's got to go. It's very important."

"Oh, of course, if you want to kill father with all your beastly services—" he broke in furiously.

"It won't be—" Amy began, and then, as though she did not trust herself to continue, got up and left the room.

"Mother," he said, "why on earth don't you do something?"

"I, dear?" she looked at him placidly. "In what way?"

"They're killing father between them with all these services and the rest of the nonsense."

"Your father doesn't listen to anything I say, dear."

"He ought to go away for a long rest."

"Well, dear, perhaps he will soon. You know I have nothing to do with the Chapel. That was settled years ago. I wouldn't interfere for a great deal."

Martin turned fiercely upon her saying:

"Mother, don't you care?"

"Care, dear?"

"Yes, about father—his living and getting well again and being happy as he used to be. What's happened to this place?"

She looked at him in the strangest way. He suddenly felt that he'd never seen her before.

"There are a number of things, Martin, that you don't understand—a number of things. You are away from us for years, you come back to us and expect things to be the same."

"You and Amy," he said, "both of you, have kept me out of everything since I came back. I believe you both hate me!"

She got up slowly from her seat, slowly put her spectacles away in their case, rubbed her fat little hands together, then suddenly licked inquisitively one finger as an animal might do. She spoke to him over her shoulder as she went to the door:

"Oh no, Martin, you speak too strongly."

Left then to his own devices he, at last, wandered out into the foggy streets. After a while he found himself outside a public-house and, after a moment's hesitation, he went in. He asked the stout, rubicund young woman behind the counter for a whisky. She gave him one; he drank that, and then another.

Afterwards he had several more, leaning over the bar, speaking to no one, seeing no one, hearing nothing, and scarcely tasting the drink. When he came out into the street again he knew that he was half drunk—not so drunk that he didn't know what he was doing. Oh dear, no. HE could drink any amount without feeling it. Nevertheless he had drunk so little during these last weeks that even a drop ... How foggy the streets were ... made it difficult to find your way home. But he was all right, he could walk straight, he could put his latch-key into the door at one try, HE was all right.

He was at home again. He didn't stop to hang up his hat and coat but went straight into the dining-room, leaving the door open behind him. He saw that the meal was still on the table just as they'd left it. Amy was there too.

He saw her move back when he came in as though she were afraid to touch him.

"You're drunk!" she said.

"I'm not. You're a liar, Amy. You've always been a liar all your life."

She tried to pass him, but he stood in the middle of the door.

"No, you don't," he said. "We've got to have this out. What have you been spreading scandal about me and Maggie Cardinal for?"

"Let me go," she said again.

"Tell me that first. You've always tried to do me harm. Why?"

"Because I hate the sight of you," she answered quickly. "As you've asked me, you shall have a truthful answer. You've never been anything but a disgrace to us ever since you were a little boy. You disgraced us at home and then abroad; now you've come back to disgrace us here again."

"That's a lie," he repeated. "I've not disgraced anybody."

"Well, it won't be very long before you finish ruining that wretched girl. The best you can do now is to marry her."

"I can't do that," he said. "I'm married already." She did not answer that hut stared at him with amazement.

"But never mind that," he went on. "What if I am a bad lot? I don't know what a bad lot is exactly, but if you mean that I've lived with women and been drunk, and lost jobs because I didn't do the work, and been generally on the loose, it's true, of course. But I meant to live decently when I came home. Yes, I did. You can sneer as much as you like. Why didn't you help me? You're my sister, aren't you? And now I don't care what I do. You've all given me up. Well, give me up, and I'll just go to bits as fast as I can go! If you don't want me there are others who do, or at any rate the bit of money I've got. You've kept me from the only decent girl I've ever known, the one I could have been straight with—"

"Straight with!" Amy broke in. "How were you going to be straight if you're married already?"

He would have answered her but a sound behind him made him turn. He wheeled round and saw his father standing almost up against him. He had only time for a horrified vision of the ghostlike figure, the staring eyes, the open mouth, the white cheeks. The old man caught his coat.

"Martin, what was that? What did you say? ... No, no ... I can't bear that now. I can't, I can't."

He turned and made as though he would run up the stairs, catching about him like a child the shabby old dressing-gown that he was wearing. At the first step he stumbled, clutching the bannister to save himself.

Martin rushed to him, putting his arms round him, holding him close to him. "It's all right, father ... It's not true what you heard ... It's all right."

His father turned, putting his arms round his neck.

Martin half helped, half carried him up to his bedroom. He laid him on his bed and then, holding his hand, sat by his side all through the long dim afternoon.

About, five Warlock suddenly revived, sat up, arid with the assistance of Martin dressed properly, had some tea, and went down to his study. He sat down in his chair, then suddenly looking up at his son he said:

"Did you and Amy have a quarrel this afternoon?"

"No, father," said Martin.

"That's right. I thought—I thought ... I don't know ... My head's confused. You've been a good boy, Martin, haven't you? There's no need for me to worry, is there?"

"None, father," Martin said.

After a while Martin said:

"Father, don't go to Chapel to-night."

Warlock smiled.

"I must go. That's all right ... Nothing to worry about."

For some while he sat there, Martin's hand in his; Martin did not know whether he were asleep or not.

At about ten he ate and drank. At eleven he started with Amy and Thurston for the Chapel.

THE CHARIOT OF FIRE

When Jane, scolded by Aunt Anne for an untidy appearance, gave notice and at once departed, Maggie felt as though the ground was giving way under her feet.

A week until the New Year, and no opportunity of hearing from Martin during that time. Then she laughed at herself:

"You're losing your sense of proportion, my dear, over this. Laugh at yourself. What's a week?"

She did laugh at herself, but she had not very much to base her laughter upon. Martin's last letters had been short and very uneasy. She had already, in a surprising fashion for one so young, acquired a very wise and just estimate of Martin's character.

"He's only a boy," she used to say to herself and feel his elder by at least twenty years. Nevertheless the thought of his struggling on there alone was not a happy one. She longed, even though she might not advise him, to comfort him. She was beginning to realise something of her own power over him and to see, too, the strange mixture of superstition and self-reproach and self-distrust that overwhelmed him when she was not with him. She had indeed her own need of struggle against superstition. Her aunts continued to treat her with a quiet distant severity. Aunt Elizabeth, she fancied, would like to have been kind to her, but she was entirely under the influence of her sister, and there, too, Maggie was generous enough to see that Aunt Anne behaved as she did rather from a stern sense of duty than any real unkindness. Aunt Anne could not feel unkindly; she was too far removed from human temper and discontent and weakness. Nevertheless she had been deeply shocked at the revelation of Maggie's bad behaviour, and it was a shock from which, in all probability she would never recover.

"WE'LL never be friends again." Maggie thought, watching her aunt's austere composure from the other side of the dining-table. She was sad at the thought of that, remembering moments—that first visit to St. Dreot's, the departure in the cab, the night when she had sat at her aunt's bedside—that had given glimpses of the kind human creature Aunt Anne might have been had she never heard of the Inside Saints.

Maggie, during these last days, did everything that her aunts told her. She was as good and docile as she could be. But, oh! there were some dreary hours as she sat, alone, in that stuffy drawing-room, trying to sew, her heart aching with loneliness, her needle always doing the wrong thing, the clock heavily ticking, Thomas watching her from the mat in front of the fire, and the family group sneering at her from the wall-paper.

It was during these hours that superstitious terrors gained upon her. Could it be possible that all those women whom she had seen gathered together in Miss Avies's room really expected God to come when the clock struck twelve on the last night of the year? It was like some old story of ghosts and witches that her nurse used to tell her when she was a little girl at St. Dreot's. And yet, in that dark dreary room, almost anything seemed possible. After all, if there was a God, why should He not, one day, suddenly appear? And if He wished to spare certain of His servants, why should He not prepare them first before He came? There were things just as strange in the Old and New Testament. But if He did come, what would His Coming be like? Would every one be burnt to death or would they all be summoned before some judgment and punished for the wicked things they had done? Would her father perhaps return and give evidence against her? And poor Uncle Mathew, how would he fare with all his weaknesses? Her efforts at laughing at herself rescued her from some of the more incredible of these pictures. Nevertheless the uncertainty remained and only increased her loneliness. Had Martin been there in five minutes they would, together, have chased all these ghosts away. But he was not there. And at the thought of him she would have to set her mouth very firmly, indeed, to prevent her lips from trembling. She took out her ring and kissed it, and looked at the already tattered copy of the programme of the play to which they had been, and recalled every minute of their walks together.

Christmas Day was a very miserable affair. There were no presents and no festivities. They went to Chapel and Mr. Thurston preached the sermon. Maggie did, however, receive one letter. It was from Uncle Mathew. He wrote to her from some town in the north. He didn't seem very happy, and asked her whether she could possibly lend him five pounds. Alluding with a characteristic vagueness to "business plans of the first importance that were likely to mature very shortly."

She told Aunt Anne that she wanted five pounds of her money, but she did not say for what she needed them.

Aunt Anne gave her the money at once without a word—as though she said: "We have given up all control of you except to see that you behave decently whilst you are still with us."

When the fog arrived it seemed to penetrate every nook and corner of the house. The daily afternoon walk that Maggie took with Aunt Elizabeth was cancelled because of the difficulty of finding one's way from street to street and "because some rude man might steal one's money in the darkness," and Maggie was not sorry. Those walks had not been amusing, Aunt Elizabeth having nothing to say and being fully occupied with keeping an eye on Maggie, her idea apparently being that the girl would suddenly dash off to freedom and wickedness and be lost for ever. Maggie had no such intention and developed during these weeks a queer motherly affection for both the aunts, so lost they were and helpless and ignorant of the world! "My dear," said Maggie to herself, "you're a bit of a fool as far as common-sense goes, but you're nothing to what they are, poor dears." She tried to improve herself in every way for their benefit, but her memory was no better. She forgot all the things that were, in their eyes, the most important—closing doors, punctuality for meals, neat stitches, careful putting away of books and clothes.

Once, during a walk, she said to Aunt Elizabeth:

"I am trying, Aunt Elizabeth. Do you think Aunt Anne sees any improvement?"

And all Aunt Elizabeth said was:

"It was a great shock to her, what you did. Maggie—a great shock indeed!"

When the last day of the year arrived Maggie was surprised at the strange excitement that she felt. It was excitement, not only because of the dim mysterious events that the evening promised, but also because she was sure that this day would settle the loneliness of herself and Martin. After this they would know where they stood and what they must do. Old Warlock loomed in front of her as the very arbiter of her destiny. On his action everything turned. Oh! if only after this he were well enough for Martin to be happy and at ease about him! She was tempted to hate him as she thought of all the trouble that he had made for her. Then her mind went back to that first day long ago when he had spoken to her so kindly and bidden her come and see him as often as she could. How little she had known then what the future held for her! And now around his tall mysterious figure not only her own fate but that of every one else seemed to hang. Her aunts, Amy, Miss Pyncheon, Miss Avies, Thurston, that strange girl at the meeting, with them all his destiny was involved and they with his.

As the day advanced and the silver fog blew in little gusts about the house, making now this corner now that obscure, drifting, so that suddenly, when the door opened, the whole passage seemed full of smoke, clearing, for a moment, in the street below, showing lamp-posts and pavements and windows, and then blowing down again and once more hiding the world, she felt, in spite of herself, that she was playing a part in some malignant dream. "It can't be like this really," she told herself. "If I were to go to tea now with Mrs. Mark and sit in her pretty drawing-room and talk to that clergyman I wouldn't believe a word of it." And yet it was true enough, her share in it. As the afternoon advanced her sensations were very similar to those that she had had when about to visit the St. Dreot's dentist, a fearsome man with red hair and hands like a dog's paws. She saw him now standing over her as she sat trembling in the chair, a miserable little figure in a short untidy frock. She used to repeat to herself then what Uncle Mathew had once told her: "This time next year you'll have forgotten all about this," but when it was a question of facing the immensities of the Last Day that consolation was strangely inapt. It was dusk very early and she longed for Martha to bring the lamp.

At last it came and tea and Aunt Elizabeth. Aunt Anne had not appeared all day. Then long dreary hours followed until supper, and after that hours again until ten o'clock.

She had not been certain, all this time, whether the aunts meant to take her to the service with them. She had supposed that her introduction to the meeting at Miss Avies's meant that they intended to include her in this too, but now, as the evening advanced, in a fit of nervous terror she prayed within herself that they would not take her. If the end of the world were coming she would like to meet it in her bed. To go out into those streets and that ugly unfriendly Chapel was a horrible thing to do. If this were to be the end of the world how she did wish that she might have been allowed to know nothing about it. And those others—Miss Pyncheon and the rest who devoutly believed in the event—how were they passing these last hours?

"Oh, it isn't true! It can't be true!" she said to herself. "It's a shame to frighten them so!"

By eleven o'clock the excitement of the day had wearied her so that she fell fast asleep in the arm-chair beside the fire. She woke to find Aunt Anne standing over her.

"It's a quarter past eleven. It's time to put on your things," she said. So she was to go! She rose and, in spite of herself, her limbs were trembling and her teeth chattered. To her surprise Aunt Anne bent forward and kissed her on the forehead.

"Maggie," she said, "if I've been harsh to you during these weeks I'm sorry. I've done what I thought my duty, but I wouldn't wish on this night that we should have any unkindness in our hearts towards one another."

"Oh, that's all right," Maggie said awkwardly.

She went up to put on her things; then the three of them went out into the dark foggy street together.

Because it was New Year's Eve there were many people about, voices laughing and shouting through the mist and then some one running with a flaring light, then some men walking singing in chorus. The aunts said nothing as they went. Maggie's thoughts were given now to wondering whether Martin would be there. She tied her mind to that, but behind it was the irritating knowledge that her teeth were chattering and her knees trembling and that she did not maintain her courage as a Cardinal should.

As they entered the Chapel the hoarse ugly clock over the door grunted out half-past eleven. The Chapel seemed on Maggie's entering it to be half in darkness, there was a thin splutter of gas over the reading-desk at the far end and some more light by the door, but the centre of the building was a shadowy pool. Only a few were present, gathered together in the middle seats below the desk, perhaps in all a hundred persons. Of these three-quarters were women. The aunts and Maggie went into their accustomed seat some six rows from the front. When Maggie rose from her knees and looked about her she recognised at once that only the Inside Saints were here.

Amongst the men she recognised Mr. Smith, Caroline's father, two old men, brothers, who had followed Mr. Warlock from their youth, and a young pale man who had once been to tea with her aunts. Martin she saw at once was not there.

For some time, perhaps for ten minutes, they all sat in silence, and only the gruff comment of the clock sounded in the building. Then the lights went up with a flare and Thurston, followed by Mr. Warlock, entered. It was at that moment that Maggie had a revelation. The faces around her seemed to be suddenly gathered in front of her, and it was with a start of surprise that she suddenly realised: "Oh, but they don't believe in this any more than I do!" The faces around her were agitated, with odd humble beseeching looks, as though they were helpless utterly and were hoping that some one would suddenly come and lead them somewhere that they might be comfortable again and at ease.

There was not to-night, as there had been on other occasions (and especially during that service that Mr. Crashaw had conducted), any sign of religious and mystical excitement. The people seemed huddled together in the cold and draughty place against their will, and the very fact that the Chapel was only half full chilled the blood. No drama of exultation here, no band of God's servants gloriously preparing to meet Him, only the frightened open-mouthed gaze of a little gathering of servant girls and old maids. That was Maggie's first impression; then, when the service began, when the first hymn had been sung and Thurston had stumbled into his extempore prayer. Maggie found herself caught into a strange companionship with the people around her. Not now ecstasy nor the excitement of religious fanaticism nor the superstitious preparation for some awful events—none of these emotions now lifted her into some strained unnatural sphere—no, nothing but a strange sympathy and kindness and understanding that she had never known in all her life before. She felt the hunger, the passionate appeal: "Oh God come! Prove Thyself! We have waited so long. We have resisted unbelievers, we have fought our own doubts and betrayals, give us now a Sign! something by which we may know Thee!" and with that appeal the conviction in the hearts of almost all present that nothing would happen, that God would give no sign, that the age of miracles was past.

"Oh, why did He want to be so definite," she thought. "Why couldn't He have left them as they were without forcing them to this."

They were sitting down now, and Thurston, with his cheap sense of the dramatic and false emphasis, was reading from the New Testament. Maggie looked to where Mr. Warlock was, a little to the right of Thurston, in his black gown, his head a little lowered, his hands on his lap.

When she saw him she was touched to the very heart. Why, he had aged in the last month a hundred years! He looked, sitting there, so frail and helpless that it seemed wonderful that he should have been able to get there at all.

His hair seemed to have an added intensity of whiteness to-night, and his beard lay against the black cloth of his gown with a contrast so sharp that it was unreal. Maggie fancied, as she watched him, that he was bewildered and scarcely knew where he was. Once he looked up and round about him; he put his hand to his brow and then let it fall as though he had no longer any control over it.

She was now so touched by the pathos of his helplessness that she could think of nothing else and longed to go to him and comfort him. Time stole on and it was now ten minutes to twelve. They sang another hymn, but the voices were very weak and feeble and the words quivered round the building in a ghostly whisper. Then Thurston came to the Master and gave him his arm and led him to the reading-desk. The old man seemed for a moment as though he would fall, then, holding to the front of the desk, he spoke in a very weak and faltering voice. Maggie could not catch many of his words: "My children— only a little time—Our preparation now is finished ... God has promised ... Not the least of these His little ones shall perish ... Let us not fear but be ready to meet Him as our Friend ... our Friend ... God our Father ..." Then in a stronger voice: "Now during these last minutes let us kneel in silent prayer."

They all knelt down. Maggie had no thoughts, no desire except that the time might pass; she seemed to kneel there asleep waiting for the moment when some one should tell her that the time had gone and she was safe. The moments dragged eternally; a thrilling suspense like a flood of water pouring into an empty space had filled the Chapel. No one moved. Suddenly into the heart of the silence there struck the first note of the clock tolling the hour. With Maggie it was as though that sound liberated her from the spell that had been upon her. She looked up; she saw the master standing, his hands stretched out, his face splendid with glory and happiness.

He looked beyond them all, beyond the Chapel, beyond the world. He gave one cry:

"My God, Thou art come." Some other words followed but were caught up and muffled. He fell forward, collapsing in a heap against the desk. His head struck the wood and then he lay there perfectly still.

Maggie could only dimly gather what happened after the sound of that fall. There seemed to her to be a long and terrible silence during which the clock continued remorselessly to strike. The Chapel appeared to be a place of shadows as though the gas had suddenly died to dim haloes; she was conscious that people moved about her, that Aunt Anne had left them, and that Aunt Elizabeth was saying to her again and again: "How terrible! How terrible! How terrible!"

Then as though it were some other person, Maggie found herself very calmly speaking to Aunt Elizabeth.

"Are we to wait for Aunt Anne?" she whispered.

"Anne said we were to go home."

"Then let's go," whispered Maggie.

They went to the door, pushing, it seemed, through shadows who whispered and forms that vanished as soon as one looked at them.

Out in the open air Maggie was aware that she was trembling from head to foot, but a determined idea that she must get Aunt Elizabeth home at once drove her like a goad. Very strange it was out here, the air ringing with the clamour of bells. The noise seemed deafening, whistles blowing from the river, guns firing and this swinging network of bells echoing through the fog. Figures, too, ran with lights, men singing, women laughing, all mysteriously in the tangled darkness.

They were joined at once by Aunt Anne, who said:

"God has called him home," by which Maggie understood that Mr. Warlock was dead.

They went home in silence. Inside the hall Aunt Elizabeth began to cry. Aunt Anne put her arm around her and led her away; they seemed completely to forget Maggie, leaving her standing in the dark hall by herself.

She found a candle and went up to her room. The noise in the streets had ceased quite suddenly as though some angry voice had called the world to order.

Maggie undressed and lay down in her bed. She lay there staring in front of her without closing her eyes. She watched the grey dawn, then the half-light, then, behind her blind, bright sunshine. The fog was no more.

The strangest fancies and visions passed through her brain during that time. She saw Mr. Warlock hanging forward like a sack of clothes, the blood trickling stealthily across his beard. Poor old man! What were the others all thinking now? Were they sorry or glad? Were they disappointed or relieved? After all, he had, perhaps, spoken the truth so far as he was himself concerned. God had come for him. He was now it might be happy somewhere at peace and at rest. Then like a flash of lightning across the darkness came the thought of Martin. What had he said? "If anything happened to his father—"

The terror of that made her heart stop beating. She wanted instantly to go to him and see what he was doing. She even rose from her bed, stumbled in the darkness towards her dressing-table, then remembered where she was and what time and went back and sat upon her bed.

She sat there, her fingers tightly pressed together, staring in front of her until the morning came. She felt at her heart a foreboding worse than any pain that she had ever known. She determined that, directly after breakfast, whatever the aunts would say, she would go to his house and demand to see him. She did not mind who might try to prevent her, she would fight her way through them all. Only one look, one word of assurance from him, and then she could endure anything. That she must have or she would die.

At last Martha knocked on the door; she had her bath, dressed, still with this terrible pain at her heart.

She was alone at breakfast, she drank some coffee, then went up to the drawing-room to think for a moment what course she should pursue. The room was flooded with sunlight that struck the fire into a dead, lifeless yellow.

As she stood there she heard through the open door voices in the hall. But before she had heard the voices she knew that it was Martin.

Martha was expostulating, her voice following his step up the hall.

"I shall go and tell my mistress," Maggie heard.

Then Martin came in.

When she saw him she stood speechless where she was. The change in him terrified her so that her heart seemed to leap into her throat choking her. The colour had drained from his face, leaving it dry and yellow. He had an amazing resemblance to his father, his eyes had exactly the same bewildered expression as though he were lost and yet he seemed quite calm, his only movement was one hand that wandered up and down his waistcoat feeling the buttons one after the other.

He looked at her as though he did not know her, and yet he spoke her name.

"Maggie," he said, "I've come to say good-bye. You know what I said before. Well, it's come true. Father is dead, and I killed him."

With a terrible effort, beating down a terror that seemed personally to envelop her, she said:

"No, Martin. I saw him die. It wasn't you, Martin dear."

"It was I," he answered. "You don't know. I came into the house drunk and he heard what I said to Amy. He nearly died then. The doctor in the evening said he must have had some shock."

She tried to come to him then. She was thinking: "Oh, if I've only got time I can win this. But I must have time. I must have time."

He moved away from her, as he had done once before.

"Anyway, it doesn't matter," he said. "I've killed him by the way I've been behaving to him all these months. I'm going away where I can't do any harm."

She desperately calmed herself, speaking very quietly.

"Listen, Martin. You haven't done him any harm. He's happier now than he's been for years. I know he is. And that doesn't touch us. You can't leave me now. Where you go I must go."

"No," he answered. "No, Maggie. I ought to have gone before. I knew it then, but I know it absolutely now. Everything I touch I hurt, so I mustn't touch anything I care for."

She put her hands out towards him; words had left her. She would have given her soul for words and she could say nothing.

She was surrounded with a hedge of fright and terror and she could not pass it.

He seemed to see then in her eyes her despair. For an instant he recognised her. Their eyes met for the first time; she felt that she was winning. She began eagerly to speak: "Listen, Martin dear. You can't do me any harm. You can only hurt me by leaving me. I've told you before. Just think of that and only that."

The door opened and Aunt Anne came in.

He turned to her very politely. "I beg your pardon for coming, Miss Cardinal," he said. "I know what you must think of me, but it's all right. I've only come to say good-bye to Maggie. It's all right. Neither you nor Maggie will be bothered with me again."

He turned to the open door. Aunt Anne stood aside to let him pass. Maggie said:

"Martin, don't go! Martin, don't leave me! Don't leave me, Martin!"

He seemed to break then in his resolution.

"It's better. It's better," he cried, as though he were shouting himself down, and then pushing Aunt Anne with his arm he hurried out almost running, his steps stumbling down the stairs.

Maggie ran to the door. Her aunt stopped her, holding her back.

"It's better, Maggie dear," she said very gently, repeating Martin's words.

The sound of the hall door closing echoed through the house.

Maggie struggled, crying again and again: "Let me go! Let me go! I must go with him! I can't live without him! Let me go!"

She fought then, and with one hand free hit Aunt Anne's face, twisting her body. Then, suddenly weak, so that she saw faintness coming towards her like a cloak, she whispered:

"Oh, Aunt Anne, let me go! Oh, Aunt Anne, let me go! Please, please, let me go!"

Suddenly the house was darkened, at her feet was a gulf of blackness, and into it she tumbled, down, far down, with a last little gasping sigh of distress.

PART III

CHAPTER I

THE THREE VISITS

On a spring day, early in March of the next year, 1908, Mathew Cardinal thought that he would go and discover how his niece was prospering. He had seen nothing of her for a very long time.

He did not blame himself for this, but then he never blamed himself for anything. A fate, often drunken and always imbecile, was to blame for everything that he did, and he pitied himself sincerely for having to be in the hands of such a creature. He happened to be just now very considerably frightened about himself, more frightened than he had been for a very long time, so frightened in fact that he had drunk nothing for weeks. For many years he had been leading a see-saw existence, and the see-saw had been swung by that mysterious force known as Finance. He had a real gift for speculation, and had he been granted from birth a large income he might have ended his days as a Justice of the Peace and a Member of Parliament. Unfortunately he had never had any private means, and he had never been able to make enough by his mysterious speculations to float him into security—"Let me once get so far," he would say to himself, "and I am a made man." But drink, an easy tolerance of bad company, and a rather touching conceit had combined to divorce him from so fine a destiny. He had risen, he had fallen, made a good thing out of this tip, been badly done over that, and missed opportunity after opportunity through a fuddled brain and an overweening self-confidence.

Last year for several months everything had succeeded; it was during that happy period that he had visited Maggie. Perhaps it was well for his soul that success had not continued. He was a man whom failure improved, having a certain childish warmth of heart and simplicity of outlook when things went badly with him. Success made him abominably conceited, and being without any morality self-confidence drove him to disastrous lengths. Now once more he was very near destruction and he knew it, very near things like forging and highway robbery, and other things worse than they. He knew that he was very near; he peered over into the pit and did not wish to descend. He was not a bad man, and had he not believed himself to be a clever one all might yet have been well. The temptation of his cleverness lured him on. A stroke of the pen was a very simple thing...

To save his soul he thought that he would go and see Maggie. His affection for her, conceited and selfish though it was, was the most genuine thing in him. For three-quarters of the year he forgot her, but when life went badly he thought of her again—not that he expected to get anything out of her, but she was good to him and she knew nothing about his life, two fine bases for safety.

"What have they been doing to her, those damned hypocrites, I wonder," was his thought. He admired, feared, and despised his sisters. "All that stuff about God" frightened him in spite of himself, and he knew, in his soul, that Anne was no hypocrite.

He rang the bell and faced Martha. He had dressed himself with some care and was altogether more tidy just then, having a new mistress who cared about outside appearances. Also, having been sober for nearly two months, he looked a gentleman.

"Is my niece at home?" he asked, blinking because he was frightened of Martha.

She did not seem to be prepared to let him in.

"Miss Maggie has been very ill," she said, frowning at him.

"Ill?" That really hurt him. He stammered, "Why? ... When?"

She moved aside then for him to pass into the hall. He came into the dark stuffy place.

"Yes," said Martha. "Just after Christmas. Brain-fever, the doctors said. They thought she'd die for weeks. Had two doctors ... You can't see her, sir," she ended grumpily.

Then Aunt Anne appeared, coming through the green-baize door.

"Why, Mathew," she said. Mathew thought how ill she looked.

"They're all ill here," he said to himself.

"So Maggie's ill," he said, dropping his eyes before her as he always did.

"Yes," Aunt Anne answered. "She was very ill indeed, poor child. I'm glad to see you, Mathew. It's a long time since you've been."

He thought she was gentler to him than she had been, so, mastering his fear of her, fingering his collar, he said:

"Can't I see her?"

"Well, I'm not ... I think you might. It might do her good. She wants taking out of herself. She comes down for an hour or two every day now. I'll go and see." She left him standing alone there. He looked around him, sniffing like a dog. How he hated the house and everything in it! Always had ... You could smell that fellow Warlock's trail over everything. The black cat, Tom, came slipping along, looked for a moment as though he would rub himself against Mathew's stout legs, then decided that he would not. Mysterious this place like a well, with its green shadows. No wonder the poor child had been ill here. At the thought of her being near to death Mathew felt a choke in his throat. Poor child, never had any fun all her life and then to die in a green well like this. And his sisters wouldn't care if she did, hard women, hard women. Funny how religion made you hard, darn funny. Good thing he'd been irreligious all his life. Think of his brother Charles! There was religion for you, living with his cook and preaching to her next morning. Bad thing religion!

Aunt Anne returned, coming down the stairs with that queer halting gait of hers.

"Maggie's in the drawing-room," she said. "She'll like to see you."

As they went up, Aunt Anne said: "Be careful with her, Mathew. She's still very weak. Don't say anything to upset her?"

He mumbled something in his throat. Couldn't trust him. Of course they couldn't. Never had ... Fine sort of sisters they were.

Maggie was sitting by the fire, a shawl over her shoulders. By God, but she looked ill. Mathew had another gulp in his throat. Poor kid, but she did look ill. Poor kid, poor kid.

"Sorry you've been bad, Maggie," he said.

She looked up, smiling with pleasure, when she saw who it was. Yes, she was really pleased to see him. But how different a smile from the old one! No blood behind it, none of that old Maggie determination. He was filled with compassion. He took a chair close beside her and sat down, leaning towards her, his large rather sheepish eye gazing at her.

"What's been the matter?" he asked.

"I don't know," Maggie said. "I was suddenly ill one day, and after that I didn't know any more for weeks. But I'm much better now."

"Well, I'm delighted to hear that anyway," he said heartily. He was determined to cheer her up. "You'll be as right as rain presently."

"Of course I shall. I've felt so lazy, as though I didn't want to do anything. Now I must stir myself."

"Have the old women been good to you?" he asked, dropping his voice.

"Very," she answered.

"Not bothering you about all their religious tommy-rot?"

She looked down at her hands.

"No," she said.

"And that hypocritical minister of theirs hasn't been at you again?"

"Mr. Warlock's dead," she answered very quietly.

"Warlock dead!" Uncle Mathew half rose from his chair in his astonishment. "That fellow dead! Well, I'm damned, indeed I am. That fellow—! Well, there's a good riddance! I know it isn't good form to speak about a man who's kicked the bucket otherwise than kindly, but he was a weight on my chest that fellow was, with his long white beard and his soft voice ... Well, well. To be sure! Whatever will my poor sisters do? And what's happened to that young chap, his son, nice lad he was, took dinner with us that day last year?"

"He's gone away," said Maggie. Mathew, stupid though he was, heard behind the quiet of Maggie's voice a warning. He flung her a hurried surreptitious look. Her face was perfectly composed, her hands still upon her lap. Nevertheless he said to himself, "Danger there, my boy! Something's happened there!"

And yet his curiosity drove him for a moment further.

"Gone, has he? Where to?"

"He went abroad," said Maggie, "after his father's death. I don't know where he's gone."

"Oh, did he? Pity! Restless, I expect—I was at his age."

There was a little pause between them when Maggie sat very quietly looking at her hands. Then, smiling, she glanced up and said:

"But tell me about yourself, Uncle Mathew. You've told me nothing."

He fidgeted a little, shifting his thick legs, stroking his nose with his finger.

"I don't know that I've anything very good to tell you, my dear. Truth is, I haven't been doing so very well lately."

"Oh, Uncle, I'm sorry!"

"It's nothing to make yourself miserable about, my dear. I always turn my corners. Damn rocky ones they are sometimes too. Everything's turned itself wrong these last weeks, either too soon or too late. I don't complain, all the same it makes things a bit inconvenient. Thank you for that five pounds you sent me, my dear, very helpful it was I can tell you."

"Do you want another five pounds?" she asked him. He struggled with himself. His hesitation was so obvious that it was quite touching. She put her hand on his knee.

"Do have another five pounds, Uncle. It won't be difficult for me at all. I've been spending nothing all these weeks when I've been ill. Please do."

He shook his head firmly.

"No, my dear, I won't. As I came along I said to myself, 'Now, you'll be asking Maggie for money, and when she says "Yes" you're not to take it'—and so I'm not going to. I may be a rotter—but I'm not a rotten rotter."

He clung to his decision with the utmost resolve as though it were his last plank of respectability.

"I can't believe," he said to her with great solemnity, "that things can really go wrong. I know too much. It isn't men like me who go under. No. No."

He saw then her white face and strange grey ghostly eyes as though her soul had gone somewhere on a visit and the house was untenanted. He felt again the gulp in his throat. He bent forward, resting his fat podgy hand on her knee.

"Don't you worry, Maggie dear. I've always noticed that things are never bad for long. You've still got your old uncle, and you're young, and there are plenty of fish in the sea ... there are indeed. You cheer up! It will be all right soon."

She put her hands on his.

"Oh I'm not—worrying." But as she spoke a strange strangled little sob had crept unbidden into her throat, choking her.

He thought, as he got up, "It's that damned young feller I gave dinner to. I'd like to wring his neck."

But he said no more, bent closer and kissed her, said he was soon coming again, and went away.

After he had gone the house sank into its grey quiet again. What was Maggie thinking? No one knew. What was Aunt Anne thinking? No one knew ... But there was something between these two, Maggie and Aunt Anne. Every one felt it and longed for the storm to burst. Bad enough things outside with Mr. Warlock dead, members leaving right and left, and the Chapel generally going to wrack and ruin, but inside!

Old Martha, who had never liked Maggie, felt now a strange, uncomfortable pity for her. She didn't want to feel pity, no, not she, pity for no one, and especially not for an ugly untidy girl like that, but there it was, she couldn't help herself! Such a child that girl, and she'd been as nearly dead as nothing, and now she was suffering, suffering awful ... Any one could see ... All that Warlock boy. Martha had seen him come stumbling down the stairs that day and had heard Maggie's cry and then the fall. Awful noise it made. Awful. She'd stood in the hall, looking up the stairs, her heart beating like a hammer. Yes, just like a hammer! Then she'd gone up. It wasn't a nice sight, the poor girl all in a lump on the floor and Miss Anne just as she always looked before one of her attacks, as though she were made of grey glass from top to toe ...

But Martha hadn't pitied Maggie then. Oh, no. Might as well die as not. Who wanted her? No one. Not even her young man apparently.

Better if she died. But slowly something happened to Martha. Not that she was sentimental. Not in the least. But thoughts would steal in—steal in just when you were at your work. The girl lying there so good and patient—all the pots and pans winking at you from the kitchen-wall. Must remember to order that ketchup—cold last night in bed—think another blanket ... yes, very good and patient. Can't deny it. Always smiles just that same way. Smiles at every one except Miss Arne. Won't smile at her. Wonder why not? Something between those two. What about dinner? A little onion fry—that's the thing these damp days—Onion fry—Onion Fry. ONION FRY ... One last look back before the world is filled with the sense, smell, and taste of it.—Poor girl, so white and so patient—the young man will never come back—never ... never ... ONION FRY.

No; no one knew what Maggie was thinking. No one found out until Maggie had her second visitor, Miss Avies.

When Martha opened the door to Miss Avies she was astonished. Miss Avies hadn't been near the house since old Warlock died. What was she wanting here now, with her stiff back and bossy manner.

"I don't know whether you can see—"

"Oh nonsense, it's Maggie Cardinal I want to see. She's now in the drawing-room sitting on a chair with a shawl on by the fire. Don't tell me!"

Martha quivered with anger. "The doctor's orders is—"

"I'm going to be doctor to-day," she said, and strode inside. She went upstairs and found Aunt Elizabeth sitting with Maggie.

"How do you do, Miss Cardinal?" They shook hands, Miss Avies standing over Aunt Elizabeth like the boa constrictor raised above the mouse.

"That's all right ... No, I don't want to see your sister. And to be quite honest, I don't want to see you either. It's your niece I want to see. And alone—"

"Certainly—it's only the doctor said—"

"Not to excite her. I know. But I'm not going to excite her. I'm going to give her some medicine. You come back in half an hour from now. Will you? That's right. Thank you so much."

Aunt Elizabeth, unhappy, uncomfortable, filled with misgivings, as in these days she always was, left the room.

"Well, there ... that's right," said Miss Avies, settling herself in the opposite side of the fire from Maggie and looking at her with not unfriendly eyes. "How are you?"

"Oh much better, thank you," said Maggie. "Ever so much better."

"No, you're not," said Miss Avies. "And you're only lying when you say you are. You'll never get better unless you do what I tell you—"

"What's that?" asked Maggie.

"Face things. Face everything. Have it all out. Don't leave a bit of it alone, and then just keep what's useful."

"I don't quite know what you mean," said Maggie—but the faint colour had faded from her cheeks and her hands had run together for protection.

Miss Avies's voice softened—"I'm probably going away very soon," she said, "going away and not coming back. All my work's over here. But I wanted to see you before I went. You remember another talk we had here?"

"Very well," said Maggie.

"You remember what I told you?"

"You told me not to stay here," said Maggie.

"Yes, I did," said Miss Avies, "and I meant it. The matter with you is that you've been kept here all this time without any proper work to do and that's been very bad for you and made you sit with your hands folded in front of you, your head filling with silly fancies."

Maggie couldn't help smiling at this description of herself.

"Oh, you smile," said Miss Avies vigorously, "but it's perfectly true."

"Well, it's all right now." said Maggie, "because I am going away—as soon as ever I'm well enough."
"What to do?" asked Miss Avies.

"I don't quite know yet," said Maggie.

"Well, I know," said Miss Avies. "You're going away to brood over that young man."

Maggie said nothing.

"Oh I know ... It seems cruel of me to speak of it just when you've had such a bad time, but it's kindness really. If I don't force you to think it all out and face it properly you'll be burying it in some precious spot and always digging it up to look at it. You face it, my girl. You say to yourself—well, he wasn't such a wonderful young man after all. I can lead my life all right without him—of course I can. I'm not going to be dependent on him and sigh and groan and waste away because I can't see him. I know what it is. I've been through it myself."

Then there was a pause; then Maggie suddenly looked up and smiled.

"But you're quite wrong, Miss Avies. I've no intention of not facing Martin, and I've no intention either of having my life ruined because he's not here. At first, when I was very ill, I was unhappy, and then I saw how silly I was."

"Why?" said Miss Avies with great pleasure. "You've got over it already! I must say I'm delighted because I never thought much of Martin Warlock if you want to know, my dear. I always thought him a weak young man, and he wouldn't have done you any good. I'm delighted—indeed I am."

"That's not true either," said Maggie quietly. "If by getting over it you mean that I don't love Martin you're quite wrong. I loved him the first moment I saw him and I shall love him in just the same way until I die. I don't think it matters what he does or where he is so far as loving him goes. But that doesn't mean I'm sitting and pining. I'm not."

Miss Avies looked at her with displeasure.

"It's the same thing then," she said. "You may fancy you're going to lead an ordinary life again, but all the time you'll just be waiting for him to come back."

"No," said Maggie, "I shall not. I've had plenty of time for thinking these last weeks, and I've made up my mind to his never coming back—never at all. And even if he did come back he mightn't want me. So I'm not going to waste time about it. I shall find work and make myself useful somewhere, but I shall always love Martin just as I do now."

"You're very young," said Miss Avies, touched in spite of herself. "Later on you'll find some one much better than young Warlock."

"Perhaps I shall," said Maggie. "But what's the use of that if he isn't Martin? I've heard people say that before—some one's 'better' or 'stronger' or 'wiser.'—But what has that got to do with it? I love Martin because he's Martin. He's got a weak character you say. That's why he wants me, and I want to be wanted more than anything on earth."

"Why, child," said Miss Avies, astonished. "How you've grown these last weeks!"

"Do you want to know how I love Martin," said Maggie, "so that there shall be no mistake about it? Well, I can't tell you. I couldn't tell any one. I don't know how I love him, but I know that I shall never change or alter all my life—even though he never comes back again. I've given over being silly," she went on. "There were days and days at first when I just wanted to die. But now I'm going to make my own life and have a good time—and never stop loving Martin for one single second."

"Supposing," said Miss Avies, "some one wanted to marry you? Would you?"

"It would depend," said Maggie; "if I liked him and he really wanted me and I could help him I might. Only, of course, I'd tell him about Martin first."

She went on after a little pause: "You see, Miss Avies, I haven't been very happy with my aunts, and I always thought it was their fault that I wasn't. But during these weeks when I've been lying in bed I saw that it was my own fault for being so gloomy about everything. Now that I've got Martin—"

"Got him!" interrupted Miss Avies; "why, you've only just lost him!"

"No, I haven't," answered Maggie. "He didn't go away because he hated me or was tired of me, he went away because he didn't want to do me any harm, and I think he cared for me more just at that minute than he'd ever done before. So I've nothing to spoil my memory of him. I daresay we wouldn't have got on well, together, I don't think I would ever have fascinated him enough to keep him with me for very long—but now I know that he loved me at the very moment he went away and wasn't thinking how ugly I was or what a nasty temper I had or how irritating I could be."

"But, my dear child," said Miss Avies, astonished. "How can you say you loved one another if you were always quarrelling and expecting to part?" "We weren't always quarrelling," said Maggie. "We weren't together enough, but if we had been it wouldn't have meant that we didn't love one another. I don't think we'd ever been very happy, but being happy together doesn't seem to me the only sign of love. Love seems to me to be moments of great joy rising from every kind of trouble and bother. I don't call tranquillity happiness."

"Well, you have thought things out," said Miss Avies, "and all of us considering you so stupid—"

"I'm not going to squash myself into a corner any more," said Maggie. "Why should I? I find I'm as good as any one else. I made Martin love me—even though it was only for a moment. So I'm going to be shy no longer."

"And here was I thinking you heart-broken," said Miss Avies.

"I'm going out into the world," said Maggie half to herself. "I'm going to have adventures. I've been in this house long enough. I'm going to see what men and women are really like—I know this isn't real here. And I want to discover about religion too. Since Martin went away I've felt that there was something in it. I can't think what and the aunts can't think either; none of you know here, but some one must have found out something. I'm going to settle what it all means."

"You've got your work cut out," said Miss Avies. "I'll come and see you again one day soon."

"Yes, do," said Maggie.

When Miss Avies had gone Maggie realised that she had been talking with bravado—in fact she hid her head in the cushion of the chair and cried for at least five minutes. Then she sat up and wiped her eyes because she heard Aunt Anne coming. When Aunt Anne came towards her now she was affected with a strange feeling of sickness. She told herself that that was part of her illness. She did not hate Aunt Anne. For some weeks, when she had risen slowly from the nightmare that the first period of her illness had been, she hated Aunt Anne, hated her fiercely, absorbingly, desperately. Then suddenly the hatred had left her, and had she only known it she was from that moment never to hate any one again. A quite new love for Martin was suddenly born in her, a love that was, as yet, like the first faint stirring of the child in the mother's womb. This new love was quite different from the old; that had been acquisitive, possessive, urgent, restless, and often terribly painful; this was tranquil, sure, utterly certain, and passive. The immediate fruit of it was that she regarded all human creatures with a lively interest, an interest too absorbing to allow of hatred or even active dislike. Her love for Martin was now like a strong current in her soul washing away all sense of irritation and anger. She regarded people from a new angle. What were they all about? What were they thinking? Had they too had some experience as marvellous as her meeting with and parting from Martin? Probably; and they too were shy of speaking of it. Her love for Martin slowly grew, a love now independent of earthly contact and earthly desire, a treasure that would be hers so long as life lasted, that no one could take from her.

She no longer hated Aunt Anne, but she did not intend to live with her any more. So soon as she was well enough she would go. That moment of physical contact when Aunt Anne had held her back made any more relation between them impossible. There was now a great gulf fixed.

The loneliness, the sense of desperate loss, above all the agonising longing for Martin, his step, his voice, his smile—she faced all these and accepted them as necessary companions now on her life's journey, but she did not intend to allow them to impede progress. She wondered now about everybody. Her own experience had shown her what strange and wonderful things occur to all human beings, and, in the face of this, how could one hate or grudge or despise? She had a fellowship now with all humanity.

But she was as ignorant about life as ever. The things that now she wanted to know! About Aunt Anne, for instance. How had she been affected by Mr. Warlock's death and the disappointment of her expectations? The Chapel now apparently was to be taken over by Thurston, who had married Amy Warlock and was full of schemes and enterprises. Maggie knew that the aunts went now very seldom to

Chapel, and the Inside Saints were apparently in pieces. Was Aunt Anne utterly broken by all this? She did not seem to be so. She seemed to be very much as she had been, except that she was in her room now a great deal. Her health appeared, on the whole, to be better than it had been. And what was Aunt Elizabeth thinking? And Martha? And Miss Avies? And Caroline Smith? ...

No, she must get out into the world and discover these things for herself. She did not know how the way of escape would come, but she was certain of its arrival.

It arrived, and through her third visitor. Her third visitor was Mrs. Mark.

When Katherine Mark came in Maggie was writing to Uncle Mathew. She put aside her writing-pad with a little exclamation of surprise. Mrs. Mark, the very last person in all the world whom she had expected to see! As she saw her come in she had a swift intuition that this was Destiny now that was dealing with her, and that a new scene, involving every sort of new experience and adventure, was opening before her. More than ever before she realised how far Katherine Mark was from the world in which she, Maggie, had during all these months been living. Katherine Mark was Real—Real in her beautiful quiet clothes, in her assurance, her ease, the sense that she gave that she knew life and love and business and all the affairs of men at first hand, not only seen through a mist of superstition and ignorance, or indeed not seen at all.

"This is what I want," something in Maggie called to her.

"This will make me busy and quiet and sensible—at last—"

When Katherine Mark sat down and took her hand for a moment, smiling at her in the kindliest way, Maggie felt as though she had known her all her life.

"Oh! I'm so glad you've come!" she cried spontaneously; and then, as though she felt she'd gone too far, she blushed and drew back.

But Katherine held her hand fast.

"I wrote," she said, "some weeks ago to you, and your aunt answered the letter saying you were very ill. Then, as I heard nothing of you, I was anxious and came to see what had happened. You've not kept your word, Maggie, you know. We were to have been great friends, and you've never been near me."

At the use of her Christian name Maggie blushed with pleasure.

"I couldn't come," she said. "I didn't want to until—until—until some things had settled themselves."

"Well—and they have?" asked Katherine.

"Yes—they have," said Maggie.

"What's been the matter?" asked Katherine.

"I was worried about something, and then I was ill," said Maggie.

"And you're not worried now?" said Katherine.

"I'm not going to give in to it, anyway," said Maggie. "As soon as I'm well, I'm off. I'll find some work somewhere."

"I've got a plan," said Katherine. "It came into my head the moment I saw you sitting there. Will you come and stay with us for a little?"

That sense that Maggie had had when she saw Katherine of fate having a hand in all of this deepened now and coloured her thoughts, so that she could feel no surprise but only a curious instinct that she had been through all this scene before.

"Stay with you!" she cried. "Oh, I should love to!"

"That's good," said Katherine. "Your aunts won't mind, will they?"

"They can't keep me," said Maggie. "I'm free. But they won't want to. Our time together is over—"

"I'll come and fetch you to-morrow," said Katherine. "You shall stay with us until you're quite well, and then we'll find some work for you."

"Why are you good to me like this?" Maggie asked.

"I'm not good to you," Katherine answered, laughing. "It's simply selfish. It will be lovely for me having you with me."

"Oh, you don't know," said Maggie, throwing up her head.

"No, I don't think I'll come. I'm frightened. I'm not what you think. I'm untidy and careless and can't talk to strangers. Perhaps I'll lose you altogether as a friend if I come."

"You'll never do that," said Katherine, suddenly bending forward and kissing her. "I don't change about people. It's because I haven't any imagination, Phil says."

"I shall make mistakes," Maggie said. "I've never been anywhere. But I don't care. I can look after myself."

The thought of her three hundred pounds (which were no longer three hundred) encouraged her. She kissed Katherine.

"I don't change either," she said.

She had a strange conversation with Aunt Anne that night, strange as every talk had always been because of things left unsaid. They faced one another across the fireplace like enemies who might have been lovers; there had been from the very first moment of this meeting a romantic link between them which had never been defined. They had never had it out with one another, and they were not going to have it out now; but Maggie, who was never sentimental, wondered at the strange mixture of tenderness, pity, affection, irritation and hostility that she felt.

"Aunt Anne, I'm going away to-morrow," said Maggie.

"To-morrow!" Aunt Anne looked up with her strange hostile arrogance. "Oh no, Maggie. You're not well yet."

"Mrs. Mark," said Maggie, "the lady I told you about, is coming in a motor to fetch me. She will take me straight to her house, and then I shall go to bed."

Aunt Anne said nothing.

"You know that it's better for me to go," said Maggie. "We can't live together any more after what happened. You and Aunt Elizabeth have been very very good to me, but you know now that I'm a disappointment. I haven't ever fitted into the life here. I never shall."

"The life here is over," said Aunt Anne. "Everything is over—the house is dead. Of course you must go. If you feel anger with me now or afterwards remember that I have lost every hope or desire I ever had. I don't want your pity. I want no one's pity. I wanted once your affection, but I wanted it on my own terms. That was wrong. I do not want your affection any longer; you were never the girl I thought you. You're a strange girl, Maggie, and you will have, I am afraid, a very unhappy life."

"No, I will not," said Maggie. "I will have a happy life."

"That is for God to say," said Aunt Anne.

"No, it is not," said Maggie. "I can make my own happiness. God can't touch it, if I don't let Him."

"Maggie, you're blasphemous," said Aunt Anne, but not in anger.

"I'm not," said Maggie. "When I came here first I didn't believe in God, but now—I'm not sure. There's something strange, which may be God for all I know. I'm going to find out. If He has the doing of everything then He's taken away all I cared for, and I'm not going to give Him the satisfaction of seeing that it hurt; if He didn't do it, then it doesn't matter."

"You'll believe in Him before you die, Maggie," said Aunt Anne. "It's in you, and you won't escape it. I thought it was I who was to bring you to Him, but I was going too fast. The Lord has His own time. You'll come to Him afterwards."

"Oh," cried Maggie. "I'm so glad I'm going somewhere where it won't be always religion, where they'll think of something else than the Lord and His Coming. I want real life, banks and motor-cars and shops and clothes and work ..."

She stopped suddenly.

Aunt Anne was doing what Maggie had never seen her do before, even in the worst bouts of her pain—she was crying ... cold solitary lonely tears that crept slowly, reluctantly down her thin cheeks.

"I meant to do well. In everything I have done ill ... Everything has failed in my hands—"

Once again, as long before at St. Dreot's, Maggie could do nothing.

There was a long miserable silence, then Aunt Anne got up and went away.

Next day Katherine came in a beautiful motor-car to fetch Maggie. Maggie had packed her few things. Bound her neck next her skin was the ring with three pearls ...

She said good-bye to the house: her bedroom beneath which the motor-omnibuses clanged, the sitting-room with the family group, the passage with the Armed Men, the dark hall with the green baize door ... then good-bye to Aunt Elizabeth (two kisses), Aunt Anne (one kiss), Martha, Thomas the cat, the parrot ... all, everything, good-bye, good-bye, good-bye!

May I never see any of you again. Never, never, never, never! ...

She was helped into the car, rugs were wrapped round her, there was a warm cosy smell of rich leather, a little clock ticked away, a silver vase with red and blue flowers winked at her, and Katherine was there close beside her ...

Never again, never again! And yet how strange, as they turned the corner of the street down into the Strand, Maggie felt a sudden pang of regret, of pathos, of loneliness, as though she were leaving something that had loved her dearly, and leaving it without a word of friendliness.

"Poor dear!" She wanted to return, to tell it ... to tell it what? She had made her choice. She was plunging now into the other half of the world, and plunging not quite alone, because she was taking Martin with her.

"I do hope you won't mind, dear," said Katherine. "My cousin Paul—the clergyman you met once—is staying with us. He and his sister. No one else."

"Oh, I shan't mind," said Maggie. Her fingers, inside her blouse, tightly clutched the little pearl ring.

CHAPTER II

PLUNGE INTO THE OTHER HALF

For a week Maggie was so comfortable that she could think of nothing but that. It must be remembered that she had never before known what comfort was, never at St. Dreot's, never at Aunt Anne's, and these two places had been the background of all her life.

She had never conceived of the kind of way that she now lived. Her bedroom was so pretty that it made her almost cry to look at it: the wall-paper scattered with little rosy trees, the soft pink cretonne on the chairs, the old bureau with a sheet of glass covering its surface that was her dressing-table, the old gold mirror—all these things were wonders indeed. She was ordered to have breakfast in bed; servants looked after her with a kindliness and ease and readiness to help that she had never dreamed of as possible. The food was wonderful; there was the motor ready to take her for a drive in the afternoon, and there was the whole house at her service, soft and cosy and ordered so that it seemed to roll along upon its own impulse without any human agency.

"I believe if every one went away and left it," she thought, "it would go on in exactly the same way."

Figures gradually took their places in front of this background. The principals at first were Katherine and Philip, Henry and Millicent, Katherine's brother and sister, Mr. Trenchard senior, Katherine's father, Lady Rachel Seddon, Katherine's best friend, and Mr. Faunder, Katherine's uncle. She saw at once that they all revolved around Katherine; if Katherine were not there they would not hold together at all. They were all so different—so different and yet so strangely alike. There was, for instance, Millicent Trenchard, whom Maggie liked best of them all after Katherine. Millie was a young woman of twenty-one, pretty, gay, ferociously independent, enthusiastic about one thing after another, with hosts of friends, male and female, none of whom she took very seriously. The love of her life, she told Maggie almost at once, was Katherine. She would never love any one, man or woman, so much again. She lived with her mother and father in an old house in Westminster, and Maggie understood that there had been some trouble about Katherine's marriage, so that, although it happened three years ago, Mrs. Trenchard would not come to see Katherine and would not allow Katherine to come and see her.

Then there was Henry, a very strange young man. He was at Cambridge and said to be very clever. He did indeed seem to lead a mysterious life of his own and paid very little attention to Maggie, asking her once whether she did not think The Golden Ass wonderful, and what did she think of Petronius; and when Maggie laughed and said that she was glad to say she never read anything, he left her in an agitated horror. Lady Rachel Seddon was very grand and splendid, and frightened Katherine. She was related to every kind of duke and marquis, and although that fact did not impress Maggie in the least, it did seem to remove Lady Rachel into quite another world.

But they were all in another world—Maggie discovered that at once. They had, of course, every sort of catch-word and allusion and joke that no one but themselves and the people whom they brought into the house understood; Katherine was kindness itself. Philip too (he seemed to Maggie a weak, amiable young man) took a lot of trouble about her, but they did not belong to her nor she to them.

"And why should they?" said Maggie to herself. "I must look on it as though I were staying at a delightful hotel and were going on with my journey very soon."

There was somebody, however, who did not belong any more than Maggie did, and very soon he became Maggie's constant companion—this was the Rev. Paul Trenchard, Katherine's cousin.

From the very moment months ago, when Maggie and he had first met in Katherine's drawing-room, they had been friends. He had liked her, Maggie felt, at once. She on her side was attracted by a certain childlike simplicity and innocence. This very quality, she soon saw, moved the others, Philip and Henry and Mr. Trenchard senior, to derision. They did not like the Rev. Paul. They chaffed him, and he was very easily teased, because he was not clever and did not see their jokes. This put Maggie up in arms in his defence at once. But they had all the layman's distrust of a parson. They were all polite to him, of course, and Maggie discovered that in this world politeness was of the very first importance, so that you really never said what you thought nor did what you wanted to. They frankly could not understand why Katherine asked the parson to stay, but because they loved Katherine they were as nice to him as their natures would allow them to be. Paul did not apparently notice that they put him outside their life. He was always genial, laughed a great deal when there WAS no reason to laugh at all, and told simple little stories in whose effect he profoundly believed. He was supported in his confidence by his sister Grace, who obviously adored him. She too was "outside" the family, but she seemed to be quite happy telling endless stories of Paul's courage and cleverness and popularity. She did indeed believe that Skeaton-on-Sea, where Paul had his living, was the hub of the universe, and this amused all the Trenchard family very much indeed. It must not be supposed that Paul and his sister were treated unkindly. They were shown the greatest courtesy and hospitality, but Maggie knew that that was only because it was the Trenchard tradition to do so, and not from motives of affection or warmth of heart.

They could be warm-hearted; it was wonderful to see the way that they all adored Katherine, and they had many friends for whom they would do anything, but the Rev. Paul seemed to them frankly an ass, and they would be glad when he went away.

He did not seem to Maggie an ass. She thought him the kindest person she had ever known, kinder even than Katherine, because with Katherine there was the faintest suspicion of patronage; no, not of patronage—that was unfair ... but of an effort to put herself in exactly Maggie's place so that she might understand perfectly what were Maggie's motives. With Paul Trenchard there was no effort, no deliberate slipping out of one world into another one. He was frankly delighted to tell Maggie everything—all about Skeaton-on-Sea and its delights, about the church and its marvellous east window, about the choir and the difficulties with the choir-boys and the necessity for repairing the organ, about the troubles with the churchwardens, especially one Mr. Bellows, who, in his cantankerous and dyspeptic objections to everything that any one proposed, became quite a lively figure to Maggie's imagination, about the St. John's Brotherhood which had been formed to keep the "lads" out of the public-houses and was doing so well, about the Shakespeare Reading Society and a Mrs. Tempest (who also became a live figure in Maggie's brain), "a born tragedian" and wonderful as Lady Macbeth and Katherine of Aragon. Skeaton slowly revealed itself to Maggie as a sunny sparkling place, with glittering sea, shining sand, and dark cool woods, full of kindliness, too, and friendship and good-humour. Paul and Grace Trenchard seemed to be the centre of this sunshine. How heartily Paul laughed as he recounted some of the tricks and escapades of his "young scamps." "Dear fellows," he would say, "I love them all ..." and Grace sat by smiling and nodding her head and beaming upon her beloved brother.

To Maggie, fresh from the dark and confused terrors of the Chapel, it was all marvellous. Here was rest indeed, here, with Martin cherished warmly in her heart, she might occupy herself with duties and interests. Here surely she would be useful to "somebody." She heard a good deal of an old Mr. Toms, "a little queer in his head, poor man," who seemed to figure in the outskirts of Skeaton society as a warning and a reassurance. ("No one in Skeaton thinks of him in any way but tenderly.") Maggie wondered whether he might not want looking after ...

The thought gradually occurred to her that this kindly genial clergyman might perhaps find her some work in Skeaton. He even himself hinted at something ... She might be some one's secretary or housekeeper.

About Grace Trenchard Maggie was not quite so sure. She was kindness itself and liked to hold Maggie's hand and pat it—but there was no doubt at all that she was just a little bit tiresome. Maggie rebuked herself for thinking this, but again and again the thought arose. Grace was in a state of perpetual wonder, everything amazed her. You would not think to look at her flat broad placidity that she was a creature of excitement, and it might be that her excitement was rather superficial. She would say: "Why! Just fancy, Maggie! ... To-day's Tuesday!" Then you wondered what was coming next and nothing came at all. She had endless stories about her adventures in the streets of London, and these stories were endless because of all the details that must be fitted in, and then the details slipped out of her grasp and winked at her maliciously as they disappeared. The fact was perhaps that she was not very clever, but then Maggie wasn't very clever either, so she had no right to criticise Miss Trenchard, who was really as amiable as she could be. Henry Trenchard said once to Maggie in his usual scornful way:

"Oh, Grace! ... She's the stupidest woman in Skeaton, which means the stupidest woman in the world."

The Trenchards, Maggie thought, were rather given to scorning every one save themselves. Even Philip, who was not a Trenchard, had caught the habit. Katherine, of course, despised no one and liked every one, but that was rather tiresome too.

In fact at the end of her first week Maggie thought that as soon as possible she would find a room for herself somewhere and start to earn her living. She discovered that she was developing a new sensitiveness. When she was living with the aunts she had not minded very seriously the criticisms made upon her; she had indeed been disappointed when Aunt Anne had not admired her new dress, and she had hated Amy Warlock's rudeness, but that was because Martin had been involved. This new sensitiveness worried her; she hated to care whether people laughed at the way she came into a room or whether she expressed foolish opinions about books and pictures. She had always said just what she thought, but now, before Philip's kindly attention and Mr. Trenchard senior's indulgence (he wrote books and articles in the papers), she hated her ignorance. Paul Trenchard knew frankly nothing about Art. "I know what I like," he said, "and that's enough for me." He liked Watts's pictures and In Memoriam and Dickens, and he heard The Messiah once a year in London if he could leave his parish work. He laughed about it all. "The souls of men! The souls of men!" he would say. "That is what I'm after, Miss Cardinal. You're not going to catch them with the latest neurotic novel, however well it's written."

Oh, he was kind to her! He was kinder and kinder and kinder. She told him everything—except about Martin. She told him all about her life at St. Dreot's and her father and Uncle Mathew, the aunts and the Chapel.

He was frankly shocked by the Chapel. "That's not the way to get into heaven," he said. "We must be more patient than that. The daily round, the daily task, that's the kind."

His physical presence began to pervade all her doings. He was not handsome, but so clean, so rosy, and so strong. No mystery about him, no terrors, no invasions from the devil. Everything was clear and certain. He knew just where he was and exactly whither he was going. One afternoon, when they were out in the motor together, he took Maggie's hand under the rug and he held it so calmly, so firmly, with so kindly a benevolence that she could not be frightened or uncomfortable. He was like a large friendly brother ...

One day he called her Maggie. He blushed and laughed. "I'm so sorry," he said. "It slipped out. I caught it from Katherine."

"Oh, please, ... never mind," she answered. "Miss Cardinal's so stiff."

"Then you must call me Paul," he said.

A little conversation that Maggie had after this with Millicent showed her in sharp relief exactly where she stood in relation to the Trenchard family. They had been out in the motor together. Millie had been shopping and now they were rolling back through the Park.

"Are you happy with us, Maggie?" Millicent suddenly asked.

"Very happy," Maggie answered.

"Well, I hope you are," said Millicent. "I don't think that as a family we're very good at making any one happy except ourselves. I think we're very selfish."

"No, I don't think you're selfish," said Maggie, "but I think you're sufficient for yourselves. I don't fancy you really want any one from outside."

"No, I don't think the others do. I do though. You don't suppose I'm going to stay in the Trenchard bosom for ever, do you? I'm not, I assure you. But what you've said means that you don't really feel at home with us."

"I don't think I want to feel at home with you," Maggie answered. "I don't belong to any of you. Contrast us, for instance. You've got everything—good looks, money, cleverness, position. You can get what you like out of life. I've got nothing. I'm plain, poor, awkward, uneducated—and yet you know I wouldn't change places with any one. I'd rather be myself than any one alive."

"Yes, you would," said Millicent, nodding her head. "That's you all over. I felt it the moment you came into the house. You're adventurous. We're not. Katherine was adventurous for a moment when she married Philip, but she soon slipped back again. But you'll do just what you want to always."

"I shall have to," said Maggie, laughing. "There's no one else to do it for me. It isn't only that I don't belong to you—I've never belonged to any one, only one person—and he's gone now. I belong to him—and he'll never come back."

"Were you frightfully in love?" asked Millie, deeply interested.

"Yes," said Maggie.

"He oughtn't to have gone away like that," said Millicent.

"Yes, he ought," said Maggie. "He was quite right. But don't let's bother about that. I've got to find some place now where I can work. The worst of it is I'm so ignorant. But there must be something that I ran do."

"There's Paul," said Millie.

"What do you mean?" asked Maggie.

"Oh, he cares like anything for you. You must have noticed. It began after the first time he met you. He was always asking about you. Of course every one's noticed it."

"Cares for me," Maggie repeated.

"Yes, of course. He's wanted to marry for a long time. Tired of Grace bossing him, I expect. That doesn't sound very polite to you, but I know that he cares for you apart from that—for yourself, I mean. And I expect Grace is tired of housekeeping."

Maggie's feelings were very strange. Why should he care about her? Did she want him to care? A strange friendly feeling stole about her heart. She was not alone then, after all. Some one wanted her, wanted her so obviously that every one had noticed it—did not want her as Martin had wanted her, against his own will and judgment. If he did offer her his home what would she feel?

There was rest there, rest and a real home, a home that she had never in all her life known. Of course she did not love him in the least. His approach did not make her pulses beat a moment faster, she did not long for him to come when he was not there—but he wanted her! That was the great thing. He wanted her!

"Of course if he asked you, you wouldn't really think of marrying him?" said Millicent.

"I don't know," said Maggie slowly.

"What! Marry him and live in Skeaton!" Millicent was frankly amazed. "Why, Skeaton's awful, and the people in it are awful, and Grace is awful. In the summer it's all nigger-minstrels and bathing-tents, and in the winter there isn't a soul—" Millicent shivered.

Maggie smiled. "Of course it seems dull to you, but my life's been very different. It hasn't been very exciting, and if I could really help him—" she broke off. "I do like him," she said. "He's the kindest man I've ever met. Of course he seems dull to you who have met all kinds of brilliant people. I hate brilliant people."

The car was in Bryanston Square. Just before it stopped Millie bent over and kissed Maggie.

"I think you're a darling," she said.

But Millie didn't think Maggie "a darling" for long—that is, she did not think about her at all for long; none of the family did.

So quiet was Maggie, so little in any one's way that, at the end of a fortnight, she made no difference to any one in the house. She was much better now, looking a different person, colour in her cheeks and light in her eyes. During her illness they had cut her hair and this made her look more than ever like a boy. She wore her plain dark dresses, black and dark blue; they never quite fitted and, with her queer odd face, her high forehead, rather awkward mouth, and grave questioning eyes she gave you the impression that she had been hurried into some disguise and was wearing it with discomfort but amusement. Some one who met her at the Trenchards at this time said of her: "What a funny girl! She's like a schoolboy dressed up to play a part in the school speeches." Of course she was not playing a part, no one could have been more entirely natural and honest, but she was odd, strange, out of her own world, and every one felt it.

It was, perhaps, this strangeness that attracted Paul Trenchard. He was, above everything, a kindly man-kindly, perhaps a little through laziness, but nevertheless moved always by distress or misfortune in others. Maggie was not distressed—she was quite cheerful and entirely unsentimental—nevertheless she had been very ill, was almost penniless, had had some private trouble, was an orphan, had no friends save two old aunts, and was amazingly ignorant of the world.

This last was, perhaps, the thing that struck him most of all. He, too, was ignorant of the world, but he didn't know that, and he was amazed at the things that Maggie brushed aside as unimportant. He found that he was beginning to think of her as "my little heathen." His attitude was the same as that of a good missionary discovering a naked but trusting native.

The thought of training this virgin mind was delightful to him.

He liked her quaintness, and one day suddenly, to his own surprise, when they were alone in the drawing-room, he kissed her, a most chaste kiss, gently on the forehead.

"Oh. my dear child—" he said in a kind of dismay.

She looked up at him with complete confidence. So gentle a kiss had it been that it had been no more than a pressure of the hand.

A few days later Katherine spoke to her. She came up to her bedroom just as Maggie was beginning to undress. Maggie stood in front of the glass, her evening frock off, brushing her short thick hair before the glass.

"Have you made any plans yet, dear?" asked Katherine.

Maggie shook her head.

"No." she said. "Not yet."

Katherine hesitated.

"I've got a confession to make," she said at last.

Maggie turned to look at her with her large childish eyes.

"Oh, I do hope you've done something wrong," she said, laughing, "something really bad that I should have to 'overlook.'"

"What do you mean?" asked Katherine.

Maggie only said: "We'd be more on a level then."

"I don't think it's anything very bad. But the truth is, Maggie, that I didn't ask you here only for my own pleasure and to make you well. There was a third reason."

"I know," said Maggie; "Paul."

"My dear!" said Katherine, amazed. "How did you guess? I never should have done."

"Paul's asked you to find out whether I like him," said Maggie.

"Yes," said Katherine.

"Well, I do like him." said Maggie.

"Don't think that I've been unfair," said Katherine. They were sitting now side by side on Maggie's bed and Katherine's hand was on Maggie's knee. "I'll tell you exactly how it happened. Paul was interested in you from the moment that he saw you at my house ever so long ago. He asked ever so many questions about you, and the next time he stayed he wanted me to write and ask you to come and stay. Well, I didn't. I knew from what you told me that you cared for somebody else, and I didn't want to get Paul really fond of you if it was going to be no good. You see, I've known Paul for ages. He's nearly ten years older than I, but he used to come and stay with us at Garth, when he was at Cambridge and before he was a clergyman."

"I'm very fond of him. I know the others think he's stupid simply because he doesn't know the things that they do, but he's good and kind and honest, and just exactly what he seems to be."

"I like him," repeated Maggie, nodding her head.

"He's been wanting to be married," went on Katherine, "for some time. I'm going to tell you everything so that I shall have been perfectly fair. Grace wants him to be married too. All her life she's looked after him and he's always done exactly what she told him. He's rather lazy and it's not hard for some one to get an influence over him. Well, she's not really a very good manager. She thinks she is, but she isn't. She arranges things and wants things to stay just where she puts them, but she arranges all the wrong unnecessary things. Still, it's easy to criticise, and I'm not a very good manager myself. I think she's growing rather tired of it and would like some one to take it off her hands. Of course Paul must marry the right person, some one whom she can control and manage, and some one who won't transplant her in Paul's affection. That's her idea. But it's all nonsense, of course. You can't have your cake and eat it. She simply doesn't understand what marriage is like. When Paul marries she'll learn more about life in a month than she's learnt in all her days. Well, Maggie, dear, she thinks you're just the girl for Paul. She thinks she can do what she likes with you. She thinks you're nice, of course, but she's going to 'form' you and 'train' you. You needn't worry about that, you needn't really, if you care about Paul. You'd manage both of them in a week. But there it is—I thought I ought to warn you about Grace."

"As to Paul, I believe you'd be happy. You'd have your home and your life and your friends. Skeaton isn't so bad if you live in it, I believe, and Paul could get another living if you weren't happy there."

Did Katherine have any scruples as she pursued her argument? A real glance at Maggie's confiding trustful gaze might have shaken her resolve. This child who knew so little about anything—was Skeaton the world for her? But Katherine had so many philanthropies that she was given to finishing one off a little abruptly in order to make ready for the next one.

She was interested just now in a scheme for adopting illegitimate babies. She thought Maggie an "angel" and she just longed for her to be happy. Nevertheless Maggie was very ignorant, and it was a little difficult to see what trade or occupation she would be able to adopt. She was nearly well now and Katherine did not know quite what to do with her. Here was an admirable marriage, something that would give a home and children and friends. What could be better? She had just passed apparently through a love affair that could have led to no possible good—solve the difficulty, make Maggie safe for life, and pass on to the illegitimate babies!

"Of course, I don't love him," said Maggie, staring in front of her.

"But you like him," said Katherine. "It isn't as though Paul were a very young man. He wouldn't expect anything very romantic. He isn't really a romantic man himself."

"And I shall always love Martin," pursued Maggie.

Katherine's own romance had fulfilled itself so thoroughly that it had almost ceased to be romantic. The Trenchard blood in her made her a little impatient of unfulfilled romances.

"Don't you think, Maggie, dear," she said gently, "that it would be better to forget him?"

"No, I don't," said Maggie, moving away from Katherine. "And I should have to tell Paul about him. I'd tell Paul the exact truth, that if I married him it was because I liked him and I thought we'd be good friends. I see quite clearly that I can't sit for ever waiting for Martin to come back, and the sooner I settle to something the better. If Paul wants a friend I can be one, but I should never love him—even though Martin wasn't there. And as to the managing, I'm dreadfully careless and forgetful."

"You'd soon learn," said Katherine.

"Do you think I should?" asked Maggie. "I don't know, I'm sure. As to Grace, I think we'd get on all right. There's a greater difficulty than that though."

"What?" asked Katherine as Maggie hesitated.

"Religion," said Maggie. "Paul's a clergyman and I don't believe in his religion at all. Two months ago I'd have said I hated all religion—and so would you if you'd had a time like me. But since Martin's gone I'm not so sure. There's some-thing I want to find out... But Paul's found out everything. He's quite sure and certain. I'd have to tell him I don't believe in any of his faith."

"Tell him, of course," said Katherine. "I think he knows that already. He's going to convert you. He looks forward to it. If he hadn't been so lazy he'd have been a missionary."

"Tell me about Skeaton," said Maggie.

"I've only been there once," said Katherine. "Frankly, I didn't like it very much, but then I'm so used to the Glebeshire sea that it all seemed rather tame. There was a good deal of sand blowing about the day I was there, but Paul's house is nice with a garden and a croquet-lawn, and—and—Oh! very nice, and nice people next door I believe."

"I'm glad it's not like Glebeshire," said Maggie. "That's a point in its favour. I want to be somewhere where everything is quiet and orderly, and every one knows their own mind and all the bells ring at the right time and no one's strange or queer, and—most of all—where no one's afraid of anything. All my life I've been with people who were afraid and I've been afraid myself. Now Paul and Grace are not afraid of anything."

"No, they're not," said Katherine, laughing.

Suddenly Maggie broke out:

"Katherine! Tell me truly. Does Paul want me, does he need me? Does he indeed?"

The storm of appeal in Maggie's voice made Katherine suddenly shy; there was a hint at loneliness and desolation there that was something beyond her reach. She wanted to help. She was suddenly frightened at her urging of Paul's suit. Something seemed to say to her: "Leave this alone. Don't take the responsibility of this. You don't understand ..."

But another voice said: "Poor child ... all alone, penniless, without a friend. What a chance for her! Paul such a kind man."

So she kissed Maggie, and said: "He wants you dreadfully, Maggie dear."

Maggie's cheeks flushed.

"That's nice," she said in her most ordinary voice. "Because no one ever has before, you know."

Paul's proposal came the very next day. It came after luncheon in a corner of the drawing-room.

Maggie knew quite well that it was coming. She was lying in a long chair near the fire, a shawl over her knees. It was a blustering day at the end of February. The windows rattled, and the wind rushing down the chimney blew the flame into little flags and pennants of colour.

Paul came and stood by the fire, warming his hands, his legs spread out. Maggie looked at him with a long comprehensive glance that took him in from head to foot. She seemed to know then that she was going to marry him. A voice seemed to say to her: "Look at him well. This is the man you're going to live with. You'd better realise him."

She did realise him; his white hair, his rosy cheeks, his boyish nose and mouth and rounded chin, his broad chest, thick long legs and large white hands—soft perhaps, but warm and comfortable and safe. Maggie could think of little else as she looked at him but of how nice it would be to lay her head back on that broad chest, feel his arms around her, and forget—forget—forget!

That was what she needed—forgetfulness and work ... She did not love him—no, not one little atom. She had never felt less excitement about anybody, but she liked him, respected him, and trusted him. And he wanted her, wanted her desperately, Katherine had said, that was the chief thing of all.

"Maggie!" he said suddenly, turning round to her. "Would you ever think of marrying me?"

She liked that directness and simplicity, characteristic of him.

She looked up at him.

"I don't think I'd be much of a success, Paul," she said.

He saw at once from that that she did not intend instantly to refuse him. His rosy cheeks took on an added tinge of colour and he caught a chair, drew it up to her long one and sat down, bending eagerly towards her.

"Leave that to me," he said.

"I oughtn't to think of it," she answered, shaking her head. "And for very good reasons. For one thing I'm not in love with you, for another I'm not religious, and for a third I'm so careless that I'd never do for your wife."

"Of course I knew about the first," he said eagerly. "I knew you didn't love me, but that will come, Maggie. It MUST come ..."

Maggie shook her head. "I love some one else," she said, "and I always will. But he's gone away and will never come back. I've made up my mind to that. But if he did come back and wanted me I couldn't promise that I wouldn't—" She broke off. "You can see that it wouldn't do."

"No, I can't see," he said, taking her hand. "I can see that you like me, Maggie. I can see that we're splendid friends. If your other—friend—has left you altogether, then—well, time makes a great difference in those things. I think after we'd been together a little—Oh, Maggie, do!" he broke off just like a boy. "Do! We suit each other so well that we MUST be happy, and then Grace likes you—she likes you very much. She does indeed."

"Let's leave Grace out of this," Maggie said firmly. "It's between you and me, Paul. It's nobody else's affair. What about the other two objections? I don't believe in your faith at all, and I'm unpunctual and forgetful, and break things."

Strangely she was wanting him urgently now to reassure her. She realised that if now he withdrew she would be faced with a loneliness more terrible than anything that she had known since Martin had left her. The warm pressure of his hand about hers reassured her.

"Maggie dear," he said softly, "I love you better because you're young and unformed. I can help you, dear, and you can help me, of course; I'm a dreadful old buffer in many ways. I'm forty, you know, and you're such a child. How old are you, Maggie?"

"Twenty," she said.

"Twenty! Fancy! And you can like an old parson—well, well ... If you care for me nothing else matters. God will see to the rest."

"I don't like leaving things to other people," Maggie said slowly. "Now I suppose I've shocked you. But there you are; I shall always be shocking you."

"Nothing that you can say will shock me," he answered firmly. "Do you know that that's part of the charm you have for me, you dear little wild thing? If you will come and live with me perhaps you will see how God works, how mysterious are His ways, and what He means to do for you—"

Maggie shivered: "Oh, now you're talking like Aunt Anne. I don't want to feel that I'm something that some one can do what he likes with. I'm not."

"No. I know you're not," Paul answered eagerly. "You're very independent. I admire that in you—and so does Grace—"

"Would Grace like us to marry?" asked Maggie.

"It's the desire of her heart," said Paul.

"But how can you want to marry me when you know I don't love you?"

"Love's a strange thing. Companionship can make great changes. You like me. That is enough for the present. I can be patient. I'm not an impetuous man."

He was certainly not. He was just a large warm comfortable creature far, far from the terrified and strangely travelled soul of Martin ... Insensibly, hardly realising what she did, Maggie was drawn towards Paul. He drew close to her, moved on to the sofa, and then with one arm about her let her head rest against his chest. Maggie could neither move nor speak. She only felt a warm comfort, an intense desire for rest.

Very, very gently he bent down and kissed her forehead. The clock ticked on. The flames of the fire spurted and fell. Maggie's eyes closed, she gave a little sigh, and soon, her cheek against his waistcoat, like a little child, was fast asleep.

The engagement was a settled thing. Every one in the house was relieved. Maggie herself felt as though she had found lights and safety, running from a wood full of loneliness and terror. She was sharp enough to see how relieved they all were that she was 'settled.' They were true kindly people, and now they were more kind to her than ever: that showed that they had been uneasy about her. She was 'off their hands now.'

Maggie, when she saw this in the faces of Philip and Mr. Trenchard, and even of Millicent, was glad that she was engaged. She was somebody's now; she had friends and a home and work now, and she would banish all that other world for ever. For ever? ... How curious it was that from the moment of her engagement her aunts, their house, the Chapel, and the people around it began to press upon her attention with a pathos and sentiment that she had never felt before. She went to see the aunts, of course, and sat in the old drawing-room for half-an-hour, and they were kind and distant. They were glad that she was to be married; they hoped that she would be happy. Aunt Anne looked very ill, and there was a terrible air of desertion about the house as though all the life had gone out of it. Maggie came away very miserable. Then she said to herself: "Now, look here. You're in a new house now. You've got to think of nothing but that—nothing, nothing, nothing ..."

She meant Martin. She might think of Martin (how indeed could she help it?) but she was not to long for him. No, no ... not to long for him. She did wish that she could go to sleep more quickly when she went to bed.

Paul and Grace were very kind to her. Paul was just the big elder brother that she loved him to be. No more sentiment than that. A kiss morning, a kiss evening, that was all. Grace behaved to them both with a motherly indulgence. Maggie saw that she considered that she had arranged the whole affair. There were signs that she intended to arrange everything for Maggie. Well, it was rather pleasant just now to have things arranged for you. Maggie had only one wish—that Grace would not take so long to explain everything. Maggie always ran ahead of her long before she had finished her involved sentences and then had to curb her impatience. However one would get used to Grace; one would have to because she was going to live with them after they were married. Maggie had hoped that it would be otherwise, but it was at once obvious that neither Paul nor Grace dreamt of being separated.

The wedding was to be as soon as possible, and very, very quiet. In a little church close by, no bridesmaids, everything very simple. Maggie was glad of that. She would have hated a church full of staring people. She enjoyed immensely buying her trousseau. Paul was very generous with his money; it was evident that Grace thought him too generous. Maggie and Katherine went together to buy things, and Katherine was a darling. Maggie fancied that Katherine was not quite easy in her mind about her share in the affair.

"You won't expect Skeaton to be wildly exciting, Maggie dear, will you?" she said. "You'll find plenty to do and there are lots of nice people, I'm sure, and you'll come up and stay with us here."

"I think it sounds delightful," said Maggie. "If you'd lived for years in St. Dreot's, Katherine, you wouldn't talk about other places being dull. It isn't excitement I want. It's work."

"Don't you let Grace bully you," said Katherine.

"Bully me? Grace?" Maggie was very astonished. "Why, she's the kindest old thing. She wants me to do everything."

"So she says," said Katherine doubtfully. "But she's very jealous of Paul. How much she'll really like giving up her authority when it comes to the point I don't know. You stick up to her. Paul's weak."

"I don't think he is." said Maggie rather indignantly. "Grace always does what he says." "Yes, just now," said Katherine.

And Maggie had one funny little conversation with Henry Trenchard. That wild youth catching her alone one day said abruptly:

"What the devil have you done it for?"

"Done what?" asked Maggie, her heart beating a little faster. Strangely Henry reminded her of Martin. He alone of all the Trenchards had something that was of that other world.

"Engaged yourself to Paul," said Henry.

"Why shouldn't I?" asked Maggie.

"You don't love him—of course you couldn't. You're not his sort in the least. You're worth a million Pauls."

This was so odd for Henry, who was certainly not given to compliments, that Maggie burst out laughing.

"Yes, you may laugh," said Henry. "I know what I'm talking about. Have you ever seen Paul asleep after dinner?"

"No," said Maggie.

"I wish you had. That might have saved you. Have you ever seen Grace lose her temper?"

"No," said Maggie, this time a little uneasily.

"Look here," he came close to her, staring at her with those eyes of his that could be very charming when he liked. "Break it off. Say you think it's a mistake. You'll be miserable."

"Indeed I shan't," said Maggie, tossing her head. "Whatever happens I'm not going to be miserable. No one can make me that."

"So you think," Henry frowned. "I can't think what you want to be married for at all. These days women can have such a good time, especially a woman with character like you. If I were a woman I'd never marry."

"You don't understand," said Maggie. "You haven't been lonely all your life as I have, and you're not afraid of making yourself cheap and—and—looking for some one who doesn't want—you. It's so easy for you to talk. And Paul wants me—really he does—"

"Yes, he does," said Henry slowly. "He's in love with you all right. I'm as sorry for Paul as I am for you."

Maggie laughed. "It's very kind of you to be sorry," she said, "but you needn't trouble. I believe we can look after ourselves."

For a quarter of an hour after this conversation she was a little uneasy. He was a clever boy, Henry; he did watch people. But then he was very young, It was all guesswork with him.

She became now strangely quiescent; her energy, her individuality, her strength of will seemed, for the time, entirely to have gone. She surrendered herself to Grace and Paul and Katherine and they did what they would with her.

Only once was she disturbed. Two nights before the wedding she dreamt of Martin. It did not appear as a dream at all. It seemed to her that she had been asleep and that she suddenly woke. She was gazing, from her bed, into her own room, but at the farther end of it instead of the wall with the rosy trees and the gold mirror was another room. This room was strange and cheerless with bare boards, a large four-poster bed with faded blue hangings, two old black prints with eighteenth-century figures and a big standing mirror. In front of the bed, staring into the mirror, was Martin, He was dressed shabbily in a blue reefer coat. He looked older than when she had seen him last, was stouter and ill, with white puffy cheeks and dark shadows under his eyes. She saw him very clearly under the light of two candles that wavered a little in the draught.

He was staring into the mirror, absorbed apparently in what he saw there. She cried his name and he seemed to start and turn towards the door listening. Then the picture faded. She woke to find herself sitting up in bed crying his name ...

In the morning she drove this dream away from her, refusing to think of it or listen to it, but somewhere far down in her soul something trembled.

The wedding was over so quickly that she scarcely realised it. There was the stuffy little church, very empty and dusty, with brass plates on the wall. She could hear, in the street, rumblings of carts and the rattle of wheels; somewhere a barrel-organ played. The clergyman was a little man who smiled upon her kindly. When Paul put the ring on her finger she started as though for a moment she awoke from a dream. She was glad that he looked so clean and tidy. Grace was wearing too grand a hat with black feathers. In the vestry Paul kissed her, and then they walked down the aisle together. She saw Katherine and Millie and Henry. Her fingers caught tightly about Paul's stout arm, but she would have been more at home she thought with Uncle Mathew just then.

It was a nice bright spring day, although the wind blew the dust about. They had a meal in Katherine's house and some one made a speech, and Maggie drank some champagne. She hoped she looked nice in her grey silk dress, and then caught sight of herself in a glass and thought she was as ever a fright.

"My little wild thing—mine now," whispered Paul. She thought that rather silly; she was not a wild thing, but simply Maggie Cardinal. Oh, no! Maggie Trenchard ... She did not feel Maggie Trenchard at all and she did not suppose that she ever would.

They were to have a fortnight alone at Skeaton before Grace came. Maggie was glad of that. Paul was really nicer when Grace was not there.

They were all very kind to her. They had given her good presents—Millie some silver brushes, Henry some books, Philip a fan, and Katherine a most beautiful dressing-bag. Maggie had never had such things before. But she could have wished for something from her own people. She had written to Uncle Mathew but had not heard from him.

At the very last moment, on the morning of the wedding day, a present came from the aunts—an old box for handkerchiefs. The cover was inlaid with sea-shells and there was a little looking-glass inside.

Very soon it was all over and then to her own intense surprise she was alone in the train with Paul. What had she expected? She did not know—but somehow not this.

They were in a first-class carriage. Paul was doing the thing nobly. He sat close to her, his broad knee against her dress. How broad his knee was, a great expanse of black shining cloth. He took her hand and rested it on the expanse, and, at the touch of the stuff and the throb of the warm flesh beneath it, she shivered a little and would wish to have drawn her hand away. He seemed so much larger than she had expected; from his knee to his high shining white collar was an immense distance and midway there was a thick gold watch-chain rising and falling as he breathed. He smelt very faintly of tooth-powder.

But on the whole she was comfortable; only the thin gold ring round her finger felt strange. Deep in a little pocket inside her blouse was the ring with the three little pearls.

"I do hope, Maggie darling," he said, "you don't think it strange our not going somewhere else for our honeymoon. My lads will be expecting me back—I was kept longer in London than I should have been—by you, you little witch. My witch now—"

He put his arm round her waist and urged her head towards his coat. But her hat, her beautiful hat that had cost so much more than she had ever spent on a hat before, was in the way. It struck into his chin. They were both uncomfortable and then, thank heaven, the train slowed down; they were at a station and some one got into their carriage, a stout man, all newspaper and creases to his trousers. That, in the circumstances, was a great relief and soon Maggie dozed, seeing the telegraph wires and the trees like waving hands through a mist of sleep.

As she fell asleep she realised that this was only the second time in all her life that she had been in a train. Some one bawled in her ear "Skeaton! Skeaton!" and she looked up to find a goat-faced porter gazing at her through the window. She was on a storm-driven platform, her husband's arm was through hers, she was being helped into an old faded cab. Now they were driving down a hill, under a railway-arch, along a road with villas and trees, trees and villas, and then villas alone. What a wind! The bare branches were in a frenzy, and from almost every villa blew little pennons of white curtains. "They like to have their windows open any way," she thought. Paul said very little; he was obviously nervous of how she would take it all. She took it all very well.

"What pretty houses!" she said. "And here are the shops!"

Only a few—a sweet-shop, a grocer's, a stationer's with "Simpson's Library" on the door, a post-office.

"The suburbs," said Paul.

What a wind! It rolled up the road like a leaping carpet, you could almost see its folds and creases. No one about—not a living soul.

"The cab I ordered never came. Lucky thing there was one there," said Paul.

Not a soul about. Does any one live here? She could not see much through the window, and she could hear nothing because the glass rattled so.

"Here we are!" The cab stopped with a jerk. Here they were then. A gate swung to behind them, there was a little drive with bushes on either side of it and then the house.

Not a very handsome house, Maggie thought. A dull square grey with chimneys like ears in exactly the right places. Some pieces of paper were whirled up and down by the wind, they danced about the horse's feet. She noticed that the door-handles needed polishing. A cavernous hall, a young girl with untidy hair and a yelping dog received them.

"That's Mitch!" said Paul. "Dear old Mitch. How are you, dear old fellow? Down Mitch! Down! There's a good dog."

The young girl was terrified of Maggie. She gulped through her nose.

"I've put tea in the study, sir," she said.

"Tea at once, little woman, eh?" said Paul. "I'm dying for some. Thank you, Emily. All well? That's right. Dear, dear, It IS nice to be home again."

Yes, he was nervous, poor Paul. She felt a great tenderness for him, but she could not say the right words. She should have said: "It is nice," but it was not. The hall was so cold and dark, and all over the house windows were rattling.

They went straight into the study. What a room! It reminded Maggie at once, in its untidiness and discomfort, of her father's, study, and that thought struck a chill into her very heart, so that she had to pause for a moment and control herself. There were piles of newspapers heaped up against the shelves; books run to the ceiling, old, old books with the covers tumbling off them. On the stone mantelpiece was a perfect litter—old pipes, bundles of letters, a ball of string, some yellow photographs, a crucifix and a small plant dead and shrivelled in its pot.

"Now then, darling. Hurrah for some tea!"

She poured it out and he watched her in an ecstasy. Strangely she began to be frightened and a little breathless, as though the walls of the room were slowly closing in. The tea had been standing a long time, it was very strong and chill.

The house was a firing-ground of rattle and whirs, but there were no human sounds anywhere. There was dust all over the room.

They had said nothing for some time.

He spoke suddenly, his voice husky and awkward, as though he were trying a new voice for the first time.

"Maggie!" he said. "Don't sit so far away. Come over here."

She crossed over to him. He, with an arm that seemed to be suddenly of iron, pulled her on to his knee. She was rebellious. Her whole body stiffened. She did not want this, she did not want this! Some voice within cried out: "Take care! Take care!" ... He pressed her close to him; he kissed her furiously, savagely, her eyes, her mouth, her cheek. She could feel his heart pounding beneath his clothes like a savage beast. His hands were all about her; he was crushing her so that she was hurt, but she did not feel that at all; there was something else ...

With all her might she fought down her resistance. This was her duty. She must obey. But something desolate and utterly, utterly lonely crept away and cried bitterly, watching her surrender.

CHAPTER III

She was swinging higher, higher, higher—swinging with that delightful rhythm that one knows best in dreams, lazily, idly, and yet with purpose and resolve. She was swinging far above the pain, the rebellion, the surrender. That was left for ever; the time of her tears, of her loneliness was over. Above her, yet distant, was a golden cloud, soft, iridescent, and in the heart of this lay, she knew, the solution of the mystery; when she reached it the puzzle would be resolved, and in a wonderful tranquillity she could rest after her journey. Nearer and nearer she swung; the cloud was a blaze of gold so that she must not look, but could feel its warmth and heat already irradiating about her. Only to know! ... to connect the two worlds, to find the bridge, to destroy the gulf!

Then suddenly the rhythm changed. She was descending again; slowly the cloud diminished, a globe of light, a ball of fire, a dazzling star. The air was cold, her eyes could not penetrate the dark; with a sigh she awoke.

It was early morning, and a filmy white shadow pervaded the room. For a moment she did not know where she was; she saw the ghostly shadows of chairs, of the chest of drawers, of a high cupboard. Then the large picture of "The Crucifixion," very, very dim, reminded her. She knew where she was; she turned and saw her husband sleeping at her side, huddled, like a child, his face on his arm, gently breathing, in the deepest sleep. She watched him. There had been a moment that night when she had hated him, hated him so bitterly that she could have fought him and even killed him. There had been another moment after that, when she had been so miserable that her own death seemed the only solution, when she had watched him tumble into sleep and had herself lain, with burning eyes and her flesh dry and hot, staring into the dark, ashamed, humiliated. Then the old Maggie had come to her rescue, the old Maggie who bade her make the best of her conditions whatever they might be, who told her there was humour in everything, hope always, courage everywhere, and that in her own inviolable soul lay her strength, that no one could defeat her did she not defeat herself.

Now, most strangely, in that early light, she felt a great tenderness for him, the tenderness of the mother for the child. She put out her hand, touched his shoulder, stroked it with her hand, laid her head against it. He, murmuring in his sleep, turned towards her, put his arm around her and so, in the shadow of his heart, she fell into deep, dreamless slumber.

At breakfast that morning she felt with him a strange shyness and confusion. She had never been shy with him before. At the very first she had been completely at her ease; that had been one of his greatest attractions for her. But now she realised that she would be for a whole fortnight alone with him, that she did not know him in the least, and that he himself was strangely embarrassed by his own discoveries that he was making.

So they, both of them, took the world that was on every side of them, put it in between them and left their personal relationship to wait for a better time.

Maggie was childishly excited. She had, for the first time in her life, a house of her own to order and arrange; by the middle of that first afternoon she had forgotten that Paul existed.

She admitted to herself at once, so that there should be no pretence about the matter, that the house was hideous. "Yes, it's hideous," she said aloud, standing in the middle of the dining-room and looking about her. It never could have been very much of a house, but they (meaning Paul and Grace) had certainly not done their best for it.

Maggie had had no education, she had not perhaps much natural taste, but she knew when things and people were sympathetic, and this house was as unsympathetic as a house could well be. To begin with, the wall-papers were awful; in the dining-room there was a dark dead green with some kind of pink flower; the drawing-room was dressed in a kind of squashed strawberry colour; the wall-paper of the staircases and passages was of imitation marble, and the three bedrooms were pink, green, and yellow, perfect horticultural shows.

It was the distinctive quality of all the wall-papers that nothing looked well against them, and the cheap reproductions in gilt frames, the religious prints, the photographs (groups of the Rev. Paul at Cambridge, at St. Ermand's Theological College, with the Skeaton Band of Hope) were all equally forlorn and out of place.

It was evident that everything in the house was arranged and intended to stay for ever where it was, the chairs against the walls, the ornaments on the mantelpieces, the photograph-frames, the plush mats, the bright red pots with ferns, the long blue vases, and yet the impression was not one of discipline and order. Aunt Anne's house had been untidy, but it had had an odd life and atmosphere of its own. This house was dead, utterly and completely dead. The windows of the dining-room looked out on to a lawn and round the lawn was a stone wall with broken glass to protect it. "As though there were anything to steal!" thought Maggie. But then you cannot expect a garden to look its best at the beginning of April. "I'll wait a little," thought Maggie. "And then I'll make this house better. I'll destroy almost everything in it."

About mid-day with rather a quaking heart Maggie penetrated the kitchen. Here were gathered together Alice the cook, Emily the housemaid, and Clara the between maid.

Alice was large, florid, and genial. Nevertheless at once Maggie distrusted her. No servant had any right to appear so wildly delighted to see a new mistress. Alice had doubtless her own plans. Emily was prim and conceited, and Clara did not exist. Alice was ready to do everything that Maggie wanted, and it was very apparent at once that she had not liked "Miss Grace."

"Ah, that'll be much better than the way Miss Grace 'ad it, Mum. In their jackets, Mum, very well. Certainly. That would be better."

"I think you'd better just give us what seems easiest for dinner, Cook," said Maggie, thereby handing herself over, delivered and bound.

"Very well, Mum—I'm sure I'll do my best," said Alice.

Early on that first afternoon she was taken to see the Church. For a desperate moment her spirits failed her as she stood at the end of the Lane and looked. This was a Church of the newest red brick, and every seat was of the most shining wood. The East End window was flaming purple, with a crimson Christ ascending and yellow and blue disciples amazed together on the ground. Paul stood flushed with pride and pleasure, his hand through Maggie's arm.

"That's a Partright window," he said with that inflection that Maggie was already beginning to think of as "his public voice."

"I'm afraid, Paul dear," said Maggie, "I'm very ignorant."

"Don't know Partright? Oh, he's the great man of the last thirty years—did the great East window of St. Martin's, Pontefract. We had a job to get him I can tell you. Just look at that purple."

"On the right you'll see the Memorial Tablet to our brave lads who fell in the South African War—Dulce et decorum est pro patria mori—very appropriate. Brave fellows, brave fellows! Just behind you, Maggie, is the Mickleham Font, one of the finest specimens of modern stone-work in the county—given to us by Sir Joseph Mickleham—Mickleham Hall, you know, only two miles from here. He used to attend morning service here frequently. Died five years ago. Fine piece of work!"

Maggie looked at it. It was enormous, a huge battlement of a font in dead white stone with wreaths of carved ivy creeping about it.

"It makes one feel rather shivery," said Maggie.

"Now you must see our lectern," said Paul eagerly.

And so it continued. There was apparently a great deal to be said about the Lectern, and then about the Choir-Screen, and then about the Reredos, and then about the Pulpit, and then about the Vestry, and then about the Collecting-Box for the Poor, and then about the Hassocks, and finally about the Graveyard ... To all this Maggie listened and hoped that she made the proper answers, but the truth of the matter was that she was cold and dismayed. The Chapel had been ugly enough, but behind its ugliness there had been life; now with the Church as with the house there was no life visible. Paul, putting his hand on her shoulder, said:

"Here, darling, will be the centre of our lives. This is our temple. Round this building all our happiness will revolve."

"Yes, dear," said Maggie. She was taken then for a little walk. They went down Ivy Road and into Skeaton High Street. Here were the shops. Mr. Bloods, the bookseller's, Tunstall the butcher, Toogood the grocer, Father the draper, Minster the picture-dealer, Harcourt the haberdasher, and so on. Maggie rather liked the High Street; it reminded her of the High Street in Polchester, although there was no hill. Out of the High Street and on to the Esplanade. You should never see an Esplanade out of the season, Katherine had once said to Maggie. That dictum seemed certainly true this time. There could be no doubt that this Esplanade was not looking its best under the blustering March wind. Here a deserted bandstand, there a railway station, here a dead haunt for pierrots, there a closed and barred cinema house, here a row of stranded bathing-machines, there a shuttered tea-house—and not a living soul in sight. In front of them was a long long stretch of sand, behind them to right and left the huddled tenements of the town, in front of them, beyond the sand, the grey sea—and again not a living soul in sight. The railway line wound its way at their side, losing itself in the hills and woods of the horizon.

"There are not many people about, are there?" said Maggie. Nor could she wonder. The East wind cut along the desolate stretches of silence, and yet how strange a wind! It seemed to have no effect at all upon the sea, which rolled in sluggishly with snake-like motion, throwing up on the dim colourless beach a thin fringe of foam, baring its teeth at the world in impotent discontent.

"Oh! there's a boy!" cried Maggie, amazed at her own relief. "How often do the trains come in?" she asked.

"Well, we don't have many trains in the off-season," said Paul. "They put on several extra ones in the summer."

"Oh, what's the sand doing?" Maggie cried.

She had seen sand often enough in her own Glebeshire, but never sand like this. Under the influence of the wind it was blowing and curving into little spirals of dust; a sudden cloud, with a kind of personal animosity rose and flung itself across the rails at Maggie and Paul. They were choking and blinded—and in the distance clouds of sand rose and fell, with gusts and impulses that seemed personal and alive.

"What funny sand!" said Maggie again. "When it blows in Glebeshire it blows and there's a perfect storm. There's a storm or there isn't. Here—" She broke off. She could see that Paul hadn't the least idea of what she was speaking.

"The sand is always blowing about here," he said. "Now what about tea?"

They walked back through the High Street and not a soul was to be seen.

"Does nobody live here?" asked Maggie.

"The population," said Paul quite gravely, "is eight thousand, four hundred and fifty-four."

"Oh, I see," said Maggie.

They had tea in the dusty study again.

"I'm going to change this house," said Maggie.

"Change it?" asked Paul. "What's my little girl going to do?"

"She's going to destroy ever so many things," said Maggie.

"You'd better wait," said Paul, moving a little away, "until Grace comes back, dear. You can consult with her."

Maggie said nothing.

Next day Mrs. Constantine, Miss Purves, and Mrs. Maxse came to tea. They had tea in the drawing-room all amongst the squashed strawberries. Three large ferns in crimson pots watched them as they ate. Maggie thought: "Grace seems to have a passion for ferns." She had been terribly nervous before the ladies' arrival—that old nervousness that had made her tremble before Aunt Anne at St. Dreot's, before the Warlocks, before old Martha. But with it came as always her sense of independence and individuality.

"They can't eat me," she thought. It was obvious at once that they did not want to do anything of the kind. They were full of kindness and curiosity. Mrs. Constantine took the lead, and it was plain that she had been doing this all her life. She was a large black and red woman with clothes that fitted her like a uniform. Her hair was of a raven gleaming blackness, her cheeks were red, her manner so assured and commanding that she seemed to Maggie at once like a policeman directing the traffic. The policeman of Christian Skeaton she was, and it did not take Maggie two minutes to discover that Paul was afraid of her. She had a deep bass voice and a hearty laugh.

"I can understand her," thought Maggie, "and I believe she'll understand me."

Very different Miss Purves. If Mrs. Constantine was the policeman of Skeaton, Miss Purves was the town-crier. She rang her bell and announced the news, and also insisted that you should tell her without delay any item of news that you had collected.

In appearance she was like any old maid whose love of gossip has led her to abandon her appearance. She had obviously surrendered the idea of attracting the male, and flung on her clothes—an old black hat, a grey coat and skirt—with a negligence that showed that she cared for worthier things. She gave the impression that there was no time to be lost were one to gather all the things in life worth hearing.

If Mrs. Constantine stood for the police and Miss Purves the town-crier, Mrs. Maxse certainly represented Society. She was dressed beautifully, and she must have been very pretty once. Her hair was now grey, but her cheeks had still a charming bloom. She was delicate and fragile, rustling and scented, with a beautiful string of pearls round her neck (this, in the daytime, Maggie thought very odd), and a large black hat with a sweeping feather. Her voice was a little sad, a little regretful, as though she knew that her beautiful youth was gone and was making the best of what she had.

She told Maggie that "she couldn't help" being an idealist.

"I know it's foolish of me," she said in her gentle voice, smiling her charming smile. "They all tell me so. But if life isn't meant to be beautiful, where are we? Everything must have a meaning, mustn't it, Mrs. Trenchard, and however often we fail—and after all we are only human—we must try, try again. I believe in seeing the best in people, because then they live up to that. People are what we make them, don't you think?"

"The woman's a fool," thought Maggie. Nevertheless, she liked her kindness. She was so strangely driven. She wished to think of Martin always, never to forget him, but at the same time not to think of the life that was connected with him. She must never think of him as some one who might return. Did that once begin all this present life would be impossible—and she meant to make this new existence not only possible but successful. Therefore she was building, so hard as she could, this new house; the walls were rising, the rooms were prepared, every window was barred, the doors were locked, no one from outside should enter, and everything that belonged to it—Paul, Grace, the Church, these women, Skeaton itself, her household duties, the servants, everything and every one was pressed into service. She must have so much to do that she could not think, she must like every one else so much that she could not want any one else—that other world must be kept out, no sound nor sight of it must enter ... If even she could forget Martin. What had he said to her. "Promise me whatever I am, whatever I do, you will love me always"—and she had promised. Here she was married to Paul and loving Martin more than ever! As she looked at Mrs. Constantine she wondered what she would say did she know that. Nevertheless, she had not deceived Paul ... She had told him. She would make this right. She would force this life to give her what she needed, work and friends and a place in the world. Her face a little white with her struggle to keep her house standing, she turned to her guests. She was afraid that she did not play the hostess very well. She felt as though she were play-acting. She repeated phrases that she had heard Katherine Mark use, and laughed at herself for doing so. She suspected that they thought her very odd, and she fancied that Mrs. Constantine looked at her short hair with grave suspicion.

Afterwards, when she told Paul this, he was rather uncomfortable.

"It'll soon be long again, dear, won't it?" he said.

"Don't you like it short then?" she asked.

"Of course I like it, but there's no reason to be unusual, is there? We don't want to seem different from other people, do we, darling?"

"I don't know," said Maggie. "We want to be ourselves. I don't think I shall ever grow my hair long again. It's so much more comfortable like this."

"If I ask you, dear," said Paul.

"No, not even if you ask me," she answered, laughing.

She noticed then, for the first time, that he could look sulky like a small school-boy.

"Why, Paul," she said. "If you wanted to grow a beard I shouldn't like it, but I shouldn't dream of stopping you."

"That's quite different," he answered. "I should never dream of growing a beard. Grace won't like it if you look odd."

"Grace isn't my teacher," said Maggie with a sudden hot hostility that surprised herself.

She discovered, by the way, very quickly that the three ladies had no very warm feelings for Grace. They showed undisguised pleasure at the thought that Maggie would now be on various Committees instead of her sister-in-law.

"It will be your place, of course, as wife of the vicar," said Mrs. Constantine. "Hitherto Miss Trenchard—"

"Oh, but I couldn't be on a Committee," cried Maggie. "I've never been on one in my life. I should never know what to do."

"Never been on a Committee!" cried Miss Purves, quivering with interest. "Why, Mrs. Trenchard, where have you been all this time?"

"I'm only twenty," said Maggie. They certainly thought it strange of her to confess to her age like that. "At home father never had any Committees, he did it all himself, or rather didn't do it."

Mrs. Constantine shook her head. "We must all help you," she said. "You're very young, my dear, for the responsibilities of this parish."

"Yes, I am," said Maggie frankly. "And I'll be very glad of anything you can tell me. But you mustn't let me be Treasurer or Secretary of anything. I should never answer any of the letters, and I should probably spend all the money myself."

"My dear, you shouldn't say such things even as a joke," said Mrs. Constantine.

"But it isn't a joke," said Maggie. "I'm terribly muddleheaded, and I've no idea of money at all. Paul's going to teach me."

Paul smiled nervously.

"Maggie will soon fit into our ways," he said.

"I'm sure she will." said Mrs. Constantine very kindly, but as though she were speaking to a child of ten.

The bell rang and Mr. Flaunders the curate came in. He was very young, very earnest, and very enthusiastic. He adored Paul. He told Maggie that he thought that he was the very luckiest man in the world for having, so early in his career, so wonderful a man as Paul to work under. He had also adored Grace, but very quickly showed signs of transferring that adoration to Maggie.

"Miss Trenchard's splendid," he said. "I do admire her so, but you'll be a great help to us all. I'm so glad you've come."

"Why, how do you know?" asked Maggie. "You've only seen me for about two minutes."

"Ah, one can tell," said Mr. Flaunders, sighing.

Maggie liked his enthusiasm, but she couldn't help wishing that his knees wouldn't crack at unexpected moments, that he wasn't quite so long and thin, and that he wouldn't leave dried shaving-soap under his ears and in his nostrils. She was puzzled, too, that Paul should be so obviously pleased with the rather naif adoration. "Paul likes you to praise him," she thought a little regretfully.

So, for the moment, these people, the house and the Church, fitted in her World. For the rest of the fortnight she was so busy that she never went on to the beach nor into the woods. She shopped every morning, feeling very old and grown-up, she went to tea with Mrs. Constantine and Mrs. Maxse, and she sat on Paul's knee whenever she thought that he would like her to. She sat on Paul's knee, but that did not mean that, in real intimacy, they approached any nearer to one another. During those days they stared at one another like children on different sides of a fence. They were definitely postponing settlement, and with every day Maggie grew more restless and uneasy. She wanted back that old friendly comradeship that there had been before their marriage. He seemed now to have lost altogether that attitude to her. Then on the very day of Grace's return the storm broke. It was tea-time and they were having it, as usual, in his dusty study. They were sitting someway apart—Paul in the old leather armchair by the fire, his thick body stretched out, his cheerful good-humoured face puckered and peevish.

Maggie stood up, looking at him.

"Paul, what's the matter?" she asked.

"Matter," he repeated. "Nothing."

"Oh yes, there is ... You're cross with me."

"No, I'm not. What an absurd idea!" He moved restlessly, turning half away, not looking at her. She came close up to him.

"Look here, Paul. There is something the matter. We haven't been married a fortnight yet and you're unhappy. Whatever else we married for we married because we were going to be friends. So you've just got to tell me what the trouble is."

"I've got my sermon to prepare," he said, not looking at her, but half rising in his chair. "You'd better go, darling."

"I'm not going to," she answered, "until you've told me why you're worrying."

He got up slowly and seemed then as though he were going to pass her. Suddenly he turned, flung his arms round her, catching her, crushing her in his arms, kissing her wildly.

"Love ... love me ... love me," he whispered. "That's what's the matter. I didn't know myself before I married you, Maggie. All these years I've lived like a fish and I didn't know it. But I know it now. And you've got to love me. You're my wife and you've got to love me."

She would have given everything that she had then to respond. She felt an infinite tenderness and pity for him. But she could not. He felt that she could not. He let her go and turned away from her. She thought for a moment wondering what she ought to say, and then she came up to him and gently put her hand on his shoulder.

"Be patient, Paul," she said. "You know we agreed before we married that we'd be friends at any rate and let the rest come. Wait ..."

"Wait!" he turned round eagerly, clutching her arm. "Then there is a chance, Maggie? You can get to love me—you can forget that other man?"

She drew back. "No, you know I told you that I should never do that. But he'll never come back nor want me again and I'm very fond of you, Paul—fonder than I thought. Don't spoil it all now by going too fast—"

"Going too fast!" he laughed. "Why, I haven't gone any way at all. I haven't got you anywhere. I can hardly touch you. You're away from me all the time. You're strange—different from every one ..."

"I don't know anything about women. I've learnt a lot about myself this week. It isn't going to be as easy as I thought."

She went up to him, close to him, and said almost desperately: "We MUST make this all right, Paul. We can if we try. I know we can."

He kissed her gently with his old kindness. "What a baby you are. You didn't know what you were in for ... Oh, we'll make it all right."

They sat close together then and drank their tea. After all, Grace would be here in an hour! They both felt a kind of relief that they would no longer be alone.

Grace would be here in an hour! Strange how throughout all these last days Maggie had been looking forward to that event with dread. There was no definite reason for fear; in London Grace had been kindness itself and had shown real affection for Maggie. Within the last week she had written two very affectionate letters. What was this, then, that hung and hovered? It was in the very air of the house and the garden and the place. Grace had left her mark upon everything and every one, even upon the meagre person of Mitch the dog. Especially upon Mitch, a miserable creeping fox-terrier with no spirits and a tendency to tremble all over when you called him. He had attached himself to Maggie, which was strange, because animals were not, as a rule, interested in her. Mitch followed her about, looking up at her with a yellow supplicating eye. She didn't like him and she would be glad when Grace collected him again—but why did he tremble?

She realised, in the way that she had of seeing further than her nose, that Grace was going to affect the whole of her relations with Paul, and, indeed, all her future life. She had not realised that in London. Grace had seemed harmless there and unimportant. Already here in Skeaton she seemed to stand for a whole scheme of life.

Maggie had moved and altered a good many of the things in the house. She had discovered a small attic, and into this she had piled pell-mell a number of photographs, cheap reproductions, cushions, worsted mats, and china ornaments. She had done it gaily and with a sense of clearing the air.

Now as Grace's hour approached she was not so sure.

"Well, I'm not afraid," she reassured herself with her favourite defiance. "She can't eat me. And it's my house."

Paul had not noticed the alterations. He was always blind to his surroundings unless they were what he called "queer."

There was the rattle of the cab-wheels on the drive and a moment later Grace was in the hall.

"Dear Paul—Maggie, dear ..."

She stood there, a very solid and assured figure. She was square and thick and reminded Maggie to-day of Mrs. Noah; her clothes stood cut out around her as though they had been cut in wood. She had her large amiable smile, and the kiss that she gave Maggie was a wet, soft, and very friendly one.

"Now I think I'll have tea at once without taking my hat off. In Paul's study? That's nice ... Maggie, dear, how are you? Such a journey! But astonishing! Just fancy! I got into Charing Cross and then—! Why! Here's the study! Fancy! ... Maggie, dear, how are you? Well? That's right. Why, there's tea! That's right. Everything just as it was. Fancy! ..." She took off her gloves, smiled, seated herself more comfortably, then began to look about the room. Suddenly there came: "Why, Paul, where's the Emmanuel football group?"

There was a moment's silence. Maggie felt her heart give a little bump, as it seemed to her, right against the roof of her mouth. Paul (so like him) had not noticed that the football group had vanished. He stared at the blank place on the wall where it had once been.

"Why, Grace ... I don't know. I never noticed it wasn't there."

"I took it down," said Maggie. "I thought there were too many photographs. It's in the attic."

"In the attic? ... Fancy! You put it away, did you, Maggie? Well, fancy! Shan't I make the tea, Maggie, dear? That tea-pot, it's an old friend of mine. I know how to manage it."

They changed seats. Grace was as amiable as ever, but now her eyes flashed about from place to place all around the room.

"Why, this is a new kind of jam. How nice! As I was saying, I got into Charing Cross and there wasn't a porter. Just fancy! At least there was a porter, an old man, but when I beckoned to him he wouldn't move. Well, I was angry. I can tell you, Paul, I wasn't going to stand that, so I-what nice jam, dear. I never knew Mitchell's had jam like this!"

"I didn't get it at Mitchell's," said Maggie. "I've changed the grocer. Mitchell hasn't got anything, and his prices are just about double Brownjohn's ..."

"Brownjohn!" Grace stared, her bread and jam suspended. "Brownjohn! But, Maggie dear, he's a dissenter."

"Oh. Maggie!" said Paul. "You should have told me!"

"Why!" said Maggie, bewildered. "Father never minded about dissenters. Our butcher in St. Dreot's was an atheist and—"

"Well, well," said Grace, her eyes still flashing about like goldfish in a pool. "You didn't know, dear. Of course you didn't. I'm sure we can put it right with Mitchell, although he's a sensitive man. I'll go and see him in the morning. I am glad I'm back. Well, I was telling you ... Where was I? ... about the porter—"

Something drove Maggie to say:

"I'd rather have a good grocer who's a dissenter than a bad one who goes to church—"

"Maggie," said Paul, "you don't know what you're saying. You don't realise what the effect in the parish would be."

"Of course she doesn't," said Grace consolingly. "She'll understand in time. As I was saying, I was so angry that I caught the old man by the arm and I said to him, 'If you think you're paid to lean up against a wall and not do your duty you're mightily mistaken, and if you aren't careful I'll report you—that's what I'll do,' and he said—what were his exact words? I'll remember in a minute. I know he was very insulting, and the taxi-cabman—why, Paul, where's mother's picture?"

Grace's eyes were directed to a large space high above the mantelpiece. Maggie remembered that there had been a big faded oil-painting of an old lady in a shawl and spectacles, a hideous affair she had thought it. That was now reposing in the attic. Why had she not known that it was a picture of Paul's mother? She would never have touched it had she known. Why had Paul said nothing? He had not even noticed that it was gone.

Paul stared, amazed and certainly—yes, beyond question—frightened.

"Grace—upon my word—I've been so busy since my return—"

"Is that also in the attic?" asked Grace.

"Yes, it is," said Maggie. "I'm so sorry. I never knew it was your mother. It wasn't a very good painting I thought, so I took it down. If I had known, of course, I never would have touched it. Oh Grace, I AM so sorry."

"It's been there," said Grace, "for nearly twenty years. What I mean to say is that it's always been there. Poor mother. Are there many things in the attic, Maggie?"

At that moment there was a feeble scratching on the door. Paul, evidently glad of anything that would relieve the situation, opened the door.

"Why, it's Mitch!" cried Grace, forgetting for the moment her mother. "Fancy! It's Mitch! Mitch, dear! Was she glad to see her old friend back again? Was she? Darling! Fancy seeing her old friend again? Was she wanting her back?"

Mitch stood shivering in the doorway, then, with her halting step, the skin of her back wrinkled with anxiety, she crossed the room. For a moment she hesitated, then with shamefaced terror, slunk to Maggie, pressed up against her, and sat there huddled, staring at Grace with yellow unfriendly eyes.

CHAPTER IV

GRACE

 Not in a day and not in a night did Maggie find a key to that strange confusion of fears, superstitions, and self-satisfactions that was known to the world as Grace Trenchard. Perhaps she never found it, and through all the struggle and conflict in which she was now to be involved she was fighting, desperately, in the dark. Fight she did, and it was this same conflict, bitter and tragic enough at the time, that transformed her into the woman that she became ... and through all that conflict it may be truly said of her that she never knew a moment's bitterness—anger, dismay, loneliness, even despair-bitterness never.

It was not strange that Maggie did not understand Grace; Grace never understood herself nor did she make the slightest attempt to do so. It would be easy enough to cover the ground at once by saying that she had no imagination, that she never went behind the thing that she saw, and that she found the grasping of external things quite as much as she could manage. But that is not enough. Very early indeed, when she had been a stolid-faced little girl with a hot desire for the doll possessed by her neighbour, she had had for nurse a woman who rejoiced in supernatural events. With ghost stories of the most terrifying kind she besieged Grace's young heart and mind. The child had never imagination enough to visualise these stories in the true essence, but she seized upon external detail-the blue lights, the white shimmering garments, the moon and the church clock, the clanking chain and the stain of blood upon the board.

These things were not for her, and indeed did she allow her fancy to dwell, for a moment, upon them she was besieged at once by so horrid a panic that she lost all control and self-possession. She therefore very quickly put those things from her and thenceforth lived in the world as in a castle surrounded by a dark moat filled with horrible and slimy creatures who would raise a head at her did she so much as glance their way.

She decided then never to look, and from a very early age those quarters of life became to her "queer," indecent, and dangerous. All the more she fastened her grip upon the things that she could see and hold, and these things repaid her devotion by never deceiving her or pretending to be what they were not. She believed intensely in forms and repetitions; she liked everything to be where she expected it to be, people to say the things that she expected them to say, clocks to strike at the right time, and trains to be up to the minute. With all this she could never be called an accurate or careful woman. She was radically stupid, stupid in the real sense of the word, so that her mind did not grasp a new thought or fact until it had been repeated to her again and again, so that she had no power of expressing herself, and a deep inaccuracy about everything and every one which she endeavoured to cover by a stream of aimless lies that deceived no one. She would of course have been very indignant had any one told her that she was stupid. She hated what she called "clever people" and never had them near her if she could help it. She was instantly suspicious of any one who liked ideas or wanted anything changed. With all this she was of an extreme obstinacy and a deep, deep jealousy. She clung to what she had with the tenacity of a mollusc. What she had was in the main Paul, and her affection for him was a very real human quality in her.

He was exactly what she would have chosen had she been allowed at the beginning a free choice. He was lazy and good-tempered so that he yielded to her on every possible point, he was absolutely orthodox and never shocked her by a thought or a word out of the ordinary, he really loved her and believed in her and said, quite truly, that he would not have known what to do without her.

It seems strange then that it should have been in the main her urgency that led to the acquisition of Maggie. During the last year she had begun to be seriously uneasy. Things were not what they had been. Mrs. Constantine and others in the parish were challenging her authority, even the Choir boys were scarcely so subservient as they had been, and, worst of all, Paul himself was strangely restive and unquiet. He talked at times of getting married, wondered whether she, Grace, wouldn't like some one to help her in the house, and even, on one terrifying occasion, suggested leaving Skeaton altogether. A momentary vision of what it would be to live without Paul, to give up her kingdom in Skeaton, to have to start all over again to acquire dominion in some new place, was enough for Grace.

She must find Paul a wife, and she must find some one who would depend upon her, look up to her, obey her, who would, incidentally, take some of the tiresome and monotonous drudgery off her shoulders. The moment she saw Maggie she was resolved; here was just the creature, a mouse of a girl, no parents, no money, no appearance, nothing to make her proud or above herself, some one to be moulded and trained in the way she should go. To her great surprise she discovered that Paul was at once attracted by Maggie: had she ever wondered at anything she would have wondered at this, but she decided that it was because she herself had made the suggestion. Dear Paul, he was always so eager to fall in with any of her proposals.

Her mind misgave her a little when she saw that he was really in love. What could he see in that plain, gauche, uncharming creature? See something he undoubtedly did. However, that would wear off very quickly. The Skeaton atmosphere was against romance and Paul was too lazy to be in love very long. Once or twice in the weeks before the wedding Grace's suspicions were aroused.

Maggie seemed to be an utter little heathen; also it appeared that she had had some strange love affair that she had taken so seriously as actually to be ill over it. That was odd and a little alarming, but the child was very young, and once married-there she'd be, so to speak!

It was not, in fact, until that evening of her arrival in Skeaton that she was seriously alarmed. To say that that first ten minutes in Paul's study alarmed her is to put it mildly indeed. As she looked at the place where her mother's portrait had been, as she stared at the trembling Mitch cowering against Maggie's dress, she experienced the most terrifying, shattering upheaval since the day when as a little girl of six she had been faced as she had fancied, with the dripping ghost of her great-uncle William. Not at once, however, was the battle to begin. Maggie gave way about everything. She gave way at first because she was so confident of getting what she wanted later on. She never conceived that she was not to have final power in her own house; Paul had as yet denied her nothing. She moved the pictures and the pots and the crochet work down from the attic and replaced them where they had been-or, nearly replaced them. She found it already rather amusing to puzzle Grace by changing their positions from day to day so that Grace was bewildered and perplexed.

Grace said nothing—only solidly and with panting noises (she suffered from shortness of breath) plodded up and down the house, reassuring herself that all her treasures were safe.

Maggie, in fact, enjoyed herself during the weeks immediately following Grace's return. Paul seemed tranquil and happy; there were no signs of fresh outbreaks of the strange passion that had so lately frightened her. Maggie herself found her duties in connection with the Church and the house easier than she had expected. Every one seemed very friendly. Grace chattered on with her aimless histories of unimportant events and patted Maggie's hand and smiled a great deal. Surely all was very well. Perhaps this was the life for which Maggie was intended.

And that other life began to be dim and faint-even Martin was a little hidden and mysterious. Strangely she was glad of that; the only way that this could be carried through was by keeping the other out of it. Would the two worlds mingle? Would the faces and voices of those spirits be seen and heard again? Would they leave Maggie now or plan to steal her back? The whole future of her life depended on the answer to that ...

During those weeks she investigated Skeaton very thoroughly. She found that her Skeaton, the Skeaton of Fashion and the Church, was a very small affair consisting of two rows of villas, some detached houses that trickled into the country, and a little clump of villas on a hill over the sea beyond the town. There were not more than fifty souls all told in this regiment of Fashion, and the leaders of the fifty were Mrs. Constantine, Mrs. Maxse, Miss Purves, a Mrs. Tempest (a large black tragic creature), and Miss Grace Trenchard—and they had for their male supporters Colonel Maxse, Mr. William Tempest, a Mr. Purdie (rich and idle), and the Reverend Paul. Maggie discovered that the manners, habits, and even voices and gestures of this sacred Fifty were all the same. The only question upon which they divided was one of residence. The richer and finer division spent several weeks of the winter abroad in places like Nice and Cannes, and the poorer contingent took their holiday from Skeaton in the summer in Glebeshire or the Lake District. The Constantines and the Maxses were very fine indeed because they went both to Cannes in the winter and Scotland in the summer. It was wonderful, considering how often Mrs. Constantine was away from Skeaton, how solemn and awe-inspiring an impression she made and retained in the Skeaton world. Maggie discovered that unless you had a large house with independent grounds outside the town it was impossible were to remain in Skeaton during the summer months. Oh! the trippers! ...Oh! the trippers! Yes, they were terrible-swallowed up the sands, eggshells, niggers, pierrots, bathing-machines, vulgarity, moonlight embracing, noise, sand, and dust. If you were any one at all you did not stay in Skeaton during the summer months-unless, as I have said, you were so grand that you could disregard it altogether.

It happened that these weeks were wet and windy and Maggie was blown about from one end of the town to the other. There could be no denying that it was grim and ugly under these conditions. It might be that when the spring came there would be flowers in the gardens and the trees would break out into fresh green and the sands would gleam with mother-of-pearl and the sea would glitter with sunshine. All that perhaps would come. Meanwhile there was not a house that was not hideous, the wind tore screaming down the long beaches carrying with it a flurry of tempestuous rain, whilst the sea itself moved in sluggish oily coils, dirt-grey to the grey horizon. Worst of all perhaps were the deserted buildings at other times dedicated to gaiety, ghosts of places they were with torn paper flapping against their sides and the wind tearing at their tin-plated roofs. Then there was the desolate little station, having, it seemed, no connection with any kind of traffic-and behind all this the woods howled and creaked and whistled, derisive, provocative, the only creatures alive in all that world.

Between the Fashion and the Place the Church stood as a bridge.

Centuries ago, when Skeaton had been the merest hamlet clustered behind the beach, the Church had been there-not the present building, looking, poor thing, as though it were in a perpetual state of scarlet fever, but a shabby humble little chapel close to the sea sheltered by the sandy hill.

The present temple had been built about 1870 and was considered very satisfactory. It was solid and free from draughts and took the central heating very well. The graveyard also was new and shiny, with no bones in it remoter than the memories of the present generation could compass. The church clock was a very late addition—put up by subscription five years ago-and its clamour was so up to date and smart that it was a cross between the whistle of a steam-engine and a rich and prosperous dinner-bell.

All this was rightly felt to be very satisfactory. As Miss Purves said: "So far as the dear Church goes, no one had any right to complain about anything."

When Maggie had first arrived in Skeaton her duties with regard to the Church were made quite plain to her. She was expected to take one of the classes in Sunday school, to attend Choir practice on Friday evening, to be on the Committees for Old Women's Comforts, Our Brave Lads' Guild, and the Girls' Friendly Society, to look after the flowers for the Altar, and to attend Paul's Bible Class on Wednesdays.

She had no objection to any of these things-they were, after all, part of her "job." She found that they amused her, and her life must be full, full, full. "No time to think—No time to think," some little voice far, far within her cried. But on Grace's return difficulties at once arose. Grace had, hitherto, done all these things. She had, as she called it, "Played a large part in the life of our Church." She was bored with them all, the Choir practices, the Committees, the Altar flowers, and the rest; she was only too pleased that Maggie should do the hard work—it was quite fair that she, Grace, should have a rest. At the same time she did not at all want to surrender the power that doing these things had given her. She did not wish Maggie to take her place, but she wanted her to support the burden-very difficult this especially if you are not good at "thinking things out."

Grace never could "think things out." It seemed as though her thoughts loved wilfully to tease and confuse her. Then when she was completely tangled, and bewildered, her temper rose, slowly, stealthily, but with a mighty force behind it; suddenly as a flood bursts the walls that have been trying to resist it, it would sweep the chambers of her mind, submerging, drowning the flock of panic-stricken little ideas.

She then would "lose her temper" so much to her own surprise that she at once decided that some one else must be responsible. A few days after her return she decided that she "must not let these things go," so she told Maggie that she would attend the Committee of Old Women's Comforts and be responsible for the Choir practice. But on her return to these functions she found that she was bored and tired and cross; they were really intolerable, she had been doing them for years and years and years. It was too bad that Maggie should suffer her to take them on her shoulders. What did Maggie think she was a clergyman's wife for? Did Maggie imagine that there were no responsibilities attached to her position?

Grace did not say these things, but she thought them. She did not of course admit to herself that she wanted Maggie both to go and not to go. She simply knew that there was a "grievance" and Maggie was responsible for it. But at present she was silent ...

The next factor in the rapidly developing situation was Mr. Toms. One day early in April Maggie went for a little walk by herself along the lane that led to Marsden Wood. Marsden Wood was the most sinister of all the woods; there had once been a murder there, but even had there not, the grim bleakness of the trees and bushes, the absence of all clear paths through its tangles and thickets made it a sinister place. She turned at the very edge of the wood and set her face back towards Skeaton.

The day had been wild and windy with recurrent showers of rain, but now there was a break, the chilly April sun broke through the clouds and scattered the hedges and fields with primrose light.

Faintly and with a gentle rhythm the murmur of the sea came across the land and the air was sweet with the sea-salt and the fresh scent of the grass after rain. Maggie stood for a moment, breathing in the spring air and watching the watery blue thread its timid way through banks of grey cloud. A rich gleam of sunlight struck the path at her feet.

She saw then, coming towards her, a man and a woman. The woman was ordinary enough, a middle-aged, prim, stiffly dressed person with a pale shy face, timid in her walk and depressed in mouth and eyes. The man was a stout, short, thick-set fellow with a rosy smiling face. At once Maggie noticed his smile. He was dressed very smartly in a black coat and waist-coat and pepper-and-salt trousers. His bowler was cocked a little to one side. She passed them and the little round man, looking her full in the face, smiled so happily and with so radiant an amiability that she was compelled to respond. The woman did not look at her.

Long after she had left them she thought of the little man's smile. There was something that, in spite of herself, reminded her both of Uncle Mathew and Martin. She felt a sudden and warm kinship, something that she had not known since her arrival in Skeaton. Had she not struggled with herself every kind of reminiscence of her London life would have come crowding about her. This meeting was like the first little warning tap upon the wall ...

On her return she spoke of it.

"Oh," said Paul, "that must have been poor little Mr. Toms with his sister."

"Poor?" asked Maggie.

"Yes. He's queer in his head, you know," said Paul. "Quite harmless, but he has the strangest ideas."

Maggie noticed then that Grace shivered and the whole of her face worked with an odd emotion of horror and disgust.

"He should have been shut up somewhere," she said. "It's disgraceful letting him walk about everywhere just like any one else."

"Shut up!" cried Maggie. "Oh, no! I don't think any one ought to be shut up for anything."

"My dear Maggie!" said Paul in his fatherly protecting voice. "No prisons? Think what would become of us all."

"Oh!" said Maggie impatiently, "I'm not practical of course, I don't know what one should do, but I do know that no one should be shut up."

"Chut-chut—" said Grace.

Now this "Chut, chut," may seem a very little thing, but very little things are sometimes of great importance. Marriages have been wrecked on an irritating cough and happy homes ruined by a shuffle. Grace had said "Chut, chut," for a great many years and to many people. It expressed scorn and contempt and implied a vast store of superior knowledge. Grace herself had no idea of the irritating nature of this exclamation, she would have been entirely amazed did you explain to her that it had more to do with her unpopularity in Skeaton than any other thing. She had even said "Chut, chut," to Mrs. Constantine.

But she said it to Maggie more than to any other person. When she had been in the house a few days she said to her brother:

"Paul, Maggie's much younger than I had supposed."

"Oh, do you think so?" said Paul.

"Yes, I do. She knows nothing about anything. She's been nowhere. She's seen nobody ... Poor child."

It was the "poor child" position that she now, during these first weeks, adopted. She was very, very kind to Maggie. As she explained to Mrs. Maxse, she really was very fond of her—she was a GOOD girl. At the same time ... Well! ... Mrs. Maxse would understand that Paul can hardly have known what he was marrying. Ignorance! Carelessness! Strange ideas! Some one from the centre of Africa would have known more ... and so on. Nevertheless, she was a GOOD girl ... Only she needed guidance. Fancy, she had taken quite a fancy to poor Mr. Toms! Proposed to call on his sister. Well, one couldn't help that. Miss Toms was a regular communicant ... Nevertheless ... she didn't realise, that was it. Of course, she had known all kinds of queer people in London. Paul and Grace had rescued her. The strangest people. No, Maggie was an orphan. She had an uncle, Grace believed, and two aunts who belonged to a strange sect. Sex? No, sect. Very queer altogether.

Mrs. Maxse went home greatly impressed.

"The girl's undoubtedly queer," she told her husband.

"The parson's got a queer sort of wife," Colonel Maxse told his friends in the Skeaton Conservative Club. "He rescued her from some odd sort of life in London. No. Don't know what it was exactly. Always was a bit soft, Trenchard."

Maggie had no idea that Skeaton was discussing her. She judged other people by herself. Meanwhile something occurred that gave her quite enough to think about.

She had understood from Grace that it was expected of her that she should be at home on one afternoon in the week to receive callers. She thought it a silly thing that she should sit in the ugly drawing-room waiting for people whom she did not wish to see and who did not wish to see her, but she was told that it was one of her duties, and so she would do it. No one, however, had any idea of the terror with which she anticipated these Friday afternoons. She had never been a very great talker, she had nothing much to say unless to some one in whom she was interested. She was frightened lest something should happen to the tea, and she felt that they were all staring at her and asking themselves why her hair was cut short and why her clothes didn't fit better. However, there it was. It was her duty.

One Friday afternoon she was sitting alone, waiting. The door opened and the maid announced Mrs. Purdie. Maggie remembered that she had been told that Mr. Alfred Purdie was the richest man in Skeaton, that he had recently married, and was but now returned from his honeymoon.

Mrs. Purdie entered and revealed herself as Caroline Smith. For a moment, as Maggie looked upon that magnificent figure, the room turned about her and her eyes were dim. She remembered, as though some one were reminding her from a long way off, that Caroline had once told her that she was considering the acceptance of a rich young man in Skeaton.

She remembered that at the time she had thought the coincidence of Caroline and Paul Trenchard strange. But far stronger than any such memory was the renewed conviction that she had that fate did not intend to leave her alone. She was not to keep the two worlds apart, she was not to be allowed to forget.

The sight of Caroline brought Martin before her so vividly that she could have cried out. Instead she stood there, quietly waiting, and showed no sign of any embarrassment.

Caroline was dressed in peach-coloured silk and a little black hat. She was not confused in the least. She seized Maggie's hand and shook it, talking all the time.

"Well now, I'm sure you're surprised to see me," she said, "and perhaps you're not too glad either. Alfred wanted to come too, but I said to him, 'No, Alfred, this will be just a little awkward at first, for Maggie Trenchard's got a grievance, and with some reason, too, so you'd better let me manage it alone the first meeting.' Wasn't I right? Of course I was. And you can just say right out now, Maggie, exactly what's in your mind. It's not my fault that we're both in the same town. I'm sure you'd much rather never set eyes on me again, and I'm sure I can quite understand if you feel like that. But there it is. I told you long ago in London that Alfred was after me, and I was in two minds about it-but of course I didn't dream you were going to marry a parson. You could have knocked me down with less than a feather when I saw it in the Skeaton News, 'That can't be my Margaret Cardinal,' I said, and yet it seemed so strange the two names and all. Well, and then I found it really WAS the same. I WAS astonished. You of all people the wife of a parson! However, you know your own mind best, and I'm sure Mr. Trenchard's a very lucky man. So you can just start off and curse me, Maggie, as much as you like."

The strange thing was that as Maggie listened to this she felt a desire to embrace rather than curse. Of course Caroline had done her harm, she had, perhaps ruined Martin's life as well as her own, but the mistake had been originally Maggie's in trusting Caroline with more confidence than her volatile nature would allow her to hold. And now, as she looked at Caroline and saw that pretty pink and white face, the slim beautiful body, the grace and gaiety, and childish amiability, her whole soul responded. Here was a friend, even though an indiscreet one, here was some one from home, the one human being in the whole of Skeaton who knew the old places and the old people, the Chapel, and the aunts—and Martin. She knew at once that it would have been far safer had Caroline not been there, that the temptation to discuss Martin would be irresistible, that she would yield to it, and that Caroline was in no way whatever to be trusted-she realised all these things, and yet she was glad.

"I don't want to curse you, Caroline," said Maggie. "Sit down. Tea will be here in a minute. I was very unhappy about what you did, but that's all a long time ago now, and I was to blame too."

"Oh, that's just sweet of you," said Caroline, running over and giving Maggie an impulsive kiss. "I said to Alfred, 'Maggie may be angry. I don't know how she'll receive me, I'm sure. She had the sweetest nature always, and it isn't like her to bear a grudge. But whatever way it is, I'll have to take it, because the fact is I deserve it.' But there you are, simply angelic and I'm ever so glad. The fact is I was ridiculous in those days. I don't wonder you lost your patience with me, and it was just like your honest self to be so frank with me. But marriage has just taught me everything. What I say is, every one ought to be married; no one knows anything until they're married. It's amazing what a difference it makes, don't you think so? Why, before I was married I used to chatter on in the most ridiculous way (Caroline always said ridiculous) and now-but there I go, talking of myself, and it's you I want to hear about. Now, Maggie, tell me—" But the sudden entrance of Grace and Paul checked, for the moment, these confidences. Caroline did not stay long this first time. She talked a little, drank some tea, ate a biscuit, smiled at Paul and departed. She felt, perhaps, that Grace did not approve of her. Grace had not seen her before, certainly she would not approve of the peach-coloured dress and the smile at Paul. And then the girl talked too much. She had interrupted Grace in the middle of one of her stories.

When Caroline had departed (after kissing Maggie affectionately) Grace said:

"And so you knew her before, Maggie?"

"I knew her in London," said Maggie.

"I like her," said Paul. "A bright young creature."

"Hum!" said Grace.

That was a wonderful spring evening, the first spring evening of the year. The ugly garden swam in a mist faintly cherry-colour; through the mist a pale evening sky, of so rich a blue that it was almost white, was shadowing against a baby moon sharply gold. The bottles on the wall were veiled by the evening mist; a thrush sang in the little bush at the end of the lawn.

Paul whispered to Maggie: "Come out into the garden."

She went with him, frightened; she could feel his arm tremble against her waist; his cold hard fingers caught hers. No current ran from her body to his. They were apart, try as she may. When they had walked the length of the lawn he caught her close to him, put his hand roughly up to her neck and, bending her head towards his, kissed her. She heard his words, strangled and fierce.

"Love me, Maggie-love me-you must—"

When he released her, looking back towards the dark house, she saw Grace standing there with a lamp in her hand.

Against her will she shared his feeling of guilt, as, like children caught in a fault, they turned back towards the house.

CHAPTER V

THE BATTLE OF SKEATON

FIRST YEAR

Afterwards, when Maggie looked back she was baffled. She tried to disentangle the events between that moment when Grace, holding the lamp in her hand, blinked at them as they came across the lawn, and that other most awful moment when, in Paul's study, Grace declared final and irrevocable war.

Between those two events ran the history of more than two years, and there was nothing stranger than the way that the scene in the garden and the scene in the study seemed to Maggie to be close together. What were the steps, she used to ask herself afterwards, that led to those last months of fury and tragedy and disaster? Was it my fault? Was it hers? Was it Paul's? What happened? If I had not done this or that, if Grace had not said—no, it was hopeless. She would break off in despair. Isolated scenes appeared before her, always bound, on either side, by that prologue and that finale, but the scenes would not form a chain. She could not connect; she would remain until the end bewildered as to Grace's motives. She never, until the day of her death, was to understand Grace.

"She was angry for such little things," she said afterwards.

"She hated me to be myself." The two years in retrospect seemed to have passed with incredible swiftness, the months that followed them were heavy and slow with trouble. But from the very first, that is, from the moment when Grace saw Paul kiss Maggie in the evening garden, battle was declared. Maggie might not know it, but it was so-and Grace knew it very well.

It may be said, however, in Grace's defence that she gave Maggie every chance. She marvelled at her own patience. For two years after that moment, when she decided that Maggie was "queer," and that her beloved Paul was in real danger of his losing his soul because of that "queerness," she held her hand. She was not naturally a patient woman-she was not introspective enough to be that—and she held no brief for Maggie. Nevertheless for two whole years she held her hand...

They were, all three, in that ugly house, figures moving in the dark. Grace simply knew, as the months passed, that she disliked and feared Maggie more and more; Paul knew that as the months passed—well, what he knew will appear in the following pages. And Maggie? She only knew that it needed all her endurance and stubborn will to force herself to accept this life as her life. She must-she must. To give way meant to run away, and to run away meant to long for what she could not have, and loneliness and defeat. She would make this into a success; she would care for Paul although she could not give him all that he needed. She would and she could... Every morning as she lay awake in the big double-bed with the brass knobs at the bed-foot winking at her in the early light she vowed that she would justify her acceptance of the man who lay sleeping so peacefully beside her. Poor child, her battle with Grace was to teach her how far her will and endurance could carry her...

Grace, on her side, was not a bad woman, she was simply a stupid one. She disliked Maggie for what seemed to her most admirable reasons and, as that dislike slowly, slowly turned into hatred, her self-justification only hardened.

Until that moment, when she saw a faded patch of wall-paper on the wall instead of her mother's portrait, she had no doubts whatever about the success of what she considered her choice. Maggie was a "dear," young, ignorant, helpless, but the very wife for Paul. Then slowly, slowly, the picture changed. Maggie was obstinate, Maggie was careless, Maggie was selfish, idle, lazy, irreligious—at last, Maggie was "queer."

Then, when in the dusk of that summer evening, she saw Paul kiss Maggie, as the moths blundered about her lamp, her stolid unimaginative heart was terrified. This girl, who was she? What had she been before they found her? What was this strange passion in Paul isolating him from her, his sister? This girl was dangerous to them all-a heathen. They had made a terrible mistake. Paul had been from the first bewitched by some strange spell, and she, his sister, had aided the witch.

And yet, to her credit be it remembered, for two years, she fought her fears, superstitions, jealousies, angers. That can have been no easy thing for a woman who had always had her own way. But Maggie helped her. There were many days during that first year at any rate when Grace thought that the girl was, after all, only the simple harmless child that she had first found her.

It was so transparently clear that Maggie bore no malice against any one in the world, that when she angered Grace she did so always by accident, never by plan-it was only unfortunate that the accidents should occur so often.

Maggie's days were from the very first of the utmost regularity. Breakfast at 8.30, then an interview with the cook (Grace generally in attendance here), then shopping (with Grace), luncheon at 1.30, afternoon, paying calls or receiving them, dinner 7.45, and after dinner, reading a book while Paul and Grace played bezique, or, if Paul was busy upon a sermon or a letter (he wrote letters very slowly), patience with Grace. This regular day was varied with meetings, choir practices, dinner-parties, and an occasional Penny Reading.

In this framework of the year it would have appeared that there was very little that could breed disturbance. There were, however, little irritations. Maggie would have given a great deal could she have been allowed to interview the cook in the morning alone.

It would seem impossible to an older person that Grace's presence could so embarrass Maggie; it embarrassed her to the terrible extent of driving every idea out of her head.

When Maggie had stammered and hesitated and at last allowed, the cook to make a suggestion, Grace would say. "You mustn't leave it all to cook, dear. Now what about a nice shepherd's pie?"

The cook, who hated Grace, would toss her head.

"Impossible to-day, Mum ... Quite impossible."

"Oh, do you think so?" Maggie would say.

This was the cook's opportunity.

"Well, for you, Mum, I'll see if it can't be managed. Difficult as it is."

Grace's anger boiled over.

"That woman must go," she insisted.

"Very well," said Maggie.

Cook after cook appeared and vanished. They all hated Grace.

"You're not very good at keeping servants, are you, Maggie, dear?" said Grace.

Then there was the shopping. Grace's conversation was the real trouble here. Grace's stories had seemed rather a joke in London, soon, in Skeaton, they became a torture. From the vicarage to the High Street was not far, but it was far enough for Grace's narrative powers to stretch their legs and get a healthy appetite for the day's work. Grace walked very slowly, because of her painful breathing. Her stout stolid figure in its stiff clothes (the skirt rather short, thick legs in black stockings and large flat boots), marched along. She had a peculiar walk, planting each foot on the ground with deliberate determination as though she were squashing a malignant beetle, she was rather short-sighted, but did not wear glasses, because, as she said to Maggie, "one need not look peculiar until one must." Her favourite head-gear was a black straw hat with a rather faded black ribbon and a huge pin stuck skewer-wise into it. This pin was like a dagger.

She peered around her as she walked, and for ever enquired of Maggie, "who that was on the other Bide of the road." Maggie, of course, did not know, and there began then a long cross-questioning as to colour, clothes, height, smile or frown. Nothing was too small to catch Grace's interest but nothing caught it for long. Maggie, at the end of her walk felt as though she were beset by a whirl of little buzzing flies. She noticed that Paul had, from, long habit, learnt to continue his own thoughts during Grace's stories, and she also tried to do this, but she was not clever at it because Grace would suddenly stop and say, "Where was I, Maggie?" and then when Maggie was confused regard her suspiciously, narrowing her eyes into little thin points. The shopping was difficult because Grace would stand at Maggie's elbow and say: "Now, Maggie, this is your affair, isn't it? You decide what you want," and then when Maggie had decided, Grace simply, to show her power, would say: "Oh, I don't think we'd better have that ... No, I don't think we'll have that. Will you show us something else, please?"-and so they had to begin all over again.

Nevertheless, throughout their first summer Maggie was almost happy; not QUITE happy, some silent but persistent rebellion at the very centre of her heart prevented her complete happiness. What she really felt was that half of her-the rebellious, questioning, passionate half of her-was asleep, and that at all costs, whatever occurred, she must keep it asleep. That was her real definite memory of her first year-that, through it all, she was wilfully, deliberately drugged.

Every one thought Paul very strange that summer. Mr. Flaunders, the curate, told Miss Purves that he was very "odd." "He was always the most tranquil man-a sunny nature, as you know, Miss Purves. Well now, I assure you, he's never the same from one minute to another. His temper is most uncertain, and one never can tell of what he's thinking. You know he took the Collects in the wrong order last Sunday, and last night he read the wrong lesson. Two days ago he was quite angry with me because I suggested another tune for 'Lead Kindly Light'-unlike himself, unlike himself."

"To what do you attribute this, Mr. Flaunders?" said Miss Purves. "You know our vicar so well."

"I'm sure I can't tell what it is," said Mr. Flaunders, sighing.

"Can it be his marriage?" said Miss Purves.

"I'm sure," said Mr. Flaunders, flushing, "that it can be nothing to do with Mrs. Trenchard. That's a fine woman, Miss Purves, a fine woman."

"She seems a little strange," said Miss Purves. "Why doesn't she let her hair grow? It's hardly Christian as it is."

"It's her health, I expect," said Mr. Flaunders.

Paul was very gentle and good to Maggie all that summer, better to her than any human being had ever been before. She became very fond of him, and yet it was not, apparently, her affection that he wanted. He seemed to be for ever on the verge of asking her some question and then checking himself. He was suddenly silent; she caught him looking at her in odd, furtive ways.

He made love to her and then suddenly checked himself, going off, leaving her alone. During these months she did everything she could for him. She knew that she was not satisfying him, because she could give him only affection and not love. But everything that he wanted her to do she did. And they never, through all those summer months, had one direct honest conversation. They were afraid.

She began to see, very clearly, his faults. His whole nature was easy, genial, and, above all, lazy. He liked to be liked, and she Was often astonished at the pleasure with which he received compliments. He had a conceit of himself, not as a man but as a clergyman, and she knew that nothing pleased him so much as when people praised his "good-natured humanity."

She saw him "play-acting," as she called it, that is, bringing forward a succession of little tricks, a jolly laugh, an enthusiastic opinion, a pretence of humility, a man-of-the-world air, all things not very bad in themselves, but put on many years ago, subconsciously as an actor puts on powder and paint. She saw that he was especially sensitive to lay opinion, liked to be thought a good fellow by the laymen in the place. To be popular she was afraid that he sometimes sacrificed his dignity, his sincerity and his pride. But he was really saved in this by his laziness. He was in fact too lazy to act energetically in his pursuit of popularity, and the temptation to sink into the dirty old chair in his study, smoke a pipe and go to sleep, hindered again and again his ambition. He had, as so many clergymen have, a great deal of the child in him, a remoteness from actual life, and a tremendous ignorance of the rough-and-tumble brutality and indecency of things. It had not been difficult for Grace, because of his laziness, his childishness, and his harmless conceited good-nature to obtain a very real dominion over him, and until now that dominion had never seriously been threatened.

Now, however, new impulses were stirring in his soul. Maggie saw it, Grace saw it, before the end of the summer the whole parish saw it. He was uneasy, dissatisfied, suffering under strange moods whose motives he concealed from all the world. In his sleep he cried Maggie's name with a passion that was a new voice in him. When she awoke and heard it she trembled, and then lay very still ...

And what a summer that was! To Maggie who had never, even in London, mingled with crowds it was an incredible invasion. The invasion was incredible, in the first place, because of the suddenness with which it fell upon Skeaton. One day Maggie noticed that announcements were pasted on to the Skeaton walls of the coming of a pierrot troupe ... "The Mig-Mags." There was a gay picture of fine beautiful pierrettes and fine stout pierrots all smiling together in a semi-circle. Then on another hoarding it was announced that the Theatre Royal, Skeaton, would shortly start its summer season, and would begin with that famous musical comedy, "The Girl from Bobo's."

Then the Pier Theatre put forward its claim with a West End comedy. The Royal Marine Band announced that it would play (weather permitting) in the Pergola on the Leas every afternoon, 4.20-6. Other signs of new life were the Skeaton Roller-Skating Rink, The Piccadilly Cinema, Concerts in the Town Hall, and

Popular Lectures in the Skeaton Institute. There was also a word here and there about Wanton's Bathing Machines, Button's Donkeys, and Milton and Rowe's Char-a-bancs.

Then, on a sunny day in June the invasion began. The little railway by the sea was only a loop-line that connected Skeaton with Lane-on-Sea, Frambell, and Hooton. The main London line had its Skeaton station a little way out of the town, and the station road to the beach passed the vicarage. Maggie soon learnt to know the times when the excursion trains would pour their victims on to the hot, dry road. Early in the afternoon was one time, and she would see them eagerly, excitedly hurrying to the sea, fathers and mothers and babies, lovers and noisy young men and shrieking girls. Then in the evening she would see them return, some cross, some too tired to speak, some happy and singing, some arguing and disputing, babies crying-all hurrying, hurrying lest the train should be missed. At first she would not penetrate to the beach. She understood from Paul and Grace that one did not go to the beach during the summer months; at any rate, not the popular beach. There was Merton Sand two miles away. One might go there ... it was always deserted. This mysterious "one" fascinated Maggie's imagination. So many times a day Grace said "Oh, I don't think one ought to." Maggie heard again and again about the trippers, "Oh, one must keep away from there, you know."

In fact the Skeaton aristocracy retired with shuddering gestures into its own castle. Life became horribly dull. The Maxses, the Constantines, and the remainder of the Upper Ten either went away or hid themselves in their grounds.

Once or twice there would be a tennis party, then silence ...

This summer was a very hot one; the little garden was stifling and the glass bottles cracked in the sun.

"I want to get out. I want to get out," cried Maggie-so she went down to the sea. She went surreptitiously; this was the first surreptitious thing she had done. She gazed from the Promenade that began just beyond the little station and ran the length of the town down upon the sands. The beach was a small one compared with the great stretches of Merton and Buquay, and the space was covered now so thickly with human beings that the sand was scarcely visible. It was a bright afternoon, hot but tempered with a little breeze. The crowd bathed, paddled, screamed, made sand-castles, lay sleeping, flirting, eating out of paper bags, reading, quarrelling. Here were two niggers with banjoes, then a stout lady with a harmonium, then a gentleman drawing pictures on the sand; here again a man with sweets on a tray, here, just below Maggie, a funny old woman with a little hut where ginger-beer and such things were sold. The noise was deafening; the wind stirred the sand curiously so that it blew up and about in little wreaths and spirals. Everything and everybody seemed to be covered with the grit of this fine small sand; it was in Maggie's eyes, nose, and mouth as she watched.

She hated the place—the station, the beach, the town, and the woods—even more than she had done before. She hated the place—but she loved the people.

The place was sneering, self-satisfied, contemptuous, inhuman, like some cynical, debased speculator making a sure profit out of the innocent weaknesses of human nature. As she turned and looked she could see the whole ugly town with the spire of St. John's-Paul's church, raised self-righteously above it.

The town was like a prison hemmed in by the dark woods and the oily sea. She felt a sudden terrified consciousness of her own imprisonment. It was perhaps from that moment that she began to be definitely unhappy in her own life, that she realised with that sudden inspiration that is given to us on occasion, how hostile Grace was becoming, how strange and unreal was Paul, and how far away was every one else!

Just below her on the sand a happy family played-some babies, two little boys digging, the father smoking, his hat tilted over his eyes against the sun, the mother finding biscuits in a bag for the youngest infant. It was a very merry family and full of laughter. The youngest baby looked up and saw Maggie standing all alone there, and crowed. Then all the family looked up, the boys suspended their digging, father tilted back his hat, the mother shyly smiled.

Maggie smiled back, and then, overcome by so poignant a feeling of loneliness, tempted, too, almost irresistibly to run down the steps, join them on the sand, build castles, play with the babies, she hurried away lest she should give way.

"I must be pretending at being married," she thought to herself. "I don't feel married at all. I'm not natural. If I were sitting on the sand digging I'd be quite natural. No wonder Grace thinks me tiresome. But how does one get older and grown up? What is one to do?"

She did not trust herself to go down to the sands again that summer. The autumn came, the woods turned to gold, the sea was flurried with rain, and the Church began to fill the horizon. The autumn and the winter were the times of the Church's High Festival. Paul, as though he were aware that he had, during these last months, been hovering about strange places and peering into dark windows, busied himself about the affairs of his parish with an energy that surprised every one.

Maggie was aware of a number of young women of whom before she had been unconscious. Miss Carmichael, Misses Mary and Jane Bethel, Miss Clarice Hendon, Miss Polly Jones ... some of these pretty girls, all of them terribly modern, strident, self-assured, scornful, it seemed to Maggie. At first she was frightened of them as she had never been frightened of any one before. They did look at her, of course, as though they thought her strange, and then they soon discovered that she knew nothing at all about life.

Their two chief employments, woven in, as it were, to the web of their church assistance, were Love and Mockery-flirtations, broken engagements, refusals, acceptances, and, on the other hand, jokes about everybody and everything. Maggie soon discovered that Grace was one of their favourite Aunt Sallies; this made her very angry, and she showed so plainly her indignation on the first occasion of their wit that they never laughed at Grace in Maggie's presence again.

Maggie felt, after this, very tender and sympathetic towards Grace, until she discovered that her good sister-in-law was quite unaware that any one laughed at her and would have refused to believe it had she been told. At the same time there went strangely with this confidence an odd perpetual suspicion. Grace was for ever on guard against laughter, and nothing made her more indignant than to come into a room and see that people suddenly ceased their conversation. Maggie, however, did try this autumn to establish friendly relations with Grace. It seemed to her that it was the little things that were against the friendliness rather than the big ones. How she seriously blamed herself for an irritation that was really childish. Who, for instance, a grown woman and married, could do other than blame herself for being irritated by Grace's habit of not finishing her sentences. Grace would say:

"Maggie, did you remember to-oh well, it doesn't matter—"

"Remember what, Grace?"

"No, really it doesn't matter. It was only that—"

"But Grace, do tell me, because otherwise you'll be blaming me for something I ought to have done."

"Blaming you! Why, Maggie, to hear you talk any one would think that I was always scolding you. Of course if that's what you feel—"

"No, no, I don't. But I'm so careless. I forget things so. I don't want to forget something that I ought to do."

"Yes, you are careless, Maggie. That's quite true. It's one of your faults."

(Strange how willing we are ourselves to admit a fault and irritated when a friend agrees about it with us.)

"Oh, I'm not always careless," said Maggie.

"Often you are, dear, aren't you? You must learn. I'm sure you'll improve in time. I wonder whether-but no, I decided I wouldn't bother, didn't I? Still perhaps, after all—No, I daresay it's wiser to leave it alone."

Another little thing that the autumn emphasised was Grace's inability to discover when a complaint or a remonstrance was decently deceased. One evening Paul, going out in a hurry, asked Maggie to give Grace the message that Evensong would be at 6.30 instead of 7 that day. Maggie forgot to give the message and Grace arrived at the Church during the reading of the second lesson.

"Oh Grace, I'm so sorry!" said Maggie.

"It doesn't matter," said Grace; "but how you could forget, Maggie, is so strange! Do try not to forget things. I know it worries Paul. For myself I don't care, although I do value punctuality and memory—I do indeed. What I mean is that it isn't for my own happiness that I mind—"

"I don't want to forget," said Maggie. "One would think to hear you, Grace, that you imagine I like forgetting."

"Really, Maggie," said Grace, "I don't think that's quite the way to speak to me."

And again and again throughout the long winter this little episode figured.

"You'll remember to be punctual, won't you, Maggie? Not like the time when you forgot to tell me."

"You'll forgive me reminding you, Maggie, but I didn't want it to be like the time you forgot to give me—"

"Oh, you'd better not trust to Maggie, Paul. Only the other day when you gave her the message about Evensong—"

Grace meant no harm by this. Her mind moved slowly and was entangled by a vast quantity of useless lumber. She was really shocked by carelessness and inaccuracy because she was radically careless and inaccurate herself but didn't know it.

"If there's one thing I value it's order." she would say, but in struggling to remember superficial things she forgot all essentials. Her brain moved just half as slowly as everything else.

That winter was warm and muggy, with continuous showers of warm rain that seamed to change into mud in the air as it fell.

The Church was filled with the clammy mist of its central heating. Maggie, as she sat through service after service, watched one headache race after another. The air was full of headache; she asked once that a window might be kept open. "That would mean Death in Skeaton. You don't understand the Skeaton air," said Grace.

"That's because I don't get enough of it," said Maggie. She found herself looking back to the Chapel services with wistful regret. What had there been there that was not here? Here everything was ordered, arranged, in decent sequence, in regular symmetry and progression. And yet no one seemed to Maggie to listen to what they were saying, and no one thought of the meaning of the words that they used.

And if they did, of what use would it be? The affair was all settled; heaven was arrayed, parcelled out, its very streets and courts mapped and described. It was the destination of every one in the building as surely as though they were travelling to London by the morning express. They were sated with knowledge of their destiny—no curiosity, no wonder, no agitation, no fear. Even the words of the most beautiful prayers had ceased to have any meaning because the matter had been settled so long ago and there was nothing more to be said. How that Chapel had throbbed with expectation, with amaze, with curiosity, with struggle! Foolish much of it perhaps, stifling it had seemed then in its superstition. Maggie had been afraid then, so afraid that she could not sleep at nights. How she longed now for that fear to return to her!

At this point she would discover that she was beckoning back to her the figures of that other world. They must not come ... the two worlds must not join or she was lost ... she turned her back from her memories and her desires.

During this winter there were the two affairs of Mr. Toms and Caroline.

Maggie carried out her resolve of calling on Mr. Toms. She did it one dark afternoon a few days before Christmas, moved, it must be confessed, partly by a sense of exasperation with Grace. Grace had been that day quite especially tiresome. She had a cold, and a new evening dress had cost twice as much as it ought to have done. Mitch had broken into eczema, and Mrs. Constantine had overruled her at a committee meeting. With a flood of disconnected talk she had overwhelmed Maggie until the girl felt as though her head had been thrust into a bag of flour. Through it all there had been an undercurrent of complaint as though Maggie were responsible.

Early in the afternoon Grace declared that her head was splitting and retired to her bedroom. Maggie, in a state of blinded and deafened exasperation, remembered Mr. Toms and decided to call on him. She found a neat little house standing in a neat little garden near the sea just beyond the end of the Promenade, or The Leas, as the real Skeatonian always called it. Miss Toms and Mr. Toms were sitting in a very small room with a large fire, a pale grey wallpaper, and a number of brightly-painted wooden toys arranged on a shelf running round the room. The toys were of all kinds—a farm, cows and sheep, tigers and lions, soldiers and cannon, a church and a butcher's shop, little green tufted trees, and a Noah's ark. Mr. Toms was sitting, neat as a pin, smiling in an armchair beside the fire, and Miss Toms near him was reading aloud.

Maggie saw at once that her visit embarrassed Miss Toms terribly. It was an embarrassment that she understood perfectly, so like her own feelings on so many occasions. This put her at once at her ease, and she was the old, simple, direct Maggie, her face eager with kindness and understanding. Mr. Toms smiled perpetually but shook hands like the little gentleman he was.

Maggie, studying Miss Toms' face, saw that it was lined with trouble—an ugly face, grave, severe, but brave and proud. Maggie apologised for not coming before.

"I would have come—" she began.

"Oh, you needn't apologise," said Miss Toms brusquely. "They don't call on us here, and we don't want them to."

"They don't call," said Mr. Toms brightly, "because they know I'm queer in the head, and they're afraid I shall do something odd. They told you I was queer in the head, didn't they?"

Strangely enough this statement of his "queerness," although it brought a lump into Maggie's throat, did not disturb or confuse her.

"Yes," she said, "they did. I asked who you were after I had seen you in the road that day."

"I'm not in the least dangerous," said Mr. Toms. "You needn't be afraid. Certain things seem odd to me that don't seem odd to other people—that's all."

"The fact is, Mrs. Trenchard," said Miss Toms, speaking very fast and flushing as she spoke, "that we are very happy by ourselves, my brother and I. He is the greatest friend I have in the world, and I am his. We are quite sufficient for one another. I don't want to seem rude, and it's kind of you to have come, but it's better to leave us alone—it is indeed."

"Well, I don't know," bald Maggie, smiling. "You see, I'm a little queer myself—at least I think that most of the people here are coming to that conclusion. I'm sure I'm more queer than your brother. At any rate I can't do you any harm, and we may as well give it a trial, mayn't we?"

Mr. Toms clapped his hands with so sudden a noise that Maggie jumped.

"That's right," he said. "That's the way I like to hear people talk. You shall judge for yourself, and WE'LL judge for ourselves." His voice was very soft and pleasant. The only thing at all strange about him was his smile, that came and went like the ripple of firelight on the wall. "You'd like to know all about us, wouldn't you? Well, until ten years ago I was selling corn in the City. Such a waste of time! But I took it very seriously then and worked, worked, worked. I worked too hard, you know, much too hard, and then I was ill—ill for a long time. When I was better corn didn't seem to be of any importance, and people thought that very odd of me. I was confused sometimes and called people by their wrong names, and sometimes I said what was in my head instead of saying what was in my stomach. Every one thought it very odd, and if my dear sister hadn't come to the rescue they would have locked me up—they would indeed!"

"Shut me up and never let me walk about—all because I didn't care for corn any more."

He laughed his little chuckling laugh. "But we beat them, didn't we, Dorothy? Yes, we did—and here we are! Now, you tell us your history."

Miss Toms had been watching Maggie's face intently while her brother spoke, and the clear steady candour of Maggie's eyes and her calm acceptance of all that the little man said must have been reassuring.

"Now. Jim," she said, "don't bother Mrs. Trenchard. You can't expect her to tell us her history when she's calling for the first time."

"Why not expect me to?" said Maggie. "I've got no history. I lived in Glebeshire most of my life with my father, who was a clergyman. Then he died and I lived with two aunts in London. Then I met Paul and he married me, and here I am!"

"That's not history," said Mr. Toms a little impatiently. "However, I won't bother you now. You're only a child, I see. And I'm very glad to see it. I don't like grown up people."

"How do you like Skeaton?" asked Miss Toms, speaking more graciously than she had done.

"Oh I shall like it, I expect," said Maggie. "At least I shall like the people. I don't think I shall ever like the place—the sand blows about, and I don't like the woods."

"Yes, they're greasy, aren't they?" said Mr. Toms, "and full of little flies. And the trees are dark and never cool—"

They talked a little while longer, and then Maggie got up to say good-bye. When she took Mr. Tom's hand and felt his warm confident pressure, and saw his large trusting eyes looking into hers, she felt a warmth of friendliness, also it seemed to her that she had known him all her life.

Miss Toms came with her to the door. They looked out into the dark. The sea rustled close at hand, far on the horizon a red light was burning as though it were a great fire. They could hear the wave break on the beach and sigh in the darkness as it withdrew.

"I shall come again," said Maggie.

"Don't you be too sure," said Miss Toms. "We shall quite understand if you don't come, and we shan't think the worse of you. Public opinion here is very strong. They don't want to be unkind to Jim, but they think he ought to be shut up ...Shut up!" Maggie could feel that she was quivering. "Shut up!"

Maggie tossed her head.

"Anyway, they haven't shut me up yet," she said.

"Well—good-night," said Miss Toms, after a little pause in which she appeared to be struggling to say more.

She told Grace and Paul at supper that night that she had been to see the Toms. She saw Grace struggling not to show her disapproval and thought it was nice of her.

"Do you really think—?" said Grace. "Oh, perhaps, after all—"

"Paul," said Maggie, "do you not want me to see the Toms?"

Paul was distressed.

"No, it isn't that ...Miss Toms is a very nice woman. Only—"

"You think it's not natural of me to take an interest in some one who's a little off his head like Mr. Toms."

"Well, dear, perhaps there is something—"

Maggie laughed. "I'm a little off my head too. Oh! you needn't look so shocked, Grace. You know you think it, and every one else here thinks it too. Now, Grace, confess. You're beginning to be horrified that Paul married me."

"Please, Maggie—" said Paul, who hated scenes. Grace was always flushed by a direct attack. Her eyes gazed in despair about her while she plunged about in her mind.

"Maggie, you mustn't say such things—no, you mustn't. Of course it's true that you've got more to learn than I thought. You ARE careless, dear, aren't you? You remember yesterday that you promised to look in at Pettits and get a reel of cotton, and then of course Mr. Toms is a good little man—every one says so—but at the same time he's QUEER, you must admit that, Maggie; indeed it wasn't really very long ago that he asked Mrs. Maxse in the High Street to take all her clothes off so that he could see what she was really made of. Now, that ISN'T nice, Maggie, it's odd—you can't deny it. And if you'd only told me that you hadn't been to Pettits I could have gone later myself."

"If it isn't one thing," said Maggie, "it's another. I may be a child and careless, and not be educated, and have strange ideas, but if you thought, Grace, that it was going to be just the same after Paul was married as before you were mistaken. Three's a difficult number to manage, you know."

"Oh, if you mean," said Grace, crimsoning, "that I'm better away, that I should live somewhere else, please say so openly. I hate this hinting. What I mean to say is I can leave to-morrow."

"My dear Grace," said Paul hurriedly, "whoever thought such a thing? We couldn't get on without you. All that Maggie meant was that it takes time to settle down. So it does."

"That isn't all I meant," said Maggie slowly. "I meant that I'm not just a child as you both think. I've got a life of my own and ideas of my own. I'll give way to you both in lots of things so long as it makes you happy, but you're not—you're not going to shut me up as you'd like to do to Mr. Toms."

Perhaps both Grace and Paul had a sharp troubling impression of having caught some strange creature against their will. Maggie had risen from the table and stood for the moment by the door facing them, her short hair, standing thick about her head, contrasting with her thick white neck, her body balanced clumsily but with great strength, like that of a boy who has not yet grown to his full maturity. She tossed her head back in a way that she had and was gone.

The Caroline affair was of another sort. Some days after Christmas, Maggie went to have tea with Caroline. She did not enjoy it at all. She felt at once that there was something wrong with the house. It was full of paintings in big gold frames, looking-glasses, and marble statues, and there was a large garden that had an artificial look of having been painted by some clever artist in the course of a night. Maggie did not pay a long visit. There were a number of men present; there was also a gramophone, and after tea they turned up the carpet in the dining-room and danced.

Caroline, in spite of her noise and laughter, did not seem to Maggie to be happy. She introduced her for a moment to the master of the house, a stout red-faced man who looked as though he had lost something very precious, but was too sleepy to search for it. He called Caroline "Sweet," and she treated him with patronage and contempt. Maggie came away distressed, and she was not surprised to hear, a day or two later, from Grace that Mrs. Purdie was "fast" and had been rude to Mrs. Constantine.

One day early in the spring Grace announced that Maggie ought not to go and see Mrs. Purdie any more. "There are all sorts of stories," said Grace. "People say—Oh, well, never mind. They have dancing on Sunday."

"But she's an old friend of mine," said Maggie.

"You have others to think of beside yourself, Maggie," said Grace. "And there is the Church."

"She's an old friend of mine," repeated Maggie, her mouth set obstinately.

"I will ask Paul what he thinks," said Grace.

"Please," said Maggie, her colour rising into her cheeks, "don't interfere between Paul and me. I'll speak to him myself."

She did. Paul maintained the attitude of indifference that he had adopted during the last six months.

"But would you rather I didn't go?" asked Maggie, aggravated.

"You must use your judgment," said Paul.

"But don't you see that I can't leave a friend just because people are saying nasty things."

"There's your position in the parish," said Paul.

"Oh, Paul!" Maggie cried. "Don't be so aggravating! Just say what you really think."

"I'm sorry I'm aggravating," said Paul patiently.

It was this conversation that determined Maggie. She had been coming, through all the winter months, to a resolution. She must be alone with Paul, she must have things out with him. As the months had gone they had been slipping further and further apart. It had been Paul who had gradually withdrawn into himself. He had been kind and thoughtful but reserved, shy, embarrassed. She understood his trouble, but at her first attempt to force him to speak he escaped and placed Grace between them. Well, this summer should see the end of that. They must know where they stood, and for that they must be alone ...

One day, early in June, Paul announced that he thought of exchanging duties, for the month of August, with a Wiltshire clergyman. This was Maggie's opportunity. Finding him alone in his study, she attacked.

"Paul, did you mean Grace to come with us to Little Harben in August?"

"Of course, dear. She has nowhere else to go."

"Well, she mustn't come. I've given way about everything since we were married. I'm not going to give way about this. That month we are to be alone."

"Alone!" said Paul. "But we're always alone."

"We're never alone," said Maggie, standing with her legs apart and her hands behind her back. "I don't mean to complain about Grace. She's been very good to me, I know, and I've got much to be grateful for. All the same she's not coming to Little Harben. She's got you all the rest of the year. She can give you up for a month."

"But Maggie—" said Paul.

"No, I'm quite determined about this. I may be a child and a fool, but I know what I'm talking about this time. You're not happy. You never talk to me as you used to. There are many things we ought to have out, but Grace is always there in the daytime and at night you're too tired. If we go on like this we'll be strangers in another six months."

He turned round to stare at her, and she saw in his eyes an odd excited light.

"Maggie," he said in a low voice. "If we go alone to Little Harben does it mean that you think—you can begin to love me?"

She turned her eyes away. "I don't know. I don't know about myself, I only know that I want us to be happy and I want us to be close together—as we were before we were married. It's all gone wrong somehow; I'm sure it's my fault. It was just the same with my father and my aunts. I couldn't say the things to them I wanted to, the things I really felt, and so I lost them. I'm going to lose you in the same way if I'm not careful."

He still looked at her strangely. At last, with a sigh, he turned back to his desk.

"I'll speak to Grace," he said. That night the storm broke.

During supper Grace was very quiet. Maggie, watching her, knew that Paul had spoken to her. Afterwards in the study the atmosphere was electric. Grace read The Church Times, Paul the Standard, Maggie Longfellow's Golden Legend, which she thought foolish.

Grace looked up. "So I understand, Maggie, that you don't want me to come with you and Paul this summer?"

Maggie, her heart, in spite of herself, thumping in her breast, faced a Grace transfigured by emotion. That countenance, heavily, flabbily good-natured, the eyes if stupid, also kind, was now marked and riven with a flaming anger.

But Maggie was no coward. With her old gesture of self-command she stilled her heart. "I'm very sorry, Grace," she said. "But it's only for a month. I want to be alone with Paul."

Grace, her hands fumbling on the arms of her chair as though she were blind, rose.

"You've hated my being here, Maggie ... all this time I've seen it. You've hated me. You don't know that you owe everything to me, that you couldn't have managed the house, the shops, the servants— nothing, nothing. This last year I've worked my fingers to the bone for you and Paul. What do you think I get out of it? Nothing. It's because I love Paul ... because I love Paul. But you've hated my doing things better than you, you've wanted me to fail, you've been jealous, that's what you've been. Very well, then, I'll go. You've made that plain enough at any rate. I'll leave to-morrow. I won't wait another hour. And I'll never forgive you for this—never. You've taken Paul away from me ... all I've ever had. I'll never forgive you—never, never, never."

"Grace, Grace," cried Paul.

But she rushed from the room.

Maggie looked at her husband.

"Why, Paul," she said, "you're frightened. Grace doesn't mean it. She won't go to-morrow—or ever. There's nothing to be frightened of."

His red cheeks were pale. His hands trembled.

"I do so hate quarrels," he said.

Maggie went up to him and rather timidly put her hand on his arm.

"We'll have a lovely time at Harben," she said. "Oh, I do want you to be happy, Paul."

CHAPTER VI

Strangely enough Maggie felt happier after this disturbance. Grace, in the weeks that followed, was an interesting confusion of silent and offended dignity and sudden capitulations because she had some news of fussing interest that she must impart. Nevertheless she was deeply hurt. She was as tenacious of her grievances as a limpet is of its rock, and she had never been so severely wounded before. Maggie, on her side, liked Grace better after the quarrel. She had never really disliked her, she had only been irritated by her.

She thought it very natural of her to be angry and jealous about Paul. She was determined that this month at Little Harben should put everything right. Looking back over these past years she blamed herself severely. She had been proud, self-centred, unfeeling. She remembered that day so long ago at St. Dreot's when Aunt Anne had appealed for her affection and she had made no reply. There had been many days, too, in London when she had been rebellious and hard. She thought of that night when Aunt Anne had suffered so terribly and she had wanted only her own escape. Yes—hard and unselfish that was what she had been, and she had been punished by losing Martin.

Already here, just as before in London, she was complaining and angry, and unsympathetic. She did care for Paul—she could even love Grace if she would let her. She would make everything right this summer and try and be a better, kinder woman.

Then, one morning, she found a letter on the breakfast table. She did not recognise the handwriting; when she opened it and saw the signature at the end for a moment she also did not recognise that. "William Magnus." ... Then—why, of course! Mr. Magnus! She saw him standing looking down at her with his mild eyes, staring through his large spectacles.

Her heart beat furiously. She waited until breakfast was over, then she took it up to her bedroom.

The letter was as follows:

Dear Miss Maggie,

I know you are not "Miss Maggie" now, but that is the only way that I can think of you. I expect that you have quite forgotten me, and perhaps you don't want to hear from me, but I must not lose sight of you altogether. I haven't so many friends that I can lose one without a word. I don't know quite what to begin by telling you. I ought to ask you questions about yourself, I suppose, but I know that your aunts hear from you from time to time and they give me news from your letters. I hear that you are happily married and are quite settled down to your new life. I'm very glad to hear that, although it isn't quite the life that I would have prophesied for you. Do you like Skeaton? I've never cared much for seaside resorts myself, but then I'm a queer cranky old man, and I deserve all I get. I wish I could tell you something cheerful about all your friends here, but I'm afraid I can't. Your aunt is so brave and plucky that probably she said nothing to you in her last letter about how ill she has been, but she's just had a very bad bout, and at one time we were afraid that we were going to lose her. You can imagine how anxious we all were. But she is better again now, although very much shattered. The Chapel is closed. There's a piece of news for you! It never recovered from poor Warlock's death; he was the spirit that gave it life, and although he may have had his dreams and imaginations that deceived him, there was some life in that building that I have never found anywhere else and shall never find again. You remember that Amy Warlock married that scamp Thurston. Well, she has left him and has come back to live with her mother. She had a rather bad experience, I'm afraid, poor woman, but she says nothing to any one about it. She and the old lady have moved from this part of London and have gone to live somewhere in Kensington. Some one saw Martin Warlock in Paris the other day. I hear that he has been very seriously ill and is greatly changed, looking years older. I can say, now that you are happily married, that I am greatly relieved that you were not engaged to him. You won't think this presumptuous of a man old enough to be your father, will you? I am sure he had many good things in him, but he was very weak and not fitted to look after you. But he had a good heart, I'm sure, and his father's death was a great shock to him. Thurston, I hear, is having revival meetings up and down the country. Miss Avies, I believe, is with him. You remember Miss Pyncheon? She and many other regular attendants at the Chapel have left this neighbourhood. The Chapel is to be a cinematograph theatre, I believe. There! I have given you all the gossip. I have not said more about your aunts because I want you to come up one day to London, when you have time, and see them. You will do that, won't you? I expect you are very busy—I hope you are. I would like to have a line from you, but please don't bother if you have too much to do.

Always your friend,

WILLIAM MAGNUS.

When Maggie saw Martin's name the other writing on the page transformed itself suddenly into a strange pattern of webs and squares. Nevertheless she pursued her way through this, but without her own agency, as though some outside person were reading to her and she was not listening.

She repeated the last words "Always your friend, William Magnus" aloud solemnly twice. Her thoughts ran in leaps and runs, hurdle-race-wise across the flat level of her brain. Martin. Old. Ill. Paris. Those walls out there and the road-man with a spade—little boy walking with him—chattering—it's going to be hot. The light across the lawn is almost blue and the beds are dry. His room. The looking-glass. Always tilts back when one tries to see one's hair. Meant to speak about it. Martin. Ill. Paris. Paris. Trains. Boats. How quickly could one be there? No time at all. Paris. Never been to Paris. Perhaps he isn't there now ...

At that definite picture she controlled her mind again. She pulled it up as a driver drags back a restive horse. Her first real thought was: "How hard that this letter should have come now when I was just going to put everything right with Paul." Her next: "Poor Paul! But I don't care for him a bit ... I don't care for any one but Martin. I never did." Her next: "Why did I ever think I did?" And her next: "Why did I ever do this?" She knew with a strange calm certainty that from this moment she would never be rid of Martin's presence again. She had maintained for more than a year a wonderful make-believe of indifference. She had fancied that by, pushing furiously with both hands one could drive things into the past. But Fate was cleverer than that. What he wanted to keep he kept for you—the weaving of the pattern in the carpet might be your handiwork, but the final design was settled before ever the carpet was begun. Not that any of these fine thoughts ever entered Maggie's head. All that she thought was "I love Martin. I want to go to him. He's ill. I've got to do my duty about Paul." She settled upon that last point. She bound her mind around it, fast and secure like thick cord. She put Mr. Magnus' letter away in the shell-covered box, the wedding-present from the aunts; in this box were the programme of the play that she had been to with Martin, the ring with the three pearls, Martin's few letters, and some petals of the chrysanthemum, dry and faded, that she had worn on the great day of the matinee. Something had warned her that it was foolish to keep Martin's letters, but why should she not? She had never hidden her love for Martin. Then, standing in the middle of the room, close beside the large double-bed, with a football-group and "The Crucifixion" staring down upon her, she had her worst hour. Nothing in all life could have moved her as did that picture of Martin's loneliness and sickness. Wave after wave of persuasion swept over her: "Go! Go now! Take the train to Paris. You can find out from Mr. Magnus where he was living. He is sick. He needs you. You swore to him that you would never desert him, and you have deserted him. They don't want you here. Grace hates you, and Paul is too lazy to care!"

At the thought of Paul resolution came to her. She looked up at the rather fat, amiable youth with the stout legs and the bare knees in the football photograph, and prayed to it: "Paul, I'm very lonely and tempted. Care for me even though I can't love you as you want. Don't give me up because I can't let you have what some one else has got. Let's be happy, Paul—please."

She was shivering. She looked back with a terrified, reluctant glance to the drawer where Mr. Magnus' letter was, then she went downstairs.

Soon after they started for Little Harben. The last days in Skeaton had scarcely been happy ones. Grace had erected an elaborate scaffolding of offended dignity and bitter misery. She was not bitterly miserable, indeed she enjoyed her game, but it was depressing to watch Paul give way to her. He was determined to leave her in a happy mind. Any one could have told him that the way to do that was to leave her alone altogether. Instead he petted her, persuading her to eat her favourite pudding, buying her a new work-box that she needed, dismissing a boy from the choir (the only treble who was a treble) because he was supposed to have made a long-nose at Grace during choir-practice.

He adopted also a pleading line with her. "Now, Grace dear, don't you think you could manage a little bit more?"

"Do you think you ought to go out in all this rain, Grace dear?"

"Grace, you look tired to death. Shall I read to you a little?"

He listened to her stories with a new elaborate attention. He laughed heartily at the very faintest glimmer of a joke. Through it all Grace maintained an unreleased solemnity, a mournful superiority, a grim forbearance.

Maggie, watching, felt with a sinking heart that she was beginning to despise Paul.

His very movement as he hurried to place a cushion for Grace sent a little shiver down her back. "Oh, don't do it, Paul!" she heard herself cry internally, but she could say nothing. She had won her victory about Harben. She could only now be silent. Still, she bore no grudge at all against Grace. She even liked her.

Grace made many sinister allusions to her fancied departure. "Ah, in November ... Oh! of course I shall not be here then!" or, "That will be in the autumn then, won't it? You'd better give it to some one who will be here at the time." With every allusion she scored a victory. It was evident that Paul was terrified by the thought that she should leave him. He did not see what he would do without her. His world would tumble to pieces.

"But she hasn't the remotest intention of going," said Maggie. "She'll never go."

"Well, I don't know. It would be strange without her, Maggie, I must confess. You see, all our lives we've been together—all our lives."

Nevertheless he felt perhaps some relief, in spite of himself, when they were safely in a train for Little Harben. It was rather a relief, just for a day or two, not to see Grace's reproachful face. Yes, it was. He was quite gay, almost like the boy he used to be. Little Harben was one of the smallest villages in Wiltshire and its Rectory one of the most dilapidated. The Rectory was sunk into the very bottom of a green well. Green hills rose on every side above it, green woods pressed in all around it, a wild, deserted green garden crept up to the windows and clambered about the old walls. There was hardly any furniture in the house, and many many windows all without curtains. Long looking-glasses reflected the green garden at every possible angle so that all the lights and shadows in the house were green. There was a cat with green eyes, and the old servant was so aged and infirm that she was, spiritually if not physically, covered with green moss.

From their bedroom they could see the long green slope of the hill. Everywhere there was a noise of birds nestling amongst the leaves, of invisible streams running through the grass, of branches mysteriously cracking, and, always, in the distance some one seemed to be chopping with an axe. If you pushed a window open multitudes of little insects fell in showers about you. All the roses were eaten with green flies.

"What a place!" said Maggie; nevertheless it was rather agreeable after the sand of Skeaton.

During the first three days they preserved their attitude of friendly distance. On the fourth evening Maggie desperately flung down her challenge. They were sitting, after supper, in the wild deserted garden. It was a wonderful evening, faintly blue and dim crocus with flickering silver stars. The last birds twittered in the woods; the green arc of the hill against the evening sky had a great majesty of repose and rest. "Now, Paul!" said Maggie.

"What is it, dear?" but he slowly changed colour and looked away from her, out into the wood.

"We've got to face it some time," she said. "The sooner, then, the better—"

"Face what?" he asked, dropping his voice as though he were afraid that some one would overhear.

"You and me." Maggie gathered her resources together. "Before we were married we were great friends. You were the greatest friend I ever had except Uncle Mathew. And now I don't know what we are."

"Whose fault is that?" he asked huskily. "You know what the matter is. You don't love me. You never have ... Have you?" He suddenly ended, turning towards her.

She saw his new eagerness and she was frightened, but she looked at a little bunch of stars that twinkled at her above the dark elms and took courage.

"I'm very bad at explaining my feelings," she said. "And you're not very good either, Paul. I know I am very fond of you, and I feel as though it ought to be so simple if I were wiser or kinder. I've been thinking for weeks about this, and I want to say that I'm ready to do anything that will make you happy."

"You'll love me?" he asked.

"I'm very fond of you, and I always will be."

"No, but love."

"A word like that isn't important. Affection—"

"No. It's love I want."

She turned away from him, pressing her hands together, staring into the wood that was sinking into avenues of dark. She couldn't answer him. He came over to her. He knelt on the dry grass, took her head between his hands, and kissed her again and again and again.

She heard him murmur: "Maggie ... Maggie ... Maggie. You must love me. You must. I've waited so long. I didn't know what love was. God in His Mercy forgive me for the thoughts I've had this year. You've tormented me. Tantalised me. You're a witch. A witch. You're so strange, so odd, so unlike any one. You've enchanted me. Love me. Maggie ... Love me ... Love me."

She caught his words all broken and scattered. She felt his heart beating against her body, and his hands were hot to the touch of her cold cheek. She felt that he was desperate and ashamed and pitiful. She felt, above all else, that she must respond—and she could not. She strove to give him what he needed. She caught his hands, and then, because she knew that she was acting falsely and the whole of her nature was in rebellion, she drew back. He felt her withdraw. His hands dropped.

She burst into tears, suddenly hiding her face in her hands as she used to do when she was a little girl.

"Oh, Paul," she wept. "I'm so sorry. I'm so sorry. I'm wicked. I can't—"

He got up and stood with his back to her, looking towards the night sky that flashed now with stars.

She controlled herself, feeling desperately that their whole future together hung on the approaching minutes. She went up to him, standing at first timidly behind him, then putting her hand through his arm.

"Paul. It isn't so hopeless. If I can't give you that I can give you everything else. I told you from the first that I couldn't help loving Martin. All that kind of love I gave to him, but we can be friends. I want a friend so badly. If we're both lonely we can come together closer and closer, and perhaps, later on—"

But she could not go on. She knew that she would never forget Martin, that she would never love Paul. These two things were so clear to her that she could not pretend. As the darkness gathered the wood into its arms and the last twitter of the birds sank into silence, she felt that she too was being caught into some silent blackness. The sky was pale green, the stars so bright that the rest of the world seemed to lie in dim shadow. She could scarcely see Paul now; when he spoke his voice came, disembodied, out of the dusk.

"You'll never forget him, then?" at last he asked.

"No."

"You're strange. You don't belong to us. I should have seen that at the beginning. I knew nothing about women and thought that all that I wanted—oh God, why should I be so tempted? I've been a good man ..." Then he came close to her and put his hand on her shoulder and even drew her to him. "I won't bother you any more, Maggie. I'll conquer this. We'll be friends as you want. It isn't fair to you—"

She felt the control that he was keeping on himself and she admired him. Nevertheless she knew, young though she was, that if she let him go now she was losing him for ever. The strangest pang of loneliness and isolation seized her. If Paul left her and Martin wasn't there, she was lonely indeed. She saw quite clearly how his laziness would come to his aid. He would summon first his virtue and his religion, and twenty years of abstinence would soon reassert their sway; then he would slip back into the old, lazy, self-complacent being that he had been before. Staring into the dark wood she saw it all. She could completely capture him by responding to his passion. Without that she was too queer, too untidy, too undisciplined, to hold him at all. But she could not lie, she could not pretend.

She kissed him.

"Paul, let's be friends, then. Splendid friends. Oh! we will be happy!"

But as he kissed her she knew that she had lost him.

Paul was very kind to her during their stay at Little Harben, but they recovered none of that old friendship that had been theirs before they married. Too many things were now between them. By the end of that month Maggie longed to return to Skeaton. It was not only that she felt crushed and choked by the strangling green that hemmed in the old house—the weeds and the trees, and the plants seemed to draw in the night closer and closer about the windows and doors—but also solitude with Paul was revealing to her, in a ruthless, cruel manner, his weaknesses. They were none of them, perhaps, very terrible, but she did not wish to see them. She would like to shut her eyes to them all. If she lost that friendly kindness that she felt for him then indeed she had lost everything. She felt as though he were wilfully trying to tug it away from her.

Why was it that she had never shrunk from the faults of Martin and Uncle Mathew—faults so plain and obvious—and now shrunk from Paul's? Paul's were such little ones—a desire for praise and appreciation, a readiness to be cheated into believing that all was well when he knew that things were very wrong, an eagerness to be liked even by quite worthless people, sloth and laziness, living lies that were of no importance save as sign-posts to the cowardice of his soul. Yes, cowardice! That was the worst of all. Was it his religion that had made him cowardly? Why was Maggie so terribly certain that if the necessity for physical defence of her or some helpless creature arose Paul would evade it and talk about "turning the other cheek"? He was so large a man and so soft—a terrific egoist finally, in the centre of his soul, an egoist barricaded by superstitions and fears and lies, but not a ruthless egoist, because that demanded energy.

And yet, with all this, he had so many good points. He was a child, a baby, like so many clergymen. Even her father could have been defended by that plea ...

He was not radically bad, he was radically good, but he had never known discipline or real sorrow or hardship. Wrapped in cotton wool all his life, spoilt, indulged, treated by the world as men treat women. His effeminacy was the result of his training because he had always been sheltered. Now his contact with Maggie was presenting him for the first time with Reality. Would he face and grapple with it, or would he slip away, evade it, and creep back into his padded castle?

The return to Skeaton and the winter that followed it did not answer that question. Maggie, Grace, and Paul were figures, guarded and defended, outwardly friendly. Grace behaved during those months very well, but Maggie knew that this was a fresh sign of hostility. The "Chut-Chut," "My dear child," and the rest that had been so irritating had been after all signs of intimacy. They were now withdrawn. Maggie made herself during that winter and the spring that followed as busy as possible. She ruthlessly forbade all thoughts of Martin, of the aunts, of London; she scarcely saw Caroline, and the church was her fortress. She seemed to be flung from service to service, to be singing in the choir (she had no voice), asking children their catechism, listening to Paul's high, rather strained, voice reading the lessons, talking politely to Mrs. Maxse or one of the numerous girls, knitting and sewing (always so badly), and above all struggling to remember the things that she was for ever forgetting. Throughout this period she was pervaded by the damp, oily smell of the heated church, always too hot, always too close, always too breathless.

She had many headaches; she liked them because they held back her temptation to think of forbidden things.

Gradually, although she did not know it, the impression gained ground that she was "queer." She had not been to the Toms' often, but she was spoken of as their friend. She had seen Caroline, who was now considered by the church a most scandalous figure, scarcely at all, but it was known that she was an old friend. Above all, it was understood that the rector and his wife were not happy.

"Oh, she's odd—looks more like a boy than a woman. She never says anything, seems to have no ideas. I don't believe she's religious really either."

She knew nothing of this. She did not notice that she was not asked often to other houses. People were kind (the Skeaton people were neither malicious nor cruel) but left her more and more alone. She said to herself again and again: "I must make this a success—I must"—but the words were becoming mechanical. It was like tramping a treadmill: she got no further, only became more and more exhausted. That spring and summer people noticed her white face and strange eyes. "Oh, she's a queer girl," they said.

The summer was very hot with a little wind that blew the sand everywhere. Strange how that sand succeeded in penetrating into the very depth of the town. The sand lay upon the pavement of the High Street so that your feet gritted as you walked. The woods and houses lay for nearly two months beneath a blazing sun. There was scarcely any rain. The little garden behind the Rectory was parched and brown; the laurel bushes were grey with dust. They saw very few people that summer; many of their friends had escaped.

Maggie, thinking of the green depths of Harben a year ago, longed for its coolness; nevertheless she was happy to think that she would never have to see Harben again.

As she had foretold, laziness settled upon Paul. What he loved best was to sink into his old armchair in the dusty study and read old volumes of Temple Bar and the Cornhill. He had them piled at his side; he read article after article about such subjects as "The Silkworm Industry" and "Street Signs of the Eighteenth Century." He was very proud of his sermons, but now he seldom gave a new one. He always intended to. "Don't let any one disturb me to-night, Maggie," he would say at supper on Fridays. "I've got my sermon." But on entering the study he remembered that there was an article in Temple Bar that he must finish. He also read the Church Times right through, including the advertisements. Grace gradually resumed her old functions.

She maintained, however, an elaborate pretence of leaving everything to Maggie. Especially was she delighted when Maggie forgot something. When that happened she said nothing; her mouth curled a little. She treated Maggie less and less to her garrulous confidences. They would sit for hours in the drawing-room together without exchanging a word. Maggie and Paul had now different bedrooms. Early in the autumn Maggie had a little note from Mr. Magnus. It said:

"You have not written to any of us for months. Won't you come just for a night to see your aunts? At least let us know that you are happy."

She cried that night in bed, squeezing her head into the pillow so that no one should hear her. She seemed to have lost all her pluck. She must do something, but what? She did not know how to deal with people. If they were kind and friendly there were so many things that she could do, but this silent creeping away from her paralysed her. She remembered how she had said to Katherine: "No one can make me unhappy if I do not wish it to be." Now she did not dare to think how unhappy she was. She knew that they all thought her strange and odd, and she felt that strangeness creeping upon her. She MUST be odd if many people thought her so. She became terribly self-conscious, wondering whether her words and movements were strange.

She was often so tired that she could not drag one foot after another.

A few weeks before Christmas something happened. A terrible thing, perhaps—but she was delivered by it ...

She was sitting one afternoon a few weeks before Christmas in the drawing-room alone with Grace. It was her "At Home" day, a Friday afternoon. Grace was knitting a grey stocking, a long one that curled on her lap. She knitted badly, clumsily, twisting her fingers into odd shapes and muddling her needles. Now and then she would look up as though she meant to talk, and then remembering that it was Maggie who was opposite to her she would purse her lips and look down again. The fire hummed and sputtered, the clock ticked, and Grace breathed in heavy despairing pants over the difficulties of her work. The door opened and the little maid, her eyes nervously wandering towards Grace, murmured, "Mr. Cardinal, mum."

The next thing of which Maggie was conscious was Uncle Mathew standing clumsily just inside the door shifting his bowler hat between his two hands.

The relief of seeing him was so great that she jumped up and ran towards him crying, "Oh, Uncle Mathew! I'm so glad! At last!"

He dropped his bowler in giving her his hand. She noticed at once that he was looking very unhappy and had terribly run to seed.

He was badly shaved, his blue suit was shabby and soiled. He was fatter, and his whole body was flabby and uncared for. Maggie saw at once that he had been drinking, not very much, but enough to make him a little uncertain on his feet and unsteady in his gaze. Maggie, when she saw him, felt nothing but a rush of pity and desire to protect him. Very strangely she felt the similarity between him and herself. Nobody wanted either of them—they must just love one another because there was no one else to love them.

She was aware then that Grace had risen and was standing looking at them both.

She turned round to her saying, "Grace, this is my uncle. You've heard me speak of him, haven't you? He was very kind to me when I was a little girl ... Uncle, this is my sister-in-law, Miss Trenchard."

Uncle Mathew smiled and, rather unsteadily, came forward; he caught her hand in both his damp, hot ones. "Very pleased to meet you, Miss Trenchard. I know you've been very good to my little Maggie; at least when I say 'my little Maggie' she's not mine any longer. She belongs to your brother now, doesn't she? Of course she does. I hope you're well."

Maggie realised then the terrified distress in Grace's eyes. The grey stocking had fallen to the ground, and Grace stared at Uncle Mathew in a kind of fascinated horror. She realised of course at once that he was what she would call "tipsy." He was not "tipsy," but nevertheless "tipsy" enough for Grace. Maggie saw her take in every detail of his appearance—his unshaven cheeks, the wisps of hair over the bald top of his head, the spots on his waistcoat, the mud on his boots, and again as she watched Grace make this summary, love and protection for that unhappy man filled her heart. For unhappy he was! She saw at once that he had had a long slide downhill since his last visit to her. He was frightened—frightened immediately now of Grace and the room and the physical world—but frightened also behind these things at some spectre all his own. Grace sat down and tried to recover herself. She began to talk in her society voice. Maggie knew that she was praying, over and over again, with a monotony possible only to the very stupid, that there would be no callers that afternoon.

"And so you know Glebeshire, Mr. Cardinal! Fancy! I've never been there—never been there in my life. Fancy that! Although so many of my relations live there. I once nearly went down, one wet Christmas, and I was going to stay with my aunt, but something happened to prevent me. I think I caught a cold at the time. I can't quite remember. But fancy you knowing Glebeshire so well!"

All this came out in a voice that might have issued from a gramophone, so little did it represent Grace's real feelings or emotions. Maggie knew so well that inside her head these exclamations were rising and falling: "What a horrible man! What a dreadful man! Maggie's uncle! We're lost if any one calls! Oh! I do hope no one calls!"

It was obvious meanwhile that Mathew was urgently wishing for a moment alone with Maggie. He looked at her with pleading eyes, and once he winked towards Grace. He talked on, however, running some of his words into one another and paying very little attention to anything that Grace might say:

"No, I haven't seen my little niece, Miss Trenchard, for a long time—didn't like to interfere, in a way. Thought she'd ask for me when she wanted me. We've always been the greatest friends. I'm a bachelor, you see—never married. Not that I'd like you to fancy that I've no interest in the other sex, far from it, but I'm a wanderer by nature. A wife in every port, perhaps. Well, who knows? But one's lonely at times, one is indeed. A pretty tidy little place you've got here. Yes, you have—with a garden too."

Paul came in, and Maggie saw him start as Mathew's stout figure surprised him. She felt then a rush of hostility against Paul. It was as though, at every point, she must run in fiercely to defend her uncle.

Meanwhile Grace's worst fears were realised. The little maid announced Miss Purves and Mrs. Maxse. A terrible half-hour followed. Miss Purves, as soon as she understood that this strange man was Mrs. Trenchard's uncle, was all eager excitement, and Uncle Mathew, bewildered by so many strangers, confused by a little unsteadiness in his legs that would have been nothing had he not been in a small room crowded with furniture, finally clasped Mrs. Maxse by the shoulder in his endeavour to save himself from tumbling over the little table that held the cakes and bread-and-butter. His hot, heavy hand pressed into Mrs. Maxse's flesh, and Mrs. Maxse, terrified indeed, screamed.

He began to apologise, and in his agitation jerked Miss Purves' cup of tea from the table on to the floor.

After that he realised that it would be better for him to go. He began elaborate apologies. Paul saw him to the door. He gripped Paul by the hand. "I'm delighted to have met you," he said in full hearing of the trembling ladies. "You've given me such a good time. Give my little Maggie a good time too. She's not looking over well. Send her up to London to stay with me for a bit."

Maggie saw him to the gate. In the middle of the little drive he stopped, turning towards her, leaning his hands heavily upon her. "Maggie dear," he said, "I'm in a bad way, a very bad way. You won't desert me?"

"Of course I won't," she answered. "I may want your help in a week or two."

He looked dismally about him, at the thick, dull laurel bushes and the heavy, grey sky. "I don't like this place, Maggie," he said, "and all those women. It's religion again, and it's worse than that Chapel. You don't seem to be able to get away from religion. You're not happy, my dear."

"Yes, I am," she answered firmly.

"No, you're not. And I'm not. But it will be all right in the end, I've no doubt. You'll never desert me, Maggie."

"I'll never desert you," Maggie answered.

He bent down and kissed her, his breath whisky-laden. She kissed him eagerly, tenderly. For a moment she felt that she would go with him, just as she was, and leave them all.

"Uncle," she said, "you understand how it is, don't you? We'd have asked you to stay if we'd known."

"Oh, that's all right." He looked at her mysteriously. "That new sister-in-law of yours was shocked with me. They wouldn't have me in the house. I saw that. And I only had one glass at the station. I'm not much of a man in society now. That's the trouble ... But next time I'll come down and just send you a line and you'll come to see me in my own little place—won't you? I'm in the devil of a mess, Maggie, that's the truth, and I don't know how to get out of it. I've been a bit of a fool, I have."

She saw the look of terror in his eye again.

"Would some money—" she suggested.

"Oh, I'm afraid it's past five pounds now, my dear." He sighed heavily. "Well, I must be getting along. You'll catch your death of cold standing out here. We ought to have been together all this time, you know. It would have been better for both of us."

He kissed her again and left her. She slowly returned into the house. Curiously, he had made her happier by his visit. Her pluck returned. She needed it. Grace was now stirred by the most active of all her passions—fear.

Nevertheless Grace and Paul behaved very well. Maggie understood the shock that visit must have given them. She watched Grace imagining the excited stories that would flow from the lips of Miss Purves and Mrs. Maxse. She was determined, however, that Grace and Paul should not suffer in silence—and Uncle Mathew must be vindicated.

At supper that night she plunged:

"Uncle Mathew's been very ill," she began, "for a long time now. He wasn't himself this afternoon, I'm afraid. He was very upset at some news that he'd just had. And then meeting so many strangers at once—"

Maggie saw that Grace avoided her eyes.

"I don't think we'll discuss it, Maggie, if you don't mind. Mr. Cardinal was strange in his behaviour, certainly. It was a pity that Miss Purves came. But it's better not to discuss it."

"I don't agree," said Maggie. "If you think that I'm ashamed of Uncle Mathew you're quite wrong. He's very unhappy and lonely—" She felt her voice tremble. "He hasn't got any one to look after him—"

Grace's hand was trembling as she nervously crumbled her bread. Still without looking at Maggie she said:

"By the way, you did the church flowers this morning didn't you, eh?"

Maggie turned white and, as always on these occasions, her heart thumped, leaping, as it seemed, into the very palms of her hands.

"But it was to-morrow—" she began.

"You remember that I told you three days ago that it was to be this morning instead of the usual Thursday because of the Morgans' wedding."

"Oh, Grace, I'm so sorry! I had remembered, I had indeed, and then Lucy suddenly having that chill—."

Paul struck in. "Really, Maggie, that's too bad. No flowers to-morrow? Those others were quite dead yesterday. I noticed at evensong ... Really, really. And the Morgans' wedding!"

Maggie sat there, trembling.

"I'm very sorry," she said, almost whispering. Why did fate play against her? Why, when she might have fought the Uncle Mathew battle victoriously, had Grace suddenly been given this weapon with which to strike?

"I'll go and do them now," she said. "I can take those flowers out of the drawing-room."

"It's done," Grace slowly savouring her triumph. "I did them myself this afternoon."

"Then you should have told me that!" Maggie burst out. "It's not fair making me miserable just for your own fun. You don't know how you hurt, Grace. You're cruel, you're cruel!"

She had a horrible fear lest she should burst into tears. To save that terrible disaster she jumped up and ran out of the room, hearing behind her Paul's admonitory "Maggie, Maggie!"

It is to be expected that Mrs. Maxse and Miss Purves made the most of their story. The Rector's wife and a drunken uncle! No, it was too good to be true ... but it was true, nevertheless. Christmas passed and the horrible damp January days arrived. Skeaton was a dripping covering of emptiness—hollow, shallow, deserted. Every tree, Maggie thought, dripped twice as much as any other tree in Europe. It remained for Caroline Purdie to complete the situation. One morning at breakfast the story burst upon Maggie's ears. Grace was too deeply moved and excited to remember her hostility. She poured out the tale.

It appeared that for many many months Caroline had not been the wife she should have been. No; there had been a young man, a Mr. Bennett from London. The whole town had had its suspicions, had raised its pointing finger, had peeped and peered and whimpered. The only person who had noticed nothing was Mr. Purdie himself. He must, of course, have seen that his house was filled with noisy young men and noisier young women; he must have realised that his bills were high, that champagne was drunk and cards were played, and that his wife's attire was fantastically gorgeous. At any rate, if he noticed these things he said nothing. He was a dull, silent, slow-thinking man, people said. Then one day he went up to London or rather, in the manner of the best modern problem play, he pretended to go, returned abruptly, and discovered Caroline in the arms of Mr. Bennett.

He flung Mr. Bennett out of the bedroom window, breaking his leg and his nose, and that was why every one knew the story. What he said to Caroline was uncertain. He did not, however, pack her off, as Miss Purves said he should have done, but rather kept her in the big ugly house, just as he had done before, only now without the young men, the young women, the champagne and the flowers.

"I must go and see her," said Maggie when she heard this story.

Grace turned the strange pale yellow that was her colour when she was disturbed.

"Maggie," she said, "I warn you that if you go to see this abandoned woman you will be insulting Paul and myself before the whole town."

"She is my friend," said Maggie.

"She is a wicked woman," said Grace, breathing very heavily, "and you're a wicked woman if you go to see her. You have already made Paul miserable."

"That is untrue," Maggie said fiercely. "It is I that have been miserable. Not that it hasn't been my own fault. I should never have married Paul."

"No, you should not," said Grace, breathing as though she had been running very hard. "And for that I was partly to blame. But fancy what you've done since you've been with us! Just fancy! It's terrible ... never a greater mistake ... never, never."

Maggie tossed her head. "Well, if it was a mistake," she said, "the end of pretending has come at last. I've been trying for nearly two years now to go your way and Paul's. I can't do it. I can't alter myself. I've tried, and I can't. It's no use. Grace, we'd never get on. I see it's been hopeless from the first. But you shan't make Paul hate me. You've been trying your hardest, but you shan't succeed. I know that I'm stupid and careless, but it's no use my pretending to be good and quiet and obedient. I'm not good. I'm not quiet. I'm not obedient. I'm going to be myself now. I'm going to have the friends I want and do the things I want."

Grace moved back as though she thought that Maggie were going to strike her.

"You're wicked," she said. "What about those letters in your drawer? You've never loved Paul."

"So you've been opening my drawers?" said Maggie. "You're worse than I, Grace. I never opened any one's drawers nor read letters I shouldn't. But it doesn't matter. There's nothing I want to hide. Paul knows all about it. I'm not ashamed."

"No, you're not," Grace's eyes were large with terror. "You're ashamed at nothing. You've made every one in the place laugh at us. You've ruined Paul's life here—yes, you have. But you don't care. Do you think I mind for myself? But I love Paul, and I've looked after him all his life, and he was happy until you came—yes, he was. You've made us all laughed at. You're bad all through, Maggie, and the laws of the Church aren't anything to you at all."

There was a pause. Maggie, a little calmer, realised Grace, who had sunk into a chair. She saw that stout middle-aged woman with the flat expressionless face and the dull eyes. She saw the flabby hands nervously trembling, and she longed suddenly to be kind and affectionate.

"Oh, Grace," she cried. "I know I've been everything I shouldn't, only don't you see I can't give up my friends? And I told Paul before we married that I'd loved some one else and wasn't religious. But perhaps it isn't too late. Let's be friends. I'll try harder than ever before—"

Then she saw, in the way that Grace shrank back, her eyes staring with the glazed fascination that a bird has for a snake, that there was more than dislike and jealousy here, there was the wild unreasoning fear that a child has for the dark.

"Am I like that?" was her own instinctive shuddering thought. Then, almost running, she rushed up to her bedroom.

CHAPTER VII

DEATH OF AUNT ANNE

Maggie, after that flight, faced her empty room with a sense of horror. Was there, truly, then, something awful about her? The child (for she was indeed nothing more) looked into her glass, standing on tip-toe that she might peer sufficiently and saw her face, pale, with its large dark eyes rimmed by the close-clipped hair. Was she then awful? First her father, then her aunts, then the Warlocks, now Grace and Paul—not only dislike but fright, terror, alarm!

Her loneliness crushed her in that half-hour as it had never crushed her since that day at Borhedden. She broke down altogether, kneeling by the bed and her head in her pillow sobbing: "Oh, Martin, I want you! Martin, I want you so!"

When she was calmer she thought of going down to Paul and making another appeal to him, but she knew that such an appeal could only end in his asking her to change herself, begging her to be more polite to Grace, more careful and less forgetful, and of course to give up such people as the Toms and Caroline, and then there would come, after it all, the question as to whether she intended to behave better to himself, whether she would be more loving, more ... Oh no! she could not, she could not, she could not!

She saw the impossibility of it so plainly that it was a relief to her and she washed her face and brushed her hair and plucked up courage to regard herself normally once more. "I'm not different," she said to the looking-glass. "There's no reason for Grace to make faces." She saw that the breach between herself and Grace had become irreparable, and that whatever else happened in the future at least it was certain that they would never be friends again.

She went downstairs prepared to do battle ...

Next morning she paid her visit to Caroline. It was a strange affair. The girl was sitting alone in her over-gorgeous house, her hands on her lap, looking out of the window, an unusual position for her to be in.

Caroline was at first very stiff and haughty, expecting that Maggie had come to scold her. "I just looked in to see how you were," said Maggie.

"You might have come before," answered Caroline. "It's years since you've been near me."

"I didn't like all those people you had in your house," said Maggie. "I like it better now there's no one in it."

That was not, perhaps, very tactful of her. Caroline flushed.

"I could have them all here now if I wanted to ask them," she answered angrily.

"Well, I'm very glad you'd rather be without them," said Maggie. "They weren't worthy of you, Caroline."

"Oh! What's the use going on talking like this!" Caroline broke out. "Of course you've heard all about everything. Every one has. I can't put my nose outside the door without them all peering at me. I hate them all—all of them—and the place too, and every one in it."

"I expect you do—" said Maggie sympathetically.

"Nasty cats! As though they'd never done anything wrong all their days. It was mostly Alfred's fault too. What does he expect when he leaves me all alone here week after week eating one's heart out. One must do something with one's time. Just like all men! At first there's nothing too good for you, then when they get used to it they can't be bothered about anything. I wonder what a man thinks married life is? Then to listen to Alfred, you'd think we were still living in the days of the Good Queen Victoria—you would indeed. Wouldn't let me go up to London alone! There's a nice thing for you. And all because he did let me go once and I meant to stay with mother and mother was away. So I had to sleep at a hotel. Why shouldn't I sleep at a hotel! I'm not a baby. And now he keeps me here like a prisoner. Just as though I were in jail."

"Is he unkind to you?" asked Maggie.

"No, he isn't. It's his horrible kindness I can't stand. He won't divorce me, he won't let me go away, he just keeps me here and is so kind and patient that I could kill him. I shall one day. I know I shall." She stood for a moment, pouting and looking out of the window. Then suddenly she turned and, flinging her arms around Maggie, burst into tears.

"Oh, Maggie! I'm so miserable ... I'm so miserable, Maggie! Why did I ever come here? Why did I ever marry? I was so happy at home with mother."

Maggie comforted her, persuading her that all would soon be well, that people very quickly forgot their little pieces of scandal, and that so long as she did not run away or do anything really desperate all would come right. Maggie discovered that Caroline had escaped from her crisis with an increased respect and even affection for her husband. She was afraid of him, and was the sort of woman who must be afraid of her husband before her married life can settle into any kind of security.

"And I thought you'd altogether abandoned me!" she ended.

"I wasn't coming while all those people were about," said Maggie.

"You darling!" cried Caroline, kissing her. "Just the same as you used to be. I was angry I can tell you when month after month went by and you never came near me. I used to tell people when they asked me that you were odd. 'She's not a bit like other people,' I would say; 'not a bit and it's no use expecting her to be. She's always been queer. I used to know her in London.' They do think you odd here, darling. They do indeed. No one understands you. So odd for a clergyman's wife. Well, so you are, aren't you? I always tell them you had no bringing up."

Caroline in fact very quickly recovered her flow. As soon as she found that Maggie was not shocked she reasserted her old superiority. Before the visit was over she had rather despised Maggie for not being shocked. At Maggie's departure, however, she was very loving.

"You will come soon again, darling, won't you? It's no use asking you to dinner because, of course, your husband won't come. But look in any afternoon—or we might go for a drive in the motor. Good-bye—good-bye."

Maggie, on her return, found Grace looking at the mid-day post in the hall. She always did this in a very short-sighted way, taking up the letters one by one, holding each very close to her eyes, and sniffing at it as though she were trying to read through the envelope. This always irritated Maggie, although her own letters were not very many. To-night, when she heard the hall door open, she turned and dropped the letters, giving that especial creaking little gasp that she always did when she was startled.

"Oh, it's you, Maggie, is it? Where've you been?"

"I've been to see Mrs. Purdie," Maggie said defiantly.

Grace paused as though she were going to speak, then turned on her heel. But just as she reached the sitting-room door she said, breathing heavily:

"There's a telegram for you there."

Maggie saw it lying on the table. She picked it up and hesitated. A wild beating of the heart told her that it must be from Martin. She didn't know what told her this except that now for so long she had been expecting to see a telegram lying in just this way on the table, waiting for her. She took it up with a hand that trembled. She tore it open and read:

"Come at once. Your aunt dying. Wishes to see you. Magnus."

No need to ask which aunt. When one aunt was mentioned it was Aunt Anne—of course. Oh, poor Aunt Anne! Maggie longed for her, longed to be with her, longed to be kind to her, longed to comfort her. And Mr. Magnus and Martha and Aunt Elizabeth and the cat—she must go at once, she must catch a train after luncheon.

She went impetuously into her husband's study.

"Oh, Paul!" she cried. "Aunt Anne's dying, and I must go to her at once."

Paul was sitting in his old armchair before the fire; he was wearing faded brown slippers that flapped at his heels; his white hair was tangled; his legs were crossed, the fat broad thighs pressing out against the shiny black cloth of his trousers. He was chuckling over an instalment of Anthony Trollope's "Brown Jones and Robinson" in a very ancient Cornhill.

He looked up, "Maggie, you know it's my sermon-morning—interruptions—" He had dropped the Cornhill, but not fast enough to hide it from her.

She looked around at the dirty untidiness of the study. "It's all my fault, this," she thought. "I should have kept him clean and neat and keen on his work. I haven't. I've failed."

Then her next thought was: "Grace wouldn't let me—"

The study, in fact, was more untidy than ever, the pictures were back in their places whence Maggie had once removed them.

Husband and wife looked at one another. If she felt: "I've not managed my duty," he felt perhaps: "What a child she is after all!" But between them there was the gulf of their past experience.

"I'm sorry to hear that," he said, yawning. "Is she an old lady?"

"No, she's not," said Maggie, breathing very quickly. "I love her very much. I've been thinking, Paul, I've not been good about my relations all this time. I ought to have seen them more. I must go up to London at once."

"If your aunt's bad and wants you, I suppose you must," he answered. He got up and came over to her. He kissed her suddenly.

"You'll be wanting some money," he said. "Don't be long away. I'll miss you."

She caught the 2.30 train. It seemed very strange to her to be sitting in it alone after the many months when she had been always either with Grace or Paul. An odd sense of adventure surrounded her, and she felt as though she were now at last approaching the climax to which the slow events of the last two years had been leading. When she had been a little girl one of the few interesting books in the house had been The Mysteries of Udulpho. She could see the romance now, with its four dumpy volumes, the F's so confusingly like S's, the faded print, and the yellowing page.

She could remember little enough of it, but there had been one scene near the beginning of the story when the heroine, Emily, looking for something in the dusk, had noticed some lines pencilled on the wainscot; these mysterious pencilled lines had been the beginning of all her troubles, and Maggie, as a small girl, had approached sometimes in the evening dusk the walls of her attic to see whether there too verses had been scribbled. Now, obscure in the corner of her carriage, she felt as though the telegram had been a pencilled message presaging some great event that would shortly change her life.

It was a dark and gloomy day, misty with a gale of wind that blew the smoke into curls and eddies against the sky. There seemed to be a roar about the vast London station that threatened her personally, but she beat down her fears, found a taxi, and gave the driver the well-remembered address.

As they drove along she felt how much older, how much older she was then than when she was last in London. Then she had been ignorant of all life and the world, now she felt that she was an old, old woman with an infinite knowledge of marriage and men and women and the way they lived. She looked upon her aunts and indeed all that world that had surrounded the Chapel as something infinitely childish, and for that reason rather sweet and touching. She could be kind and friendly even to Amy Warlock she thought. She wished that she had some excuse so that she might stay in London a week or two. She felt that she could stretch her limbs and breathe again now that she was out of Grace's sight.

And she would find out Uncle Mathew's address and pay him a surprise visit ... She laughed in the cab and felt gay and light-hearted until she remembered the cause of her visit. Poor, poor Aunt Anne! Oh, she did hope that she would be well enough to recognise her and to show pleasure at seeing her. The cab had stopped in the well-remembered street before the same old secret-looking house. Nothing seemed to have changed, and the sight of it all brought Martin back to her with so fierce a pang that for a moment breath seemed to leave her body. It was just near here, only a few steps away, that he had suddenly appeared, as though from the very paving-stones, when she had been with Uncle Mathew, and then had gone to supper with him. It was from this door that he had run on that last desperate day. She looked up at the windows; the blinds were not down; her aunt was yet alive; she paid the taxi and rang the bell.

The door was opened by Martha, who seemed infinitely older and more wrinkled than on the last occasion, her old face was yellow like drawn parchment and her thin grey hairs were pasted back over her old skull; she was wearing black mittens.

"Miss Maggie!" and there was a real welcome in her voice. Maggie was drawn into the dark little hall that smelt of cracknel biscuits and lamp oil, there was the green baize door, and then suddenly the shrill cry of the parrot, and then, out of the dark, the fiery eyes of Thomas the cat.

"Oh, Miss Maggie!" said Martha. "Or I suppose I should say 'Mrs.' now. It's a long, long time ..."

"Yes, it is," said Maggie. "How is my aunt?"

"If she lives through the night they'll be surprised," Martha answered, wheezing and sighing. "Yes, the doctor says—' If Miss Cardinal sees morning,' he says—" Then as Maggie hesitated at the bottom of the staircase. "If you'd go straight to the drawing-room, Miss, Mum, Mr. Magnus is waiting tea for you there."

Maggie went up, past the Armed Men into the old room. She could have kissed all the things for their old remembered intimacy and friendliness, the pictures, the books, the old faded carpet, the fire-screen, the chairs and wall-papers. There, too, was Mr. Magnus, looking just as he used to look, with his spectacles and his projecting ears, his timid smile and apologetic voice. He did seem for a moment afraid of her, then her boyish air, her unfeigned pleasure and happiness at being back there again, and a certain childish awkwardness with which she shook hands and sat herself behind the little tea-table reassured him:

"You're not changed at all," he told her. "Isn't that dreadful?" she said; "when all the way in the cab I've been telling myself how utterly different I am."

"I suppose you feel older?" he asked her.

"Older! Why, centuries!"

"You don't look a day," he said, smiling at her.

"That's my short hair," she answered, smiling back at him, "and not being able to wear my clothes like a grown woman. It's a fact that I can't get used to long skirts, and in Skeaton it's bad form to cross your knees. I try and remember—" she sighed. "The truth is I forget everything just as I used to."

"How is Aunt?" she asked him. He looked very grave, and behind his smiles and welcome to her she saw that he was a tired and even exhausted man.

"They don't think she can live through the night," he answered her, "but, thank God, she's out of all pain and will never suffer any more. She's tranquil in her mind too, and the one thing she wanted to put her quiet was to see you. She's been worrying about you for months. Why didn't you come up to see us all this time, Maggie? That wasn't kind of you."

"No, it wasn't," said Maggie. "But I didn't dare."

"Didn't dare?" he asked, astonished.

"No, there were things all this would have reminded me of too badly. It wasn't safe to be reminded of them."

"Haven't you been happy, then, there?" he asked her almost in a whisper.

"Oh, I don't know," she didn't look up at him. "I made a mistake in doing it. It was my fault, not theirs. No, I haven't been happy if you want to know. And I shan't be. There's no chance. It's all wrong; they all hate me. I seem to them odd, mad, like a witch they used to burn in the old days. And I can't alter myself. And I don't want to."

It was amazing what good it did her to bring all this out. She had said none of it to any one before.

"Oh dear, oh dear," sighed Mr. Magnus. "I hadn't known. I thought it was all going so well. But don't tell your aunt this. When she asks you, say you're very, very happy and it's all going perfectly. She must die at peace. Will you, my dear, will you?"

His almost trembling anxiety touched her.

"Why, dear Mr. Magnus, of course I will. And I am happy now that I'm back with all of you. All I want is for people to be fond of me, you know, but there's something in me—" She jumped up and stood in front of him. "Mr. Magnus! You're wise, you write books, you know all about things, tell me—tell me the absolute truth. Am I odd, am I queer, am I like a witch that ought to be burnt at the stake?"

He was deeply touched. He put his hands on her shoulders, then suddenly drew her to him and kissed her.

"I don't find you odd, my dear, but then, God forgive me, I'm odd myself. We're all rather odd in this house, I'm afraid. But don't you worry, Maggie. You're worth a wagon-load of ordinary people."

She drew slowly away. She sighed.

"I wish Paul and Grace only thought so," she said.

They had a quiet little tea together; Maggie was longing to ask Mr. Magnus questions about himself, but she didn't dare to do so. He wrapped himself in a reserved friendly melancholy which she could not penetrate. He looked so much older, so much more faded, as though the heat and fire had gradually stolen away from him and left him only the grey ghost of what he had been.

"Are you writing any books, Mr. Magnus?" she asked him.

"Any books?" he answered smiling. "Surely one would be enough, my dear. I have one half-finished as a matter of fact, but it's not satisfactory. If it weren't for the bread and butter I don't think I'd ever tackle it again. Or rather the bread, I should say. It's precious little butter it brings in."

"What's it called?" she asked.

"'The Toad in the Hole,'" he said.

"What a funny name! What does it mean?"

"I don't know." He shook his head. "It meant something when I began it, but the meaning doesn't seem important now."

In a little while he left her, saying: "Now if I were you I'd take a little nap, and later on I'll wake you and we'll go and see your aunt."

She slept, lying back in the blue armchair in front of the fire, with only the leaping flames as light to the room. Strange and dim but unspeakably sweet were her dreams. It seemed that she had escaped for ever from Paul and Grace and Skeaton, and that in some strange way Martin was back with her again, the same old Martin, with his laugh and the light in his eyes and his rough red face. He had come into the room—he was standing by the door looking at her; she ran to him, her hands stretched out, cries of joy on her lips, but oven as she reached him there was a cry through the house: "Your Aunt Anne is dead! Your Aunt Anne is dead!" and all the bells began to toll, and she was in the Chapel again and great crowds surged past her. Aunt Anne's bier borne on high above them all. She cried aloud, and woke to find Mr. Magnus standing at her side; one glance at him told her that he was in terrible distress.

"You must come at once," he said. "Your aunt may have only a few minutes to live."

She followed him, still only half-awake, rubbing her eyes with her knuckles, and feeling as though she were continuing that episode when Martha had led her at the dead of night into her aunt's bedroom.

The chill of the passages however woke her fully, and then her one longing and desire was that Aunt Anne should be conscious enough to recognise her and be aware of her love for her.

The close room, with its smell of medicines and eau-de-Cologne and its strange breathless hush, frightened her just as it had done once before. She saw again the religious picture, the bleeding Christ and the crucifix, the high white bed, the dim windows and the little table with the bottles and the glasses. It was all as it had been before. Her terror grew. She felt as though no power could drag her to that bed. Something lurked there, something horrible and unclean, that would spring upon her and hold her down with its claws ...

"Maggie!" said the clear faint voice that she knew so well. Her terror left her. She did not notice Aunt Elizabeth, who was seated close to the bed, nor Mr. Magnus, nor the nurse, nor the doctor. She went forward unafraid.

"Doctor, would you mind ..." the voice went on. "Three minutes alone with my niece ..." The doctor, a stout red-faced man, said something, the figures, all shadowy in the dim light, withdrew.

Maggie was aware of nothing except that there was something of the utmost urgency that she must say. She came close to the bed, found a chair there, sat down and bent forward. There her aunt was lying, the black hair in a dark shadow across the pillow, the face white and sharp, and the eyes burning with a fierce far-seeing light.

They had the intense gaze of a blind man to whom sight has suddenly been given: he cries "I see! I see!" stretching out his arms towards the sun, the trees, the rich green fields. She turned her head and put both her hands about Maggie's; she smiled.

Maggie said, "Oh, Aunt Anne, do you feel bad?"

"No dear. I'm in no pain at all. Now that you've come I'm quite happy. It was my one anxiety." Her voice was very faint, so that Maggie had to lean forward to catch the words.

"You'll have thought me unkind all this time," said Maggie, "not to have come, but it hasn't been unkindness. Many times I've wanted, but there seemed to be so much to do that it wasn't RIGHT to come away."

"Are you happy, dear?" Aunt Anne said in her ghostly whisper.

"Very, very happy," said Maggie, remembering what Mr. Magnus had said to her.

Aunt Anne sighed. "Ah, that's good. It was my one worry that you mightn't be happy. I was all wrong about you, Maggie, trying to push you my way instead of letting you go your own. I should have waited for God to show His direction. But I was impatient—and if you were unhappy—" She broke off and for a moment Maggie thought that she would speak no more. She lay there, with her eyes closed, like a waxen image.

She went on again: "I've always loved you, Maggie, from the very first, but I was so impatient for you to come to God. I thought He would reveal Himself and you not be ready. He did reveal Himself, but not as I had thought. He came that night and took Mr. Warlock with Him—that was true, Maggie, that night. All true—All true. God will show you His way. It will be revealed to you. Heaven and its glories. God and His dear Son ..."

She stopped again and lay with her eyes closed.

Maggie timidly, at last, said:

"Aunt Anne, I want you to forgive me for all my wickedness. I didn't mean to be wicked, but I just couldn't say my feelings out loud. I was shy of them somehow. I still am, perhaps. Maybe I always will be. But I just want to say that I know now how good you were to me all that time and I'm grateful from my heart."

"You'll get better won't you, Aunt Anne, and then I'll come often? I'm shy to say my feelings, but I love you. Aunt Anne, for what you've been to me."

She stopped. There was a deathly stillness in the chamber. The lamp had sunk low and the fire was a gold cavern. Dusk stole on stealthy feet from wall to wall. Aunt Anne did not, it seemed, breathe. Her hands had dropped from Maggie's and her arms lay straight upon the sheet. Her eyes were closed.

Suddenly she whispered:

"Dear Maggie ... Maggie ... My Lord and my God ... My Master ..."

Then very faintly: "The Lord is my Shepherd ... My Shepherd ... He shall lead me forth ... beside the pastures ... my rod and my staff ... The Lord ..."

She gave a little sigh and her head rolled to one side.

Maggie, with a startled fear, was suddenly conscious that she was alone in the room. She went to the door and called for the doctor. As they gathered about the bed the caverns of the fire fell with the sharp sound of a closing door.

Next morning Maggie wrote to Paul telling him that her aunt was dead, that the funeral would be in two days' time, and that she would stay in London until that was over. She had not very much time just then to think of the house and the dead woman in it, because on the breakfast-table there was this letter for her.

23 CROMWELL RD., KENSINGTON, March 12, 1912.

DEAR MRS. TRENCHARD,

I hear that you have come to London to visit your aunt. I have been hoping for some time past to have an opportunity of seeing you. I am sure that you will have no wish at all to see me; at the same time I do beg you to give me half an hour at the above address. Five o'clock to-morrow would be a good time. Please ask for Miss Warlock.

Believe me, Yours faithfully, AMY WARLOCK.

Maggie stared at the signature, then, with a thickly beating heart, decided that of course she would go. She was not afraid but—Martin's sister! What would come of it? The house was strangely silent; Aunt Elizabeth sniffed into her handkerchief a good deal; Mr. Magnus, his face strained with a look of intense fatigue, went out about some business. The blinds of the house wore down and all the rooms were bathed in a green twilight.

About quarter past four Maggie went down into the Strand and found a cab. She gave the address and off they went. Sitting in the corner of the cab she seemed to be an entirely passive spectator of events that were being played before her. She knew, remotely, that Aunt Anne's death had deeply affected her, that coming back to the old house had deeply affected her, and that this interview with Amy Warlock might simply fasten on her the fate that she had for many months now seen in front of her. She could not escape; and she did not want to escape.

They found the house, a very grimy looking one, in the interminable Cromwell Road. Maggie rang a jangling bell, and the door was ultimately opened by a woman with sleeves turned up at the elbows and a dirty apron.

"Is Miss Warlock at home?" The woman sniffed.

"I expect so," she said. "Most times she is. What name?"

"Mrs. Trenchard," Maggie said.

She was admitted into a hall that smelt of food and seemed in the half-light to be full of umbrellas. The woman went upstairs, but soon returned to say that Miss Warlock would see the lady. Maggie found that in the sitting-room the gas was dimly burning. There was the usual lodging-house furniture, and on a faded red sofa near the fire old Mrs. Warlock was lying. Maggie could not see her very clearly in the half-light, but there was something about her immobility and the stiffness of her head (decorated as of old with its frilly white cap) that reminded one of a figure made out of wax. Maggie turned to find Amy Warlock standing close to her.

"Mrs. Thurston—" Maggie began, hesitating.

"You may not know," said Amy Warlock, "that I have retained my maiden name. Sit down, won't you? It is good of you to have come."

The voice was a little more genial than it had been in the old days. Nevertheless this was still the old Amy Warlock, stiff, masculine, impenetrable.

"I hope your aunt is better," she said.

"My aunt is dead," answered Maggie.

"Dear me, I'm sorry to hear that. She was a good woman and did many kind actions in her time."

There was something very unpleasant about that room, with the yellow light, the hissing gas, and the immobile figure on the sofa. Maggie looked in the direction of old Mrs. Warlock.

"You needn't mind mother," said Amy Warlock. "For some time now she's been completely paralysed. She can't speak or move. But she likes to be downstairs, to see the world a bit. It's sad after the way that she used to enjoy life. Father's death was a great shock to her."

It was sad. Maggie remembered how fond she had been of her food. Like a waxen image! Like a waxen image! The whole room was ghoulish and unnatural.

"I've asked you to come and see me, Mrs. Trenchard," continued Miss Warlock, "not because we can have any wish to meet, I am sure. We have never liked one another. But I have something on my conscience, and I may not have another opportunity of speaking to you. I don't suppose you have heard that very shortly I intend to enter a nunnery at Roehampton."

"And your mother?" asked Maggie.

"Mother will go into a Home," answered Miss Warlock.

There was a strange little sound from the sofa like a rat nibbling behind the wainscot.

"I must tell you," said Miss Warlock, speaking apparently with some difficulty, "that I have done you a wrong. Shortly after my father's death my brother wrote to you from Paris."

"Wrote to me?" repeated Maggie.

"Yes—wrote to you through me. I destroyed the letters. He wrote then five times in rather swift succession. I destroyed all the letters."

Maggie said nothing.

"I destroyed the letters," continued Amy Warlock, "because I did not wish you and my brother to come together. I did not wish you to, simply out of hatred for you both. I thought that my brother killed my father—whom—whom—I loved. I knew that the one human being whom Martin had ever loved beside his father was yourself. He did love you, Mrs. Trenchard, more truly than I had believed it in his power to love any one. I think you could have made him happy—therefore I did not wish you to meet again."

There was a pause. Maggie said at last:

"Were there no other letters?"

"Yes," said Miss Warlock. "One this summer. For more than a year there was nothing; then this summer, a little one. I destroyed that too."

"What did it say?" asked Maggie.

"It said that the woman to whom he had been married was dead. He said that if you didn't answer this letter he would understand that you would not want to hear from him any more. He had been very ill."

"Where did he write that?"

"In Paris."

"And where is he now?"

"I don't know. I have heard from him no more."

Maggie got up and stood, her head raised as though listening for something.

"You've been very cruel, Miss Warlock," she said.

"Perhaps I have," said Miss Warlock. "But you cannot judge until you know with what reason I hated my brother. It is a very old story. However, now I hate no one. I will not apologise for what I have done. I do not want your forgiveness. I had to absolve my conscience."

"And you have no idea where he is now?"

"I have no idea. He may be dead for all I know."

Maggie shivered. "If you have any more information you will give it me?"

"I will give it you."

"This is my address." Maggie gave her a card.

They said good-day, looking for one moment, face to face, eye to eye.

Then Maggie turned and went. Her eyes were dim so that she stumbled on the stairs. In the street she walked, caring nothing of her direction, seeing only Martin.

CHAPTER VIII

DEATH OF UNCLE MATHEW

Grace, during the days that Maggie was in London, regained something of her old tranquillity. It was wonderful to her to be able to potter about the house once more mistress of all that she surveyed and protected from every watching eye. She had had, from her very earliest years, a horror of being what she called "overlooked."

She had a habit of stopping, when she had climbed halfway upstairs, of suddenly jerking her head round to see whether any one were looking at her. You would have sworn, had you seen her, that she was deeply engaged upon some nefarious and underhand plot; yet it was not so-she was simply going to dust some of her hideous china treasures in her bedroom.

Always after breakfast there was this pleasant ritual. She would plod all round the house, duster in hand, picking things up, giving them a little flick and putting them back again, patting treasures that she especially loved, sighing heavily with satisfaction at the pleasant sight of all her possessions tranquilly in their right places. As she looked around the ugly sitting-room and saw the red glazed pots with the ferns, the faded football-groups, the worsted mats and the china shepherdesses, a rich warm feeling rose in her heart and filled her whole body. It was like a fine meal to a hungry man: every morning at half-past nine she was hungry in this fashion, and every morning by eleven o'clock she was satisfied. Her thick body thus promenaded the house; she was like a stolid policeman in female attire, going his rounds to see that all was well. From room to room she went, pausing to pant for breath on the stairs, stumbling always because of her short sight at the three dark little steps just outside Paul's bedroom, always sitting down on her bed "to take a breath" and to get a full gaze at the crucifix of bright yellow wood, that hung just under her mother's picture. Tramp, tramp, tramp round the house she went.

It was incredible how deeply Maggie had interfered with this ritual. She had certainly not intended to do so. After that first effort to change certain things in the house she had retired from the battle, had completely capitulated. Nevertheless she had interfered with all Grace's movements and, as the terror of her grew, it seemed to pervade every nook and corner of the house, so that Grace felt that she could go nowhere without that invasion. Oh, how she resented it, and how afraid she was! After Paul and Maggie returned from that summer holiday she saw that Paul too felt Maggie's strangeness. To Grace, from the beginning of that autumn, every movement and gesture of Maggie's was strange. The oddity of her appearance, her ignorance of everything that seemed to Grace to be life, her strange, half-mocking, half-wondering attitude to the Church and its affairs ("like a heathen in Central Africa"), her dislike of the Maxses and the Pynsents and her liking for the Toms and Caroline Purdie, her odd silences and still odder speeches, all these things increased the atmosphere that separated her from the rest of the world.

Then came the day when Grace, dusting in Maggie's bedroom, discovered the bundle of letters. She read them, read them with shame at her own dishonesty and anger at Maggie for making her dishonest. To her virgin ignorance the passion in them spoke of illicit love and the grossest immorality. Her heart burnt with a strange mingling of envy, jealousy, loneliness, shame, and eagerness to know more ...

Then came Uncle Mathew's visit; then Caroline Purdie's disgrace. The count was fully charged. Maggie, that strange girl found in the heart of London's darkness, alone, without friends or parents, was a witch, a devilish, potion-dealing witch, who might, at any time, fly through the night-sky on a broom-stick as surely as any mediaeval old hag. These visions might be exaggerated for many human beings, not so for Grace. Having no imagination she was soaked in superstition. She clung to a few simple pictures, and was exposed to every terror that those pictures could supply.

Maggie now haunted her day and night. Everywhere she could feel Maggie's eyes piercing her. A thousand times an hour she looked up to see whether Maggie were not there in the room watching her. She hated her now with terror that was partly fear for her own safety, partly love and jealousy for Paul, partly outraged modesty and tradition, partly sheer panic.

She had, as yet, said very little to Paul. She waited the right moment. Maggie's absence showed her how deep and devastating this fear had been. She saw that it embraced the whole life of Paul and herself in Skeaton. She had grown fond of Skeaton; she was a woman who would inevitably care for anything when she had become thoroughly accustomed to its ways and was assured that it would do her no harm.

She liked the shops and the woods, the sand and the sea. Above all, she adored the Church. During a large part of every day she was there, pottering about, talking to the caretaker, poking her nose into the hymn-books to see whether the choir-boys had drawn pictures in them, rubbing the brasses, making tidy the vestry. The house too she loved, and the garden and the bottles on the wall. She might have known that she was not popular in the place, she cannot have failed to realise that she had no woman friend and that she was seldom invited to dinner. This did not matter to her. Her affections—and they were very real and genuine—were all for her brother. Had she Paul she wanted no one else. That was enough.

And now it might be that they would have to leave the place. Already the talk about Maggie was intolerable. Grace heard it on every side. After Mathew Cardinal's visit the talk rose to a shriek. Grace knew that those sudden silences on her entrance into the room meant lively and excited discussion. "How terrible for the poor rector!" "Such an odd girl—taken out of the slums." "Yes, quite drunk. He knocked Mrs. Maxse down." "Oh I assure you that she went to see Caroline Purdie the very day after. She did indeed ..."

Yes. Grace knew all about it. Unless things changed Paul would have to go. His life was ruined by this girl.

Nevertheless for a whole happy week the world seemed to sink back into its old accustomed apathy. The very house seemed to take on its old atmosphere. Paul came out of his study and went about paying calls. That hour, from six to seven, when he was at home to his parishioners seemed once again to be crowded with anxious old women and men out of work and girls in trouble. He took Grace with him on his rounds. Every one was very friendly. Grace was able to reassume some of her old importance.

Her old flow of conversation—checked recently by the sense of Maggie's strangeness—returned to her. In the morning she would stand by her brother's study-table, duster in hand, and pour out her heart.

"You know, Paul, it's all very well, you may say what you like, but if Mrs. Maxse thinks she's going to have the whole of that second pew she's mistaken. It's only for a week or two that she's got the Broadbents staying with her, and I know what she's after. Just fancy! What she wants is to put the Broadbents in that second seat the two Sundays they're here and then stick to it after they're gone. Just fancy what Miss Beats and Miss Hopwood will feel about it! What I mean is that they've had that seat for nearly eight years and now to be turned out! But I assure you, Paul, from what Linda Maxse said to me yesterday I believe she intends that, I do indeed. She thinks Miss Beats and Miss Hopwood will get used to sitting somewhere else after two Sundays. 'I'm sure they won't mind—poor old things,' she said only yesterday. 'Poor old things.' Just fancy! Why, Mary Beats is very little older than I. You'll have to put your foot down about it, you will, indeed, Paul. Yes, you will. Give Linda Maxse an inch and she takes a mile, I always said—and this is just the kind of thing ..."

So happily Grace ran on and Paul looked up from his desk at her, digging his fingers into his white hair, smiling at her in just the old confidential way that he used to have before Maggie came.

She revived, too, her old habit of talking to herself. This had always been an immense relief to her—it had helped her to feel reassurance. Lately she had felt that Maggie was overhearing her and was laughing at her; this had checked her and made her suspicious. Now as she began to mount the stairs she would murmur to herself: "It might be better to tell Jenny to go to Bartletts. After all, it's quicker that way, and she'll be able to tell the boy to bring the things back. She needn't wait. All the same she's stupid, she'll make a muddle of it as likely as not. And Womball's boy is livelier than Bartletts'. That's something after all. But if she goes out at two-thirty she'll never be back by four—unless she went by Smith's lane of course—she might do that ... Oh, dear, these stairs are a trial ... yes, she might do that, and then she'd only be an hour altogether. I'll suggest that ..."

Her murmur was a cheerful monotonous sound accompanying her as she went. She would stop and rub the side of her nose with her thumb, considering. In the house, when there was no fear of callers, she wore large loose slippers that tap-tapped as she went. In the evenings she sat in Paul's study all amongst the Cornhills, The Temple Bars, and The Bible Concordances. They were very cosy and happy, and she talked incessantly. For some reason she did not dare to ask him whether he were not happier now that Maggie was away. She did not dare. There was not the complete confidence that there had been. Paul was strange a little, bewitched by Maggie's strangeness ... There was something there that Grace did not understand. So she said nothing, but she tried to convey to him, in the peculiar warmth of her good-night kiss, what she felt.

Then Maggie returned. She came back in her black clothes and with her pale face. Her aunt had died. She was more alone even than before. She was very quiet, and agreed to everything that Grace said. Nevertheless, although she agreed, she was more antagonistic than she had been. She had now something that intensely preoccupied her. Grace could see that she was always thinking about something that had nothing to do with Skeaton or Paul or the house. She was more absent-minded than ever, forgot everything, liked best to sit in her bedroom all alone.

"Oh, she's mad!" said Grace. "She's really mad! Just fancy if she should go right off her head!" Grace was now so desperately frightened that she lay awake at night, sweating, listening to every sound. "If she should come and murder me one night," she thought. Another thought she had was: "It's just as though she sees some one all the time who isn't there."

Then came 13th March, that dreadful day that would be never forgotten by Grace so long as she lived. During the whole of the past week Skeaton had been delivered up to a tempest of wind and rain. The High Street, emptied of human beings, had glittered and swayed under the sweeping storm. The Skeaton sea, possessing suddenly a life of its own, had stormed upon the Skeaton promenade, and worried and lashed and soaked that hideous structure to within an inch of its unnatural life. Behind the town the woods had swayed and creaked, funeral black against the grey thick sky. Across the folds the rain fell in slanting sheets with the sibilant hiss of relentless power and resolve.

After luncheon, on this day the 13th, Maggie disappeared into the upper part of the house and Grace settled down on the drawing-room sofa to a nice little nap. She fell asleep to the comforting patter of rain upon the windows and the howling of the storm down the chimney. She dreamt, as she often did, about food.

She was awakened, with a sudden start, by a sense of apprehension. This happened to her now so often that there was nothing strange in it, but she jumped up, with beating heart, from the sofa, crying out: "What's happened? What's the matter?"

She realised that the room had grown darker since she fell asleep, and although it was early still there was a sort of grey twilight that stood out against a deeper dusk in the garden beyond.

"What is it?" she said again, and then saw that Jenny, the maid, was standing in the doorway.

"Well, Jenny?" she asked, trying to recover some of her dignity.

"It's a man, mum," said the little girl. (Grace had got her cheap from an orphanage.) "A gentleman, mum. He's asking for Mrs. Trenchard. 'E give me 'is card. Oh, mum, 'e is wet too!"

She had scarcely finished, and Grace had only taken the card, when Mathew Cardinal came forward out of the hall. He was a dim and mysterious figure in that half-light, but Grace could see that he was more battered and shabby than on his last visit. His coat collar was turned up. She could only very vaguely see his face, but it seemed to her strangely white when before it had been so grossly red.

She was struck by his immobility. Partly perhaps because she had been roused from sleep and was yet neither clear nor resolved, he seemed to her some nightmare figure. This was the man who was responsible for all the trouble and scandal, this was the man who threatened to drive Paul and herself from her home, this was the blackguard who had not known how to behave in decent society. But behind that was the terror of the mystery that enveloped Maggie—the girl's uncle, the man who had shared in her strange earlier life, and made her what she now was. As he stood there, motionless, silent, the water dripping from his clothes, Grace was as frightened as though he had already offered her personal violence or held a pistol to her head.

"What do you want?" she asked hoarsely, stepping back to the sofa. Jenny had left the room.

"I want to see my niece," he answered, still without moving. She recognised then, strangely, in his voice a terror akin to her own. He also was afraid of something. Of what? It was not that his voice shook or that his tongue faltered. But he was terrified ... She could feel his heart thumping behind the words.

"I'm sorry," she said. "You can't see her. She's upstairs resting."

She did not know whence the resolution had come that he was not, in any case, to see Maggie; she did not know what catastrophe she anticipated from their meeting. She was simply resolved, as though acting under the blind orders of some other power, that Maggie should not see him and that he should leave the house at once.

"I must see her," he said, and the desperate urgency in his voice would have touched any one less terrified than Grace. "I must."

"I'm sorry," she answered. The fear in his voice seemed now to give her superiority over him. "It's impossible."

"Oh no," he said. "If she's here it can't be impossible. She'd want to see me. We have things ... I must ... You don't understand, Miss Trenchard."

"I only know," said Grace, "that after what occurred on your last visit here, Mr. Cardinal, Maggie said that she would never see you again."

"That's a lie!" he said.

She made no answer. Then at last he said pitifully:

"She didn't really say that, did she?"

"Yes. I'm sorry. But you can understand after what occurred—"

He came suddenly forward, the water trickling from him on to the carpet.

"You swear that's true?"

She could see now his face and realised that he was, indeed, desperate—breathless as though he had been running from some one.

"Yes, that's true," she answered.

"Maggie said that."

"Those were Maggie's words."

"Oh, well, I'm done ..." He turned away from her as though her announcement had settled something about which he had been in doubt. "It isn't like Maggie ... But still she hasn't written. She saw I was hard up last time. All I deserve ... All I deserve." He turned round to Grace again. "I can't quite believe it, Miss Trenchard. It doesn't sound like Maggie, but perhaps you've influenced her ... That's likely. If she should change her mind I'm at the 'Sea Dog.' Not much of a place. Quiet though. Yes, well. You might tell her not to bother. I'm finished, you see, Miss Trenchard. Yes, down. You'll be glad to hear it, I've no doubt. Well, I mustn't stay talking. I wish Maggie were happier though. She isn't happy, is she?"

The question was so abrupt that Grace was startled.

"I should hope so—Mr. Cardinal," she said.

"Oh, no, she isn't. I know. Always this religion she gets into. If it isn't one sort it's another. But she's a good girl. Don't you forget that. Well, I must be going. Good day. Good day."

He was actually gone, leaving a little pool of water on the carpet behind him. Grace sat down on the sofa again. What a horrible man! What a horrible man! But she had been wrong to say that about Maggie. Yes, she had. But he had taken her by surprise. Oh dear! How her heart was beating! And how strange he had looked. She could scarcely breathe. She sat there lost in stupefied wonder. At last tea came in, and with it Paul and Maggie. Grace felt ashamed and frightened. Why was Maggie always making her do things of which she was ashamed? It was as though the girl had power over her ... absurd, of course. Nevertheless, as she poured out the tea she was haunted by that man's eyes. Yes, he had undoubtedly been very unhappy. Yes, in great trouble.

Maggie sat quietly there. Paul was preoccupied with a letter that must, he had decided, be written to The Church Times. It was a letter about Churchwardens and their growing independence. He finished his tea hurriedly, but before he left the room, looking at Maggie rather wistfully, suddenly he bent down and kissed her. She glanced up at him, smiling.

"Is there anything I can do for you, Grace?" she asked.

Then, as it were without her own desire, Grace was compelled to speak. "There's something I ought to tell you—" she began awkwardly. Then she stopped. Maggie was troubled. She knew that when Grace was uncomfortable every one else was uncomfortable.

"What have I done now?" she said rather sharply.

"It's nothing that you've done," answered Grace also sharply. "I'm sure I don't know, Maggie, why you should always think that I'm scolding you. No, I don't indeed. It's nothing that you've done. Your uncle came to see you this afternoon."

"Uncle Mathew?" Maggie jumped up from her chair. "Came here?"

"Yes."

"And wanted to see me? Oh, Grace, why didn't you tell me?"

"I have told you ... There's nothing to make a fuss about, Maggie. Really, you needn't look like that—as though I were always doing something wrong. I only did it for your sake."

"For my sake? But why? I wanted to see him. I was trying to see him in London. Oh, Grace, what did he say?"

"What did he say? Well, fancy! As though I could remember. He said he'd come to see you, and when I said he couldn't, he went away again."

"Said he couldn't? But why couldn't he?"

"Really, Maggie, your tone is extraordinary. Fancy what Paul would say if he heard you. He wouldn't like it, I'm sure. I said that after the way he'd behaved last time he came here you didn't want to see him again."

"You said that? Oh, Grace! How did you dare!" "Now, Maggie, don't you look like that. I've done nothing, I'm sure."

"Did you say that I'd said that I didn't want to see him again?"

Grace shrank back behind the tea-things.

"Yes, I did ... Maggie, you frighten me."

"I hope I do ... You're wicked, you're wicked. Yes, you are. Where is he now?"

"He's at the 'Sea Dog.' That dirty public house on the sea-front—near Tunstalls—Where are you going?"

"I'm going to him of course." Maggie turned and looked at Grace. Grace was fascinated as a rabbit is by a snake. The two women stared at one another.

"How strange you are, Grace," Maggie said. "You seem to like to be cruel!" Then she went out. When the door was closed Grace found "that she was all in a perspiration." Her hand trembled so that when she tried to pour herself another cup of tea—just to fortify herself—she poured it into the saucer. And the tea was cold—no use now.

When she rose at last to go in and seek consolation from Paul her knees were trembling so that she staggered across the floor. This couldn't go on. No, it could not. To be frightened in one's own house! Absurd ... Really the girl had looked terrible ... Murder ... That's what it had looked like. Something must be done.

Murmuring aloud to herself again and again "Something must be done" as she crossed the hall, she walked slowly, her hand to her heart, ponderously, as though she were walking in the dark. Then, as soon as she had opened the study door she began, before she could see her brother: "Oh, Paul, I'm so frightened. It's Maggie. She's very angry. Fancy what she said."

Maggie meanwhile had gone straight up to her bedroom and found her black hat and her waterproof. Her one thought now was lest he should have caught the five o'clock train and gone back to London. Oh! how hurt he would be with her, how terribly hurt! The thought of the pain and loneliness that he would feel distressed her so bitterly that she could scarcely put on her hat, she was so eager to run and find him. She felt, at the thought of his fruitless journey through the rain, the tenderest affection for him, maternal and loving, so that she wanted to have him with her at once and to see him in warm clothes beside the fire, drinking whisky if he liked, and she would give him all the money she possessed.

She had still touched very little of her own three hundred pounds. He should have as much of that as he liked. The death of Aunt Anne had shown her how few people in the world there were for her to love. After all, the aunts and Uncle Mathew had needed her as no one else had done. She made little plans; she would, perhaps, go back with him to London for a little time. There was, after all, no reason why she should remain in this horrible place for ever. And Paul now seemed not to care whether she went or stayed.

She ran out into the wind and the rain. She was surprised by the force and fury of it. It would take time and strength to battle down the High Street. Poor Uncle Mathew! To walk all the way in the rain and then to be told that she would not see him! She could imagine him turning away down the drive, bitterly disappointed ...

Probably he had come to borrow money, and she had promised that she would not fail him. When she reached the High Street she was soaked. She felt the water dripping down her neck and in her boots. At the corner of the High Street by the bookseller's she was forced to pause, so fiercely did the wind beat up from the Otterson Road, that runs openly to the sea. Maggie had not even in Glebeshire known so furious a day and hour when the winds tossed and raged but never broke into real storm. It was the more surprising. She had to pause for a moment to remember where Turnstall's the butcher was, then, suddenly recalling it, she turned off the High Street and found her way to the mean streets that ran behind the Promenade. Still she met no one. It might have been a town abandoned by all human life and given over to the wind and rain and the approaching absorption of the sea. It was now dark and the lamp at the end of the street blew gustily and with an uncertain flare.

Maggie found Turnstall's, its shop lit and Mr. Turnstall himself, stout and red-faced, behind his bloody counter. She went in and asked him where "The Sea Dog" might be. He explained to her that it was close at hand, on the right, looking over the Promenade. She found it at last because it had an old-fashioned creaking wooden sign with a blue sailor painted on it. Timidly she stepped into the dark uneven passage. To the right of her she could see a deserted room with wooden trestles and a table. The bar must be near because she could hear voices and the clinking of glasses, but, in spite of those sounds the house seemed very dead. Through the walls and rooms she could hear the pounding beat of the sea. She walked to the end of the passage and there found an old wrinkled man in riding breeches and a brightly-coloured check shirt.

"Can you tell me where a gentleman, Mr. Cardinal, is staying?" she asked.

He was obviously very deaf; she had to shout. She repeated her question, adding. "He came from London to-day."

A stout middle-aged woman appeared. "What is it?" she asked. "The old man's stone deaf. He can't hear at all."

"I was wondering," said Maggie, "whether you could tell me where I could find a Mr. Cardinal. He came down from London to-day and is staying here."

"Cardinal ... Cardinal?" The woman thought, scratching her head. "Was it Caldwell you meant?"

"No," said Maggie. "Cardinal."

"I'll go and see." The woman disappeared, whilst the old man brushed past Maggie as though she were a piece of furniture; he departed on some secret purpose of his own.

"What a horrible place!" thought Maggie. "Uncle must be in a bad way if he comes here. I never should sleep for the noise of the sea."

The woman returned. "Yes. 'E's here. No. 5. Come this afternoon. Up the stairs and second door on the right."

The stairs to which she pointed offered a gulf of darkness. The woman was gone. The noises from the bar had ceased. The only sound in the place was the thundering of the sea, roaring, as it seemed, at the very foot of the house.

Maggie climbed the stairs. Half-way up she was compelled to pause. The darkness blinded her; she had lost the reflection from the lamp below and, above her, there was no light at all. She advanced slowly, step by step, feeling her way with a hand on the rickety bannisters. At the top of the stair there was a gleam of light and, turning to the right, she knocked on the second door. There was no answer and she knocked again. Listening, the noise of the sea was now so violent that she fancied that she might not have heard the answer so she turned the handle of the door and pushed it open. She was met then by a gale of wind, a rush of the sea that seemed as imminent as though she were on the shore itself and a dim grey light that revealed nothing in the room to her but only shapes and shadows.

She knew at once that the windows must be wide open; she could hear some papers rustling and something on the wall tapped monotonously.

"Uncle Mathew!" she whispered, and then she called more loudly.

"Uncle Mathew! Uncle Mathew!"

There was no answer and suddenly a strange, quite unreasoning terror caught her by the throat. It was all that she could do not to cry out and run down to the gas-lit passage. She held herself there by sheer force; the smell of the sea was now very strong; there was a tang of rotten seaweed in it.

As she remained there she could see more clearly, but it seemed that the room was full of some dim obscuring mist. She moved forward into the room, knocked her knee against a table, and then as the panic gained upon her called more loudly, "Uncle... Uncle. Are you in? Where are you? It's I, Maggie."

"Oh well... of course he isn't here," she said to herself. "He's downstairs." And yet, strangely, something seemed to persuade her that he was there; it was as though he were maliciously hiding from her to tease her.

Feeling her way cautiously, her hands before her face, she moved forward to close the windows, thinking that she must shut out that abominable sound of the sea and the stale stink of the seaweed. She was suddenly caught by a sweep of rain that wetted her hair and face and neck. She started back and touched a piece of damp cloth. She turned, and there, very close to her but above her and staring over her head, was Uncle Mathew's face. It was so close to her that she could have touched it by putting up her hand. It was white-grey and she would not have seen it at all had she not been very near to it.

She realised nothing, but she felt that her knees were trembling and that she would fall if she did not steady herself. She put out her hand and clutched damp heavy thick cloth, cloth that enwrapped as it seemed some weighty substance like stone or brick.

She passed her hand upwards and suddenly the damp cloth gave way beneath her fingers, sinking inwards against something soft and flabby. She sprang away. She stood for one shuddering moment, then she screamed again and again, shrieking and running, as it were for her life, out of the room, down the passage. She could not find the staircase. Oh! she could not find the staircase! She stood there, leaning against the damp wall, crying: "Oh help! Help! Quickly!"

There were steps and voices, then the woman whom she had seen before appeared at the turn of the stair holding a lamp.

"What is it?" she asked, raising the light high. Maggie did not answer, only leaning there and staring down.

"You'd better come, Bill," the woman said. "There's something wrong up 'ere."

The woman came up the stairs followed by two men; they moved cautiously as though, they expected to find something terrible round the next corner.

"What is it?" said the woman again when she came up to Maggie. But Maggie made no answer. They pushed past her and went into the room. Maggie followed them. She saw the room obscured by mist; she heard some whispering and fumbling, then a match was struck; there was a bead-like flare followed suddenly by the flaming of a candle. In the quick light the room was bright. Maggie saw her uncle hanging from some projection in the rough ceiling. A chair was overturned at his feet. His body was like a bag of old clothes, his big boots turning inwards towards one another. His face was a dull grey and seemed cut off from the rest of his body by the thick blue muffler that encircled his neck. He was grinning at her; the tip of his tongue protruded at her between his teeth. She noticed his hands that hung heavily like dead fish.

After that she knew no more save that the sea seemed to rush in a great flood, with a sudden vindictive roar, into the room.

CHAPTER IX

SOUL OF PAUL

Nothing so horrible had ever happened to Paul before, nothing ...

He felt as though he had committed a murder; it was as though he expected arrest and started at every knock on the door. Nothing so horrible ...

It was, of course, in all the Skeaton papers. At the inquest it appeared that Mathew Cardinal had imitated the signature of a prosperous City friend; had he not chosen his own way out he would have discovered the arduous delights of hard labour. But he had chosen suicide and not "while of unsound mind." Yes, the uncle of the Rector's wife ... Yes, The Rector's Wife's Uncle ... Yes, The Rector's Wife's Uncle!

Sho discovered him, bumped right into him in the dark. What a queer story—like a novel. Oh, but she had always been queer—Trenchard had picked her up somewhere in a London slum; well, perhaps not a slum exactly but something very like it. Why did he marry her? Perhaps he had to. Who knows? These clergymen are sly dogs. Always the worst if the truth were known ...

So it went on. For nine whole days (and nights) it was the only topic in Skeaton. Paul caught the fringe of it. He had never known very much about his fellow-beings. He had always taken the things that they said to him as the true things, when they smiled he had thought that they meant their smiles. And why not? ... since he always meant his. He had always been too lazy to dislike people, and his digestion had been too good and his ambition too slender to urge him towards spite and malice. He had believed that he was on excellent terms with all the world.

Now that was changed. He was watched, he knew, with curious, inquisitive, critical glances. Through no fault of his own he was soiled and smirched. That hearty confident laugh of his must be checked. He was afraid. Yes, he was afraid. He sat in his study and trembled at the thought of meeting his congregation. He had done nothing and yet his reputation was no longer clean. But he was afraid, also, of something else. He saw, desperately against his will, the central picture. He saw the body hanging in the dark room, Maggie tumbling against it, the cries, the lights, the crowd ... He saw it all, hour after hour. He was not an imaginative man, but it seemed to him that he had actually been present at this scene. He had to attend the inquest. That had been horrible. With all eyes upon him he stood up and answered their detestable questions. He had trembled before those eyes. Suddenly the self-confidence of all his life had left him. He had stammered in his replies, his hands had trembled and he had been forced to press them close to his sides. He had given his answers as though he were a guilty man.

He came then slowly, in the silence of his study, to the consideration of Grace and Maggie. This would kill Grace. She had altered, in a few days, amazingly; she would meet nobody, but shut herself into her bedroom. She would not see the servants. She looked at Paul as though she, like the rest of the world, blamed him. Paul loved Grace. He had not known before how much. They had been together all their lives and he had taken her protection and care of him too much for granted. How good she had been to him and for how many years! When they were happy it seemed natural that she should look after him, but now, in the middle of this scandal he saw that it should have been he who looked after her. He had not looked after her. Of course, now they would have to leave Skeaton and he knew what that departure would mean to Grace. She was suspicious of new places and new people. Strange to think now that almost the only person of whom she had not been suspicious was Maggie.

Maggie! His mind slowly wheeled round to her. He rose from his chair and began clumsily to parade the room. He walked up and down the study as though with closed eyes, his large body bumping against corners of tables and chairs. Maggie! He looked back, as of late he had often done, to those days in his cousin's house in London. What had happened to the Maggie whom he had known there?

He saw her again, so quiet, so ready to listen and learn, so modest, and yet with a humour and sense of appreciation that had promised well for the future. A child—an ignorant, charming, uneducated child, that is what she had seemed. He admitted now that his heart, always too soft and too gentle perhaps, had been touched beyond wisdom. She had seemed to need just the protection and advice that he had been fitted to give her. Then, as though in the darkness of the night, the change had been made; from the moment of entering into Skeaton there had been a new Maggie. He could not tell himself, because he was not a man clever at psychology, in what the change consisted. Had he been pressed he would have said perhaps that he had known the old Maggie intimately, that nothing that she could say or do astonished him, but that this new Maggie was altogether a stranger. Time had not altered that; with the passing months he had known her less and less. Why, at their first meeting long ago in Katherine's house he had known her better than he knew her now. He traced the steps of their history in Skeaton; she had eluded him always, never allowing him to hold her for more than a moment, vanishing and appearing again, fantastic, in some strange lighted distance, hurting him and disappointing him ... He stopped in his walk, bewildered. He saw, with a sudden flash, that she had never appeared so fascinating to him as when she had been strangest. He saw it now at the moment when she seemed more darkly strange, more sinister and dangerous than ever before.

He realised, too, at the same sharp moment the conflict in which he was engaged. On the one side was all his life, his sloth and ease and comfort, his religion, his good name, his easy intercourse with his fellow-men, Grace, intellectual laziness, acceptance of things as they most easily are, Skeaton, regular meals, good drainage, moral, physical and spiritual, a good funeral and a favourable obituary in The Skeaton Times. On the other hand unrest, ill-health, separation from Grace, an elusive and never-to-be-satisfied pursuit, scandal and possible loss of religion, unhappiness ... At least it was to his credit that he realised the conflict; it is even further to his credit that he grasped and admitted the hopelessness of it. He knew which way he would go; even now he was tired with the thought of the struggle; he sank into his shabby chair with a sigh of weariness; his hand stretched out instinctively for an easy volume. But oh, Maggie! how strange and fascinating at that moment she appeared to him, with her odd silences, her flashes of startled surprise, her sense of being half the day in another world, her kindness to him and then her sudden terror of him, her ignorance and then the conviction that she gave suddenly to him that she knew more than he would ever know, above all, the way that some dark spirit deep down in him supported her wild rebellions, her irreverences, her irreligion, her scorn of tradition. Oh! she was a witch! Grace's word for her was right, but not Grace's sense of it. The more Grace was shocked the more tempting to him the witch became. It had seemed to him, that day in Katherine's drawing-room, so slight a thing when she had said that she did not love him, he had no doubt but that he could change that. How could a child, so raw and ignorant, resist such a man? And yet she had resisted. That resistance had been at the root of the trouble. Whichever way things went now, he was a defeated man.

The door opened and Grace came in. Looking at her he realised that she would never understand the struggle through which he had been timorously wading, and saw that she was further away from him than she had ever been before. He blamed her too. She had had no right to refuse that man to Maggie. Had she allowed Maggie to see him none of this might have occurred. The man was a forger and would, had he lived, have gone to prison, but there would not then have been the same open scandal. No, he blamed Grace. It might be that their old absolutely confident intimacy would never be renewed. He felt cold and lonely. He bent forward, putting some coal on the fire, breaking it up into a cheerful blaze. Then he looked up at her, and his heart was touched. She looked to-day an old woman. Her hair was untidy and her face was dull grey in colour. Her eyes moved restlessly round the room, wandering from picture to picture, from the mantelpiece to the chairs, from the chairs to the book-shelves, as though she sought in the sight of these well-remembered things some defence and security.

"Is your head better?" he asked her, not meeting her eyes, because the dull pain in them disturbed him.

"Not much," she said. "It's very bad, my head. I've taken aspirin. I didn't eat anything yesterday. Nothing at all except some bread and milk, and very little of that ... I couldn't finish it. I felt I'd be sick. I said to Emily, 'Emily, if I eat any more of that I'll be sick,' and Emily advised me not to touch it. What I mean is that if I'd eaten any more I'd have been really sick—at least that's what I felt like."

Her restless eyes came suddenly to a jerking pause as though some one had caught and gripped them. She was suddenly dramatic. "Oh. Paul, what are we going to do?" she cried.

Paul was irritated by that. He hated to be asked direct questions as to policy.

"What do you mean what are we going to do?" he asked.

"Why, about this—about everything. We shall have to leave Skeaton, you know. Fancy what people are saying!"

Suddenly, as though the thought of the scandal was too much for her, her knees gave way and she flopped into a chair.

"Well, let them say!" he answered vigorously. "Grace, you're making too much of all this. You'll be ill if you aren't careful. Pull yourself together." "Of course we've got to go," she answered. "If you think that we can go on living here after all that's happened—"

"Well, why not?" he interrupted. "We haven't done anything. It's only—"

"I know what you're going to say." (It was one of Grace's most irritating habits that she finished other people's sentences for them in a way that they had not intended) "that if they look at it properly they'll see that it wasn't our fault. But will they look at it properly? Of course they won't. You know what cats they are. They're only waiting for a chance. What I mean is that this is just the chance they've been waiting for."

"How can you go on and every time you preach they'll be looking up at you and saying 'There's a brother of a murderer'? Why, fancy what you'd feel!"

Paul jumped in his chair. "What do you mean, Grace? The brother of a murderer?"

"What else am I?" Grace began to warm her podgy hands. "It came out at the inquest that I wouldn't see the man, didn't it? Maggie thinks me a murderer. I see it in her eyes every time. What I mean to say, Paul, is, What are you going to do about Maggie?"

Grace's voice changed at that question. It was as though that other trouble of the scandal were nothing to her compared with this matter of Maggie's presence. Paul turned and looked at her. She dropped her voice to a whisper and went on:

"I won't stay with Maggie any more. No, no, no! You must choose, Paul, between Maggie and me. What I mean is that it simply isn't safe in the same house with her. You may not have noticed it yourself, but I've seen it coming on a long time. I have indeed. She isn't right in her head, and she hates me. She's always hated me. She'd like to do me an injury. She follows me round the house. She's always watching me, and now that she thinks that I killed her uncle it's worse. I'm not safe, Paul, and that's the truth. She hides in my room behind the curtains waiting for me. It's my safety you've got to consider. It's me or her. I know she's your wife, but what I mean is that there'll be something awful happening if you aren't careful."

Grace, as she spoke, was a woman in the very heart of a desperate panic. Her whole body trembled; her face was transfixed as though she saw Maggie standing in front of her there with a knife. No one looking at her could deny that she was in mortal terror—no affectation here. And Paul loved her. He came over to her and put his arm round her; she caught hold of his hand, clutched it desperately. When he felt the trembling of her body beneath his hand his love for her and protective care of her overwhelmed him.

"Grace, dear, it's all right," he said. "You're exaggerating all this. Maggie wouldn't hurt a fly—indeed, she wouldn't. She has her faults, perhaps, but cruelty isn't one of them. You must remember that she's had a bad time lately losing her aunt and then finding her uncle in that horrible way. After all, she's only a child. I know that you two haven't got on well together, and I daresay that it has been very largely my fault; but you mustn't be frightened like that. No harm shall come to you so long as I am alive—no harm whatever."

But she stared in front of her, like a woman in a dream, repeating—

"No, no, Paul. Either she goes or I go. She's your wife. She must stay. Then I must go. I can't stand it; I can't indeed. I'm not sleeping; I'm not indeed. It isn't fair to ask it. What I mean is that it isn't fair to me."

Although he had known Grace for years he still believed her threats and promises. "My sister's an obstinate woman," he would say, although had he looked truly into his experience he must have seen that she changed her mind more frequently by far than she changed her clothes. He thought that now she meant what she said; indeed, on his own side he really did not see how in the future Maggie and Grace could continue to live in the same house. But, as Grace had said, he was married to Maggie and therefore it was Grace that must go. Then when he confronted the fact of Grace's departure he could not endure it. No, he could not. Had Maggie been everything to him that she might have been, bad she been his true wife, had she loved him, had she—oh! a thousand things she might have been!—then perhaps life would be possible without Grace. But now! ... at the thought of being alone for ever with Maggie a strange passion, mingled of fascination and fear, affection and sensuality, cowardice and excitement, pervaded him. What would their life together be? Then he turned to Grace as the very rock of his safety.

"Oh, Grace, you mustn't go—you mustn't think of going. Whatever should I do without you?"

A dull flush of gratification coloured her cheeks.

"Either she goes or I," she repeated. "It can't go on. You must see that it can't. Fancy what people must be thinking!"

As always, he postponed the issue. "We'll settle something. Don't you worry, dear. You go and lie down. That's what you want—a thorough good rest."

She plodded off. For himself he decided that fresh air was what he needed. He went for a stroll. As soon as he was in the Charleston Road that led to the High Street he was pleased with the day. Early spring; mild, faint haze, trees dimly purple, a bird clucking, the whisper of the sea stirring the warm puddles and rivulets across the damp dim road. Warm, yes, warm and promising. Lent ... tiresome. Long services, gloomy sermons. Rebuking people, scolding them—made them angry, did them no good. Then Easter. That was better. Jolly hymns. "Christ is risen! Christ is risen!" Jolly flowers—primroses, crocuses—(no, they were earlier). They'll have forgotten about Maggie's uncle by then. Live it down—that's the thing. Give them a good genial sermon this Sunday. Show them he wasn't caring ... If only the women would get on together. Women—women. How difficult they were! Yes, Sunday would be difficult—facing them all. He knew what they'd be thinking. He wanted to be jolly again. Jolly. That was the thing. Joking with Grace, jolly even with Maggie. Jolly with his congregation. Jolly with God. Why wasn't he left alone? Had been until Maggie came. Maggie like a stone flung into a frosty pool! Broke everything up, simply because she was unlike other people. He'd married her because he thought he could make her into what he pleased. Well, it had been the other way. Oh, she was queer, queer, queer.

He stopped, his large boots in a warm puddle. He felt the warm sun hot through the damp mist. He wanted to take her into his arms, to hug her, above all to feel her response. To feel her response, that was what, for years now, he had been wanting, and never once had she responded. Never once. She let him do as he pleased, but she was passive. She didn't love him. Grace loved him, but how dull Grace was! Dull—it was all dull! Grace was dull, Skeaton was dull, the church was dull—God was dull! God? Where was God? He looked around. There was no God. To what had he been praying all these years? He had not been praying. His congregation had not been praying. They were all dead and God was dead too.

He looked up and saw that his boots were in a puddle. He walked on. For a moment, the mists of sloth and self-indulgence that had for years obscured his vision had shifted and cleared, but even as he moved they settled down and resolved themselves once more. The muscles of Paul's soul were stiff with disuse. Training is a lengthy affair and a tiresome business to the stout and middle-aged.

The hedges gave way to houses; he was in the High Street. He saw then, plastered at intervals on the hoardings, strange phenomena. It was the colour that first attracted him—a bright indecent pink with huge black lettering. Because it was the offseason in Skeaton other announcements were few. All the more prominent then the following:

THE KINGSCOTE BEETHEEN WILL HOLD A RELIGIOUS FESTIVAL IN THE TOWN OF SKEATON-ON-SEA FROM APRIL 10 TO 16.—SERVICES 10 A.M., 3 P.M. SPECIAL SONG SERVICE, 7.30 P.M. DAILY All are Cordially Invited. ADDRESSES BY REV. JOHN THURSTON. REV. WILLIAM CRASHAW. SISTER AVIES.

Paul stared at this placard with horror and disgust in his soul. For the moment Maggie and Grace and all the scandal connected with them was forgotten. This was terrible. By temperament, tradition, training, he loathed and feared every phase of religion known to him as "Methodistic." Under this term he included everything that was noisy, demonstrative, ill-bred and melodramatic. Once when an undergraduate at Cambridge he had gone to some meeting of the kind. There had been impromptu prayers, ghastly pictures of hell-fire, appeals to the undergraduates to save themselves at once lest it be too late, confessions and appeals for mercy. The memory of that evening still filled him with physical nausea. It was to him as though he had seen some gross indecent act in public or witnessed some horrible cruelty.

Maggie had told him very little about the Chapel and its doings, and he had shrunk from asking her any questions, but everything that was odd and unusual in her behaviour he attributed to her months under that influence. As he stared at the flaunting pink sheet he felt as though it were a direct personal assault on himself and his church.

And yet he knew that he could do nothing. Once before there had been something of the kind in Skeaton and he had tried with others to stop it. He had failed utterly; the civic authorities in Skeaton seemed almost to approve of these horrors. He looked at the thing once more and then turned back towards home. Something must be done... Something must be done ... but, as on so many earlier occasions in his life, he could face no clear course of action.

That Saturday evening he tried to change his sermon. He had determined to deliver a very fine address on "Brotherly Love" and then, most fortunately, he had discovered a five-years' old sermon that would, with a little adaptation, exactly fit the situation.

To-night he was sick of his adaptation. The sermon had not been a good one at the first, and now it was a tattered thing of shreds and patches. He tried to add to it some sentences about the approaching "Revival." No sentences would come. What a horrible fortnight it had been! He looked back upon his district visiting, his meetings, his choir-practices with disgust. Something had come in between himself and his people. Perhaps the relationship had never been very real? Founded on jollity. An eagerness to accept anybody's mood for one's own if only that meant jollity. What had he thought, standing in the puddle that afternoon? That they were all dead, he and his congregation and God, all dead together? He sank into his chair, picked up the Church Times, and fell asleep.

Next morning as he walked into the choir this extraordinary impression that his congregation was dead persisted. As he recited the "Confession" he looked about him. There was Mr. Maxse, and there Miss Purves. Every one was in his and her appointed place; old Colonel Rideout with the purple gills not kneeling because of his gout; young Edward Walter, heir to the sugar factory, not kneeling because he was lazy; sporting Mr. Harper, whose golf handicap was +3, not kneeling because to do so would spoil the crease of his trousers; old Mrs. Dean with her bonnet and bugles, the worst gossip in Skeaton, her eyes raised to heaven; the Quiller girls with their hard red colour and their hard bright eyes; Mr. Fortinum, senior, with his County Council stomach and his J.P. neck; the dear old Miss Fursleis who believed in God and lived accordingly; young Captain Trent, who believed in his moustache and lived accordingly ... Oh yes, there they all were—and there, too, were Grace and Maggie kneeling side by side.

Maggie! His eyes rested upon her. Her face suddenly struck him as being of extraordinary beauty. He had never thought her beautiful before; very plain, of course. Every one knew that she was plain. But to-day her face and profile had the simplicity, the purity, the courage of a Madonna in one of the old pictures—or, rather, of one of those St. John the Baptist boys gazing up into the face of the Christ—child as it lay in its mother's arms. He finished the "Confession" hurriedly—Maggie's face faded from his view; he saw now only a garden of hats and heads, the bright varnished colour of the church around and about them all.

He gave out the psalms; there was a rustle of leaves, and soon shrill, untrained voices of the choir-boys were screaming the chant like a number of baby steam-whistles in competition.

When he climbed into the pulpit he tried again to discover Maggie's face as he had already seen it. He could not; it had been, perhaps, a trick of light and, in any case, she was hidden now behind the stout stolidity of Grace. He looked around at the other faces beneath him and saw them settle themselves into their customary expressions of torpor, vacuity and expectation. Very little expectation! They knew well enough, by this time, the kind of thing to expect from him, the turn of phrase, the rise and fall of the voice, the pause dramatic, the whisper expostulatory, the thrust imperative, the smile seductive.

He had often been told, as a curate, that he was a wonderful preacher. His round jolly face, his beaming smile, a certain dramatic gift, had helped him. "He is so human," he had heard people say. For many years he had lived on that phrase. For the first time in his life, this morning he distrusted his gift. He was out of touch with them all—because they were dead, killed by forms and repetitions and monotony. "We're all dead, you know, and I'm dead too. Let's close the doors and seal this church up. Our day is over." He said of course nothing of the kind. His sermon was stupid, halting and ineffective.

"Naturally," as Colonel Rideout said over his port at lunch, "when a feller's wife's uncle has just hung himself in public, so to speak, it does take the wind out of you. He usen't to preach badly once. Got stale. They all do."

As Paul dismissed the congregation with the Blessing he felt that everything was over. He was more completely miserable than he had ever been. He had in fact never before been really miserable except when he had the toothache. And now, also, the custom of years made it impossible for him to be miserable for long. He had had no real talk with Maggie since the inquest. Maggie came into his study that afternoon. Their conversation was very quiet and undemonstrative; it happened to be one of the most important conversations in both their lives, and, often afterwards, Paul looked back to it, trying to retrace in it the sentences and movements with which it had been built up. He could never recover anything very much. He could see Maggie sitting in a way that she had on the edge of her chair, looking at him and looking also far beyond him. He knew afterwards that this was the last moment in his life that he had any contact with her. Like a witch, like a ghost, she had come into his life; like a witch, like a ghost, she went out of it, leaving him, for the remainder of his days, a haunted man.

As he looked at her he realised that she had aged in this last fortnight. Yes, that horrible affair had taken it out of her. She seemed to have recovered self-control at some strange and unnatural cost—as though she had taken some potion or drug.

She began by asking Grace's question:

"Paul, what are we going to do?"

But she did not irritate him as Grace had done. His one idea was to help her; unfortunately he had himself thought out nothing clearly.

"Well, Maggie," he answered, smiling, "I thought you might help me about that. I want your advice. I thought—well, as a matter of fact I hadn't settled anything—but I thought that I might get a locum for a month or two and we might go abroad for a trip perhaps. To Paris, or Venice, or somewhere."

"And then come back?" she asked.

"For a time—yes—certainly," he answered.

"I don't think I can ever come back to Skeaton," she said in a whisper, as though speaking to herself. He could see that she was controlling herself and steadying her voice with the greatest difficulty. "Of course I must come, Paul, if you want me to. It's been all my fault from the very beginning—"

"Oh no," he broke in, "it hasn't."

"Yes, it has. I've just spoilt your life and Grace's. You were both very happy until I came. I had no right to marry you when I didn't love you. I didn't know then all I know now. But that's no excuse. I should have known. I was younger than most girls are, though."

Paul said:

"But Maggie, you're not to blame yourself at all. I think if we were somewhere else than Skeaton it would be easier. And now after what has happened—"

Maggie broke in: "You couldn't leave Skeaton, Paul. You know you couldn't. It would just break your heart. All the work of your life has been here—everything you've ever done. And Grace too."

"No, no, you're wrong," said Paul vigorously. "A change is probably what I need. I've been too long in the same place. Time goes so fast that one doesn't realise. And for Grace, too, I expect a change will be better."

"And do you think," said Maggie, "that Grace will ever live with me now in the same house when she knows that I've driven you from Skeaton? Grace is quite right. She's just to feel as she does about me."

"Then Grace must go," said Paul firmly, looking at Maggie and feeling that the one thing that he needed was that she should be in his arms and he kissing her. "Maggie, if we go away, you and I, right away from all of this, perhaps then you can—you will—" he stopped.

She shook her head. "Never, Paul. Never. Do you know what I've seen this last week? That I've left all those who really wanted me. My aunts, very much they needed me, and I was selfish and wouldn't give them what they wanted, and tried to escape from them. You and Grace don't need me. Nobody wants anything here in Skeaton. You're all full. It isn't my fault, Paul, but everything seems to me dead here. They don't mean anything they say in Church, and the Church doesn't mean anything either. The Chapel was wrong in London too, but it was more right than the Church here is. I don't know what religion is or where it is: I don't know anything now except that one ought to be with the people who want one and not with the people who don't. Aunt wanted me and I failed her. Uncle wanted me and I—I—I—"

She broke down, crying, her head in her arms. He went over to her and put his arms around her. At his touch she shrank a little, and when he felt that he went away from her and stood, silently, not knowing what to do.

"Maggie, don't—don't, Maggie. I can't bear to hear you cry."

"I've done all wrong—I've done all wrong," she answered him. "I've been wrong always."

His helplessness was intolerable. He knew that she would not allow him to touch her. He went out closing the door softly behind him.

CHAPTER X

THE REVIVAL

Maggie cried for a little while, then, slowly recovering, realised that she was alone in the room. She raised her head and listened; then she dried her eyes and stood up, wondering what she should do next.

During the last week she had spent all her energy on one thing alone—to keep back from her the picture of Uncle Mathew's death. That at all costs she must not see. There it was, just behind her, hovering with all its detail, at her elbow. All day and most of the night she was conscious of it there, but she would not turn and look. Uncle Mathew was dead—that was all that she must know. Aunt Anne was dead too. Martin had written to her, and then, because she had not answered, had abandoned her. Paul and Grace were to be driven out of Skeaton because of her. Grace hated her; Paul would never love her unless she in return would love him—and that she would never do because she loved Martin. She was alone then.

She had made every one unhappy—Aunt Anne, Uncle Mathew, Paul, Grace; the best thing that she could do now was to go away and hide herself somewhere.

That, at least, she saw very clearly and she clung to it. If she went away Paul and Grace need not leave Skeaton; soon they would forget her and be happy once more as they had been before she came. But where should she go? All her life she had depended upon her own self-reliance, but now that had left her. She felt as though she could not move unless there was some one somewhere who cared for her. But there was no one. Katherine Mark. No, she certainly could never go there again. Behind all this was the constant preoccupation that she must not look, for an instant, at Uncle Mathew's death. If she did everything would break ... She must not. She must not. She must not.

She went up to her bedroom, took from their box Martin's letters and the ring with the three pearls, and the tattered programme. She sat on her bed and turned them over and over. She was bewildered and scarcely knew where she was. She repeated again and again: "I must go away at once ... I must go away at once."

Then as though moved by some compelling force that she did not recognise she fell on her knees beside the bed, crying: "Martin, Martin, I want you. I don't know where you are but I must find you. Martin, tell me where you are. I'll go to you anywhere. Martin, where are you? Where are you?"

It may not have been a vocal cry; perhaps she made no sound, but she waited, there on her knees, hearing very clearly the bells ringing for evening service and seeing the evening sun steal across her carpet and touch gently, the pictures on the wall. Gradually as she knelt there, calm and reassurance came back to her. She felt as though he, somewhere lost in the world, had heard her. She laid her cheek upon the quilt of the bed and, for the first time since Uncle Mathew's death, her thoughts worked in connected order, her courage returned to her, and she saw the room and the sun and the trees beyond the window as real objects, without the mist of terror and despair that had hitherto surrounded her.

She rose from her knees as though she were withdrawing from a horrible nightmare. She could remember nothing of the events of the last week save her talk with Paul that afternoon. She could recall nothing of the inquest, nor whether she had been to Church, nor any scene with Grace.

"So long as I'm alive and Martin's alive it's all right," she thought. She knew that he was alive. She would find him. She put away the things into the box again; she had not yet thought what she would do, but, in some way, she had received during those few minutes in her room a reassurance that she was not alone.

She went out into the spring dusk. She chose the road towards Barnham Wood because it was lonely there and the hedges were thin; you could feel the breath of the sea as it blew across the sparse fields. The hush of an English Sunday evening enfolded the road, the wood, the fields. The sun was very low and the saffron light penetrated the dark lines of the hedges and hung like a curtain of misty gold before the approaches to the wood. The red-brown fields rolled to the horizon and lay, like a carpet, at the foot of the town huddled against the pale sky.

She was near the wood, and could see the little dark twisted cone-strewn paths that led into the purple depths, when a woman came out of it towards her. She saw that it was Miss Toms. It seemed quite natural to see her there because it was on this same road that she had first met the lady and her brother. Miss Toms also did not seem at all surprised. She shook Maggie warmly by the hand.

"You said that I wouldn't come often to see you," said Maggie.

"And it's been true. Things have been more difficult for me than I knew at the time."

"That's all right," said Miss Toms.

"But I ought to tell you," said Maggie, "that although I haven't been to see you, I've felt as though you and your brother were my friends, more than any one in this place. And that's been a great help to me."

They started to walk down the road together.

"You've been in trouble," said Miss Toms. "Of course I've heard about it. I would have liked to come and see you but I didn't know how your sister-in-law would like it."

She put her arm through Maggie's.

"My dear," she said, "don't be discouraged. Because Skeaton is dead it doesn't mean that all the world is. And remember this. The world's view of any one is never the right one. I know that the world thinks my brother's mad, but I know that he's a lot saner than most people. The world thinks your uncle was a rascal, but if you can remember one good thing he did you know he wasn't, and I'm sure you can remember many good things."

"It isn't that," said Maggie. "It is that I seem to have done everything wrong and made every one I had to do with unhappy."

"Nonsense," said Miss Toms. "I'm sure if they've been unhappy it's their own fault. Isn't the evening air lovely? At times like these I wonder that Skeaton can dare to exist. You'll come and see us one day, won't you?"

"I think—I don't know," said Maggie; "I may be going away."

Miss Toms gave her a penetrating look.

"I daresay you're right. Skeaton's not the place for you. I saw that the first time we met. Well, whatever you do, don't lose your pluck. You're yourself, you know, and you're as good as anybody else. Don't you forget that. Because a lot of people say a thing it doesn't mean it's true, and because a set of idiots think a thing shocking it doesn't mean that it's shocking. Think how wrong people have always been about everything!"

They turned down a side lane and arrived in the High Street. The street was very empty. In the fading light a large pink poster attracted Maggie's attention. She went close to it and read the announcement of the Revival services.

When she read the names of Thurston and Mr. Crashaw and Miss Avies it seemed to her incredible, and then at the same time as something that she had always expected.

"Oh," she cried, "it's coming here!" She was strangely startled as though the sign of Thurston's name was strange forewarning.

"What's coming?" asked Miss Toms.

She read the notice.

"I don't know what you think," said Miss Toms, "but that kind of thing's humbug if you ask me."

"Oh!" Maggie cried. "It's so strange. I knew those people in London. I used to go to their services. And now they're coming here!"

She could not explain to Miss Toms the mysterious assurance that she had of the way that her former world was drawing near to her again. She could see now that never for a moment since her arrival in Skeaton had it let her alone, slowly invading her, bit by bit driving in upon her, forcing her to retire ...

It was quite dark now. Because it was Sunday evening the shops were closed. Only behind some of the curtained windows dim lights burned. Very clearly the sea could be heard breaking upon the shore. The last note of the bell from the Methodist Chapel echoed across the roofs and stones.

"Good-night," said Miss Toms.

"Good-night," said Maggie.

She turned back towards home hearing, as she went, Thurston's voice, seeing beyond all the thick shadow of Martin's body, keeping pace with her, as it seemed, step by step with her as she went.

She turned into the Rectory drive. She heard with a startled shiver the long gate swing screaming behind her, she could smell very faintly the leaves of the damp cold laurel bushes that pressed close in upon her. It was as though some one were walking with her and whispering in her ear: "They're coming! They're coming! They've got you! They've got you!"

She opened the hall door; the hall was all dark; some one was there. Maggie gave a little cry. A match was struck and revealed the white face of Grace. The two women stared at one another.

Grace had returned from Church; she was wearing her ugly black hat with the red velvet.

"It's all right," said Maggie, "I've been for a walk."

"Oh—I didn't know," gasped Grace, still staring. "I thought—yes, of course. Fancy, you've been for a walk!"

Still staring as though she could keep Maggie at bay only by the power of her vision she backed on to Paul's study door, turned the handle, and disappeared. The hall was in darkness again. Maggie stumbled her way towards the staircase, then, seeing Grace's terrified eyes, filled with a horror that she, Maggie Cardinal, should cause any one to look at her like that, she ran clumsily upstairs, shutting herself into her bedroom.

During the next fortnight the dominant element in the situation was Grace's terror. Skeaton was already beginning to forget the story of the suicide. Maggie was marked for ever now as "queer and strange," but Paul was not blamed; he was rather, pitied and even liked the more. But Grace could not forget. Maggie intended perhaps to murder her in revenge for her uncle's death; well, then, she must be murdered ... She would not leave her brother. She could not consider the future. She knew that she could not live in the same house with Maggie for long, but she would not go and Maggie would not go ... What was to happen?

Poor Grace, the tortures that she suffered during those weeks will not be understood by persons with self-confidence and a hearty contempt for superstition.

She paid the penalty now for the ghosts of her childhood—and no one could help her.

Maggie saw that Paul was, with every day, increasingly unhappy. He had never been trained to conceal his feelings, and although he tried now he succeeded very badly. He would come into her room in the early morning hours and lie down beside her. He would put his arms around her and kiss her, and, desperately, as though he were doing it for a wager, make love to her. She felt, desperate also on her side, that she could comfort and make him happy, if only he would want something less from her than passion. But always after an hour or a little more, he crept away again to his own room, disappointed, angered, frustrated. These hours were the stranger because, during the day, he showed her nothing of this mood, but was kindly and friendly and distant.

She would have done anything for him; she tried sometimes to be affectionate to him, but always, at once, he turned upon her with a hungry, impassioned look ...

She knew, without any kind of doubt, that the only way that she could make him happy again was to leave him. His was not a nature to brood, for the rest of his days, on something that he had lost.

Only once did he make any allusion to the coming Revival services. He burst out one day, at luncheon: "The most scandalous thing!" he said. "We had them here once, years ago, and the harm they did no one would believe. I've been to Tamar about it; he can do nothing, unless they disturb the public peace, of course. He had the impertinence to tell me that they behaved very well last time they were here!"

"I don't like that man," said Grace. "I don't believe he makes his money properly. Look at the clothes Mrs. Tamar wears! What I mean is, I don't like his wife at all."

"It's very hard," said Paul, his voice trembling with indignation, "that when men and women have been working for years to bring Christ into the hearts of mankind that mountebanks and hypocrites should be allowed to undo the work in the space of a night. I know this man Thurston. They've had letters in the Church Times about him." "Fancy!" said Grace, "and still he dares show his face."

"But do they really do so much harm?" asked Maggie. "I should have thought if they only came once for a week in ten years they couldn't make any real effect on anybody—"

"Maggie, dear," said Paul gently, "you don't understand."

As the day of the Revival approached, Maggie knew that she would go to one of the services. She was now in a strange state of excitement. The shock of her uncle's death had undoubtedly shaken her whole balance, moral, physical, and mental. The fortnight that had followed it, when she had clung like a man falling from a height and held by a rocky ledge to the one determination not to look either behind or in front of her, had been a strain beyond her strength.

She did not know; she did not feel any weakness; she felt rather a curious atmosphere of light and expectation as though that cry to Martin in her bedroom had truly been answered. And she felt more than this. Old Magnus had once said to her: "I don't know what religion is except that it is a fight—and some people join in because they want to, some are forced to join in whether they want to or no, some just leave it alone, and some (most) don't know there's one going on at all. But if you don't join in you seem to me to have wasted your time."

She had not understood in the least what he meant; she did not understand now; but, thinking of his words, it did seem to her that she was sharing in some conflict. The vast armies hidden from her by mist, the contested ground also hidden, but the clash of arms clearly to be heard. Her own part of a struggle seemed to be round her love for Martin; it was as though, if she could get some realisation of that, she would have won her way to a vantage-point whence she could visualise the next place. She did not think this out. She only felt in her heart a little less lonely, a little less wicked and selfish, a little less deserted, as though she were drawing nearer to some hidden fire and could feel the first warm shadow of the flames.

She made one more appeal to Grace on the very morning of the first day of the Revival.

After breakfast Maggie came into the drawing-room and found Grace sitting there sewing.

She stood, timidly, in her old attitude, her hands clasped in front of her, like a child saying her lesson.

"I beg your pardon, Grace."

Grace looked up. She had of course been conscious of Maggie ever since her entrance into the room. Her hands had trembled and her heart leapt furiously.

"Why, Maggie—" she said.

"I'm afraid I'm disturbing you," said Maggie, "but we haven't really said anything to one another for the last fortnight. I don't suppose that you want me to say anything now, but things get worse and worse if no one says anything, don't they?" Now that she had begun she went on quickly: "I wanted to say, Grace, how sorry I am for the trouble and unhappiness that you and Paul have had during the last fortnight through me. I've been nothing but a trouble to you since I first came here, but it wasn't that that I wanted to say. I couldn't bear that you should think that I was just selfishly full of my own affairs and didn't understand how you and Paul must feel about—about my uncle. Not that I mean," she went on rather fiercely, raising her head, "that he was to blame. No one ever understood him. He could have done great things if—if—some one had looked after him a little. But he hadn't any one. That was my fault. I didn't want you and Paul to think I don't blame myself. I do all the time. I can't promise to be better in the future because I've promised so often and I never am. But I am sorry."

Grace said nothing for a moment. Her hands trembled more than ever. Then, without looking up, she murmured as though to her sewing:

"Oh no. Maggie ... no one blames you, I'm sure."

There was another pause, then Grace said:

"I think I'm not well. No, I can't be well because I'm not sleeping, although I've taken aspirin more, I'm sure, than I ought to. What I mean is that they say it's bad for your heart. Of course things have been very unfortunate, from the beginning one might say, but I'm sure it's not been any one's fault exactly. What I mean is that these things never are ... No, they aren't really. I expect we all want a change."

"What are you frightened of me for, Grace," asked Maggie.

Grace started as though Maggie had indeed dropped a bomb at her feet. She looked up at Maggie, wildly, her eyes staring about the room as though she were looking for some exit of escape.

"Frightened?" she repeated.

"Yes, you are," said Maggie. "That's what worries me most. No one's ever been frightened of me before—at least I don't think any one has." Maggie laughed. "Why, Grace, it seems so funny any one being frightened of me. I couldn't hurt any one if I wanted to, and I'm sure I never want to unless it's Mrs. Maxse. Be angry with me as much as you like, Grace, but don't be frightened of me. Why, that's ridiculous!"

It was the worst word to have chosen. Grace flushed a dull unwholesome purple.

"I'm sorry you think me ridiculous, Maggie," she said. "Perhaps I am. I'm sure I don't know. Yes, perhaps I am. What I mean is that what's ridiculous to one is not ridiculous to another. You're a strange girl, Maggie, and you and I will never get on. No, never. But all I ask is that you should make Paul happy. That is enough for me. I care for nothing else. He isn't very happy just now. What I mean is that any one can see he isn't eating his meals properly."

"Oh, Grace," cried Maggie. "I didn't mean that you were ridiculous. I meant that any one being frightened of me was ridiculous. Anyway, I'm very sorry that I've made you and Paul unhappy. That's all."

She turned and went.

It was the most lovely of April days, soft, primrose-coloured, the sea-breeze gently tempered by mist-veiled sun. Maggie sat at her bedroom window overlooking the drive and the blue-grey field that ran to the woods. She knew that there would be no difficulty about her escape to the Revival meeting. Paul had arranged that there should be an evening service at the Church at the same hour, an act of rather Un-Christian defiance. Maggie sat there, looking down in a condition of strange bewildering excitement on to the laurel bushes. It was wonderful to think that in another half-hour she would see Miss Avies once more, hear those wild hymns again, catch the stridency of Thurston's voice; all these things spoke of Martin. She felt as though he were stealing towards her out of the dusk, it was as though, without any reason, she expected to find him at the service ... although she knew that he could not be there.

She heard the Church bell begin to ring, then the hall-door opened and Paul came out. He had on his soft black hat, he was carrying his Bible and prayer-book under his arm. He stood, for a moment, beside the hall-door as though he were listening or expecting something. She had a strange impulse to run down to him; so strong was it that she got up and moved to the door. Then slowly she came back to the window and stood looking down upon him. Suddenly, as though he felt her gaze, he glanced up, saw her, and waved to her. She waved back to him. He turned and walked quickly away, she heard the gate swing, screaming behind him.

She waited for a little, then put on her hat and coat and went out. She knew the Flower Street Hall, a place occasionally used by touring Companies, Wandering Lecturers, Charitable Concerts, and other casual festivals. It was at the far end of the town towards the end of the Promenade.

The town, dim in the first dusk, hummed with loiterers, girls released from the shops walking with their young men, middle-aged couples sauntering out to take a last whiff of the sea before going in to the evening meal, one or two visitors from the Hotel strolling across to the beach to watch the first evening stars and the rising moon. Pianos were playing, children shouting over the last game of the day; all hushed into a coloured mild tranquillity. In the fields beyond the houses the quiet was absolute.

Maggie found the building. The facade was blazing with electric light. A huge poster, of the now familiar pink, declared:

GRAND RELIGIOUS FESTIVAL. All are invited. IS ALL WELL WITH YOU, BROTHER?

There was a crowd about the doors, and continually, with giggles and shamefaced laughter, couples broke away and climbed the steps into the Hall. Maggie, feeling that all eyes were upon her, entered the building. In the vestibule two grave-faced women in black bonnets handed papers with prayers and hymns to every newcomer. Maggie took hers, a door was opened in front of her, and she went in. The auditorium was a large one, semicircular in shape, with tiers of seats rising circus-fashion to a ceiling decorated with silver stars and pink naked cherubs. The stage had upon it a table, some chairs, and a reading-desk draped in crimson cloth. Below the stage was a small orchestra, consisting of two fiddles, a cornet, drum, and a piano. There was also what seemed to Maggie a small choir, some women dressed in white and some men in black coats and white bow ties. Across the stage were suspended broad white bands of cloth with "Come to Jesus!" "Come now!" "He is waiting for you!" in big black letters.

The hall seemed very full, and was violently illuminated with electric light. Maggie took this in as she stood very timidly just inside the door. A steward came forward and showed her a corner-seat. She saw, then, with a dramatic flash of recognition, Thurston and Mr. Crashaw sitting behind the table; then, with a still stranger emotion, Miss Avies as one of the white-robed choir. The sight of those three familiar faces seemed to close, finally and definitely, the impression that she had had during all those last weeks. They had "got" her again, and yet not they, but the power behind them. It seemed only five minutes ago that she had sat in the London Chapel and heard old Crashaw scream "Punishment! Punishment! Punishment!" She turned half in her seat as though she expected to see Aunt Anne and Aunt Elizabeth sitting one on either side of her. She looked at Thurston; he had coarsened very much since she had seen him last. He was fatter, his cheeks stained with an unnaturally high colour, his eyes brighter and sharper and yet sensual too. He was smarter than he had been, his white bow tie stiff and shapely, his cuffs clean and shining, his hair very carefully brushed back from his high and bony forehead. His sharp eyes darted all over the building, and Maggie felt as though at any moment she would be discovered. Crashaw looked more like a decrepit monkey than ever, huddled up in his chair, his back bow-shaped. He breathed into his hands as though he wanted to warm them, and looked at nobody. Miss Avies Maggie could not see clearly.

Her eyes wandered over the audience. She saw many townspeople whom she knew, and she realised, for the first time, that tomorrow everywhere it would be said that the Rector's wife had been at the Revival meeting.

And how different an audience from the old London one. Every one had come on this occasion to see a show, and it was certainly a show that they were going to see. Maggie had entered during a pause, and all the faces that were there wore that look of expectation that demands the rising of the curtain. Soon, Maggie felt, they would stamp and whistle did the play not begin.

Thurston rose and announced:

"My brothers, we will sing hymn No. 14 on the paper."

Maggie looked and discovered that it was the hymn that had once moved her so dramatically in London with the words

By all Thy sores and bloody pain   Come down and heal our sins again.

and with the last refrain:

 By the blood, by the blood, by the blood of the Lamb   We beseech Thee.

Already, in spite of herself, in spite of her consciousness of the melodrama and meretricious glitter of the scene, her heart was beating. She was more deeply moved, even now, than she had ever been by all the services of the Skeaton Church.

And Thurston had learnt his job by this time. Softly one of the violins played the tune. Then Thurston said:

"The first verse of this hymn will be sung by the choir alone. The congregation is asked to stand and then to join in the second verse. The fourth verse will be sung by the soloist."

The audience rose. There was a hush of expectation throughout the building. The choir, to the accompaniment of the fiddlers alone, sang the first verse. They had been well selected and trained. Thurston obviously spared no expense. For the second verse, the whole orchestra combined, the drum booming through the refrain. At first the congregation was timid, but the tune was simple and attractive. The third verse was sung by every one, and Maggie found herself, almost against her will, joining in. At the fourth verse there was again the hush of expectation, then a soprano, thin and clear, accompanied again by one violin, broke the silence.

There was no doubt that this was very moving. Men and women sat down at the hymn's close quite visibly affected.

Thurston got up then and read a lesson from the Bible. He read from the Revelations:

"After this I looked, and, behold, a door was opened in heaven: and the first voice which I heard was as it were of a trumpet talking with me; which said, Come up hither, and I will show thee things which must be hereafter."

"And immediately I was in the Spirit: and, behold, a throne was set in heaven, and one sat on the throne."

"And he that sat was to look upon like a jasper and a sardine stone: and there was a rainbow round about the throne, in sight like unto an emerald. And round about the throne were four and twenty seats: and upon the seats I saw four and twenty elders sitting, clothed in white raiment; and they had on their heads crowns of gold."

Thurston had worked hard during these last years, he had immensely improved his accent, and his h's were all in their right places. He read very dramatically, dropping his voice to a whisper, then pausing and staring in front of him as though he saw God only a few yards away. The people of Skeaton had had few opportunities of any first-class dramatic entertainment. When Thurston finished there passed through the building a wave of excitement, a stir, a faint murmur. An old woman next to Maggie wiped her eyes. "Lovely!" Maggie heard her whisper. "Lovely!"

They sang, then, another hymn, accompanied by the orchestra. This was a dramatic hymn with a fiery martial tune:

The Lord of War He cometh down With Sword and Shield and Armour Bright, His armies all behind him Frown, Who can withstand His Light?

Chorus. Trumpets Blare, The drum-taps Roll, Prepare to meet Thy God, Oh Soul! Prepare! Prepare! Prepare to meet Thy God, oh Soul!

Never before had the men and women of Skeaton heard such hymns. The Revival of ten years ago, lacking the vibrant spirit of Mr. John Thurston, had been a very different affair. This was something quite new in all Skeaton experience. Red-hot expectation flamed now in every eye. Maggie could feel that the old woman next to her was trembling all over.

Thurston announced:

"Brother Crashaw will now deliver an address."

Brother Crashaw, his head still lowered, very slowly got up from his seat. He moved as though it were only with the utmost difficulty and power of self-will that his reluctant body could be compelled into action. He crept rather than walked from his chair to the reading-desk, then very very painfully climbed on to the high platform. Maggie, watching him, remembered that earlier time when he had climbed into just such another desk. She remembered also that day at her aunts' house when he had flirted with Caroline and shown himself quite another Brother Crashaw. He had aged greatly since then. He seemed now to be scarcely a man at all. Then suddenly, with a jerk, as though a string had been pulled from behind, he raised his face and looked at them all. Yes, that was alive. Monkey's mask you might call it, but the eyes behind the yellow lids flamed and blazed. No exaggeration those words. A veritable fire burned there, a fire, it might be, of mere physical irritation and savage exasperation at the too-rapid crumbling of the wilfully disobedient body, a glory, perhaps, of obstinate pride and conceit, a fire of superstition and crass ignorance, but a fire to be doubted of no man who looked upon it.

When he spoke his voice was harsher, angrier, more insulting than it had been before. He spoke, too, in a hurry, tumbling his words one upon another as though he were afraid that he had little mortal time left to him and must make the most of what he had got.

From the first he was angry, rating the men of Skeaton as they had never been rated before. And they liked it. They even revelled in it; it did them no harm and at the same time tickled their skins. Sometimes a preacher at the Methodist Chapel had rated them, but how mild and halting a scolding compared with the fury of this little man. As he continued they settled into their seats with the conviction that this was the best free show that they had ever enjoyed in all their lives. They had been afraid at first that it would not keep up its interest. They had agreed with one another that they would go in "just for a quarter of an hour to see what it was like." Now they were willing that it should continue all night.

"What came ye out for to see?" he screamed at them. "Came out to see? Ye didn't come out at all. None of you. That's what I've come to tell you. For years you've been leading your lazy, idle, self-indulgent lives, eating and drinking, sleeping, fornicating, lying with your neighbours' wives, buying and selling, living like hogs and swine. And is it for want of your being told? Not a bit of it. You are warned again and again and again. Every day gives you signs and wonders had you got eyes to see them and you will not see. Well, be it on your own heads. Why should I care for your miserable, shrivelled-up, parched little souls? Why should I care when I watch you all, with your hanging stomachs and your double chins, marching straight into such a hell as you've never conceived of. I know what's coming to you. I know what's in store for those well-filled stomachs of yours. I can see you writhing and screaming and wailing, 'Why didn't somebody tell us? Why didn't somebody tell us?' Somebody has told you. Somebody's telling you now. And will you listen? Not a bit of it. You'll have heard the music to-night, the drums and the trumpets, you'll have joined in the singing, and to-night you'll go back and tell your friends: 'Yes, we had a fine evening. You ought to go. It's worth while and costs you nothing.' And to-morrow you will have forgotten everything. But I tell you that every man, woman, and child in this building stands in as desperate peril as though his house was on fire over his head and there was no way out."

He stopped for a moment to get breath, leaning forward over the desk and panting. Over the building there was a great silence. Maggie was stirred beyond any earlier experience. She did not know whether he were charlatan or no. She did not care. She had lived for more than two years in Skeaton, where everything and every one was dead. Now here was life. The evidence of it reassured her, whispering to her that Martin still lived, that he could be found, even that he was coming to her. Her nervous excitement increased. The emotion of the people around her, the bands, the singing, all seemed to cry to her, "He is coming! He is coming! He is coming!" ... but it was Martin now and not God.

Old Crashaw, having recovered his breath, went on: he continued for some time to abuse them all, screaming and beating the wooden desk with his fists—then suddenly he changed, his voice softened, his eyes were milder, there was something wistful and pathetic in his old ugly yellow face.

"I know that you came in here to-night, all of you, just as you might into a picture-house or a theatre. Entrance free. Well, then, why not? Had we charged half-a-crown there wouldn't have been one of you. Half-a-crown and the most important thing in life. I say the most important—I say the only important thing in life. A man's soul, its history and growth. What do you know of the soul, you ask me? How do you know there is one? Well, I can only tell you my news. If a man comes into your town and tells you that there is an army marching down upon it to destroy it he may be true or he may not. If he is true then, when you don't listen to him you are doomed. If you do listen the preparation to meet that army will at any rate do you no harm even though the army doesn't exist."

"I tell you that the Soul exists, that God exists, and that one day God and the Soul will meet. You say that hasn't been proved, and until it is proved you will spend your time over other things that you know to be true. Try it at least, give it a chance. Why not? You give other things a chance, marriage, doctors, trades, amusements. Why not the Soul? Don't listen to any one else's definition of religion. Don't believe in it. Make your own. Find out for yourself. My children, I am an old man, I am shortly to die. If I have scolded forgive me. Let me leave with you my blessing, and my earnest prayer that you will not pass by God on the other side. The day will come when you cannot pass Him by. Meet Him first of your own accord and then when that other day comes He will know you as a friend ..."

The old man's voice faltered, failed, stopped. He himself seemed to be deeply affected. Was it acting? Maggie could not tell. At any rate he was old and ill and very shortly to die ...

The woman next her was crying rubbing the knuckles of her shabby old gloves in her eyes, the bugles on her bonnet shaking like live things.

She snuffled through her nose to Maggie "Beautiful—beautiful—I 'aven't 'eard such preaching since I don't know when."

Thurston again rose.

"A solo will now be sung," he said. "After the singing of the solo there will be a prayer offered, then a procession, headed by the choir, will be formed to march, with lanterns, through the town, as a witness to the glory of God. It is hoped that those of the congregation who have received comfort and help during this service will join in the procession. There will be a collection for the expenses of the Mission at the door."

Maggie watching him wondered. Of what was he thinking? Was there any truth in him? Had he, perhaps, behind the sham display and advertisement that he had been building felt something stirring? Was he conscious, against his own will, of his falsehood? Had he, while building only his own success, made a discovery? She looked at him. The dramatic mask hid him from her. She could not, tell what he was.

The soprano, who had sung a verse of the hymn earlier in the evening, now undertook "Hear my Prayer." Very beautifully she sang it.

"Hear my prayer, Oh, God, incline Thine ear, Thyself from my distresses do not hide ..."

The voice rose, soaring through the building to meet the silver stars and the naked cherubs on the ceiling. "The enemy shouteth ... The enemy shouteth ..."

Skeaton sat enraptured. Women let the tears stream down their faces, men blew their noses.

Once again the voice arose.

"Hear my prayer, Oh, God, incline Thine ear ..."

It was Maggie's voice, Maggie's cry. From the very heart of the charlatanism she cried out, appealing to a God who might exist or no, she could not tell, but who seemed now to be leading her by the hand. She saw Aunt Anne at St. Dreot's whispering "The Lord is my Shepherd. He shall lead me ..."

In a dream she shared in the rest of the ceremony. In a dream she passed with the others out of the building. The sea air blew about her; down the promenade she could see the people, she could see the silver stars in the sky, the faint orange light of the lanterns, the dim stretch of the sand, and then the grey sea. She heard the splash and withdrawal of the tide, the murmur of many voices, the singing of the distant hymn, the blare of the trumpet.

Strange and mysterious, the wind blowing through it all like a promise of beauty and splendour to come ...

She turned in the starlit dark, separated herself from the crowd, and hurried home.

In the hall on the table under the lamp she saw a letter. She saw that it was addressed to her and that the writing was Amy Warlock's. Before she picked it up she stood there listening. The house was very still. Grace and Paul had probably begun supper. She picked up the letter and went up to her bedroom.

As though she were scanning something that she had already seen, she read:

I made you a promise and I will now fulfil it.

My brother, Martin, arrived in London three days ago. He is staying at No. 13A Lynton Street, King's Cross.

I have seen him but he has told me that he does not wish to see me again. He is very ill; his heart is bad and his lungs are affected. He has also spent all his money. I mentioned your name but he did not seem to be at all interested. I think it fair to tell you this lest you should have a fruitless journey. I have now kept my promise to you, unwisely perhaps. AMY WARLOCK.

Maggie sat down on the bed and considered. There was a train at 10.30 reaching London about midnight. She could just catch it if she were quick. She found a pencil and a piece of paper and wrote:

DEAR PAUL—I have to go to London suddenly on very urgent business. I will write to you from there. Good-bye. MAGGIE.

She propped this up against the looking-glass. She put a few things, including the box with Martin's letters and the ring into a little bag, put on her hat and coat and went downstairs. She waited for a moment in the hall but there was no sound anywhere. She went out down the dark drive.

As she passed along the lonely road she heard the gate, screaming faintly, behind her.

PART IV

THE JOURNEY HOME AGAIN

CHAPTER I

THE DARK ROOM

It was after midnight when Maggie was turned out on to the long grim platform of the London station. On that other London arrival of hers the terminus had been a boiling cauldron of roar and rattle. Now everything was dead and asleep. No trains moved; they slept, ancient monsters, chained down with dirt and fog. Two or three porters crept slothfully as though hypnotised. The face of the great clock, golden in the dusk, dominated, like a heathen god, the scene. Maggie asked a porter the way to the Station Hotel. He showed her; she climbed stairs, pushed back swing doors, trod oil-clothed passages, and arrived at a tired young woman who told her that she could have a room.

Arrived there, herself somnambulistic, she flung off her clothes, crept into bed, and was instantly asleep.

Next morning she kept to her room; she went down the long dusty stairs before one o'clock because she was hungry, and she discovered the restaurant and had a meal there; but all the time she was expecting Martin to appear. Every step seemed to be his, every voice to have an echo of his tones. Then in the dusky afternoon she decided that she would be cowardly no longer. She started off on her search for No. 13A Lynton Street, King's Cross.

She searched through a strange blue opaque light which always afterwards she recollected as accompanying her with mystery, as though it followed her about deliberately veiling her from the rest of the world. She felt different from them all; she found an omnibus that was going to King's Cross, but when she was inside it and looked at the people around her she felt of them all that they had no reality beside the intensity of her own search. She, hot like a fiery coal, existed in a land of filmy ghosts. She repeated to herself over and over, "No. 13A Lynton Street, King's Cross."

She got out opposite the huge station and looked about her. She saw a policeman and went across to him.

"Can you tell me where Lynton Street is, please?" she asked him.

He smiled. "Yes, miss. Down on your right, then first to your right again."

She thanked him and wanted for a silly moment to remain with him. She wanted to stand there where she was, on the island, she couldn't go back, she was afraid to go forward. Then the moment left her and she moved on. When she saw Lynton Street written up her heart gave a strange little whirr and then tightened within herself, but she marched on and found 13A. A dirty house, pots with ferns in the two grimy windows, and the walls streaky with white stains against the grey. The door was ajar and, pushing it a little, she saw a servant-girl on her knees scrubbing the floor. At the noise of her step the girl looked up.

"Is Mr. Warlock here?" Maggie asked, but the words were choked in her throat.

"Wot d'ye sye?" the girl asked.

Maggie repeated her question.

"Yes—'e's upstairs. Always is. Fust floor, second door on yer left."

Maggie went up. She found the door. She knocked. There was no answer. She pushed the door, peered through and looked in. She saw a room with a dirty grimy window, a broken faded red sofa, a deal table. No one there.

She entered and stood listening. A door beyond her opened and a man came in. She knew at once that it was Martin. Her thoughts followed one another in strange flurried inconsequence. Yes, it was Martin. He was fatter than he had been—fat and ill. Very ill. His face was pale, his hair, thinner than before, unbrushed. He was wearing an old dirty blue suit with a coat that buttoned over the waistcoat like a seaman's jacket. Yes, he was ill and fat and unkempt, but it was Martin. At that reiterated assurance in the depths of her soul she seemed to sink into a marvellous certain tranquillity—so certain that she shed, as it were with a gesture, all the unhappiness and doubt and desolation with which the last years had burdened her.

She had "touched" Martin again, and with that "touch" she was safe. It did not matter how he treated her nor whether he wanted her. She was sane and happy and whole again as she had not been since he left her.

Meanwhile he looked at her across the dark room, frowning.

"Who is it?" he asked. "What do you want?"

The sound of his voice moved her passionately. For how long she had ached and yearned for it! He spoke more huskily, with a thicker tone than he had done, but it was the same voice, rough a little and slow.

"Don't you know me, Martin?" she said, laughing for sheer happiness. She saw before she spoke that he had recognised her. He said nothing, staring at her across the table; and she, held by some safe instinct, did not move from where she was.

At last he said:

"Well ... What do you want?"

"Oh, Martin, don't you recognise me? I'm Maggie."

He nodded. "Yes, I know. You mustn't come here, though. We've nothing to say to one another nowadays—no, nothing." He didn't look at her; his eyes were turned towards the grimy window.

She had an astonishing sense of her possession of him. She laughed and came close to the table.

"I'm not going away, Martin ... not until we've had a talk. Nothing can make me. So there!"

He was looking at her again.

"Why, you've cut your hair!" he said.

"Yes." she said.

Then he turned roughly right round upon her as though he meant to end the matter once and for all.

"Look here! ... I do mean what I say—" He was cut off then by a fit of coughing. He leant back against the wall and fought with it, his hand against his chest. She made no movement and said no word while the attack lasted.

He gasped, recovering his breath, then, speaking in a voice lower than before: "I mean what I say. I don't want you. I don't want any one. There's nothing for us to say to one another. It's only waste of time."

"Yes," she answered. "That's your side of the question. There's also mine. Once before you had your own way and I was very miserable about it. Now it's my turn. I'm going to stay here until we've talked."

He turned, his face working angrily, upon her.

"You can't stay here. It's impossible. What do you do it for when I tell you I don't want you? First my sister ... then you ... come here spying. Well, now you're seen what it's like, haven't you? Very jolly, isn't it? Very handsome? You'd better go away again, then. You've seen all you've wanted to."

"i'm not going away," repeated Maggie, "I didn't come to spy. You know that. Of course you can turn me out, but you'll have to use force."

"Oh, no, I won't," he answered. "There are other ways."

He disappeared into the other room. A moment later he returned; he was wearing a soft black hat and a shabby grey overcoat.

"You'll get tired of waiting, I expect," he said, and, without looking at her but just touching her arm as he brushed past her, he left the room. She heard him descend the stairs. Then the street-door closed.

She sat down upon the shabby red sofa and looked about her. What a horrible room! Its darkness was tainted with a creeping coldness that seemed to steal in wavering gusts from wall to wall. The carpet was faded to a nondescript colour and was gashed into torn strips near the fireplace. No pictures were on the walls from which the wall-paper was peeling. He had done nothing whatever to make it more habitable.

He must have been staying there for several weeks, and yet there were no signs of any personal belongings. Nothing of himself to be seen! Nothing! It was as though in the bitterness of his spirit he had said that he would not touch such a spot save, of necessity, with his body. It should remain, so far as he might go, for ever tenantless.

She felt that. She seemed to be now marvellously perceptive. Until an hour ago she had been lost, ostracised; now she was at home again, clear in purpose, afraid of no one and of nothing. Strangely, although his sickness both of body and soul touched her to the very depths of her being, her predominant sensation was of happiness. She had found him again! Oh, she had found him again! Nothing, in this world or the next, counted in comparison with that. If she were close to him she would make him well, she would make him rich, she would make him happy. Where he had been, what he had done, mattered nothing. Where she had been, what she had done, nothing. Nothing in their two lives counted but their meeting again, and she who had been always so shy and so diffident felt no doubt at all about his returning to her. There would be a fight. As she looked around the gradually darkening room she realised that. It might be a long fight and a difficult one, but that she would win she had no doubt. It had been preordained that she should win. No one on this earth or above it could beat her.

Gradually she became more practical. Slowly she formed her plans. First, what had Martin done? Perhaps he had told the woman of the house that she, Maggie, was to be turned out, did she not, of herself, go away. No, Martin would not do that. Maggie knew quite confidently that he would never allow any one to insult her. Perhaps Martin would not come back at all. Perhaps his hat and his coat were his only possessions. That was a terrible thought! Had he gone, leaving no trace, how would she ever find him again? She remembered then that he had gone straight downstairs and out of the house. He had not spoken to the landlady. That did not look like a permanent departure. But she would make certain.

She pushed open the other door and peeped into the further room. She saw a dirty unmade bed, a tin washhand stand, and an open carpet-bag filled with soiled linen. No, he would come back.

She sat there thinking out her plans. She was suddenly clear, determined, resourceful, all the things that she had never been in her life before. First she must see the landlady; next she must go to the shops— but suppose he should return while she was there, pack his bag and leave for ever? She must risk that. She thought that he would not return at once because he would want, as he said, "to tire her out." "To tire her out!" She laughed at that. She looked about the room and decided how she would improve it. She nodded to herself. Yes, and the bedroom too. All this time she was so happy that she could scarcely prevent herself from singing aloud.

She went out, down the dark stairs, and found the maid, under a swinging candle-flame, still scrubbing. How strange that in that short space of time, when the whole of life had altered for her, that girl had been on her knees scrubbing!

"Could you tell me, please," she asked, "whether I could see somebody who is in charge of this house— the landlady or—"

"Is there anything I can do?" said a voice behind her.

She turned to find a short stout woman in voluminous black—black bonnet, black cape, black gloves— watching her with sharp bright eyes.

"Are you the landlady?" Maggie asked.

"I ham," said the woman. "Mrs. Brandon—ma'am."

The servant-girl had suspended operations, kneeling up and watching with open mouth developments.

"I'm very glad to meet you," said Maggie. "How do you do?"

"How do you do, ma'am?" said Mrs. Brandon.

"The point is just this," said Maggie, speaking rather fast as though she were confused, which she was not. "Mr. Warlock is a very old friend of mine and I'm afraid he's very ill indeed. He's very ill and there's nobody to look after him. What I was wondering was whether there was a bedroom in your house that I could have—so that I could look after him, you see, and get him anything he wants."

Mrs. Brandon overlooked Maggie from head to foot—very slowly she did it, her eyes passing over the rather shabby black hat, the short hair, the plain black dress, the shoes worn and soiled. She also looked at Maggie's wedding-ring.

"Well, Mrs.—" she began.

"Mrs. Trenchard is my name," said Maggie, blushing in spite of herself at the long scrutiny.

"I 'ope you're not reproaching anybody with neglect of the gentleman." She had an action, as she talked, of flinging a very seedy-looking black boa back across her neck vindictively. "Wot I mean to say is that gentleman lodgers must take their chance and e's two weeks overdue with 'is rent as it is ... but of course I'm not saying I couldn't oblige. 'E's a nice gentleman too, although not talkative so to speak, but if it would give 'im 'appiness to 'ave a lady friend close at 'and as you might say, why I wouldn't like to be one to stand in 'is way. 'Live and let live,' 'as always been my motter, and a very good one too."

She said all this very slowly, with a good many significant pauses. Maggie, however, felt nothing but happiness at the prospect of getting her way. She had gone far beyond all personal sensations of shame or fear or hesitation.

"Would you show me the room, please?" she asked.

They pushed past the servant-girl, whose eyes followed them up the stairs with hungry curiosity.

They climbed to the top of the house. Mrs. Brandon displayed a dark sulky little room with damp of the tomb clinging to its wall.

"Ten bob a week," she said. She sunk her voice to a confidential whisper. "The best of this 'ouse is that you can do what you like. No one minds and no one sees. 'Them as lives in glass 'ouses.' That's what I say."

"I'll take it," said Maggie.

"You'll be wanting a key, my dear," said Mrs. Brandon, suddenly very friendly. "To let yerself in an' out at nights. I'll fetch yer one."

She did. Maggie thanked her.

"I wonder," she said, "whether you have such a thing as a small basket you could lend me. I'm going out to buy one or two necessaries."

"Certingly," said Mrs. Brandon, all smiles. "Certingly, and anythink else you'll be needing. All you've got to do is ter ask."

This settled, Maggie departed on her shopping expedition. She was still driven by a curious clarity and decision as to what she wanted to do. She felt as though she could conquer the world to-day and then parcel it out equitably and with success amongst the greedy kings of the earth. What were kings to her now that she had found Martin? Less than the dust ...

Lynton Street offered her nothing but dirty and grime-stained windows, but she found her way into King Edward Street, and here there were many shops. She had not very much money actually upon her, and the remainder of her precious three hundred was locked up in a bank in Skeaton, but it was a bank that had, she knew, branches in London. She looked in her purse and found that she had three pounds, twelve shillings and sixpence. Martin must have his meals upon something other than paper, so the probability was that there was crockery of a kind in his room—or perhaps Mrs. Brandon supplied it. Nevertheless Maggie's first purchases were a blue teapot, two blue plates, and two blue cups and saucers.

As to food she must get something that could be cooked easily on his fire. She bought three of the freshest possible eggs, half a dozen sausages, a loaf of bread, half a pound of butter, two pots of jam, one pot of marmalade, some apples, a pound of tea, a pound of sugar.

"This will do as a start," she said to herself.

She was just about to turn into Lynton Street when she stopped at a flower shop. In the window, smiling at her most fragrantly under the gas-light was a white hyacinth in a blue pot. It seemed to speak to her with, the same significance as once the ring with the three pearls; as though it said: "You've got to use me. I'm a link in the chain."

She went in and asked its price; not very much, considering the splendour of the blue pot. She bought it. She was glad that 13A was not far, because now the basket and the flower weighed heavily upon her.

She climbed the stairs to Martin's room with beating heart. Suppose he had returned and was there and would not let her in? Or suppose, worse than that, that he had returned, packed his bag and gone away again? Her heart was beating so terribly when at last she had arrived outside the door that she had to put down the hyacinth and the basket and stand for a minute there, panting.

She pushed back the door; the room was lit by the reflection from a lamp in a window on the opposite side of the road; this flickered with a pale uncertain glow across the floor. He was not here. She opened the bedroom door. He had not packed his bag. She sighed with relief. She found a bell and pressed it. To her great surprise the scrubbing maid almost instantly presented herself; curiosity had undoubtedly hastened her steps.

"What's your name?" asked Maggie, smiling.

"Emily," said the girl.

"The first thing I want is a box of matches," said Maggie. "You'll light the gas for me, won't you. The truth is, I'm not quite tall enough to reach it."

Emily lit the gas.

"Thank you so much," said Maggie. "I must have a fire. That's the next thing. This cold room must have been a bad thing for Mr. Warlock with his cough."

"Yes, 'e 'as got a corf," said Emily, watching Maggie with all her eyes.

"Well, do you think I could have a fire?" asked Maggie.

Emily considered.

"I'll ask the missus," she said; "I shouldn't wonder."

She returned soon with coal, wood and newspaper. She also informed Maggie that Mrs. Brandon would like to have a "little in advance if convenient, that being the custom."

Maggie delivered up ten and sixpence and was left with exactly two shillings in her pocket. But how beautiful the room appeared! Emily, whose ugly bony countenance now wore a look of excited breathlessness as though she were playing a new kind of game, discovered a piece of dark sad cloth somewhere in the lower region and this was pinned up over the window. The fire was soon blazing away as though the fireplace rejoiced to have a chance of being warm once more. A shabby but clean table-cloth was discovered and placed upon the table, and in the middle of this the hyacinth was triumphantly stationed.

"Now I tell you what would be nice," said Maggie, also by this time breathless, "and that's a lamp. This gas isn't very pleasant, is it, and it DOES make such a noise."

"It DOES make a noise," said Emily, looking at the gas as though she were seeing it for the first time.

"Well, do you think there's a lamp somewhere?"

Emily licked her finger.

"I'll ask the missus," she said and disappeared. Soon she returned with a lamp, its glories hidden beneath a bright pink paper shade.

Maggie removed the paper shade, placed the lamp on the table, then the blue plates, the blue cups and saucers, the blue teapot.

A shrill voice was heard calling for Emily. Maggie had then her kingdom to herself.

She stood there, waiting and listening. The approaching interview must have seemed to her the climax of her whole life. She stood, clasping and unclasping her hands, going to the table, moving the plates, then moving them back again. Perhaps he would not return at all that night, perhaps not until midnight or later. He might be drunk, he might be violent. She did not care. It was enough for her that he should be there.

"Oh I do wish he'd come," she whispered aloud.

She had looked at her watch and seen that it was just eight o'clock when she heard a step on the stair. She had already borrowed from Emily a frying-pan. Quickly she put the sausages into it, placed them on the fire and then stood over them.

The door opened. She knew who it was because she heard him start suddenly with a little exclamation of surprise. She turned and looked at him. Her first thought was that he seemed desperately weary, weary with a fatigue not only physical. His whole bearing was that of a man beaten, defeated, raging, it might be, with the consciousness of his defeat but beyond all hope of avenging it. Her pity for him made her tremble but, with that, she realised that the worst thing that she could do was to show pity. What had he expected? To find her gone? To find her still sitting defiantly where he had left her? To see her crying, perhaps on her knees before him, beseeching him? Anything but not this.

She could see that he was astonished and was resolved not to let her know it.

He moved past her without a word, and went into the other room. She said nothing, but bent over the sausages. They were sizzling and flung out a splendid smell.

He came back without his hat and coat. He stood by the bedroom door and slowly looked round the room, taking everything in.

"I thought you'd have gone," he said; "I warned you."

She looked up at him, laughing:

"I haven't," she said. "Whatever happens afterwards, Martin, we may as well have one meal together. I'm very hungry. I know you'll forgive my using your room like this, but I didn't want to go to a shop. So I just brought the things in here."

His eyes lighted on the hyacinth.

"I know what your game is," he said huskily. "But it isn't any good. You may as well chuck it."

"All right," she said. "After we've had a meal."

Straightening herself up from the heat of the fire she had a terrible temptation then to go to him. It overwhelmed her in a flood; her knees and hands trembled. She wanted just to touch his arm, to put her hand on his shoulder. But she knew that she must not.

"Sit down for a bit," she said very quietly, "and let's have our meal. There's nothing terrible in that, Martin. I've not put poison in your food or anything and the sausages do smell nice."

To her surprise he sat down, suddenly collapsing as though he were too tired to stand any longer. He said nothing more. She finished the sausages, put them on the table, then took a saucepan (also Emily's gift), filled it with water and put in the eggs.

"Come on," she said gently, "or the sausages will get cold."

He went then to the table, cut off some bread and began to eat ravenously. Her heart felt a dim distant triumph when she saw that he was so hungry, but it was too early to feel triumph yet.

She came to the table and began to eat, although she felt no hunger.

"You're married, aren't you?" he asked suddenly.

"Yes," she answered.

"Where's your husband?"

"A place called Skeaton."

"Well, you'd better get back there to-night—"

"I'm staying in London for a day or two."

"Where?"

"Here. I've got a bedroom upstairs."

"You can do what you damn well please," he said. "It doesn't matter to me. I'm going away from here to-morrow morning." Then, after another pause, he said:

"What sort of a man's your husband?"

"A clergyman," she answered.

"A clergyman ... good Lord!" He laughed grimly. "Still religious, I see."

All this time she was thinking how ill he was. Every breath that he drew seemed to hurt him. His eyes were dull and expressionless. He moved his hands, sometimes, with a groping movement as though he could not see. He drank his tea thirstily, eagerly.

At last he had finished. He bent forward, leaning on his hands, looking her steadily in the face for the first time.

"It was clever of you to do this," he said; "damn clever. I was hungry, I don't mind confessing ... but that's the last of it. Do you hear? I can look after myself. I know. You're feeling sorry for me. Think I'm in a dirty room with no one to look after me. Think I'm ill. I bet Amy told you I was ill. 'Oh, poor fellow,' you thought, 'I must go and look after him.' Well, I'm not a poor fellow and I don't want looking after. I can manage for myself very nicely. And I don't want any women hanging round. I'm sick of women, and that's flat."

"I'm not pretending it's not all my own fault. It is. ALL my own fault, but I don't want any one coming round and saying so. AND I don't want any pity. You've had a nice romantic idea in your head, saving the sinner and all the rest of it. Well, you can get back to your parson. He's the sort for that kind of stuff."

"Indeed I haven't," said Maggie. "I don't care whether you're a sinner or not. You're being too serious about it all, Martin. We were old friends. When I heard you were in London I came to see you. That's all. I may as well stay here as anywhere else. Aunt Anne's dead and—and—Uncle Mathew too. There's nowhere else for me to go. I don't pity you. Why should I? You think too much about yourself, Martin. It wasn't to be clever that I got these things. I was hungry, and I didn't want to eat in an A.B.C. shop."

"Oh, I don't know," he said, turning away from the table.

He stood up, fumbling in his pocket. He produced a pipe and some tobacco out of a paper packet. As he filled it she saw that his hand was trembling.

He turned finally upon her.

"Whatever your plan was it's failed," he said. "I'm going to bed straight away now. And to-morrow morning early I'm off. Thank you for the meal and—good-night and good-bye."

He gave her one straight look. She looked up at him, calmly. He dropped his eyes; then, clumsily he walked off, opened his bedroom door, closed it behind him, and was gone.

She sat there, staring in front of her, thinking. What was she to do now? At least she might clear up. She had nowhere to wash the things. She would put them ready for the morning. She tidied the table, put the plates and cups together, then, overcome by a sudden exhaustion, she sat down on the sofa.

She realised then the fight that the day had been. Yes, a fight! ... and she was still only at the beginning of it. If he really went away in the morning what could she do? She could not follow him all round London. But she would not despair yet. No, she was far from despair. But she was tired, tired to death.

She sat on there in a kind of dream. There were no sounds in the house. The fire began to drop very low. There were no more coals. The room began to be very chilly. She laid her head back on the sofa; she was half asleep. She was dreaming—Paul was there and Grace—the Skeaton sands—the Revival procession with the lanterns—the swish of the sea...

Suddenly she was wide awake. The lamp had burnt down to a low rim of light. Martin was coughing in the other room. Coughing! She had never heard such a cough, something inhuman and strange. She stood up, her hands clutched. She waited. Then, as it continued, growing fiercer and fiercer, so that in spite of the closed door it seemed to be in the very room with her, she could bear it no longer.

She opened the door and went in. The room was lit by a candle placed on a chair beside the bed. Martin was sitting up, his hands clenched, his face convulsed. The cough went on—choking, convulsing, as though some terrible enemy had hands at his windpipe. He grasped the bedclothes, his eyes, frightened and dilated, staring in front of him.

She went to him. He did not look at her, but whispered in a voice that seemed to come from miles away:

"Bottle ... over there ... glass."

She saw on the wash-hand stand a bottle with a medicine glass behind it. She read the directions, poured out the drops, took it over and gave it to him. He swallowed it down. She put out her arm to steady him and felt his whole body tremble beneath her hand. Gradually he was quieter. Utterly exhausted he slipped back, his head on the pillow.

She drew her chair close to the bed. He was too exhausted to speak and did not look at her at all. After a while she put her hand on his forehead and stroked it. He did not draw away from her. Slowly his head turned towards her. He lay there in the crook of her arm, she bending forward over him.

Her heart beat. She tried not to be conscious of his closeness to her, but her hand trembled as it touched his cheek.

Still he did not move away. After, as it seemed to her, a long time he was asleep. She listened to his breathing, and only then, when she knew that he could not hear, she whispered:

"Oh, Martin, I love you so! Dear Martin, I love you so much!"

She blew out the candle and, her arm beneath his head, sat there, watching.

CHAPTER II

HOBGOBLINS

The dawn had made the dark room grey when Maggie, stiff and sore from the strained position in which she had been sitting, went up to her room. She had intended not to go to bed, but weariness overcame her; she lay down on her bed, dressed as she was, and fell into a deep, exhausted slumber.

When she woke it was broad daylight. She was panic-stricken. How could she have slept? And now he might have gone. She washed her face and hands in the horrible little tin basin, brushed her hair, and then, with beating heart, went downstairs. His sitting-room was just as she had left it, the unwashed plates piled together, the red cloth over the window, the dead ashes of the fire in the grate. Very gently she opened his bedroom door. He was still in bed. She went over to him. He was asleep, muttering, his hands clenched on the counterpane. His cheeks were flushed. To her inexperienced eyes he looked very ill.

She touched him on the shoulder and with a start he sprang awake, his eyes wide open with terror, and he crying:

"What is it? No ... no ... don't. Don't."

"It's all right, Martin. It's I, Maggie," she said.

He stared at her; then dropping back on to the pillow, he muttered wearily as though he were worn out after a long struggle:

"I'm bad ... It's my chest. There's a doctor. They'll tell you ... He's been here before."

She went into the other room and rang the bell. After a time Mrs. Brandon herself appeared.

"I'm afraid Mr. Warlock is very ill," said Maggie, trying to keep her voice from trembling. "He's asked me to fetch the doctor who's been here to see him before. Can you tell me who he is and where he lives?"

Mrs. Brandon's bright and inquisitive eyes moved round the room, taking in the blue china, the hyacinth and the lamp. "Certingly," she said. "That must be Dr. Abrams. 'E lives in Cowley Street, No. 4—Dr. Emanuel Abrams. A good doctor when 'e's sober, and the morning's the best time to be sure of 'im. Certingly 'e's been in to see your friend several times. They've been merry together more than once."

"Where is Cowley Street?" asked Maggie.

"First to the right when you get out of the 'ouse, and then second to the left again. No. 4's the number. It's most likely 'e'll be asleep. Yes, Dr. Abrams, that's the name. 'E's attended a lot in this 'ouse. Wot a pretty flower! Cheers the room up I must say. Will you be wanting another fire?"

"Yes," said Maggie. "Could Emily see to that while I'm away?"

"Certingly," said Mrs. Brandon, looking at Maggie with a curious confidential smile—a hateful smile, but there was no time to think about it.

Maggie went out. She found Cowley Street without any difficulty. Dr. Abrams was up and having his breakfast. His close, musty room smelt of whisky and kippers. He himself was a little, fat round Jew, very red in the face, very small in the eye, very black in the hair, and very dirty in the hands.

He was startled by Maggie's appearance—very different she was from his usual patients.

"Looked just a baby," he informed Mrs. Brandon afterwards.

"Mrs. Warlock?" he asked.

"No," said Maggie defiantly. "I'm a friend of Mr. Warlock's."

"Ah, yes—quite so." He wiped his mouth, disappeared into another room, returned with a shabby black bag and a still shabbier top hat, and declared himself ready to start.

"It's pneumonia," he told her as they went along. "Had it three weeks ago. Of course if he was out in yesterday's fog that finished him."

"He was out," said Maggie, "for a long time."

"Quite so," said Dr. Abrams. "That's killed him, I shouldn't wonder." He snuffled in his speech and he snuffled in his walk.

Before they had gone very far he put his hand on Maggie's arm; she hated his touch, but his last words had so deeply terrified her that nothing else affected her. If Martin were killed by going out yesterday then she had killed him. He had gone out to escape her. But she drove that thought from her as she had driven so many others.

"The pneumonia's bad enough," said the little man, becoming more confidential as his grip tightened on her arm, "but it's heart's the trouble. Might finish him any day. Tells me his father was the same. What a nice warm arm you've got, my dear—it's a pleasant day, too."

They entered the house and Dr. Abrams stayed chatting with Emily in the passage for a considerable time. Any one of the opposite sex seemed to hare an irresistible attraction for him.

When they went upstairs the doctor was so held by his burning curiosity that it was difficult to lead him into Martin's bedroom. Everything interested him; he bent down and felt the tablecloth with his dirty thumb, then the soil round the hyacinth, then the blue china. Between every investigation he stared at Maggie as though he were now seeing her for the first time. At last, however, he was bending over Martin, and his examination was clever and deft; he had been, like his patient, used to better days. Martin was very ill.

"The boy's bad," he said, turning sharply round upon Maggie.

From the speaking of that word, for six days and six nights he was Maggie's loyal friend and fellow-combatant. They fought, side by side, in the great struggle for Martin's life. They won; but when Maggie tried to look back afterwards on the history of that wrestling, she saw nothing connectedly, only the candle-light springing and falling, the little doctor's sharp eyes, the torn paper of the wall, the ragged carpet, and always that strange mask that was Martin's face and yet the face of a stranger, something tortured and fantastic, passing from Chinese immobility to frenzied pain, from pain to sweating exhaustion, from exhaustion back to immobility.

On the eighth day she rose, as a swimmer rises from green depths, and saw the sunshine and the landscape again.

"He'll do if you're careful," said Dr. Abrams, and suddenly became once more the curious, dirty, sensual little creature that he had been at first. Her only contact with the outer world had been her visits to the neighbouring streets for necessaries and one journey to the bank (the nearest branch was in Oxford Street) to settle about her money. But now, with the doctor's words, the rest of the world came back to her. She remembered Paul. She was horrified to realise that during these days she had entirely forgotten him. He, of course could not write to her because he did not know her address. When she saw that Martin was quietly sleeping she sat down and wrote the following letter:

13A LYNTON STREET, KING'S CROSS, April 28th, 1912.

MY DEAR PAUL,—I have been very wrong indeed not to write to you before this. It's only of a piece with all my other bad behaviour to you, and it's very late now to saw that I am ashamed. I will tell you the truth, which is that on the day I left you I had received a letter telling me that the friend of whom I have often told you was in England, very ill, and with no one to care for him. I had to go. I don't know whether it was right or wrong—wrong I suppose—but I always knew that if he ever wanted me I SHOULD go. I've always been truthful to you about that. When I came here I found that he was in horrible lodgings, very ill indeed, and with no one to look after him. I HAD to stay, and now for a week he has been between life and death. He had pneumonia some weeks ago and went out too soon. His heart also is bad. I believe now he can get well if great care is taken.

Dear Paul, I don't know what to say to you. I have a bedroom in this house and every one is very kind to me, but you will think me very wicked. I can't help it. I can't come back to you and Grace. Perhaps later when he is quite well I shall be able to, but I don't think so. You don't need me; I have never been satisfactory to you, only a worry. Grace will never be able to live with me again, and I can't stay in Skeaton any more after Uncle Mathew's death. It has all been a wretched mistake, Paul, our marriage, hasn't it? It was my fault entirely. I shouldn't have married you when I knew that I would always love Martin. I thought then that I should be able to make you happy. If now I felt that I could I would come back at once, but you know as well as I do that, after this, we shall never be happy together again. I blame myself so much but I can't act differently. Perhaps when Martin is well he will not want me at all, but even then I don't think I could come back. Isn't it better that at least I should stay away for a time? You can say that I am staying with friends in London. You will be happier without me, oh, much happier—and Grace will be happier too. Perhaps you will think it better to forget me altogether and then your life will be as it was before you met me.

I won't ask you to forgive me for all the trouble I have been to you. I don't think you can. But I can't do differently now. Your affectionate MAGGIE.

She felt when she had finished it that it was miserably inadequate, but at least it was truthful. As she wrote it her old feelings of tenderness and affection for Paul came back in a great flood. She saw him during the many, many times when he had been so good to her. She was miserable as she finished it, but she knew that there was nothing else to do. And he would know it too.

A day later a long letter came from Paul. It was very characteristic. It began by saying that of course Maggie must return at once. Throughout, the voice was that of a grieved and angry elder talking to a wicked and disobedient child. She saw that, far beyond everything else, it was his pride that was wounded, wounded as it had never been before. He could see nothing but that. Did she realise, he asked her, what she was doing? Sinning against all the laws of God and man. If she persisted in her wickedness she would be cut off from all decent people. No one could say that he had not shown her every indulgence, every kindness, every affection. Even now he was ready to forgive her, but she must come back at once, at once. Her extreme youth excused much, and both he and Grace realised it.

Through it all the strain—did she not see what she was doing? How could she behave so wickedly when she had been given so many blessings, when she had been shown the happiness of a Christian home? ...

It was not a letter to soften Maggie's resolve. She wrote a short reply saying that she could not come. She thought then that he would run up to London to fetch her. But he did not. He wrote once more, and then, for a time, there was silence.

She had little interval in which to think about Paul; Martin soon compelled her attention. He was well enough now to be up. He would lie all day, without moving except to take his meals, on the old red sofa, stretched out there, his arms behind his head, looking at Maggie with a strange taunting malicious stare as though he were defying her to stand up to him. She did stand up to him, although it needed all her strength, moral and physical. He was attacking her soul and she was saving his ...

He said no more about his going away. He accepted it as a fact that she was there and that she would stay there. He had changed his position and was fighting her on another ground.

Maggie had once, years before, read in a magazine, a story about a traveller and a deserted house. This traveller, lost, as are all travellers in stories, in a forest, benighted and hungry, saw the lights of a house.

He goes forward and finds a magnificent mansion, blazing with light in every window, but apparently deserted. He enters and finds room after room prepared for guests. A fine meal is laid ready and he enjoys it. He discovers the softest of beds and soon is fast asleep; but when he is safely snoring back creep all the guests out of the forest, hideous and evil, warped and deformed, maimed and rotten with disease. They had left the house, that he might be lured in it, knowing that he would never come whilst they were there. And so they creep into all the rooms, flinging their horrible shadows upon the gleaming walls, and gradually they steal about the bed ...

Maggie forgot the end of the story. The traveller escaped, or perhaps he did not. Perhaps he was strangled. But that moment of his awakening, when his startled eyes first stared upon those horrible faces, those deformed bodies, those evil smiles! What could one do, one naked and defenceless against so many?

Maggie thought of this story during Martin's convalescence. She seemed to see the evil guests, crowding back, one after the other into his soul, and as they came back they peeped out at her, smiling from the lighted windows. She saw that his plan was to thrust before her the very worst of himself. He said: "Well, I've tried to get rid of her and she won't go. That's her own affair, but if she stays, at least she shall see me as I am. No false sentimental picture. I'll cure her."

It was the oldest trick in the world, but to Maggie it was new enough. At first she was terrified. In spite of her early experience with her father, when she had learnt what wickedness could be, she was a child in all knowledge of the world. Above all she knew very little about her own sex and its relation with men. But she determined that she must take the whole of Martin; in the very first days of her love she had resolved that, and now that resolution was to be put to the test. Her terrified fear was lest the things that he told her about himself should affect her love for him. She had told him years before: "It isn't the things you've done that I mind or care about: it's you, not actions that matter." But his actions were himself, and what was she to do if all these things that he said were true?

Then she discovered that she had indeed spoken the truth. Her love for him did not change; it rather grew, helped and strengthened by a maternal pity and care that deepened and deepened. He seemed to her a man really possessed, in literal fact, by devils. The story of the lighted house was the symbol, only he, in the bitterness and defiance of his heart, had invited the guests, not been surprised by them.

He pretended to glory in his narration, boasting and swearing what he would do when he would return to the old scenes, how happy and triumphant he had been in the midst of his filth—but young and ignorant though she was she saw beneath this the misery, the shame, the bitterness, the ignominy. He was down in the dust, in a despair furious and more self-accusing than anything of which she had ever conceived.

Again and again, too, although this was never deliberately stated, she saw that he spoke like a man caught in a trap. He did not blame any one but himself for the catastrophe of his life, but he often spoke, in spite of himself, like a man who from the very beginning had been under some occult influence. He never alluded now to his early days but she remembered how he had once told her that that "Religion" had "got" him from the very beginning, and had weighted all the scales against him. It was as though he had said: "I was told from the very beginning that I was to be made a fighting-ground of. I didn't want to be that. I wasn't the man for that. I was chosen wrongly."

He only once made any allusion to his father's death, but Maggie very soon discovered that that was never away from his mind. "I loved my father and I killed him," he said one day, "so I thought it wise not to love any one again."

Gradually a picture was created in Maggie's mind, a picture originating in that dirty, dark room where they were. She saw many foreign countries and many foreign towns, and in all of them men and women were evil. The towns were always in the hour between daylight and dark, the streets twisted and obscure, the inhabitants furtive and sinister.

The things that those inhabitants did were made quite plain to her. She saw the dancing saloons, the women naked and laughing, the men drunken and besotted, the gambling, the quarrelling, drugging, suicide—all under a half-dead sky, stinking and offensive.

One day, at last, she laughed.

"Martin," she cried, "don't let's be so serious about it. You can't want to go back to that life—it's so dull. At first I was frightened, but now!—why it's all the same thing over and over again."

"I'm only telling you," he said; "I don't say that I do want to go back again. I don't want anything except for you to go away. I just want to go to hell my own fashion."

"You talk so much about going to hell," she said. "Why, for ten days now you've spoken of nothing else. There are other places, you know."

"You clear out and get back to your parson," he said. "You must see from what I've told you it isn't any good your staying. I've no money. My health's gone all to billyoh! I don't want to get better. Why should I? Perhaps I did love you a little bit—once—in a queer way, but that's all gone now. I don't love any one on this earth. I just want to get rid of this almighty confusion going on in my head. I can't rest for it. I'd finish myself off if I had pluck enough. I just haven't."

"Martin," she said, "why did you write all those letters to me?"

"What letters?" he asked.

"Those that Amy stopped—the ones from abroad."

"Oh, I don't know," he looked away from her. "I was a bit lonely, I suppose."

"Tell me another thing," she said. "These weeks I've been here have I bored you?"

"I've been too ill to tell ... How do I know? Well, no, you haven't. You're such a queer kid. You're different from any other human—utterly different. No, you haven't bored me—but don't think from that I like having you here. I don't—you remind me of the old life. I don't want to think of it more than I must. You'll admit I've been trying to scare you stiff in all I've told you, and I haven't scared you. It's true, most of it, but it isn't so damned sensational as I've tried to make it ... But, all the same, what's the use of your staying? I don't love you, and I'm never likely to. I've told you long ago you're not the sort of woman to attract me physically. You never did. You're more like a boy. Why should you ruin your own life when there's nothing to gain by it? You will ruin it, you know, staying on here with me. Every one thinks we're living together. Have you heard from your parson?"

"Yes," said Maggie.

"What does he say?"

"He says I've got to go back at once."

"Well, there you are."

"But don't you see, Martin, I shouldn't go back to him even if I left you. I've quite decided that. He'll never be happy with me unless I love him, which I can't do, and there's his sister who hates me. And he's just rooted in Skeaton. I can't live there after Uncle Mathew!"

"Tell me about that."

"No," she said, shrinking back. "I'll never tell any one. Not even you."

"Now, look here," he went on, after a pause. "You must see how hopeless it is, Maggie. You've got nothing to get out of it. As soon as I'm well enough I shall go off and leave you. You can't follow me, hunting me everywhere. You must see that."

"Yes, but what you don't, Martin, see," she answered him, "is that I've got some right to think of my own happiness. It's quite true what you say, that if you get well and decide you don't want to see me I won't follow you. Of course I won't. Perhaps one day you will want me all the same. But I'm happy only with you, and so long as I don't bore you I'm going to stay. I've always been wrong with every one else, stupid and doing everything I shouldn't. But with you it isn't so. I'm not stupid, and however you behave I'm happy. I can't help it. It's just so."

"But how can you be happy?" he said, "I'm not the sort for any one to be happy with. When I've been drinking I'm impossible. I'm sulky and lazy, and I don't want to be any better either. You may think you're happy these first few weeks, but you won't be later on."

"Let's try," said Maggie, laughing. "Here's a bargain, Martin. You say I don't bore you. I'll stay with you until you're quite well. Then if you don't want me I'll go and not bother you until you ask for me. Is that a bargain?"

"You'd much better not," he said.

"Oh, don't think I'm staying," she answered, "because I think you so splendid that I can't leave you. I don't think you splendid at all. And it's not because I think myself splendid either. I'm being quite selfish about it. I'm staying simply because I'm happier so."

"You'd much better not," he repeated.

"Is that a bargain?"

"Yes, if you like," he answered, looking at her with puzzled eyes. It was the first long conversation that they had had. After it, he was no nicer than before. He never kissed her, he never touched her, he seldom talked to her; when she talked, he seemed to be little interested. For hours he lay there, looking in front of him, saying nothing. When the little doctor came they wrangled and fought together but seemed to like one another.

Through it all Maggie could see that he was riddled with deep shame and self-contempt and haunted, always, by the thought of his father. She longed to speak to him about his father's death, but as yet she did not dare. If once she could persuade him that that had not been his fault, she could, she thought, really help him. That was the secret canker at his heart and she could not touch it.

Strangely, as the days passed, the years that had been added to him since their last meeting seemed to fall away. He became to her more and more the boy that he had been when she had known him before. In a thousand ways he showed it, his extraordinary youth and inexperience in spite of all that he had been and done. She felt older now than he and she loved him the more for that. Most of all she longed to get him away from this place where he was. Then one day little Abrams said to her:

"He'll never get well here."

"That's what I think," she said.

"Can't you carry him off somewhere? The country's the place for him—somewhere in the South."

Her heart leapt.

"Oh, Glebeshire!" she cried.

"Well, that's not a bad place," he said. "That would pick him up."

At once she thought, night and day, of St. Dreot's. A very hunger possessed her to get back there. And why not? For one thing, it would be so much cheaper. Her money would not last for ever, and Mrs. Brandon robbed her whenever possible. She determined that she would manage it. At last, greatly fearing it, she mentioned it to him, and to her surprise he did not scorn it.

"I don't care," he said, looking at her with that curious puzzled expression that she often saw now in his eyes, "I'm sick of this room. That's a bargain, Maggie, you can put me where you like until I'm well. Then I'm off."

She had a strange superstition that Borhedden was fated to see her triumph. She had wandered round the world and now was returning again to her own home. She remembered a Mrs. Bolitho who had had the farm in her day. She wrote to her, and two days later received a letter saying that there was room for them at Borhedden if they wished.

She was now all feverish impatience. Dr. Abrams said that Martin could be moved if they were very careful. All plans were made. Mrs. Brandon and the ugly little doctor both seemed quite sorry that they were going, and Emily even sniffed and wiped her eye with the corner of her apron. The world seemed now to be turning a different face to Maggie. Human beings liked her and were no longer suspicious to her as they had been before.

She felt herself how greatly she had changed. It was as though, until she had found Martin again, everything had been tied up in her, constrained. She had been some one lost and desolate. Nevertheless, how difficult these days were! Through all this time she spoke to him no affectionate word nor touched him with an affectionate gesture. She was simply a good-humoured companion, laughing at him, assuming, through it all, an off-hand indifference that meant for her so difficult a pretence that she thought he must discover it. He did not; he was in many ways more simple than she. She laid to sleep his suspicions. She could feel his relief that she was not romantic, that she wanted nothing whatever from him. He was ill—therefore was often churlish. He tried to hurt her again and again with cruel words and then waited to see whether she were hurt. She never showed him. He treated her with contempt, often not answering her questions, laughing at her little stupidities, complaining of her forgetfulness and, sometimes, her untidiness—telling her again and again to "go back to her parson."

She gave no sign. She fought her way. But it hurt; she could not have believed that anything could hurt so much. She was being always drawn to him, longing to put her arm around him, to dare to kiss him, risking any repulse. He seemed so young, so helpless, so unhappy. Every part of him called to her, his hair, his eyes, his voice, his body. But she held herself in, she never gave way, she was resolute in her plan.

On their last evening in Lynton Street, for five minutes, he was suddenly kind to her, almost the old Martin speaking with the old voice. She held her breath, scarcely daring to let herself know how happy she was.

"What do you think about God, Maggie?" he asked, turning on the sofa and looking at her.

"Think about God?" she said, repeating his words.

"Yes ...Is there one?"

"I don't know. I haven't any intelligence about those things."

"Is there immortality?"

"I don't know."

"I hope not. Your parson thinks there is, doesn't he?"

"Of course he does."

"Did he have lots of services and did you hare to go to them?"

"Yes."

"Poor Maggie—always having to go to them. Well, it's queer. Funny if there isn't anything after all when there's been such a fight about it so long. Did they make you very religious at Skeaton or wherever the place was?"

"No," said Maggie. "They thought me a terrible heathen. Grace was terrified of me, I seemed so wicked to her. She thought I was bewitching Paul's soul—"

"Perhaps you were."

"No. So little did I that he hasn't even come up to London to fetch me."

"Which did you like best—Skeaton or the Chapel?"

"I don't know. I was wrong in both of them. They were just opposite." Maggie waited a little. Then she said: "Martin there must be something. I can feel it as though it were behind a wall somewhere—I can hear it and I can't see anything. Aunt Anne and—and—your father, and Paul, and Mr. Magnus were all trying ... It feels like a fight, but I don't know who's fighting who."

Her allusion to his father had been unfortunate.

"It's all damned rot if you ask me," he said, turned his face to the wall and wouldn't say another word.

Next morning they started. Mrs. Brandon's bill was as large as she could make it and still not very large. Dr. Abrams, to Maggie's immense surprise, would not take a penny.

"I'm not wantin' money just now," he said. "I'm robbing a rich old man who lives near here. I'm a sort of highway man, you know, rob the rich and spend it how I like. Now don't you press me to make up a bill or I shall change my mind and give you one and it will be so large that you won't be able to go down to Glebeshire. How would you like that? Oh, don't think I'm doing it from fine motives. You're both a couple of babies, that's what you are, and it would be a shame to rob you. How you're ever going to get through the world don't know. The Babes in the Wood weren't in it. He thinks he's wicked, doesn't he?"

"Yes, he does," said Maggie.

"Wicked! Why, he doesn't know what wickedness is. A couple of children. Look after his heart or he'll be popping off one fine morning."

Maggie turned pale. "Oh no," she said, her voice trembling.

"He's going to get well."

Abrams sniffed. "If he doesn't drink and leads a healthy life he may. But leopards don't change their spots. He's worrying over something. What is it?"

"His father's death," said Maggie. "He loved his father more than any one and he's got it into his head that he gave him a shock and killed him."

"Well, you get it out of his head," said Abrams. "He won't be better until you do."

Next morning they were at Paddington, Martin very feeble but indifferent to everything. They had a third-class compartment to themselves until they got to Exeter, and all that while Martin never spoke a word. During this time Maggie did a lot of quiet thinking. She was worried, of course, about many things but especially finances. She knew very little about money. She gathered from Martin that he had not only spent all that his and had left him, but had gone considerably beyond it, that he was badly in debt and saw no way of paying. This did not seem to worry him but it worried Maggie. Debts seemed to her awful things, and she could not imagine how any one lived under the burden of them. Supposing Martin were ill for a long time, how would they two live? Her little stock of money would not last very long. She must get work, but she knew more about the world after her years at Skeaton. She knew how ignorant she was, how uneducated and how unsophisticated. She did not doubt her ability to fight her way, but there might be weary months first, and meanwhile what of Martin?

She looked at him, asleep now in a corner of the carriage, his soft hat pulled down over his eyes, his head sunk, his hands heavy and idle on his lap. A fear caught at her heart as she watched him; he looked, indeed, terribly ill, exhausted with struggle, and now, with all the bitterness and despair drowned in sleep, very gentle and helpless. She bent over and folded the rug more closely round his knees. Had he woken then and seen her gaze! Her hand" routed for an instant on his, then she withdrew back into her own corner.

That coming back into Glebeshire could not but be wonderful to her. She had been away for so long and it was her home.

The tranquillity and peace of the spring evening clothed her like a garment, the brown valleys, the soft green of the fields, the mild blue of the sky touched her until she could with difficulty keep back her tears.

"Oh, make it right!" she whispered; "make it right! Give him to me again—I do love him so!"

It was dusk when they arrived at Clinton St. Mary's.

The little station stood open to all the winds of heaven blowing in from the wide expanses of St. Mary's Moor. Maggie remembered, as though it were yesterday, her arrival at that station with Aunt Anne. Yes, she had grown since then.

A trap was waiting for them. Martin was still very silent, but he liked the air with the tang of the sea in it, and he asked sometimes about the names of places. As they drew nearer and nearer to all the old—remembered scenes, Maggie's heart beat faster and faster—this lane, that field, that cottage. And then, at last, there was the Vicarage perched on the top of the hill, with its chimneys like cats' ears!

She thought of Uncle Mathew. The sight of the tranquil evening the happiness and comfort of the fields enabled her to think of him, for the first time, quietly. She could face deliberately his death. It was as though he had been waiting for her here and had come forward to reassure her.

They drove through the quiet little village, out on to the high road, then down a side lane, the hedges brushing against the sides of the jingle, then through the gates, into the yard, with Borhedden Farm, bright with its lighted windows, waiting for them.

Mrs. Bolitho was standing in the porch and greeted them warmly.

"You'll be just starved," she said. "It's wisht work driving in an open jingle all the way from Clinton. Supper's just about ready."

They were shown up to the big roomy bedroom, smelling of candles and clover and lavender. Martin stood there looking about, then—

"Oh, Martin, isn't it nice!" Maggie cried. "I do hope you'll be happy here!"

The emotion of returning home, of seeing the old places, sniffing the old scents, reviving the old memories was too much for her. She flung her arms round his neck and kissed him on the lips. For a moment, for a wonderful moment it seemed that he was going to respond. She felt him move towards her. His hands tightened about hers. Then, but very gently, he drew away from her and walked to the window.

CHAPTER III

THE TRIUMPH OF LIFE

Maggie, before she left London, had written both to Paul and Mr. Magnus giving them her new address. She had intended to see Magnus, but Martin's illness had absorbed her so deeply that she could not proceed outside it. She told him quite frankly that she was going down to Glebeshire with Martin and that she would remain with him there until he was well. She did not try to defend herself; she did not argue the case at all; she simply stated the facts.

Mr. Magnus wrote to her at once. He was deeply concerned, he did not chide her for what she had done, but he begged her to realise her position. She felt through every line of his letter that he disapproved of and distrusted Martin. His love for Maggie (and she felt that he had indeed love for her) made him look on Martin as the instigator in this affair. He saw Maggie, ignorant of the world, led away by a seducer from her married life, persuaded to embark upon what his own experience had taught him to be a dangerous, lonely, and often disastrous voyage. He had never heard of any good of Martin; he had been always in his view, idle, dissolute, and selfish. What could he think but that Martin had, most wickedly, persuaded her to abandon her safety?

She answered his letter, telling him in the greatest detail the truth. She told him that Martin had done all he could to refuse, that, had he not been so ill, he would have left her, that he had threatened her, again and again, with what he would do if she did not the him.

She showed him that it had been her own determination and absolute resolve that had created the situation—and she told him that she was happy for the first time in her life.

But his letter did force her to realise the difficulties of her position. In writing to Mrs. Bolitho she had spoken of herself as Martin's wife, and now when she was called "Mrs. Warlock" she tacitly accepted that, hating the deceit, but wishing for anything that might keep the situation tranquil and undisturbed. She asked Mrs. Bolitho to let her have a small room near the big one, telling her that Martin was so ill that he must be undisturbed at night. Then Mr. Magnus's letter arrived addressed to "Miss Cardinal," and she thought that Mrs. Bolitho looked at her oddly when she gave it to her. Martin's illness, too, seemed to disturb the household. He cried out in his dreams, his shouts waking the whole establishment. Bolitho, once, thinking that murder was being committed, went to his room, found him sitting up in bed, sweating with terror. He caught hold of Bolitho, flung his arms around him, would not let him go, urging him "not to help them, to protect him. They would catch him ... they would catch him. They would catch him."

The stout and phlegmatic farmer was himself frightened, sitting there on the bed, in his night-shirt, and "seeing ghosts" in the flickering light of the candle. Martin's conduct during the day was not reassuring. He had lost all his ferocity and bitterness; he was very quiet, speaking to no one, lying on a sofa that over-looked the moor, watching.

Mrs. Bolitho's really soft heart was touched by his pallor and weakness, but she could not deny that there was something queer here. Maggie almost wished that his old mood of truculence would return. She was terrified, too, of these night scenes, because they were so bad for his heart. The local doctor, a clever young fellow called Stephens, told her that he was recovering from the pneumonia, but that his heart was "dickey."

"Mustn't let anything excite him, Mrs. Warlock," he said.

There came then gradually over the old house and the village the belief that Martin was "fey." Mrs. Bolitho was in most ways a sensible, level-headed, practical woman, but like many of the inhabitants of Glebeshire, she was deeply superstitious. It was not so very many years since old Jane Curtis had been ducked in the St. Dreot's pond for a witch, and even now, did a cow fall sick or the lambs die, the involuntary thought in the Glebeshire "pagan mind" was to look for the "evil eye." But Mrs. Bolitho herself had had a very recent example in her own family of "possession." There had been her old grandfather, living in the farm with them, as hale and hearty a human of sixty-five years as you'd be likely to find in a day's march through Glebeshire. "He lost touch with them," as Mrs. Bolitho put it. In a night his colour failed him, his cheerful conversation left him, he could "do nought but sit and stare out o' window." A month later he died.

Martin had not been long at Borhedden before she came to her conclusions about him, told them to her James, and found that his slow but sure brains had come to the same decision. In the sense of the tragedy overhanging the poor young man she forgot to consider the possible impropriety of his relations with Maggie. He was removed at once from human laws and human judgment. He became "a creature of God" and was surrounded with something of the care and reverence with which the principal "softie" in the village was regarded.

It was not that Martin's behaviour was in any way odd. After a few days in the utter peace and quiet of the moor and farm he screamed no more at night. He was gentle and polite to every one, ate his meals, took little walks out on to the moor and into the village, but liked best to sit in front of the parlour window and look out on to the heath and grass, watching the shadows and the sunlight and the driving sheets of rain.

Mrs. Bolitho had a tender heart and Maggie shared in her superstitious pity. Looking back to her youth she had always thought Maggie a "wisht little thing." "Poor worm," what chance had she ever had with that great scandalous chap of a father? She saw her still in her shabby clothes trying to keep that dilapidated house together. No, what chance had she ever had? She was still a "wisht little thing."

Nor did it need very shrewd eyes to see how desperately devoted Maggie was to Martin. The sight of that touched the hearts of every human being in the farm. Not that Maggie was foolish; she did not hang about Martin all the time, she never, so far as Mrs. Bolitho could see, kissed him or fondled him, or was with him when he did not want her. She was not sentimental to him, not sighing nor groaning, nor pestering him to answer romantic questions. On the contrary, she was always cheerful, practical, and full of common sense, although she was sometimes forgetful, and was not so neat and tidy as Mrs. Bolitho would have wished. She always spoke as though Martin's recovery were quite certain, and Dr. Stephens told Mrs. Bolitho that he did not dare to speak the truth to her. "The chances against his recovery," Stephens said, "are about one in a hundred. He's been racketing about too long. Too much drink. But he's got something on his mind. That's really what's the matter with him."

Mrs. Bolitho was as naturally inquisitive as are most of her sex, and this knowledge that Martin was a doomed creature with a guilty conscience vastly excited her curiosity. What had the man done? What had been his relations with Maggie? Above all, did he really care for Maggie, or no? That was finally the question that was most eagerly discussed in the depths of the Bolitho bedchamber. James Bolitho maintained that he didn't care "that" for her; you could see plain enough, he asserted, when a man cared for a maid—there were signs, sure and certain, just as there were with cows and horses.

"You may know about cows and horses," said Mrs. Bolitho; "you're wrong about humans." The way that she put it was that Martin cared for Maggie but "couldn't get it out." "He doesn't want her to know it," she said.

"Why shouldn't he?" asked James.

"Now you're asking," said Mrs. Bolitho.

"Nice kind of courtin' that be," said James; "good thing you was a bit different, missus. Lovin' a lass and not speaking—shouldn't like!"

Mrs. Bolitho's heart grew very tender towards Maggie. Married or not, the child was in a "fiery passion of love." Nor was it a selfish passion, neither—wanted very little for herself, but only for him to get well. There was true romance here. Maggie, however, gave away no secrets. She had many talks with Mr. Bolitho: about the village, about the new parson, about Mrs. Bolitho's son, Jacob, now in London engineering, and the apple of her eye,—about many things but never about herself, the past history nor her feeling for Martin.

The girl never "let on" that she was suffering, and yet "suffering she must be." You could see that she was just holding herself "tight" like a wire. The strange intensity of her determination was beautiful but also dangerous. "If anything was to happen—" said Mrs. Bolitho. She saw Martin, too, many times, looking at Maggie in the strangest way, as though he were travelling towards some decision. He certainly was a good young man in his behaviour, doing now exactly what he was told, never angry, never complaining, and that, Mrs. Bolitho thought, was strange, because you could see in his eye that he had a will and a temper of his own, did he like to exercise them. After all, he himself was the merest boy, scarcely older than Jacob. She could, herself, see that he must have been a fine enough lad when he had his health—the breadth of his shoulders, the thick sturdiness of his shape, the strength of his thighs and arms. Her husband had seen the boy stripped, and had told her that he must have been a "lovely man." Drink and evil women—ay, they'd brought him down as they'd brought many another—and she thought of her Jacob in London with a catch at her heart. She stopped in her cooking and prayed there and then, upon her kitchen floor, that he might be kept safe from all harm.

Nearly every one in the village, of course, remembered Maggie, and they could not see that she was "any changed." "Cut 'er 'air short—London fashion" they supposed. They had liked her as a child and they liked her now. She was more cheerful and friendly, they thought, then she used to be.

Nevertheless all the village awaited, with deep interest, for what they felt would be a very moving climax. The young man was "fey." God had set His mark upon him, and nothing that any human being could do would save him. In old days they would have tried to come near him and touch him to snatch some virtue from the contact. They did not do that, but they felt when they had spoken to him that they had received some merit or advantage. The new parson came to call upon Martin and Maggie, but he got very little from his visit.

"Poor fellow," he said to his wife on his return. "His days are numbered, I fear."

To every one it was as though Martin and Maggie were enclosed in some world of their own. No one could come near them, no one could tell of what they were really thinking, of their hopes or fears, past or future.

"Only," as Mrs. Bolitho said to her husband, "one thing's certain, she do love 'im with all her heart and soul—poor lamb."

When Martin and Maggie had been at the farm about a fort-night, there came to St. Dreot's a travelling circus. This was a very small affair, but it came every year, and provided considerable excitement for the village population. There were also gipsies who came on the moor, and telling the fortunes of any who had a spare sixpence with which to cross their palms. The foreign and exotic colour that the circus and the gipsies brought into the village was exactly suited to the St. Dreot blood. Many centuries ago strange galleys had forced their way into bays and creeks of the southern coast, and soon dark strangers had penetrated across the moors and fields and had mingled with the natives of the plain. Scarcely an inhabitant of St. Dreot but had some dark colour in his blood, a gift from those Phoenician adventurers; scarcely an inhabitant but was conscious from time to time of other strains, more tumultuous passions, than the Saxon race could show.

This coming of the circus had in it, whether they knew it or no, something of the welcoming of their own people back to them again. They liked to see the elephant and the camel tread solemnly the uneven stones of the village street, they liked to hear the roar of the wild beasts at night when they were safe and warm in their own comfortable beds, they liked to have solemn consultations with the gipsy girls as to their mysterious destinies. The animals, indeed, were not many nor, poor things, were they, after many years' chains and discipline, very fierce—nevertheless they roared because they knew it was their duty so to do, and when the lion's turn came a notice was hung up outside his cage saying: "This is the Lion that last year, at Clinton, bit Miss Harper." There were also performing dogs, a bear, and two seals.

The circus was quite close to the farm.

"I do hope," said Mrs. Bolitho to Martin, "that the roaring of the animals won't disturb you."

It did not disturb him. He seemed to like it, and went out and stood there watching all the labours of the gipsies and the tent men, and even went into "The Green Boar" and drank a glass of beer with Mr. Marquis, the proprietor of the circus.

On the third day after their arrival there was a proper Glebeshire mist. It was a day, also, of freezing, biting cold, such a day as sometimes comes in of a Glebeshire May—cold that seems, in its damp penetration, more piercing than any frost.

The mist came rolling up over the moor in wreaths and spirals of shadowy grey, sometimes shot with a queer dull light as though the sun was fighting behind it to beat a way through, sometimes so dense and thick that standing at the door of the farm you could not see your hand in front of your face. It was cold with the chill of the sea foam, mysterious in its ever-changing intricacies of shape and form, lifting for a sudden instant and showing green grass and the pale spring flowers in the border by the windows, then charging down again with fold on fold of vapour thicker and thicker, swaying and throbbing with a purpose and meaning of its own. Early in the afternoon Mrs. Bolitho took a peep at her lodgers. She did not intend to spy—she was an honest woman—but she shared most vividly the curiosity of all the village about "these two queer ignorant children," as she called them. Standing in the bow-window of her own little parlour she could see the bow-window and part of the room on the opposite side of the house-door. Maggie and Martin stood there looking out into the mist. The woman could see Maggie's face, dim though the light was, and a certain haunting desire in it tugged at Mrs. Bolitho's tender heart. "Poor worm," she thought to herself, "she's longing for him to say something to her and he won't." They were talking. Then there was a pause and Martin turned away. Maggie's eyes passionately besought him. What did she want him to do—to say? Mrs. Bolitho could see that the girl's hands were clenched, as though she had reached, at last, the very limits of her endurance. He did not see. His back was half turned to her. He did not speak, but stood there drumming with his hands on the glass.

"Oh, I could shake him," thought Mrs. Bolitho's impatience. For a time Maggie waited, never stirring, her eyes fixed, her body taut.

Then she seemed suddenly to break, as though the moment of endurance was past. She turned sharply round, looking directly out of her window into Mrs. Bolitho's room—but she didn't see Mrs. Bolitho.

That good woman saw her smile, a strange little smile of defiance, pathos, loneliness, cheeriness defeated. She vanished from her window although he stood there. A moment later, in a coat and hat, she came out of the front door, stood for a moment on the outskirts of the mist looking about her, then vanished on to the moor.

"She oughtn't to be out in this," thought the farmer's wife. "It's dangerous."

She waited a little, then came and knocked on the door of the other sitting-room. She met Martin in the doorway.

"Oh, Mrs. Bolitho," he said, "I thought I'd go to the circus for half an hour."

"Very well, sir," she said.

He too disappeared. She sat in her kitchen all the afternoon busily mending the undergarments of her beloved James. But her thought were not with her husband. She could not get the picture of those two young things standing at the window facing the mist-drunk moor out of her head. The sense that had come to the farm with Martin's entry into it of something eerie and foreboding increased now with every tick of the heavy kitchen clock. She seemed to listen now for sounds and portents. The death-tick on the wall—was that foolish? Some men said so, but she knew better. Had she not heard it on the very night of her grandfather's death? She sat there and recounted to herself every ghost-story that, in the course of a long life, had come her way. The headless horseman, the coach with the dead travellers, the three pirates and their swaying gibbets, the ghost of St. Dreot's churchyard, the Wailing Woman of Clinton, and many, many others, all passed before her, making pale her cheek and sending her heart in violent beats up and down the scale.

The kitchen grew darker and darker. She let the underclothes lie upon her lap. Soon she must light the lamp, but meanwhile, before the oven she let her fancies overwhelm her, luxuriating in her terror.

Suddenly the kitchen-door was flung open. She started up with a cry. Martin stood there and in a voice, so new to her that she seemed never to have heard it before, he shouted, "Where's Maggie?"

She stood up in great agitation. He came towards her and she saw that his face was violent with agitation, with a kind of rage.

"Where's Maggie?" he repeated.

She saw that he was shaking all over and it was as though he did not know who she was.

"Maggie?" she repeated.

"My wife! My wife!" he cried, and he shouted it again as though he were proclaiming some fact to the whole world.

"She went out," said Mrs. Bolitho, "about three hours back I should think."

"Went out!" he stormed at her. "And in this?"

Then, before she could say another word, he was gone. It was in very truth like an apparition.

She sat there for some time staring in front of her, still shaken by the violence of his interruption. She went then to the kitchen-door and listened—not a sound in the house. She went farther, out through the passage to the hall-door. She opened it and looked out. A sea of driving mist, billowing and driving as though by some internal breeze, met her.

"Poor things," she said to herself. "They shouldn't be out in this." She shut the door and went back into the house. She called, "Jim! Jim! Where are you?" At last he came, stumping up from some mysterious labour in the lower part of the house.

"What is't?" he said, startled by her white face and troubled eyes.

"The two of them," she said, "have gone out on to the moor in this mist. It isn't safe."

"Whatever for?" he asked.

"How should I know? She went out first and now he's after her. 'Tisn't safe, Jim. You'd best follow them."

He didn't argue with her, being an obedient husband disciplined by many years of matrimony.

"Well, I'll go," he said slowly. "Best take William, though."

He went off in search of his man.

But Bolitho need not trouble. Half an hour later Maggie returned, stood in the sitting-room looking about her, took off her jacket and hat, then, pursuing her own thoughts, slowly put them on. She was then about to leave the room when the door burst open and Martin tumbled in. He stood at the doorway staring at her, his mouth open. "Why!" he stammered. "I thought ... I thought ... you were out—" She looked at him crossly.

"You shouldn't have gone out—an afternoon like this. If I'd been here—"

"Well, you weren't. You shouldn't have gone out either for the matter of that. And I was at the circus—a damned poor one too. Your things are soaking," he added, suddenly looking up at her. "You talk about me. You'd better go and change."

"I'm going out again," she said.

"Out again?"

"Yes ... There's a train at Clinton at seven. I'm catching that."

"A train?" He stared at her, completely bewildered.

"Yes. That's what I went out to get my head clear about. Martin, you've beaten me. After all these years you have. After all my fine speeches, too."

He began to drum on the window. He tried to speak casually.

"I haven't beaten you, Maggie."

"Yes, you have. I said you wouldn't be able to send me away. Well, you've managed to and in the only way you could—by your silence. You haven't opened your mouth for a fortnight. You're better now, too, and Mrs. Bolitho will look after you. I was determined to hang on to you, but I find I can't. I'm going back to London to get some work."

His hand dropped from the window. Then, with his head turned from her and his voice so low that she could scarcely hear the—

"No, Maggie, don't go."

She smiled across at him. "There's no need to be polite, Martin. We're both of us beyond that by this time. I'll come back if you really want me. You know that I always will, but at last, after all these years, I've found a scrap of self-respect. Here am I always bundling about—first the aunts, then you, then Paul, then you again, and nobody wanting me. I don't suppose," she said laughing, "that there can be anybody less wanted in the world. So I'm just going to look after myself now. It's quite time I did."

"But I want you," he said, his voice still very low. She looked up, her eyes lit as though with some sudden recognition.

"If you really mean that," she said, "say it again. If you don't mean it, don't humbug me. I won't be humbugged any more."

"I haven't humbugged you—ever," he answered. "You're the only person I've always been absolutely straight with. I've always, from the very beginning, told you to have nothing to do with me. It's more true than ever now. I've been trying ever since you came back to me in London to get you to leave me. But it's too late. I can't fight it any more ... I loved you all the time I was abroad. I oughtn't to have written to you, but I did. I came back to London with the one hope of seeing you, but determined not to."

"I loved you more than ever when you came into my lodging there, but I was sick and hadn't any money, besides all my other failings ... It's the only decent thing I've ever really tried to do, to keep you away from me, and now I've failed in that. When I came in and found you were gone this afternoon I thought I'd go crazy."

"I'm not going to struggle any more. If you go away I'll follow you wherever you go. I may as well try to give up keeping you out of it. It's like keeping myself out of it."

Slowly she took her hat and coat off again.

"Well, then," she said, "I'd better stay, I suppose."

He suddenly sat down, his face white. She came across to him.

She put her hand on his forehead.

"You'd better go to bed, Martin, dear. I'll bring your tea in."

He caught her hand. She knelt down, put her arms round him, and so they stayed, cheek to cheek, for a long time.

When he had gone to his room she sat in the arm-chair by the fire, her hands idly folded on her lap. She let happiness pour in upon her as water floods in upon a dried and sultry river-bed. She was passive, her tranquillity was rich and full, too full for any outward expression.

She was so happy that her heart was weighted down and seemed scarcely to beat. It was not, perhaps, the exultant happiness that she had expected this moment to bring her.

When, in after days, she looked back to that quiet half-hour by the fire she saw that it was then that she had passed from girlhood into womanhood. The first chapter of her life was, at that moment's laying of her hand on Martin's forehead, closed. The love for him that filled her so utterly was in great part maternal. It was to be her destiny to know the deep tranquil emotions of life rather than the passionate and transient. She was perhaps the more blessed in that.

Even now, at the very instant of her triumph, she deceived herself in nothing. There were many difficulties ahead for her. She had still to deal with Paul: Martin was not a perfect character, nor would he suddenly become one. Above all that strange sense of being a captive in a world that did not understand her, some one curious and odd and alien—that would not desert her. That also was true of Martin. It was true—strangely true—of so many of the people she had known—of the aunts, Uncle Mathew, Mr. Magnus, of Paul and of Grace, of Mr. Toms, and even perhaps of Thurston and Amy Warlock—all captives in a strange country, trying to find the escape, each in his or her own fashion, back to the land of their birth.

But the land was there. Just as the lion, whose roar very faintly she could hear through the thick walls, remembered in his cage the jungles and mountains of his happiness, so was she aware of hers. The land was there, the fight to get hack to it was real.

She smiled to herself, looking back on the years. Many people would have said that she had had no very happy time since that sudden moment of her father's death, but it did not seem to her, in retrospect, unhappy. There had been unhappy times, tragic times, but life was always bringing forward some magnificent moment, some sudden flash of splendour that made up for all the rest. How could you be bitter about people when you were all in the same box, all as ignorant, as blind, as eager to do well, as fallible, as brave, as mistaken?

The thoughts slipped dimly through her mind. She was too happy to trace them truly. She had never been one for conscious philosophy.

Nevertheless she did not doubt but that life was worth while, that there was something immortal in her, and that the battle was good to fight—but what it really came to was that she loved Martin, and that at last some one needed her, that she need never be lonely any more.

Mrs. Bolitho stepped in with the tea.

"I'll take it in to him," Maggie said, standing up and stretching out her arms for the tray.

The woman looked at her and gave a little "Ah!" of satisfaction, as though, at length, she saw in Maggie's eyes that for—which she had been searching.

"Why, I do believe," she said, "that walk's done 'ee good."

"I do believe," Maggie said, laughing, "it has."

Carrying the tray carefully she went through into Martin's room.

Hugh Walpole – A Short Biography

Sir Hugh Seymour Walpole, CBE was born in Auckland, New Zealand, on March 13th, 1884.

His parents had moved to New Zealand in 1877, but his mother, Mildred, unable to settle there, eventually persuaded, in 1889, her husband, Somerset, an Anglican clergyman, to accept another post, this time in New York.

Walpole's early years involved being educated by a Governess until, in 1893, his parents decided he needed an English education and the young Walpole was sent to England.

He first attended a preparatory school in Truro. He naturally missed his family but was reasonably happy. A move to Sir William Borlase's Grammar School in Marlow in 1895, found him bullied, frightened and miserable. He later said, "The food was inadequate, the morality was 'twisted', and Terror—sheer, stark unblinking Terror—stared down every one of its passages ... The excessive desire to be loved that has always played so enormous a part in my life was bred largely, I think, from the neglect I suffered there".

In 1896 Somerset Walpole, hearing of his son's unhappiness, moved him to the King's School, Canterbury. For two years he settled but was undistinguished as a pupil. The following year, 1897, Walpole senior was appointed principal of Bede College, Durham, and his son was moved again; to be a day boy for four years at Durham School. Day boys were regarded as the underclass by boarders, and Bede College was the subject of snobbery within the university. His sense of isolation increased. He continually took refuge in the local library, where he read all the novels of Austen, Fielding, Scott and Dickens and many others. He was voracious in reading.

Walpole wrote in 1924: "I grew up ... discontented, ugly, abnormally sensitive, and excessively conceited. No one liked me—not masters, boys, friends of the family, nor relations who came to stay; and I do not in the least wonder at it. I was untidy, uncleanly, excessively gauche. I believed that I was profoundly misunderstood, that people took my pale and pimpled countenance for the mirror of my soul, that I had marvellous things of interest in me that would one day be discovered".

From 1903 to 1906 Walpole studied history at Emmanuel College, Cambridge and there, in 1905, had his first work published, the critical essay "Two Meredithian Heroes". Here he met and fell under the spell of A C Benson. Walpole's religious beliefs, previously sacrosanct, were fading, and Benson helped him through that personal crisis. Walpole was also attempting to cope with his homosexual feelings, which, for a while, focused on Benson.

Benson gently declined Walpole's advances. They remained friends, but Walpole, feeling rebuffed, gradually downgraded the relationship. Two years later Benson's diary entry on Walpole's subsequent social career reveals his thoughts on his protégé's progress: "He seems to have conquered Gosse completely. He spends his Sundays in long walks with H G Wells. He dines every week with Max Beerbohm and R Ross ... and this has befallen a not very clever young man of 23. Am I a little jealous?—no, I don't think so. But I am a little bewildered ... I do not see any sign of intellectual power or perception or grasp or subtlety in his work or himself. ... I should call him curiously unperceptive. He does not, for instance, see what may vex or hurt or annoy people. I think he is rather tactless—though he is himself very sensitive. The strong points about him are his curiosity, his vitality, his eagerness, and the emotional fervour of his affections. But he seems to me in no way likely to be great as an artist.

Somerset Walpole, himself the son of an Anglican priest, hoped that his eldest son would follow him into the ministry. Walpole was concerned for his father's feelings. So much so that on graduation from Cambridge in 1906 he took a post as a lay missioner at the Mersey Mission to Seamen in Liverpool. He described that as one of the "greatest failures of my life". Walpole resigned after six months.

From April to July 1907 Walpole was in Germany, privately tutoring children before returning, in 1908, to teach French at Epsom College.

Walpole now found the desire to fully immerse himself in the literary world. He moved to London to become a book reviewer for The Standard and to write fiction in his spare time. He had by this time come to terms with his homosexuality. His encounters were discreet, as they were illegal in Britain. He was constantly searching for "the perfect friend".

In 1909, Walpole published his first novel, The Wooden Horse, the story of a staid, snobbish English family shaken by the return of one of their own from a more out-going New Zealand. The book received good reviews but sold little.

Better was to come in 1911 when he published Mr Perrin and Mr Traill. The Guardian observed that "the setting of Mr Perrin and Mr Traill was clearly drawn from life". The boys of Epsom College were delighted with the thinly disguised version of their school, but the authorities were not, and Walpole was persona non grata there for many years. It was an early illustration of his capacity, noted by Benson, for unthinkingly giving offence, though being hypersensitive to criticism himself.

In early 1914 Henry James wrote an article for The Times Literary Supplement surveying the younger generation of British novelists and comparing them with their eminent elders. In the latter category James put Bennett, Conrad, Galsworthy, Hewlett and H G Wells. The four new authors were Walpole, Gilbert Cannan, Compton Mackenzie and D H Lawrence. From Walpole's point of view one of the greatest living authors had publicly ranked him among the finest young British novelists.

As war approached, Walpole realised that his poor eyesight would disqualify him from serving in the armed forces. He volunteered for the police, but was turned down. He then accepted an appointment, based in Moscow, reporting for The Saturday Review and The Daily Mail. Although he was allowed to visit the front in Poland, these dispatches were not enough to stop hostile comments at home that he was not doing his bit for the war effort.

Walpole was ready with a counter; an appointment as a Russian officer, in the Sanitar. He explained they were "part of the Red Cross that does the rough work at the front, carrying men out of the trenches, helping at the base hospitals in every sort of way, doing every kind of rough job. They are an absolutely official body and I shall be one of the few Englishmen in the world wearing Russian uniform".

While training Walpole spent many hours gaining fluency in Russian, and writing a literary biography of Joseph Conrad.

In the summer of 1915 he worked on the Austrian-Russian front, assisting at operations in field hospitals and retrieving the dead and wounded from the battlefield. Writing home to Arnold Bennett he said "A battle is an amazing mixture of hell and a family picnic—not as frightening as the dentist, but absorbing, sometimes thrilling like football, sometimes dull like church, and sometimes simply physically sickening like bad fish. Burying the dead afterwards is worst of all."

During a skirmish in June 1915 Walpole rescued a wounded soldier; his Russian comrades refused to help and this meant Walpole had to carry one end of a stretcher, dragging the man to safety. He was awarded the Cross of Saint George.

In October 1915 he returned to England to visit family and friends and to stay at a cottage he had purchased in Cornwall. In January 1916 he was asked by the Foreign Office to return to Petrograd.

Before going his novel, The Dark Forest, was published. It drew on his experiences in Russia, and was more sombre than much of his earlier fiction. Reviews were highly favourable; The Daily Telegraph commented on "a high level of imaginative vision ... reveals capacity and powers in the author which we had hardly suspected before."

Back in Petrograd his diary entry for March 13th records "Thirty two today! Should have been a happy day but was completely clouded for me by reading in the papers of Henry James' death. This was a terrible shock to me."

By late 1917 it was clear to Walpole and the authorities that his work was at an end. On November 7th he left, missing the Bolshevik Revolution, which began that very day.

In London Walpole was appointed to a post at the Foreign Office and remained there until resigning in February 1919. For his wartime work he was awarded the CBE in 1918.

Walpole continued to write and publish and now also began a career on the highly lucrative lecture tour in the United States.

He made his first lecture tour in 1919, receiving an enthusiastic welcome wherever he went. It was noted that Walpole's "genial and attractive appearance, his complete lack of aloofness, his exciting fluency as a speaker and his obvious and genuine liking for his hosts" combined to win him a large American following. The success of his talks led to an increase in lecturing fees, greater sales of his books, and large sums from American publishers keen to print his latest fiction.

A keen music lover, Walpole, in 1920, heard a new tenor at the Proms, impressed he sought him out. Lauritz Melchior became one of the most important friendships of his life, and Walpole did much to foster the singer's budding career. Wagner's son Siegfried engaged Melchior for the Bayreuth Festival in 1924 and succeeding years. Walpole attended, and met Adolf Hitler, then recently released from prison after an attempted putsch.

In 1924 Walpole moved to a house, Brackenburn, near Keswick in the Lake District. His large income enabled him to maintain his London flat in Piccadilly, but Brackenburn was his main home for the rest of his life.

At the end of 1924 Walpole met Harold Cheevers, who soon became his friend and companion and remained so for the rest of his life. Cheevers, a policeman, with a wife and two children, left the police force and entered Walpole's service as his chauffeur. Walpole trusted him completely, and gave him extensive control over his affairs. Whether Walpole was at Brackenburn or Piccadilly, Cheevers was almost always with him, and often accompanied him on overseas trips. Walpole provided a house in Hampstead for Cheevers and his family.

During the mid-twenties Walpole produced two of his best-known novels in the macabre vein that he drew on from time to time, exploring the fascination of fear and cruelty. The Old Ladies (1924) is a study of a timid elderly spinster exploited and eventually frightened to death by a predatory widow. Portrait of a Man with Red Hair (1925) depicts the malign influence of a manipulative, insane father on his family and others.

Walpole continued a series of stories for children, begun in 1919 with Jeremy, taking the young hero's story forward with Jeremy and Hamlet (the boy's dog) in 1923, and Jeremy at Crale in 1927.

In 1930 Walpole wrote possibly his best-known work, Rogue Herries, a historical novel set in the Lake District. The Daily Mail considered it "not only a profound study of human character, but a subtle and intimate biography of a place." He followed it with four sequels and an almost finished fifth.

Hollywood, in the shape of MGM, invited him in 1934 to write the script for a film of David Copperfield. Walpole enjoyed life in Hollywood, but as one who rarely revised any of his work he found it a bore to produce sixth and seventh drafts at the behest of the studio. He also had a small acting role in the film; he played the Vicar of Blunderstone delivering a boring sermon that sends David to sleep.

Walpole's performance was a success. The sermon was improvised and the producer, David O Selznick, had mischievously called for retake after retake to try to make him dry up, but Walpole fluently delivered a different extempore address each time.

The critical and commercial success of the film led to a return in 1936. Arriving, he found the studio had no idea which films they wanted him to work on, and he had eight weeks of highly paid leisure, during which he wrote a short story and worked on a novel. He was eventually asked to write the script for Little Lord Fauntleroy. He spent most of his fees on paintings; he was an avid collector and left many to the Tate in London on his death. His last lecture tour, also in 1936, was primarily to raise funds to pay US taxes which he had neglected to pay earlier.

In 1937 Walpole was offered a knighthood. He accepted although Kipling, Hardy, Galsworthy had all refused. "I'm not of their class... Besides I shall like being a knight," he said.

Walpole's taste for adventure did not diminish in his last years. In 1939 he was commissioned to report for William Randolph Hearst's newspapers on the funeral in Rome of Pope Pius XI, the conclave to elect his successor, and the subsequent coronation. In the weeks between the funeral and Pius XII's election Walpole, with his customary fluency, wrote much of Roman Fountain, a mixture of fact and fiction about the city. It was his last overseas visit.

After the outbreak of the Second World War Walpole remained in England, dividing his time between London and Keswick, where he continued to write with his usual speed. He completed a fifth novel in the Herries series and began work on a sixth.

Unfortunately his health was undermined by diabetes. He overexerted himself at the opening of Keswick's fund-raising "War Weapons Week" in May 1941, making a speech after taking part in a lengthy march.

Sir Hugh Seymour Walpole, CBE died of a heart attack at Brackenburn, aged 57 on June 1st, 1941. He was buried in St John's churchyard in Keswick.

Hugh Walpole – A Concise Bibliography

Books
The Wooden Horse (1909)
Maradick at Forty: A Transition (1910)
Mr Perrin and Mr Traill (1911) (Revised for the US version as The Gods and Mr Perrin)
The Prelude to Adventure (1912)
Fortitude (1913)
The Duchess of Wrexe, Her Decline and Death (1914)

The Golden Scarecrow (Short Stories) (1915)
Prologue
Hugh Seymour
Henry Fitzgeorge Strether
Ernest Henry
Angelina
Bim Rochester
Nancy Ross
'Enery
Barbara Flint
Sarah Trefusis
Young John Scarlet
Epilogue
The Dark Forest (1916)
Joseph Conrad (1916)
The Green Mirror (1918)
The Secret City (1919)
Jeremy (1919)
The Art of James Branch Cabell (1920)
The Captives (1920)
The Thirteen Travellers (Short Stories) (1920)
Absalom Jay
Fanny Close
The Hon Clive Torby
Miss Morganhurst
Peter Westcott
Lucy Moon
Mrs Porter and Miss Allen
Lois Drake
Mr Nix
Lizzie Rand
Nobody
Bombastes Furioso
The Young Enchanted (1921)
The Cathedral (1922)
Jeremy and Hamlet (1923)
The Crystal Box (1924) Privately published by Walpole – limited edition of 150 copies
The Old Ladies (1924)
The English Novel: Some Notes on its Evolution (1924)
Portrait of a Man with Red Hair (1925)
Harmer John (1926)
Reading: An Essay (1926)
Jeremy at Crale (1927)
Anthony Trollope (1928)
My Religious Experience (1928)
The Silver Thorn (Short Stories) (1928)
The Little Donkeys with the Crimson Saddles
The Tiger

No Unkindness Intended
Ecstasy
A Picture
Old Elizabeth (A Portrait)
The Etching
Chinese Horses
The Tarn
Major Wilbraham
A Silly Old Fool
The Enemy
The Enemy in Ambush
The Dove
Bachelors
Wintersmoon (1928)
Farthing Hall (1929) With J B Priestley
Hans Frost (1929)
Rogue Herries (1930)
Above the Dark Circus (1931) Published in the US as Above the Dark Tumult
Judith Paris (1931)
The Apple Trees: Four Reminiscences (1932) Limited edition of 500 copies
The Fortress (1932)
A Letter to a Modern Novelist (1932)
All Souls' Night (Short Stories) 1933
The Whistle
The Silver Mask
The Staircase
A Carnation for an Old Man
Tarnhelm – or The Death of my Uncle Robert
Mr Oddy
Seashore Macabre – A Moment's Experience
Lilac
The Oldest Talland
The Little Ghost
Mrs Lunt
Sentimental but True
Portrait in Shadow
The Snow
The Ruby Glass
Spanish Dusk
Vanessa (1933)
Extracts from a Diary (1934) Privately published by Walpole
Captain Nicholas (1934)
Cathedral Carol Service (1934) An episode from "The Inquisitor"
The Inquisitor (1935)
Claude Houghton: Appreciations (1935) With Clemence Dane
A Prayer for My Son (1936)
John Cornelius: His Life and Adventures (1937)
Head in Green Bronze and Other Stories (1938)

Head in Green Bronze
The German
The Exile
The Train
The Haircut
Let The Bores Tremble
The Honey-Box
The Fear of Death
The Field with Five Trees
Having No Hearts
The Conjurer
The Joyful Delaneys (1938)
The Sea Tower (1939)
Roman Fountain (1940)
The Bright Pavilions (1940)
The Blind Man's House (1941)
Open Letter of an Optimist (1941)
The Killer and the Slain (1942)
Katherine Christian (1943)
Mr Huffam and Other Stories (1948)
The White Cat
The Train to the Sea
The Perfect Close
Service for the Blind
The Faithful Servant
Miss Thom
Women are Motherly
The Beard
The Last Trump
Green Tie
The Church in the Snow
Mr Huffam – A Christmas Story

Short Stories
The following stories appeared in the Windsor Magazine

The Dog and the Dragon In Reminiscence (October 1923)
Red Amber (December 1923)
The Garrulous Diplomatist (December 1924)
The Adventure of Mrs Farbman (January 1925)
The Adventure of the Imaginative Child (February 1925)
The Happy Optimist (March 1925)
The Dyspeptic Critic (April 1925)
The Man Who Lost His Identity (May 1925)
The Adventure of the Beautiful Things (June 1925)
The War Babies are Growing Up! (November 1934)

The Young Huntress (1933)
The Cathedral (adaptation of his 1922 novel) (1936)
The Haxtons (1939)

In 1932 Walpole edited The Waverley Pageant: Best Passages from the Novels of Sir Walter Scott. In 1937 he edited a compilation of short stories, A Second Century of Creepy Stories (Hutchinson, 1937), by a range of writers including Guy de Maupassant, M. R. James, Henry James, Walter de la Mare, Oliver Onions, Walpole himself ("Tarnhelm") and twenty-one others.

www.ingramcontent.com/pod-product-compliance
Lightning Source LLC
Chambersburg PA
CBHW070533260626
47161CB00002B/358